Praise for

THE LOST SUMMER OF LOUISA MAY ALCOTT

"McNees discovered in reading biographies of Alcott that there was one summer about which very little was known—the summer of 1855, right before Louisa went off to Boston to become a writer. Here, McNees gives us that summer, creating a bittersweet love affair for Louisa and presenting her with the choice of marriage or career. We already know which she chose—there are all those lovely books—and so McNees's challenge was to get us there in a believable and satisfying way. And so she did."

—*Minneapolis Star Tribune*

"McNees gets the period details just right: the crinolines and carriages; the spare, aesthetic plainness of nineteenth-century New England. And although the love affair with Joseph is invented, she remains faithful to the broad outlines of Alcott's biography. In fact, *The Lost Summer* is the kind of romantic tale to which Alcott herself was partial, one in which love is important but not a solution to life's difficulties. Devotees of *Little Women* will flock to this story with pleasure."

—*The Washington Post*

"Even if readers have never read *Little Women*, they will enjoy this historical novel—a compelling, heart-wrenching story about the difficult choices women face. It resonates with themes that are as timely today as they were in Alcott's day."

—*Bookpage*

continued . . .

The

LOST SUMMER

of

LOUISA MAY ALCOTT

Kelly O'Connor McNees

Berkley Books, New York

THE BERKLEY PUBLISHING GROUP
Published by the Penguin Group
Penguin Group (USA) Inc.
375 Hudson Street, New York, New York 10014, USA
Penguin Group (Canada), 90 Eglinton Avenue East, Suite 700, Toronto, Ontario M4P 2Y3, Canada
(a division of Pearson Penguin Canada Inc.)
Penguin Books Ltd., 80 Strand, London WC2R 0RL, England
Penguin Group Ireland, 25 St. Stephen's Green, Dublin 2, Ireland (a division of Penguin Books Ltd.)
Penguin Group (Australia), 250 Camberwell Road, Camberwell, Victoria 3124, Australia
(a division of Pearson Australia Group Pty. Ltd.)
Penguin Books India Pvt. Ltd., 11 Community Centre, Panchsheel Park, New Delhi—110 017, India
Penguin Group (NZ), 67 Apollo Drive, Rosedale, Auckland 0632, New Zealand
(a division of Pearson New Zealand Ltd.)
Penguin Books (South Africa) (Pty.) Ltd., 24 Sturdee Avenue, Rosebank, Johannesburg 2196,
South Africa

Penguin Books Ltd., Registered Offices: 80 Strand, London WC2R 0RL, England

This is a work of fiction. Names, characters, places, and incidents either are the product of the author's imagination or are used fictitiously, and any resemblance to actual persons, living or dead, business establishments, events, or locales is entirely coincidental. The publisher does not have any control over and does not assume responsibility for author or third-party websites or their content.

PRINTING HISTORY
Amy Einhorn Books hardcover edition / April 2010
Berkley trade paperback edition / May 2011

Berkley trade paperback ISBN: 978-0-425-24083-0

The Library of Congress has catalogued the Amy Einhorn Books hardcover edition of this book as follows:

McNees, Kelly O'Connor.
The lost summer of Louisa May Alcott / Kelly O'Connor McNees.
    p.   cm.
    ISBN 978-0-399-15652-6
    1. Alcott, Louisa May, 1832–1888—Fiction.   2. Alcott, Louisa May, 1832–1888—Homes
and haunts—New Hampshire—Fiction.   3. Alcott, Louisa May, 1832-1888—Family—Fiction.
4. Walpole (N.H.)—Fiction.   I. Title.
    PS3613.C58595L67   2010   2009046024
    813'.6—dc22

PRINTED IN THE UNITED STATES OF AMERICA

10 9 8 7 6 5 4 3 2 1

For my family

Don't laugh at the spinsters, dear girls, for often
very tender, tragical romances are hidden
away in the hearts that beat so quietly
under their sober gowns.

—*Little Women*

BOSTON, MASSACHUSETTS,
TO WALPOLE, NEW HAMPSHIRE

October 25, 1881

Louisa May Alcott approached the ticket window of the Boston passenger station clutching a large case and a black parasol. She asked for the tickets on hold under her name—she'd written a week before to reserve them. The clerk's forehead gleamed, wet in the heat of his cramped booth. He held her gaze a moment longer than was proper and began to ask a question, then stopped. He seemed to decide that if this well-dressed woman *was* who he thought she was, he probably shouldn't ask for confirmation. He took the money she offered and gave her back the change.

It was a brisk autumn day and the platform was blustery. Louisa felt the skirts of her slim black dress swirl around her ankle boots, the pair she'd had for years, the pair she'd worn in Rome in the cathedrals, in Nice, in the parlor of the Paris inn where she'd shared wine with a Polish revolutionary as he described the deaths of all his friends. The boots were sturdy but the leather was cracked. She could afford to buy new ones—she could afford to buy just about anything she wanted now, though it hadn't always been that way. In her childhood poverty she had looked with breathless guilty glee at the fashion plates in *Godey's Lady's*, memorized every ruffle, collar, and bow the Paris girls wore. Now that she finally had the money to dress like a proper lady, she felt she was too old to do it. At forty-eight, she'd grown accustomed to her spinster's garb: black dresses, white lace collars fastened high around her neck. Corsets, bustles, scarlet French-heeled boots that buttoned up with pearls—those were for the younger set, still upright, with color in their cheeks, anticipating life instead of looking back on it.

She expected a smooth journey, provided they did not encounter engine trouble or problems with the track. Winter ice sometimes pried rail ties loose, but by May all the damage to the track had been repaired. Now fall was upon them once again, the destructive ice not far away, and anticipation of the looming chill filled her with weariness.

Once in the rail car, she glanced around at her fellow travelers. At the front of the car two little girls sat together, their spindly legs swinging in time with the rocking train. One girl held her doll in the crook of her elbow and stroked its carefully braided hair of gold yarn. She turned to the side and whispered something in her sister's ear. The girls broke into a shrill giggle before their mother turned to them and thrust her index finger to her lips. Quiet now, they grinned at each other, their eyes dancing.

A few men sat at the other end of the car, reading the newspaper and smoking while they watched trees and cranberry bogs replace Boston's dusty, crowded bustle. She didn't recognize anyone and they didn't seem to recognize her, which helped relax the tightness in her chest. But only a little.

It had been twenty-six years since she had seen the tidy houses and storefronts lined up along Washington Square in Walpole, the lilacs buzzing with honeybees. Twenty-six years, but the place was seared in her brain. The tracks curved through a dense stand of white birch and she realized she was wistful, an emotion in which she rarely allowed herself to indulge.

Louisa reached inside the case at her feet and pulled out the thick envelope of folded paper. She ran her fingers along the irregular edges of the letters she had tried so many times but never quite managed to destroy. Before she could restrain them, images flooded her mind and something cinched tightly around her heart. It was all right to think about it one last time, she supposed, as she unfolded the letters on her lap. Very soon these letters would be nothing more than embers. Her intention that day, the very reason for her journey, was to ensure the letters, and all other traces of that long ago summer, were destroyed.

In Bellows Falls, Vermont, she would hire a Rockaway to take her the rest of the way to Walpole, where Joseph Singer would be waiting.

For now, the train swayed on.

WALPOLE, NEW HAMPSHIRE

July–November 1855

Jo . . . was eager to be gone, for the homenest was growing too narrow for her restless nature.

—*Little Women*

Chapter One

It didn't take long for the Alcott sisters to finish unpacking their clothes. Anna, Louisa, Lizzie, and May didn't have many bonnets or dresses, both because they couldn't afford them and because their father, Bronson, believed a penchant for lace and silk revealed a weakness in one's character.

"It feels so nice to put things away," Anna said as she smoothed a worn quilt at the foot of her bed. The narrow wardrobe at her back contained six dresses Louisa and Anna shared between them, though the fabric stretched a bit across Anna's slightly wider shoulders. "Should we not find something to dress these windows?"

Anna and Louisa would also share the stuffy attic room that ran the length of the borrowed house. The sisters' small beds were nestled opposite each other in the cozy—or constrictive, depending on the mood—corner made by the steep angle of the roof. On stormy nights Louisa and Anna would be forced to raise their voices over the wind whistling through the poorly insulated walls. This room would be uninhabitable in a New England winter, but for the mild summer months it would do, and they were happy to have a room of their own away from the others. Near the head of each bed, a cushioned perch in the twin dormers provided just the right amount of light for reading or sewing.

Anna twisted up her mouth. "Oh, I forgot—Marmee put the drapes from Hillside up in Lizzie and May's room." She swung open the lid of her trunk and bent down to dig through the pile of folded fabric. A moment later she stood upright and turned to her sister. "Louisa, are you listening to me?"

"Hmm?" Louisa turned her body toward the direction of Anna's voice, but her eyes remained fixed in the book she held in front of her face. It was Longfellow's *Hyperion*, a tale of a man's travels through Germany. Mr. Emerson had urged her to borrow it for the summer. Louisa knew that Longfellow admired Goethe, as she did—her ostensible reason for wanting to read the book. She also knew that the book's romance came from Longfellow's real-life fumblings with love. Something about that fact made the story all the more sensational and impossible to put down.

Anna scoffed as she tipped the trunk's lid closed. "You read too much. Sometimes I think I can't remember what your face looks like from the cheekbones down."

Louisa looked up, finally, and lowered the book. She registered the question that had so far failed to penetrate her mind, as if it were a bird colliding with a windowpane. The mention of Hillside called up an image of the cozy house in Concord where they'd lived for three whole years until she was fifteen and financial woes had forced them back to Boston. The memory of it made her glum.

"I'm sorry, Anna. I *did* hear you." She felt her flushed cheek with the back of her hand. The attic room was unbearably hot and it was only ten in the morning. "If the Hillside drapes are in use, we may have to make some new ones."

Anna nodded. "Singer Dry Goods—Margaret Lewis said we might try there for the things we need to get settled. They'll have fabric. I believe it's across from the post office."

Louisa retrieved their bonnets from the top shelf of the wardrobe. They fastened them as they descended the stairs, calling out clipped good-byes in the hopes of escaping the house before May heard about the outing and insisted on tagging along.

But they weren't quick enough to thwart their youngest sister, who had lost "the whole of society," as she put it, when the family left Boston, and was desperate for a little adventure.

"Louy, I'm coming along with you," May cried from the parlor as she threw down her needlework. "Just give me a minute to arrange my hair."

Louisa sighed as May dashed toward her room. Louisa loved her sister, but she sometimes felt May came by that love in spite of herself. It was hardly her fault. May was only fifteen, and the time before she was born had been the most difficult for the family. Bronson's determination to live out his philosophies—transcending material pleasure, developing the soul through tireless self-examination—had never been stronger, and consequently the Alcott women lived without many domestic comforts. Over time, Bronson was forced to concede that some of his beliefs worked better in the abstract than on the ground. May was born after the family had overcome the worst of its poverty and privation, and Louisa resented that the youngest Alcott walked through the world with the posture of a girl who hadn't known true sacrifice.

"May," Anna called after her, anxious to be on their way. "Another day—tomorrow. I promise. I'll take you with me into town tomorrow."

They closed the heavy front door against May's shrill protests and made their way down the path. Louisa thought about how she missed the familiar woods of Concord. As a girl, she ran there every day, darting through the narrow spaces between the trees on a path Henry Thoreau had shown her years before, when he'd taken her to see a family of whip-poor-wills he'd discovered at dusk. She ran, she said, to keep up her strength, but in truth she was desperate to escape the crowded house and chores that always waited for her. Washing, knitting, mending, baking, weeding. She longed for quiet so that she could read and spin her tales, but sometimes even that required more concentration than her vibrating brain could muster. Running calmed and focused her thoughts. While she thudded along, her skirts rustled the leaves at her feet, picking up burrs and spiders she'd later have to shake off before going into the house. Louisa felt a pang as she thought back on those carefree days. A girl of twelve could be odd and sullen and race through the woods without fear of reproach; a woman of twenty-two had to concern herself with matters of propriety.

The family hadn't wanted to leave Boston and Concord. Bronson liked living near Emerson and his Transcendental friends, like Theodore Parker, the Boston minister, and the provocative abolitionist William Lloyd Garrison, and the girls had finally managed to make friends after years of moving from place to place. But they could not stay.

Bronson had not earned a regular income in sixteen years, so he and Abigail May—"Abba" to her husband and friends and "Marmee" to her daughters—depended on the charity of family and friends.

The Alcotts worried most about how Lizzie would adjust to another upheaval. One summer five years back, Abba's ever-present charity work brought her into contact with an impoverished family suffering from smallpox. She and Bronson became desperately ill. The girls' infection had seemed mild in comparison, but this consolation was short-lived. Though the other three bounced back after a few days, Lizzie never fully recovered her strength and had since suffered from a weakened constitution. Any stress was enough to send her to bed for a week. Though moving was sure to be a trial, Bronson and Abba knew they had little choice and only prayed they could find a suitable situation.

Financial mercy came when Abba's brother-in-law Benjamin Willis offered the use of a house he owned in Walpole, a New Hampshire town of fifteen hundred souls, and Bronson did not have the luxury of refusing. The house was known in town as Yellow Wood. Originally a saddler's shop, it was admired for its lilacs and golden autumn maples. Yellow Wood sat on a hill at the top of Wentworth Road, which snaked a quarter mile north and bisected the town center. Uncle Willis filled the shed with firewood and wrote to the family promising they could stay until Bronson's fortunes changed.

The first meager supper the night before had not satisfied bellies hungry from a long day of travel and unpacking, but they had to make do with the hard rolls and preserved vegetables in the pantry. When Louisa was writing, she could forget about every worldly thing, including food. The previous night she had begun a new story about a woman named Natalie, rejected and cast out by her lover when he discovered she had worked as an actress and could bring shame to his wealthy family. She filled her pages with ink late into the night, when her rumbling stomach finally broke her concentration.

Soon Abba would visit the orchard they'd passed on their way into town and establish a line of credit for food. They had no money to pay for it now, but Bronson had promised to embark on a new tour of conversations, his name for speeches he made in parlors across New England about famous philosophers. He refused to sell tickets to the events, as he was morally opposed to all acts of commerce, but he had in the past been unable to refuse donations. So a new tour held the tenuous promise of a little income. Abba knew better than to count on it, though. She knew all too well that her husband's lofty aims rarely deigned to find their way down to earth. His philosophies were concerned with ideals and symbols but rarely realities. Two winters ago he had set out for a tour of New York and Ohio, promising to earn enough to pay off their debts and finally provide a comfortable life for his family. Six months later he returned home with only one dollar.

It was true providence that Mr. Emerson had been their neighbor in Concord. He and Bronson were friends and intellectual equals, but Emerson was shrewd in pecuniary affairs. It was well known that he received a fortune when his tubercular first wife died at the age of twenty, and he and his second wife, Lidian, did not want for money. Though Bronson was proud of his refusal to sully himself with base economic affairs, he accepted Emerson's assistance with a surprising lack of protest. And the Alcott women thanked God for that small mercy.

Louisa had been to Walpole only once before, when she was quite young, so she tried to notice each storefront and memorize its contents to report back to her mother. The sisters were experienced at moving. As children they'd lived in several different houses, and they knew all about the work each move made for the women—stocking the kitchen, dressing the windows, planting a new vegetable garden. It helped to get the lay of the land and meet the shopkeepers early—especially, Louisa thought with dread, since they would soon be testing those shopkeepers' generosity by asking to buy things on credit.

As they descended the hill, they turned west on Middle Street and then north into Washington Square, where the town's few shops were clustered. The butcher's shop occupied the southwest corner of the square. Bronson's aversion to meat made Anna and Louisa a little skittish about the carcasses hanging in the windows, and they looked away as they passed by. The square contained two village bookstores that were local centers of political discussion. On the west side of the square, men interested in the philosophy of the waning Whig party argued over what to do about slavery and how modern technology like the railroads might change the country. Directly opposite, on the east side of the square, Democrats stood with their arms crossed, some pensively fingering their beards, as they lamented the death of the idyllic farming society President Jefferson had envisioned in their grandfathers' time. And the men who cared for neither politics nor books gathered at the tavern that sat between the stores, to imbibe and gamble until their wives prevailed upon them to return home for supper. Abba was at least lucky on one account: Bronson was a temperate man and never once set foot in *that* place of temptation.

Louisa fought back the welling irritation that made her jaw feel tight. Walpole seemed to her wholly unremarkable. Over the last few years she had felt herself growing restless, yearning for freedom from the domestic obligations that came with continuing to live at home. Though the chaos of Boston frightened her—the noise and heat of the trains, the looming shadow of steamers discharging immigrants at India Wharf, where vendors sold peppered oysters soaked in vinegar near the overcrowded tenements—she loved the excitement and freedom of the city. With her family she had bounced between Boston and Concord over the years but never had the chance to live in the city on her own, to have the space and time to think and write.

Since her father had announced the solution to their current financial woes, his plan to move the family here to Walpole, Louisa had been scheming for a way to get back to the city as soon as possible. She had promised herself she would accompany them to her uncle's house, help unload the trunks and be on the train from Bellows Falls back to Boston by the end of the first week. She still had most of the money left from the ten dollars she earned for "The Rival Prima Donnas," a story she wrote under the name Flora Fairfield, and the advance on *Flower Fables*, her collection of fairy tales published in a tiny local run the previous fall. The publisher had sent her a mere thirty-two dollars for that work, though even this small sum had astonished her at the time. She gave a portion to her father for the good of the household and squirreled the rest away, professing an oath to Anna and her mirror that she would safeguard the money for one express purpose.

"I, Louisa Alcott, do swear—"

"—do *solemnly* swear," Anna offered, her hands cradling the green leather Bible on which Louisa rested her palm.

"—do solemnly swear to resist temptations large and small, be they in the form of particularly bewitching bonnets, slippers . . ."

"Gloves?" Anna asked with her eyebrows raised.

Louisa nodded. "Gloves . . ."

Anna was quick to test her sister's conviction. "Even if they happen to be the sort that close with those tiny pearl buttons?"

"*Especially* if they have pearl buttons. As well as chocolates, pecans, new books, fine pens . . ."

"And cream laid writing paper. Don't forget that." Anna pressed her lips together to suppress a smile.

Louisa groaned and closed her eyes. "The very thought of it tests me this moment! Yes, yes—no fine writing paper. Now, where was I? Oh, yes . . . resist temptations large and small, so noted, in the service of my especial aim: to secure for myself in the city of Boston a *place apart* and a room in which I might write my stories and sell them to the highest bidder."

"Well done!" cried Anna. And the oath was sealed.

The savings was enough to pay her room and board for a few weeks until she sold a story or two, or found some other way to earn her bread. She pictured a cozy rooming house, perhaps a little dilapidated, with a long dining table full of boarders swapping tales of their travels. It wouldn't be hard to convince her father to let her go. Obtaining her mother's blessing would be the more difficult task.

But now that they had arrived in Walpole, Louisa could see the route to freedom wouldn't be smooth. Her uncle's house hadn't been lived in for some time. Linens moldered in a damp cabinet; spiders nested in the corners of the parlor; and the kitchen was in lamentable shape. How could she leave all this work for her mother and sisters while she went off on her own to spin her tales and merely hope to earn a little income? Louisa fought hard against her rising despair and tried to muster the patience that often eluded her. *I'll stay on until they get settled,* Louisa promised herself. *Until the house is fit to live in and Marmee has her kitchen up and running. It won't be so very long. And then I'll be on my way.*

They passed the Elmwood Inn and at last came to Singer Dry Goods. When the bell jingled as Louisa first stepped inside, it took her eyes a moment to adjust to the dim light after the searing July sunshine. The floor creaked under her boots as she followed her sister, who had already scurried over to the rows of dress fabrics, ribbons, and lace. Despite their father's warnings, Anna couldn't help being enamored with the beautiful dresses her wealthier cousins had. The fashions seemed to change so quickly, and she felt hopelessly left out of the running. She ran her hand along a bolt of shot silk and noticed a few magazine pages pinned on the wall featuring crinolines so wide she wondered how the wearer traversed a doorway.

Louisa rolled her eyes and found the shelf of calicos that would make a simple set of drapes. She didn't dare admit, even to herself, that she ached to touch the pale mousseline the color of an eggshell and imagine her broad shoulders slimmed by a flattering sleeve. The spirit of self-denial that colored every aspect of her family's life was strong in her, but so was a yearning to, just once, have the things others had.

"Good afternoon, Miss. Have you found something you like?"

Louisa looked up. She felt her cheeks color, as if she had been speaking her thoughts aloud. A freckled young man stood tall in brown suspenders and grinned at her. She shook her head, feeling suddenly shy, and turned quickly back to the fabric to avoid his eyes.

He shrugged and turned toward the counter, where a woman stood waiting to place an order. Louisa peered at her from behind a post. She wore a light cotton dress and a straw spoon bonnet with a cluster of daisies over her left ear.

"Good afternoon, Miss Daniels," the clerk said. "Is that a new bonnet? It's awfully becoming."

Miss Daniels tilted her head to the side and preened with a demure smile. "Why, thank you, Mr. Singer. It was a gift."

He clutched theatrically at his chest. "Not from some wealthy suitor, I hope. Don't tell me you've gone and given your heart away. After I've been waiting here pining for you all these years!"

She giggled, clearly enjoying the attention, Louisa noted, and touched the curls that hung beneath her bonnet. "You know very well Mr. Ross and I are to be married in a few months' time."

He gave a dramatic sigh, then narrowed his eyes at her. "I'd swear all you beautiful women are in on the conspiracy. The way you break hearts for sport—it's cruel and unusual!"

"Joseph Singer!" Miss Daniels pretended to be scandalized. "Does your father know what a terrible flirt you've become?"

Joseph chuckled. "He should—he taught me himself."

Miss Daniels rolled her eyes. "Well, if you are quite recovered from your broken heart, might I trouble you for six yards of that gray gabardine?"

The clerk chuckled and walked over to the bolts of fabric, glancing at Louisa as he passed. "Still deciding?"

Young men like this were the worst sort, Louisa thought. Flippant and casual, utterly amused with themselves.

"I only *just* arrived," she snapped.

His eyes widened with surprise and he pressed his lips together to conceal a grin. "Of course, take your time." He carried the gabardine back to the counter to fulfill Miss Daniels's order. A few moments later the bell on the door gave a cheerful ring as she exited the shop and Joseph took up his post near—but not too near—where Louisa browsed.

Anna appeared at her side. "Oh, Louy, you must come see this yellow silk. It's just divine." Anna noticed the young man waiting patiently and took a step toward him. "Oh, how rude of me. Good afternoon." He returned Anna's demure nod. "Is this your store?"

"My father's. But I help from time to time and . . ." He trailed off for a moment. "Well, he has been ill. So here I am."

"I'm Anna Alcott, and this is my sister Louisa. We just arrived in town." Louisa felt a sting of envy at Anna's bravery. "I'm sorry to hear about your father's health, but I'm happy to meet you," Anna said.

"Joseph Singer," he said, nodding. "Yes, it has been a difficult time for my sister and me. We want to keep the business in the family if . . . You see, I haven't any brothers. I'm doing my best for now and hope he will soon recover."

Anna nodded sympathetically. "Well, I'm glad to see that you stock grains and spices as well as the dry goods," she said, gesturing to the barrels in the corner. "That must help your business."

Joseph nodded. "We just began selling those in the spring. Used to be people ordered the spices from Boston and the deliveries came once a week. But when the Boston train started running all the way to Bellows Falls—that's just across the river there into Vermont—" he said, gesturing vaguely west, "people in town came around asking about them more often. And we like to keep our customers happy."

"Well, you've just earned some new ones. Our family has let a house down the road," Anna said, the lie tumbling easily from her lips.

"Is it Yellow Wood? That place is a beauty."

Anna smiled. "It is, though the windows seem quite bare."

"Ah, so it's drapes you'd like to make? I tried to inquire with your sister here, but she seems a bit shy." Louisa felt Joseph's eyes on her again and fixed her face into an indisputable scowl.

"Louy, shy? Wait until I tell our mother you said so— we'll all have a good laugh about that. Won't we, Lou?" Anna nudged Louisa with an elbow and she forced a smile.

Louisa tried to think of something clever to say in

response, but charm had abandoned her for the moment. She kept her eyes safely trained on her sister's face. "Nan, what do you think of this one?" Louisa said, pointing out a blue floral print.

"Oh, I don't really care for cornflowers. Isn't there anything with lily of the valley? It's my favorite."

"We just got some of the new designs in this morning. They're in the back." Joseph walked around the counter and through the open door of the stockroom. Louisa watched his back arch as he tilted his head back and reached for a wooden crate on a high shelf. His face didn't have a hint of a beard, but as he eased the heavy shipment from the shelf his shirt pulled taut across the muscles in his back. He was older than she'd first suspected, but only just.

"Lou, do you think that room will have much of a draft?" Anna rubbed the fabric between her thumb and index finger. "Will we need something heavier than these cottons?"

Louisa stared out the window to Washington Street, which was empty except for a few pigeons fighting over an abandoned crust of bread. Her fingers grazed the bolts of fabric, as if they contained some message only discernable through touch.

"*Louisa*—I'm talking to you."

She looked up, blinking. "Sorry, Anna. What was that? I drifted off for a second."

"What were you thinking about just then?" Anna looked at her sister and then at the stockroom door, where Joseph crouched inside, removing brown paper wrappings from the new fabrics.

"A story I'm working on," Louisa blurted. This was her standard excuse. When her first book had been published the year before, her family was quite taken aback that all Louisa's dreamy afternoons holed up in her room with a stack of paper had actually led to something—and they'd all been a bit penitent ever since.

Anna looked her over carefully. "I thought perhaps you were thinking that Joseph Singer is handsome. That's what *I* was thinking."

Louisa looked her dead in the eye and whispered her reply as Joseph approached them, the lily-of-the-valley print atop a pile of fabric in his arms. "No. I was thinking about people who aren't even real. As always."

"What do you think of this one?" Joseph asked, holding the sample out for Louisa to touch. Before she thought to stop herself, she looked up and met his eyes. They were a pale smoke blue but seemed to change even as she looked at them.

Her eyes darted to the fabric. "It's up to my sister, really." Louisa turned to Anna.

"This is perfect," Anna said. "We'll need five yards— what's the price?"

"I'll have to check the list," Joseph said, turning back toward the counter. "If you'll just follow me over here . . ."

While Anna went to settle the payment with Joseph, Louisa hovered near the door contemplating her sudden skittishness as she pretended to assess the selection of ribbons and trim. She was simply tired, she supposed, and unaccustomed to meeting new people after many safely predictable years amongst friends in Boston and Concord. She heard Anna's footsteps on the broad plank floor and pulled open the door without turning around. The bell mounted on the frame announced their departure.

"Very pleased to meet both of you," Joseph called out as they left. Only Anna turned back to wave.

Back outside, the sun was blinding once again. Anna clutched the package of fabric to her chest.

"Well, so far this seems like a friendly town."

"Nice enough." Louisa touched one of the pins that held her raven mane in place to make sure it was secure.

"Oh, Lou, be reasonable. I think Mr. Singer was friendly, though not for any reason I can see—you were quite rude. What's come over you?"

"*I* was rude to *him*? *He* was rude to *me*. I was simply trying to browse in peace. It's startling to be spoken to by strangers. We *knew* everyone in Concord," she muttered.

Anna rolled her eyes. "Well, we aren't in Concord anymore."

"That's right—we aren't. We never would have been buying fabric for drapes in Concord, because we wouldn't have had any windows to put them in." Louisa could feel her speech taking a turn toward the dramatic. "We would have been homeless, cast out by debtors. If only Father would have tried a *little* harder to find work."

Anna stopped dead and turned to Louisa, her face a mixture of astonishment and an older sister's reproach.

Louisa put her hand on Anna's forearm. "Of course, you *know* I think Father is more brilliant than just about anyone else. But aren't you tired of worrying about money? I would say we see it differently now that we are older, but doesn't it seem like we've always worried about the debts more than he has? And, of course, Marmee has worried too. God only knows how much."

Anna nodded and took her sister's arm. "It won't always be this way. It's lucky we're girls, I guess."

Louisa furrowed her brow in confusion and Anna smiled. "What do you mean?" Louisa asked.

Anna leaned against her sister and for a moment rested her cheek on Louisa's shoulder. "Well, my dear, it's not as if we'll be living with Father and Marmee forever."

A short hard laugh escaped from Louisa's lips. "Well, I certainly don't intend to do *that*." She thought again of Boston, rolled the calendar forward in her mind to the date when she might be able to leave.

The two strolled in silence up Main Street and then east along the woods at the edge of the square, taking the long way back to Yellow Wood. Louisa continued to brood. They were in this unfamiliar town, Louisa knew, because her father was a man of many grand ideas and little common sense. As a child, she had revered him, and never doubted that the problem lay with a world unwilling to comprehend his brilliance. But eventually she had come to see him in a different light, one that revealed his flaws. For a time, in response to Emerson's urgings, Bronson had worked at becoming a writer, but he found the public either wouldn't or couldn't accept his ideas. His affected prose had earned many polite nods and one harsh critique that his writing conjured an image of fifty boxcars rattling by containing only one passenger. After that he abandoned literary pursuits, though he continued to journal extensively and focused his efforts on teaching. A great lot of money was invested by others in his schools, which promised to transform children's minds and souls through Transcendental teachings. Each had temporary success, but ultimately Bronson would reach too far outside acceptable boundaries and offend a wealthy contributor. The Quakers had influenced his philosophy and he came to believe that no religious ritual or temple could substitute for direct communication with God. Bronson was reluctant to accept dogma of any kind and told his students that Jesus was a great teacher but was not divine. None of this sat well with the Episcopalian and Unitarian ministers who contributed to his school fund. But the theological disagreements were nothing compared to what came later on, when Bronson tried to engage his young students in a discussion of where babies came from. It was brave for Bronson to speak his mind to Boston's powerful interests, Louisa knew, but he had never learned how to choose his battles.

Of course, *he* believed the world did not understand what he was trying to tell it. His ventures would fail and the family would soon be back to living in poverty. In Bronson's estimation, his family's money troubles weren't his fault—they were the fault of a world too cowardly to consider new ways of thinking. After all, Louisa thought bitterly, what would we have him do? Put his philosophy aside and *work*?

They passed a cluster of white pines, impossibly tall and sturdy on their slender trunks. Anna pointed toward a bench nestled beneath the outermost trees. "Let's rest a moment."

Louisa looked worriedly at her. "Are you well, Nan?" All the Alcotts worried constantly about illness since Lizzie had become so frail after her bout of smallpox.

Anna rolled her eyes. "Fine, fine. I just want to sit a moment and look at these trees."

They pulled their skirts up at the knee to keep the hems out of the dirt. The pale blue of Anna's dress made Louisa think of a robin's egg in a nest of dark leaves and branches. They shared the same dark hair. All the sisters swapped clothes, particularly the older two, which contributed to Louisa's feeling that she was looking into a mirror when she looked at Anna. A prettier, sunnier mirror, she thought, but in truth while Anna was noble, measured, and plain, Louisa's deep-set eyes were magnetic, appraising the world with brazen intensity.

"Lou," Anna began in a serious tone, then laughed out loud.

"What? Why are you laughing?"

"I just realized the futility of the conversation I was about to start."

Louisa felt a burning in her chest as she strained to withhold her frustration. "Am I really so predictable?" As a young girl she'd been given to angry explosions and had to work hard to keep her sudden changes in mood concealed from the people around her. A fiery twelve-year-old was amusing, perhaps even charming, but a woman of twenty-two wasn't given nearly so much license. "Perhaps I will surprise you," Louisa said weakly.

Anna grinned. "Louy, do you ever think about getting married?"

Her eyes widened and she drew in a sharp breath. *"Married?"*

Anna laughed again. "Yes, married. Don't act as if you've never heard of it."

"Oh, I've heard all about it. I've watched it my whole life." She pictured their mother, straining over the arm of her chair toward the oil lamp as she mended the heels of their father's stockings, her shoulders tense from hours at the washtub. When Abba wasn't tending to her family's endless needs, she spent her time knitting or baking bread or collecting medicine for Boston's poor. Bronson was deeply committed to one man's charity for another, though practical implementation of the notion seemed to escape him.

"I suppose no one is lamenting our prospects just yet, but it's about time we start thinking about it—we've reached the conventional age." Anna looked down. "It wouldn't have to be like Marmee and Father, you know."

"No, I don't know." Louisa sat stiffly, her body aware of the conversation's direction before her mind could catch up. At twenty-four, Anna had so far been content to resist any attachments that might take her away from home and instead remained with the parents who adored her.

"There are choices. There are different sorts of men. Different from Father."

Louisa looked at her, surprised to hear this veiled criticism from her angelic sister, their father's favorite.

"There's love. That's something. Wouldn't you like to be in love, Lou?"

Henry Thoreau appeared in her mind, his sodden boots, his beard snagged with leaves, a notebook clutched in the black half-moons of his fingertips. He had been another of their Concord neighbors. Love was a foreign country Louisa didn't care to visit, and the only time she'd ever come close to the feeling was developing a pupil's adoration for her teacher. Henry could peel a wide strip of birch bark with one deft slice of his knife and fold it into a box to hold the leaves and flowers and stones they collected on their explorations. Once, they found a store of Indian spearheads poking out of the earth beneath a huckleberry bush. They would walk all afternoon until the sun baked them red. When she shrank from the delicate brush of a cobweb, he told her it was a handkerchief dropped by a fairy.

From the time she first walked alone with Henry as a girl, she dared to hope he saw in her a like mind, a ruminator.

But Henry only loved his trees, his work, his solitude. Louisa had heard through the Concord gossip that her tutor Sophia, a young woman closer to Henry's age, confessed her love and hopes to marry him. She'd left town the following year, shattered by his rejection. Henry grew still more reclusive then, no longer inviting the children to walk with him. When Louisa's breasts began to fill out, he hardly spoke to her at all, except to wave from a distance.

"I didn't know it was as simple as deciding to do it. Why are you bringing this up now, Anna?" Louisa's voice was cross.

"Because I'm trying to tell you about me. About what I want."

"And what is that?"

"Oh, Louisa, you are so *trying* sometimes. *I* want to be in love. *I* want to get married. I want to have a different kind of life than this one. My own life."

Louisa turned to her, softening her voice with all her might. "You believe getting married is going to let you have your own life? Don't you think the way to do that is to *avoid* marriage?" For Louisa, marriage and love had almost nothing to do with each other. Love, or at least what she had been able to glean about love from books, represented a kind of sweet and everlasting acceptance, a companionship, an adoration that aimed to preserve its object, not wrestle it to the ground. Marriage was something else altogether. Once Abba had told Louisa, "Wherever I turn, I see that women are like beasts of burden, under the yoke, dragging their lengthening chain." Louisa had never forgotten that image, the hopelessness of it. Marriage was no kind of freedom.

Anna struggled to be patient with her sister, who always seemed to make the simplest things difficult. "It depends on what kind of 'own life' you mean, I suppose. I want a husband. I want children. My own home, even if it is a humble little place. And rugs and china and furniture."

Louisa was quiet a moment. "Well, I want to be a writer. I *am* a writer. Did you ever hear of a married woman writer?"

"I'm sure there are plenty." Anna sighed. "Why should you have to choose, if you find the right sort of husband? One who would indulge your interests."

"I don't want to be indulged," Louisa shot back, rankled. "I want to *work*. And besides, when, amongst all the birthing and bathing and china washing and rug sweeping and fire stoking do you think I'd have time to write? Or should I let my family go hungry and languish in frayed clothes while I place my work above their needs, as Father has done to us?"

"*Louisa!*"

Anna's scolding was more provocation than her restrained temper could resist. She flew to her feet. "Well, why shouldn't I say it? It's the truth! It's selfish and neglectful. Marmee has done her best for us, but in *spite* of him, not with his help. I could never put my children through that, knowing how it felt to me as a child." She sat back down, her eyes full of tears. "Don't you see? I do have to choose. I have inherited Father's love of ideas and books but I also know how that love can separate you from the people who need you most. And yet, I can't imagine my life without books. I don't even know who I'd *be* then."

"Oh, poor Louy." Anna put her arm around her sister, pulling Louisa's head down onto her shoulder. "To me you'd still be you—exactly the same. Funny and kind and working yourself into a frenzy."

"As *soon* as I can—as *soon* as you're all settled in—I'm

leaving for Boston. It's as if—" Her voice had taken on a childish whine that embarrassed her, and she stopped short.

"What?" Anna asked. "As if what?"

". . . as if my life depended on getting out on my own, away from all this. And I intend to send home my wages, but . . . well, do you think wanting to go is awfully selfish?" Louisa felt her cheeks grow hot with shame.

Anna shook her head. "No, I don't. I think it is honest. But it doesn't matter what I think."

"Of course it does!" Louisa exclaimed, looking up at her.

Anna shook her head. "No, it doesn't. Not when it comes to deciding how to make a happy life for yourself. And you will."

Though Louisa faced the trees, Anna knew just the look that was on her face: brows wrenched skeptically, her lips a twisted prune.

"You will," she said again.

My definition [of a philosopher] is of a man up in a balloon, with his family and friends holding the ropes which confine him to earth and trying to haul him down.

—Louisa May Alcott: Her Life, Letters, and Journals

Leaves of Grass . . . is too frequently reckless and indecent. . . . His words might have passed between Adam and
Eve in Paradise, before the want of fig-leaves brought no
shame; but they are quite out of place amid the decorum of
modern society.

—CHARLES A. DANA,
New York Daily Tribune,
July 23, 1855

Bronson balanced his weight on one knee and patted the
soil into place around the delicate sprout of a pumpkin
vine, newly emerged from the ground just that morning. It had
been ten days since he drew up his plan for the garden, and
he was pleased to see the plants taking root. He chose not to
dwell on the fact that it was nearly August; this vine would
not produce fruit until at least November, assuming there was
no frost before then. No matter—he felt a provider's pride. He
was making food for his family out of a few seeds and a patch
of earth.

Louisa stood nearby, hanging laundry on the line. Tuesday mornings they washed the linens, and she'd volunteered
for the chore of hanging the wet laundry out of sheer self-
preservation. She felt if she did not get out of the washroom,

away from the bubbling vat of soap, she might pick up a chair and hurl it across the room. She didn't trust herself to keep her temper. It seemed she was getting less patient, less able to accept her duties, despite the fact that she wanted desperately to be good. All her life she had observed Anna as a scientist observes the object of his experiment; she watched for patterns that might reveal how Anna was able to move through life with ease while Louisa trailed behind her in fits and starts. But Louisa couldn't seem to discern Anna's secrets. She doubted Anna herself understood them.

And now Anna wanted to get *married*. How she could come to that conclusion after watching their mother suffer all these years was baffling to Louisa. Abba's entire adult life was one test of endurance after another. She'd birthed five children, one too early to survive, and had the misfortune of a husband who floated through the world, his feet rarely touching the ground. When she fell in love with Bronson and his ideas, she knew his philosophy and teaching would not provide the means for a life full of fine things. It mattered not to her—dresses and fine furniture were dull compared to Plato and Shakespeare. But Abba had underestimated just how little he thought of practical things, like how they might pay for a place to live, or how they would raise healthy children on a diet of vegetables and bread alone. Abba tried for her daughters' sakes to bear up, but the strain showed. Louisa had decided from an early age that she wanted her life to be nothing like her mother's.

Bronson stood up and arched his back, his eyes closed a moment to the glare of the sun. He glanced over at Louisa as she stretched to pin a sheet on the line. "You make a lovely tableau, my daughter."

Louisa noticed a bit of dirt trapped in the cloud of his wiry sideburn and smiled, feeling her heart swell in response to this rare bit of praise. No matter what she wanted to achieve, who she wanted to be, it was her father's love and approval she wanted more than anything else in the world.

"Ho, Alcott!"

Father and daughter looked up to see the familiar gait of their Concord neighbor Mr. Emerson as he moved up the path, clutching a large glass jar between his elbow and ribs.

Bronson stepped forward to shake his hand. "Hello, my friend. I knew this promised to be a pleasant day."

Emerson smiled, the deep creases in the outer corners of his eyes stretching to his temples. "I've come to see how you're settling in." He held out the jar. "Lemon preserves for your wife, with best wishes from Mrs. Emerson. Good morning, Miss Louisa," he said, tipping his hat in her direction.

"Good morning," she replied, her voice barely louder than a whisper. Mr. Emerson was sober and polite to most, but the Alcotts awakened a joviality in him. When Louisa was fourteen, he patiently read her writing and offered encouraging words. The attention astonished her and she began to wrestle with the question that would trouble her all her life: Why would God give a woman talent if He meant her to be confined to the kitchen and washtub? Though to her father he was simply Waldo, Louisa never forgot she was in the presence of a great man and couldn't help but be self-conscious around him. Bronson placed his hand on Emerson's shoulder and turned him toward the house.

"Let's go inside to talk." Bronson pulled his handkerchief from his pocket and used it to mop his face. "Perhaps Louisa will be kind enough to get us something cool to drink."

Bronson and Emerson retired to the parlor and Louisa

turned toward the kitchen carrying the preserves. Abba stood at the sink, her knife poised above a half-peeled potato. A mountain of the knobby root vegetables and a large cabbage that looked to be half rotten lay heaped at her elbow. She gazed out the window toward the woods at the edge of the garden. Louisa looked out in the same direction to see what had captured her mother's attention, but nothing was there. She reached for the metal pitcher that hung on a rusty hook above where Abba worked.

Abba's knife clattered to the floor. "God in *heaven*—you startled me!"

Louisa touched her mother's arm. "I'm sorry, Marmee. You looked lost in thought—I didn't want to interrupt you."

Abba blinked at her daughter, as if she knew she should recognize her but didn't. Then the vacant expression disappeared and Abba stooped to pick up the knife. "Did you finish hanging the laundry?"

"Yes. Father was working in the garden and Mr. Emerson has come. He brought you some of Mrs. Emerson's preserves." Louisa placed the jar on the worktable. "I was going to take them something to drink in the parlor."

Abba already had turned back to the sink and was digging a black spot out of a potato with the tip of the blade. Louisa observed Abba's stooped posture and the silver streaks in her hair. Abba spoke over her shoulder. "It's nearly eleven. Perhaps they would like something to eat as well."

Louisa brought the pitcher of water into the parlor a few moments later, along with half a loaf of brown bread and some butter from the larder, and placed the tray on the low table between the sofa and armchairs that faced the hearth. Behind the sofa was a narrow shelf with two chairs and

Louisa slipped into one, quietly taking up a stocking from the mending basket and hoping for a chance to listen to the men talk without being noticed by them or by Abba, who would likely find a chore for Louisa to do.

"Well, my friend, how do you find Walpole so far?" Emerson's face was dominated by his Roman nose and prominent brow. "Have you gone much into town?"

"I have stopped in at the village store but haven't spent much time there," Bronson said. "In general I find the men here have a tendency to pontificate endlessly."

Louisa bit her bottom lip and jabbed the needle into the toe seam to stifle a giggle.

She could see the irony of the comment did not escape Emerson either, but he continued kindly. "What have you been reading lately? I have something intriguing that I think you'll quite enjoy."

"All my old texts—*Pilgrim's Progress*, *Aids to Reflection*, Plato. You know how I feel that one must read the same works again and again to truly extract the meaning. But let no one say Alcott's mind is closed to the new."

Emerson grinned at the proclamation. Bronson fancied himself a grand man, and though his lofty way of speaking endeared him to Emerson, it sometimes earned him ridicule from others.

"This appeared just a few weeks ago, out of the ether." Emerson pulled a volume the size of a prayer book from his jacket pocket. The book was bound in green cloth with gold-stamped type on the front cover and spine, and Louisa strained to see the title. "The poet calls it *Leaves of Grass*. And—you will not believe this when I tell you—his name is nowhere to be found on the cover."

Bronson's eyes widened. "He doesn't identify himself?" To two men quite enamored of the sight of their own names in print, the news was shocking.

"None. Only this." Emerson opened to the frontispiece. "A daguerreotype of the poet. Dressed like a scoundrel, I might add."

He handed the book to Bronson, who flipped slowly through its pages. "And what is the nature of the verse?"

"It is the most extraordinary piece of wit and wisdom an American has ever contributed."

Bronson, who knew his friend was not prone to exaggeration, raised his eyebrows.

"His words and form are *transcendental* in every meaning of the word. There's nothing else like it I've ever seen."

Louisa realized she had been holding her breath. The hole in the much-darned stocking remained, the needle pinched between her index finger and thumb. She had never heard Mr. Emerson talk this way before. He sat on the edge of his chair, his typically sober demeanor alive with excitement.

"You will find, I think . . ." Emerson hesitated. " . . . that his subject matter is . . . peculiar. A bit shocking." He gave a quick glance in Louisa's direction. "And certainly not meant for the eyes of our counterparts." Louisa realized glumly that he'd been aware of her presence all along. "In any case, they wouldn't be able to make much sense of it, I don't think. This is the poet of the man, the American man, and the meaning and responsibilities of his radical freedom."

Bronson turned the volume in his hands. "And you know nothing of his identity?"

"Aha." Emerson raised an index finger. "I did not, until a few nights ago. I saw an advertisement with a picture of the book, and beneath that, for the first time, the poet's name. Mr. Walt Whitman, of Brooklyn, New York. You must read it as soon as you can, my friend. I am anxious to hear your thoughts on his work."

"I will begin it as soon as we part. Your recommendation is enough to convince me." Bronson smeared butter on a slice of bread he'd been eyeing throughout the conversation. "And your own work—does it go well?"

Emerson nodded. "I am finishing a volume of essays on my visits to England." He pulled his watch from his waist pocket and squinted at it. "In fact, I should be on my way now. It is nearly afternoon."

The men rose. Bronson walked his friend to the front door and shook his hand. Emerson nodded to Louisa and asked Bronson to wish Mrs. Alcott well. When Bronson turned back, his eyes registered Louisa's presence, but he took no notice of her. His mind was far away on something else. He reached for the strange volume of poetry Emerson had been so eager to show him and turned toward his study.

Louisa set down her mending and followed him. "Father?"

Bronson turned, startled. "Yes, child?"

She had to think quickly now. "Do you think . . . do you think Mr. Emerson will be thought of in the future as a philosopher? The way we think of Plato now?" She hadn't actually meant to ask that, but now that the question was out, she did want to know the answer. Just as she'd hoped, he began walking slowly toward his study. She walked alongside, her hands clasped in front of her.

He thought a moment before he spoke. "There is no question that Emerson's mind knows no equal. But he is too interested in fame and scholarship, not enough in the divine."

Bronson squared his shoulders, forever at the podium. "He sees all but doesn't always feel. Do you understand my meaning? He has a capital intellect but an undeveloped soul."

Louisa nodded, surprised to hear her father speak so critically. They reached his study and he walked around to his desk, pulling out the chair and settling in to shuffle through the disorganized stacks of papers. His face glowed in the light of the green-shaded brass lamp on the corner of his desk. He laid the mysterious volume of poetry off to the side and placed his journal on top of it, then looked up, surprised to see Louisa still standing in the room.

As he opened his mouth to speak, they both turned toward soft footfalls in the hallway. Lizzie appeared at the door holding a small tray that held a tarnished coffeepot. She entered the room behind Louisa and placed the tray on a table under the window, then turned to Bronson. "Father, I'm sorry to interrupt your conversation."

"No need to apologize, little bird. What is it?"

Louisa wondered at her sister's ethereal appearance, the dove-gray cotton of her dress doing nothing to enliven her pale complexion and light hair. She seemed at times like a slender ghost who fluttered from room to room, enamored with the textures of domesticity: the smooth bone of the knitting needle, the snap and flutter of a sheet in the breeze. They called her their little bird, little housewife, though Lizzie brushed off this praise.

"Marmee says there's a family on River Road that has the scarlet fever?"

Bronson nodded. "Yes, I believe I heard something about that in town just yesterday."

Lizzie reached into the right pocket of her apron and pulled out a handful of coins. A bulge in the left pocket squirmed and two orange ears poked out.

Louisa giggled, pointing at the kitten. "I see you've already taken on a new charge," she whispered. The sisters had long joked that stray kittens throughout the northeast flocked to Lizzie, knowing she wouldn't refuse them. Once, in Concord, Bronson finally put his foot down and ordered them out of the house when he found a whole litter scattered in the spaces on his bookshelf. Louisa had helped Lizzie hide them under the bed until he forgot about his prohibition.

Lizzie smiled, putting her finger to her lips. Bronson was flipping through a hefty book and failed to notice the feline interloper. Lizzie pushed the fuzzy head back into her pocket and held out the money. "Father, I'd like to send this to them, and I have some brown bread cooling. Marmee says they have no flour."

He looked up. "This is a kind gesture, Elizabeth, and it gives me pride to see it."

She smiled. "It wouldn't be right *not* to give, when we can." Louisa felt humbled by her sister's generosity, though she wondered about whether they truly had anything to spare. Lizzie floated out into the hallway but then turned back. Bronson sighed impatiently.

"Will you be going into town today?" she asked.

"Yes," Bronson said with a little irritation. "Just as soon as I have a moment to complete this letter. I will deliver your gifts then."

Lizzie nodded. "Thank you, Father."

Bronson turned back to Louisa, who stood waiting

patiently to reclaim the thread of their conversation. "And now to you. Did I answer your question about Mr. Emerson well, my child? It is time for me to work."

"Yes, Father. Very well." Louisa marked the place on the desk where Whitman's book lay concealed, already calculating the hours until her father's evening constitutional when the study would be empty and she might slip in and claim it. "Very well indeed."

That evening, Louisa climbed wearily up the steps under the strain of a feigned headache and waited until she was safely ensconced in the attic room before liberating the book from the waistband of her dress. She settled upon the sagging bed and leaned back against the wall, feeling her chignon press against the faded wallpaper.

The book felt smaller than she'd expected after dreaming about it all afternoon. She stared at the frontispiece image of the poet. He did indeed look like a scoundrel, with his hat tipped to the side and a rumpled shirt, open at the collar. He reminded her of the vagrants she'd seen lurking in Boston Common when she crossed the park on walks with her father. All the poets she'd ever seen had gray hair, wore neat, if not new, frock coats and top hats, and took their tea in parlors. Whitman looked like the sort who might tear across a parlor like a maniac, frightening the ladies and overturning all the furniture. She thought back to Mr. Emerson's warning that the book was not meant for a woman's eyes, though she didn't for a second consider retreating from her investigations.

And then she turned past the introduction to the opening verse.

I celebrate myself,
And what I assume you shall assume,
For every atom belonging to me as good belongs to you.

She turned the pages and a glowing candle on the table beside the bed sank into its pricket. The verse was at once crude and reverent, panoramic and microscopic. With a kinetic rhythm, the poet wrote of an America Louisa scarcely knew, of bodies at work, sweating, cursing, praying; of slaves; of lovers; of buds folded in the earth. Line by line, the words lapped at her like waves crawling the shore. When she finally slept she dreamed of train whistles and the rhythmic clang of a blacksmith's hammer, her hand clutched as if it held a pen.

All I have to say is, that you men have more liberty than
you know what to do with, and we women haven't enough.

—"The King of Clubs and the Queen of Hearts"

Chapter Three

Wednesday

To the Misses Alcott:

If you find you can set your sewing aside, please join me and the other young Walpoleans for an afternoon of picnicking and swimming at the riverbank near the Arch Bridge, this Saturday at one o'clock.

Yours,

J. Singer

New Englanders spent much of the year shrouding their bodies from winter's frigid gloom, but August, hot and fragrant, drew them into the open. Out-of-doors became a state of mind as well as a place. In the meadows, vanilla-scented wildflowers the locals called "joe pye weed" broke into pink feathering blossoms and were soon papered with monarchs. Spicy bergamot edged the woods. In the shadow of the canopy, the crisp scent of teaberry filled the air; beneath its waxy leaves, white flowers draped like a string of pearls. A week passed in which no rain fell and the heat stretched from mid-morning until late into the evening. All that sunlight was cultivating something in Louisa as well, though she wouldn't know it for a while.

Louisa and Anna walked with Margaret Lewis along the narrow forest path that led from town to the muddy bank of the Connecticut River. Besides the relatives who had provided their accommodations, Margaret was the only other person in town the sisters had known before they arrived. Margaret's uncle lived in Concord with his wife and children, and she had visited the relatives for a fortnight each spring and fall. Unfortunately, she could scarcely bear the company of her cousins, three dreadfully dull and pious young ladies who shunned music, dancing, and parties as works of the devil they lived to thwart. Margaret often found her way across the two yards that separated the Lewis home from Hillside. She was Anna's age and found in the Alcott girls a bit more spirit of adventure.

Louisa carried a bundle that contained their lunch and clothes for swimming. She had been hunched over a meandering draft—a story about a vicious family feud that finally ends one New Year's Eve because of a child called Alice—late into the previous night, and her back ached. With her free hand she slapped away a cloud of mosquitoes that seemed to be following them all the way through the damp woods.

Anna clapped her hands. "Girls, what do you think about putting on a play?"

Margaret squealed with unencumbered delight. "That's a wonderful idea! Assuming I get to play the lead, of course."

Louisa felt a small wave of dread. A play would take months to arrange and would interfere with her Boston plans. But she tried to cover her feelings with wary enthusiasm. "It could be fun."

"Do you think anyone else would be interested?" Anna asked her.

"Oh, yes," Margaret said. The quiver in her substantial bosom threatened to settle once and for all the ongoing battle between her flesh and the seams of her dress. "There is little to interest the young people of this town in the way of entertainment." Margaret had an affected way of speaking that Louisa found irritating but tried to ignore.

"Well," Louisa said, "we will have to ask the others about it today."

They reached a bright clearing where the ground sloped toward the river. Anna and Margaret, uncertain how to appear dignified, slowly descended the steep path down to the bank where the rest of the group lounged in the sunlight mottled with shadows the shape of birch leaves. Louisa, who didn't mind her manners as well as her sister, let her momentum build untempered and nearly careened into a girl with curly red hair who sat with her back to the path, eating a handful of blueberries.

"Please excuse me," Louisa said, embarrassed.

The girl smiled. "It's all right." She offered a friendly smile. "I'm Nora. You must be one of these Alcott girls I've been hearing about."

Louisa stuck out her hand. "Louisa Alcott," she said. After a surprised look, Nora took her hand and gave it an awkward shake. In her experience, only men shook hands.

Louisa resisted the urge to roll her eyes. So many girls, especially in the small towns, were still being raised in the old
way—demure bows and curtsies. But why shouldn't they
shake hands, the way men did, with dignity?

"And this," Louisa gestured behind her as her sister and
Margaret approached, "is my sister Anna."

Anna tilted her head and smiled. "It's a pleasure to meet
you, Nora."

"That's my brother over there," Nora said, pointing
toward a pair of boys struggling to secure a tent between two
trees. "Nicholas. The one with the dark hair. He's older than
I am—closer in age to you and your sister. That is, I think
so—well, how old are you?" Nicholas was a full head shorter
than his friend. He sported the bushy sideburns just coming
into fashion and his hair was precisely combed and greased.

"I'm twenty-two," Louisa said.

"Our little Nora's but nineteen," Margaret said, then
sighed. "That's Samuel next to Nicholas. Is he not the tallest
young man you've ever seen?"

The girls laughed and walked together toward the water.
Margaret had confided in Anna earlier that morning that she
was smitten with Samuel Parker and believed he returned her
favor. Louisa could see now from his wistful gaze in Margaret's
direction that he was indeed a man in love. In a rare moment of
courage the previous Sunday, Samuel had suggested the swimming party when Margaret told him that the Alcotts were in
Walpole for the summer. As they stood on the lawn beneath
the arched windows of the Unitarian church, the pale pink
and yellow panes glinting in the morning sun, he had suddenly grown shy. Margaret tried to put him at ease by suggesting whom he might invite and how they might send around

the invitations. Samuel seemed only too happy to oblige her wishes. She had told Anna that though he wouldn't admit it, welcoming the Alcott sisters was for him the perfect pretense for a gathering he could be sure Margaret would attend.

She had then further divulged that at a party the previous fall, after Samuel drank three glasses of champagne punch, he'd told Margaret, haltingly, that her blond curls reminded him of corn silk at a husking bee. Or, rather, that corn silk reminded him of Margaret's curls, since he had touched the slick fibers many times but could only dream of touching her hair. Anna had giggled and rolled her eyes, but Margaret nearly went into a swoon as she relived the encounter. Louisa just shook her head, amazed at the nonsense to which young women her age seemed devoted.

Once the tent was fixed securely between the trees, Samuel and Nicholas waved the girls over. Inside, the swimmers could change from their Saturday clothes into proper swimming attire, which for the boys meant wool tunics with short sleeves and wool breeches that stopped below the knee, and for the girls a heavy flannel dress with pantalettes beneath, swimming boots, and a cap for their hair. All the girls but Louisa emerged from the tent one by one, shapeless, bobbing along like bald old men toward the water.

Louisa peeked out of the tent to see the group gathered on the water's edge, splashing in the warm current and pointing out a red deer that eyed them from the opposite bank. She crept out and folded her dress into a neat square, then rested it atop her boots, which she placed in the modest line the other girls' boots formed. Their laces were cinched into bows, as if leaving them untied signified less than total commitment to matters of propriety. She'd been unsure just what to do about her feet. She had only one pair of boots, and it had taken her all morning to help Anna fashion something *she* could wear in the water, a pair of slippers their father had abandoned, which the girls cut down with a kitchen knife and sewed into rough shape, the laces jutting in irregular zigzag down the front. Anna had refused to go to the party at all until Louisa convinced her that no one would be looking at her feet.

Since their conversation on the bench at the edge of town, Anna had grown demure, reticent. She was thinking now about impressions, taking note of the names of important families in town, particularly the ones with sons. Louisa had no choice but to leave her own feet bare. She didn't care at all whether the others thought the Alcotts were poor—they probably knew it anyway, since why else would they drag themselves to Walpole for the summer, unless it was to live as another family's charge? But Louisa knew it mattered to Anna.

Better to be called brazen than destitute, she thought, forsaking her bathing cap. She pulled the long steel comb out of her coiled hair, shaking the dark waves free until they hung to her waist, skimming the gray flannel belt of the swimming costume Margaret had lent her. At times like these, Louisa felt quite proud of her ability to rise above the frivolous material trappings of feminine existence. She did not have dresses with lace bodices or bonnets decorated with velvet ribbon; she did not own jewels or cashmere shawls. It simply was not possible in their current circumstances to attire all four girls as well as most young women would have liked. But Louisa knew she had something far more luxurious within reach: a thick stack of paper and ink in the well. In the quiet of the evening she could hold the blotched sheets in her hands and marvel that she had once again captured and set down in words the thoughts and images that careened through her mind. There was something deliciously permanent about those sentences on the page. The world could take an awful lot from her, but it couldn't take those words. As long as she had her ink, her paper, she told herself, she was content with her lot and yearned for nothing.

She stalked to the river, her shoulders back, her head held high. The other girls stood in the river, the water lapping at their waists. The echoing chatter halted as she approached, and Nora, a few tangerine curls poking out along the edge of her swim cap, stared at first Louisa's hair and then down to her bare feet, white and cold, like two stones. Nora pointed a slender finger; the skin on her hands was nearly translucent. "Your feet—" she began.

"It's simply too warm—I just couldn't *bear* to put on my swimming boots," Louisa replied, too loudly. She forced herself to slow her pace, though she longed to rush into the water before anyone else looked too closely at her feet. Anna watched as Louisa's thick hair floated away from her torso where it met the surface of the water, then Anna closed her eyes, willing her mortification down deep in her chest, away from her face where everyone would see it.

A girl with fine black hair like moss and round toad eyes gasped. "Aren't you going to turn up your hair?" she asked in a superior tone. There was one in every group, Louisa reflected, who relished rules and the chance to police those who dare to defy them. It seemed this one had generously volunteered for that task.

Louisa shook her head and shrugged. "I don't mind if it gets wet. I'm Louisa, by the way." This time she didn't offer a handshake.

"I know. I'm Harriet Palmer," the girl said, eyeing Louisa like she might be daft. Harriet stood with her shoulders hunched severely forward, her back curved like a lady's fan. Louisa tried to conjure some compassion for the unfortunate girl but felt only irritation.

An uncomfortable silence fermented as the others looked away and tried to gather the fragments of their interrupted conversations. A sharp whistle came from the top of the hill and they all turned to look.

"Ho, swimmers!"

Joseph Singer waved his arm above his head, descending the hill on his heels, a paper sack wedged between his elbow and ribs. Louisa felt her chest tighten and was glad for the river's cold swell against her torso, glad to turn and face the opposite bank long enough to arrange her face in bemused calm. Turning back she saw Anna's eyebrows climb and a social smile unfold.

Margaret's cheeks were full of color. She whispered to Anna and Louisa as Joseph made his way to the water. "That's Joseph Singer. His father owns the dry goods store on Washington—"

"Yes," Anna cut her off. "He is very charming. We met him last week on our errands. Remember, Louisa?"

"Of course I remember," Louisa replied. "He seemed like quite the dullard to me." She felt instinctive dislike for Joseph as she heard her sister praise him, but she hadn't intended to speak quite so loudly. Joseph stood shaking hands with Nicholas, but his face whipped in the direction of her voice. When he saw Louisa, he broke into a wide grin and waved.

Anna and Margaret whispered in unison: "Louisa!" Nora

and Harriet moved closer and the five girls stood in a cluster, their hands undulating in the river's miniature whirlpools.

Margaret rolled her eyes and continued softly. "The Singers are one of the oldest families in this town. But people are saying the father—"

Splash. Louisa tucked her feet beneath her and plunged her head into the river's murky surface, feeling her scalp tingle as the water spread through her hair. She didn't want to hear Margaret's gossip, didn't want to watch her sister prudently cataloging details about Joseph's suitability as a prospective match. Louisa's own impressions were enough for her. He was skinny and smug, and anyone who married him would have to suffer his company for years to come.

"Good afternoon, ladies," Joseph called to them with a wave. "What a lovely painting you'd make, perched there in the sunshine."

Margaret stopped talking immediately and preened while the other girls giggled, then Nora began chattering about a harvest party her parents were planning. Louisa, standing apart from them, ignored Joseph's attempts at charm and watched a turtle climbing onto the opposite bank.

Joseph joined the other boys a little way down the bank. Louisa peered furtively at him as he walked slowly into the current, his eyes closed against the bright light reflecting off the water. He stopped when the water reached his waist and spread his palms across its surface. Nicholas and Sam stood behind him setting up their fishing poles. Much as Joseph irritated her, Louisa perceived that something made him different from his friends, who fumbled with their tackle boxes and argued the merits of earthworms over grubs.

Joseph seemed to be somewhere apart, absorbing the river's stillness, taking it inside himself.

It was rude and strange to stare and Louisa looked away. She decided it was an opportune moment to exit the water without attracting too much attention and climbed to the bank, sheets of water cascading off the layers of fabric in her swimming costume. She gathered her long hair out to the side of her body, twisting it like a rope to wring out the water, and walked over to where her dry clothes lay folded next to her sister's to fish her comb out of her boot and refasten her chignon. But her hair was too heavy to arrange now, wet up to her ears—if she tried it would give her a headache. She decided to let it dry a little in the sun. She chose a flat rock and sank wearily onto it, her body becoming aware of the fatigue that comes from fighting to stand still in a swift current. She closed her eyes, the late summer heat on her cheeks, and nosed the scent of syrupy mud lumpy with buried frogs, the verdant, mossy side of tree trunks untouched by the sun. This was the smell of *outside*, the smell of endless re-creation, the only place, her father and Mr. Emerson would say, where man can seek to transcend the confines of body and rational mind.

"Hungry?" A cheerful voice pried its way into her reverie.

Louisa opened one eye and squinted. Joseph stood barefoot in the grass, a fragrant pear proffered in his hand. She blinked at him a few times and glanced over at the bank. His fishing rod was lodged between two rocks, bobbing gently with the current.

"Oh," she blurted, struggling to steer her focus back into the present. Seeing him took her by surprise and her thoughts scattered. "Thank you, but that's all right. We brought our own lunch." She gestured to the basket containing hard rolls, deviled eggs, and cake made with the preserves Mr. Emerson had brought for Abba. Louisa noticed the icing had melted and smeared against the newsprint wrapping, and she fumbled with it, trying to tuck the cake under the rolls and out of the sun. Her hands felt clumsy—she realized she was nervous.

"Well, would you like to join me? I'm famished."

She grimaced—imperceptibly, she hoped—and nodded. "Just let me call my sister."

He nodded. "Of course. The more the merrier."

"Nan!" Louisa called out to the covey of girls now perched on the bank, their hems still floating in the water. Nicholas had gone over to them and sat on the bank with his legs outstretched, leaning back on his palms. When Anna saw Louisa and Joseph waving her over, she moved toward the bank. Nicholas offered her his hand and helped pull her to her feet. Louisa felt the ache of conflicting emotions. Once Anna became enmeshed in the world of courting, dances, dressing the part, Louisa felt she'd lose her sister forever. But she knew Anna wasn't happy in the family home, waiting for her life to begin, dreaming of what it was to be in love.

Anna joined them on the rocks, her dress now dry from the waist up, and tucked her strangely fashioned slippers beneath her heavy skirt.

"Mr. Singer has invited us to eat with him." Louisa affected a strained smile. She wondered whether Anna fancied Joseph, whether she should try to prod the two of them toward conversation.

Joseph chortled at her formal tone. "Please," he said. "Call me Joseph. Mr. Singer is my father."

"And how is he, your father?" Anna practiced compassion like an art form. She knew how to apply it with a delicate hand, knew its gradations and nuances, could distinguish its authentic form from imposters like sympathy and voyeurism. It came naturally to her, almost a physical impulse. Louisa had always admired this ability. She felt in comparison like some kind of lumbering boar, unwieldy, slow, low to the ground. She wasn't any better with others' emotions than she was with her own and often felt a thrashing within her she struggled to contain. But Anna was serene.

Joseph smiled gratefully. "How kind of you to ask. He has recovered a great deal in the last few days, is up out of bed, and came to the table for dinner yesterday noon." His lips tightened slightly, a somber quality deepening his voice. "We fear, though, that he'll never fully recover. His lungs were quite weakened with last year's bout of pneumonia. He seems to get ill more frequently. I've taken over most of the work at the store."

"I'm sure he is grateful to have such a dutiful son," Anna said, breaking her square of lemon cake in two and handing him a piece. "Did you tell us that you don't have any brothers?"

Joseph shook his head, fixing a steady gaze on Anna's eyes, her lashes turned down as she brushed crumbs from her lap. Louisa took note of it and felt the twin pangs of vicarious excitement and jealousy, to her dismay.

"I have one sister, Catherine. She is not yet fifteen and most of the time seems even younger than that. I wonder why it is that the expectations are so different for the youngest child in the family." He was thinking aloud and, once he realized what he had said, looked embarrassed at his frankness.

Louisa and Anna grinned at each other. They knew something about this phenomenon. "Your sister Catherine must meet our youngest sister May," Anna said. "I believe they will find they have some things in common."

A breeze rustled the umber fringe of Joseph's hair. He waved his hand as if to brush away his frustration. "Why should I begrudge her her childhood? She could be as serious and straight as an arrow, and it wouldn't change the fact that our father is going to die."

They sat silently for a long moment. Joseph's embarrassment was palpable—he seemed to be wishing for a way to withdraw his words. Up on the road at the top of the hill they heard a carriage pass, the hooves of the horses pounding the dusty path. Louisa was grateful when Anna spoke.

"It must feel at times like a great burden, but it snaps life into focus, does it not? We know we must appreciate all that we have been given. It isn't ours to keep." Even the tone of Anna's voice was a balm.

He nodded in agreement, gazing at a squirrel, its cheeks loaded with food, frozen halfway down the trunk of a nearby tree. "Thank you for your kind words." Joseph noticed the cake, his voice bright once again. "This looks delicious."

Anna seemed amused by how quickly he flitted from the weighty topic of his father's illness to the frivolity of dessert. He was indeed scarcely more than a boy.

"And how are you liking Walpole so far?" he asked. "Are you happy with your new drapes?"

"They aren't finished yet." Anna tucked a now-dry and unruly curl behind her ear. "It seems we've had too many distractions the last few days."

"Is that so? What have you been up to?"

"Well, Margaret has been so nice to take me along when she calls on friends, and Louisa too, *when* she'll agree to come." Anna elbowed Louisa teasingly. "It has been hard to tear her away."

"And what is it that has such a hold on your attention, Miss Louisa?" Joseph inquired, affecting his own formal mode of address, to her chagrin.

Off at the edge of the clearing, where the changing tent stood, Nora and Margaret were wringing out their swimming costumes and refastening their hair, preparing to head home for supper. "Please—call me Louisa. It's probably nothing you'd be interested in," she replied curtly, eager to turn the focus away from herself. *Blast Anna and her loose lips!* she thought.

"Don't be so sure," Joseph replied with a grin. "We dullards can surprise you."

Louisa colored, her pulse beating like a hummingbird in her throat. She couldn't decide if she should apologize for the rude comment he'd overheard, or if that would only draw more attention to it. After a few perilous seconds she managed to croak out, "I've been reading a new collection of poetry. It only just appeared last month."

Joseph swallowed the last bite of the cake, licking the icing from his fingers. "Would this be the work of the indecorous Mr. Whitman?"

Louisa's jaw fell. "How do *you* know about that?"

"Miss Alcott, as I get the distinct impression that you dislike being proven wrong, you'll be disappointed to know that your initial judgment of my character is turning out to be incorrect. I am a ravenous reader and have a cousin in New York who sends me all the new volumes. But how did *you* come by yours?"

"Mr. Emerson is our neighbor—well, *was* our neighbor, when we lived in Concord. He is a close friend of my father's and . . . has taken an interest in my literary education." It wasn't really a lie. Mr. Emerson *had* given her books in the past. Just not this one.

Joseph's eyebrows leapt. "Emerson was your neighbor? How fortunate you are!"

"Louisa is a published author herself," Anna said, reliably eager to bolster her sister. "Perhaps you have heard of *Flower Fables*?"

Joseph shook his head. "I can't say that I have, but nonetheless, how intriguing. Perhaps you will be so kind as to lend me a copy."

"I'm sure I don't have the book here in Walpole," said Louisa, her chin raised. "But perhaps you could secure one at the bookshop in town."

Joseph chuckled. "Protecting your sales numbers, I see. Well, I can hardly blame you for that. Authorship is not a lucrative career. You must make the most of it."

"On the contrary." The late afternoon sun cast long shadows behind them and Louisa paused to check her defensive tone. "My work is going quite well, and I have a few more irons in the fire. I'll be off to Boston soon to get some real writing done." Anna smiled, amused as usual by her sister's stubbornness.

Louisa tried once again to redirect the conversation. "Anna is an avid reader as well. And she also loves the theater."

"Really?" Joseph turned toward Anna and Louisa breathed a silent sigh of relief. "Do you put on plays yourself?"

Anna nodded. "I *adore* the theater. If it weren't for my bad ear, I would have tried to make it on the stage in New York. There's just nothing like it. As a substitute we do like to put on plays for fun. In fact, we were just discussing on the way here that we might like to stage something in Walpole. Do you think the others would be interested?"

"Certainly. You could call it the 'Amateur Dramatic Company of Walpole.' Which play were you thinking of taking on?"

Louisa piped up then, as she hoped to have her say before Margaret tried to take over and boss them into some unbearably frivolous charade. "What about *The Jacobite* by J. R. Planché? That's an old favorite." As she said it she wondered why she should even bother pressing for a particular play. She didn't plan to be around by the time it was performed. "Have you read it?"

Joseph nodded and gave an indifferent shrug.

"You don't share my sister's good opinion of it, I see," Anna said with a grin.

"It's fine. Probably just right for this group. Anyway, you shouldn't consult me. I probably will not be able to participate. The store takes up all of my time these days." He crumpled up the empty newsprint. "Have you ever staged *Hamlet*? It's my favorite play."

"Why, that's Louy's favorite as well. Isn't it, Lou?" Anna and Joseph turned back to her once again. Louisa felt exasperated that the focus of the conversation kept returning to her, and for some reason it rankled her to know Joseph had read all the same books she had.

Joseph surveyed her face and broke into the infuriating grin Louisa was beginning to realize he wielded like a weapon. "I think I've got you figured out, Miss Louisa: the more I impress you, the angrier you get," he said. Anna suppressed a giggle with her slender fingers.

Louisa's jaw ached from clenching it against one of a few

biting replies careening through her mind. She summoned a benevolent smile and a calm tone, reminding herself that the only thing that could trump her pride was her desire to keep from embarrassing her sister in front of this young man she obviously favored.

"Anna, Marmee will be wondering where we are. We should be getting home."

The three of them stood, brushing crumbs from their laps and shaking hands good-bye. Louisa and Anna began up the steep hill, still wearing their mostly dry swimming costumes, as the other boys had folded up the changing tent and taken it with them. Joseph lingered a moment, inspecting the clearing to ensure that nothing had been left behind. He glanced up at the girls, happily chatting with their backs to him, then to the rock where they'd sat to eat their lunches. As Louisa would discover many years later, her comb, adorned with a steel chrysanthemum, lay forgotten by her in the grass. Joseph crouched down and slipped it in his pocket.

"I am angry nearly every day of my life, Jo;

but I have learned not to show it."

—*Little Women*

Chapter Four

When Louisa and Anna arrived back at Yellow Wood, they found Abba in a distressed state. Bronson had spent the day in his study sketching elaborate plans for the garden he'd begun planting. He whistled and plotted space on the paper for corn, asparagus, and beets, with sweet william for decoration. Louisa and Anna exchanged a glance, wondering when he would realize it was too late in the season for planting the vegetables.

Meanwhile, Abba continued the overwhelming task of scrubbing the floors, beating the dust out of the furniture, and airing the rooms. No one could settle in comfortably until these tasks were completed. May, full of resentment that she was too young to have been invited to the swimming party, reluctantly joined Anna and Louisa in coming to Abba's aid. Lizzie was feeling the early signs of a cold and had retired to her room to rest.

As the evening breeze dried the floors, Abba and May hung the woolen carpets out on the line to be beaten, though Louisa suspected it was Abba who did most of the work. May had been blessed with a slender physique and petite shoulders. Anna and Abba would say that her features were simply God's design, but Louisa sometimes wondered if they resulted from a lack of hard work. No matter who did the chores, once the carpets were sufficiently free of dust, someone would have to roll them to be stored in the attic and lay the simple painted oilcloth across the boards until the weather cooled again.

Anna and Louisa began the particularly smelly task of dipping candles. The family's present budgetary constraints put whale oil for lamps out of reach, and candles were the next best thing. Anna heated a kettle of sheep tallow on the stove until the acrid smell of burning fat engulfed the kitchen.

"Did you know," Anna began, stirring the burping sludge with a flat piece of wood reserved for the task, "that the brick house at the corner of River Road and Westminster Street belongs to the Sutton family? The house with the two chimneys?"

Louisa worked a dull knife through the cotton cord, cutting equal lengths for the wicks. "Oh, that house is lovely."

"As a boy, Nicholas's grandfather built it with his father."

"Is that so? How lucky to be a Sutton!"

"Indeed."

Louisa counted the pieces of cord. "Does Marmee want us to make the extra this time, for the charity collection?"

"I think Mrs. Parker organizes it here. I wonder whether Marmee has met her." The last solid hunks of fat had dissolved in the pot.

"I'd better go ask her before we begin." Louisa looked into the parlor but Abba wasn't there. She passed back through the kitchen and down the hall. The door to Bronson's study was open, and she heard the voices of her parents within.

Abba's grew sharp and Louisa froze, a few steps away and out of sight.

"I do not see how working for *bread* implies unworthy gains."

Louisa heard the familiar sound of her father absently shuffling through his papers. He did not like any of them to come into his study when he was working, certainly not to question or criticize him. "Wife, I must be true to this philosophy, no matter what the cost."

Abba responded with an irritated sigh. "Give me one day of practical philosophy. It is worth a century of speculation and discussion."

Bronson's voice was measured. He rarely lost his temper. "I know this is the righteous path."

"What could be righteous about taking food out of the mouths of your own children?"

"I am teaching them that acts of commerce divide man from man, lead to greed and selfishness," he explained, as if he were speaking to a small child. "I am teaching them not to let their bellies lead them through life. When we abstain from physical comforts, inside we are made whole. If I work for pay, I violate my conscience."

"If you don't work, you violate mine."

"And God in his wisdom made the *husband* the head of the household."

It was silent a long moment. Louisa bit her lip in antici- pation of her mother's reply. She had heard her father talk at length on the "woman question," advocating for the rights to vote and be educated the same as men. She had never heard him evoke his supremacy in this way. Perhaps he had shocked Abba into silence.

"It's August," she said. "We always manage in the summer with vegetables and fruit. People here have been very generous indeed. But it is a sin to rely on charity when you can do for yourself—that is *my* philosophy. When winter comes, we will not have enough wood to keep that fire going." Louisa thought of the cherished little coin purse concealed in the lining of her trunk and felt a wave of guilt. How could she let her mother suffer under the burden of this worry when that money from her advance could help the family, at least for a little while? But behind the guilt was despair—how could she let the money go when the dream of her freedom in Boston meant everything in the world?

Louisa heard Bronson clear his throat. "You would have me write to Emerson again, I suppose . . ."

"No—I would have you work enough to feed our family."

"God will provide, if we trust . . ."

Louisa backed quietly down the hall away from Bronson's study. In the past her mother had always deferred to his wisdom on matters of housing and provision. Louisa had never heard her speak so bluntly before, but she was glad Abba was questioning his decisions. After all, it was easy for Bronson to claim allegiance to his philosophy when it was Abba who suffered, Abba who had to quietly ask the neighbor to spare a few eggs, Abba who arranged free housing from a sympathetic relation. Why should they eat potatoes for every meal when they had a healthy father who *could* work but instead sat reading in his study all day?

And yet Louisa knew better than most that it wasn't so simple. She couldn't bear to give up the money that would buy her the freedom to write, just as her father would not consent to set aside his philosophy to work as a clerk in a stifling office. Men in Boston respected her father not only because of his ideas but because of the ways in which he challenged himself and others to go beyond the talking and *live* them. She had heard the story from Mr. Emerson of the previous May, when Bronson proved his allegiance to ideas of equality and compassion. Anthony Burns, a twenty-year-old runaway slave from Virginia, was arrested in Boston and taken to jail. President Pierce was hell-bent on enforcing his pet law, the Fugitive Slave Act, which dictated that northern states must return runaway slaves to the southern states from which they'd escaped, or face federal sanction. Despite the protests of Massachusetts officials, Pierce sent a federal marshal to Boston to retrieve Burns.

Bronson heard of the case and immediately began to organize a group of abolitionists to free Anthony Burns. Bronson led the mob to the jailhouse steps. They broke down the door and forced their way in, but the sheriff and his men fought them back out into the street.

Bronson looked at the defeated crowd and said, "Why are we not within?"

He then ascended another staircase alone, unarmed. Even when pistol shots could be heard within, he stood firm before the massive oak doors. Though there was nothing the men could do to stop the captured slave's prosecution, Bronson proved that night that he was a man of more than just words. When the case was lost, the president sent two thousand troops to ensure that Burns was returned to slavery in Virginia. They lined the path to the courthouse with their bayonets drawn. Louisa would never forget the scene—the windows of Boston draped with black crepe in silent protest, as she stood in the early summer heat holding her mother's hand. Burns was led to his ship in shackles. It surprised her to see that Burns was just a boy, his eyes wide with fear, his cheeks smooth, save for the deep scar of his master's branding. Bronson watched the scene with his jaw clenched tight, his anger barely contained. For the next twenty-four hours he did not speak, except when the family gathered for a solemn supper of cold vegetables and hard rolls.

"Lord, bless this food to our use and us to Thy service," Bronson murmured, his voice near breaking. "And make us ever mindful to the needs of others. Amen."

Anna looked up, annoyed, when Louisa came back to the kitchen. "Well, that took long enough. What does she say?"

Louisa knew her mother would tell them to make the extra candles—she always gave to charity, even when they had nothing to spare. But they would need every penny this winter, and someone—Louisa perhaps—had to be the voice of reason. "She says we do not need to make the extras. Mrs. Parker received a large donation just last month."

"Well, that's a blessing," Anna said. "I can scarcely stand this smelly job long enough to make the candles *we* need." She turned back to the stove and began stirring again. "So, as I was going to say before, despite having this wonderful house of his grandfather's, Nicholas is building his own."

"Ah, to be a man," Louisa said wistfully. "To be able to say, 'I would like a house,' and simply begin to build it."

"Well, he won't be able to do it *all* on his own. Samuel and Joseph are helping him with the construction."

Joseph sprang into her mind like a bird roused from a bush. She remembered how he had stalked to the river's edge but entered the water almost reverently, walking in up to his waist, smoothing his palms in two arcs over its surface. She recalled a line of Mr. Whitman's. *As he swims through the salt transparent greenshine . . .*

"It is just down the lane from the first. They started on it back in the spring. It sounds like they're a little crowded over at the elder Mr. Sutton's, now that Nora is back home for good, probably. That poor girl." Anna held the center of the length of wick and dipped the two ends into the tallow, pausing a moment and pulling them back out. She waited for the tallow to harden, then plunged them back into the kettle. "Did you know she was meant to be married to a man from New York City?"

Louisa shook her head absently.

"Anyway, Nicholas told me about the house today at the party. Don't you think that's interesting?"

Anna draped the finished candle over the wooden rack to dry and put out her hand to take the next wick. Louisa stared out the window over the sink, thinking of the saturated folds of Joseph's shirt . . . *lies on his back and rolls silently with the heave of the water.*

"Louy?" Anna touched her arm. "Did you hear me?"

Louisa shook off the reverie. Why on earth was her mind floating off this way? Perhaps there was such a thing as too much poetry. It was making a mess of her thoughts. "I'm sorry, Anna. Yes, I did hear you. Building his own house. Joseph must be so pleased."

"Joseph? Louisa, I don't think you *are* listening to me. I was talking about Nicholas Sutton, not Joseph."

"Of course—Nicholas. That's what I meant to say. I'm sorry, Nan. I think I had too much sun today."

Anna looked curiously at her. "I think it's *who* was sitting near you in the sun that's got you out of sorts," she simpered. "Miss Lou, I think you have a little crush."

Louisa gave her a scandalized stare. "I don't know to *what* or *whom* you are referring, but if it has anything to do with Joseph Singer, you can leave off right there. Even if we were the last two left on earth, I'd still remain a happy spinster."

Anna rolled her eyes. "This is all part of it, you know—the defensiveness, insulting him, telling me how he is the *last* man on earth you'd consider. Come now—I know you have read more romances than I."

Louisa shook her head. "Anna, I assure you that Joseph Singer is too much in love with himself to begin to dream of loving anyone else. And if he ever did, I should take pity on the object of his affections. This short life would be unendurably long with him by your side."

Anna gave her a skeptical glance, then turned her attention back to the bubbling tallow. She wiped a film of sweat from her forehead. Both of them had grown pale from the smell of the burning fat. "You may be in for trouble, then. He seemed quite taken with you."

"Nonsense—have you not noticed that he talks that way to every young lady who crosses his path? Don't put any stock in it—your sister is safe with you at home, and at home I will *stay*."

"Love will change you," Anna said.

Louisa shook her head. "Perhaps you, my dear. But not me. For me it is a disease I am lucky not to catch."

She believed what she said, but Anna's comment needled its way into her mind. Louisa felt a fluttering in her ribs like the pages of a book fanning out in a breeze, a sensation that something was beginning that she wouldn't be able to stop. She rushed to divert the conversation.

"And now to more important matters. When shall we begin rehearsing the play?"

When the candles hung drying and the supper dishes were washed, Louisa and Anna joined Bronson, Abba, Lizzie, and May in the small parlor off the kitchen. Bronson held his Bible open on his lap—he often read passages to them in the evening and asked for his daughters' thoughts on the quandaries of Christian theology. Louisa plucked at the front of her dress a few times to cool her damp underarms. The heat from the kitchen had been stifling, and the small parlor window let in only a hint of a breeze.

"My daughters," Bronson began, his high forehead gleaming in the light of a candle, "what have you written today about our journey?" Abba turned expectantly to them, her face revealing a bit of sympathy. When would they have had time to write on this of all days? But Bronson believed in the importance of self-discipline above everything else, and he often asked to read his daughters' reflections to ensure they were adhering to the routine of writing each day.

And in truth, this chore seemed small in comparison to what he had asked them to do in the past in the service of his philosophical searching. Years back, Bronson had dragged his wife and daughters into an experiment in communal living. He envisioned building a new Eden, where his natural family and new chosen family, Abba and the girls as well as other like-minded people, could live according to Transcendental ideals. As pioneers, they would abstain from commerce of any kind and spare animals the enslavement he believed they suffered. This meant no meat or milk or eggs, no leather, wax, or manure. No ox would work the plow, and Bronson forbade the planting of root vegetables for fear they would upset the worms in the soil. Though he spent a great deal of time searching for just the right site and participants, Bronson failed to plan for the practical aspects of such a harsh life. When the group was established at Fruitlands, a rocky farm fifteen miles from Concord, it became clear that keeping the children warm and free from hunger would be Abba's burden. Several months into the experiment, as the winter descended, Bronson had to accept that the experiment had failed. Around Christmas, the Alcotts moved back to Concord.

Devastated, Bronson began to contemplate the idea of setting himself free from his family obligations. He was interested in the ideas of free love, a philosophy that cast doubt on whether traditional marriage could or should be sustained. True to form, rather than leave in the night or hold a private conversation with his wife on the matter, Bronson called a family meeting to discuss whether the family should split up. Anna was only thirteen, Louisa twelve, Lizzie only eight, and May just a toddler. In the end he hadn't left, though the knowledge that he had even considered it was a betrayal from which the Alcott women never quite recovered.

After surviving this difficult chapter, keeping a journal now hardly seemed like something to complain about. Bronson began with May, whom they all freely admitted was already more beautiful than her three older sisters combined. Unlike the others', her tawny hair held a natural curl, and she tied it back from her face with a ribbon.

"May writes about a woman in our train car on the

journey here," he said, skimming over the pages. "She wore fine lace that 'must have been from France' and carried a basket covered with a cloth. May wondered what delicious treasures might have been inside."

Bronson smiled tolerantly at his youngest daughter. His full gray hair and wiry brows gave him a stern appearance, but his blue eyes softened his face. "You have an artist's eye for detail, my dear, but your words reveal a covetous nature. Remember that fine things make us their prisoner. It is in having nothing that true freedom can be found, freedom as *we* are blessed to experience it."

May nodded, her blue eyes far away and a sweet smile on her lips that Louisa knew meant his warnings passed out of her head the moment they were issued. Louisa herself felt amused by her father's claim that the hunger they had experienced on the train, the hunger that still rumbled unsated in their bellies, represented freedom.

Bronson turned his attention to Lizzie, who rested her cheek on Abba's shoulder. She stifled a small yawn as she sat upright and tucked a wisp of her fine hair back into its plain bun. Lizzie moved to retrieve her journal from the table but Abba clutched at her elbow.

"Rest, child. You've had plenty of exertion for today."

"But Marmee, I've written something as well. Shouldn't I read along with my sisters?" Louisa often had to remind herself that her younger sister was a woman of twenty. Lizzie still had the voice and mien of a much younger girl.

Bronson hesitated a moment as if he were weighing the risk of taxing his soft-spoken daughter against enabling any self-indulgence. Abba spoke before his mind was settled.

"No, little bird. Your sisters are strong and healthy, but

your burden is a weaker constitution. We must at all times be cautious."

"But Marmee," Lizzie said, touching her forehead to prove she did not have a fever. "I'm well."

"It may seem so, but you've only just recovered from that dreadful spring cough. Please—rest."

Lizzie looked at Bronson and he nodded, giving her a gentle smile Louisa rarely saw. Lizzie seemed to think it over a moment longer and relented. "Perhaps tomorrow, then," she said.

"You can read mine now, Father." Anna handed over her journal and sat back with her hands folded on her lap. They were white and fine like two little doves.

Bronson glanced over her pages, his eyes full of pride. "Anna writes that she was sad to leave Pinckney Street but eager for the challenge of a new town. 'Hard work,' she says, 'is God's design for our bodies and minds, and we must not question His will.' She is grateful for the new embroidery needles from Mrs. Emerson and longs to put them to use in readying the new home."

Anna beamed as she saw she had won his coveted approval once more. It was among these sisters nearly as important as water or oxygen.

Bronson looked in turn at each of his daughters. "I wish we were all as diffident and unpretending as this sister of yours."

Louisa nodded with a clenched jaw and thought about how her father had approached child-rearing like a scientific study. He collected evidence, keeping written observations of his subjects and, as the girls grew, reviewing their own journals. And like any scientist worth his salt, Bronson formed theories and then constructed experiments to test their veracity. One of Louisa's earliest memories was of such a test, designed to assess his young daughters' moral fortitude.

Bronson sat five-year-old Anna and four-year-old Louisa in two chairs in his study that faced his desk, on which he placed a polished apple. He glanced deliberately at the fruit to ensure the girls had noticed it, then addressed Anna. "Anna, should little girls take things that do not belong to them, things they might like to eat or drink?"

Anna's face grew solemn. "No, Father, they should not."

He nodded and turned to Louisa. "And you, little one—would you do such a thing?" Louisa shook her head.

"Very good," Bronson said, then crossed the room toward the door. "Now I must go fetch some wood for the fire. I shall return in a moment. Please keep your seats—and remember what you said."

"Yes, Father," the girls replied in unison. Bronson closed the door softly behind him and Anna and Louisa were alone with the beguiling fruit. When he returned with an armload of cedar the girls remained in their places, but the apple had been reduced to a spindly core.

Bronson pressed his lips into a line, more intellectually intrigued than angry. He pointed at the apple core. "What is this?"

Louisa's legs were too short to reach the floor and they swung beneath the seat of her chair. "Apple," she said.

"Well," Anna added, her linguistic abilities slightly more developed, "it *was* an apple."

Bronson nodded. "And what happened to it?"

Louisa looked blankly at her father. Anna spoke up. "Louisa took it. I told her she must not, but she did. And then I took a little bite but I knew I was naughty. So I threw it on the floor, but *Louisa*," she said, pointing her finger at her sister, "*Louisa* picked it up and ate the rest."

"Is this true?" Bronson questioned his younger child. Louisa nodded. The notion of telling a lie to cover her misdeeds had not occurred to her.

"I was naughty, wasn't I, Father?" Anna asked, twisting her fingers together. "I *stole*, didn't I? Will you punish me for it?"

Bronson thought a moment. "I will answer your question with a question of my own, something I am anxious to know. Did you think you were doing right when you took a bite?"

Anna shook her head. "No, my conscience told me I was not."

"And next time you will obey that precious voice inside, instead of ignoring it?"

"Yes, Father. I think I shall."

"Then I shall not punish you." He sat down in the wide armchair behind his desk and motioned with his index finger for Louisa to approach. She hopped down and toddled around to him, the back of her dress caught up in her lace-edged pantalettes. Bronson pulled Louisa onto his lap. "And what about you, my little hoyden? Why did you take the apple before Father said you could?"

Louisa looked up at her father, surprised by his question. "Because I wanted it."

Bronson had learned much from his experiment that held true as his daughters grew, and he never declined an opportunity to remind Louisa of how she differed from her older sister. And he was right—Anna was skilled in the womanly art of self-sacrifice. For as long as she could remember, Louisa had prayed for God to change her into someone more like Anna: a reasonable girl ruled by her intellect and sentiment rather than her passion. Anna had never despaired that she had been born a girl. Perhaps it helped that she was beautiful. Louisa wanted with all her heart to be good like Anna, but she knew she wasn't.

Bronson turned to Louisa. "And last, my little hoyden. What have you written today, Louisa?"

Louisa felt a grim smile stretch across her face. Indeed, how little had changed! She handed over the journal, its pages mashed together with the haste that indicates a disorganized mind. A disintegrating black-eyed Susan, pressed between the pages since the previous summer, fell out on the floor. Bronson took no notice—he had scolded her on her untidy habits many times. He opened to the place she had marked with her thumb, then turned the page forward and back again, drawing his eyebrows together like two dark curtains. "Louisa has written only two sentences: complaints about doing her share of the work and the size of this home we're lucky to have at all."

Bronson pressed his lips into a taut line. "While the rest of us feel gratitude for our good fortune, Louisa finds fault in her new surroundings." He turned to her. "Do you agree that you have indulged in self-pity?"

Louisa looked down at her lap and nodded, shame burning along the edges of her ears.

"Father," Anna said. "I think what Louisa was *trying* to say is that though she will have to adjust to a new place, she intends to hold herself to a high standard and keep accomplishing her work, even if it is difficult." She glanced at Louisa, tilting her head tenderly.

"Loyalty is a lovely trait in a sister, but it will not help her improve." He turned to Louisa once more. "Do you know why I ask the four of you to write?" He waited until their eyes all blinked expectantly at him, save Lizzie's, which were now drawn in sleep. "The evils of life are not so much social and political as personal, and so we must work toward personal reform. Through writing we reveal what is in our minds. If goodness and selflessness be there, the words will show it. If evil lurks, the words reveal it, and all the better, for we must root it out and improve. Always, always work to improve, my girls." He closed his Bible and rose, indicating that the evening was ending and in a moment all would go to bed. "It is the very reason we're alive."

He shuffled toward his study to begin the work that would keep him awake long into the night while the women slept. Abba kissed each of her girls good night. She was a plump woman with a round face, and her daughters resembled her. When she embraced Louisa, she held her an extra moment and whispered, "You are full of promise and vitality, my darling. Do not let his words discourage you. Bear up under them and resolve to be the best of who you are." She kissed her daughter's temple and sent her off toward bed.

"Is this the stage? How dusty and dull it is by daylight!" said Christie next day, as she stood by Lucy on the very spot where she had seen Hamlet die in great anguish two nights before.

—*Work: A Story of Experience*

Chapter Five

Despite Louisa's reluctance to commit to another project that would keep her away from Boston, Anna's enthusiasm prevailed and the Walpole Amateur Dramatic Company assembled a few days later for its first rehearsal. Mrs. Ferguson, keeper of the Elmwood Inn on Washington Square, offered her attic to the company in exchange for free tickets, acknowledgment in the program, and a promise that her son Paul could have a role in the performance.

The Elmwood was a Georgian beauty built in 1762, and the grand old home towered above the neighboring buildings with three full stories and two massive chimneys. The attic proved to be the perfect spot for rehearsals. It formed one open room, spanning the length of the house, and was sparsely furnished with a few chairs, a long table, and decaying velvet drapery. The six dormers, three on either side, let in plenty of light, and there was no chance of anyone peeping in at the clumsy first steps the actors would take as they worked to refine their performances.

Nora had refused to come, saying she couldn't shake the feeling that they would be laughed at. The others waved off this assertion with slight nervousness. Nicholas and Samuel extracted a commitment from Joseph on the grounds that if they had to be there, he did too. That first day, Louisa, Anna, May, along with Margaret, Harriet, the boys, and Paul Ferguson, climbed the creaking stairs to the attic.

Though Louisa dreaded getting caught up in a lengthy project, she also couldn't bear to take direction from a Walpolean who couldn't possibly know as much as she did about the theater. So as she usually did, she took charge and appointed herself director. She brought the group to order with a few claps of her hands. "Thank you for coming. I know with hard work and dedication we will put on an excellent performance. I thought we could try *The Jacobite*. How many have read it?"

A few hands went up, including Joseph's. Margaret pursed her lips. "I thought we might do something Greek."

Louisa groaned. She supposed no one could mount a successful argument against the classics, but she felt Planché's light comedy would have a wider appeal. "My sisters and I have done those tragedies dozens of times. They're so *sober*. I thought it might be a lark to do something new. Something modern and comical." Louisa handed her the play. "Just read it over—you'll see."

They waited while Margaret scanned the first scene. Samuel shifted his weight from one foot to another. May patted the curls along her forehead to ensure they were in place. Harriet scoffed, annoyed at the delay, and sat down in a chair that scarcely creaked under her paltry weight.

Margaret giggled over a line, then flipped the page closed. "You're right, Louisa. This *is* quite amusing. Let's try it." She stepped toward the center of the room. "So, who will assign the parts?"

Joseph could see vexation rising in Louisa's face and broke in to stop Margaret from running roughshod over the enterprise. "Louisa knows the story better than anyone else," Joseph said.

"Well, I suppose that's true," said Margaret, unconvinced. She stepped back. Louisa reclaimed the reins.

She flipped to the first page. "There are three male and three female parts," Louisa said. "Let's see . . . Lady Somerford. She is the gentlewoman caught up in an affair."

"Louy, please don't give me a part. I want to be the prompter," May said.

Louisa and Anna turned to their youngest sister in surprise.

May giggled, embarrassed. "I know your thoughts—it's rare indeed that I would pass up the chance to be the center of attention. But this way if Lizzie feels well enough to come, we can work together."

Anna kissed May on the cheek. "What a kind little sister I have."

Louisa nodded her approval. "Speaking of roles offstage, we're going to need someone to work on the sets." She looked over at Paul Ferguson, who hovered at the back of the group. He looked mortified when all the eyes in the room turned in his direction. "Paul, I happen to know that you are quite the artist yourself. Your mother told me those paintings in the parlor are yours."

Paul looked down at his shoes and nodded.

"Would you be willing to design and build some sets for us?"

"It would be my pleasure," he mumbled, his voice scarcely above a whisper. "But perhaps—d-do you know Alfie Howland?"

May's eyebrows went up. "The painter? Yes! I *worship* his work."

"He was born in Wa . . . Walpole. Comes here for the summers, though he lives in Boston now." He took a long breath, as if getting through the last sentence without his stutter had winded him. "Maybe we could ask him to help."

"Oh, that would be a dream," said May with her hands clutched at her breast.

Paul gave her a shy smile. "I'll see what I can do."

"Thank you, Paul," said Louisa. "Now, then—back to Lady Somerford . . ."

"I'll take that part," Harriet said. "I don't really *want* to be in the play at all. But I suppose I could play a noble-woman. Provided the costume is something rather fine."

Louisa blinked at Harriet and contemplated spontane-ously adding a new role to the play: irritating girl who looks like a toad. Instead she decided to ignore Harriet for the moment. "Lady Somerford is engaged to be married to Sir Richard. Samuel, perhaps you could play that role?"

"My pleasure, Miss Louisa," he said, anxious to be agreeable.

"Samuel, please call me Louisa." He nodded.

"I wonder," Margaret piped up, "if it might not be bet-ter that *I* play Lady Somerford." Harriet began to pout. Her hunched shoulders and sallow complexion made her seem like a deflated example of womanhood next to Margaret, who was pure fleshy vivacity. Margaret turned to her with mock solicitude. "Harriet, dear, it's *only* that, as you know, I have *been* to London—my grandmother was British—and, well, perhaps I can render the upper-class accent a bit more . . . authentically. It's not *your* fault that you haven't traveled."

Harriet pursed her lips and thought a moment. She knew

better than to challenge Margaret. "Well, what other female parts are left?"

Louisa glanced at the list. "The Widow Pottle. She owns the tavern. And her daughter Patty."

"No. I don't like the sound of either of those," Harriet said.

"Harriet," May said. "Why don't you help with the prompting? We have to copy out the parts for all the characters and whisper their lines to them if they forget." Harriet nodded reluctantly and went to stand by May.

"Very well," Louisa said. "Margaret will play Lady Somerford. As I said, she is engaged to be married to Sir Richard—that's Samuel," Louisa said, caught up in making her notes on the page, unaware that this statement caused both Samuel and Margaret to blush. "But Sir Richard is cruel to her and she doesn't love him. Secretly, Major Murray is the *true* object of her affections."

Margaret's face fell—she wanted *Samuel* to play the true object of her affections. Louisa looked up at the remaining young men. "Nicholas," she said, "perhaps you could play the Major?"

Margaret broke in. "Louisa, I don't mean to *insert* myself where I'm not needed . . ."

"Certainly not," Louisa said with a sarcasm Margaret ignored.

". . . but doesn't it say here that the Major is a 'tall, fair man'?"

Louisa looked back at the description, exasperated. "Yes. Indeed, it does."

"Well," Margaret said. "Perhaps, then, would it not be better if Samuel played the role of the Major? After all, he is a head taller than both Nicholas and Joseph."

Louisa looked at Samuel. He nodded, smirking at Joseph

and Nicholas. "It is true that I am *far* taller than either of my friends."

"Not very bright, though," Joseph shot back with a grin. "Without a doubt, you have the feeblest intellect of the three of us."

"Why don't *you* take Sir Richard, you lout?" Samuel said, chuckling. "Miss Louisa, didn't you say he is the villain?"

Louisa nodded, ignoring the formal mode of address he seemed unable to abandon. She turned to Joseph. "You don't mind?"

He shook his head. "Mind a role that asks me to thwart the intentions of Mr. Parker? I believe I was born to play it!"

Louisa rolled her eyes. "Well, now that we finally have *that* settled . . . Anna, will you play Patty Pottle?" Anna nodded. "Oh, thank goodness. And I will take the role of the foulmouthed widow—I suppose no one will argue with me about that." Joseph smiled. "And that just leaves . . . John Duck. Nicholas, you're left. Would you mind?"

"Not at all, Louisa."

"Right then. Let's read through the first scene. I have only two copies here. So until May and Harriet finish the rest, we'll have to pass it back and forth. Will you set up the scene for us, May?" Louisa asked, handing her the play.

May nodded. "This scene takes place in the parlor of a public house or roadside inn called the Crooked Billet. Patty and Lady Somerford enter first." May handed the script to Anna. She and Margaret stepped forward. Margaret assumed the posture she imagined to be a staple of the genteel class, though Louisa observed that she looked rather like she'd injured her neck.

Patty Pottle spoke first. *"It's all safe, my lady. There's nobody down here, and mother and John are down in the cellar bottling cider."* Anna passed the script to Margaret.

"Then tell me quickly. Did you put the note where I told you?"

"No, my lady."

"No!"

"Pray forgive me, my lady; but I couldn't help it. It was all along of John Duck."

"John Duck?"

"Yes, my lady, our man—he—he—would try to . . ." Anna stared at the page, blinking furiously. Nicholas examined the skin around his thumb. Anna rushed quietly through the remainder of the line. *". . . kiss me, my lady . . . and I ran away and he ran after me, and somehow or another, I lost it, my lady."*

"Anna—" Louisa broke in, oblivious, as usual, to subtexts of any sort, particularly those of the romantic variety. She took her role as director very seriously. "You must speak up."

Anna nodded, her cheeks flushed. Louisa noticed their color, and, as she glanced at Nicholas, it dawned on her why her sister was losing her nerve. "Cast, let me explain a little more about what is happening in this scene," she said, turning the attention away from the skittish pair for a moment. "Lady Somerford is fretting over this lost note. Sir Richard is a possessive and powerful man"—Joseph straightened his shoulders and tipped his chin in the air—"and he already suspects the Lady's love is not true. The lost note was meant to reach Major Murray and urge him come to the Crooked Billet at eight o'clock so the lovers might safely meet. But Lady Somerford fears that if Sir Richard happens upon the note, it will confirm his suspicions."

"And he intends to challenge the Major to a duel if he finds out about the affair?" Margaret asked.

Louisa shook her head. "It's not only her secret affair that she means to protect. The Major is an accused Jacobite. Only Sir Richard can pardon him and spare his life, but he'd speed the Major to the executioner if he had an atom of proof that the Lady loves him."

May shimmied with excitement. "This sounds *very* romantic!"

Nicholas cleared his throat, summoning his nerve. "May I ask you to summarize the plot surrounding John Duck and Patty?" Anna appeared to chomp down on the insides of her cheeks.

"Well, John works for Patty's mother, helping out around the inn since her husband died. John is in love with Patty"— Margaret gave Anna's forearm a furtive pat—"but because he hasn't any money, her mother won't let her marry him. So Patty won't own that she loves him and he makes a fool of himself again and again to win her affections. Soon, the widow—that's me—agrees to consider the marriage *if* John can come up with a sum of one hundred pounds. The widow believes, of course, that it will be an impossible task and Patty will be rid of him forever."

May gave a little gasp. "Does he get the money? Does he win her in the end?"

"We shall see," said Louisa, who was fond of a little suspense. As she was drawn in to rehearsing the first scene, long moments passed in which she could scarcely hear the incessant voice in her head urging her toward Boston and freedom.

There is no fairy-book half so wonderful as the lovely

world all about us, if we only know how to read it.

—"Morning-Glories"

Chapter Six

The following Saturday afternoon, Louisa sat at a narrow table in the sweltering attic room she shared with Anna. Bronson had gone to the village store, apparently poised to withstand the endless pontification of the locals if they would let him sit all day without buying anything. The Alcott women had been invited to lunch with Eliza Wells, Abba's niece, who was the object of much sympathy amongst the town's women. It was well known that Eliza's father was partial to drink, and between his episodes and her husband's ragged temper, she was rarely able to leave the house. Abba urged the girls to come along and try to cheer her, but Louisa was always keen to get an afternoon to herself—no interruptions, no guilt for reading while the others dutifully washed and sewed and baked—and so she asked to stay behind. They didn't mind granting her request. It was a relief sometimes to leave their moody, pensive sister behind with her thoughts and conduct their social lives in peace.

Once a week the stores in town stocked the newspapers from New York, and occasionally Bronson brought them home. Louisa had the previous week's edition of the *New York*

Daily-Times spread open on the tabletop. She skimmed the page for notices about *Leaves of Grass,* but this edition carried no news of the book. Despite herself, she loved to read about the outrageous crimes of passion sometimes reported—a woman in a jealous rage confronts her husband's mistress and they both end up dead; a man kidnaps his child to save her from spending her childhood with a heartless mother. As she searched for the scandalous details, an article caught her eye.

> Mrs. Butler, or Miss Fanny Kemble, as she prefers to be known since her much-publicized divorce, gave three of her lauded readings of *Othello* this week at the Stuyvesant Institution on Broadway to a room of six or seven hundred persons. The audience members flocked to the space two or three hours before the time of the lady's appearance to procure seats and sat in tedious anticipation, the delicate women displaying their rich taffeta or shot silk dresses and intricate lace gloves while their grave gentlemen companions filled their pipes and reclined in the hard wooden chairs as they waited. They were compensated for this long wait by the performance Miss Kemble calls a "labor of love." And she is well-compensated for her efforts. Shakespeare never earned as much for writing his plays as Miss Kemble does for reading them.

Louisa leaned back in her chair and closed her eyes, imagining herself sitting in the front row of that crowded room on Broadway. Like everyone else in America—and England, for that matter—the Alcotts had followed the story of Fanny Kemble's divorce and emancipation, which unfolded throughout Louisa's teenage years.

The Kemble family had dominated the British stage for generations. Fanny's mother, father, aunt, and uncle built livelihoods and fame on Shakespeare's plays, and when her father's share in the Royal Opera House at Covent Garden looked like it might be in danger, he thrust his twenty-year-old daughter onto the stage. From then on she bounced back and forth between London and New York, living in a hotel with her parents while she was performing away from home. It was well known that Fanny found America to be a little less refined than her native country, though she loved to ride her horse along the Hudson River north out of New York City. An incident at the Park Theater amused her American fans, who liked to see British visitors' delicate sensibilities challenged by what the Brits still thought of as the frontier. During a quiet soliloquy, a rat emerged from a hole in the stage floor and scampered through the orchestra pit, eliciting quite a scream from poor Fanny.

Fanny's romantic life caused great speculation amongst Louisa and her sisters. She had many admirers, but one in particular finally convinced her that becoming his wife offered more happiness than a life on the stage. Pierce Butler was the son of wealthy landowners who lived in Philadelphia, and the grandson of one of the founding fathers, his namesake. After they married, Pierce inherited his family's sea-island cotton and rice plantations in Georgia, and he took Fanny there to live. To the satisfaction of New England abolitionists like Bronson, Fanny was appalled when she saw firsthand the conditions under which the slaves lived and suffered. She found in her conscience that she was opposed to slavery and began to write about her beliefs.

The drama continued to fill the papers when she publicly

implored her husband to consider the morality of enslaving fellow human beings, but he refused to be swayed and began to regret having married a woman with so fiery a personality. She agitated the situation further by writing an anti-slavery treatise with descriptions of what she had witnessed on the plantation. Pierce resented her insolence and forbade her to publish it. Eventually, she left the plantation for England to return to the stage, leaving her daughters behind with their father. It was this final act of independence that prompted Pierce to file for divorce. Louisa never forgot the press statement Pierce made, in which he explained that the relationship had failed because of Fanny's peculiar view that marriage should be "companionship on equal terms."

What Louisa really admired was Fanny's determination to go on after the marriage dissolved. She worked and traveled, she made her own money, and she lived her life independently, on her own terms. To Louisa, Fanny's view of marriage was not brazen and shocking but simply logical— not to mention the only guiding philosophy under which both parties could expect to find happiness. But rather than encourage Louisa to look for a husband with enlightened views, Fanny's experience seemed to prove the impossibility of equality in marriage.

A sweating glass of cold tea sat beside the newspaper and Louisa's open journal on the table. She always kept a stack of paper and an inkwell nearby just in case a lightning bolt of a thought struck. It was known to happen, and then she'd be off again into her vortex, where she could work without stopping for days on end, to the point of total exhaustion.

The fantasy of imagined characters and events gave her a kind of temporary euphoria. She couldn't choose when to enter that furious state, so she had to be ready to seize it when it flashed by, like a runaway carriage headed for the Commons.

She took up *Leaves of Grass* once again, though she knew soon she would have to slip it back onto her father's desk or risk being caught with it and having to explain. The room was sweltering and the pages clung to her damp fingertips. She had read the volume straight through once and had begun again that morning. Now she reached the end of the first poem: *Failing to fetch me at first keep encouraged, / Missing me one place search another, / I stop somewhere waiting for you.*

Suddenly she heard a soft tapping on the first-floor window. She had every intention of pretending not to hear, so she rose and moved carefully toward the window, shifting the new drapery to the side ever so slightly. It was Joseph Singer.

Louisa froze, her hand still on the fabric. Should she answer the door? No one else was home, and surely he wanted to see Anna. Just as she'd resolved to slink back to her desk and wait for him to go away, he looked up and grinned at her figure in the window.

She reluctantly descended the stairs, drawing her sleeve across her damp forehead before opening the door.

"Good afternoon, Miss Louisa."

"Hello, Joseph. We weren't expecting you."

"I hope you don't mind."

She clutched the door with both hands, willing her nerves away from her tongue and into her fingers. "Oh, of course not. But everyone is out. Anna is with my mother and sisters at our cousin's for lunch. I know she will be disappointed that she missed your visit."

Joseph smiled, amused by how flustered she was. "It's always a pleasure to see your sister, and I hope you'll tell her I said so. But I didn't come to see Anna. I came to see you."

Louisa processed this information through her sluggish brain. Perhaps he was coming to inquire after her sister's feelings. Should she tell him that Anna seemed to favor Nicholas Sutton, at least for the moment?

"Would it be all right if I came inside? I'm likely to melt out here."

"Of course! Oh, forgive me," she said, throwing open the door. "Please, come in."

The skin of his temples was pink and his eyes were bright. The heat from outside wafted in after him. Louisa tried to think of what she was supposed to do next.

"If you don't mind," Joseph began, "I would love something cold to drink."

"Of course!" Louisa knew she was going to have to calm down if she had any hope of carrying on a conversation with him. She felt at any moment she might take wing and crash right through the glass of the front window. *What has come over me?* she thought, angry at herself. Over the years she'd received plenty of her father's friends, and Abba had trained her well on the duties of a hostess. Perhaps she had felt shy in the presence of some of these men, like Mr. Emerson, who seemed to her like royalty. But never before had she found herself so . . . *flustered* by anyone.

She handed him the cold tea and they sat down on opposite ends of the horsehair sofa. His cheeky self-assurance seemed to have dissolved. He drank a few nervous sips and they sat in silence.

Joseph cleared his throat. "Do I remember your saying

you will be leaving for Boston soon? We'll all be awfully sorry to see you go."

Louisa sat up straighter, folding her hands in her lap. "Yes, that's right. Probably just another few weeks and I'll be on my way."

"And you'll go . . . all on your own?"

She disliked his tone; it seemed to question her willingness or determination to follow through with her plan. "Yes, alone. Freedom and independence—that is my aim. Nothing else means anything to me."

He clamped his lips closed and nodded, chastened. She checked the pride in her voice and decided to change the subject. Louisa had watched Anna fill awkward social pauses with tidbits of gossip. "My mother told me this morning that Samuel Parker has proposed to our friend Margaret and she has accepted," she said.

Joseph brightened. "Ah, that's wonderful news! You know that whole swimming party was an elaborate ruse designed to give him an afternoon with her. I don't mind admitting I was a coconspirator. All for a good cause, I can now say."

Louisa grinned. She loved a good conspiracy. "Samuel's parents must be happy about the match?"

Joseph hesitated. "Yes, I believe they are. Mr. Parker is, anyway. Mrs. Parker—well, she can be a tough one to please, especially when it comes to convincing her a young lady is good enough for her son. But I won't say a thing against her—she has been like a mother to me since my own died."

Louisa pressed her lips together. "Well, that is wonderful to hear, though I'm sorry to know about your mother." Her curiosity prompted her to ask more, but she refrained.

Joseph shrugged. "Thank you—it was a long time ago.

But my father and sister and I were blessed to have Mrs. Parker. When Mother died, we moved to the apartment above the store so Father could keep an eye on us while he was working. We were quite small then. And Samuel's mother brought us our dinner each afternoon. I don't know how she did it, but my father was grateful. And Mother too, I'm sure." He trailed off. "But happy news should be our focus. And Samuel is the happiest of all today, I think."

"I'm sure he will make a devoted husband. Our friend deserves only the best." Something gave a quarter turn in Louisa's belly as she thought of Anna and their talk on the walk home from the store. "But it's all so soon, don't you think? It seems only last summer we were all romping around together and having larks," she thought, but found she had said out loud.

"I don't know. I don't think age has anything to do with it. Of course, it is a serious endeavor, and one must treat it as such. But more years don't necessarily better prepare one, I imagine."

"I suppose we never know what life is going to send our way."

Joseph considered her remark. "Some people just seem to know what they want and go after it full steam ahead."

She nodded, thinking that not every woman was so free to pursue what she wanted, if her object went against convention. An awkward moment passed.

Joseph reached for his pocket and pulled out the thin volume. "Since we talked about these poems the other day at the party, I cannot stop rereading them. They really are remarkable."

Louisa cheered a bit. Here was something she could

speak freely about; here was a subject that had nothing to do with her.

"I wonder, what do you think of his punctuation?" Joseph flipped forward a few pages with his index finger and pointed to several ellipses that dotted the page like a strange kind of Morse code. "I've never seen poetry set on the page this way."

"Neither have I. It is odd—as if the poem is one long sentence. You can scarcely stop for breath as you read it. Perhaps he wanted the appearance of the page to match the content of its message. His philosophy is unorthodox, so why shouldn't his grammar be as well?"

Joseph nodded. "He certainly has a way of shocking his reader, does he not?" Louisa looked at her knees. The poetry was full of talk of the body. The first time she read some of the passages, she had blushed to the ends of her hair. "In fact, I wasn't sure I should bring it with me today. I don't wish to make you uncomfortable."

Louisa felt her temper rear like a colt. "Because I am a woman, you mean?" She snatched his copy of the book from his hand, flipped to the page she'd reread ten times to imprint it on her brain, and recited: "*I am the poet of the woman the same as the man, / And I say it is as great to be a woman as to be a man.* What do you say to that? Is he wrong?"

Joseph tried to hide his amused smile and gazed admiringly at her. "No, Miss Louisa, I do not think he is wrong," he replied softly. "If anything, I think he may be underestimating *you.*"

Her eyes darted around his face, trying to discern whether he spoke sincerely or was teasing her. She sighed, exhausted by her own defensiveness. She knew her temper made her silly and childish. But it was as easily triggered as ever.

The coy demeanor dropped from his face. "Miss Louisa—"

"Just Louisa, please," she interrupted.

"—I don't believe I ever have encountered a woman quite like you."

Louisa's eyes darted back to that safe place on her knees. It was a wonder she had not stared a hole straight through them.

"I feel I could talk to you about anything and you would understand. Do you feel the same?"

She did not nod or shake her head or move her lips. She felt she heard the top and bottom rows of her eyelashes crashing together, so silent was the air in the room as he spoke.

"And a writer yourself, with success at so young an age. Think what a long career you have to look forward to, all the stories you will bring to the world."

Louisa grimaced. "Nothing is guaranteed. Some interests are more easily carried over into adulthood than others. Women have many responsibilities that fill their time—they cannot depend on the luxury of hours on end to write."

"But what a *shame* it would be to let your talents languish."

Louisa gave a short, sad-sounding laugh. "You haven't read a word I've written and yet you fret over the loss of my talent. Take care not to heap on too much praise until you are familiar with its object."

"I'll soon change that. I wrote to my cousin Edward asking him to send me a copy of your *Flower Fables*."

"Oh, dear," Louisa said, her face full of dread. "Please remember—I wrote most of those tales when I was just a girl. I like to think, to hope, that my writing has improved *somewhat* since then."

"I know I will enjoy your work. I can hear it in our conversations. You have a gift."

"I fear some people believe it should be a youthful amusement and nothing more. Perhaps you have heard that the singular preoccupation of a young woman's life is to find a husband." Louisa gave him a wry smile.

A strain passed across Joseph's pale eyebrows a moment, as if her comment called forth an unpleasant thought, but as soon as the troubled look appeared it vanished. His freckles dotted the apples of his cheeks like spilled wheat. "Yes, I believe I am acquainted with the idea," he said, grinning.

Louisa sighed. "And when he is found, the work has only begun. Take Margaret, for example. Soon she will be a wife, keeping a home for her husband, nursing his relatives and her own, preparing for children, God willing. She won't have time for anything else."

Joseph scoffed. "Hardly! Margaret lives for parties and gossip—two things she'll be able to pursue just as well, if not better, in marriage."

"I beg your pardon—I don't like your tone." Louisa's voice surprised her by sounding sharp. She softened it. "Please don't speak about her that way. Margaret is my friend."

"And mine. I only meant that she is very different from you, is interested in different things."

"We may be unlike each other, but the duties of a wife are the same for each."

"I disagree. Husbands vary just as wives do. The possibility of a happy marriage hinges on the choosing, though most girls are so eager to make the pact, they do not take the time for careful consideration."

His smug tone needled her. "Is that so? You seem to have thought an awful lot about this matter."

"Not at all—it's just that the facts of it are very clear. You, for example. It will be very important that you marry the right sort of man—"

"And I suppose *you* think you know what sort of man that is." Louisa felt her cheeks get hot.

He nodded and broke into that infuriating grin, his playfulness returning. "I do. Primarily, he will have to be the sort of man who does not mind being interrupted. You know—the sort who would rather *listen* than talk. With you, one is apt to do a lot of listening."

Louisa felt her temper swing inside her head like the tongue of a bell. "When someone has graciously accepted your visit—an unannounced visit, I might add—do you always put such *effort* into insulting her?"

Her anger only compounded his amusement. "On the contrary—finding things to say that you will interpret as insults takes very little effort at all."

Before she could stop herself, Louisa was on her feet. "Aren't you clever? Well, here is something that will surprise you: 'Conventionality is not morality.' Miss Charlotte Brontë wrote that, and it is as true for me as it was for her. To do things just because others do is cowardly. Not that it is any business of yours, but I have *no* intention of marrying."

He watched her, his lips pressed into a line. "You are wrong. *That* doesn't surprise me at all."

Louisa ignored his quip. "I could never love anyone better than I love my independence."

"And you shouldn't. Your independence suits you." Joseph's face grew serious. "You know, Louisa, there are some men out there who are *charmed* by an independent woman, who feel that marriage can be an equal partnership of head and heart. Who would love you just as you are—fiery, overwrought, as passionate as any man."

Louisa felt something snatch her breath down deep into her lungs. She'd never met a person who spoke so bluntly, even to people he barely knew. She couldn't think of a thing to say.

"And to those men," Joseph said as he clapped his hands together and broke into a grin, "I say, God be with you, friends!"

The blood drained from Louisa's face and was replaced by hot mortification. Louisa took a slow breath.

"All this," she said, recovering as she gestured from his head to his feet, "*and* a sense of humor. How fortunate for the young ladies of this town."

Joseph grimaced at her bitter tone. "Miss Louisa, I have taken up too much of your lovely afternoon. I should leave you to your books."

She stood up and walked with him to the door, afraid to speak for fear of betraying how much he'd rankled her.

"Well, then . . ." He tucked *Leaves of Grass* into the crook of his elbow. "Thank you for the . . . *lively* discussion."

She nodded. He stepped across the threshold into the blinding sun.

"And I . . ." he continued as he placed his hat on his head and wiggled it into place by the brim. "Well, I'm . . . perhaps we could meet to talk again sometime."

"Perhaps," she said in a tone assuring him they would *not*, and closed the door. She started toward the stairs, eager to take advantage of the last quiet moments the afternoon promised, but she turned first down the narrow hall leading away from the parlor. The door to Bronson's study stood open an inch, and as Louisa pushed, its hinges creaked. Lizzie had been in to tidy the room earlier that morning. Books Louisa had seen stacked in piles of various sizes across the floor like buildings in a cityscape had been returned to their place on the shelf between the room's two windows. The surface of the desk was clean, save for two piles of paper.

Louisa shook her head as she touched the cream-colored stock. One stack was blank and the other contained Bronson's writing, a scant four or five sentences scrawled across the center of each page, leaving inches of unused space. Her father insisted on the most expensive paper and was determined to use it as wastefully as he could, she thought bitterly. Up in the attic room her own journals were bursting at the seams, each page full to the corners, front and back, until the ink bled through and rendered the text unreadable. The green-shaded lamp sat in the center of the desk next to a vase of pale purple verbena, the tart perfume of the flowers filling the space. Another of Lizzie's silent gestures.

Her father hadn't discovered that the book was missing, and Louisa wanted to keep it that way. The top shelf held books he rarely read but liked to keep at hand, and there was a space at the end of the row for one more slim volume. If he did notice it, perhaps he would conclude that Lizzie had moved it there. She pressed the book into place with her index finger. With its spine facing out it looked just like any other of the black, gray, and green books in the shadowed rectangle of the shelf. How strange, she thought, as she scanned the titles of his library. That paper and board and ink could work such alchemy.

She shut the door to the study and turned toward the stairs, passing the front door on her way. Something on the floor caught her eye. The white corner of a folded piece of paper was wedged under the door. Louisa crouched down and pulled gently to avoid tearing it. She unfolded the paper as she stood.

Dear Louisa,

Lest you persist in your belief that I am a dim-witted country boy, here is a letter to prove that I can write as well as read. I know these rare talents will astonish you.

Perhaps I only wanted an excuse to thank you for receiving me this afternoon. The cold tea was welcome comfort from the heat, but the conversation scarcely allowed my mind a moment of leisure. There isn't another person in this town, perhaps in the whole of New Hampshire, with whom I could discuss the work of Mr. Whitman.

You have the spirit of one who will let nothing separate her from her object. Do not let your visitors, eager as they are to share your company, get in the way of your work.

Yours,

Joseph

Money is the root of all evil, and yet it is such a useful root that we cannot get on without it any more than we can without potatoes.

—*Little Men*

Chapter Seven

Singer Dry Goods

WALPOLE, NEW HAMPSHIRE

ITEM	
Miss Louisa Alcott, credit for flour, ten pounds	*$1.75 (of which 50 cents has been paid)*
Balance Owed	*$1.25*

Louisa, did you set aside the candles for the collection?" Abba's voice startled Louisa, and the steel brush she was using to scour the soot from the stove door clattered to the floor.

"I'm sorry, Marmee. What did you say?"

"The charity candles—I can't seem to find them." Anna

glanced up from the peas she was shelling into a bowl, her fingers glistening wet and green at the tips. She gave Louisa a confused look.

"No, Marmee. It's my fault—I think I forgot to make them."

Abba pulled a week's worth of the slender brown sticks from the bin under the sink, wrapped them in a stiff rag, and tied them with twine. Louisa felt a disappointed pang in her stomach as she tried to calculate just how many late-night writing hours she would lose without those candles.

"Take these to Mrs. Parker," Abba said, handing the parcel to Anna. She pried the lid off a tin box and shook a few coins into her hand. "And here's the rag money. We have only a dusting of flour left, so you'll have to see how far you can make this stretch."

Louisa felt a vibration whisk through her veins. They would buy the flour at the dry goods store. "Please, Marmee—can't May go? I find that Joseph Singer *intolerable*."

Anna looked at Louisa and rolled her eyes. "Don't mind her, Marmee. We'll go."

Abba nodded. "Wipe your face, my dear—you've soot on your chin."

Louisa nodded, putting the money in the pocket of her dress and dabbing at her chin with a rag from the sink.

"I'll finish the peas, Anna." As they turned to go, Abba took note of the creases in Louisa's forehead and her voice turned sharp. "I will not abide self-pity, Louisa."

Louisa cast her eyes down to the floor. "Yes, Marmee."

"I know we do without—I know better than any of you just how much we do without. But I hope I never live to see the day when we have too little to share with those who are worse off than we are. God has blessed us in so many ways, and in return we must give with an open heart. And we don't do it for a reward, even though the Bible says we *will* be rewarded, tenfold."

Louisa nodded at the toe of her boot. The floor was bare and clean. She had swept it that morning.

Abba smiled faintly, finally letting her stern façade retreat just a little. "All right, off with you. When you return we will make the stew."

Outside, Louisa inhaled a giant gulp of air and imagined it could cleanse away all her selfish feelings.

Anna cinched the string on her bonnet. "What was that all about? I thought you said Marmee told you *not* to make the extra candles." They moved along the dusty path in the late morning sun. Lizzie's marmalade kitten poked its nose out of a shrub and watched them, slipping silently out after they had passed and following behind their footsteps.

"When I went to ask Marmee the other day I overheard a . . . tense discussion she was having with Father. It certainly wasn't meant for our ears."

"What did they say?"

"Some of it was muffled—listen to me, speaking so easily about eavesdropping on our parents!"

"Well, if they won't tell us the truth, what choice do we have?"

Louisa eyed Anna carefully. In recent days something had changed in her. The slightest whiff of haughtiness put an edge on her comments. It was so unlike the Anna she had always known. "Yes, perhaps that is true. Marmee questioned Father's choice to refuse work and accept charity from

Mr. Emerson instead. He explained that his philosophy and beliefs were the very foundation of his character—that violating them was . . . well, out of the question."

Anna said nothing but exhaled sharply as they approached the lane where the Parkers lived.

"So, as I was not going to interrupt the discussion, I crept back down the hallway the way I came. Certainly we cannot afford to give candles away, and I thought I would try to be the voice of reason on Marmee's behalf."

"No chance of reason when it comes to money in this family," Anna said, exasperated. "Father doesn't think of it at all, and Marmee gives it away as fast as we can get it."

"One thing's certain," Louisa said, pointing to Anna's pocket. "That rag money won't get us more than a half-pound of flour."

Anna sighed. "I know."

Louisa couldn't bear the guilt that weighed on her heart. She stopped in the road and turned to her sister. "You know, Anna, there is that money I've been saving back for Boston. It just doesn't seem right—"

"Louisa Alcott, don't you say it." Anna's voice was fierce as she fixed her eyes on her sister. "That is *your* money, and I won't let you chip away at it. You'll never get to Boston without it. I won't even discuss it."

Louisa opened her mouth to protest as they approached the Parkers' house. Anna shut her up by raising her palm to their friends. "Hello, Mrs. Parker! Hello, Margaret!"

The women, future mother- and daughter-in-law, sat on the porch sipping cold tea. The humidity was already thick in the air—anyone could see it would be a sweltering day. Anna and Louisa lingered a moment to join their conversation about the details of Margaret's trousseau. Both she and Mrs. Parker looked uneasy. They were just beginning the process of forming a friendship based on mutual adoration of the same man—for very different reasons. They seemed relieved to be interrupted.

"Miss Louisa, you're of at least reasonable intelligence," Mrs. Parker said, turning to her. She was a birdlike woman with a pointed nose and fragile-looking wrists. "I heard about your book—well done. Tell me, what do you think of this crinoline business? I myself think they are outrageous."

Louisa smiled at what Mrs. Parker clearly believed to be her neutral presentation of the topic. "I must agree that they certainly aren't practical. I've heard appalling stories about the largest ones overturning in a brisk breeze, exposing the lady's petticoats. Why do you ask, Mrs. Parker?"

"My future daughter-in-law was just telling me how much she admired the fashion. Taste is a curious thing, I suppose."

Margaret's eyes flashed with anger and she opened her mouth to respond.

Anna, always aware, always nimble, spoke just in time to smooth Margaret's quills. "Crinolines are very dignified, though—you must admit. Of course, I wouldn't want to wear one to weed the garden, but I can't imagine wearing anything else to the theater or a dance." She laughed. "That is, if I ever went to a dance, a crinoline is what I would want to wear. Wouldn't you agree, Margaret?"

Margaret looked up at Anna, the flush subsiding from her cheeks. "Yes. That is what I meant, of course. You see these things in the ladies' books, but we know they aren't meant to be worn all the time. Only for special occasions."

Mrs. Parker nodded. "I see. Well, that seems reasonable

enough. I suppose you feel one of these special occasions might arise in association with the wedding?"

Margaret nodded, the blond coils of her hair trembling from her exertion at keeping her temper. Louisa watched in awe. Once again Anna was three steps ahead of her. Louisa hadn't picked up on the subterranean tension between the two until it nearly exploded. Her mind had been on other things.

"I suppose that is acceptable. I will speak to your mother about it. Heaven knows your parents won't be able to afford it." Anna put her hand inconspicuously on Margaret's back, willing her not to take the bait. "But with Mr. Parker's assistance, we should be able to make it so."

Louisa observed that the women's appearances had little in common. Mrs. Parker was stern and almost disturbingly thin, as if she believed any additional tissue to be a frivolity. Margaret was plump and fleshy, and her faded dress stretched to contain her curves. Louisa wondered if Mrs. Parker was offended that her son had chosen someone so unlike herself as his wife. Or perhaps it was that one could not look at Margaret without the mind drifting, however briefly, to the more carnal aspects of marriage. Louisa thought of the skin of Joseph's neck that sloped along the top of his collar, brown from the sun with a narrow white strip along his hairline. As soon as the image appeared, she banished it, recoiling. Perhaps it was all the heat that was making her behave so queerly.

The sisters said their good-byes to Mrs. Parker and Margaret, and turned down Washington Street toward the shops. When they entered Singer Dry Goods, the bell above the door jangled, summoning Joseph from the back room. Louisa couldn't help but be buoyed by the smell of cinnamon and nutmeg that permeated the shop.

"Well, it's the Misses Alcott. Good morning." He wore a half-apron around his waist, and a pair of dusty boots. His face was pink and the tips of his ears looked tender. "What brings you here today?"

Louisa felt her voice wither in her throat like a cluster of drying leaves and it filled her with frustration. She had been around plenty of young men as a girl and thought nothing of it. In fact, she'd always *preferred* the company of boys over other girls—boys loved to run and shout; they carried pocket-knives and knew how to coax shad and speckled trout out of the river. What could girls do that compared with that? So what was it about *this* young man that made her so nervous?

Anna squared her shoulders and placed the rag money on the counter with all the dignity she could muster.

"We'll be needing some flour, if it's not too much trouble."

"No trouble at all." He wiped his hands on a cloth. "How much would you like?"

"Well, you see," she began, clearing her throat to eke out the lie. "We'd already walked halfway here when I realized I forgot my purse. This is just what I had in my pocket." She slid the coins toward him. "Will it stretch to cover a few pounds?"

"Well," Joseph stalled. "Ah . . . let me see what I can do." He disappeared behind the canvas curtain between the front of the store and the back room. Anna grimaced, and Louisa gave her a weak smile.

A moment later Joseph reappeared, ten pounds of flour in a cloth sack cinched closed with twine. "Here we are. Is there anything else I can get you today?"

Anna's mouth made a small red circle. "Surely ten pounds of flour costs more than what is here on the counter."

"Well, it's your lucky day. We are having a sale." He winked at the sisters, his hands on his hips.

Louisa twisted her mouth to the side. To stand in the shadow of his pity, to see his self-satisfied ease, transformed her shame into fury. Stepping up to the counter, she asked, "How much is the discount?"

"What's that?" Joseph asked, busying himself with sliding the coins into his palm and dropping them into the sections of the drawer.

"The sale. What percentage have you deducted from the total cost?"

He looked uneasily between the two of them and rubbed his palms together. "Ah, I've never been one for math. It all works out in the end—that's what my father always says."

"Well," Anna said, shoving in front of Louisa to take the flour. "I'm glad we didn't wait until tomorrow to come."

Louisa pushed her sister's hand away from the bag. "Anna, we can't take this." She turned back to Joseph. "You are generous, but we cannot accept charity."

"Please don't think of it as charity. Anna forgot her purse—she said so herself. You can make up for it next time."

Louisa sighed. "Anna doesn't even own a purse." In her peripheral vision she saw Anna close her eyes, radiating embarrassment. "I suppose it's all over town that we can't pay for things. Well, I won't be pitied." Her voice had grown louder and two elderly women examining folded cotton scraps stopped and looked in their direction.

"Louisa, please," Anna hissed into Louisa's ear. "You are making a scene." She composed her face and turned back to the counter. "Thank you, Joseph. We will, of course, pay the balance next week." She clamped her hand on Louisa's forearm and wrenched her toward the door, the sack of flour perched on her hip like a baby.

They were a hundred yards down the lane when he came running up behind them. He put his hand on Louisa's shoulder and turned her to face him.

"Here." He held up a yellow paper and then pressed it into her hand. "This is what you owe. You can pay it next time you come in. Do you understand? It's not charity." Eagerness raised the pitch of his voice and his eyes searched her face for pardon.

Louisa stared at him a moment, and when no words would come she nodded. She tried to call up the righteousness that had propelled her to anger a moment before, but the weight of his palm on her shoulder had caused it to evaporate.

"Agreed?" he asked, his forehead still creased with concern.

"Yes."

"All right." He nodded as if that settled the matter and turned back toward the store. "Good afternoon, ladies."

"Good afternoon," Anna called. Louisa felt the oxygen coming back into her brain. Anna twisted her lips into a coy smile. "Well, he was certainly worried about upsetting *you*."

Louisa gave her a blank look.

"My brilliant sister, the idiot. *He likes you*."

In the evening the family sat in the parlor. A book lay facedown and open over Bronson's knee like a tent. He stared into the fire. The expression on his face had in Louisa's mind always been associated with *silence*, from the first time the word's sibilant pronunciation skated across her tongue. As a little girl she had asked him about it.

"Father," she whispered, appearing at the side of his chair, twisting the end of her braid between her fingers. "Why do you stare so?"

He had turned to her with a startled look on his face, his eyes softening into his temples as his mind returned to the present and he recognized this sprite as his daughter. "My child, I am thinking about grand ideas, enormous ideas with a collection of smaller ideas inside them. And so I must be still to allow my mind to work."

"But you are so quiet."

"My body and voice are silent. But the noise inside my head is like a carnival. A cacophony."

Louisa had nodded, solemn. "What is *cacophony*?"

"Tomorrow, my dear. I will tell you all about it tomorrow." He had taken her on his knee and she watched him fade back into his faraway place. She stared at the fire then and yearned for some grand ideas of her own, but all she could think of was a hand mirror she'd seen that day at school. Rebecca Carson, a clerk's daughter, held it in her palm as the other girls crowded around her to look, the silver flowers etched along its handle glinting in the sun. Louisa had wanted to touch it but stayed behind the other girls, her hands pressed to her sides. Knowing the pretty little mirror existed filled her with a kind of grief she had never known before. Something so exquisite was in the world, and she would never, ever be able to have it. Sitting on Bronson's knee, she held fast to her whimper until it died in her throat.

And now here she was so many years later, and she understood little more about the workings of her father's mind. She turned her needlework on her lap and smoothed the stitches of the nosegay she was embroidering on a handkerchief. A lady in Boston who knew Mrs. Emerson bought them by the dozen. Anna and Abba sat beside her knitting caps for the newborn babies in town. Lizzie sat near the fire at Abba's insistence to avoid a chill, though the balmy August night held little chance of that.

Suddenly May galloped into the room, her voice bursting through the peaceful parlor.

"Catherine Singer is having her birthday! She is turning fifteen, and guess where her father gave her permission to go?"

"May," Abba scolded. "Please don't shout."

"It's the circus, Marmee. She is going to the circus in Keene, and she has invited me and Anna and Louisa—I mean, Anna and Louisa and me—along. And Lizzie too, if she is well enough. May we go? Please, Marmee?"

Lizzie snapped her book closed and pressed it to her chest. "The circus?" She exhaled a plaintive sigh that tugged at Louisa's heart. "I have always wanted to see the circus."

Abba looked at Lizzie in surprise and then turned to May. "My dear, you know how I feel about those dreadful displays. The people and animals are filthy, they travel from place to place doing so many . . . unnatural things."

"But . . . everyone from town will be there."

"Everyone? Is that so."

"Well, everyone who is anyone, of course. I simply *must* go."

An amused smile flashed across Abba's face. "I see. Well, only if your sisters go with you."

"Does that mean," Lizzie ventured tentatively, "that *I* may go along?" She reached into a basket on the hearth and removed a pair of tattered slippers, edging on her knees to the foot of Bronson's chair, and placed them gently on his feet. His gaze never wavered from the fire.

Abba grimaced. "Oh, my darling, I didn't mean . . . Well, I was thinking of Anna and Louisa. I fear you aren't well enough for a long journey in an open carriage."

Lizzie's face fell, her eyes filling as she looked away. "Of course. I suppose I would ruin everyone's fun if I were to have a spell."

Louisa watched her carefully, then looked at Anna. She could see from her older sister's expression that they shared a common thought.

"That's nonsense, Lizzie," Louisa said. "I think you're well enough for an afternoon—and whose health can't be improved by fresh air and a day out with friends? Please, Marmee—reconsider. Lizzie can accompany May."

Abba clutched her hands together in her lap. "I don't know. . . . Let me think about it."

Lizzie gave Abba a pleading look and Louisa felt a surge of compassion. It was true that as a girl Lizzie hadn't loved to run and play like her sisters, but when had she ever been given the chance? Abba held on to her so tightly, protecting her, limiting her exposure to the world. It was important to Abba to be needed.

"Marmee, you are too protective. Lizzie is not a child!"

"Louisa, that's enough. I said I will consider it."

"What is there to consider? As an adult she should not *need* your permission."

"*Louisa.*" Anna's mouth was agape. "Do not be insolent. You've made your view clear. Now, leave off. Marmee, forgive her. You know how her mouth can run away from her." Louisa glared at Anna.

Abba looked silently between her two older daughters and then over at Lizzie, whose eyes were trained on her lap. "I hope I never see the day when my protection and care are unwelcome."

Louisa's righteousness subsided and remorse took its place. "Oh, Marmee, I'm sorry. It is only my passion getting in the way of my mind again. You know we would be lost without you."

Abba gave her a steely expression and sighed. She turned to May. "As to the general outing, I could not consent unless your older sisters accompanied you."

"Oh," Anna broke in. "Please don't ask it. I have so little freedom as it is, and Saturdays are my only day . . ." May turned to her, her hands clasped beatifically.

"When is the party, May?" Louisa bristled. May often asked for, and got, all the things she wanted.

"Next Saturday."

Anna relaxed. "Then I cannot go. I've promised Margaret I will help her shop for fabric."

"Louy, then," May said, turning to her. "My dear, dear, lovely older sister."

Louisa rolled her eyes. "May, I do not wish to spend my Saturday with a bunch of children and smelly elephants."

"*Marmee,*" May squealed in desperation. She made her final desperate appeal. "Last year, Rose Wilson had the tiniest of fevers and her mother made her stay home from the school picnic. She missed out on everything, and all the other girls stopped talking to her. She told me later she would rather have gone to the picnic and died the next day than suffer the ostrich-iza . . . ostrich-era . . ."

A grin burst through Louisa's worried expression. "May, do you mean to say *ostracism?*"

She looked puzzled. "You mean it has nothing at all to do with the bird?"

Anna giggled beside her and placed her arm across May's shoulders. "No, nothing at all."

"Well, anyway, they did give her an os-tra-cism, and—"

Louisa broke in. "Oh, for *heaven's* sake!" She looked at Abba, whose dour demeanor had been washed away by May's charm. Perhaps because she was younger, perhaps because she was the prettiest, the one who demanded that the world take notice of her, May seemed to represent for Abba the possibility that the family might one day transcend its humble circumstances. Louisa knew her mother had come from a family of Sewalls and Quincys—good New England stock with a history and station. Abba's own marriage had been an imprudent match in the eyes of her family, and she liked to boast of this fact, as proof, Louisa supposed, that the things of the world meant nothing to her. Yet it was plain to see that she had ambitions for her youngest daughter.

Louisa ventured tentatively back to the subject she'd left off, as if it were a scab she couldn't help but pick. "Abba, if I agree, then Lizzie may come along as well?" Lizzie sat forward, clutching at the book in her lap, the ends of her fingers gone white with the pressure.

"That I cannot promise. We must wait until next Saturday morning to see that she is feeling strong and the weather is fair."

Lizzie turned to Louisa. "I am feeling quite strong now— I'm *sure* I will be well."

Abba rubbed her arm. "We will see, my darling."

Louisa gave her youngest sister a weary look. "Very well, May. You have won your prize. I'll go with you to Keene."

May squealed and clapped her hands, then danced

around the room to kiss her mother and each of her sisters on the cheek.

"May, how will you girls travel to Keene?" Abba asked.

"Ah, I can't believe I forgot to tell you the *best* part," she said, placing her palm on her chest for dramatic effect. "We will travel in Catherine's father's new carriage. Her brother will drive us."

"Joseph?" Anna said with eyebrows raised. She looked coyly at Louisa.

Louisa dropped her eyes to the fabric pinched between her fingers.

Abba's eyes darted from Anna to Louisa, instantly sensing what passed between them. "Has this information helped ease your reluctance to spend an afternoon with—what was it you said? 'Children and smelly elephants'?"

Anna nodded. "Yes, I believe that *is* what she said."

Louisa tipped her nose toward the ceiling. "Not in the slightest. If anything, I have something else to dread."

Lizzie looked worriedly at Louisa.

"Oh, don't worry, Lizzie. Joseph Singer may be the most presumptuous, disagreeable—"

Anna cut her off, laughing. "Take care not to say anything you'll regret, Louisa."

"—insufferable young man," she continued, "but I wouldn't let *that* stand in the way of making sure you get to see the circus."

Lizzie beamed.

"Provided you are well," Abba cautioned, as she placed her hand on Lizzie's. "Provided the day is warm and dry."

May pirouetted around the parlor. Passing the table next to Bronson's chair, her knee upset his saucer, and the lukewarm tea splashed across his lap. He jumped to his feet and, for the first time since they'd settled in the parlor two hours before, acknowledged the existence of his family.

"What the *devil* is going on?" he barked.

"May has prevailed upon Louisa to perform the chore of chaperoning her to the circus with her friends," Abba said, accustomed to Bronson's tendency to arrive late to conversations taking place right in front of him. She looked knowingly at Anna, all the while maintaining the rhythm of her knitting needles. "But we do not believe Louisa will suffer *over*much."

The acre on which Nicholas Sutton's partially constructed house stood had a rocky western edge and sloped away from the river, cresting in a broad hill. The site was a quarter mile up River Road from the much larger property where Nicholas had grown up, the home where his parents and sister still lived, shaded by a stand of beech trees edging the meadow where their horses nosed the grass in fair weather.

June had been a productive month, as Nicholas had explained to Anna at the swimming party. With his father's help, as well as Joseph and Samuel's, Nicholas had drawn up plans for the house, a two-story Italianate like the ones springing up all over Boston. By the first day of summer they'd raised the frame and amassed all the materials needed to complete the job—shingles for the roof, glass for the windows, and wood for the trim. If the weather cooperated, Nicholas said he thought he'd be finished by summer's end.

Anna and Louisa decided to walk the long way to the Elmwood Inn for rehearsal on Friday morning, heading west toward the river instead of northwest toward Washington Square, so they might walk by and see the project for themselves.

They heard hammering and the wheezing rasp of a saw before the house came into view. Then they passed a stand of trees and it appeared. The sun shining between the ribs of the frame made a shadow like a railroad track across the ground. Samuel noticed the girls first. He stood at the base of a tall ladder leaned against the side of the house, holding it steady for Nicholas, who was perched on the top rung hammering a board into place.

"Good morning," Samuel said with a friendly nod meant to substitute for a wave. He didn't take his hands from the ladder.

"Isn't it?" Anna said. "I try to imprint this sunshine in my mind and save it for January. It never does seem to work, though." Samuel smiled.

"Ho, there!" Nicholas called from above, waving his hammer. "Where are the pretty ladies off to today?"

Louisa cupped her hands around her mouth and shouted, "To the same place you should be going. Rehearsal."

"Rehearsal! Of course!" Nicholas called down. "We were just about to finish up here and head over."

Louisa laughed, shielding her eyes from the sun. "Yes, I've no doubt of that. All the same, perhaps it *is* fortunate we happened to pass by."

Nicholas affected the mien of the wrongly accused. "I hope you don't mean to imply we *forgot* about rehearsal."

"Oh, never." Louisa and Anna giggled.

Nicholas held his hammer to his breast. "And disobey our commanding officer? We wouldn't think of it."

"I should hope not," Anna said. "Louisa does not look kindly on dissent in the ranks."

They heard a rhythmic thudding above as Joseph made his way across the open slats in the roof to their side of the house. He scuttled on all fours like a crab, his boots on one slat and his palms on another, moving two boards at a time. Louisa felt her body tense up when he came into view. It was thrilling to see him in the yellow morning light, his shirt cuffs rolled up to the elbows, his skin brown. But just behind the excitement was her dread of what it all could mean.

He peered down at them. "What's all this racket over here?"

"Joe, I was just explaining to the young ladies that we fully intended to repair to rehearsal at the designated time."

"Oh, yes," said Joseph, catching on. "We planned to arrive just when we were told."

"And what time was that?" Louisa asked, willing confidence into her voice.

"Why," Joseph replied, "the very time you instructed and not a second later. You are the director after all, Miss Louisa. Your word is law."

Louisa relished the praise a moment, then rolled her eyes. "Yes, but *what* time was it?"

Joseph looked at his friend. "Well, that would be Nick's department. I believe we put *you* in charge of the schedule."

"No, sir. It was Mr. Parker," Nicholas replied, then shouted down, solemnly shaking his head. "Samuel is in charge of all appointments."

Samuel chuckled, looking first at Louisa and Anna and then tipping his head up toward his accuser. "It seems unwise to sell a man down the river when he is holding your ladder, friend."

Nicholas pressed his lips into a line. "That's a good point, lad. Ladies, it was Joseph. He has a corrupting influence on us all, and I hope you'll forgive our weak wills."

Joseph shifted his weight onto his heels to free his hands, one of which held a hammer. He smiled, a half-dozen nails glinting between his teeth. "Look—no hands."

Louisa gasped. "Are you soft in the head, Joseph Singer?"

He thought for a moment. "Yes, that is quite likely. But what does that have to do with the matter at hand?"

"You are two stories up, teetering like an inebriate. One gust of wind and you'd be finished. Will you please be careful?"

"For you, Miss Louisa? Anything. We'll even come down right now and walk with you the rest of the way to the inn."

"Splendid," Anna said, and they waited as the boys made their way down the creaking ladder.

I don't waste ink in poetry and pages of rubbish now. I've begun to live, and have no time for sentimental musing.

—*Louisa May Alcott: Her Life, Letters, and Journals*

Chapter Eight

Louisa woke in the early morning to a pale sky and the whisper of raindrops. In the half-light, her mind cluttered with the images of a retreating dream, she felt a pang of disappointment. Surely Abba would now insist on Lizzie staying home. She sat up and swung her feet to the floor, pulling the drape aside to assess the weather. The rain was steady, gaining strength. Perhaps none of them would go to the circus. Anna slept soundly in the bed next to her, her hair fanned across her face and the cotton blanket. Louisa rose and descended to the kitchen to put on the water for tea.

As it boiled, the others rose. Bronson went into his study. Anna scoured the floor, then dressed and left to meet Margaret in town. Abba entered the kitchen and put on a pot to cook down plums for jam.

Louisa dreaded asking the question she felt she already knew the answer to. "Marmee, where is Lizzie?"

Abba clucked sympathetically as she sliced the plums and pried out the stones. "Still in bed, I fear. She was restless in the night—perhaps she was overwrought with the possibility of coming with you girls—and did not sleep well. We shouldn't have gotten her hopes up. By the looks of that rain, none of you may be going."

Poor Lizzie, Louisa thought.

By noon the rain had subsided but Lizzie remained in bed in the room she shared with May. Louisa knocked softly on the door and stuck her head inside. Lizzie wore a night-gown cinched around her collarbone with a blue ribbon and sat in bed reading a book, a stack of pillows propping her up.

"How is my little patient?" Louisa asked, crossing the room to sit on the edge of the bed.

Lizzie sighed and closed the book over her finger to hold her place. "Sleepy. And more than a little disappointed. I'm sorry to have caused all this trouble."

Louisa put her hand on Lizzie's. "I only wish you could come. Are you sure Marmee isn't being a little too cautious?"

Lizzie shrugged. "I feel fine, but I know she is right that I tire easily. Keene *is* a long carriage ride away. I think it is best that I stay home." Lizzie reached toward the floor and pulled her orange kitten into her lap. "Say you will wave hello to the tigers for Ginger and me. I promised her I'd tell her all about her wild ancestors." Since Louisa had first seen Ginger poking her head out of Lizzie's apron, the kitten had grown lanky, her fine puff of fur now sleek.

"I promise, my dear, if you're sure you won't try to come? Wouldn't you like to have just a *little* adventure?"

Lizzie looked at Louisa a moment, as if mulling this over. Finally, she shook her head, though her eyes were a little sad. "There is nothing I love better than home, wherever home happens to be."

Louisa nodded. "Then I will leave you to it. Good-bye,

Ginger." Louisa rubbed the kitten's ears. "I'll bring you both a souvenir."

Louisa and May sat down to eat a light luncheon before walking into town to join Joseph and Catherine. May flitted about the room, scarcely ingesting a bite.

Exasperated, Abba took her by the waist and guided her into a chair. "Abigail May, you *must* eat something, or you will pass out from hunger somewhere along the road."

Afterward, they set out for the Singers' store. The sky remained gloomy but the rain held off, and Louisa couldn't help feeling cheerful on her sister's behalf, though at the same time her heart pounded in her ears. What would she and Joseph say to each other?

They were a few minutes early coming up the road. Catherine sat on a bench in front of the store in a new dress, her hair pulled tightly away from her face. Her brow was just like Joseph's—fair and freckled—but her hair was darker, arranged for this special occasion in intricate coils just behind her ears. May sighed reflexively when she saw the ribbon edging on Catherine's dress. It was a blinding white, the way only new clothes can be. The girls began a vigorous conversation about the other young people from town they expected to see at the circus. Louisa decided to go inside the store to find Joseph. She expected to hear the jangle of the bell when she entered, but the door slipped open silently. She looked up to see the bell bent off its bracket, as if it had been broken when someone slammed the door. No one was behind the counter. She walked toward the curtained doorway that led to the back room but stopped short when she heard Joseph's voice take on a sharp tone.

"Isn't there any other way?"

"I don't see one. There just isn't time."

"So that is how it will be? 'The sins of the father are to be laid upon the children'?"

"You've let your anger bring you so low you'd use the Bible—"

"I was thinking of Shakespeare, Father. *The Merchant of Venice.*"

It was silent for a moment then. Louisa heard a rustling, the scrape of a stool across the worn planks of the floor.

"Sit down, Father. Rest a moment. I'm sorry for what I said."

"You think I don't know God will judge me for my sins? Why don't you leave it to Him and let it be? Think of your sister, Joseph. If she had inherited her mother's measured temperament, I would not worry. But I'm afraid she is just like her father—frivolous, impulsive. Easily led astray. We have the chance to protect her. We must take it."

"We? You mean *I* must take it—"

"I cannot stop death from coming for me, boy. I can do many things, but I cannot do that."

Louisa backed quietly toward the door, opened it, and shook it on its hinges so the bell, mangled as it was, produced a small sound. The voices in the back room stopped. She heard a shuffling of feet and Joseph emerged.

"Well, then. Are we all set to go?" Joseph's jaw moved slightly under his skin as he worked deliberately to relax his expression.

Louisa smiled at him with bare kindness for the first time. There was no pride in it, no defensive edge like before, when she'd felt overwhelmed by the competing desires to be near him and not to let him know that she thought of him at all. Hearing his conversation with his father broke through all that. He looked calm enough now, but instinctively she knew he was writhing inside, like a butterfly on a pin before the life goes out of it.

"Yes, before our sisters start walking to Keene on their own." She watched him gathering his things—two blankets for their feet in case of a chill, umbrellas, a bag of lemon candies from one of the glass jars behind the counter. She wondered if he thought of her as his friend. She wanted very much to be his friend just then.

Out behind the store, Mr. Singer's new phaeton rocked back and forth on its wheels as its two harnessed horses shifted in place, anxious to move. Joseph stretched open the extension-top and secured it in place. It was covered in fine leather dyed the blue of a church hymnal.

He felt along the harness, making sure it was secure, then smoothed his hand over the blond mane of one of the horses. "This here's Juliet, and that one's Romeo. But we call the back half of Romeo 'President Pierce.'"

Louisa laughed and the girls rolled their eyes. To them, nothing was duller than politics, and they were bored to death by the recent griping about how the first president to hail from New Hampshire seemed to be protecting the interests of slave owners over the good people of New England.

Joseph swung the half-moon–shaped door open and gestured for the Alcott sisters to climb into the more comfortable and well-covered seats in the rear. May grinned and nearly bounced inside. Louisa realized May probably had not ever been in a carriage this nice, then admitted to herself she hadn't either. Louisa moved to climb in after May but paused when Catherine conspicuously cleared her throat.

"I believe since it is *my* birthday, I should sit in the rear. This *is* a new dress, after all, and if it rains again, there will be mud." She gestured toward Louisa's dress, which she and Anna had worked on into the early morning hours, sewing on a new flounce cut from some leftover cloth, scrubbing stains along the hem out with a worn wire brush. "Your dress is so old, you won't mind, will you?"

Before she could stop herself, she turned to look at Joseph, her eyebrows arched. He closed his eyes and shook his head. "Forgive my sister. Catherine, these are our *guests*."

May sat in the shadow of the carriage with her hands clasped, silently pleading with Louisa not to make a scene.

"Of course I don't mind," Louisa replied, plastering a smile on her face and moving out of the way. Her nerves were returning and she was uncertain again. Catherine climbed in next to May and settled her skirts around her knees. Joseph offered Louisa his hand to help her climb over the wheel into the front seat. She felt a fluttering in her chest as their hands touched, and tried to avoid his eyes. He seemed unfazed, reminding her to tuck her hem behind her boots so that it did not get caught in the spokes of the wheel. Louisa watched him climb in after her and take up the reins. Her eye followed the line of his coat, where it was faded and frayed along the collar.

They started off, lurching and chugging down Main Street. This was the long way around to the road that led out of town, but Catherine and May begged Joseph to take it so that any of their friends who happened to pass by would see the manner in which they were traveling.

"This is a lovely carriage," May said, her breath in her voice. She ran her hand along the buff-colored seat, touched the gold ties that held the drapes up.

"It is, isn't it?" Joseph said. And then he half muttered, "It's a shame we'll have to give it back soon."

Catherine whipped her head in his direction. "Give it *back*? What do you mean?"

"Carriages aren't free, my sister. One must pay for them."

"But can't Father pay—"

"I shouldn't have said a thing. Let's not talk of family matters now. Besides, it's your birthday! This is a celebration!"

Louisa sat turned sideways. She could see Catherine's face in profile and recognized the familiar pouted lips made by one who still had the emotions of a girl, despite looking very much the part of a young lady. May had made the very same expression days before when begging to come on this trip.

"Must we walk everywhere from now on?" Catherine whined.

Joseph slowed the horses to a stop so that he could turn and look her square in the eyes. Louisa and May shifted uncomfortably. "I asked you not to talk of family matters now. I will ask you once more, and then I will turn us around and take our friends home. You are too old now to behave in this way. Do you understand me?"

Catherine looked down at her lap and nodded.

"Right then. Let's go." Joseph started off again and they rode along in silence. Louisa could tell by the look of the sky that the weather would taunt them all day. A placid blue seemed now to be breaking through the clouds, but a slate-colored cloud loomed on the horizon like a steamship chugging slowly across the ocean. It was lovely to ride along in silence, though this moment of silence felt charged with anticipation. She realized she spent much of her life searching for quiet, trying to determine when she would next have the chance to sink into its intoxicating comfort. Even when she was with other people—especially when she was with other people.

May, on the other hand, could not abide silence. It was true she loved to talk, but she was also sensitive to tension. She needed constant reassurance that the people in her vicinity were enjoying themselves so that she felt she had permission to enjoy herself too.

"How many elephants do you think they'll have?" May asked.

Catherine turned to May and watched her brother from the corner of her eye to discern when his anger had subsided. "Three or four at least. Have you ever seen one before?"

May shook her head.

"As big as you expect them to be, they'll be bigger. *I've* been to the circus lots of times, so I won't be surprised. But—"

Joseph smiled, in spite of himself. "'Lots of times' is an exaggeration, don't you think?"

She looked at him, a haughty expression turning down the corners of her mouth. "I'd rather walk the rest of the way than have you interrupting me every time I try to speak and ruining our good time. It is my *birthday*, after all."

Joseph held up a hand. "Fine, fine. Never mind." Louisa smiled. Catherine and May certainly seemed to have a few things in common.

They could smell the animals before they crossed into Keene, the acrid aroma of manure mixed with the smell of wet fur closed into train cars. The road into town sloped up and then down again, and when they crested the hill Catherine spotted the yellow flags on top of the circus tent. "There it is!" she cried, forgetting for a moment she meant to display a veteran's disinterest in the novelty of the day.

They descended into town and pulled the carriage into line behind the dozens of others parked outside an old barn. Joseph hopped down and circled around to Louisa, offering his hand to help her descend. Her stomach leapt when she allowed her eyes to meet his. His gaze was unflinching and he seemed to be searching her face, though she wondered at what he hoped to find there. She reached for his arm, her hands feeling constricted in their borrowed gloves.

They made their way across the field. To the left of the main tent stood an elephant, tied to an iron spike driven into the dirt. The beast siphoned water up his trunk, then extended it into the air and sprayed it across the bony ridge of his back. A cloud of flies circled the elephant's head and it flapped its ears like giant paper fans to shoo them away.

"What a beast," Joseph said, his eyes wide in admiration as they approached the animal. "Magnificent."

Louisa assessed the stake: a piece of iron six inches thick was all that stood between a jolly afternoon and a stampede. But the elephant didn't appear to be struggling against its constraints. "Look at his eyes," Louisa said. The lashes were long and pale. "They look like an old man's. Sad." She wanted to reach up and touch the leathery skin, but she was afraid.

Joseph pulled the gold chain connected to the watch in his vest pocket. "If we hurry we can catch the show starting in a few minutes. Or we can go see the rest of the animals and the marvels tent first, and see the later show."

"Now, now. Let's go now!" Catherine said, tugging his arm toward the main tent.

He grinned and turned to Louisa and May. "What do you say?"

May nodded vigorously.

"I am happy to oblige the birthday girl," Louisa said.

"All right. Let's find our seats." May took Louisa's arm and they followed Joseph and Catherine. A crowd amassed at the wide entrance as a few hundred people streamed up the hill from Keene's train station and the muddy lot where rows of carriages rocked slightly in the breeze. Catherine's father had purchased four tickets for the fifty-cent seats, which offered a better view than the spots in the pit that went for a quarter. They climbed the creaking steps of the hastily constructed stands to a bench about halfway up.

"Not too much higher," Joseph said, glancing toward the railless end of the row, which dropped off into the dark. "This is high enough."

Catherine scoffed but didn't argue. Joseph went in first, followed by his sister and May, with Louisa settling near the middle of the bench. She turned her attention to the bright center of the tent, where two men on stilts bobbed unsteadily in opposite directions around a circle that had been formed by plowing the earth up two feet high all around. One by one they lit tall torches that marked the perimeter of the ring. In the far corner, half in shadow, a steam trumpet blared out a hypnotic song.

The fidgeting in the audience subsided, and they began to clap as they heard the music. Stagehands closed the flaps at the entrance of the tent, blocking out the last of the natural light. The torches burned a bright amber. Suddenly, off to the left, Louisa saw a flash of white. A small man, dressed in a white tunic and close-fitting trousers covered all over with large red dots, ran toward a springboard that catapulted him, tumbling through the air, into the ring. His head was covered with a cap made of the same dotted white fabric and he had a large black mustache and exaggerated eyebrows painted above his eyes.

The clown stood with his arms outstretched and the quiet audience broke into applause.

"Good afternoon, ladies and gentlemen and members of the colored population." Louisa glanced toward the pit, where a small cluster of black audience members stood. She noted that none of them sat in the stands. "I am Billy, but you can call me your fool for the afternoon."

The audience laughed. Billy turned toward the dark corner from which he had emerged and whistled. After a slight delay, a small pony cantered toward the ring and jumped over the earthen divider. The pony's mane was long and pale, like straw.

"Folks, this is Blind Jim, my trusty steed. He is mighty faithful, but he can't see his hoof in front of his face, if you see what I mean."

Blind Jim pranced in a circle around the clown, then stretched out his front hooves on the ground and lowered his head in a kind of bow. The audience clapped.

"How are you today, Blind Jim?" Billy asked. The pony nickered.

"Is that so?"

The audience laughed.

"You know, Jim, I'm awful tired. What do you say we lie down a moment and have a little rest?"

Blind Jim didn't take a moment to think it over. He

lowered his weight down onto his hindquarters and then rolled onto his side. He rested his cheek in the dirt and swished his tail a few times. "That's a good friend, Jim," Billy said. He lay down beside the horse, snuggling against its ribs so that the horse's left front leg draped across his shoulder in a kind of embrace. Catherine and May giggled, their hands over their mouths. A man sitting a few rows below them cupped his hands around his mouth and shouted, "Why don't you give him a kiss, Billy?"

Billy lifted himself up on his elbow and looked up at the dark stands, in the general direction of the voice. "What's that, sir?"

"I said, why don't you give your pony a kiss?"

"Is your wife there with you, sir?"

"Yes," the man shouted. "She's a fine woman too."

"Ma'am," said Billy, addressing the shrouded man's wife, "you have my sympathies."

The crowd guffawed. "I'm embarrassed to have to tell you this, sir," Billy said as he scooched back into Blind Jim's arms. "But the idea of a man kissing a pony is *ridiculous*." The laughter roared out again and then subsided.

After the clowns succeeded in warming up the audience, a woman rode into the ring bareback, her blond hair trailing loose behind her. She waved her arms and a team of horses loped into view. They pranced according to her demands and leapt through a ring of fire one by one. Next came the jugglers and a team of acrobats who swung and tumbled from lines erected in the peak of the tent. Finally a mournful song played on the steam trumpet, signaling the start of the main event. A small man in formal dress appeared followed by his assistants, two small boys, who pulled a wheeled platform supporting a shrouded box. The boys maneuvered the platform through the opening in the ring and pulled it to the center. Each took a corner of the black cloth that covered the box and pulled as they backed away, revealing an iron cage that contained a massive tiger. The animal blinked as its eyes adjusted to the light. It stood up on four paws the size of platters and began to pace the small confines of its cage.

Louisa felt her chest tighten. May clutched Louisa's hand and Louisa gave her sister's arm a reassuring pat. "It's all part of the show, May," she said, though she didn't sound convinced. She shot a furtive glance over at Joseph. His eyes were wide, but when he turned to look at her, he smiled. "It's all right," he mouthed.

They watched, thunderstruck, as the man opened the door to the cage and ushered the beast out. For the next ten minutes not one breath could be heard in the tent as the audience watched the tamer crack his whip, moving in circles around the tiger. At first the animal reared up on its hind legs, growling, but soon the tamer lulled it back onto all fours, then into a seated position. The tiger lay down, resting its massive head on its front paws. At last it rolled onto its back, exposing its white belly, and purred like a barn cat in a patch of sun. The tamer took a bow and the people leapt to their feet, cheering.

After the tiger was locked safely back in its cage, the assistants wheeled it away and opened the flaps at the entrance of the tent, revealing a triangle of daylight. The show was over. The party made its way down the steps along with the rest of the crowd. Exiting was a slow process, and Catherine and May grew impatient to see the remainder of the attractions. They obtained reluctant permission from Joseph to go off on their own and flitted away as Louisa and Joseph moved through the excited crowd.

Outside they traversed the perimeter of the tent to the back side, where a smaller tent stood, the sailcloth flaps that flanked its entrance undulating in the breeze. A sign on an easel read *Martin's Marvels*. Louisa looked up and saw that the dark cloud that had seemed so far away was now overtaking the sky. "Shall we go inside?"

A man with hair that sprung from his head in all directions like a mane greeted them and gestured to a semicircle of tables and a crowd of people moving slowly from one to the next. "Welcome, folks. Welcome to Martin's Marvels, where you will see things that will shock your mind and disturb your sense of the natural order. Be the first of your friends to see the pig-faced lady in her prettiest dress, the world's smallest man and his giantess wife, the 'two-headed nightingale' singing slave songs from her plantation in North Carolina. Ten cents, folks."

Joseph and Louisa looked at each other and raised their eyebrows. Finally she shrugged and Joseph fished two dimes from his pocket. As they passed, the man turned his attention to a group of boys filing in at the entrance. "One at a time, now, boys, one at a time. The half-woman isn't going anywhere—she can't move very fast without any legs." He chuckled. "Get out your dimes now, please."

First they passed a table with a basket of eggs. A man held one out to Louisa. "Miss, could you tell me what this is, please?"

She looked at him, uncertain. "An egg?"

"And, if you don't mind, where do eggs come from?"

"From chickens, sir."

"Since the egg came from a chicken, would you not expect to find a little yellow chick inside it?"

"Yes, sir, I would."

"Would you crack the egg open, please?"

Louisa shook her head. "The chick will die if you crack it open before it's ready."

"That so?" He looked steadily at her, then at Joseph, as if to challenge him to question the next bit. He slammed the egg too hard against the tabletop. Louisa winced, then reeled as a full-grown pigeon careened toward her face. Several ladies cried out as it swerved, teetering around the tent, then circled back and landed on the table, folding its wings and pecking at the seed the man sprinkled at its feet.

"Well, that's a dirty trick," Joseph said. "You should be more careful."

"I had no idea that was in there," the man said. He winked at them and grinned. Three of his front teeth were missing, and he stuck his tongue out at them through the gap.

Louisa moved closer to Joseph and he pulled her away to the next exhibit. A perfectly demure woman sat on a throne raised above the floor on a platform. She wore a vaguely rococo dress from the previous century, made of gold and burgundy brocade, and her waist was tightly corseted so that her bosom nearly spilled out at the top in a way that seemed obscene to the ladies in the tent, though they knew from paintings in museums and their grandmothers' stories that this had once been the fashion. Members of the crowd stood gaping at her, not because of her décolletage, but because every inch of the woman's skin was covered in silky black hair. It sprouted from the bridge of her nose, grew in tendrils from her ears, bristled along her shoulders. When she spoke, the people standing on either side of Joseph and Louisa reeled back.

"I am Madame Clofullia. Gaze upon me," she said, looking around. "I do not mind. I am a real woman, flesh and blood. I have a son. He is like me." She lifted the edge of her heavy skirt on one side and a small boy emerged from its dome. He wore a dusty black suit and his face was covered with hair the color of corn silk. He removed his hat and took a bow, then stood at his mother's side, clutching her downy hand.

"Sometimes I feel like life is one long string of exploitations," Louisa said. "Use or be used." Joseph had sensed that Louisa wanted to escape the disturbing sights of the marvels tent and suggested a walk. They headed out across the open field, their steps rustling crickets out of the grass and up into the air.

"I know what you mean."

"I listen to my father's friends talk about their ideas of what we *could* be, how we *could* live, and I feel hopeful. But then I go out into the world. I see a man putting these poor people on display for money. I hear that our own president agrees to let new states decide for themselves the question of slavery, when he should make their entrance into the Union contingent on an outright ban. It just doesn't end. So much needs to change."

"I think *we* will change it," Joseph said. "The men in your father's parlor—and don't misunderstand me, because I admire some of them more than anyone in the world—but all those men have done is talk and write, talk and write. Now it's time to act. It's going to be up to our generation to act."

"But how? So much of it seems to be human nature. Inevitable." Louisa was surprised to hear such a pessimistic statement come out of her mouth. Sometimes she felt so overwhelmed by managing her own existence, there wasn't anything left for other matters.

"That is why we have laws. Without them, the country becomes the sum of its citizens' impulses. We must make sure the laws represent the best of us, what we should always strive to be." The tall weeds and scrub of the field brushed his shins and fanned away.

"But in Georgia, the law says one man can own another."

"Then we must change the laws. Or break them. 'An unjust law is no law at all.'"

"Saint Augustine?" Louisa asked, smiling to herself that once again she had underestimated Joseph's knowledge of letters and ideas. "Do you mean you believe we will go to war?" She thought about that a moment. "I think I would like to fight. Do you think they would let me?"

Joseph smiled. "Those rednecks wouldn't stand a chance against you. But perhaps it won't come to that. There are other ways to take action. Do you know about what some folks have been doing over in Ohio? And right here in New Hampshire and Massachusetts? A secret transport operation. Helping slaves get to Canada." The expression on his face looked strangely familiar: eyebrows pulled high, mouth taut with the passion of his argument. It took her a moment to realize why she recognized it—it was just like an expression she'd seen in the mirror many times.

Louisa nodded. Everyone in Concord knew that Henry Thoreau was involved, though they never spoke of it. At night he guided the runaways through the dense woods, giving them food and finding them a place to hide when the daylight came. Most thought what he was doing was courageous but dangerous. He *was* breaking the law, after all, even if the law was wrong. Once, when she was about twelve, he took her out walking near his cabin to find where the scarlet tanagers were keeping their nest. The sun shining through the trees made a mottled pattern on the pine needle floor. Henry placed her palm on the cool, mossy side of a dead tree trunk.

"This is how they *know*," he'd said.

She'd lost her last baby molar the night before and the tip of her tongue rooted around in the empty space. "Know what?"

"Which way is north."

Joseph put his hand on her elbow and it wrenched her back to the present. "The most dangerous thing we can believe is that we are not the authors of our fate. God gave us reason, conscience. We must use it. To say that our life, our world, just *is* the way that it is, that we do not play a part—I think it is the worst kind of cowardice."

Dark circles began to appear along Joseph's shoulders. The light shifted like a lamp turning down and the sky opened. They turned around to see how far they had walked. The tent was a hundred yards away, and they saw the man at the entrance pull the flaps closed and cinch the rope to keep the wind and water out. The crowd that hadn't made it inside in time huddled just inside the entrance to the tent of marvels. Louisa felt goose bumps crawl across the back of her neck as the wind whipped over it. Joseph looked east. A gray barn slumped against a hill, its roof sinking in the middle from neglect. He motioned to her and they ran toward it. She felt the heels of her boots sinking into the mud and arched her feet as high as she could to run on her toes.

The wet hay in the doorway was slick beneath her feet, but a few steps inside, it was dry and rustled as they walked over it. Her hair was soaked through under her flimsy bonnet and she felt droplets crawling along her scalp. She longed to unfasten her chignon and shake the water out but she was self-conscious.

"Where do you suppose our sisters are?" Louisa asked, looking out across the field to the circus tent.

"Somewhere where their curls will stay dry." Joseph sat on an overturned crate and pulled an apple from his pocket. Louisa realized she was ravenous. He plucked his knife from his other pocket and unfolded it, pressing the blade into the fruit's russet skin. "Would you like some?"

She felt suddenly alarmed by how comfortable she felt around him and busied herself with untying her bonnet. Throughout the day they had become increasingly easy around each other. Louisa had forgotten to monitor her words and expressions. She wondered if she had grown too familiar with him. "No, thank you."

He grinned. "Yes, you would. I *saw* you looking at it."

Louisa felt her cheeks flush and turned away. "You must be mistaken."

"You are a puzzle to me, Miss Louisa. It seems we circle each other, become friends, speak openly . . ." He carved the core out of each of the four quarters. The rain droned on outside, forcing him to raise his voice to be heard. "But then—suddenly, it seems to me—you pull away. And it's as if we are strangers again."

He was exactly right, of course. She didn't know what to say and didn't dare look back at him.

"There's only one thing for me to do, and that's to stop paying any attention to the things you say." He pulled another crate from the stack and set it on the floor next to his, then pointed at it. "Sit," he ordered, an amused smile on his face.

Louisa smiled in spite of herself and relented. When she lowered herself onto the crate, she felt the small of her back press into the damp fabric of her dress. She suppressed a shiver. "It's only that . . ." She scanned his face and noticed a bump on the bridge of his nose where he must have broken it as a child. She longed to touch it. "I believe you are a puzzle to me as well."

He handed her a piece of the apple. "What do you want to know?"

She chewed a fragrant bite. "What were you like as a boy?"

"Just about the same, I suppose. Only shorter." He grinned.

"I think that grin comes from the devil himself."

"My mother used to say that to me. She never could stay mad if I was smiling at her. Even the time I stomped out all the beets in her garden. I disliked beets more than any other food. Still do."

Louisa hesitated. "What happened to her? Your mother."

"I was to have another sister. When Catherine was just three. But our mother died giving birth to her and the baby died a few days later. Her name was Elizabeth." He examined his palms. "Like my mother."

She felt something open in her chest and her eyes grew damp. "Forgive me—I shouldn't have intruded. . . ."

He shook his head. "It was a long time ago."

Louisa didn't know what to say. She put her hands on her knees, then clasped them together, worrying the skin around her thumbnails.

He touched her hand. "Anything else you'd like to know?" She looked up into his eyes. They seemed almost to be challenging her.

"I think I know it all now."

Joseph hesitated, his forehead creased. "You nearly do, though there *is* something else. . . ."

"Nearly is just fine, I think," Louisa said, dropping her gaze back to her lap, hoping to ease his worries.

The rain pummeled the side of the barn; the noise was deafening. They sat so close together their shoulders nearly touched. Joseph leaned toward her and she felt the fabric of his shirt make contact with her sleeve. He turned to face her, then reached up and swept his index finger across her cheek, along her earlobe, down her hairline to the nape of her neck. The toes of his shoes touched the outside edge of her left boot. She kept her eyes on the dark shape they made in the hay.

"Are you cold, Louisa?"

She tried to breathe. "No," she whispered, just as a chilly shiver cascaded down her back. She thought of the poem: *This is the touch of my lips to yours . . . this is the murmur of yearning.*

Joseph grinned again, amused by her stubbornness, and she looked up at him. A moment of delicious tension passed and she thought of the circus tumblers suspended in midair, their bodies arched, coiled like springs.

Joseph took a breath and spoke. "I wonder, do you think . . ." He looked away, raked his fingers through his hair, then looked back at Louisa. "Do you think I might kiss you?"

Her eyes widened and she felt her body arch away from

him before her mind had time to catch up. "This is . . . I . . ." she fumbled, trying to regain her footing.

Joseph's face fell and contrition came over it like a cloud. "I'm so sorry—please, Louisa, forgive me for overstepping . . ."

Louisa shook her head quickly, the way one might to scatter the remnants of a dream. Her face was hot with mortification. She didn't want him to apologize. She wanted to retreat in time, wanted the chance to react some other way, but she knew she couldn't. Her mind raced in search of a diversion. "Don't you think we should check on Catherine and May? This is a terrible storm."

The rain pounded the saturated ground outside and the barn seemed to sway in the wind. Joseph joined Louisa in the doorway and looked out to see the darkest part of the sky receding to reveal a pale blue patch.

"I believe the storm has nearly wrung itself out, and I'm sure the girls are safe inside the tent." He folded his hands in a gesture of prayer. "If I promise to be very, very good, will you stay just a little while longer?"

Louisa examined Joseph's face—the arched brows, the beguiling grin. The awkwardness that had passed between them a moment before was melting away. In spite of herself Louisa smiled, then nodded. She turned back into the dim interior of the barn, where the air was sweet with the scent of hay, and Joseph followed.

To live for one's principles, at all costs,

is a dangerous speculation.

—"Transcendental Wild Oats:
A Chapter from an Unwritten Romance"

Chapter Nine

When Mr. and Mrs. Alcott and their two older daughters were invited to dine at the Suttons' to celebrate the harvest, Louisa faced her scant dress options with a slightly heavy heart but dignified resolve. She'd simply make the best of what she had, borrowing an expensive shawl sent to May by an aunt. For Anna, on the other hand, the situation was grave. Louisa could see that she felt this was her chance to make a good impression on the Sutton family, and particularly to sustain the impression she hoped she'd made on Nicholas. Louisa reassured her sister that it was her pink cheeks and dark eyes he was after, not the quality of her dress fabric. Those were the sorts of details noticed only by other women, Louisa told her. And *they* would be jealous of Anna, no matter what she wore, since she was so kindhearted and wise that no man could help falling in love with her.

"If only my sister's good opinion could act as decree!" Anna proclaimed as the four of them set out, finally, for the Sutton house.

This time of year the imposing trees on Washington

Square blocked a pedestrian's view of many of its buildings. Some of the trees were hundreds of years old, with foliage so thick, hardly any light came through. Consequently, the Alcotts did not see the façade of the Sutton home until they were nearly upon it. It sat on the corner of Westminster and River Road, set apart from its neighbors by a regal white fence and gate that now hung invitingly open.

They were received by an efficient, unsmiling servant, who ushered them through the entryway, which faced the back side of the ascending staircase, rising from the rear toward the front of the first floor. Louisa tried not to gawk at the elaborate carving work around the ceiling, up the banister, and along the arches between one room and the next. The entryway and first parlor walls were covered in a pale blue paper featuring majestic-looking pheasants. She could sense her sister's surprise at just how well off Nicholas Sutton might be.

Charles Sutton stood in the center of the parlor with his thumbs hooked on his suspenders, a corpulent figure with scarlet cheeks and a bellowing laugh. Margaret had told Louisa and Anna that Mr. Sutton was born in Boston to a well-known family who built ships for the navy. The War of 1812 had the Suttons building ships faster than the British could fill them with cannonballs. By the time Charles's father passed away, he had amassed quite a fortune. Though Charles knew he was fortunate to have been born into such wealth, he had always felt his father pressured him into taking over the family business, when in truth Charles had little interest in matters of money and commerce. As an act of somewhat cowardly rebellion, considering the man it intended to irk was dead, Charles took the money with him and left Boston for the New Hampshire countryside. No one was quite sure what he did with his time now. He was said, depending on whom you asked, to be alternately writing poetry, tinkering in his workshop with a machine that boiled water without fire, or chronicling the migration patterns of New England bird species. Perhaps it was all three. People only knew that there must have been quite a bit of money to sustain his family on no income.

He had caused quite a scandal soon after his arrival in Walpole in 1830 by falling feverishly in love with the governess of his neighbors' children, a working-class girl from Dublin named Clara McCarron, who, shrewdly, did not waste time marveling at her good fortune and agreed immediately to be his wife. Hence, their children, Nicholas and Nora, who came along in quick succession, had a most unusual New England upbringing of sensitivity to all economic classes and watered-down Catholicism, though Mrs. Sutton did not hold fast to it. She was a practical sort of person, and she reasoned that if the Divine Father had cast this loving and quite wealthy man in her path, He *must* have wanted her to marry him. The small matter of his being a Protestant could be overlooked.

Nicholas wore a butternut frock coat over a silk waistcoat secured with steel buttons. An Albert chain looped around one of the buttons and connected to the watch in his pocket. He stood off to the side with the newly engaged Samuel and Margaret. They seemed to be floating just a bit above the ground, glancing every few moments at each other with a look of pure pleasure. A similar expression crossed Nicholas's face when he saw Anna enter the room. He had the features some described as "black Irish"—dark hair and countenance with clear blue eyes—but Anna's appearance lightened his features. He glided over toward the Alcotts, taking her hand.

"Mr. Sutton, this is my father and mother, Mr. and Mrs. Alcott. And of course, you know my sister Louisa."

Nicholas nodded, smiling as he took each of their hands. Louisa felt a rush of pride that her father had dressed so carefully for the evening. His coat was a little faded and his cravat not starched quite as stiffly as it could have been, but his attire was entirely appropriate for the occasion. No one in the room would have guessed that Bronson's ideas about clothing had once been a source of mortification for his daughters. Not so many years ago he had insisted on strict adherence to his philosophies in even the mundane arena of dress. He rejected anything made from an animal's hide, including leather for shoes and belts, and eschewed cotton because of its connection to the slave trade. Fleece belonged to the sheep, and man had no right to take it. Linen was nearly the only material that did not carry with it the burden of some sort of oppression, and his daughters spent many New England winters chilled to the bone in the name of his peculiar morality. Fortunately, in recent years Bronson had relaxed on matters of dress, compelled to accept gifts and hand-me-downs of all kinds. But Louisa would take this rather dusty and rumpled father over his more severe former self any day, especially because tonight he appeared so jolly. As much as he claimed to loathe the trappings of society, Bronson loved a good party.

Anna had refused to tell her mother and father much about Nicholas and her feelings for him. She told Louisa she felt it was premature, since he had not yet pledged himself to her or come to speak to Bronson. Louisa could see, though, watching them talk together, that there was no question of what was to come. She felt her heart give way, a wilted flower finally dropping from its stem. Nicholas's affections were wonderful news for Anna. She would be able to leave home and have a secure future. She would be a mother and have a garden and nice dresses—all the things she wanted.

Louisa knew that her own anguish on the matter was pure selfishness at best. Perhaps it even revealed slight jealousy. It wasn't that she was jealous of Anna's prospects; in fact, Louisa's chest tightened at the very thought of spending her days as mistress of an enormous house like this one. Rather, she envied the way Anna so effortlessly complied with others' expectations of how she should live, what she should dream about. Anna yearned for things, but they were all within the boundaries of acceptability. What Louisa wanted—to have freedom and money of her own, lots of it, so that she could control her fate and take care of her parents, to come and go as she pleased, to have an apartment of her own, with big bright windows and a desk so wide she could curl up to sleep on top of it when the words wouldn't come—these weren't the sorts of yearnings one discussed at parties. Anna was a blade of grass, swaying in the wind in concert with all the other blades. Louisa was a rare bird poking its head above them, a thing with purple feathers and a strangely hooked beak. She just could not, would not, adhere to convention when it went against her own heart.

Becoming a spinster didn't bother her. In fact, it appealed to the part of her that ached to go against the grain. Spinsterhood seemed a powerful position. At Louisa's age of twenty-two, people still asked questions, still hoped that she would find a husband. But in a few more years, certainly by her thirtieth birthday, the clamor would die down and her position would set, like the hardening of sculptor's clay. After all, *someone* has to be the governess; *someone* has to teach school and nurse the sick. No, Louisa didn't mind being a spinster, but the prospect of being completely alone troubled her. In her mind, marriage and love had little to do with one another, and she wished there could be some kind of middle ground. A few lucky people saw the two states coincide, but when they did, it was a complete accident, for it seemed marriage by its very design was meant to seek out love and destroy it. Seen with a cold, practical eye, the state of marriage was nothing more than indentured servitude, legal dependence, a claiming of property. One surrendered her mind and her autonomy when she pledged her fidelity. It was as simple as that.

Louisa's thoughts were interrupted as the party guests were called to take their seats. She felt the scuffed toes of her boots sink into the red carpet of the octagonal dining room. The table stretched toward the fireplace, recently stoked, with flames leaping up the chimney. A servant showed the Alcotts to their places and Louisa eased into her chair, her eyes roving the collage of ivory china, silver, and glass that adorned the table.

Mr. Charles Sutton stood at the head of the table, a forearm resting on his great shelf of a belly. He waited patiently for the rest of the guests to take their seats, then raised his glass in the air. The loud talking subsided, though a few of the women could be heard expressing a last giggle before he had the room's attention. He appeared to be poised to make an announcement or propose a toast. Louisa looked over at Samuel and Margaret. It seemed odd that Mr. Sutton should be the one to offer public congratulations, since Margaret's parents hadn't yet had time to organize a gathering of their own, and it was only proper that *they* should announce their own daughter's engagement.

"My friends," Mr. Sutton began, his baritone a viscous liquid oozing into every corner of the room, "as you well know, the book of Genesis, that splendid chronicle of beginnings large and small, beginnings of man, yes, but also the sun and planets, our oceans and rivers, from the thundering Nile to our stately Connecticut to the stream that bisects this very property, it is from that book of Genesis that we learn the story of Adam and Eve, the first example of that holy companionship . . ."

Louisa and the other guests continued to hold their glasses suspended above the table, though it seemed Mr. Sutton was only beginning a somewhat lengthy speech. She cut her eyes at Anna, seated beside her, and Anna raised an eyebrow, a substitute for a shrug, as if to say, *oh dear*.

". . . that we call marriage. Adam, you see, was lonely. Despite the paradise that surrounded him, which we only can imagine and will not know until we enter that heavenly place when our last breaths leave us, despite the beauty and tranquillity—no money, no death or sin or shame—he was lonely. That is how elemental our need for companionship can be. And God made the animals, all the beasts of the world, 'all things bright and beautiful, all creatures great and small,' but it was not enough for Adam . . ."

Louisa wondered wryly whether she had accidentally stumbled upon a Sunday service. She glanced around the long table, which held at least twenty guests. Mrs. Sutton and Nora looked more like sisters than mother and daughter.

Each had a porcelain face framed by orange hair and they had the same delicate hands. Mrs. Sutton clasped hers in the pose of prayer and tilted her chin up toward her husband, her face full of adoring dotage. It appeared she was the only one enthralled with his speech. Next to Mrs. Sutton, Nora and Nicholas fingered their cutlery, a little embarrassed of their loquacious father. Next was Margaret with her mother and father, then Samuel Parker with his parents. Louisa continued around to a family she did not recognize, which exhausted the list of guests sitting opposite her. Those on the same side of the table, down at the other end from her sister and parents, were too hard to see without the kind of stretching and straining that would appear rude.

". . . and so God created woman. Beautiful, mild, steadfast, gentle . . ."

Margaret bugged her eyes and Louisa suppressed a giggle. She nodded her head in the direction of her father, whose eyelids fluttered on the verge of sleep, his cup of wine tilting dangerously sideways as he faded from consciousness.

". . . and it has always been thus, two people bound together by God to stand against the tyrannies, disappointments, illnesses of mind and body that are the signatures of this world. And the joys too. We can only hope and pray for many of those . . ."

Louisa's wrist ached from holding her glass aloft. She considered setting it down when she heard the familiar sound of tapping fingertips, this time on the underside of the dining chair a few guests down from her. Before she could think what to do she leaned back in her chair slightly, looking in the direction of the sound. Joseph was looking back at her, a beguiling grin on his face. Louisa would always think back on his expression, the look of a boy, really, just a boy, unaware that in a moment his life would change forever.

Mr. Sutton had gone on, though Louisa's heart seemed to fill her mouth and plug up her ears. She couldn't get her brain to focus on what he was saying. Suddenly, Mr. Singer was standing, looking quite ill, his face grave.

"And so it is with hearts full of joy"—apparently not in Mr. Singer's case, Louisa noted—"that we announce the engagement of my Nora to Mr. Joseph Singer. We wish them all the happiness God can bestow."

Louisa sat frozen in place, her eyes tracing the outline of a flower embroidered on the tablecloth. A great cry of surprise and relief disguised as good cheer went up among the guests and they drank, finally, a sip from the heavy glasses they were so glad to place back on the table. Louisa turned to see Joseph standing slowly, the color gone from his face, as Mr. Sutton pressed Joseph's hand to Nora's. She was stunning in an emerald-green dress—the perfect complement to her hair—with a white lace overskirt. The wide neckline wreathed her delicate shoulders, and a tiny locket hung over her collarbone. She is in every way, Louisa reflected, my complete opposite—petite, fair, delicate, soft-spoken. Joseph looked stricken and glanced to his father with wide eyes. The infirm man shook his head slightly, some kind of inadequate apology perhaps, and sat back down, looking away. Mr. Sutton pounded Joseph heartily on the back a few times, and Nora beamed at her father and then her intended, nearly bursting with pride at her luck in men.

And Joseph looked at Louisa. But she turned and kept her eyes on the table and clutched her napkin as if it were the rope that kept the sea from washing her away.

When women set their hearts on anything it is a known fact that they seldom fail to accomplish it.

—"Mrs. Podgers' Teapot"

Chapter Ten

The meal passed quickly in celebratory spirit. Two engaged couples in one week was big news in such a small town. The talk was boisterous and ongoing, despite mouths full of food, and guests gulped their wine mid-sentence and prattled on. They were clearly enjoying themselves, but there was also a kind of urgency to their conversation, as if they felt compelled to fill every lull in the talking, in case Charles Sutton attempted another lengthy speech.

Louisa felt she was playing her most difficult role yet— Lighthearted Acquaintance to the Newly Engaged Couple. It was a minor part, which didn't have many lines and kept her standing upstage for most of the scene. When she'd acted in *The Captive of Castile* and *The Greek Slave*, plays she'd written as a girl to perform with her sisters, she'd found it useful to think about a particular adjective and hold it in her mind as she was speaking her lines. Words were more powerful to her than images, more precise and layered. When she played Mrs. Malaprop she thought of the word *befuddled*. Now she held the word *beatific* in her mind and tried to project its essence in her face. Pleased but distant. Out of reach of more base emotions like jealousy and betrayal. She seemed to be convincing her audience. After all, none of them had reason to suspect she would care one way or the other about whom Joseph Singer planned to marry. She'd met him only a few times and had proclaimed him insufferable within earshot of her mother and sisters. Only Anna eyed Louisa carefully, searching for signs of distress. But Anna couldn't be sure. Louisa was, after all, a very good actress.

Finally the meal was ended. The Alcotts bade good evening to the other guests and congratulations to their hosts, though Louisa abruptly volunteered to see about her mother and sister's bonnets when she saw Joseph heading across the parlor toward them. The fresh night air was sweet with summer flowers as they made their way along West-minster Street. They had talked themselves out at the party, and now they walked quietly together, noticing the sound of crickets and an obsidian sky flecked with stars. Louisa was grateful not to have to talk. It was one thing to keep up the appearance of her good mood when she was with a group of near strangers, but with her family it was a different matter. She'd never been the kind of child who kept her emotions to herself. Always wanting, yearning, for something, some intangible thing that she could not identify or understand, let alone attain.

Fast on the heels of the memory of these fits was the mem-ory of the shame that went along with them. Self-restraint, mastery of impulse—these were the qualities her father held in the highest regard, the qualities he tried to instill in his daughters from an early age. As he chronicled their early childhood in his journals, he detailed their attempts at identity, their achievements, their sins, and the corrections he made in the hopes of raising them into the best sort of women he could imagine. He was trying to prove his theory that a child came into the world blank, a sponge ready to absorb its surroundings. With Anna the theory held; she behaved just as he instructed her to, never straying or giving in to temptation. But Louisa was different, all fierceness and petulance, poised for combat, then instantly full of regret. Furthermore, he conceded that some traits probably were inherited, particularly the bad ones. He was convinced Louisa had inherited her temper from her mother. He saw in her dark features the mark of the devil and told her often that she was "not a child of light."

Abba could plainly see that Louisa was troubled but mercifully let her be. Louisa went straight up to bed. It wasn't until she pulled the light cotton summer blanket up over her head that she finally let the tears flow. She drew a mournful breath, taking care that Anna should not hear her. Images of the last few weeks thronged her mind. How, she wanted to know, could Joseph have sat with her at the picnic as he did; how could he have come to call on her to talk about Whitman, speak to her as a close friend in the barn during the rainstorm—ask to kiss her!—and not *once* mention that he was to become engaged, soon, to a girl she knew. To the sister, Louisa realized with horror, of the man Anna might very well marry. Louisa wiped angrily at her eyes. Would she spend the rest of her life watching the man she thought she might—she hesitated even to use the word, it sounded so foolish—*love*, live as husband to a sister-in-law?

But after a few minutes more of the crying, she was

through. She had been raised to believe that being denied the thing we think we want the most can make us strong and wise in ways we cannot imagine. If Louisa had anything, it was a will of iron. Once she made up her mind to do something, it was as good as done, and nothing could dissuade her. And so she made up her mind then to slough away these feelings, for as quickly as they had emerged, they could be discarded, she reasoned, and she could be free of sadness. *I cannot wish him ill*, she thought. *If he is happy, then all the better for it, and I shall be happy too, in my own way, in my own time.* But even as she told herself this, the sentiment rang hollow.

Louisa didn't fall asleep until the early morning hours, and soon the harsh light of dawn was slicing into her dream. Before she was even conscious she felt her whole body resist waking. The events of the previous night appeared in her mind like a trout surfacing in a stream. But the awareness came before she could stop it. She sat up when she heard a soft clink of something striking the window next to her bed. She looked over at Anna, who lay curled in the sheets. Louisa heard the sound again and this time saw a small stone make contact with the glass.

She slipped out of her faded nightgown and into a work dress that was in need of laundering. She pinned up her hair as she descended the steps to the front hall, smoothing the curls around her forehead flat. The bright sun stung her eyes as she pulled open the heavy door wide enough to peer out. Joseph stood with his hat in his hand. He wore the wilted white shirt from the night before, his cravat hanging untied around his neck.

It took a moment for her to summon a voice from her throat. "Why are you here?"

Joseph's eyes were red. Sandy whiskers colored the skin around his mouth. "I needed to speak with you."

"Have you been up all night?" She eyed his face carefully, wondered if he had been drinking.

"Yes. I was waiting until morning so I could come to see you. I would have come last night, but I didn't want to wake you."

"I'm sorry you came all the way here," Louisa said as she began to close the door. "But I can't talk now."

He stuck his hand through the narrow opening and grabbed her arm. "Wait."

She opened the door a few inches and sighed. She noticed he wasn't as tall as she had thought. In fact, he was about her height. She stood level with his mournful eyes.

"Please, Louisa." Desperation flashed in his eyes. "Give me a chance to explain."

"Joseph, you owe me no explanation. This is happy news for you and your family. You have my congratulations." All around them birds chirped an irritating chorus.

Exhaustion showed on Joseph's face. "But you don't *understand*," he snapped.

Louisa felt her humiliation harden into an anger that raced up the back of her neck. "I understand *perfectly*," she said, pointing her index finger at his chest. "I understand you had your fun with me while you could. I understand that you aren't who I thought you were, and now you want me to tell you it's all right. Well, I won't."

"But it's not—"

"—and if you do not leave the property this instant, I am going to scream for my father."

Joseph opened his mouth to speak but hesitated. Louisa's

eyes shone, daring him to test her. She pinned her lips into a slim line. He tipped his head down and pressed his hat slowly back on, his palm lingering on its crown a moment, as if he had to muster the energy to lift his head. Louisa watched him walk slowly down the path, then pressed the door closed and secured the latch.

He came back in the afternoon, when Bronson was tucked away in his study and Abba had gone to the orchard to trade her plum jam for summer apples. Louisa was sitting in the dormer near her bed reading and looked up from the page when a movement on the front path caught her eye. Joseph wore a clean shirt, white linen, with the sleeves rolled up to the elbows. A book was tucked between his brown forearm and his ribs. She ducked out of the window and backed onto her bed. Anna sat in her rocker by the other window, plucking at a square of embroidery.

"Anna," Louisa said as the knock sounded below. "Joseph's at the door."

Anna looked up, surprised. "Do you want to see him?"

"No. Tell him . . . tell him I'm ill. Or that I've gone out. Yes, tell him I've gone out."

Anna appraised her sister with a sympathetic frown. "Oh, Lou, what he did to you is . . ."

Joseph knocked again.

"Hush about that. Go—before Father hears him and comes out of his study." Anna hesitated a moment before she draped the embroidery over the arm of the chair and hurried toward the steps. Louisa closed her eyes and listened to Anna's dress swish across the floorboards.

She heard voices drifting up through the open windows below but couldn't make out what they said. Soon the heavy door closed. Louisa lowered herself to her knees and peered over the bottom of the window just in time to see Joseph traverse the last few feet of the path and exit the front gate. He looked back at the house and Louisa dropped her head out of sight. She climbed back onto the bed and took up her book.

It took all her strength not to look up when Anna came in.

"Well," Anna said, standing in the center of the room. "Don't you want to know what he said?"

"Not particularly," Louisa said.

Anna rolled her eyes. "I tried to give him a piece of my mind, Louisa." Anna sat back in her rocker. "But he looked so . . . bereft. I tried to ask him why, why he didn't tell us about . . . Nora, his plans. But he just shook his head. Said he had to talk to you."

Louisa finally raised her eyes from the paragraph she'd been scanning for a full minute without comprehension. "We have nothing to say to each other."

"I know. He wanted me to give you this." She extended her arm toward Louisa, offering a book with a letter tucked in its front pages.

Louisa didn't put out her hand. "Burn it."

"But don't you at least want to see what it says? Perhaps there is *some* explanation for what happened."

"I can imagine no satisfactory explanation for lying. Can you?"

Anna shook her head. "No."

Louisa crossed her arms. "I think we must see people for

who they are, not who we wish they might be. It is hard now, but it will be for the best in the end. You know I'm not one for a fairy story."

"You used to be," Anna reminded her.

"As the verse says, 'When I was a child I spake as a child'—but the time comes to put away childish things. Some people disappoint. But not my sisters," Louisa said, taking Anna's empty hand. "Never my sisters. And for that I am grateful."

Anna bit her bottom lip. "What if *I* were to read it, and then, if it contained anything other than what we already know, I could tell you about it?" she ventured.

"You wouldn't dare. Give it to me." Louisa slid the square of paper out of the book, then lit the candle at her bedside and held the corner in its flame. She tilted the paper until two sides were engulfed, then laid it in a tin tray she sometimes used to bring tea up to their room in the afternoons. The flame flared as it consumed the fibers, then subsided into the orange perimeter of the ashes. "There," Louisa said. "Has Father made the fire in the parlor yet?"

Anna shook her head. "Not the book. Louisa Alcott—how can *you* burn a book?"

Louisa sighed. "All right, I won't burn the book." She reached for it but Anna hugged it to her breast.

"I don't believe you."

"No—I promise. I won't do anything to it. You can have it if you want. I just want to look at it for a moment."

Anna handed it to her. Louisa traced the small cover, then opened it and drew her finger across Mr. Whitman's portrait on the frontispiece. The copy was identical to Mr. Emerson's—same green cloth binding, same stamped letters of the title depicted as if they sprouted roots and leaves. The only difference in Joseph's copy was an inscription on the flyleaf:

From J.S. to L.M.A. He is "the poet of the woman the same as of the man."

Over the ensuing weeks, the letters continued to come every few days. After Louisa insisted on burning the first few, Anna made sure to intercept the mail and tuck the letters into her sewing basket, safe from her sister's wrath. She didn't open them, for they weren't hers to read, but something tugged at her, convinced her to save them in case Louisa had a change of heart.

As she made her way each day through the work that kept her hands busy but left her mind free to roam, Louisa tried hard not to let it drift back to that morning when Joseph stood on the front steps, tried not to remember his lips forming the word *please* as he begged her to listen to his explanation. But many times she could not resist and then the pictures flooded the space behind her eyes and she heard the word repeating in quick succession until it sounded like the call of a weary warbler beseeching his mate.

But Alcotts did not succumb, no matter the burden. There might not be a thing to do except struggle to wobbly feet and stand in the torrent, but sometimes that was enough to wear the torrent down, to coax out its final pathetic gust. In the end, an Alcott, though raw, bruised, and worn, was still standing. Louisa was determined that this would be so. She threw herself into the activities of daily life, hoping somehow *motion* could erase the blackboard of her memory in long quick strokes. But in her secret heart she despaired: why did anyone want to love anyone, if this was what came of it?

To keep from brooding, Louisa began work on a new volume of stories, a follow-up to *Flower Fables*, imagining she would finish it and be off to Boston at last. She cringed at her juvenile subject—Christmas elves—but it seemed prudent to stick with the formula that had worked before. She dutifully locked herself in her room for hours at a time, a basket of apples by her side, to work on it. The stories were slow going and she had no guarantee they would bring income, but when she sat by the fire in the evening in her ink-stained apron, her hand aching from clutching the pen all afternoon, Louisa felt rich in other ways. May had offered to do the illustrations and she worked at rough sketches in the evenings after dinner while Anna and Louisa scrubbed and shined in the kitchen. Louisa thought the drawings lovely, though she felt exasperated that once again her youngest sister had found a way to avoid helping with the chores.

Louisa knew that it was Anna, steady and reliable as always, who continued to do the lion's share of housework, despite her preoccupation with Nicholas Sutton. He continued to work on his house with the help of his father, Samuel Parker, a couple of uncles from Boston, and, Louisa realized, his brother-in-law-to-be, Joseph Singer. Together they measured, sawed, and hammered boards into place in the late summer heat. Though Nicholas had yet to speak to Bronson, he had pledged to Anna that he would do so soon. He wanted to wait until the house was finished, so they could marry promptly and take residence. As usual, Bronson had his head in the clouds and did not in the least suspect he would soon be asked for his eldest daughter's hand. Anna felt she could scarcely contain her excitement, but she didn't express it. She thought of all the sorts of faces that existed in the world—fat, thin, round, dark, white, or freckled—and guessed that heartbreak looked the same on every one of them. One could spot it from a mile away. The last thing Louisa needed to hear about was Anna's expectation that she would soon become engaged.

The opening night of the play approached, but the cast had not rehearsed nearly as much as Louisa knew they needed to. One week Walpole saw the worst thunderstorm anyone in town could remember, and all the young people were needed at home to help clear downed tree limbs and sweep up broken glass. Then the boys called off a rehearsal to spend time on the construction project. Fall was on its way, and Nicholas wanted to be sure the house was ready for the winter well before it came. Just as it seemed they would get back on schedule, May came down with a terrible cold and said she couldn't bear to know they were all together having fun without her. So Louisa called off rehearsal once again.

Finally, just days before opening night, the cast gathered at the Elmwood to devote themselves to their roles in *The Jacobite*.

"I'm so pleased we're all finally here," Louisa said as the group filed into the attic. The anticipation of seeing Joseph had rattled her nerves, and she resisted the impulse to scan the room for him, dreaded the possibility of awkward conversation. "We have a lot of work ahead of us, but I know if we can just buckle down and really *work* today and tomorrow, we'll be ready for Tuesday's performance."

May and Harriet passed around copies of the play and the paper rustled as the cast flipped through the pages to their various parts.

"Wait a minute," Louisa said. "Where are Paul and Alfie?"

"Over at the Academy, in the great hall," Margaret said. "They've painted all the pieces of the set, and it didn't make sense to put them together up here, only to have to take them down again."

Louisa nodded. "Of course. Good—so there's some progress, then. Now, let's see . . ." She starting making arbitrary checkmarks on her notes so as to appear engrossed in her thoughts. In truth she had just realized the scene that needed work included Joseph. There would be no putting off facing him. Best to get it out of the way. "I was thinking perhaps we should run through the final scene, where the Major's secret identity is revealed to Sir Richard, and John Duck jumps down from the chimney just in time to save the pardon."

"But we don't have a Sir Richard today," Anna said, giving Louisa a curious look. "Hadn't you noticed that Joseph's not here?"

Louisa looked up in surprise, relief washing over her, then tried to cover it with irritation. "Nicholas," she demanded. "Where's Joseph?"

Nicholas cleared his throat and shifted his weight from one foot to the other. "Right. Well, it seems he's not going to be able to be in the play after all. You know, his father hasn't been well."

Louisa nodded. "Is he worse off than before?"

Nicholas shrugged his shoulders. "It's hard to say. But either way, there's too much work at the store for one man to do, especially one who's ill every other day. So Joseph is needed there."

Louisa held his gaze a moment, trying to assess the veracity of this explanation. Nicholas looked down at his shoes.

"He hasn't time for a few more days until the play is over?" Margaret chimed in. "He's already learned all his lines." Louisa wouldn't have asked a question that seemed so rude, but she was eager to hear Nicholas's response.

He hesitated. "My sister—she's asked him not to attend. She feels this is . . ."

"Is what?" Margaret challenged.

"Is . . . frivolous. Considering his father's illness and their upcoming wedding."

Margaret rolled her eyes. "She behaves as if she's the first girl on earth to get married. Nora never did have a whole lot of sense."

"I'll ask you to hold your tongue on that account," Nicholas said, his dark brows lowering into a V. Anna looked nervously between him and Margaret.

Louisa held up her hand. "This will get us nowhere. We have two days left and no Sir Richard." She rubbed circles into her forehead, struggling to concentrate. "Paul will have to play the role."

Margaret looked skeptical. "Paul can scarcely speak a sentence to four people, much less an entire crowd."

"Well," Louisa said, "he will have to overcome his fear.

We've no other choice. But let's not ask him now—let him finish the sets first. May or Harriet, would either of you be willing to stand in, just for today?"

Harriet looked incredulous. "Play a man's role? Hardly."

Though Louisa usually found Harriet's whining amusing, today it needled her. "Not onstage—just for today's rehearsal."

"I'll do it, Lou," May said.

Louisa sighed. "Thank you, May—it's nice to see someone is still interested in ensuring the quality of this performance. Now stand up very straight and do your best to act like a mustached nobleman."

There are many Beths in the world, shy and quiet, sitting in corners till needed, and living for others so cheerfully that no one sees the sacrifices.

—*Little Women*

Chapter Eleven

Louisa rose before the others and pulled on her boots. This was what she loved: quiet solitude, the restful few hours when the frenetic pace of her mind subsided and she could embrace the blank rhythm of walking. Outside, the morning was golden. The angle of the light portended the coming autumn, though the trees were verdant still and full of songbirds. Louisa watched the intermittent bursts of feathers as the birds moved about, launching themselves to higher branches.

The path snaked away from the house and down a steep hill, where the trees were denser near the ravine and the morning light scarcely penetrated. The earth felt soft under her soles. Though the hoyden within her longed to run, she settled now for swift walking, as if her stride could outpace the thoughts trying to worm their way into her mind. Sometimes life seemed to her one long assault she was never quite prepared to defend herself against. If only she could slow it down, take each strange development one at a time, examine it, find some way to control it. She approached the edge of the ravine. The water slid over the limestone without making a sound.

Her father would say that the chaos of life, its unpredictability, existed to challenge one's commitment to improvement, that one must extract himself piece by piece out of the wildness and assemble a spirit that transcends the sum of mere body parts. Mr. Whitman seemed to say, rather, that the wildness *itself* was the thing to cultivate. For him, the spirit and the flesh were one, the physical experience of the world *was* divinity. Louisa supposed they both were right. Of one thing she felt certain: men would go on arguing about these matters as long as there were people on the earth. The women, meanwhile, would continue to peel the vegetables and soak the linens in boiling tubs and mend the torn seams and bring new lives into the world. Louisa wondered if anyone would ever write poetry about that.

The sun was getting higher now and Louisa turned back toward home. There was nothing that angered Anna more than sisters who disappeared when it was time to divide up the work for the day. In addition to the regular chores, they had the preparations for the play—there was no time to spare.

As Louisa came up the back path, Anna gave a little half-wave, her elbow clutching the broom to her side. "Isn't it lovely out this morning?"

"Yes," Louisa said. "You should hear the sound of all those birds as the sun is coming up. What a racket!"

"I'm sure Lizzie loved hearing them. It was thoughtful of you to take her walking with you."

"Lizzie?"

"Yes—has she not gone back into the house already?"

Louisa frowned at her sister. "Nan, I walked by myself this morning. I have not seen Lizzie since we sat in the parlor last night after supper."

Anna's eyes widened. "That's very strange, because she isn't here."

Just then Abba appeared in the doorway. "Louisa—I'm so happy you girls are back. I know you meant well, but you must tell me when you hatch these schemes. Last night was so damp, and I've been so worried."

Anna looked at Louisa and then back at her mother. "Marmee, Lizzie isn't with Louisa."

"Isn't with her? What do you mean?"

"I mean I walked alone this morning. I hadn't any idea anyone was worried about Lizzie until I walked up just now and Anna told me she isn't here."

Abba put her hand to her mouth. "You mean . . . you don't know where she is?"

"No, Marmee."

"God in heaven." Abba closed her eyes. "What could have . . . has my child been kidnapped?"

Anna shook her head. "Marmee, let's not jump to extremes. I know she is not as strong as the rest of us and that she is more timid than most, but Lizzie *is* twenty years old. She isn't a child."

Abba's eyes darkened. "I know the age of my own daughter—I was there the day she came into this world. But Lizzie is not like other girls her age. You know she is too gentle, too easily frightened to be out on her own. . . ."

"We talked last night of cakes for the party after tomorrow's performance. Perhaps she walked down to the orchard for more apples." Anna leaned the broom against the side of the house. "Louisa and I will go look for her."

Abba nodded. "Please do. I'm going to get your father out of his study." Abba turned and disappeared back into the house. Louisa and Anna set off diagonally across the open field that stretched southeast of town. The orchard began at its outer edge, about a mile from Yellow Wood. The sisters slogged through the mud in silence, swatting at the insects stirred up by the late-morning heat.

"I have a bad feeling, Nan. Marmee's right—this *is* very strange."

Anna gave her a sympathetic glance. "You only feel that way because you were so hard on Marmee the night May asked us to go to the circus. You're afraid she was right about what Lizzie should and shouldn't do."

"If anything should happen to her . . ." Louisa looked miserable.

"Don't say, 'It will be all my fault,' because that isn't true." The sisters were almost the same height, with the same long legs and sturdy hips. They walked with one synchronized stride.

"But I told her she needed to have a little adventure. What if something *has* happened?" Louisa continued to fret. "Do you think Marmee was right?"

"No, I don't. I think Lizzie is a grown woman, even if none of us treat her as one. She is sure to be nearby, either in the orchard or down by the river, and if we let her alone I'm sure she'd be home before dinner."

"Well, for Marmee's sake we shall look now," Louisa said.

Anna put her arm around her sister's waist and replied with a gentle tease. "And for the sake of your guilty conscience."

But though they looked up and down each of the neat rows of trees, their boughs heavy with apples flecked russet and mellow green, they couldn't find Lizzie. The orchard belonged to Mr. Parsons, who was an admirer of Bronson's writing on the education of young children and had followed his career. He had promised Abba the Alcotts could have as many apples as they liked if Bronson would promise to visit and answer his questions on Plato. Anna and Louisa trekked up the hill to his barn, where the wide door stood open to let in the light. Mr. Parsons wore a heavy apron and tinkered with a tool at the gears of his cider press.

Anna knocked on the open door, and Mr. Parsons looked up and grinned when he saw he had visitors. "Good morning, girls!"

"Good morning," Anna said.

"I understand we will have the pleasure of seeing both of you perform tomorrow night. Planché, is it?"

Louisa nodded. "Yes, sir. *The Jacobite.*"

"I've read it," he said, placing the tool back in its box and taking up the oil can. "But, you know, we usually have to go to Boston to see a play performed. I am looking forward to it."

Anna smiled, waiting a polite moment before changing the subject. "Mr. Parsons, have you seen our sister Lizzie around the orchard this morning?"

He thought a moment. "Lizzie—is she the one with the wavy blond hair?"

Anna shook her head. "No, that would be May—she is the youngest. You may never have met Lizzie. She does not usually go out."

"We call her our little housewife because she so likes to bake and sew and care for our father. There's nowhere in the world she likes to be except at home." Louisa felt the dread welling up in her voice.

"Well, then," Mr. Parsons said, observing Louisa with concern. "I shouldn't know her if I did see her. But I haven't seen anyone in the orchard this morning."

"Thank you, sir. We hope you enjoy the show tomorrow night," Anna said.

"I'm sure you will find her, girls. Please let me know if I can help in any way."

Anna and Louisa walked back across the field and down to the riverbank where they had gone swimming with their friends the month before. They saw no footprints in the mud, no stump that had been brushed off for sitting on.

"Could she be in town, do you think?" Anna asked. Her confidence seemed to be wavering.

"I can't imagine that she would. Last summer, when you were away in Syracuse and I had that awful cold, I was supposed to go to the grocery one day before Marmee got home, but I felt so sick. I asked Lizzie to go and she nearly cried at the thought of doing it alone. In the end we went together." Louisa shook her head. "But we'd better check nonetheless. She may be there. How can we face Marmee if we haven't looked everywhere?"

Anna nodded. They set off walking in silence down the hill toward Main Street, afraid to give voice to their private thoughts.

Their fears only deepened as they scanned Washington Square and entered each shop to inquire whether anyone had seen Lizzie. She wasn't in either the Whig or the Democratic village store, nor the tavern, nor Slade's Meat Market. The barbershop was teeming with children crowding around to spend their pocket money on root beer and peanuts, but Lizzie was nowhere to be found. When they'd made their way all around the square, they stood in front of Singer's Dry Goods. Anna strode toward the entrance but Louisa hesitated.

Anna turned back. "Come on, let's . . ." She looked up at the sign over the door. "Oh." Louisa's eyes filled with tears as she silently admonished herself. Something terrible could have happened to Lizzie and still she could only think about her own discomfort at having to see Joseph Singer. She was a self-ish sister—if guilt was her fate, she deserved it, she thought.

"Lou, why don't you wait here, and I'll go inside to check?"

Louisa shook her head, determined. "No. I am coming with you."

They entered and the familiar bell sounded above their heads. Louisa hadn't been in since the morning of the circus, and the smell of cinnamon and spices was a bittersweet reminder of that day. Her heart pounded against her ribs and she didn't dare look toward the counter where a woman stood waiting to pay for her purchase.

"Hello, *Mr.* Singer," Anna called out, more for Louisa's benefit than to get his attention. She pulled Louisa by the sleeve toward where Joseph's father stood hunched over the cash drawer, his trembling hand spilling the coins as he tried to place them in their proper compartments. A stern woman held a cake of soap wrapped in paper and sighed impatiently. "If you drop my coins and they roll under the counter, I'm not going to give you any more."

Mr. Singer paused and steadied his hand, dropping the remaining money in place. "No, of course not, Mrs. Hawkins." He slowly pushed in the drawer. "There. All set.

I hope you have a lovely afternoon." Mrs. Hawkins scoffed and turned away without a reply.

Mr. Singer sighed, then turned to Anna. "Hello, Miss Alcott, is it? I believe I've met your sister, here."

"Yes." She nodded. "Louisa."

"Yes, hello, Miss Louisa. Joseph isn't here today. He's gone to Bellows Falls to pick up a shipment of flannel."

Louisa exhaled, relieved he would not pop out from the back room at any moment. "Sir, we're looking for our sister Lizzie. Not May—she is the one who is Catherine's age. Lizzie comes between May and me. You haven't seen her today in town, have you?"

"No, my dears. I've had only the regular customers today." He nodded toward the door, just now closing behind the haughty Mrs. Hawkins. "Though I can't say I wouldn't trade some of them for a gentle sister of yours."

Louisa smiled at the tired-looking man who seemed to have aged so far beyond his years. She felt full of sadness for him, for Joseph—for herself. And Lizzie—where could she be?

Though Anna and Louisa dreaded the scene at Yellow Wood, they knew they had better hurry to tell their parents they had no news. Back home, Abba sat in the parlor twisting a handkerchief in her lap. May sat by her side, stroking the worn sleeve of Abba's dress. Abba looked up when she saw them walk in. "My girls, have you found her?"

Anna knelt down in front of her mother. "No, Marmee. But I know we will hear something soon."

"This is dreadful," May said. "Just dreadful."

"Your father has gone to look in all the shops."

"We just came from there," Louisa said from where she stood by the fireplace, immediately regretting drawing attention to herself. Abba looked at her expectantly. "No one has seen her," Louisa said.

"Well, where else can we look?" Abba's voice was frantic. "Where else could she be? A person doesn't just vanish into thin air."

Anna looked around the room. "Have you noticed anything missing? Her bonnet? Any of her books?"

May nodded. "Her shoes are gone but her bonnet is still here. And this is very strange: *My* pink poplin dress, the one with the yellow sash that got torn on the gate at Pinckney Street—it's not in my room."

"Well, that's it," Louisa shouted a little too loudly. "She probably took it to a seamstress to have it fixed—to have a better sash sewn on. As a surprise. A belated birthday gift." May had turned fifteen in July.

"But she hasn't any money, Louisa," May said softly.

They brooded a moment, unable to think what to do next. Then, out of the silence came the *clip-clop, clip-clop* of horses out in front of the house. Louisa ran to the window and yanked the drape aside.

"It's Mr. *Singer's* carriage." The others rushed up behind Louisa and watched as the carriage slowed and a man got out. Louisa gasped and let go of the drape. It swung shut. "It's Joseph."

"Louisa," May shrieked. "Get *out* of the way—we can't see." Louisa moved away from the window, panic prickling the skin across her shoulders.

"He has a young lady with him," Abba said.

Anna was a head taller than her mother and stood behind her. "Is it Nora Sutton?"

Louisa gave her older sister a scathing look, which Anna pretended not to see.

May shrieked again. "Nora Sutton is wearing my pink poplin. Look—there's the yellow sash!"

Louisa took a breath and looked out once more. A smile spread across her face and she felt her voice wobble in her throat as she tried to speak. "That's not Nora Sutton—that's *Lizzie*. See, Anna, she has on your old bonnet. It's Lizzie—she's all right!"

"Here they come," shrieked May, dropping the drape.

Louisa ran to the front door and threw it open. "Lizzie!" She ran to her sister and folded her in her arms, pulling her inside and ignoring Joseph. Abba, Anna, and May crowded around.

"Oh, Elizabeth," Abba cried. "You don't know how we've worried." Louisa took care to lead her sister straight to the sofa and not to look up at Joseph, who stood watching the happy scene from the threshold, his hat in his hands. Soon Anna noticed their want of manners and rushed to the door.

"Joseph, please—come in." He nodded his appreciation and stepped inside, closing the heavy door.

Anna went to the window and refastened the drapes to let in the late-afternoon sun. "So we have you to thank for rescuing our sister?"

Joseph chuckled. "I don't know that she needed rescuing, but her feet *were* tired after such a long walk. I believe she did appreciate the offer of a ride home." Anna squeezed his arm and gestured to their father's armchair. "Please—sit. I will make some tea." She scurried into the kitchen.

"Long walk?" Abba said, still reeling from the shock of seeing her timid daughter dressed for her outing. "To where?"

"Bellows Falls, Marmee." Surprised, they all turned to Lizzie. She hadn't spoken a word since she arrived. A flash of orange fur darted out from the kitchen. Ginger leapt into Lizzie's lap and nudged her face into the crook of her elbow.

"You walked to Bellows Falls?" May asked, incredulous. Lizzie nodded, stroking the cat's head. "But that's five *miles* at least."

Lizzie sat up very straight on the worn sofa and slowly untied the bonnet. Her eyes were bright, though she looked tired and pale. "I just wanted to see . . ." Her voice tightened with tears. ". . . if I could do it. And I did."

Louisa knelt down on the floor in front of her and took her hand. "Of course you did."

Lizzie looked at each of her sisters. "Home is, to me, the most wonderful place. You know that I have always been content to listen to my sisters' stories, to see the world through your eyes. But sometimes . . ." She hesitated.

". . . you want to see it for yourself," Louisa said.

Lizzie nodded. "I wanted to turn up my hair and put on a nice dress—can you believe yours fit me, May?"

"Well, you *are* petite. I don't think it will be stretched out too terribly much," May said, worried.

"At first I thought I would just walk down to the shops here in Walpole," Lizzie continued. "But when I got there I felt disappointed that I wasn't going to have more of an adventure. So I crossed the river and kept walking north. It was a lovely morning."

"Oh, Lizzie," Abba moaned. "Think of all the things that could have happened to you! The river is so high from the rain last night. What if there had been a storm? What if you had turned your ankle with no one there to help you?"

Louisa, safe now from any blame she might have shared had something bad happened to Lizzie, grew irritated. "Oh, Marmee—she's fine! Can't you see? Now, Lizzie, tell us more. What did you do when you got there?"

"Well, I walked up and down the main street. Then I noticed a little bakery with a café attached, and I just stood looking at all the cakes through the window. The baker waved me in and pointed out the tarts, telling me their names in French. They looked like little sculptures. May— you would have loved them."

Anna came back with the tea tray and poured for Joseph and her mother and sisters. She settled in the chair opposite the sofa.

"Well, I hope you went in and had one," Anna said.

Lizzie smiled. "I did! The baker gave me the biggest one. It was made with plums and little currants. And I had a coffee with cream."

May sighed. "It sounds divine. You must have looked very sophisticated, sitting there alone in the café."

Lizzie rolled her eyes. "Perhaps I did, until it came time to pay the bill."

"Oh, no—you hadn't any money!" Louisa cried.

"Well, I thought I had—I took my coin purse. I've been saving my rag money. But I forgot I gave the money to Father and asked him to give it to that family on River Road that's had the scarlet fever." Lizzie's smile vanished and her voice grew sad. "The father is dead, you know—and there are three small children. All their dolls had to be burned."

"Lizzie, you're generous to a fault," Anna said.

"Well, in this case, yes—because I hadn't any money to pay the baker, and I couldn't very well return the purchase, since I'd already eaten it! I didn't know what I was going to do. I felt the panic welling up inside me and I made a show of searching through my purse over and over, even though I knew I wouldn't find a penny in it. I was going to leave him my locket, just so he believed that I *would* come back when I had the money. But then Mr. Singer walked in and I was saved."

Joseph, who had been sitting quietly as the story unfolded, interjected. "It was my pleasure to help. If only I had arrived sooner and saved her the worry of those few minutes."

Lizzie shook her head. "It was just right. He generously paid the bill—for which I *will* repay him as soon as I can—and saw me out. That's when he asked me to ride with him back to Walpole. I'm sorry, Marmee—I know it was rude to say yes."

"Nonsense," Joseph said. "The timing was perfect and we were headed to the same place. Besides, I suspected your family might have been worried."

"Well, my feet *were* very tired. And the walk home would have been long."

"You made it a lovely ride," Joseph said. He looked directly at Louisa and met her eyes before she could turn away. "The Misses Alcott make such pleasant companions. I only wish I had occasion to see them more often."

Louisa's heart felt like an old rag wrung out too many times. How could a person be at once so kind and so cruel? Why did he insist on these insinuations that only reminded her of his betrayal? She turned back to Lizzie, determined to focus on the happy news of her safety.

Abba covered her eyes with her hand and shook her head.

"I am glad this tale has a happy ending. Should we expect our Lizzie to become a woman of the world? Have you had enough adventure?"

Lizzie squeezed her mother's hand and stifled a tiny yawn. "I am so sorry I worried you, though I am glad I went. I wanted to know that I could go off for the day on my own, like any other girl my age. But I *don't* think I want to do it again."

"Well, you may, any time you like," said Louisa. "Only, please tell us first!"

Joseph stood up. "Mrs. Alcott, I thank you for your hospitality. But I should be going and let Miss Elizabeth rest."

Abba stood up and walked with him to the door. "I think we all must rest after such a scare. I am grateful to you for your help, and I know my husband will want to thank you himself when he hears what you have done for our Elizabeth."

Joseph shook his head. "Please do not think of it again— it was my pleasure." He stepped out into the sun and placed his hat on his head. Louisa sensed his gaze was fixed on her but she refused to meet it. "Good day, ladies."

The women fell into a pleasant quiet as afternoon turned to evening. It was too late in the day to start the laundry, the activity that usually consumed their Mondays and Tuesdays, but they decided they could make it up tomorrow. Abba went up to the bedrooms to collect the sheets. Lizzie stretched out on the sofa under a blanket, though the room was sweltering, and her sisters flitted about, replenishing her tea and fetching her books to keep her company. Anna declared she would mend the yellow sash once and for all and set to work, with May looking over her shoulder to watch for stitches that weren't quite as even as they could be. When Bronson arrived home soon after, his forehead creased with worry and his shoulders low, this was the scene that revived him: all four of his daughters, at home and whole, gossiping and sewing and reading as if this had been an ordinary day.

After a time Louisa noticed that Abba had been absent awfully long and wondered whether she hadn't begun the laundry after all. When Louisa saw she wasn't in the washroom, she glanced into the bedrooms. Abba sat on Lizzie's bed in the room she shared with May, looking out the window at the back lawn with the empty clothesline and the field beyond.

"Marmee, here you are." Louisa noticed the clothesline. "Don't worry—we'll finish the laundry tomorrow. I'll work double-time."

Abba nodded but didn't turn around.

"Isn't it wonderful that Lizzie is home, safe and sound?" Louisa could see her mother's shoulders were trembling. "What's the matter—are you ill?"

Abba sighed and turned to Louisa, revealing a face lined with tears. "Only in spirit."

Louisa sat down beside her. "But aren't you *happy* that everything turned out well? No one is hurt—nothing has changed."

"Everything is *always* changing," Abba said, cringing at the plaintive sound in her voice. "You couldn't possibly understand. But the way you encourage Lizzie to go off on her own so carelessly—it's as if you *want* to take her away from me." Abba's voice was hoarse from crying.

Louisa felt the guilt bloom open in her chest, just what she'd feared all day. "Of course that's not what I want! But,

Marmee, Lizzie is *not* a girl anymore and May won't let you make her your pet any longer. You have to let them grow."

"You cannot know the hardships, the exhaustion, the worry I have felt all these years . . . I've always wondered if God made woman as an afterthought—and then was ashamed of his own handiwork." Abba's voice took on the lifeless quality Louisa dreaded.

Louisa took her mother's hands. "Oh, Marmee, you sound so *wretched*." Abba sometimes descended into these "spells," as the girls called them, where despair conquered her spirit for a time. Anna always insisted their mother was only temporarily ill and would soon regain her cheerful disposition. To Anna, the despair was just a physical symptom, like a cough or a fever. But Louisa knew it ran through her mother like a current, sweeping up everything in its path and plunging down. Bronson always said that, of all the girls, Louisa was most like her mother, and he didn't mean it as a compliment. Both were mercurial, passionate, willful. Louisa had seen despair like Abba's from the inside. She had inherited it the way some daughters came into a silver tray or a set of spoons.

"When my babies were born," Abba began again, as if Louisa herself was not one of those babies, "all of their needs just . . . eclipsed me. And I was so happy. It's a cruel fate that the years I put into raising you girls are rewarded by all of you drifting away. Soon, no one will need me anymore."

Louisa pulled Abba's shoulders toward her own and held her. "We will *always* need you. And what about Father? He would be lost without you."

"Husbands and wives are not what we are discussing here."

"Marmee—you must know he is utterly devoted to you!"

Abba examined Louisa carefully for a moment. "I suppose

you will learn this soon enough on your own, but I might have understood my life a little better if someone had told me. For a man, love is just a season. For a woman it is the whole of the year—winter, spring, summer, and fall—and yet, sometimes it is not what it could be. What it seems it should be."

"What do you mean, Marmee?"

Abba turned back to the window. It faced the south. She couldn't see the setting sun, but its vivid pink light sliced through the clouds that hung over Mr. Parson's orchard in the distance. "We must never give if we are hoping for something in return."

If ever men and women are their simplest,
sincerest selves, it is when suffering softens the
one, and sympathy strengthens the other.

—"Love and Loyalty"

Chapter Twelve

With her gratitude over Lizzie's safe return and her worries over Abba's most recent spell, Louisa felt her thoughts should have been too full to be plagued by Joseph Singer. Yet he continued to appear in her mind fully formed, as real as if he had walked through the door of Yellow Wood. She woke at dawn unable to sleep and nearly leapt from bed in an attempt to keep the thoughts at bay. She woke Anna, and they descended to the washroom to begin the task of laundering the sheets, towels, and underclothes that lay heaped on the floor. Soon, May and Lizzie were awake and helping, and they worked quietly, hoping Abba would sleep late and wake to find the task completed.

Two hours before the audience would begin to arrive, Anna and Louisa met the rest of the cast at Walpole Academy, where they would perform the play. Paul Ferguson hammered away at the last piece of the set, while Alfred Howland worked at the opposite end, painting in the wood-grain detail of the two-dimensional china hutch that sat at the back of the "pub." May, who took her role as prompter quite seriously, had gathered the cast around her to go over the signals she planned to use one last time. Louisa escaped this annoyance by claiming a need to "study her lines." Anna sat near her, filling out cards with the word Reserved in her steady, feminine hand, which they would place on the chairs in the front row. Margaret sewed buttons and trim on the costumes.

Anna and Margaret chatted. Louisa appeared to be absorbed in her reading, though she listened in.

"I traveled to Boston last week to visit with my great-aunt. She is an invalid, you know," Margaret said, pulling the thread through the seam to secure it and snipping off the end with a pair of engraved embroidery scissors that hung from her wrist on a ribbon.

Anna lifted her pen from the card so as not to smudge it. "I'm sorry to hear that. I know she has been ill for some time."

Margaret nodded. "Honestly, I can't remember a time when she was well. But she bears it cheerfully enough. I, on the other hand, dread visiting, and so I walked the long way from the train station to her apartment so that I could pass the shops. You know, I have yet to find a dress that suits me and satisfies Samuel's mother."

Anna smiled. "It seems like she might be difficult to please on that account."

Margaret shook her head. "You understate the point—I don't think there is a dress or a fabric on this earth she would approve of that doesn't make me look like I'm headed for the convent."

Louisa closed her eyes and took a deep breath, working to suppress a groan. *Margaret is so tiresome,* she thought. *If I have to listen to her go on about this dress much longer I'm going to—*

"As I was walking along I saw Nora Sutton and her mother leaving a shop with the most beautiful satin silk."

"Really," said Anna. "That sounds lovely." Louisa could feel her sister's eyes sweep in her direction, hoping, she knew, that the play was fully consuming her hearing as well as her sight. "I'm sure she will make a beautiful bride."

"She is a beauty—there is no question about that. Though, of course, there is such a thing as too much beauty. It can get one into trouble." Margaret's voice took on the conspiratorial quality she embraced when she was preparing to reveal some interesting gossip.

"What do you mean?" Anna said, playing right into her game, Louisa thought.

"Were you not aware that she was previously engaged?"

Anna raised her eyebrows. "Engaged? I suppose I have heard something about that. To whom?"

"About two years ago, a man named Cecil Morris appeared in Walpole and took a job as a clerk in the town hall. He was from New York City."

"Did he have family here?" Anna asked.

"No—that was the strange part. To anyone who asked, he said he had grown tired of the noise and dust of the city. He decided one day to find a nice village in New Hampshire where he might find a wife and settle down. When he rode into Walpole in his carriage he said he knew this was the place for him."

"How interesting," Anna said.

"Telling you now, it sounds suspicious. But at the time I think we were all flattered he chose our town. The families here take a lot of pride in this place."

"As they should," Anna said.

"Word got around, and soon all the girls were talking about him. He seemed to have money, he was charming and very handsome. Of course, *I* knew there was something untrustworthy about him right from the start. But would anyone listen to me?"

"I suppose not," Anna guessed.

"No," Margaret said, shaking her head. "They wouldn't. Well, it didn't take long before he set his sights on Nora. She fell completely in love—completely lost her senses. Mr. Sutton gave his blessing and the wedding date was set. But just a few weeks before the union was to take place, Mr. Morris disappeared."

"Disappeared?"

"He said he had to travel to Boston on a business matter. Nora went to meet his train the evening he was supposed to return, but he wasn't on it. Weeks went by, the day of the wedding came and went. She heard nothing. Finally a letter came. He admitted his whole scheme—he had been married all along to a woman back in New York. He was attempting to leave her when he first came to Walpole. But the birth of his son pricked what tiny speck of a conscience he had, and he decided to return to his family."

"Poor Nora!" Anna said.

Margaret nodded. "Yes, it was unfortunate. She had made such a fool out of herself over him, flaunting her new status all over town, and all along he had no intention of following through on his pledge."

"But how could she have known? It could have happened to anyone."

Margaret pursed her lips. "Well, not anyone. Not *me*—I knew he was trouble."

"Yes," Anna said. "You mentioned that."

"Nora soon descended into a terrible state. Her nerves took over. She wouldn't leave her room. Dr. Kittredge was at the Suttons' home every day. She was convinced she had squandered her chance for a respectable life, for marriage and children. No one really blamed her, but . . . well, not everyone is as understanding as you and I are, Anna."

Anna pressed her lips together to suppress a smile. "That's true, Margaret. Well, it is fortunate, then, that she has found herself in"—she looked over at Louisa and cringed—"her current circumstances."

"Quite," Margaret said, nodding.

The two worked in silence for a moment, Margaret fastening the last gray button onto Louisa's Widow Pottle costume.

"Of course . . ." Margaret said.

"Of course what?"

Margaret leaned in toward Anna. "Well, I didn't tell you this . . ."

"Of course not," Anna said.

"Joseph Singer didn't court Nora, and I don't believe he wants to marry her."

Louisa's eyes froze on a period at the end of a sentence and refused to move.

"Margaret, that seems like an awfully salacious thing to say. How could you know?"

"I'm very observant, as you know, Anna. I pick up on these things."

Probably by listening at doors and beneath windows under the cover of night, Louisa thought. But she held her breath anticipating what Margaret would say next.

"Joseph's father is in grave financial difficulty. Joseph has helped to improve business at the store, but his father gambles the profits away on imprudent investments as quickly as Joseph can earn it."

Anna looked stricken. "That's terrible."

"Yes, it is. As you probably could see at the Suttons' dinner party, Mr. Singer is not long for this world. His lungs are weak and he probably will not make it through the winter. So he is looking to put his affairs in order. Technically Catherine is not too young to marry, but fifteen *is* awfully early."

"Our youngest sister May is fifteen as well. That is too young," Anna said firmly.

"I agree. And so does Mr. Singer. And she is a *young* fifteen. She has been coddled and spoiled her whole life. I think he doted on her out of guilt that she didn't have a mother. But because she hasn't known sacrifice or responsibility, there's no way she could be sent out as a governess or maid. She wouldn't last a week."

"I think I understand what you mean to infer," Anna said. "Mr. Singer went to see Mr. Sutton?"

Margaret nodded. "They are old friends. Each had something to gain from uniting their families. The Singer debts are repaid, Catherine is safe from a hasty marriage, and Nora's reputation is restored."

"Except that Joseph has to marry someone he doesn't love," Anna said, glancing at Louisa, who hid her face behind the play.

"Yes, Samuel says he is quite grave about it. But he admits he can't see a better way to take care of his sister. Joseph Singer's strength of character outdoes anyone's in this town, I've always said."

"I'm sure you have," Anna said with an amused smile.

Louisa's mind reeled. Was this what Joseph had meant to explain in all the letters she had refused to read?

May clapped her hands and stood on a crate at the foot of the stage. "Everyone—it's time to get dressed!"

There was no need of any more words. . . .

—*Under the Lilacs*

Chapter Thirteen

AMATEUR DRAMATIC COMPANY

FIRST PERFORMANCE

Tuesday Evening, September 11, 1855

The Company take great pleasure in producing this evening the much admired play, in two acts, by J. R. Planché, entitled

"The Jacobite."

DOORS OPEN AT 7 . . . CURTAIN RISES AT 8

The Company return their heartfelt thanks to the public for their liberal patronage, and hope, by increased exertions, to merit a continuance of their favor.

At seven in the evening, the cast members of the Walpole Amateur Dramatic Company began to hear the echoes of footsteps on the plank floors of Walpole Academy's great hall. They sequestered themselves in two empty classrooms— the young men in one, the young ladies in another—to put on their costumes and run over their lines one final time before the curtain rose at eight o'clock.

Louisa's Widow Pottle costume was a simple chintz dress and colored petticoat and took no time at all to put on. A linen cap that was more appropriate to the dress of the prior century, but was all that was available, concealed Louisa's heavy coiled braid. Though the others viewed their involvement as a light dalliance, Louisa had spent her evenings the last two weeks practicing her lines again and again in her room, relishing the chance to channel her frustrations into her character's improper pronouncements. Shouting "Impudent varlet!" and "Ragamuffin!" in any other context would have been a scandal, but onstage she could hope to garner some laughs. And now here was this unexpected piece of news that turned everything on its head. Joseph didn't love Nora. Even if he still planned on marrying her, this seemed a victory of sorts.

As the other girls fussed with their hair, Louisa crept quietly down the hall to the stage door. She entered and peeked through the gap between the old musty velvet curtain and the wall. Families and out-of-town guests crowded the rows of chairs, and the hall echoed with the chatter and laughter of friendly conversation as the audience anticipated the performance. She scanned the crowd of about a hundred for familiar faces. Her father and mother sat in the second row along with Lizzie. Three chairs in the front row sat empty, and as Louisa looked down the aisle to the entrance at the back of the hall, she discovered with astonishment the guest they had been reserved for.

Louisa had read in the New York paper that Fanny Kemble, the British actress she'd always admired, was touring New England to give her infamous Shakespeare readings. Incredibly, Louisa's idol now floated gracefully toward the front row in a gown of purple silk, her neck draped with jewels. Louisa never would have dreamed this famous actress would bother with a little community theater. Suddenly she was in the presence of a genius of her time, not to mention a woman unafraid of upsetting the dictates of propriety in order to live her life as she pleased. She wondered if God had put Fanny Kemble in her path at this moment to remind her that life held the promise of unlimited and surprising joys, if only one had the courage to pursue them.

Louisa glanced at the clock in the back of the hall to see that it was nearly time to begin. The stagehands entered and began to arrange the set pieces to form the interior of the Crooked Billet, the public house of the inn and the setting for the opening scene. Toward the back of the stage they leaned a large plank against a wedge to form the illusion of a cellar door left ajar. Anna and Margaret, as Patty and Lady Somerford, entered talking of Major Murray, secret lover of the Lady and currently imprisoned as a traitor to the king.

At last, from the "cellar," Louisa bellowed her first line: "I've told thee so a hundred times, fool; art thee deaf!" She tromped into the stage lights in an exaggerated stagger and the audience burst with laughter. Though the house lamps were dark, she imagined Fanny Kemble in the front row, laughing along with the rest. She felt truly buoyed for the first time in weeks. She had always loved the stage; she had always loved to make people laugh. One certainly could not have everything she wanted in life, but she could find the things she was good at and practice them with passion, with deep commitment, and try with all her heart to become the person the Almighty Friend intended her to be. It was a modern day. Marriage and motherhood were far from the only things a woman could seek to excel in. Just look at Fanny Kemble.

And then, as quickly as it began, the play ended. As they drew the curtain closed, it wobbled on the crude pulley system they had constructed—a comical reminder that indeed they were not acting in a Boston theater—and the cast gathered in a line across the stage to take its bows. Louisa held Anna's hand and walked forward, smiling broadly at the cheering audience members, now on their feet. As the stage lights dimmed, Louisa caught sight of Fanny's graceful clap—the movement of her slender arms, the rhythm of the fingertips on her left hand as they struck the palm of her right. The entire night had been a balm on Louisa's tender, battered heart. The world seemed to open to her then, unfolding in ways she hadn't seen before. Suddenly, a vision of herself a few years hence flashed through her mind. She walked down Beacon Street in Boston, three books in the crook of her arm, each with her name pressed into the spine. In her pocket, a fifty-dollar advance rustled against the fabric of her dress and she was headed back to her rented room, where she would put the kettle on the stove and draw a fresh sheet of paper from the drawer.

Back in the "dressing room" after their final curtain calls, the female cast members embraced joyously and chattered about the performance's best moments. They removed the pins from their hair, unfastened one another's costumes, and changed back into the dresses they had on when they arrived. The costumes lay in a heap on the floor.

Harriet, acting once again like the loudmouthed toad Louisa thought she resembled, shouted above the feminine rancor to gather their attention. "Everyone is invited to Birch Glen for a celebration. My mother and I have been baking cakes all week!"

The girls cheered and began in a flurry to fasten capes and bonnets, preparing to leave. Harriet looked at the pile of costumes on the dusty floor of the classroom. "Wait— Margaret worked so hard on these costumes—we can't just leave them to get damp and wrinkled. They'll have to be folded," she said in a tone that made it clear *she* would not be doing the folding.

The others nodded but Louisa held up her hand. "Why don't you let me do it, and I'll be just a few minutes behind you to the party?" She was desperate for a moment alone. She wasn't ready for the evening to end, wasn't ready to return to reality and all its confusions.

"And I'll help," Anna chimed in. "It will only take a moment."

"No, Anna," Harriet said. "You must come now. I have it on good authority that Mr. Nicholas Sutton will be an early guest. I think I know whom he will be anxious to see!"

The group broke into laughter and giddy chatter. Anna looked at Louisa, her cheeks pink with embarrassment, but her eyes full of yearning. Louisa clutched Anna's hand. "Go ahead," she whispered. "I'm right behind you. Will you tell Marmee and Father to go ahead without me? I'll be there soon." Anna nodded and kissed her sister's cheek, and the throng of girls poured into the school's hallway.

Louisa leaned against the teacher's desk and stood very still with her arms at her side, listening. She heard the lilting feminine voices take on a baritone accompaniment as the girls met up with the boys in the hallway. The audience waited to receive them, and she heard Harriet announce once again the invitation to the post-performance celebration. A few moments later a great silence descended on the entire building and Louisa gave a relieved sigh. Alone at last, she could finally relish the evening's successes.

She crouched down and swept the costumes up in her arms, carrying them over to the teacher's desk, where she could stand folding and letting her mind drift away. Margaret had done a beautiful job with the sewing. And she'd made them so quickly, too. She would be an excellent mistress of her new home with Samuel once they were married. Louisa felt happy for them but no longer felt the sting of envy. People were meant for different things in life, she reflected, and keeping a house, running a kitchen, sewing linens, and tending the chickens—these were not things Louisa could imagine herself doing, no matter how great the love that bound her as a wife to her husband. In that moment of unguarded reverie, an image of Joseph came into her mind and ran its course before she had time to cut it short.

It was the premonition of her future self she'd had onstage, ferrying copies of her books back to a room that was all her own, but this time she reached the parlor of the rooming house to find Joseph waiting on a settee, his hat resting on his lap. Waiting for her. He would see the books in her hands and break into a congratulatory smile, running his fingers over the covers and spines. He would flip them open to see the quality of the typesetting, but there would be no need to read them. He'd have read them all before. She would dash up to her room to place them on the shelf next to her desk and hurry back downstairs; they would set off for an afternoon walk, as they did most afternoons, and converse about the great moral issues on the minds of all thinking people: the question of slavery, the question of women's rights.

But reality broke into her reverie. If only it could be that simple! If only society were not so narrow in its notions of love and companionship! Louisa placed the last folded dress upon the pile, shaking her head in confusion. Surely it pleased God to see love grow thick and verdant in the light of equality and friendship. And yet it could not be.

She heard a floorboard creak behind her and spun around with a startled gasp. He stood in the doorway. Not the Joseph of her reverie, but Joseph flesh and bone and gentle voice.

"You're still here."

His pale eyes caressed Louisa's face like two hands. Her heart was at once exultant and rent anew.

Love bewilders the wisest, and it would make me
quite blind or mad, I know; therefore I'd rather
have nothing to do with it for a long, long while.

—*Moods*

Chapter Fourteen

It took merely a few seconds for Joseph to cross from the doorway to where Louisa stood at the front of the room, but it could have been years. Anticipation bent her like an archer's bow.

And then he was at her side. "You were wonderful," he nearly whispered. He looked tired and a little grave, two qualities she never would have imagined seeing in his face.

She felt her cheeks warming. "Wonderful as a loud-mouthed old lady. I'm not sure whether to take that as a compliment." She gave him a wry smile.

He shook his head, undeterred. "I couldn't take my eyes off you." He stood very near her now and she could feel the heat of his breath. She was afraid to touch even his hand for fear of what might happen.

"Louisa . . ." he began. She focused her eyes on his shoulder, the safest place she could find, though it too had its trappings—a wide masculine slope, the promise of slick skin beneath the cloth of his shirt. He tipped her chin up with his finger so that she could look nowhere else but his eyes. "Maybe now you will give me a moment to explain—"

"I know. Margaret told me about Nora, your father . . . all of it."

"So you understand, then?"

Louisa nodded, placing her hand on his forearm. "This is what you must do, for your family's sake. It is a great burden, but you must bear it."

"Then you *don't* understand. Listen to me—I thought I had reconciled myself to marrying Nora, but when I saw you tonight, I nearly splintered in two. I have made a grave mistake."

She closed her eyes and sighed. "Oh, why did you come? Nothing has changed since you first agreed to this arrangement. There's nothing to be done about it."

His eyes grew slightly damp and his voice broke. "I cannot bear it. I won't. Do you not feel the same?"

Before she could temper her reply, she spoke. "I do." Perhaps the evening's triumphs had made her bold. The words began tumbling out—it felt futile to try to stop them. "I've thought of little else but you these last weeks."

He exhaled with relief and placed his palm on the back of her head, drawing her face toward his. They pressed their foreheads together and she felt the sensation of contact resonate throughout her body. He brushed his thumb across her lips.

She heard a rustle of paper on the other side of the room and instinctively pulled away with a gasp. Joseph turned toward the doorway and Louisa glanced all around, but no one was there. The rustle came again and Louisa looked to see the head of a tiny mouse peeking up from beneath a pile of papers. She smiled, relieved. "We are not alone," she said, pointing. Joseph closed his eyes and shook his head, laughing at their guilty reaction to the thought of being seen together. The mouse had broken the tension between them, at least for the moment.

"Let's go outside," Louisa suggested. She didn't dare ask whether he was coming to the party at Birch Glen, and whether he would be bringing his intended wife with him. The theme of the night had been the escape from reality. Why rush back to it now? she reasoned. She placed the folded costumes in the trunk and, before she swung the lid closed, pulled a shawl from the pile. The autumn evenings had been getting cooler. She extinguished the lamp and they stood in the dark for a long moment, lacing their fingertips together. Determined to breathe, Louisa pushed past Joseph and led the way down the dark hallway toward the door.

The night air felt like a cool bath and brought her back to her senses. The thing was to keep moving, and they began to walk quickly, not along the walkway toward the street and Washington Square, as she had intended, but instead up the path that led into the woods behind the Academy and out through the dense stand of maple and elm, behind which open land stretched, patched with farms. There was no hesitation in either of their strides. A line of Whitman's lingered in her mind as she climbed the path, and she marveled at the miraculous truth of his words: *Hands I have taken, face I have kissed, mortal I have ever touched, it shall be you.*

They made their way uphill along the narrow path. Louisa walked in front, pushing low-hanging branches away, sensing the sinewy tickle of spiderwebs. They reached the last of the trail, where hunters came to take deer and pheasant. But now it was empty, save for the buttery moon hanging low in the sky.

Joseph struck out ahead, taking Louisa's hand and pulling

her along. He sat down in a feathery patch of weeds so high they almost reached his shoulders, and she sat down beside him. She felt afraid to look at him the way one does not look directly at the sun. Her left hand rested on his right palm and she felt his fingertips run along the inside of her fingers, up her wrist toward her elbow. He whispered her name and she turned toward him, her breath an imperceptible pant, to see the yellow light of the moon washing over his features.

He took her face in his hands, his thumbs pressed against her jaw, and pulled her mouth toward his. The kiss was hungry, aching, long. Louisa felt she'd like to leap into his mouth, be swallowed whole between his lips. His hands coursed her shoulders and down her back, roving frantically, taking her in. Her heart began to pound and she felt she would cry out with fear. Never had she felt her mind in such opposition to her body.

In Joseph's eyes she saw only gentle affection. He had felt her stiffen and pull away and he slowed the fumbling of his fingers at her stays, taking her fully into his arms, pressing her face to his neck, stroking her hair.

"It's all right," he said. "I only wanted to be here with you, nothing more. I only wanted to sit here beneath the moon with you, share the warmth of your kiss. Only that."

She pulled away to face him and reached to the back of her head where his hand had been, slid out a few pins and released her raven curtain of hair, which fell in waves down her back. As she began to recline onto the soft ground he stopped her, slipped out of his jacket, and spread it on the weeds beneath her head. She slid his suspender off his shoulder and he lowered himself down upon her, taking her mouth to his once again.

These hearts of ours are curious and contrary things.

—*Little Women*

Chapter Fifteen

Louisa's mind felt completely empty. She rolled on her side and felt the cool silk lining of Joseph's jacket against her cheek. A black ant ascended the sleeve of her dress, which lay rumpled on the grass beside her. He was unmoved by what he had surely witnessed from his perch on a blade of grass a few minutes before. Louisa supposed it was hard to scandalize an ant.

Joseph lay still beside her, his shirt open, and she placed her palm on his sternum to feel once again the galloping stampede of his heartbeat. He was so quiet she thought he might be asleep, but when she looked she saw that his eyes were open, scanning the sky. They lay in the tall weeds, concealed from the eyes of anyone who might pass along the path, though no one would. They seemed to be the only people in New Hampshire, in the world, for the moment.

"Are you awake?" she whispered anyway, not knowing what else to say. He did not answer but brought his hand to hers and began tracing circles on it with his fingers.

She had convinced herself that they had somehow fallen out of time, that she could lie in the grass in her shift, every inch of her skin alive with sensation, forever. She thought once again of that strange poem that seemed a cord binding the two of them together. *Press close magnetic nourishing night!* All her yearning to suspend the darkness was telescoped in that line. But as her consciousness began to return and she drifted from her body back into her mind, she saw that the moon had crossed the sky and hung above the horizon. Though dawn was only an hour away, the moon was so bright she noticed how uncovered she was for the first time. She reached for her dress.

"What time do you think it is?" she asked, sitting up, suddenly anxious. Anna would be waiting for her. They all would be. She hoped perhaps they'd have concluded that she decided at the last moment to choose a night of solitude rather than face the noise of society. She had been known to do such things.

Joseph sat up too. "I don't know." She was attempting to turn the twisted dress right side out, but he clutched her hands. "Louisa, I think I know what to do. If we leave right now they'll all still be at the party." He stood and flung his shirt over his head, attempting to button it and tuck it into his trousers at the same time. "We can walk over to Bellows Falls—it isn't far—and rent a coach. We could be in Boston just after dawn, maybe take the train to New York tomorrow. My cousin Edward—the one who sends me all the books— he could help us find accommodations, I'm sure of it."

Louisa's eyes widened. "Leave here? For how long?"

"For good." He pulled her to her feet and helped her pull her dress over her head, turning to her back to fasten it. "Don't you see—it's the only way. I can't go through with this wedding. I simply can't. I want to marry *you*, Louisa."

She took a long breath as his words penetrated her mind. Her heart wrenched within her chest. "But what about your family? What about your sister?"

"I can't think of that now. We all have to make our own way in this world."

"Joseph!" Her voice was scolding. "How can you say that? Catherine is only fifteen and a girl. How is she supposed to make her way on her own? You and I both know what can happen to girls without any means of support. She could end up a servant—or worse. I cannot let you abandon her this way!"

He stood in front of her and grabbed her shoulders hard. "Listen to me!" he shouted. His voice echoed across the empty field. "I . . . won't . . . do . . . it." With each word he shook her, his voice a low growl. Louisa grimaced with fear, her eyes swimming. Joseph seemed suddenly to realize that he was hurting her and jerked his hands away, his palms splayed open in front of him. He spoke in a meek whisper. "I'm sorry." He sank to the ground and she lowered herself down beside him.

Louisa shook her head. She knew some things about rage, for her own temper could overtake her like a hurricane when she least expected. Feeling there was something she yearned for desperately but could not have, feeling she was at the mercy of forces outside her control, forces that were determining the course of her life: these were the times she felt that hollowing anger. And she felt it now, but it was tempered by a calm that had descended on her when she looked out from the stage to see the placid, scandalous Fanny Kemble perched in the front row, a living symbol of fearlessness.

"Listen to me," she said, taking his hand. They did not look at each other but instead faced out in the same direction. "If you feel you must go away, I cannot stop you. But I will not make myself your accomplice. And if you are the person I believe you to be, you won't go at all." She was quiet a moment, measuring her words carefully. "You have to help your family, and I have to help mine. As you surely know, my own father has no grasp of or interest in finances. We only came to Walpole because my cousins were offering us a home for the summer. I can make five dollars a story in Boston, and I intend to go as soon as I can."

She glanced at Joseph but he continued to look out across the field. She saw a shadow along his jaw as he clenched it tight, and she braced herself for another angry outburst, but none came.

"And I have to go alone," she said, her voice barely above a whisper. The next words were heavy in her mouth, like marbles, for she doubted their truthfulness. "I don't think I could be married, not to anyone."

"You don't mean that." His voice broke and she realized he was not fighting back rage but tears. "It wouldn't have to be the way you think."

Louisa took a deep breath and spoke the words she believed but didn't quite own in her heart. "But it would be marriage nonetheless, and therein lies the problem. Marriage is conventional because it gives order to families, order to society. It is an exchange of property, as you well know," she said, thinking of Nora Sutton and her family's money. "Marriage does not account for love. It does not account for friendship, for independence. But what we feel for each other lives in these very things: independence of mind and spirit, ideas, each of our interests and achievements." She placed her hand against his cheek and turned his face toward hers. "Do you understand? Agreeing to marry would mean agreeing to give up everything between us that matters."

"So you would have me marry *her*? Have children with *her*?" He glanced at Louisa, gauging her reaction to the insinuation: Nora, naked in his arms.

Louisa slammed shut a door inside her mind against this image. "Your family is depending on you. You have given your word. I have seen inside the deepest part of you, and I know you are not one to go back on your word."

"If you don't love me," he said, "afford me the dignity of telling me so."

Louisa looked at him, sorrow laid bare on her face. "How dare you say this—after what happened between us just now?" She touched his arm. "How can you possibly think I don't love you?"

"I don't think it. I know it. I think you don't know what love is. If you did, you would come away with me—or let me come with you to Boston. If you loved me, you would know that nothing else matters but being together."

Louisa stared at him in disbelief. "I have been waiting my whole life for the day I would have my freedom. How can you ask me to cast it away as soon as it's finally come? Besides, it seems I am the only one who might be relied upon to earn an income for my family. I think this *real love* you talk about is only an excuse for selfishness. It is the love of an impatient boy, not a grown man. A grown man knows that in life we may not always simply have whatever we want."

"Well, you certainly had what *you* wanted tonight."

Louisa let out a cry of a wounded animal and her open

palm struck Joseph's cheek with all the force in her strong shoulder. He nearly lost his balance, and a wild look came into his eyes that made her recoil. Joseph leapt to his feet. She thought he might hit her back, but instead he stood stiff with his fists clenched at his sides. He felt she was grinding his heart under the heel of her boot, and it made him want to hurt her.

"As you wish, I will marry Nora. Soon, if I can. And you will see her on my arm; you will see her cradle our children." He pointed his index finger at her face. "And you will know regret. But I will have forgotten you by then."

Louisa looked at him with something almost like pity and in her exhaustion nearly chuckled at his words. It was impossible either of them would ever forget anything about the other, no matter how much relief it would bring them. Even then they both knew that this night would haunt them the rest of their days.

She gathered the shawl from the costume trunk around her shoulders and pulled herself to her feet, a dull pain radiating from every joint and muscle. "I cannot wish you love, for you do not love her. But I wish you the peace of duty fulfilled. Which, sometimes, can be a little *like* love."

And with that she turned and strode up the hill, her chin tipped high. Joseph followed, walking into the pitiless light of the descending moon.

It is easy to forgive, but not to forget,

words which cannot be unsaid.

—*A Modern Mephistopheles*

Chapter Sixteen

Louisa walked slowly up Wentworth Road toward Yellow Wood. If she was going to have to explain to her parents where she had been all night, ten extra minutes wouldn't change that. She reflected on how successful she'd been at convincing Joseph of the right path for him to take; her acting skills had come through for her again—or were they standing in the way of her happiness? In truth she felt nothing of the calm certainty she'd expressed to him; rather, it seemed an explosion had gone off inside her, and now tiny shards stuck all throughout her body, causing unrelenting pain. How would she ever bear it?

As the house came into view she saw that she would have to face the questions she feared right away. Anna and Nicholas sat on the front step engaged in intimate conversation. They did not see Louisa coming, so she scuffed her feet and coughed to garner their attention. She didn't want to take them by surprise.

"Louisa!" Anna exclaimed, immediately distressed to be seen so late at night alone with a caller, even if it was only by her younger sister. Anna believed deeply in the importance of propriety and would die a thousand deaths before she endured her own reputation being compromised. Women could not own property and sometimes could not even control when or whom they married or when they became mothers. Reputation was the only possession a woman had under her own control. It meant everything.

Nicholas stood up, equally embarrassed. "Well, Miss Alcott," he said, stiffly. "Now that I have seen you safely home I must be off, for the hour is late." Their eyes connected for a moment and something passed between them Louisa recognized. But their longing was tempered by a kind of tranquillity she did not know—for Anna and Nicholas looked forward to the time when they would be together, for good, in the conventional way that would cause no strife. Louisa felt her temper flare like a match. It was all so unfair! She turned away to let them have a private good-bye. Out of the corner of her eye she saw Nicholas clasp Anna's hand, which she held down at her side, and pull her toward him. He whispered something that made her giggle. Then she sighed.

"I plan to meet the boys in the morning. Which is in just a few hours, I'm afraid. We'll be working on the roof if the weather is good. But perhaps I will see you tomorrow evening."

"Please be careful," Anna said. "I've seen the way you climb around like monkeys on that roof."

"As you wish, my dear," Nicholas said, turning to Louisa and clearing his throat. "Good night, Miss Louisa." He tipped his hat in her direction.

The sisters waited until he had safely exited the front gate before speaking. Louisa steeled herself for what would come next. She could see in Anna's face that her initial embarrassment about her own circumstances had been overtaken by shock at Louisa's wandering around in the early morning hours. "Where the devil have you been?" Anna hissed, her hand at her throat. "I thought for certain you'd arrived home and were upstairs in bed."

Should she simply tell her sister the truth? Louisa wondered. It pained her to lie to Anna, the person she was closer to than anyone else in the world. And why should she lie? Nothing could be truer than what she felt for Joseph, and its truth made it an almost sacred thing. To lie about it denied this fact.

And yet she knew Anna would not understand. She would be devastated on Louisa's behalf, that her sister had behaved so foolishly and ruined any chance of future happiness with a proper husband. People talked. A young lady who was less than pure was not a suitable choice for a bride.

"I have been . . ." Louisa stalled. ". . . walking."

"All night?" Anna was incredulous. "Alone?"

Louisa nodded. Perhaps if she did not say the words aloud she would not actually be lying.

Anna examined her carefully, taking time to choose her words. "I don't know if I believe you."

"Believe what you like." Louisa's voice was sharp. "It matters not to me."

"And so *angry* too, when I merely asked a simple question, a question clearly called for by your waltzing up the path at this hour with no explanation. I certainly think I have cause to question whether you are truthful."

"Perhaps I should be asking what *you* are doing with Nicholas Sutton, alone at this hour?" Louisa felt anger overtake her sensibilities. She knew this feeling—once it came on, it was difficult to turn back, no matter how much she wanted to.

Anna's eyes filled with tears. That her sister would accuse her of something improper, knowing full well that Anna would never dream of violating her modesty outside of the safe confines of marriage, seemed a mean-spirited brutality. "Louisa, when the party at Birch Glen dragged on and you did not come . . . and Joseph Singer was noticeably absent . . . I began to fear . . ." She seemed unsure how to ask the question that burned on her lips. "I pray to God you have not done something that cannot be taken back."

"Don't worry," Louisa seethed. "I won't sully your good name in society."

"Please!" Anna began to cry. "You think that is what I care about? It isn't—I only worry that my sister will have her heart broken." She placed her hand on Louisa's arm. "Nothing good can come of it, Lou. Don't you see that? Nothing good. He is *engaged* to someone else. He will not marry you."

Louisa looked away, her own eyes brimming with hot tears, but her relentless temper flared. "And you are so certain *Nicholas Sutton's* aims are honorable? As far as I know, he has yet to speak to our father about his plans. Perhaps he does not intend to at all."

"Oh, Louisa, you know that is not true."

"Do I? It seems to me he can only sit with my sister in the dead of night, when no one else is around. Perhaps he is ashamed to associate with our family. We *are* but poor daughters of a philosopher who struts about town in tatters. When it comes to marriage, you are sorely naïve if you think money does not matter. It may be the only thing that really does."

Anna brushed aside a tear with her fingertips. She clamped her hands on the small of her back and squared her shoulders as she gazed down the path that led away from the house toward town, and beyond that Boston, New York. She knew there were thousands of other places, but she didn't need to see them for herself to know they were there. "All my life," she began, her voice low but strong, "I have tried to be good. That probably sounds silly to you, but it's true. I have. I've tried to be a good daughter to my parents, tried to keep our family together—and it hasn't always been easy. I never have asked for anything for myself, have barely hoped even in silence for the things other people take for granted. But this, the love of this man, a home of our own, my own daughters, sons, if God decides to provide them—I cannot hold my tongue and let the chance of having those things pass me by. I *will* become Mrs. Nicholas Sutton. I'm determined."

Somewhere beneath her resentment, Louisa wanted to reassure her sister that if anyone deserved the happiness of marriage and family life, it was Anna. But though it was petty and small of her, she could not do it—something she would soon regret for a long time. It wasn't jealousy Louisa felt. That very evening, though it seemed like an age ago, she'd made up her mind that marriage was not her own path, and nothing in her wanted to go back on that now, despite everything she shared with Joseph. If she was jealous of anything, it was Anna's ability to be satisfied with convention. She wasn't a prisoner of the restlessness Louisa felt, the endless questioning her mind pursued. Anna had a more typical worry: If she loved him, would he love her back? Would they be together as they hoped?

"I suppose I can hardly blame you for wanting to escape this poverty. There's certainly no end in sight."

No purer heart had contemplated the meaning of the role

of wife than Anna. The suggestion that she was clinging to Nicholas for his money cut her to the quick. "How can you say such a thing to me?" Anna cried, tears slick on her cheeks. "I *love* him."

"Well, we can love people for all sort of reasons."

"I won't hear this—I won't." Anna shook her head, her voice growing frantic. "It is only that you are envious, because your own affair cannot end happily."

"What do you know about the way that I feel? I don't envy you—I pity you. I am going to make something of my life. I am going to sell my stories and see the world. And you want to waste your life cooking and cleaning and chasing babies around the yard because a man made you his wife. Why would I be envious of that?"

Anna looked Louisa straight in the eye. "Because you can't have it."

The sisters stood still and close. Louisa turned away first, storming into the house. Anna followed silently behind. The last thing they needed now was to wake their parents.

But Abba was already awake. Or had never gone to sleep. They could hear her talking softly to Lizzie, the sound of a rag being wrung into a bowl. She was nursing her patient and took no notice of her older daughters' late arrival.

Women have been called queens for a long time,

but the kingdom given them isn't worth ruling.

—*An Old-Fashioned Girl*

Chapter Seventeen

Wednesday was reserved for baking, and as usual Anna and Louisa rose early to help their mother. May lingered in her room to "finish her mending"—and doze in the sunny window seat. In the bed beside her, Lizzie slept late, her fever in retreat after a restless night.

Baking was a hot, arduous task and it took most of the day to make the bread and pies that would get them through the week, including Sunday dinner. The kitchen was unusually silent. While they waited for the brick oven to heat, Louisa, who was best at forceful kneading, stood at the worktable. She ground the heels of her hands into the warm dough, her arms locked in the repetitive movements. Her muscles ached with exhaustion.

Anna had scarcely said good morning to her. Louisa knew she had said some hurtful things in the night, but despite the light of day she didn't exactly regret them. Her anger had been tamped down but still burned as an ember, keeping her moving. If it was jealousy that made her hate her sister at this moment, then so be it. There was no question that Anna deserved happiness, but didn't Louisa deserve it too? Didn't everyone deserve a chance to be happy?

When the last loaf was cooling, mother and daughters sat at the oak table for a moment of rest. Louisa reflected that all three of them could benefit from a long afternoon nap. Anna's face was drawn and pale and her shoulders sagged. Louisa stifled a yawn. Abba looked the worst off, sadness burning in her dark eyes.

She clasped her daughters' hands. "My girls," she whispered. "I fear for Elizabeth. She is so frail. It seems every fever or cough she contracts is worse than the last." She stifled a sob. "I don't know how much more her body can take."

The sisters comforted their mother and ushered her into the parlor to the comfort of the horsehair sofa. They never knew how much stock to put in Abba's dire predictions. To her, Lizzie was always frail, always on the verge of leaving this world for good, though the facts didn't bear that out. Louisa had to admit, though, that Lizzie seemed more like an invalid than ever as the summer waned. Since her adventure in Bellows Falls, she had spent most of her days in bed. No matter whether their mother was overreacting, Abba needed rest. Anna and Louisa promised to finish up the work in the kitchen.

A little later, as Abba's eyes fluttered on the verge of sleep, the sisters heard a sharp knock at the front door. Abba bolted up and swung the heavy door open. Samuel Parker stepped inside, the brilliant morning sun behind him throwing his face into shadow.

"Is Mr. Alcott in, ma'am?" Samuel's shirt collar hung open. A semicircle of sweat soaked his undershirt.

Abba's knuckles whitened on the doorknob. "Good morning, Samuel. Is everything all right?"

Louisa and Anna looked into the parlor, their aprons still fastened at their backs.

"Hello, Samuel," Anna called. An oblong smudge of flour marred her left cheek. "Would you like some brown bread? It's almost cool."

He glanced in her direction, then looked back at Abba. "*Please*—Mr. Alcott. Is he home, ma'am?"

"Well, yes." Abba, flustered, fussed with folds of her skirt. "He's in his study."

Without a word Samuel pushed past her and flew down the hall to the closed door. He bolted in and slammed it behind him. The two male voices ejected a few quick, indiscernible sentences, and the door flew open again. Samuel clomped noisily down the hallway in his work boots. Bronson followed at his heels, his shirt fluttering like a sail behind him.

"What the deuce is the matter with you two?" Louisa shouted, her forehead glistening in the heat of the kitchen.

Bronson turned back to Abba as Samuel sprinted down the front path and south toward the center of town. "Stay here." He clamped his hand on her upper arm, almost violently. "All of you. I mean it. I will be back as soon as I can."

He hurried awkwardly down the path after Sam.

"Wait, my husband, wait! What is the matter? Please— tell us!" Abba yelled.

But Bronson didn't turn back.

He didn't return, in fact, until the late afternoon. Abba and her daughters obeyed his command—they did not leave the house, not even to cast the dishwater into the weeds. The women were uncharacteristically silent as they worked about the house, grateful to have something to keep their hands busy. Never had the floor been quite so clean; never had the kitchen been so well scrubbed and aired.

Each held in her mind her own private speculation of what sort of disaster had befallen the town, and they prayed vague and desperate prayers against the unknown. Louisa felt an overpowering dread. Something in Bronson's demeanor betrayed his concern for his daughters in particular, and Louisa doubted the emergency involved an elderly uncle or friend of her father's. Death called on the old and sick like a guest with an appointment, but when it came for the young it barged through the door and took everyone by surprise. A frothing anxiety burned in Louisa's chest. Something had happened to Joseph. She felt she knew it for certain, could sense that he was in pain—or worse.

Oh, why hadn't she gone away with him when she had the chance? The world seemed full of poison, fear, and harm, and she began her grieving.

The clock on the mantel ticked past three when Bronson appeared in the doorway, cloaked by the shadow of the whole house now that the sun had made its way to the other side of the sky. He held his hat in his hands and stepped over the threshold with a deep sigh. He pointed toward the horsehair sofa. Louisa sat between her mother and sister, taking their hands and steeling herself for the blow to come. Bronson knelt down before them. Louisa closed her eyes and began to pray, so she did not see him take Anna's hands in his.

"My child, forgive me for what I have to tell you. Nicholas Sutton is dead."

. . .

Later they would hear the story. Halfway down the south panel of the roof, his back turned toward the breathtaking view of the Connecticut River and the verdant hills of Vermont the third-story dormer would provide, Nicholas Sutton lost his footing and felt the slate slide beneath the soles of his boots. He reached out desperately to take hold of an ill-placed shingle protruding from the pattern, an exposed beam, but there were none. The young men had crafted a smooth, even design, and there were no imperfections he could exploit. In one horrific moment his friends watched as he disappeared over the cornice, his face twisted in terror.

Samuel and Joseph clambered down the ladder as quickly as they could, throwing their own safety into jeopardy, and scrambled around to the back of the house. Joseph felt his knees buckle when he saw the contorted shape Nicholas made in the grass. His hips were squared toward the sky, his knees pointing up, but his upper body faced down into the grass. His right cheek was visible, and part of his right eye. The socket was full of blood. Samuel and Joseph sank down beside him and Nicholas emitted a small moan.

Samuel and Joseph locked eyes—they couldn't believe he was still breathing. Samuel leapt to his feet and took off running full speed toward his father's house—the first place he could think to go. Soon he would remember that his parents had gone to the next town over for a luncheon, and he would turn toward the Alcotts, two doors down, where he felt sure Mr. Alcott would be in his study. Though it was rumored he had sent his own daughters out to work rather than take on work he felt was beneath his intellectual abilities, Walpoleans also knew well the story of Bronson's effort to free the jailed runaway slave the previous summer, where his bravery and quick thinking amid the pistol shots astonished the mob. Mr. Alcott would know what to do.

Meanwhile, Joseph knelt in the blinding morning sun on the dry, caked ground, talking softly to Nicholas. "Samuel has gone to get help, Nick. Hold steady, man. Everything will be all right."

The last part was a lie, he knew. As he said it his oldest friend, who, like an older brother, had taught Joseph how to dig the thimble-sized frogs out of the muddy stream bed behind his house when they were boys, shuddered out his last breath.

We used to have such happy times

together, before we were grown up.

—*Moods*

Chapter Eighteen

September 13, 1855

Honor to the memory of our true and noble
Nicholas Charles, only son of Charles and Clara
Sutton, who died in this town on Wednesday
morning in his twenty-fourth year. The friends
of the family and classmates of the deceased
are invited to attend the funeral Saturday at
ten in the morning at the Unitarian Church.

The house was unusually quiet for a Saturday afternoon.
Typically, Bronson entertained a few of his intellectual
sparring partners from Concord or Boston while Anna, Louisa, and Lizzie looked on, sometimes chiming in, but mostly
keeping to their sewing, or in Louisa's case, escaping to the
bedroom to work on a story. May would tear through the
house just on the way to or just returned from some gathering with the friends she seemed to collect like charms on
a bracelet. And Abba, when they could convince her to let
the kitchen and the wash and the garden be, would hover a
moment in her rocking chair, her chapped and aching hands
resting in her lap like two old potatoes.

But on that morning the people of the town of Walpole
had laid Nicholas Sutton to rest in the cemetery behind
the Unitarian Church. After the service, the Sutton family

received mourners at their home. Bronson had insisted they all attend and he received little resistance. Anna entered the Suttons' parlor looking especially pale in her black dress, her hair knotted in a severe bun at the back of her head. She stood tall and did not cry, but her eyes were empty and Louisa could see she had retracted somewhere deep within herself. The neighbors greeted one another, many stopping to clutch Anna's hand a moment longer than the others', acknowledging what she alone had lost. Around midday they returned to Yellow Wood and scattered to separate corners of the house, either to contemplate the shock of the tragedy alone or to simply try to forget.

Louisa stood in the kitchen preparing a simple supper of baked apples, spider corncake steamed in molasses, and succotash. The others insisted they had no appetite, especially Anna, who ended nearly two days of silence to say so. But Louisa knew that as the nervous tension of the day subsided, they would discover they were ravenous. She reflected as she tested a half-cooked butter bean between her teeth that the grief and uncertainties that plagued the human mind drove people back into their bodies almost as a kind of refuge. Noticing the coarseness of wool against the skin, hot sun on the back of the neck, the delicious stretch of the muscle in the arch of the foot—these palpable sensations had distinct beginnings and endings, unlike the swirling chaos of the troubled mind. Louisa knew a full belly would bring unexpected comfort.

And comfort was exactly what Anna needed now. Louisa glanced out into the parlor at her sister, who sat in Abba's rocking chair gazing numbly out the window at the gray sky. Judging that the beans needed at least another quarter hour,

Louisa sighed and told herself that she could no longer put off telling Anna what had been weighing on her heart since Wednesday.

She crossed the room and stood behind her sister, looking out to see what she had been watching. The leaves of the maple tree in front of the house had begun to turn. The bright green was edged with orange, as if slow flames devoured the leaves.

"Do you remember the day we went to Singer's to buy the fabric for the drapes?" Anna's voice was scarcely above a whisper, as if sorrow itself constricted her throat. She had sensed Louisa standing near, but her gaze held steady. Louisa nodded, then said softly, "I do."

"I thought to myself that day, 'I will be engaged to be married by the time these leaves turn orange.' I remember thinking that *so* distinctly. Isn't that strange?" Louisa put her hand on Anna's shoulder. "It's not like me at all to have such a thought. The hubris—to think I had control over it all, that I could *will* it to happen. And yet I was so sure I was right. As if I were having some kind of premonition. That was before I'd even met Nicholas."

"Nan," Louisa began, her voice already quavering. "The things I said to you on Tuesday night, the way I questioned his intentions . . ." She crossed in front of Anna and sank down onto her knees and took Anna's hands. "I am so ashamed. Can you ever forgive me?"

Even in her sorrow Anna's compassion broke through. "But your *heart* is broken. You only said them because your heart is broken. Of course I forgive you."

Louisa released the sob wedged in her throat and rested her cheek on Anna's lap as she cried. Not only had she said these things and thought worse, but when the shock of their father's news about Nicholas abated, Louisa couldn't help but bemoan the fact that she would now be stranded in Walpole, taking care of Anna. She felt her dream of an independent life in Boston, the place where she could finally be herself, free from obligation, free from her heartbreak, was slipping away. Louisa's heart felt hollowed out like a melon rind. Her hair was damp from her work in the kitchen, and Anna brushed it with the tips of her fingers.

"None of it was even close to true," Louisa said. "Everyone knew how much he loved you, and you him. They treated you like a widow today, as they should. Even if you weren't married in God's eyes, you were married in your hearts."

Anna's hands stopped their absent caressing. "Please," she whispered. "Say no more about it. I cannot bear it."

Louisa sat up with a start. "Of course—I'm so sorry. I only meant—"

"Please," she said again. "Please."

Louisa nodded. "Let me make you some tea."

Anna looked out at the leaves again. "I must leave this town at once. As soon as I can find a position somewhere."

Louisa's head shot up. "Leave?"

"Argue with me all you like—it won't dissuade me. That funeral today wasn't just for Nicholas. It was for me, for the life I was meant to have as his wife, the mother of his children. Each time I pass that house I will think of the corner of the garden where my corn and beans would have grown, all the unhung Christmas wreaths. If I stay here he will die over and over again, every day. Have mercy and let me go."

How quickly everything kept changing! "I will speak with our father as soon as possible. Anything you want, my dear sister, you shall have. The Almighty Friend is looking down upon you now, one of His tenderest servants. Let Him give you comfort. Sorrow is only a season. You will be glad again—I know it."

Anna turned her vacant gaze on her sister and stared at eyes the same color as her own: dark like the soil. Louisa instantly knew she had taken her stalwart optimism too far. Anna's tone was low. "It is through the sheer force of will that I do not walk down to the river's edge right this second and throw myself under the current. I've thought of little else these last days—it seems to me the sweetest dream of relief. I know that *you* shall be glad again, and it pleases me to know it." Her voice turned cold as she looked away. "But take care not to speak of things you know nothing of."

One of the sweet things about pain and sorrow

is that they show us how well we are loved,

how much kindness there is in the world.

—*Jack and Jill*

Chapter Nineteen

Bronson secured by letter a position for Anna in Syracuse as a teacher at the newly built New York Asylum for Idiots, run by the famous Dr. Hervey Wilbur, where children born without all their faculties could go to learn a trade or simply how to read and write. Anna dreaded going and regretted asking to leave as her day of departure approached. But it was too late for changing her mind. And at work she could earn money to help the family, something she was beginning to realize her father might never be able to do. Bronson, Louisa, and May stood in front of the house while the driver loaded Anna's luggage into the carriage that would take her across the bridge to the train in Bellows Falls. She would ride the rest of the day, by train and then another carriage, to Syracuse. The trees along Wentworth Avenue had gone copper and vermilion, and a few leaves cascaded down around them. Louisa thought wistfully that no matter where Anna went, she would not be able to escape the reminder of these leaves. This thought was interrupted by a sound from behind her. Abba and Lizzie stood in the front window, knocking on the glass and waving to the traveler.

Bronson stepped forward and put his hands on his eldest daughter's shoulders.

"You break an old man's heart today, and yet I know you must go. Take an early bed, my child. And walks each day. Give yourself time for reading and other pure amusements." He kissed her forehead. "And above all, heed your conscience."

Anna gave a solemn nod in response, and Louisa noticed with a somersault of joy in her stomach that the tiniest hint of a smile crossed Anna's lips. They had laughed many times together over their father's penchant for monologues full of wise advice. How wonderful it was to see that the old Anna resided within her, dormant beneath the heavy blanket of sorrow. *Perhaps Father is right,* Louisa thought. *She must go away so that she can return to us her old self.*

Anna hugged May next. "Good-bye, little sister."

"I hope you won't wear your widow's weeds *too* long," May said worriedly. "They make your complexion look awfully pale."

Anna sighed. "Don't worry, my dear—I will take care that my fashions don't embarrass you."

May winced and grasped Anna's hand. "Forgive me— wear what you please. And know you have all my love."

Anna laughed at her inability to stay upset with May for more than a moment. "Now get inside and help Marmee. You really will have to do your share now." May nodded and turned back toward the house.

Louisa pulled Anna close and kissed her cheeks. "Work hard. But not *too* hard." She pressed an eagle into her palm and closed Anna's fingers around it. "Buy a dress or two in Syracuse. See a play."

Anna glanced at her hand and then looked up startled at Louisa. "But this is for your writing room—your little place apart. You took an oath!"

Louisa shook her head. "It's all right—I can spare it. And don't try to argue with me. It's my money and I can do what I like with it."

Anna smiled and shook her head. "You never fail to surprise me, my dear." Bronson stood talking to the driver about the route and Anna leaned in close to Louisa so he would not hear. "Now I have a surprise for you. But first you have to promise you won't be angry."

Louisa gave her a suspicious look. "I suppose that depends on what you've done. I can *try* not to be angry. . . ."

"That's the best I can hope for. I want you to go into my sewing basket—I told May I'd leave it for her to have my ribbon and trims—there's something in there for you."

"What kind of something?"

Anna hesitated, examining Louisa's face. "Letters. Probably a dozen."

"Letters from my sister, I hope," Louisa whispered back, her eyebrows drawn together.

Anna shook her head. "They just kept coming, for weeks after the Suttons' harvest party. And then they stopped. But I didn't want you to burn them, in case . . . well, in case things changed. And they have, haven't they?"

An abrupt laugh exploded from Louisa's lips and she nodded, tears pricking her eyes. Everything had changed and then changed again. Margaret's gossip had revealed the truth about Joseph and Nora, had given Louisa an excuse to yield to him when he came to her the night of the play. But that brief succumbing, sweet as it was, had nearly caused her to lose sight of what mattered, to forget that her object was freedom, not the fleeting promise of love. She thought back on that night in the field, the terrible things they'd said to each other. Joseph had nearly begged her to let him love her, to let him walk through life by her side. But she was like an animal in a trap, gnawing off a part of herself to get free.

Anna squeezed her hand. "Louy, you should talk to him. Don't leave things the way they are."

A flicker of something like hope crossed Louisa's face, but the wounded part of her, that once-tender place now grown over with the tough skin of a scar, couldn't let her take the risk of hoping. "The way they are is the way they should be. His life is his, and my life is *mine*. And that's what I always wanted, more than anything else. That my life would be my own."

Anna sighed. "And there isn't a way you could have both? Love him *and* have your freedom?"

Louisa shook her head. "It's not possible."

Anna watched her a moment. "I wish it could be different somehow. But I suppose you will do what you must."

Just then Bronson reappeared and turned the face of his pocket watch out toward Anna. "It's time to go, my dear."

Anna nodded at her father, then leaned in to Louisa, whispering, "At the very least, fish those letters out. You certainly don't want May to find them and cause a scandal."

Louisa glanced nervously at the house, then nodded.

"I'll write you every day." Anna choked on a sob.

Louisa gave a wicked smile in reply. "Well, soon you will have to send your missives to a new address. I hope to go to Boston before long."

Now Anna smiled, a real, full smile. "Write until your

fingers break. It may be the cure for everything. And don't think of this place. Pretend it was the setting in one of your stories, now finished. Perhaps one you threw in the fire."

Louisa thought for a moment of her night on the stage as the Widow Pottle, Fanny Kemble in her emeralds, Joseph's hot breath on her collarbone. "One cannot always judge things by the way they end."

"True," Anna whispered, gathering her overcoat close to her neck. "One must have faith. I want so much to believe the Psalm: '*He heals the brokenhearted and binds up their wounds.*'"

And with that she was gone. As Louisa headed back into the house, she pictured Anna speeding out of New Hampshire in the rented carriage, wrapped tight in heavy blankets to stave off the cold morning air. In the entryway she wiped her boots. May and Abba were in the back of the house, talking loudly over the clang of pots in the sink. At the foot of the armchair near the fireplace Anna's sewing basket sat, its lid askew. Louisa glanced back at the kitchen and then crossed the room to it.

The top tray, divided into sections, held a half-dozen cards wound round with various colors of thread and ribbon. A length of stiff lace had been folded into a square. Louisa pinched the center ridge of the tray and lifted it out of the basket. The deeper space below held a lone ball of yarn, a rusted pair of scissors, and the thick stack of letters. She hesitated before reaching to pull them out of the basket, as if their existence posed an actual physical threat. But once they were in her hand she almost laughed out loud. They were mere letters—paper and ink. Knowing they were in the world didn't change a thing. She stood, straightening her skirt, and stepped toward the hearth to cast them in. But then she hesitated, glancing at the flames. *Perhaps*, she reasoned with herself. *Perhaps it would be all the same if I tucked them away.* . . . She climbed the attic stairs two at a time and lifted the lid of the trunk that sat at the foot of her bed. Inside, there was a place where the lining was torn away. She tucked the letters behind the threadbare calico, placed her hand against them. Then she stood, swinging the lid shut, and began the arduous task of forgetting.

My dear Louy,

I arrived yesterday morning and was whisked straight into the care of the head teacher, a Mrs. Hutchins, who appears to be most competent, if a little stern. We are about a mile outside of Syracuse proper in a new building just opened in August. Our quarters are plain but cozy enough: a long room with five narrow beds on each side and windows along one wall. We have an efficient little stove where we can fix our tea and I've made friends already by offering Lizzie's apple cake all around.

There is room here for as many as one hundred children, but we are not yet full. My first assignment yesterday was helping to assess a new arrival, a little pale child of ten who is both deaf and dumb. Her mother hopes she can learn to write and sew, and I intend to try to teach her if I can. It is a relief to cast myself completely into my work. Heaven knows I can use the distraction.

May let slip the news that Margaret and Sam's wedding is on the horizon. I believe they waited until my departure to begin their plans. It is thoughtful of them but I am _fine_ and it will do me good to hear about their happy day. You must provide a full report. But don't do it in your way, skipping over all the details to the conversations afterward.

I want to hear about every button on her dress, the flowers—all the trifles you despise!

Ever your loving
Anna

Dear Anna,

Only an Alcott girl would believe the cure for sadness lies in reading a painstaking recitation of the joys of others. Or maybe it is just that you yearn for a beautiful dress. Have you been shopping in town? Please spend the money I gave you on something entirely impractical. It makes me mad to know that my good little lass is going around in shabby things and being looked down upon by people who are not worthy to touch the hem of her ragged old gowns.

And now you will have to bear with my faulty account of Tuesday's events. I tried to note the "trifles" as they went by, but there were so many of them!

The affair was a small one. Besides the Parkers and the Lewises, Uncle Willis and the Wellses came, along with some other folks from town. The senior Mr. Singer, I gathered from conversation, has taken a turn for the worse and his children were with him at home. Though I am saddened to hear of this news, I must admit to a little selfish relief that I did not have to face his son.

We gathered in the parlor of the Parker manse. As you know better than I, Mrs. Parker does have unimpeachable taste for fine things, but the place is not overdone. Some of the older folks sat in chairs and the rest of us stood behind in a cluster as Samuel came in from the study looking a little pale but cheered when he greeted his old friends. As I know you will want to know, he wore the checked trousers they all seem to favor, a pale silk waistcoat in a sort of butter color, white cravat tied in the loose foppish way, and a frock coat with wide lapels. He was as dashing as you can picture it, and I think we all felt a little jealous of Margaret.

Speaking of the former Miss Lewis, she made us all wait a good bit of time, as only Margaret would see fit to do, to build our anticipation before she appeared. Anna, I wish you could have seen her! Plump and lovely, her curls swept up and arranged just above her neck. She wore a wreath of white silk orange blossoms with a little veil in the back. And the dress! Words can't do it justice, but I shall try. The bodice was silk, a solid dove gray, with a snow-white lace tucker. The skirt (with a wide crinoline that Mrs. Parker must have reviled) carried the same color in a tiny flowered pattern. The bride also wore a mink pelerine. Far too early in the year for that, in my opinion, but I suppose she couldn't help but want to show it off. Father, as you would imagine, commented later that he saw no place at a ceremony dedicated to love and commitment for skin stolen from an animal. But Marmee understood, I think, and declared it "lovely."

Bride and groom made their vows in the usual way and placed the bands upon their fingers. Then commenced my favorite chapter of the day: the feast. Chicken and duck, potatoes, squash pies, corn and beans, and ice cream with champagne. It was divine and afterward I felt I could happily die in peace. Mr. and Mrs.

repaired to the apartment above the Whig store where they'll stay until they complete the purchase of the little house just out of town. The current owner is moving his family to St. Louis, and it's all taking some time. To spend the time, M and S will tour in New York City and Niagara Falls. Oh, and you will want to know: They left the party at nine. He was dashing in his top hat. She wore a white bonnet with pearls, white gloves embroidered with doves, and waved one of the pocket handkerchiefs you sent her, with lily of the valley stitched along the edge.

Have I done my duty, Nan? I hope you will be satisfied with my account. The day was incomplete without you, though I think you are just where you need to be now and speak with pride of your good works. Your prime place in Paradise has long been assured, and now you are just fluffing the pillows. If only I can work on earning my spot now—I intend to be there at your side.

Yours ever,

L

Wednesday, October 24

Dear Lou,

Oh, I am undone. Thank you for your letter—your
account was just what I hoped for. I won't conceal that
I did weep all the way through, for it was just as I had
imagined for myself. (Except for the mink pelerine,
for I agree that a fur should stay packed away until at
least December.) The dress, the feast are just what I
would have wanted for my own happy day. And will
have, I suppose, someday. I won't give up hope that the
Almighty Friend thinks of me on occasion, though His
plan does seem cruel and mysterious to me now. I only
want to be of use as He sees fit, and perhaps have a little
happiness for myself. It isn't so very bad to want that, I
don't think.

And what of your plans? Are you finding Walpole dull?

I'm off to an outing this evening. We will take some of
the children to a play in town.

Bye-bye for now,
Anna

Friday, November 2, 1855

My Dear,

Dull is a gentle way to describe this town, for what I really feel is confined and imprisoned. I've nothing here but ghosts around every corner, for my beloved sister is away, friends are married and gone, and the sight of a certain former friend is a torment. Is this a pleasant place to live besides all that? Where are the plays? There are none, unless we put them on. Is anyone here writing or arguing in parlors? No—unless it is about the virtues of a particular method for pressing cider or scouring a stove. I need to get back to the city before I weep myself a river to drown in. (And now you know your sister's flair for drama has not subsided!)

The happy news is that I shall depart presently. I had delayed my plans because of Marmee. She was so sad to see you go and I worried about burdening her with too many good-byes in one season. But last evening to my surprise she sat me down in front of the fire to tell me that she asked Uncle Willis to write to a widow in Boston who lets out rooms. So I will have my independence after all, with her blessing! As long as I can earn enough money to pay my way, I may stay in the city, and I will, for I'm not afraid of hard work when the reward is so sweet.

I must fly to preparations now. I've many letters to write.

Your sister,
Louisa

Louisa spent the weeks after Anna's departure preparing for her own. She examined her scanty wardrobe in the midday sun to locate the spots and scrub them out with a horsehair brush. Her mending basket overflowed with a few mousseline and batiste dresses handed down from a cousin, which she intended to make over, and she depleted the family's candle supply significantly in a few nights as she stayed up late sewing.

A few days after Anna's first letter arrived Louisa felt the familiar tightness in her abdomen and, the next morning, saw the red bloom of blood on her drawers. Its appearance took her breath away. Through sheer force of will she had nearly erased the memory of lying with Joseph in the tall grass. In forgetting, she did not have to acknowledge that she was at risk for a far more serious consequence than a broken heart. Her body would carry no lasting reminder of her transgression. Though she usually cursed the cotton batting and ladies' belt as a burden, reaching for it now prompted a twinge of relief.

Though she had been the one to initiate the Boston plans, Abba seemed to regret that impulse as the day of Louisa's departure approached. Suddenly, destitute families across New England were crying out for donations of candles, wool stockings, pickled vegetables. A few pieces of broken crockery urgently required gluing. Fall dresses had to be aired and pressed, sprigs of rosemary tucked in the pockets to keep them fresh until the weather turned cool. Louisa strove to make her mind still, like the surface of the river, and indulge her mother's requests. It was only a matter of time now, and she could spare a few more days.

On Louisa's last Friday in Walpole, Mr. Parsons's sow got her foot caught in some chicken wire and suffered such severe injuries from her struggling that he had to put her down. A red basket containing five pork steaks appeared on the doorstep at Yellow Wood Saturday morning, along with a note from Mrs. Parsons wishing Louisa well on her journey. Abba seized the basket and rushed to the kitchen with Bronson fast on her heels. Though she had no intention of deferring to his prohibition on meat, Abba allowed him to believe she was waiting for his approving nod. Louisa and her mother patiently weathered his speech on the sins of a carnivorous diet—the suffering of the animals, the filth of the farmyard. He frowned and weighed the consequences, finally allowing that it would be wasteful and rude not to make use of the gift.

Abba broke into a full smile and praised her husband's ardent compassion, declaring they would have a feast to send Louisa off properly. Anna had sent home a portion of her first week's wages, and for once there was enough to buy a few extra treats. Abba shooed Bronson back to his study and scratched out a list of ingredients on a scrap of the butcher paper. Louisa pulled the shopping basket from the top shelf of the pantry and wrapped a wool shawl around her shoulders. She glanced out the window to assess the sky—pale but clear—and started off for Washington Square.

The heat of the woodstove fogged the windows of the grocer's tiny shop. Inside, a table overflowed with winter squashes: the strangely shaped butternut, the warted acorn. Louisa chose a heavy squash and asked the grocer for five potatoes, two pounds of butter, and a block of cheese. As she turned to leave the shop, she felt pleased with the heft of her loaded basket. It was warm for a November day and dinner would be lovely. She nearly had her freedom.

Across the square a man in an unbuttoned coat stood leaning against the door of a carriage. He touched the brim of his hat, then reached into the pocket of his waistcoat and examined his watch. *Joseph.* Louisa stood frozen a moment, mortified at the thought of what they would say to each other if he saw her. With her free hand she pulled the collar of her shawl slowly up over the back of her head, hoping she could hide, wondering whether he was alone. Just before she turned away, he looked up. His eyes registered her presence but his expression remained cold. They stared at each other, neither of them moving to wave or nod in recognition. A figure emerged from behind the carriage, her purple skirt fluttering in the wind. Nora held her package to her chest. Joseph turned away to help her up, brushed her trailing hem into the cab, and closed the door behind her. As he stepped up and settled onto the open front seat, Louisa remembered the time she had sat there beside him while his sister pouted all the way to the circus. *He'll get to keep his carriage now,* she thought. *Catherine will be so pleased.* Joseph tossed the reins and eased the phaeton forward, his gaze fixed on the road.

The day of her departure finally arrived. Her manuscripts lined the bottom of her trunk and she piled the clothes and a few mementos on top. The savings she had guarded all summer were safe in the trunk's lining. It was time, finally, to leave everything else behind. Though she was afraid, the thought of Walpole shrinking in the distance propelled her forward.

She was edgy with anticipation when Bronson saw her to the coach parked in the road.

He shook his head. "Two of my girls gone this month," he said as he kissed her cheek.

"I'm going to write like mad and sell these stories to anyone who will have them as quickly as I can," Louisa replied.

"You must be patient, daughter. We cannot determine the pace of our accomplishments. That is for the Lord to do." Louisa knew her father doubted whether she could sell her *Christmas Elves* because it was so late in the season.

"Yes, Father, but I believe the Lord and I are in agreement that He intends me to be a writer. *Now*."

Bronson chuckled. "Well, I hope you are right. But in case the publishers are slow to respond, your mother wanted me to give you this."

He pressed a slip of paper into her hand. It said: "Mrs. Clarke, 13 Chestnut Street, Beacon Hill." She looked up at him, confused.

"This family just took in some sick relatives and is in need of new linens. Your mother was proud to recommend you to do the sewing. It is the womanly art at which you are *most* successful. Your stitches are almost as pleasing to look at as Anna's."

Louisa smoothed a smile over the face that threatened to break into a scowl. It was the same old theme: if only she could be more like Anna—womanly and docile—perhaps he would love her better.

"Thank you, Father. I will not need it, but if it makes Mother happy to know I have another way of earning money, I am happy to take it."

Bronson nodded and helped her into the carriage. "The peace and patience of the Lord be with you, my child."

To Louisa it sounded as if he were saying: Soon you will come to accept that your silly fancies are out of reach. Her confidence felt shaken, but as the carriage pulled away, she straightened up and gave her head a little shake. She'd had enough with the sadness and doubt. Enough with questioning her choices, with wondering what might have been—if it had been her purple hem trailing out the open door of Joseph's carriage instead of Nora's. Her future was in Boston. Her life was beginning.

BOSTON

November–December 1855

I'm not afraid of storms, for I'm

learning how to sail my ship.

—*Little Women*

Chapter Twenty

November 8

J. T. Fields
Publisher

Dear Mr. Fields,

If it is amenable to your schedule, could we please meet Wednesday, November 14, to discuss a story I think you might be interested in, "How I Went Out to Service." I have moved to Boston permanently and look forward to more time for writing and selling my work.

Yours truly,
Louisa May Alcott

B oston was just as Louisa remembered it: teeming with men's shouts and the chaos of horses in the dirt streets. And as she walked down Chauncey Place, southeast of the Common, a hearty autumn rain began to fall and turned the dust into a sudsy soup. She looked down to see the hem of her best dress soaked at least a good two inches with mud and laughed out loud at her futile efforts to arrive in the city with a shred of dignity.

She had the address of Mrs. David Reed's boarding-house scribbled on a paper in her pocket and, in the swampy weather, was never so glad to locate a doorway in her life. Her trunk was at the station and would be sent for once she secured her room.

Louisa knocked and a stooped woman with an out-of-date bonnet wrenched the door open just wide enough to poke her head through.

"And who might you be?"

Louisa hesitated a moment before answering what should have been a very simple question. Who *might* she be, now that she was away, on her own? She *might* be anyone. The prospect of this so seized her mind that she considered inventing a new identity, a clean slate. But there is no escaping your own skin. "Louisa May Alcott. Are you Mrs. Reed?"

The woman nodded. "Proprietress."

"Ma'am, I am the niece of Mr. Willis."

"Which Mr. Willis?" Mrs. Reed asked, narrowing her eyes.

"Mr. *Benjamin* Willis."

A change came over Mrs. Reed's face. The nose that had been upturned in distaste, giving her the appearance of a pig, relaxed and she looked human once again. "Well, why didn't you say so in the first place? Mr. Benjamin Willis was a close friend of my late husband's. I take in anyone he recommends."

Louisa exhaled with relief. "Thank goodness for that!"

Inside, Mrs. Reed showed Louisa the cramped parlor full of worn furniture. The light through the large front window was good, though, and Louisa's eye marked a chair in the corner that would be excellent for reading.

"A woman living *alone* in this big city. I shall put you in the attic—you'll be safest there."

"I thank you, ma'am." From one attic to the next, Louisa thought.

"And just what is it you're here to do, if you don't mind my asking?" Who would ever confess that in fact they *did* mind? Louisa wondered.

"I'm here to see what I can make of myself. I'm a writer."

"Gracious me! What a boring thing to do with your time."

"Yes, well, I'm a boring sort of girl, I guess you could say." Louisa grinned as she climbed the stairs behind the woman's massive rump.

"And no husband, I presume?"

Louisa felt a tug behind her ribs. The excitement of the day had managed to drown out her other thoughts. She steeled herself, remembering that all was as it should be, and the reason she was here now, with the chance to show what she could do, was that she had refused the conventional path Joseph had wanted them to take together.

"No, ma'am. Not looking for one either."

The old woman scoffed. "Gracious me," she said again under her breath. Louisa reflected that perhaps she should not have mentioned her uncle's name, in which case she would have been cast out and free to go to the next boardinghouse down the lane, where she could avoid all these questions.

The attic room was on the fourth story, cramped and stuffy. But there was a fireplace, a window that looked out on the First Church steeple, a bed and sturdy chair. Mrs. Reed told her the charge would be three dollars a week, including board and firewood. She'd have to sew an awful lot of pillow-cases to make that up if she couldn't sell her stories, but she knew it was a fair price and accepted. Mrs. Reed stood around, waiting to be asked to sit for tea by the stove, but Louisa was bold enough not to offer. She was exhausted by her travels and longed to part ways with this tiresome woman.

"Well, I'll let you get settled in, then."

"The man from the station should be bringing my trunk around soon."

"I'll send my niece Caroline up when it arrives. Supper is at five."

And with that Mrs. Reed turned and descended the steep staircase, her fingers like talons on the handrail.

The following Wednesday was sunny and warm, autumn's last hurrah before the blanket of winter descended. Louisa packed two new stories in a side bag and prepared to walk to the office of the publisher J. T. Fields, who had published Mr. Hawthorne's lurid and successful book *The Scarlet Letter.* Louisa nurtured a furtive wish to claim some literary success for her own, and Mr. Fields seemed just the sort of man to help her do it.

At the corner, Louisa stopped short to gawk in the window of Madame Garnier's boutique. It would be months before Walpole or even Concord would adopt some of the more modern trends, and she knew they'd be adopted in a sort of amateur way, with homemade touches that diminished their effect. Here she saw a painted silk fan with inlaid mother-of-pearl on the handle, a caul for the hair accented with beaded gold thread, and kid gloves in every pastel shade—pink, blue, buttery yellow. The most fashionable women now wore slightly shorter skirts, revealing a bit of ankle, and all manner of decorative hosiery was available. Horizontal stripes in the daytime, and in the evenings, slightly scandalous lace.

Though the vanity of fashion had no place in the Alcott household, Louisa observed that these garments were works of art—the texture of fine silk and lace and brocade, the pin-prick-sized stitches made by the seamstress's deft hand. If she were to admire the blacksmith, who seemed to be Whitman's hero, for pounding the perfect horseshoe, why could she not admire the seamstress for her creation and admire the creation itself? After all, just as the horse would carry the weight of all his labors on those shoes, so too would the woman carry on her shoulders the weight of her lesser status, the expectations of who she should be.

Musing on Whitman made her think of Joseph and she found herself wondering what he was doing at that very moment. Cutting fabric behind the counter at the shop? Brushing Romeo's mane? Buying a pretty bonnet for the new Mrs. Singer? Louisa nearly groaned out loud at the last image. *It's as if I'm determined to make myself miserable,* she thought. *Well, I won't do it.*

With a deliberate shake of her head, she turned away from the shop window and carried on down the street. On School Street she finally came to the Old Corner Bookshop, above which Fields had his office.

"Good morning," Louisa said to the shopkeeper, who was just cranking out the awning that protected books in the window from damage by the afternoon sun. "Is Mr. Fields in?"

"I can't say as I know," the man said. His head was covered

in tight brown curls that extended in all directions. "Sometimes he comes before I get here and lets himself in. But you can come through the store and up the back steps."

Louisa nodded and smiled, her heart too swollen in her chest with nerves for her to speak. She had written ahead to Mr. Fields to tell him she would be in the city and had some material for him. *Why should I be nervous?* she thought. *I am a published author. Of course he's going to be interested in my stories.* She threw back her shoulders in her best idea of a businessman's posture and, looking quite ridiculous, ascended the back staircase like Queen Elizabeth.

Indeed, Mr. Fields had arrived early. The main door to the offices was open. The desks in the main room were empty—his clerks did not arrive until the afternoon. The room led toward the front of the building, where an office was partitioned off by a green curtain. Long counters ran the length of the office, and books were stacked in piles taller than Louisa.

She approached the publisher's office, but she did not know how to alert him she was there. How does one knock on a curtain? She cleared her throat. "Mr. Fields?"

"Who's there?" he grunted.

"Louisa May Alcott."

"Ah, Miss Alcott, daughter of my favorite bumbling philosopher. Please come in."

Bumbling? Louisa thought, unsure of whether to take offense. It was true—her father was a bumbler. And that was far from the worst thing that could be said about him. She decided to brush the comment off.

"Yes, thank you," she said, pushing past the green curtain. "You received my letter, I hope?"

"Yes, yes," Fields said, nodding in a way that communicated he had no idea what she was talking about.

Louisa took a deep breath. "Well, I've brought the story. It is based on an experience I had a couple years ago, when I went out to service for a family in Dedham. I won't tell you their name—as you will see, their literary likeness is most unfavorable."

Fields nodded and sat back in his chair with the manuscript she'd pressed into his hand. Louisa stood uncomfortably while he read, as there was not another chair in the small office. She glanced back out into the main room. A row of gas lamps was bracketed along the walls on either side of the space. On a table in the corner, a basket of fruit stood rotting, perhaps a gift from a would-be author, ignored, gone to waste.

She turned back to Fields. His high forehead shone with perspiration in the cramped room. The noise from the street drifted in through the open window behind his desk.

Finally, he looked up and spoke. "You have been a teacher, in the past?"

"Yes, sir, I have. And a governess. But this story concerns only my time in Dedham. There I washed clothes, cooked for the family, beat the rugs. As a servant."

Fields pressed his full lips into a patient smile. "Yes," he said. "Well, I would advise you, then, to stick to teaching."

"I'm sorry, sir?"

"Stick to teaching. You have no talent for writing."

Louisa stood in the heat of the room blinking a moment before his words penetrated her mind. She felt the blood rush into her cheeks and the stays of her dress tighten as she struggled to breathe. She couldn't think of anything to say that would sound even mildly dignified. She also felt she might cry at any moment.

"Well," she choked the barely audible word and received the manuscript he handed back to her. "Good day." She made it halfway down the stairs to the street level before the tears began to flow.

Back out on the street the sky looked the color of dull homespun washed too many times. No one else seemed to be bothered by it, though. The streets were teeming with people rushing this way and that. Louisa tried to focus her eyes on individual faces—a mother and her two small daughters, covered from head to toe in silk bows, a bespectacled man with a doctor's bag, a pack of ruddy-cheeked boys with suspicious grins. She felt a pang of loneliness, as if all the rest of the world were part of a complicated waltz, moving to and fro in time, and she did not know the steps.

It occurred to her that in another two days she would have to pay Mrs. Reed the three dollars she owed for the upcoming week. She had spent some of her savings to pay the fare to Boston and to buy a kettle and a ream of paper. It wouldn't be enough merely to scrape by on her own—she needed to have something to send home to her parents.

In all her debates with herself over whether she should come to Boston to try to make her way on her own, she worried about leaving the family and feeling alone, but never once had she pondered the possibility that her stories would not sell. It seemed obvious to her that she had been put on the earth to be a writer. Nothing else held any interest for her. Teaching and housework strained her patience—they seemed the sort of occupations only a woman could do and she felt sometimes that she was very little like a woman.

Sacrifice without the expectation of anything in return was the most lauded aspiration for a woman in her father's mind, but Louisa didn't think much of it as a goal, even if she could scarcely admit that point of view to herself. Why would God give a woman the talents and abilities mostly reserved for men if He did not want her to use them?

But in Louisa's experience, no matter how much one wished and prayed, God was not going to come down and pay the rent. She reached into the pocket of her dress and felt around for the slip of paper Bronson had given her. She had only two dresses for daytime, and she'd switched back and forth between them since arriving, merely spot cleaning the front and hem to avoid the trouble and expense of laundry. The paper was right where she'd left it.

Louisa told herself to bear up, for it was all in the service of her writing. If she could earn enough money, she could stay in Boston. Back at Mrs. Reed's she wrote out a message to Mrs. Clarke, offering her services as seamstress, and sent Caroline to deliver it.

By the next evening the Clarkes had sent a bundle over. The next few days she sat in her garret surrounded by fabric, her thumb full of pinpricks. Daylight found her asleep at her desk, her cheek pressed against the page where she'd managed to record five or six meager sentences. The sewing was piled on a table by the door: one dozen pillowcases, one dozen sheets, six cambric neckties, and two dozen handkerchiefs.

I wish I had no heart, it aches so.

—*Little Women*

Chapter Twenty-one

My dear sister,

Boston is just the way we left it—filthy and full of excitement, none of which I may have, it seems. I continue to write but have no good news to share. My birthday is just weeks away. Another year gone by and I worry that I will leave this world before I have done half of what I would like to. . . .

All along as Louisa struggled to earn her room and board and stay awake long enough at the end of the day to continue writing, Joseph wound between and through and around her thoughts like a long green snake. Yet there was nothing to be done about him. Life was moving on and she approached each day the way she would cope with a rotting front tooth and no dentist nearby. One learned to smile with her lips closed.

The weather turned colder as if to impress upon her that time was indeed passing, but she did her best to ignore it. The stories piled up, along with the rejections, and she sewed more pillowcases and men's shirts than she ever had in her life. She revised *Christmas Elves*. May came to Boston for the day with a friend from school to deliver the finished drawings that would accompany the text. Louisa was surprised by how delighted she was to see her sister, to hear the news of home.

She was careful, though, to cut May off as she began prattling about what was going on in Walpole. Louisa was full of curiosity about Joseph and Nora's wedding—when it would happen, whether it had already taken place—but she was afraid of what knowing would do to her.

She tied up the manuscript and took it to Mr. Briggs, who had published *Flower Fables* the year before. He was happy to see that she continued to work but informed her that it was too late in the year for a book about the holidays because it couldn't possibly be out in time. Her father had been right after all, much as it pained her to admit it. Mr. Briggs said she could bring the manuscript back in the spring and he would see if he had the space for it then.

Though it nettled her pride after the encounter with Mr. Fields, she began to look for teaching opportunities. She knew she had to stay busy, for if she stopped to think about how differently things were working out than she had hoped, she feared she might collapse.

One Saturday morning while the rain fell in sheets out on the street, Louisa sat in the parlor of the rooming house reading *The Old Curiosity Shop*. It was a rare moment of leisure but also a practical matter: the main fireplace provided much more warmth than the tiny stove in Louisa's room, and she had spent the morning chilled to the bone. Just as she was losing herself in the image of Nell staring out at the windows of all the other houses on the lane, wondering whether those houses felt as lonely as the one she shared with her grandfather, the front door swung open with a gust, and a tall man wearing a somewhat crushed and weathered hat stepped into the entryway. Mrs. Reed's niece Caroline stood clutching the door against the wind.

"Telegram for Miss L. M. Alcott," he called to Mrs. Reed, who stood fumbling with a tea set in the dining room, preparing for the midday meal. Louisa's chest tightened. Good news usually did not arrive by telegram. She closed her eyes in prayer a moment before she spoke.

"I am Miss Alcott," Louisa said. The messenger turned to her, the shoulders of his overcoat glistening with rain.

"Yes, miss. Please sign here."

Her hand trembled as she wrote. He handed her the slender message and she thought about how a simple piece of paper could change a person's life. She ripped the message out of its envelope. It was from Joseph: *My father dead at six this morning.*

> *Saturday evening, November 24*
>
> *Dear Joseph,*
>
> *Your telegram arrived this morning in a torrent of rain that seemed choreographed to echo the tone of your message. I have thought all afternoon about what I could say to you that might provide a little comfort; of course, there is nothing. I will not say that God in His wisdom has called your father back, for you will hear it again and again in the coming days, and I know from some experience that the words ring hollow in those first days.*
>
> *I surprise myself by taking comfort in the fact that the new Mrs. Singer will be by your side through this difficult time. She is strong and true and your father will rest easy knowing his son no longer walks alone.*

Steal away a moment from your family obligations in the coming days to take up your Whitman. And look to the soil, for you will see that "the smallest sprout shows there is really no death. . . ."

Through the fullness of time, in any way I may be of use, I am ever

Yours,
Louisa

Friday, November 30, 1855

My Dearest Louisa,

Your letter came just in time to bolster me, for I was
beginning to wonder if I could endure the trial of this
week. First I must accept the death of my lifelong friend,
and now my father. My sister has lost her idol. We
are both mourning the passing of a man who, while
he did not always heed the call of his conscience in his
actions, had a full, good heart, and, always, the best of
intentions.

One mistake I must correct: there remains only one
Mrs. Singer, and that lady rests peacefully in her grave
now that her husband has been returned to her. Nora
remains a companion and I a bachelor. Hoping to express
respect for our family, she has put the nuptial plans on
hold. In fact this has caused my sister additional distress, as, though she would never admit it, she is anxious to see the covenant made and my father's financial
affairs settled. I do not know what to feel. Some days I
am tired of fighting it and wish to submit, for the good
of all those around me, including Nora, whose pure heart
deserves a happy home.

And yet there will always be a stitch in my side
emblazoned with the letters LMA. Just a few months ago
I believed things would turn out so differently. When

we were together it seemed we could have anything—
be anything—we wanted. But it has always been me
against the inkwell, has it not? At times I can scarcely
resist the urge to alight on your doorway in Boston—to
try to convince you to change your mind. But the hardest
lesson for one so stubborn as I is to learn that indeed we
are not the authors of our fate—there are greater forces
at work. I've wasted too much time believing it is so, and
I hope you will forgive me.

> *Faithfully,*
> *Joseph*

The following week Louisa sat finishing her noon meal at the long knobby table in what Mrs. Reed called the dining room. The space was scarcely more than a hallway, however, and as she ate she was forced to scrape her chair in close to the table to let people pass. Louisa tried to eat quickly. She'd had a story simmering since the early morning, and her mind felt cluttered with potions, swords, lopsided hats, old violins without any strings, as if it were some kind of gypsy cart. When she was working most feverishly, she could go for days without eating. But then she would collapse and not be able to start again until a week had gone by. She had promised her mother she would take care of herself and so she forced herself to sit and eat when she'd rather be scribbling away in the attic.

Another reason to bolt the food as quickly as possible was the lurking Mrs. Reed. She liked to find Louisa alone and pummel her with excruciating stories of fellow boarders' foibles and the trials she endured as "proprietress." Just as Louisa was chewing the last unpalatable potato, the lady entered the room with a stack of clean plates for the hutch in the corner and commenced to chat.

"Well, Louisa, there's nothing dainty about you, is there?" Mrs. Reed pointed at Louisa's empty plate and asked in what was, as far as Louisa could tell, an attempt at some kind of humor.

"The dainty ones look pretty in a sitting room, ma'am, but when a woman is making her way in the world on her own, she must resolve to take fate by the throat and shake a living out of her."

Mrs. Reed gaped at her, scandalized. "And where did you learn to talk this way? What a violent mind you have, child."

"It has always been so. My three sisters have pure hearts and gentle spirits, but all the boiling blood went into me, I'm afraid. I write it into my characters to keep it at bay."

"And your father—Mr. Alcott? He must not approve of this life you have chosen. Doesn't he wish you would marry?"

Louisa thought the question over for a moment and realized she didn't know the answer. Bronson was an unconventional man in many respects, and she knew she would be underestimating him if she categorized his disapproval as something so run-of-the-mill. Over the years, through his many parlor conversations with his friends—Mr. Emerson, Mr. Thoreau, Mr. Channing, Margaret Fuller, and others—he had developed a complex philosophy about human nature Louisa had never been able to untangle. But part of it held that a man must both marvel at the power of *and* learn to control the wildness within him. The wildness itself was not sinful—it connected man to the earth, gave him spirit and the ability to endure. But its presence was a test of his diligence. In Bronson's eyes, Louisa had never buckled a saddle on that wild mare rearing within her. Worse, she seemed almost proud of this fact and channeled the passion into writing tales of sensational drama rather than study her German, contemplate the mysteries of the divine, or somehow put her gifts to use for the greater good. In short, he thought her unashamedly feral. Whether marriage would remedy that fact was beside the point.

"Mrs. Reed, I think my father is happy to have the meager earnings my stories can bring. It is a difficult time for our family, and we all must work toward the cause of bread and decent bonnets."

She shot Louisa a skeptical look and closed the door on the hutch. "Nonsense. Every father wants his daughter to marry. When he comes to visit I will have a chat with him. From time to time, eligible bachelors come to stay at this house. I could arrange an introduction."

Louisa smiled sweetly, but inside she boiled. Was it too much to ask to simply be left alone? It seemed her very existence as a single woman invited speculation and offers of help, as if it were simply impossible that she truly might not *want* to be married.

And yet she felt a wave of doubt when she thought about the price of this freedom. The death of Joseph's father seemed to reveal the fissures in her resolve to separate herself from him. She thought of him often, felt weighed down by the grief he was suffering. It was so difficult to force herself not to love him. Joseph was *good*; he wanted to do right by his sister and Nora, didn't shy away from wrestling with the question of the proper course when what was righteous went against what was true. And there was nothing she could do to help him.

"Thank you, Mrs. Reed, but it is of no use. Even if my father was desperate for me to marry, and I don't believe he is, he couldn't get me into marriage with a shoehorn. It goes against my nature."

Mrs. Reed stared at the girl and shook her head. "This is a most unnatural way to live."

Louisa shrugged, pushing her chair back from the table one last time. "And now I'm off to write some unnatural tales. Good afternoon."

Another week of writing stories she feared no one would ever read came and died away, and Saturday morning arrived. Louisa fastened the buttons on the better of her two dresses and brushed the tangles out of her thick mane of hair. She parted it down the middle and wound the side sections into thick twists stretching from her temples to the nape of her neck. There she coiled the rest of the hair into a heavy chignon and fastened it in place with the mother-of-pearl comb Anna had sent from Syracuse as an early birthday present. The gift was just in time—Louisa never had been able to find the comb with the steel flowers that she had lost sometime over the summer.

Louisa wasn't the sort of girl to stand before the mirror contemplating her appearance, but this morning she hesitated a moment. She wished the glass could reflect more than just her deep-set eyes and round unremarkable chin and show her some clue of what was in her heart. How long should she wait to see whether anyone would show interest in her work? Perhaps it was time to consider the possibility that she might only be a writer for herself and her family. There were worse fates. She was fortunate in so many ways. She felt healthy and strong, she could work and take care of her family. And she could still write, for leisure, when she had the time. The only difference would be that she would do something else to make money. Governess, teacher. It was silly and selfish to ignore the truth.

She went out at half past eleven to deliver a stack of towels she'd finished the night before to Mrs. Clarke. Walking always had a calming influence on her. The metronomic swing of her legs cleared her mind and forced her to breathe, coaxing her courage out of its hiding place. The sun hung directly above the city. November's chill weakened its heat, but the glare was an assault on eyes accustomed to the soft light of the reading lamp. She made her way north across the Common to Chestnut Street. Soon she was rapping the iron knocker of the Clarkes' stately home, built about fifty years before by the Boston architect Charles Bulfinch. It sat among some of Boston's finest homes.

Polly, the Clarkes' stout older servant, answered the door.

"I'll take your coat, Miss Alcott," she said.

"No, thank you, Polly—I won't be but a moment. I came to bring the sewing." Louisa handed her the package of towels wrapped in paper.

"Is that Miss Alcott?" Mrs. Clarke said, coming in from the parlor. "Do come in, dear, and have some tea. What a dreadfully cold morning."

"I won't trouble you, Mrs. Clarke."

"Nonsense. Polly, would you please put on the tea? And bring us some of that wonderful sweet potato bread."

"Yes, ma'am." Polly turned and her white cap bobbed toward the kitchen.

"Let me hang your coat," Mrs. Clarke said, helping Louisa slip it off. She moved awkwardly with it to the front closet. It was clear she was inexperienced with a task of this sort. It was as if she wanted to show Louisa that though she was fortunate to afford servants, as well as a girl to do her sewing, she didn't take their work for granted. It seemed a silly show, and Louisa was almost flattered that it mattered to Mrs. Clarke what she thought.

"Now," she said with a satisfied sigh. "Let's go sit by the fire."

Mrs. Clarke was the wife of Ebenezer Clarke, a member of the Massachusetts General Court, and a lady of fine reputation in the city. She was known for her grand parties and the paintings she made of the birds and squirrels in the Public Garden.

They settled on the velvet armchairs that flanked the marble fireplace. "So tell me, Miss Alcott—how is the writing going?"

A little wave of panic came over her. Stupidly, vainly, she'd told everyone she met about her plans for a stellar writing career in Boston. The daughter of Bronson Alcott wouldn't establish herself in Boston just to be a seamstress. Now, of course, they all wanted to know how she was faring. She cleared her throat. "Well, I am determined to keep trying, though so far I haven't met with much success."

"Oh," Mrs. Clarke said, brushing Louisa's doubt away with a flick of her hand. "I am sure you will come by with good news very soon. You can't give up—that's the main thing."

"Oh, I don't intend to. But sometimes I wonder . . ."

"What's that, dear?"

"I wonder if I shouldn't be looking for a more steady type of employment. I will continue writing, of course, no matter what I'm doing with the rest of my time. But Anna is working in Syracuse now and I can't help but think I had better do my share as well."

"I see. Well, as you may know, my daughter Frances is a teacher at a school in Plymouth. Of course, it isn't that she has to work," Mrs. Clarke said, then reddened with the realization that she sounded like she was bragging about her wealth again. "But she loves teaching and Mr. Clarke and I feel it is very important for our children to learn the value of work and what the lives of others less fortunate than ourselves are like.

"Her letter from last week mentioned that one of the teachers is leaving to marry. Would you like me to inquire about the position for you?"

Polly brought in the tea tray and set it on the table between them. The china was so white it was almost blue, and the fronds of a fern splayed in the center of each saucer. *Ask and ye shall receive*, Louisa thought as Mrs. Clarke described the teaching position. But did she want to receive it? Coming from Mrs. Clarke an "inquiry" was more like a command. Probably, the job would be hers if she wanted it. She should be happy. It was just as she said—now was the time to think of others.

"That would be very generous of you, Mrs. Clarke. I would appreciate it."

"Not at all, dear. We cannot squander this bright mind of yours on sewing and other chores."

Or teaching a herd of children their letters, Louisa thought.

"The pay is quite good compared to most other schools," Mrs. Clarke said. "You'll have money left over to go to the theater, to buy a winter coat. The one you were wearing when you came in—is that all you have? Surely it can't be warm enough for the January winds. They cut right through you."

Louisa nodded, sculpting a smile for her face that she hoped was convincing. She could really help her family with a position like this. And, of course, who wouldn't love a few nicer dresses, a bonnet or two? But though she loved luxury, freedom and independence were luxury to her a thousand times over. The thought of losing them made her desolate.

By the time she arrived back at Mrs. Reed's, her mind was a tangled mess. She would have to decide, she knew; but at the moment all she wanted to do was escape into the mind of another writer. She started for the stairs up to her "garret" but she noticed the aroma of potatoes and glanced at the clock. It was nearly time for dinner. So her escape would be short-lived. She stole into a corner of the parlor with her old favorite, *Jane Eyre*, and drew a curtain on her troubles.

Mrs. Reed was in the kitchen making a lot of racket. The door on the woodstove screeching open, the rustle of the logs. The thud of a full iron pot lifted off the stove and set heavily on the worktable. The clatter of the mismatched bowls with chips around the rim.

But none of it penetrated Louisa's mind. Growing up in small apartments with three sisters and an endless stream of her father's friends visiting, a girl learned how to crouch inconspicuously in a corner and block out the noise so that she could plunge into the world of a story.

"Caroline," Mrs. Reed called into the hallway. "Please come help me serve." Mrs. Reed gave a frustrated sigh when the girl did not respond.

Jane was explaining to Mr. Rochester just why she thought he *wasn't* handsome, though in truth she thought him full of unconscious pride and at ease in his demeanor in the most beguiling way.

Mrs. Reed emerged from the kitchen, looking around the parlor for the girl. Steam had formed a patina on her sagging cheeks. She glanced over at Louisa and rolled her eyes. "Reading *again*," she muttered.

Mr. Rochester told Jane that he was in a talkative mood, and since it suited him, she should speak. But Jane was stubborn—why should she have to talk for the sake of talking, just because he was ordering her to do so? He sensed her annoyance and apologized.

Caroline rounded the corner near the banister. "There you are," Mrs. Reed began. Then she stopped short. "Caroline," she hissed. "What have I told you about letting strangers in off the street?"

Mrs. Reed put on her slightly more polite public voice. "I'm sorry, sir—all my rooms are full up. I can't take anybody new just now."

The smell of the stew was beginning to break into the world of Louisa's story. Her stomach gurgled and she realized she hadn't eaten a thing all day except for the bread she'd had at tea with Mrs. Clarke. One of the most challenging aspects of the philosophy of self-denial her father tried to teach his daughters was resisting the siren song of food. Louisa was no tender waif—she loved to eat and had a man's hunger.

Practiced in patience, Louisa kept her eye trained on the letters. She wanted to think a little more about what Mr. Rochester meant by *"remorse is the poison of life."* But it was too late—her concentration was broken. The light in the room shifted. She became aware that someone was walking toward her.

"Sir, where are you going?" Mrs. Reed cried, panic in her voice. "I told you—there's no room here."

The figure blocked the light and the page darkened. When Louisa could no longer resist it, she looked up. Joseph. Louisa blinked, staring at him, astonished. His hair had grown—it curled over his collar—and his cheeks were pink from the wind. She wondered for a moment whether her hunger was playing tricks on her, whether her mind was plagued by visions. But then the mirage opened his mouth to speak.

"You've written plenty of romantic tales," he said, taking the book from her hands and gently closing it. "Didn't you know I would come?"

"Wouldn't it be fun if all the castles in the air which we make could come true, and we could live in them?" said Jo, after a little pause.

—*Little Women*

Chapter Twenty-two

Every inch of her wanted to fly to him right there while Mrs. Reed watched, her mouth agape, and Caroline stood twirling her hair around her finger. But good sense prevailed, at least for the moment.

She stood up. "Mr. Singer," she said in an affected tone. "What a lovely surprise. Shall we go for a walk?"

His grin was full of mischief. "Yes, I believe we shall. A long walk."

"Mrs. Reed, Caroline—this is Mr. Joseph Singer." The aunt and her niece waddled over sheepishly, unsure how to account for the fact that they had been staring openly at him since he walked in the door.

"Pleased to meet you," Mrs. Reed said, shaking his hand. Then, turning to Louisa, she said, "The stew is served in just a minute."

Louisa shrugged. "I may miss it, I may not. I'm not sure."

"You're going to miss it," Joseph said.

"I'm going to miss it," Louisa parroted. Joseph broke into a smile that made Louisa a little weak with joy. Mrs. Reed harrumphed and made appalled little noises as she turned toward the kitchen.

They pushed out onto the sidewalk, which was crowded with shoppers and matinee-goers and families walking to friends' homes for dinner. Joseph grabbed her hand and began walking ahead, his long stride wrenching her along.

"Where are we going?"

He didn't turn his head to answer but strode on until near the end of the block they came to a narrow alley between two tall buildings. He pulled her sharply to the right and she followed him down the passage. One of the buildings ended before the other, creating a space that was hidden from the street. Only there did he pull her to him, so hard she felt the collision of their bodies echo through her bones. He pressed his face into the space between her neck and shoulder. His nose was cold from the wind and it sent a shiver down her arms. She was reeling. He was *here* now. Here in her arms. But why? How? What did it mean? Her hand moved of its own volition to the back of his head, her fingers touching his hair.

"I didn't know your hair was curly," she said. "You've let it grow."

He lifted up his head and looked at her, then brushed his finger across her lips, kissed her. How lovely it was to feel the very *fact* of him pressing against her. He was no reverie or vague-faced man in a book. He was real—his breath warm on her face, his coat smelling of burning leaves. But soon her mind corralled her impulses.

"What are you *doing* here?" she asked, almost angry.

He looked at her surprised, as if her stern voice had jarred him out of some half-consciousness. He opened his coat and reached into his breast pocket.

"Tickets," he said, handing them to her. "To New York. The train leaves tonight."

"Tonight?"

"Louisa, we can start again. Everything that's happened . . . we can put it behind us for good. A new city, a new beginning." He ran his thumb along her jaw. "We can be together; we can tell the truth."

She closed her eyes and listened to her heart galloping in her chest. She felt ecstatic but angry. Why now? Already she felt trapped between two choices—to stay in Boston or to face the fact of her failure and go to Plymouth to teach. Now he presented her with a third option, an appallingly selfish, dangerous, beguiling option. "It's impossible," she whispered.

"My cousin—I wrote to him. He says there is an extra room we can have. It's small, but we can manage it until I can find work. Of course, we'll be married at once. Otherwise it wouldn't be . . . proper."

She felt suddenly shy and turned her face away, thinking about just how improper they'd been together when no one was watching. Her eyes followed a cat who walked along the top of a fence at the end of the alley. It twitched its white tail and Louisa thought of Lizzie. She felt a rush of longing for home. "What did you say to Nora?"

"Don't bother yourself about that. I'll talk to her. I'll write to her."

"She doesn't know you've gone?"

"Don't you see? It doesn't matter. I don't *love* her. And she doesn't love me. She'll probably be relieved."

Louisa shot him an accusing look. "You *must* know she will be devastated."

He shook his head. "It's better this way."

"And what of your sister? Surely you can't think she will go out to service."

"We will go ahead to New York and get settled. Then we can send for her."

"But won't Catherine be angry? After all, this arrangement was meant to address your father's debts and give your sister the sort of life to which she feels . . . accustomed," Louisa said, stopping herself just before the word *entitled* slipped out instead.

He pressed his lips into a grim line. "I thought I would be able to go through with it. I thought I could make the pact despite the way that I feel about you, because it is my responsibility to take care of Catherine now—and I accept that responsibility. But there is another way to honor it. We are young and I am not afraid to work. We will live simply and, in time, pay off my father's debts. My sister will just have to become accustomed to *another* way of life."

Louisa shook her head in disbelief. She had spent so many weeks trying to crush the fantasy that her unchecked mind was eager to pursue. That he would come for her. That somehow, after everything, they could find a bridge between the two worlds she loved in equal measure.

"You can stand here all day thinking of reasons why you should not come. But eventually we will miss our train." He put the tickets back in his pocket and buttoned up his coat. "After my father died, everything became clear to me. What I need to know is, do you love me? Because if you do, we can find a solution for everything else."

Louisa was overcome by the urge to tell him she would

go anywhere to be with him, to feel the scalding sensation of his stare, the comfort of his friendship. He understood her in a way that made her feel she was being seen for the first time, really seen—the layers and layers of her public self falling away. Could she not sew or teach in New York as well as she could in Boston or Plymouth? This last month she had finally claimed her freedom, and what good had come of it? She wouldn't have to let the writing go, wouldn't have to give up on it altogether. But she could let her notion of what it meant to her shift, could let it recede. Would that be so terribly sad? She would gain so much in return.

His eyes were trained on hers as he waited for an answer. The lashes were almost translucent, his irises the blue-gray of chimney smoke on a chilly day. A moment elapsed and she realized she was nodding her head.

His eyes widened. "Is that . . . are you . . . ?"

She nodded again, more deliberately. Her voice felt strangled in her throat.

A noise, half laugh, half shout, exploded from his lungs. "My God, for a moment I thought my hopes were dashed." He laughed again and kissed her. The kiss took her by surprise and she felt her lips limp against his. He took her hand and pulled her back down the alley. "Go back to Mrs. Reed's," he said. "Pack your things and have your trunk sent ahead to the station. Will I look for you at five o'clock?"

"Yes," she said, surprised at the sound of her own voice. "Five o'clock."

Joseph nodded, his hand lingering in hers as he turned to walk in the opposite direction, toward the station. "God is good to us this day, Louisa. We can't forget it."

She nodded, then gave him a little wave and started back toward Mrs. Reed's. The incessant pounding of her heart overcame all the noises of the street. She passed some children playing a game in front of a large house. They shouted to one another but no sound came from their mouths. A carriage passed and the horses' hooves struck the road, but she did not hear the muffled thumping of their shoes. There was only the deafening, relentless pounding of her heart. She felt almost manic with the prospect of freedom. It was just as she had dreamed it the opening night of the play, when she spotted Fanny Kemble settling into the front row of the audience—she could have both. Her independence *and* the kind of love she'd given to her characters but never imagined she'd have for herself.

Mrs. Reed emerged from the kitchen when she heard the door creak open. She wiped her hands on her apron. "Miss Alcott, perhaps I should write to your father. I'm not sure he would approve of—"

Louisa clasped the old woman's hands between her own. "I'm leaving, Mrs. Reed. Tonight. We're to be married at once. I will send a telegram to my parents from the station."

Mrs. Reed's stern expression softened, though she forged ahead with disapproving prattle. "Eloping then? What will your parents think? Your poor mother!" Louisa felt a wave of guilt rising up within her, but she pushed it away. "I'm glad to see you've come to your senses," Mrs. Reed said.

"What do you mean?"

"There is no occupation more womanly and fine than the duties of wife and mother. All else is foolishness, and you are wise to let it go."

Louisa bristled. "You are mistaken. I still mean to be a writer. Somehow."

"Yes, yes," Mrs. Reed said, "I suppose it makes a lovely amusement when you have free time. Of course in the near term, you'll be going to housekeeping."

The woman seemed determined to antagonize her, but Louisa silently urged herself not to take the bait.

"My work is not simply an *amusement*," Louisa said steadily. "I intend to keep at it, despite my changing circumstances."

Mrs. Reed twisted her mouth into a wry smile. "Of course, dear."

"Watch—you'll see," Louisa said, straining to keep her temper in check. What difference did it make what an old widow believed? "I have to pack my things, Mrs. Reed." She fished in her pocket for the sewing money from Mrs. Clarke. "Here is what I owe you for the balance of the week. I want to thank you for your kindness these last months."

"This happy turn of events makes it all worth it," Mrs. Reed said, putting the money in her apron and turning back toward the kitchen. "Caroline can arrange to have your trunk sent ahead."

Louisa climbed the stairs to the attic room for the last time, taking a deep breath to try to soothe her rattled nerves. Perhaps she would have to put her work aside until they were settled in, but what was the harm in that? The living quarters would be cramped. Probably no space for a writing desk. They'd be needing linens, which meant more sewing, and then there was the wash. Until Joseph found work and they could afford some help, she'd have to do it herself. And the cooking too. Well, she had done it before and she could do it again. Hard work and sacrifice separated the true hearts from the weak, as her father was fond of saying.

Of course, there was also the matter of Catherine. Louisa cringed when she thought of Joseph's tiresome sister and her behavior the day of the circus. No one would argue that she hadn't been spoiled since birth as the baby of the family and the only girl. She was used to getting everything she wanted—clothing, parties, outings—and her unchecked extravagance was partly to blame for her father's financial ruin. Joseph had told Louisa that Catherine didn't like to read and could hardly cook or sew. It was no use counting on her help—she would have two to care for. A dull headache began radiating along Louisa's hairline.

Joseph's words came back to her: ". . . in time, we'll pay off my father's debts." That phrase, *my father's debts*, had lived in her mind for as long as she could remember, trailing the shame and anger of her own father's troubles. Married to Joseph, Louisa knew she would shoulder the debts of two fathers—one dead, with creditors lurking around his grave, the other convinced that work would sully his philosopher's soul. The burden of it, the endless grubbing for just enough money to get by, filled her with weariness.

No matter, she told herself, determined to shake off the worries as she entered the attic room. *The important thing is that we will be together. The problems will be easier to solve with the two of us.* She had been using her trunk as a table of sorts, and she cleared the piles of paper from its surface before unlatching the top and swinging it open. She surveyed the creaky wardrobe in which she hung her clothes. Mrs. Clarke had told her she could keep the fabric left over from the sheets she'd made. She'd done so happily and made a new dress and a set of underclothes from it. Aside from that, she'd acquired no new articles of clothing. Once the clothes were in the trunk, though, along with the worn quilt she'd brought along, and the Dickens and Brontë and Whitman, she could see that it would be a challenge to close the lid. She glanced at the manuscripts on the night table, shoved the books over to one side, and pressed down hard on the quilt. She placed the manuscripts on top, holding them in place with one hand while she drew the lid down with the other. It stopped a gaping six inches short of the latch, and despite her efforts to wrestle it into place, it wouldn't close.

What would she leave behind? The books? That seemed out of the question. Who knew how long it would take them to be able to afford books, and the thought of living without Dickens within easy reach was unsettling. The quilt took up the most space but it had belonged to Abba's mother, and Louisa couldn't see leaving that behind. Of course she could find a box for the stories, perhaps have them delivered to the station separately. But then she thought of all the mud puddles and gusts of wind between Mrs. Reed's and the station. If anything happened to those papers, all her work would be lost.

It would have to be the books, then. She'd read them so many times the words were burned in her brain. *Perhaps I have read them* too *many times,* she thought. *Too many books, too many times—perhaps now it's time to pull my head out of the books and realize that my real life is beginning.*

With the books removed Louisa closed the trunk and fastened the latch. She tried not to let her heart grow heavy and told herself that Mrs. Reed could send them to her when she got settled. Her father visited New York from time to time. Perhaps he would bring them.

Louisa heard light footsteps on the stairs and a rustling knock. "Miss?"

"Come in, Caroline." The pale girl slipped silently into the room.

Louisa looked behind her but no one else was there. "Surely you can't mean to carry this trunk by yourself!"

Caroline shook her head. "No, Miss. There is a man from the station downstairs. But . . ."

"What is it?" Louisa replied sharply. She had made her decisions—about everything she was going to leave behind—and she knew instinctively that motion was the only thing that would keep her from doubting. Any delay could be fatal. "I'm in a hurry, Caroline. What is it?"

Caroline stood shivering in the drafty attic, her eyes darting between Louisa's wrist and the floor. She made a sound in her throat like a bird before she spoke. "I thought . . . I thought before you go you might like to see this." Caroline pulled a letter from her apron and handed it to Louisa. "It arrived while you were out."

What now? Louisa snarled to herself. Mrs. Clarke needs some more pillowcases? May wants a new bonnet and we must all slave away until she has it? She held the letter at her side and attempted to compose herself. Her nerves were frayed—she was lashing out at all the people she blamed for putting her in this impossible situation in the first place. But it was worth remembering that she herself had chosen this path. She alone.

She took a breath and unfolded the letter.

> *Mr. William Warland Clapp*
> *Editor*
> *Saturday Evening Gazette*
>
> *Dear Miss Alcott:*
>
> *The Gazette is pleased to offer publication of your story "A New Year's Blessing" in the first edition of our Quarto Series, printing after the first of January, subject to the following terms: Stories to appear under the author's name; prompt submission of at least five additional stories by the first of December . . .*

Louisa's left hand felt for the bed behind her and she sank down onto it, resting the letter on her lap. Caroline stood blinking at her like a barn owl.

"Is everything all right, miss?"

Louisa stared blankly at her and then back at the letter. All she could think was *L.M.A.* and *Saturday Evening Gazette.* She had been published in the paper once before, but under a pseudonym, and *Flower Fables* was made of the simple fairy tales she'd dreamed up at age sixteen. This was something different. She had wanted to know whether she could write serious stories, not just fairy tales, and here was the proof. A story—six stories in all, if she could make her deadline—in one of the most widely read papers in America.

With a sinking feeling she started to realize the enormity of the housekeeping that lay ahead for her in New York. It wouldn't be like Boston, the city she had lived in off and on for most of her life. New York was massive, and she knew she would have to start at the beginning, learning her way around, finding a decent grocer, procuring the pots and dishes and other tools she would need to set up her kitchen. She saw her beloved silence slipping away—no time for work or contemplation when there were bellies to fill and linens to scrub.

She had two weeks to dash off five more stories, or Mr. Clapp would probably rescind his offer altogether. The stories she had written over the last few weeks needed editing and she doubted whether they were good enough to submit. She might have to write something new altogether. *Maybe there is some way it can all be done*, she thought weakly. *If I don't sleep . . .*

"Oh, Caroline," Louisa said. "What am I to do?" She felt her heart splitting like a piece of wet wood, its fibers clinging to the center. How could one letter be both the best and worst news you'd ever received? She thought of Joseph standing in the station, drawing his watch from his pocket to calculate the time left until they boarded their train. A sob climbed to the top of her lungs, but she was practiced at stopping the crying before it started, and this time was no different. For there was no doubt in her mind about what she would do, no matter what it cost her.

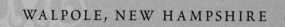

WALPOLE, NEW HAMPSHIRE

October 25, 1881

The train slowed to a stop at the station in Bellows Falls. Louisa shook herself from her reverie, closed her book, and placed it back in her case. As she adjusted her bonnet, she stooped to peer out the window of the train car to the sunny platform, where people stood waiting to greet their guests or welcome home sojourners. The passengers filed toward the front of the car and descended the stairs.

Inside the station she hired a Rockaway carriage and held her case on her lap as it thundered across the wooden bridge that spanned the Connecticut River and pulled to a stop in the center of Washington Square. The driver offered Louisa his hand and helped her step down to the road. She asked him to hold the carriage and explained that she would be back in an hour or so, and he should avail himself of the town's charms. They gave her heart a pang as she recited them: the trail along the Connecticut and up through the woods to the farms that lay beyond, the walkway through the town square to admire the autumn leaves, resplendent with their reds and golds.

As she made her way toward School Street and the

address in Joseph's recent letter, her slow pace and aching joints reminded her that much had changed since she last walked Walpole's pathways. Twenty-six years before, the town square had been surrounded on all sides by fields, full of knee-high grass that rustled Louisa's skirts, and the precise rows of orchards stretching off toward the horizon. Now the fields had been carved into plots where charming houses stood, each with its own garden and fence, each with a wreath on the door.

Louisa pressed her eyes closed, hoping that somehow she could also press away the pain in her hips that throbbed as she walked up the hill. She'd never doubted her ability to transcend the physical, to create a new reality in her mind, and she had called on this skill often in recent years as sickness took its toll on her body. She paused, ostensibly to admire the intense crimson of a sugar maple, and caught her breath. Then she set off again, tamping down the pain by remembering why she had made this journey, why she had returned to the town she had hoped to forget.

Just as Joseph had predicted the day the storm ushered the two of them away from the crowded circus and into the abandoned barn, the country did indeed lose its patience with the southern states and went to war. Louisa spent the first year lamenting the fact that she could not fight as a soldier. She was nearly thirty years old by then, a confirmed spinster and still frustrated that her writing was not generating much in the way of income. In 1862, she applied to serve as a nurse and was assigned to a temporary hospital in an old Washington, D.C., hotel, where men were hauled in each day like livestock only half slaughtered. The things she saw—heaps of legs, arms, and fingers, men turned lunatic with fear, a boy no more than fifteen, half his face shot off, still breathing enough to scream all through the night—these images were lodged in her very tissue. If she could live a hundred thousand years more, the details would be just as sharp.

She spent three weeks as a nurse and then she herself became a patient. Little rest and a poor diet had weakened her constitution and she caught typhoid. She lay raving in the infirmary for three days before Bronson came to take her home, and by then the doctors had doused her with enough calomel to replace the sickness with near catatonia. Over time she would learn that the cure was worse than the disease. The tonic made her hair and teeth fall out and seemed to settle in her joints, causing almost constant pain. In recent years during bad spells, she'd spent weeks in bed and looked forward to the relief of death.

But when she was feeling well enough, she did what she had always done—she worked. After the war, she adapted her journals and letters home into a slim volume called *Civil War Hospital Sketches*. Editors and newspapermen began paying attention to her work, and she sold her stories one after another. Bronson and her editor, Mr. Niles, urged her to write a longer story for young girls based on her childhood with her sisters. Louisa didn't want to do it. Writing about what she saw in the war hospital made her feel like she was really *living* and had finally broken free of the identity that had been thrust upon her all her life: charming authoress spinning moral tales for the young. Louisa had grown up and apart from her old self, but the people closest to her refused to recognize it.

But there was the promise of income, something poverty

had taught her never to refuse. So she gave in to her father's urgings and wrote the blasted thing. The first volume of the story she decided to call *Little Women* sold two thousand copies right away. Louisa wrote the second volume in a hurry and, soon after, went off to vacation in Quebec and Maine hoping to escape the storm. The book seemed to be taking on a life of its own, and Louisa dreaded the attention. When she finally arrived back in Boston she learned she was a wealthy woman. Suddenly she was earning more money in one month than she had over many years. Finally she could do the things she had been dreaming of: pay off the debts, keep her parents comfortable, and send May to art school in France.

But one thing she'd never thought to do was guard her privacy. After all, the details of the *Little Women* story were plucked almost entirely from her own life, and the public knew it. They seemed to believe that purchasing copies of the tale entitled them to investigate their author. Was she really just like Jo? Was she too married to a German professor? Who was the real Laurie and why hadn't Jo married him in the end? The intrusive letters and articles irritated her, and she contemplated whether the realization of her dream was worth the price. So many years she had struggled to get her work published, to establish herself as a writer of serious fiction, not just tales for young girls. So many years she worried that she was out of her mind to think she would ever know success, and now, suddenly, she had it. But at what cost?

A paper printed the location of Orchard House in Concord, where she lived most of the time with Bronson and Abba. Young girls flocked there to get a look at the real-life Jo—and were quite disappointed to see a plump old lady answer the door. It hadn't occurred to them that "Jo" would age. Soon Louisa could no longer bear the stricken looks on their faces and began to tell them that Miss Alcott had gone out of town, that she was the maid.

One particularly busy September day Louisa escaped through the back door of the house just as she saw a tour of girls coming up the path. She had a few appointments to keep, a few errands to run, and she simply could not be bothered with the nonsense. On the way to the train to Boston, she stopped to post some letters. As the heavy steel door of the letter box swung shut, a realization washed over her that nearly took her breath away: she was going to die.

This wasn't the first time Louisa had contemplated death. She'd come very close to it a few times, and after years of suffering the bad spells brought on by the calomel, the burden of constant care for her parents, she sometimes thought death would be a great comfort. But what she hadn't thought about was the fact that when she died, perfect strangers would almost surely swoop down like scavenging birds to pick through her letters and journals and find the answers to the questions she avoided. Every word she had written when she thought no one else but God was listening would now be displayed for public scrutiny and judgment.

It would be easy enough to go back through her journals and remove pages she wanted to keep private. Bronson had taught her from an early age the importance of organizing and dating the written reflections, which he believed to be the permanent record of a mind's development—like a scientist's notes. But when she thought of the years and years of letters cast across New England and beyond—to her sisters, to friends in Boston, to acquaintances made in Paris when she traveled there with a tiresome invalid woman who paid richly for her companionship—her chest tightened. There was no way to know how much she had revealed in her correspondence, no way to call it all back. Louisa had a tendency to dash off a letter when her temper flared over some injustice or oversight. Would something she wrote on impulse twenty years ago suddenly reappear?

And then the worst of it flashed in her mind: Joseph Singer. What of their correspondence of so long ago? She remembered that his letters remained in the lining of her trunk, where they had been since the day Anna left for Syracuse. She allowed herself to read them from time to time, to linger over his apologies for concealing his entanglement with Nora, his pleas for a chance to explain. After the night of the play, when Louisa and Joseph came together and broke apart once again, the letters stopped until the news of his father's death.

Louisa hadn't spoken to Joseph since the day she left him standing alone at the train station, the day she sent Caroline with her cowardly message explaining that she would not come. He never wrote her again. All these years later her heart wrenched with a fresh pang at the memory of it. It *had* been for the best, of course. She had been determined to maintain her freedom, no matter what the cost. And the cost had been higher than she ever could have anticipated. Even still, she couldn't imagine her life having turned out any other way than this—she'd had no other choice. This is what she told herself at the time, and this is what she told herself now: the fact satisfied her mind but not her heart.

It was no use questioning her decision now. Life was

nearly done, and despite some private sadnesses—never having the chance to write the sort of books she wanted to write, the loneliness of spinsterhood and, unexpectedly, of fame—life had been good to her in many ways. Almost everything she'd wished for, she'd received. It was only in the having that the objects of her wishes transfigured into something different from what she'd expected. But that was no one's fault.

She could, however, do something to protect her family and Joseph's from the truth of what had passed between them that summer in Walpole. If Nora was blissfully ignorant then, why should she have to find out now? Louisa knew they had married at Christmas, just a few short weeks after she last saw Joseph in Boston. Margaret's newsy letter described the clusters of holly that adorned the tables at the wedding feast, unaware that her benign words cut Louisa to the quick. And the children they most certainly had—why should they be given cause to question their father's fidelity? The prospect of it made her sick to her stomach.

And so she sent him a letter, a stiff, formal inquiry, requesting an appointment at his convenience and offering to travel to Walpole. Many days passed and she did not hear a reply. It occurred to her that he could be dead. He might have been a soldier. If he didn't meet his end on the battle-field, he could have died a thousand other ways: typhoid, cholera, consumption, or some vague unidentifiable illness that came on without warning and swept him away. So many others she cared about had departed this world in just that way.

But soon his reply arrived. It was only surprise at hearing from her out of the blue, he explained, that had delayed his response. He would receive her, of course, any time she liked, and though he would be willing to come to Boston to save her the trip, might she not like to see Walpole again? They agreed on a date and time. When she was young, Louisa had little patience, and the anticipation of an event like this would have driven her mad. But at forty-eight and looking and feeling much older than those years, she felt that time seemed to move much faster than she did. Soon the date arrived and now she found herself on Joseph's doorstep.

Louisa raised her hand to grasp the brass knocker shaped like a pineapple, that classic New England symbol of welcome, and hesitated. She noticed her reflection in the front window, wondered, had Joseph passed her in the street, whether he would have guessed that she was the ebullient girl he'd walked with through the woods behind his house, the target of his fierce love, anger, and regret. This woman's shoulders hunched forward, as if the weight of her mere bones strained her muscles to their limit. Beneath her bonnet, a thin froth of hair only partially covered her scalp, though she'd taken pains to arrange it as best she could. The possibility that he wouldn't recognize her—or worse, that she'd see disappointment or shock on his face—made her want to turn back. Why open this door to the past she'd closed so long ago? Sometimes it was better not to know the ways in which people had changed. Let them stay the same in your mind, preserve them as they were. She could write to him to ask about the letters. There was no need to see each other.

Just as she was turning to go, she saw a curtain move in the front window. The oak door creaked open and he was there.

A spasm of laughter escaped her lungs and she was surprised to find herself grinning. How little he had changed! Most of his hair was gone, revealing a high, noble forehead tanned from working outdoors, but his blue eyes seemed all the brighter for it. His shoulders looked as strong as they ever had, but they slumped just a little. He smiled back and they stared at each other, grinning like fools, for a long moment.

Joseph gave his head a shake, seeming to come to his senses, and pressed his lips into a dignified line. "Miss Alcott, welcome. Please come in."

She could see he wasn't sure how to address her. The first impulse for both was a familiarity that made little sense in light of the facts—they hadn't spoken in decades, they'd never had a proper good-bye. But it *felt* right to grin. She could easily imagine grabbing his hand and running down the path toward the river, walking together to see how broad and thick the forsythia had grown. Twenty years fell off her shoulders.

But if he addressed her in this way, propriety dictated she respond in kind. "Thank you, Mr. Singer. It was kind of you to receive me. I hope I'm not disturbing you." She stepped over the threshold and followed him into a parlor cluttered with the tangibles of family life. A yellowed child's drawing pressed into a frame hung above a piano with an embroidered bench worn threadbare. A shelf stuffed with books stood in a corner near twin armchairs with calico cushions, a mending basket at the foot of one chair. In the grate, a low fire burned. The last few nights had been chilly. Winter was on its way.

He motioned to the chairs. "Please—sit. Would you like some tea?"

"This chair looks as though it belongs to Mrs. Singer. Perhaps I should sit over there." She gestured toward the sofa.

"Ah." He chuckled. "I haven't had the heart to put that mending basket away, though it hasn't been touched for a year now. Nora passed on last fall."

Louisa winced at her clumsiness, then nodded. "I'm sorry to hear it—I hope she did not suffer long." Though she knew Joseph had married Nora after all, hearing him confirm it felt strange. He lived in Louisa's memory as a bachelor, as the twenty-three-year-old boy he'd been. She knew it was silly, but she felt surprise hearing that his life had continued to move forward. He had chosen correctly, she thought, glancing around at all the symbols of the family they'd built together.

"She died in her sleep. She was always the first up in the morning, bustling around, stoking up the fire, setting out the cups for tea. One day I woke up first, saw her rolled on her side, so peaceful. The doctor had warned us that her heart was weak, but I never suspected . . . I just thought, 'Let her sleep. I can manage,' and got breakfast ready myself. I went in to wake her later but she was long gone."

"Well, if we must go, that seems like a gentle way to do it," Louisa said.

"Yes. Though we'd all of us rather she had stayed here a little longer. Please excuse me a moment." He exited through a narrow passage that led to the kitchen, and in a moment she heard the sound of spoons and cups and saucers being arranged on a tray.

Hearing Joseph fumble to arrange the tea himself touched

her, and she felt keenly the loneliness of his domestic life. To have known companionship, however imperfect, and then lost it seemed more of a burden than never knowing it at all. It was plain to see that he *had* loved Nora, and Louisa chided herself for feeling surprised by that fact as well. He may have felt nothing but friendship for her when they were young, Louisa knew. But she suspected that love could grow out of time and proximity just as well as it could strike in a passionate flash. Perhaps the particularities of Nora and Joseph hardly mattered; perhaps two strangers who stood together through life's long journey would find themselves in a kind of love at the end of it.

He returned to the parlor carrying the tray and placed it on the low table between them.

"What beautiful children you have," she said, pointing at two portraits hanging side by side above the fireplace, a boy and a girl.

"Only one child now, I'm afraid. Our daughter Jane drowned in the Connecticut when she was five years old." Joseph lifted the porcelain pot and poured the steaming tea into two cups. Its lid clattered and he silenced it with his palm before setting the pot awkwardly back on the tray. "But we are blessed with a son, Timothy, though at eighteen he is no longer a child."

Louisa imagined a ginger-haired girl, like her mother, walking across a field with her arms full of wildflowers, a low sun painting the sky orange behind her. And then with dread Louisa saw the cold and heedless river that swallowed the girl. Louisa knew the physical pain of grief, knew its current could be just as deadly as a river's. She wondered how it happened that joy finally returned to Joseph and Nora's life.

Did their mourning separate them, or did the sight of Nora's silhouette unleash something wild in Joseph that allowed her body to save him? It didn't pain Louisa the way it once had to imagine his bare arms holding Nora, his palm resting on the small of her back. Life was so full of sorrow, and a body was a touchstone, a physical reminder that we are more than our grief, even if it owns us for a while.

And it was plain to see that he did know happiness again. Perhaps the day he first held his swaddled Timothy, in the yellow dawn light, the sadness subsided. Perhaps gratitude raked his veins and he thanked God for life and breath. Sometimes we are repaid for our concessions in ways we couldn't have imagined, she thought.

An uncomfortable moment passed as Louisa strained to think of the right thing to say. She shifted in the armchair, pressing against the cushion wedged behind her aching hip. "I'm sorry to hear of little Jane. That must have been a terrible time." Louisa took a sip of her tea. "But a boy of eighteen! Goodness, that makes me feel old." She felt a surge of emotion at the thought of this boy, who probably looked just like his father had that summer.

Joseph shook his head. "The time has flown. And what of the Alcotts? My condolences are long overdue for the loss of Elizabeth. I heard she passed not long after your family left Walpole."

Louisa nodded. "Scarlet fever. She picked it up from some children my mother was trying to help through one of her charities. My mother always meant well, but looking back I almost have to laugh—we were hardly in a position to be giving away bread. The six of us rarely had enough to eat ourselves."

Joseph gave her a sad smile. Louisa wondered if he was thinking back on the way she rebuked his offer of help the day she and Anna came to his father's store for flour. Or perhaps he was thinking of his own family's financial troubles. It was exhausting, the unending effort people made to shield the truth of their lives. The root of a good share of life's problems could be traced back to keeping secrets, Louisa thought.

"Elizabeth's passing must have been a trial," Joseph said. The afternoon had waned and the room was growing dim. He reached to the table behind him and turned up the lamp.

Louisa's voice softened and her heart ached to say the words aloud. "You had better save some of your condolences for more recent losses. Marmee died nearly four years ago. Her passing was a comfort, for she suffered long and was ready to go, though I miss her every day. But the worst was yet to come. May died not two years ago, in Germany."

Joseph looked stricken. "May? But she was yet so young."

"Just thirty-nine. A few years ago I sent her back to London to study, and there she met Ernest. He was still a very young man and though it seemed unlikely to the mean-spirited gossips, May wasn't too old to fall in love. They married at once and she returned with him to Germany. We were happy to hear of their good news, though we've never had the chance to meet her husband."

"He must be devastated. Was her illness sudden?"

Louisa's eyes swam as she reflected on this fresh grief. "We can't call 'illness' the travail that transfers life and spirit from one generation into the next. May gave birth after a long and difficult labor and had a month with her baby before she died. She named the little daughter Louisa May—Lulu."

"And the child?" Joseph asked, bracing himself for more tragedy.

"Rosy and blond and full of more energy than I know what to do with. The babe came to live with her Aunt Louisa and proud Grandfather Alcott just last year. May made her wishes known to Ernest before she died: she wanted Lulu to live with me. But we had to beg him to let his little one come to us. After all, she could be May's double with that blond hair and her pale eyes, and she is all Ernest has to remind him of his late wife. But caring for a child is a trying business, especially for a man who travels. If she had stayed in Germany, she would have been raised by the governess. Here, at least, she can be with family. She will be two years old next month."

Joseph broke into a relieved smile and stirred cream into his cup. "Ah, so there is some joy, then, despite the loss. Did you travel to bring Lulu home?"

Louisa shook her head. "I've been too weak for some time now for that. Seasickness makes me absolutely wretched. We enlisted the help of a friend who sailed to collect the child and bring her back to me. But I'll have you know I was the first one at the wharf, waiting to catch a glimpse of the ship as it came into the harbor."

"What a happy day it must have been! Did you know the child the moment you saw her?"

"There were so many babies in the arms of women as they came off the ship. I kept wondering as each one passed which one was our Lulu. At last the captain approached and he held in his arms a babbling little thing with yellow hair and blue eyes, just like May's. The captain placed her in my arms, and I tell you—she looked at me and she said, 'Marmar,' just as clear as a bell."

Louisa's voice wavered as her tears spilled over. She brushed them away as Joseph reached over and put his palm on her hand a moment before sitting back in his chair to muse over the happy reunion. They shared a long glance as the uneasiness that had filled the space between them fell away.

"So you are a mother now after all," Joseph said gently. "Think of everything you will teach her."

Louisa brushed away his comment with her hand. "I'm too old and sick and tired to do a proper job. I fear I will fail her when she needs me most." She hadn't realized this was what she felt until she said it out loud. She remembered Joseph had had a way of getting her to admit to thoughts she didn't know she had. Here he was, doing it again after all this time.

He looked at her carefully, noting the change that came over her demeanor with this confession. "And what of the eldest Miss Alcott? I pray that story has a happier ending, after all she went through. . . ."

A shiver snaked its way down Louisa's back at the memory of Anna rocking in her chair in front of the window, watching the leaves turn. "Thankfully, yes. After my mother and father left Walpole to return to Concord, Anna came home from Syracuse and took up acting as a hobby once again. She played in *The Loan of a Lover* opposite Mr. John Pratt. When the curtain went down, they found the role of lovers suited them. He was a poor man but proud and hardworking. He gave her two sons, my boisterous nephews. Sadly he became infirm when he was still quite a young man and left us too soon." Time had blunted Louisa's sadness for Anna's loss and she could speak of it without losing control of her emotions. She took a long breath.

"Well, what a host of difficulties the Alcotts have endured," Joseph said. "It makes my own troubles seem like nothing in comparison."

"Tragedy cannot be measured out and compared on a scale. Loss is loss. And you can never be sure how one is affected. I may speak plainly of these events, but let me assure you, my grief is quite alive just below the surface. It's only that I've learned not to let quite so many of my feelings show."

She hadn't intended to reference whatever it was that had passed between the two of them so long ago, but now that the words were out it seemed the only thing she could have meant.

Joseph locked eyes with her, the veil of formality lifting. "It has its risks—that is clear." He shifted in his chair. "But I suppose time changes the way we see these things."

"Perhaps." But Louisa wasn't sure if time had changed anything in her, other than giving her less energy to deal with more grief.

Joseph couldn't wait any longer to broach the subject. "It's wonderful to have you here, Lou—Miss Alcott. But I know you didn't come just to visit."

"Call me Louisa, please." She felt almost desperate, suddenly, to hear him say her name.

He watched her a moment, his eyes peeling away the wrinkles and the faded color of her hair. "Louisa," he said, resting on the word, drawing out its rounded vowels. "What brings you here?"

She straightened up. "I've been very fortunate to have had a little success with my writing later in life," she began.

Joseph chuckled. "I should say so."

"Why do you laugh?"

He gave an amused shake of his head, stood, and crossed the room to his desk, where he pulled open the bottom drawer and reached to the back. Beneath a pile of papers was a carved wooden box with a hinged lid. He pulled it out, set it on the desktop, and swung open the lid. He plucked up one of the folded clippings inside and his reading glasses, then stood in the middle of the room, reading, as if to a crowd. *"Miss Louisa May Alcott, who is generally regarded as the most popular and successful literary woman in America, did not at once jump into sudden fame, although the slow-developing bud bloomed into flower in a single night, as it were. . . ."* He lowered the paper and gave her a coy smile. "That was in the *Boston Herald* a few months back. It isn't the first."

Louisa felt equal parts mortification and glee. She thought it sheer vanity to read the articles that appeared from time to time—and so she never did. But she *was* proud of all her success, and not just because she had finally been able to pay off her father's lifetime of debt. A sort of astonishment dawned on her. "You saved this? Why?"

"I saved them all. That box is nearly full," he said, pointing to it, "if you'd like to hear any more."

She shook her head and put out her palms. "No—please!"

He thought for a moment before he spoke. "When you left me standing on the train platform that day in Boston, I was so angry. And hurt. Don't misunderstand me—looking back, I see now how everything was meant to turn out. But at the time I was . . ." He paused, as if he wasn't sure whether he should speak plainly. "Well, I was heartbroken. And so saving these clippings helped remind me that you had a good reason for—"

"—Joseph." The syllables of his name felt strange, like

marbles in her mouth. "I cannot tell you how sorry I am for . . . what happened."

He waved away her apology. "That's all well in the past now."

Louisa could see in his face that the long-ago summer may have been well in the past, but seeing her brought all the old thoughts back to the present. She had never stopped wondering what exactly she had given up by staying behind on her own. It was a blessing he had not come back to Mrs. Reed's after she sent Caroline to the station with her letter. If Joseph had begged Louisa to change her mind, she might have conceded. And what a lovely concession it would have been! She remembered his long brown arms, the whisper touch of his finger as it traced the curve of her hip. But where would it all have gotten her? Hanging laundry on a line in Walpole. Brimming with bitterness and untold stories. She had escaped a fate full of disappointment, and she knew it.

"I should have written to you," she said. "Or tried harder to explain."

"No." Joseph waved off the suggestion. "I knew . . . I understood."

She could see in the slant of the afternoon light that his eyes swam. "Some things just aren't meant to be. I've had a wonderful life. You have had a wonderful life. Both wonderful, just in a different way than we might have imagined."

Louisa hesitated to dredge up old memories, but her curiosity overwhelmed her manners. "What did you do? Did you go on to New York after all?"

He smiled. "Well, first I sat on a bench for a few long hours after Caroline brought your letter. I debated myself a hundred different ways about whether to go back to Mrs.

Reed's and try to win you over. But I think I knew your mind was made up. My *God*, you were stubborn."

Louisa gave him a sheepish look. "It's true. I like to think I have perhaps *some* charming qualities, but that is not one of them."

"Well, it charms me now, when I think back on it. You were like a full-speed train back then. Nothing was going to stand in your way."

"Those trains kill people all the time," Louisa said, with her hand to her brow.

"You don't have to tell me," Joseph said. "To answer your question, I did go on to New York that night. My cousin Edward was surprised to see that the rooms he'd secured for us would be occupied by just one very dour young man, but he took mercy on me and asked few questions. I spent three dark weeks roaming the streets of the city before I found a job working as a carpenter's assistant. The work was hard but I was happy to have something to do."

Louisa listened intently, feeling a rush of guilt at being the sole cause of his suffering.

"Catherine was planning to join me in the city, but I was scarcely making enough money to feed myself. I knew I couldn't go on that way much longer. I wasn't sure what I would do, but then Nora wrote me a long honest letter. She confessed she had suspected my heart belonged to someone else. She didn't know it was you, of course. . . ."

They exchanged a lingering glance. "She said she knew I didn't love her, at least not the way a husband *should* love his wife. But she also knew I was struggling in New York and said that, if I would come home and merely try, even just for a little while, she would give her best efforts to making a happy home for us. I was heartsick and she showed me true kindness. So I went back to Walpole."

"Of course you did, and what a good decision it was!" Louisa said, a bit too cheerfully. Part of her felt she should have been the one to comfort him, though of course it was a silly thought. He wouldn't have needed comforting if it hadn't been for the wounds she herself had caused him.

"I went reluctantly, but soon I accepted what my life became. God blessed me with her. Nora was a good wife and a wonderful mother." His eyes met Louisa's and he held her gaze a moment, as if he needed to be sure she understood what he was about to say. "The things I felt for you never went away, Louisa. They never even faded. But life moves on. The page has to turn."

Louisa nodded. She knew the truth of his words. As old and used up as she felt, merely sitting near Joseph now enlivened her spirit, and the intensity of all the old wishes rushed into her heart like a melted spring.

Louisa wondered what to do now. It seemed cruel to ask him for the letters, but she couldn't let these memories cloud up her thoughts and get in the way of her object in coming to Walpole this one last time. She knew she wouldn't be able to sleep until something was done about the letters to keep them from getting into the wrong hands. She had never been a patient woman, and age only made her less so.

"Joseph, I came today because of articles like the one you read," she said, pointing to the clipping from the *Boston Herald*. "Though I doubt very much that my life could be of interest to anyone, reporters come around Orchard House weekly, along with scads of young women, wanting to interview me, to take my picture. Most of them mean well and simply want to know about the writing. They want to know whether I'm Jo."

He smiled at this and she returned it with a little roll of her eyes.

"Well, aren't you?" he asked. "I recognized an awful lot of you in her character."

She nodded. "Yes—it's true, and I've never denied it. But some of these readers don't have the decency to respect my privacy. And I get the distinct feeling they're waiting for me to die so they can dig freely through my papers and turn little fragments of thought into full-blown stories that could hurt my family. And yours."

"Why would they care about me? Everything is so far in the past."

"Don't you see? They want to know who is the real-life Laurie. They all believe I am Jo, so they assume Laurie must be out in the world somewhere. They have investigated my sister May—they know *she* did not marry him, as her counterpart Amy did in the story."

Joseph nodded. "I always wondered why you made Laurie marry Amy in the end."

Louisa groaned and placed her face in her hands. "You aren't the only one!"

Joseph laughed. "Old wounds?"

"You write to please an audience, but they can turn on you—suddenly. They all wanted Jo to relent and marry Laurie, but it wasn't in Jo to do it. Those little girls never could understand that marriage is not the only thing a woman might do with her life."

"Let me make sure I understand. The young man who pursued you, who denied, pined for you, who walked around with a heart like a broken wing clutched up to his chest for months—you're afraid these meddlesome young readers will think I am he? I can't *imagine* why."

Her eyes met his and she gave him a sly smile. "Some of them are very narrow-minded. One must exercise patience."

Joseph chuckled at this. "So—am I? Am I Laurie?"

Louisa looked at him a long moment. "When I was in Paris the year before I wrote *Little Women*, I met a young man named Ladislas, a Pole. He was just nineteen, so full of spirit." Louisa took a breath. "When readers—and reporters—ask me who inspired Laurie, I tell them he did, for he is out of their reach. But that isn't the truth. Ladislas only reminded me of *you*. When I created Laurie, it was you I thought of."

"Well, I am quite honored," he said. "Laurie is very likeable. I think I can speak for an entire country of little girls when I say it would have been nice to see Jo experience a change of heart."

"And all I can say is that Jo would have ceased to be Jo if she had agreed to marry Laurie."

Joseph furrowed his brow. Louisa could see that though she wished to change the subject, he didn't want to let it go. Perhaps he had held these questions in his mind for a long time. "But she marries the professor in the end—how is that any different?"

"Eventually I gave in to the pressure of my publisher. He felt if Jo didn't marry *someone*, I'd be letting down my loyal readers. In his eyes, as a spinster, Jo would have been a tragedy. I could hardly agree, of course, given my own situation. If it had been up to me, she would have stayed happy and free, writing stories and traveling the world."

"Like you."

"Perhaps. But not so old and tired."

Joseph flashed a knowing smile. "One of the most shock-ing things about becoming an adult is the sight of your heroes growing older as well. For some reason we seem to think they should be frozen in time."

"Well, they aren't, and I have the gray hair to prove it." She paused, willing herself to lead the conversation back to her purpose, though she dreaded it. "And that's why I came here today. I have to try to protect my family, and your fam-ily, from learning anything . . . anything we'd rather keep to ourselves."

"I see."

Louisa took a breath. "I feel silly asking this question—undoubtedly they are long gone—but do you still have any of the letters I sent to you?"

He opened his mouth to answer, then closed it and walked back to his desk. He carried the wooden box from his drawer over to her chair. "See for yourself," he said.

She pulled the small stack of papers out of the box. Most were clippings from the local newspapers about her books and her involvement in suffrage speeches and conferences. Beneath those, her eye caught the familiar pattern of the stationery her uncle sent her as a Christmas gift several years in a row. The box slid forward on her lap and she heard a soft thud against the wood. She reached in and grasped an object, felt the cool steel of its three long teeth.

"My comb," she whispered, looking up at him. He nod-ded slightly. "How in the world did you come to have this?"

"Do you remember that day we had the picnic by the river, and we all went swimming? You left it on the rocks."

Mock mortification crossed Louisa's face. "Wasn't I

the picture of impropriety. Prancing around with my hair undone."

"Thank God for that impropriety." Joseph closed his eyes. "I can see it clearly in my mind at this moment. You looked like a mermaid with that hair fanning out in the water. My God, what a beauty."

"Your memory has edited out all the facts, my friend. My sister Anna was the beauty."

Joseph looked at her a moment and shook his head. "You never *could* see it. But that only made you more appealing."

She reached into the bag she'd carried on her shoulder from the train. "These are your letters," she said, holding up the sheets of paper. "And the *Leaves of Grass* you gave me. You wrote an inscription." She opened to the flyleaf.

From J.S. to L.M.A. He is "the poet of the woman the same as of the man."

Joseph held out his hand and she gave him the book. He fingered the gold words on the cover, admired the liberty Whitman had taken with the type, depicting roots and leaves growing from the letters as if they lived.

Louisa watched the tender way he held the peculiar little book that bound the two of them together. "I finally had the chance to meet him," she said. "Just last month, in fact."

Joseph's eyes widened. "Well, fame does have *some* rewards, then, does it not?"

She nodded and gave him a playful grin. "I've met the president too, you know."

"Well, I am impressed. Was Whitman the way we imagined him? A loaf and a brute?"

"Not at all. Perhaps age has mellowed him. My father and I had tea with him in Concord. Mr. Whitman wears a long white beard. Walks with a cane." Louisa recalled the way the gentle poet had asked her father endless questions about his work, Emerson's, Margaret Fuller's. Whitman had shown no ego and offered sincere compliments to them all.

"Did you tell him you blamed his poetry for causing you to fall madly in love with me?"

Louisa smiled more broadly than she had in a long time. Joseph meant the coy comment as a joke, but hearing him say those words aloud—"fall madly in love"—pried open her heart. All the inexpressible things they felt for each other that those verses allowed them to share, they could *talk* about them—they could own them now after all this time.

"I told him I never knew poetry—mere words on a page—could wreak havoc until I read his."

"And what did he say to that?"

"Well, my father was certainly puzzled—he didn't know what I could possibly be talking about. Whitman looked very wise and kind and said, 'Tell the truth and you can start a fire.' I felt he was looking right through me."

Joseph marveled at the poet's words for a moment, then looked nervously at Louisa. "What is it that you want us to do with these letters?" His fingers tightened around the book, as if he were afraid of what she would suggest.

Louisa glanced at the fireplace, where the spent logs emitted a pale glow. "Burn them."

Just the suggestion of it seemed to wound him as much as if the deed were already done. "Oh, I don't think I could."

Louisa held up her hand. "I know—it's awful. But please, let's not be sentimental about this."

"I don't consider it 'sentimental' to keep a token of—"

"Do you want your son to find these letters someday and *wonder* whether his father was unfaithful to his mother?"

Joseph closed his eyes and sighed.

"We are lucky that he hasn't already stumbled across them," she said softly.

Louisa caught a glimpse of herself in the mirror on the far wall and recalled the trepidation she'd felt standing at his front door when she first arrived. Joseph seemed to study her for a moment. She could see he thought she looked much older than her years, could see he was realizing her fears about what would happen after her death did not represent some far-off eventuality: She was dying.

Louisa carried on, desperate to convince him. "You have to believe me that these people will stop at nothing. My life is no longer my own. I must do everything I can to keep them from finding out about . . . what we had. They will make it into something tawdry and hurtful, and I couldn't bear that."

His heart cracked open like an egg. "All right," he said, nodding to the stack of letters in her hand. "But not the book."

She sighed. "I suppose the book on its own, should it be found, doesn't reveal very much. But you'll have to keep it here."

Joseph nodded and crossed the room to place the book on the shelf next to his desk. Louisa rose from the chair and lowered herself down in front of the fireplace. She felt the heft of the fire iron up to her elbow as she swung it into the pit. Joseph reached for a length of the cedar he and Timothy had chopped the day before when the temperature had turned cold.

He knelt down next to Louisa and laid the log on the freshly stoked coals. The wood was dry, and the flames climbed slowly along its fibers. She waited until the fire was high, then looked up at Joseph. He held her gaze. The apprehension that had clutched Louisa's lungs like a vise suddenly released its hold and her eyes filled as she experienced the pleasure of a full breath. What they felt for each other would be safe now; it belonged to them alone. He gave her a slight nod. Louisa cast the papers into the fire and nearly gasped at how quickly they disappeared. Joseph placed his hand on her arm and they watched the smoke that carried their secret billow up the chimney and out across the pale New Hampshire sky.

ACKNOWLEDGMENTS

My sincere thanks go to the graceful and brilliant Marly Rusoff and her associates, Michael Radulescu and Julie Mosow, who have worked tirelessly throughout this process. I am equally grateful for my editor, Amy Einhorn, whose masterly editorial skill and enthusiasm from day one have made this a better book, and for the work of her patient assistant, Halli Melnitsky. The team at Putnam is second to none. Thanks especially to Dorian Hastings, Catharine Lynch, Alaina Mauro, Meredith Phebus, Melissa Solis, Lisa D'Agostino, Krista Asadorian, Meighan Cavanaugh, Mary Schuck, Stephanie Sorensen, Claire McGinnis, Kate Stark, Lydia Hirt, Christopher Nelson, and Ashley Tucker.

I am indebted to the people who taught me about writing and reading like a writer: Hugh Spagnuolo, Fritz Swanson, Laurence Goldstein, Theresa Tinkle, and especially Tish O'Dowd. Any missteps in this book occur in spite of their efforts.

I am blessed with two loving and committed parents, Steve and Mary O'Connor, and my brother, Matt, a man of few words but a very big heart; thanks to all three of them for a lifetime of support. Thanks also to Bob Sr., Ann, Andy, and Megan McNees, my new family, for their enthusiasm. Gratitude to my first reader and dear friend Lori Nelson Spielman; to Erin Richnow Brown, for invaluable suggestions and encouragement; to John Lederman, for listening; and to Jennifer Brehl, for her support. Many thanks to Mary Bisbee-Beek, my friend who knows everybody; to Kate Emerson, for her photographic skills; and to Geoffrey Gagnon, for being in

New York seven years ago and wanting to talk about writing. It's no exaggeration to say that this book simply would not exist were it not for my wise and true friend Kelly Harms Wimmer, my deep thanks to her. And finally, out of the tree of life I picked me a plum in my husband, Bob, who has offered continuous support: thank you for taking me to Ontario, where I had nothing to do, for happily eating lima beans, and for never doubting this would happen.

AUTHOR'S NOTE

Like many American readers, I have always loved *Little Women*. But I never knew much about its author until I stumbled on Martha Saxton's *Louisa May Alcott: A Modern Biography* one day while poking around in the library. I checked it out, and for some reason as I was reading I felt compelled to mark the sections I loved with sticky notes. I just didn't want to forget any of the details. When I finished, the book looked like it was sprouting leaves—there were sticky notes on almost every page.

I read it again. I kept renewing the book until the library wouldn't let me renew it anymore. After that I went into the library through the back door so no one would corner me and try to get the book back. Finally one day my husband rolled his eyes and said, "Why don't you just *buy* it?"

So I did buy it, along with all the other biographies of Louisa I could find. And right away I noticed something strange: Each biography portrayed her differently. One painted her as a pioneering feminist; another described a reluctant spinster; yet another imagined her as little more than an extension of her father and his philosophical work. After spending so much time reading about her, I felt I had to know—who was the real Louisa?

All the biographers had drawn their details from the same primary sources—Louisa's letters and journals, among other things. So I decided to read them myself, and they simply took me over. My husband and I had recently relocated from Providence, Rhode Island, to the somewhat out-of-the-way town of Waterloo, Ontario, for his work. Leaving my job as a teacher in Rhode Island and trying to figure out what to do with myself in our new home left me feeling unsettled. I toyed with the idea of making an honest effort to write a novel, something I had wanted to do for as long as I could remember. But I was afraid. What if I wasn't any good? What if I had nothing to say? As I read Louisa's descriptions of her own anxieties about the writing process, I felt a faint twinge of hope. I knew I had to try to write, and I knew I wanted to write about her.

The final piece of the puzzle fell into place when I happened upon an excerpt from a memoir by Julian Hawthorne, the son of Nathaniel Hawthorne. Julian had been a neighbor to the Alcotts and a childhood friend of Louisa's youngest sister, May, the inspiration for *Little Women*'s Amy. Writing about Louisa, he said, "Did she ever have a love affair? We never knew. Yet how could a nature so imaginative, romantic and passionate escape it?"

And I thought, *That's it*. Biographers note that Louisa had a habit of burning letters, though it's impossible to know how many were destroyed and what they contained. Louisa herself acknowledged a childhood infatuation with Ralph Waldo Emerson that drove her to write him adoring letters, which she never sent and which she later burned. Louisa was famous in her own lifetime, and she was careful to edit the journals and papers that biographers would use to tell the story of her life after she died.

Knowing this, I didn't have to stretch too much to imagine that perhaps Louisa *did* have a love affair but erased all traces of it. Yet when would it have happened? I remembered that the biographies mentioned that the Alcotts summered in Walpole, New Hampshire, in 1855. Only a few solid facts are known about that summer—her father Bronson kept a garden, the sisters put on a few plays with local actors, and in the fall, Louisa went off to Boston to write and Anna went to Syracuse to work in an asylum. The lack of historical information made it the perfect setting for the story: a lost summer in Louisa's life.

Next I went in search of as many details as I could cull from books on nineteenth-century New England dress, cooking, house-keeping, leisure, transportation, politics, and literature. I continuously reread Louisa's letters and journals as I worked because I wanted the Louisa in my story to sound as much like the real Louisa as possible. I made a list of all the books she loved—Dickens was her favorite writer; she deeply admired *Jane Eyre*—and I pored over them looking for clues about what might have been on her mind. I tried to pull together the anecdotes that best showcased who she was. The picnic by the river, candlemaking with Anna, Bronson's insisting that his daughters read their journals aloud, J. T. Fields telling Louisa she should stick with teaching because she'd never make it as a writer—all of those things really happened in various forms. And as many readers will know, Ralph Waldo Emerson really did play a significant role in the Alcotts' lives as a source of friendship and financial support.

Despite its being rooted in fact, however, this story is without a doubt an invention, and I have taken plenty of liberties. In the interest of moving the narrative forward, I gathered episodes from Louisa's experiences living on her own in Boston from late 1855 through 1856 and beyond, and condensed them into a shorter period of time. Nicholas and Nora Sutton, Margaret Lewis, their families, the other young people in town, and, of course, Joseph Singer are entirely fictional characters, though that does not make them any less real to me.

Last summer, I traveled to Walpole for the first time. Until then I had been working from an old map of the town and some snapshots of Washington Square. It was wonderful and strange to walk through the town that seemed so vibrant in my imagination.

I pictured the characters walking to the river, rehearsing the play in the attic of a downtown inn, and shopping for fabric in the dry goods store. I felt closer to them than ever.

I was thrilled to realize that *Leaves of Grass* was published that same summer. Emerson read it immediately and probably talked about it with Bronson. Discovering the historical coincidence of Louisa's lost summer and Whitman's great work felt like a very good omen. Nothing in American literature could bind two restless hearts in love like that volume of poetry. This seemed to bring the story together, and at that point I committed to following it where it might lead.

Most of the few images of Louisa that survive show her when she was older, after the success of *Little Women* had catapulted her to almost instant fame. In them she appears tired and much older than she actually was. Her doctors, and, by extension, generations of Alcott scholars, believed she had been poisoned by the mercury-based calomel given to her as a treatment for typhoid. A biography published in 2009 cites the work of two doctors who attempted to settle remaining questions about Louisa's diagnosis.

Their investigation of her symptoms led them to posit that Louisa had developed the autoimmune disease lupus—a fascinating idea that, alas, cannot be proved. Whatever the cause of her suffering, in her later years she was in constant pain, and this is evident in the images that appear in all her biographies—one of the few things they have in common.

But there is one picture of her as a young woman in her early twenties. She isn't smiling—most people didn't smile in pictures then because they were self-conscious about the poor condition of their teeth—yet the intensity of her gaze hints at how much life resided behind those eyes. This Louisa is young, vibrant, and full of anticipation for the joys and sorrows that lie ahead. I kept the picture on my desktop as I worked, and sometimes it seemed she was nudging me, bit by bit, toward the story she wanted me to tell.

For more details about Louisa's life and writing,
visit www.kellyoconnormcnees.com.

A NOTE ON SOURCES

I am indebted to several sources for information on Louisa May Alcott's life and work, as well as the details of life in Walpole, New Hampshire, in 1855: Madeleine B. Stern's *Louisa May Alcott*, Martha Saxton's *Louisa May Alcott: A Modern Biography*, John Matteson's *Eden's Outcasts: The Story of Louisa May Alcott and Her Father*, Susan Cheever's *American Bloomsbury*, William Anderson and David Wade's *The World of Louisa May Alcott*, Ednah Dow Cheney's *Louisa May Alcott: Her Life, Letters, and Journals*, Harriet Reisen's *Louisa May Alcott: The Woman Behind* Little Women, George Aldrich's *Walpole As It Was and As It Is*, J. C. Furnas's *Fanny Kemble: Leading Lady of the Nineteenth Century Stage*, Jane Nylander's *Our Own Snug Fireside*, and John Culhane's *The American Circus: An Illustrated History*. Any factual errors or anachronisms in this story emerged from my own flawed vision and do not reflect the painstaking work of these writers.

Little Women has never been out of print since its publication in 1868, but the Louisa I have come to know—complex, ambitious, political, and, of course, a brilliant storyteller—shows herself more fully in the many other stories and novels she wrote before and after her famous novel. Those mentioned in this book include "The King of Clubs and the Queen of Hearts," "Mrs. Podgers' Teapot," and "Love and Loyalty," all collected in *Hospital Sketches and Camp Fireside Stories*; *Work: A Story of Experience*; *A Modern Mephistopheles and A Whisper in the Dark*; "Morning-Glories," from *Morning-Glories and Other Stories*; *Little Men*; "Transcendental Wild Oats:

A Chapter of an Unwritten Romance"; *Under the Lilacs*; *Moods*; *An Old-Fashioned Girl*; and *Jack and Jill*. Countless others exist, many of which were published under a pseudonym because they were deemed too sensational to be linked to Miss Alcott. Two must-reads that most certainly were *not* written for "little women" are *A Long Fatal Love Chase*, which remained unpublished until 1995, and *Behind a Mask, or A Woman's Power*, originally written under the pseudonym A. M. Barnard. I hope readers will find as much delight in their pages as I have.

*The Lost Summer
of Louisa May Alcott*

by

Kelly O'Connor McNees

READERS GUIDE

1. Have you ever read a poem or book that profoundly challenged or changed your worldview? How might the events of the novel have differed if Walt Whitman had not published *Leaves of Grass* in the summer of 1855?

2. What is Louisa's relationship like with each of her sisters? Do any of these relationships change throughout the novel? If so, how? Do you think Louisa's identity was defined by her sisters?

3. Abba says that men and women experience love differently: "For a man, love is just a season. For a woman it is the whole of the year." Is that true in *The Lost Summer of Louisa May Alcott*? Is it true in your own personal experience?

4. Bronson Alcott was a truly unusual father and man. What is your impression of him? How do you think he affected his daughters, and did he affect each one differently?

5. Describe Bronson and Abba's marriage. Do you think it influenced Louisa's view of matrimony? If so, in what way?

6. Was Louisa right not to go with Joseph Singer to New York? Why or why not? What would you have done?

7. Why was Louisa so protective of her independence? Considering the greater opportunities available to women now, but

also the frenetic pace of their lives and, in some ways, more complex obligations, do you think she would be as protective of her independence if she lived today?

8. At one point Abba tells Louisa, "We must never give if we are hoping for something in return." Why does she say that? Do you think what she says is true?

9. At the end of the novel we learn that Louisa is taking care of her niece Lulu. What kind of parent do you think Louisa would be, and why?

10. Louisa tells Joseph, "My life is no longer my own." And yet she chose to base *Little Women*, her most successful novel, on herself and her sisters. If writers use their own experiences as inspiration, are they inviting fans to pry into their personal lives? Or should their work be taken at face value?

Daily Affirmation Books from . . .
Health Communications

GENTLE REMINDERS FOR CO-DEPENDENTS: *Daily Affirmations*
Mitzi Chandler

With insight and humor, Mitzi Chandler takes the co-dependent and the adult child through the year. Gentle Reminders is for those in recovery who seek to enjoy the miracle each day brings.

ISBN 1-55874-020-1 $6.95

TIME FOR JOY: Daily Affirmations
Ruth Fishel

With quotations, thoughts and healing energizing affirmations these daily messages address the fears and imperfections of being human, guiding us through self-acceptance to a tangible peace and the place within where there is *time for joy.*

ISBN 0-932194-82-6 $6.95

AFFIRMATIONS FOR THE INNER CHILD
Rokelle Lerner

This book contains powerful messages and helpful suggestions aimed at adults who have unfinished childhood issues. By reading it daily we can end the cycle of suffering and move from pain into recovery.

ISBN 1-55874-045-6 $6.95

DAILY AFFIRMATIONS: For Adult Children of Alcoholics
Rokelle Lerner

Affirmations are a way to discover personal awareness, growth and spiritual potential, and self-regard. Reading this book gives us an opportunity to nurture ourselves, learn who we are and what we want to become.

ISBN 0-932194-47-3
(Little Red Book) $6.95
(New Cover Edition) $6.95

SOOTHING MOMENTS: Daily Meditations For Fast-Track Living
Bryan E. Robinson, Ph.D.

This is designed for those leading fast-paced and high-pressured lives who need time out each day to bring self-renewal, joy and serenity into their lives.

ISBN 1-55874-075-9 $6.95

3201 S.W. 15th Street,
Deerfield Beach, FL 33442-8190
1-800-851-9100

Health Communications, Inc.

Professional Care.
Professional Concern.
Professional Counselor . . .
just for you!

Brought to you by Health Communications, Inc., *Professional Counselor* is dedicated to serving the addictions and mental health fields. With Richard Fields, Ph.D., an authority in Dual Diagnosis, serving as editor, and in-depth articles and columns written by and for professionals, you will get the timely information you need to best serve your clients *Professional Counselor*'s coverage includes:

- Treatment advances
- Mental health and addictions research
- Family, group and special populations therapy
- The latest in counseling techniques
- Listing of upcoming workshops and events
- Managed care and employee assistance programs

Professional Counselor: Serving the Addictions and Mental Health Fields is <u>the</u> magazine for counselors, therapists, addictionologists, psychologists, managed-care specialists and employee assistance program personnel.

Order *Professional Counselor* today and take advantage of our special introductory offer: One year of *Professional Counselor* (6 bimonthy issues) for just $20.00. That's 23% off the regular subscription price!

Clip and mail to:
Professional Counselor, P.O. Box 607, Mount Morris, IL 61054-7641

YES! Enter my subscription to *Professional Counselor* for a full year (6 bimonthly issues) for only $20.00—23% off the regular subscription price. If you are not completely satisfied, simply return the subscription invoice marked CANCEL. The first issue will be yours to keep.

Name: _____

Address: _____

City: _____ State: _____ Zip: _____

❑ Payment enclosed   Charge my: ❑ Visa   ❑ MC

_____ Exp.: _____

Signature: _____

Please allow 4-6 weeks for delivery. FL residents please add $1.20 state sales tax.

The Rehnquist Court

The Rehnquist Court

JUDICIAL ACTIVISM ON THE RIGHT

Edited by Herman Schwartz

HILL AND WANG

A DIVISION OF FARRAR, STRAUS AND GIROUX

NEW YORK

Hill and Wang
A division of Farrar, Straus and Giroux
19 Union Square West, New York 10003

Copyright © 2002 by Herman Schwartz
All rights reserved
Distributed in Canada by Douglas & McIntyre Ltd.
Printed in the United States of America
Published in 2002 by Hill and Wang
First paperback edition, 2003

The Library of Congress has cataloged the hardcover edition as follows:
The Rehnquist court : judicial activism on the right / edited by Herman Schwartz.
    p.   cm.
    Includes index.
    ISBN 0-8090-8073-7 (hbk. : alk. paper)
    1. United States. Supreme Court.   2. Rehnquist, William H., 1924–   3. Conservatism—
United States.   4. Judicial process—Political aspects—United States.   I. Schwartz, Herman,
1931–

KF8742.A5 R44 2002
347.73'2635—dc21

                                                  2002068670

Paperback ISBN 0-8090-8074-5

Designed by Jonathan D. Lippincott

www.fsgbooks.com

10 9 8 7 6 5 4 3 2 1

To Justice William J. Brennan
who brought this nation a little closer to
"liberty and justice for all"

Contents

Acknowledgments

It is always a pleasure to record acknowledgments, especially since this is usually done when the book is at long last completed. In this case, it is especially pleasurable because it provides an opportunity to thank the many contributors to this volume. These hardy souls had to endure editing that was at times overly enthusiastic, had to meet pressing deadlines despite heavy schedules of their own, and even had to put up with my computer crashing. All who wrote for this book showed a remarkable patience, for which I am very grateful.

I would also like to express my appreciation to my initial editor, Elisabeth Sifton, whose encouragement and support got the book off the ground. Those who know Elisabeth are familiar with the way she provides her authors not only with the benefits of her professional experience and wisdom but also with the great pleasure of working with someone uniquely delightful and intellectually stimulating.

My second editor, Thomas LeBien, who came into the project toward its end, was also very helpful. His familiarity with the material from his previous work enabled him to take on the project without skipping a beat. His guidance in the endgame of putting the book together was invaluable.

I also want to acknowledge the support and personal friendship of Katrina vanden Heuvel, editor of *The Nation*, where shorter versions of some of these essays first appeared. Her willingness to devote virtually an entire issue of *The Nation* to those earlier pieces got the project started, and her enthusiastic backing for this book enabled it to go forward expeditiously.

As in almost every one of my publishing ventures, my agent, Milly Marmur, has been a treasure. For some fifteen years she has been not only a wise counselor, guiding me through the labyrinth of book publishing—this time through the special maze of putting together a book written mostly by others—but also a dear friend and confidante. I am deeply grateful that she has been willing to labor so tirelessly for someone who could add so little to her balance sheet.

I would also like to express my profound gratitude to my dean and dear friend, Claudio Grossman. He has been ever supportive, not just with financial support for summer grants and other assistance but with encouragement and creative suggestions whenever opportunities or problems have developed.

And finally, as always, to Mary, my wife of over four decades, who makes it all possible.

The Rehnquist Court

Foreword:

Reflections of a Court Watcher

TOM WICKER

The Supreme Court of the United States, a uniquely elitist institution
in a democratic nation, is such an accepted part of American life that
in the 2000 election it was able without much protest to force the
choice of a president who had lost the popular vote. If the justices can
choose the president, it's hard to imagine what future decision they
might make that would call forth effective resistance, much less political or constitutional retribution. And if *that's* the case, might it not be
fair to say that virtually anything the Supreme Court does—short of
ordering surrender in a time of war—is now acceptable to the American people? Maybe not. Many traumatic decisions likely await the
Court's attention—on abortion, on affirmative action, on civil liberties,
which are newly threatened by the war on terrorism. And the makeup
of the Court—no longer "nine old men" but seven suits and two
skirts—could change in such a way as to be less palatable to the public.
Still, in the wake of the Supreme Court's unprecedented—some would
say unwarranted, but certainly unchallenged—crowning of George W.
Bush as president, this proposition seems justified.

Americans now accept the authority of the Supreme Court's nine
unelected, life-tenured justices as readily as they accept the laws passed
by their chosen representatives in Congress and signed by the president. Perhaps more readily, because a law can be repealed more easily

and rapidly than practically any Supreme Court constitutional decision can be overturned.

If the Court, therefore, ever was in practice something less than decreed by the Constitution, it is now in fact a coequal branch of the government, right up there with Congress and the executive. Indeed, its perch might be just a tad higher, for it is even better able to make its judgments stick.

Two examples from history of disputed but ultimately effective Court rulings provide a context within which to judge contemporary concerns:

In 1830, a time when conflict between Indians and whites still flamed on the American frontier, the state of Georgia prohibited white men from entering "Indian country" without a license. The law, as usual in those days, was designed not to protect Indians but to answer the complaints of whites; they wanted the "racial agitators" of that day to be prevented from inciting the Cherokees to resist state laws. Two white violators, sentenced to four years at hard labor, took an appeal all the way to the Supreme Court of the United States. On March 1, 1832, Chief Justice John Marshall and his Court declared unconstitutional, "void and of no effect" *all* the laws of Georgia dealing with the Cherokee nation and ordered the two appellants freed.[1]

President Andrew Jackson, who favored the Georgia laws and was planning to deport the Eastern Indian tribes to reservations west of the Mississippi, is supposed to have replied: "Well, John Marshall has made his decision. Now let him enforce it."

Echoing down the decades, that story has exemplified Jackson's imperious style and, not too many years ago, was quoted by any number of Southern diehards to justify their resistance to court-ordered school desegregation. Unfortunately for them, Jackson said no such thing—though his biographer, Robert V. Remini, concedes that the statement *sounds* like Old Hickory and may even reflect his thoughts.

Jackson was already in conflict with South Carolina over tariff nullification, however, and eager to avoid a controversy in another state. So he quietly pulled a few strings, privately nudged Georgia officials, and within the year the imprisoned men were freed. The Supreme

Court was "upheld"—at least its ruling was made effective, however belatedly.

More than a century later, Chief Justice Earl Warren and his Court delivered a ruling confounding a large share of public opinion and over-turning what had been understood as established law, and again it did so without support from the White House. In 1954, the Court unani-mously declared in *Brown v. Board of Education of Topeka, Kansas* that racial segregation of the public schools, as then practiced in seventeen states and in certain school districts of four others, was unconstitutional.[2]

In those states, mostly Southern, the decision caused an uproar. President Dwight D. Eisenhower, who personally disapproved of the ruling, told a news conference only that he was duty bound to support a decision that he conceded had become "the law of the land." For the rest of his first term, however, and for all of his second, he failed to do so. He simply stood silent on the issue, not even acting behind the scenes to produce compliance as Jackson had done in 1832. Quite the opposite: according to Warren's memoirs, Eisenhower at a private din-ner party took ex parte action to head off what became the *Brown* rul-ing.

The ruling nevertheless was issued, and despite all outcry, progress in desegregation proceeded—though at less than a snail's pace and de-spite various forms of defiance. Not until 1957 did that defiance be-come flagrant enough to require the president to enforce the Court's ruling.

Governor Orval Faubus of Arkansas had called out his state's Na-tional Guard to prevent the court-ordered admission of nine black children to Little Rock Central High School. Even after a personal meeting with Eisenhower, Faubus refused to back down; worse, he called off his National Guard, creating a real potential for violence and loss of life as crowds of angry citizens converged on the school. Only then did the president finally send in *his* troops, the 101st Airborne Di-vision. He also federalized the Arkansas guardsmen so they were no longer under Faubus's control. The admission of the nine black young-sters finally was achieved.

In his memoirs, Attorney General Herbert Brownell said he be-lieved that the president's "decisive action" meant that "eventual en-forcement of *Brown* was assured." Depending on what the meaning of the word *eventual* is, that was true; on opening day in 1970, thirteen years later, the South's old dual school system, predicated on the "separate but equal" doctrine, had mostly disappeared, at least legally. De facto school segregation remains a virulent fact today, particularly in large cities across the nation and particularly in the South.

The stories of these two decisions vividly illustrate, in their different ways, the strengths of the Supreme Court rather than any supposed weakness. They establish the fact that the Court's unelected, life-term justices define what the Constitution means and thereby establish principles of law that most elected bodies would not be willing to consider or propound. Just as the white legislature of Georgia was obeying the mandate of that state's voters in 1832, most legislative bodies are usually too well aware of the next election to defy public opinion; and just as the Marshall Court of 1832 did not have to fear being voted out of office, the Warren Court of 1954 was able—as its successors have been—to act on constitutional "principle" rather than out of fear of vox populi.

Not, of course, that the Court always does so. A well-established conventional wisdom is that the Supreme Court follows the election returns. Which is to say, it does not too often or too egregiously defy the demonstrated will of the people—not for fear of being voted off the bench but for the less immediate, less tangible, less definable fear of a damaging loss of institutional power or influence, owing to a Congress or a population, or both, too often confounded.

It may be time to question the validity of this fear. Even after the Warren Court added controversial rulings on criminal justice to the "earthquake" of its *Brown* decision, decades of public fulmination and "Impeach Earl Warren" campaigns brought no literal change or damage to the Court or its ruling—no constitutional amendment to curtail its powers, certainly no real move to impeach Warren, no long-term revival of legally enforced school segregation. Of course, all that agitation might have influenced, and probably did, the actions of subsequent Courts. Nevertheless, *Brown* stood and in the largest sense has prevailed for half a century.

Another, more direct effort at retaliation against the Court ended in somewhat similar ambiguity, though ostensibly in a bloodied political nose for one of the most popular and effective presidents of the twentieth century. Following his landslide reelection in 1936, Franklin D. Roosevelt moved to expand membership of the Supreme Court and to force the retirement of the conservative elderly justices he held responsible for striking down some of his New Deal innovations. Unexpectedly—to FDR, at least—Congress and the public rose up in political wrath at what was seen as a power grab by the executive branch and an unwarranted rearrangement of the powers of government.

In one of Roosevelt's most resounding defeats, his "packing plan" was rejected by Congress. Ironically, the Supreme Court of the thirties seemed nevertheless to have got the president's message; from then on, it was more receptive to New Deal legislation, upholding the Wagner Act and the minimum-wage law, for instance. The congressional outcome of Roosevelt's packing plan remains a warning note for politicians, even presidents, who would try to discipline or even change an unpopular, undemocratic Supreme Court, apparently respected, after all, as the third equal branch of government.

The Court's ability to survive not just outside attack but actions of its own that seem to reflect dubious political influence was demonstrated again when the public rather quickly accepted its unprecedented decision that the deadlocked 2000 presidential election had been fairly won by the Republican candidate, Governor George W. Bush of Texas, over the Democrat, Vice President Al Gore.[3] After many decisions in which various courts had refused to get involved in the "political thicket," even the jurisdiction of the Rehnquist Court was unclear. The Court was authorized to rule on the constitutional aspects of Florida election and recount law, not—to the public's knowledge—to definitively decide the outcome of the national election. That controversial role it took upon itself. Its 5–4 decision broke along its own internal conservative/liberal partisan lines, all five justices in the majority having been nominated by Republican presidents, including Justice Clarence Thomas, who was nominated by Bush's father, George H. W. Bush.

The election of 2000 had been hard fought, Florida's vote was

marred by charges of racial and other irregularities, and few expected
the Supreme Court to do more than settle disputed points. Certainly,
few expected it to assume a responsibility no Court had taken on
before—choosing a president. The Court's chosen victor, moreover,
clearly had lost the popular vote cast in the forty-nine other states,
maybe in all fifty states, and although the "minority president" was not
unknown in American history, the victory of the popular-vote loser
was still an oddity. What is more, Bush's Court majority appeared, at
the least, to be more partisan than judicial.

Yet, though smoldering controversy remains, Bush's Court-ordered
victory was all but immediately conceded—by Al Gore, by leading
Democrats, by the general public. Not a credible voice was raised to
suggest that the Court or any of its members be impeached, or that
Bush's inaugural be stopped, or that some other method of settling the
election be found. For all practical purposes, the Court's ruling—actually, its selection of a president—was accepted by the public. Some judicial and legal experts, their image of the Supreme Court's lofty
virtues tarnished, and a few "yellow dog" Democrats did join in a faint,
continuing rumble of dissent, but Bush proceeded to select a cabinet,
take the oath, and settle unchallenged into the White House.

Despite these dramatic episodes, the Supreme Court has not always
been prominently in the public bull's-eye. For most of its history, however coequal constitutionally with Congress and the presidency, the
Court, compared with those branches, has stayed relatively in the
background. In the eighteenth and nineteenth centuries, it was rarely
even heard from and its major decisions were of more historical than
headline significance.

It was not until 1803, fourteen years after George Washington's
election as the first president, that the Court even asserted the power
for which it is best known and which gives it its most celebrated and
controversial function—that of reviewing congressional actions and
sometimes declaring them unconstitutional.[4]

Even after that, the early Court waited another half century, until
1857 and the eve of the Civil War, to act again on its review power, de-

claring in its famous *Dred Scott* decision the Missouri Compromise to be unconstitutional and holding that Negro slaves could never be citizens of the United States and that they had no rights that anyone was bound to respect.[5] Abolitionists, of course, were outraged at a decision that, in effect, upheld slavery. As a means of averting a national crisis, however, the decision was a failure. For a number of reasons, including but not limited to *Dred Scott*, the Civil War followed. But as an institution, the Court managed to survive.

Even after the Thirteenth and Fourteenth Amendments seemed to have settled the question of *slavery*, the question of *race* lingered. *Plessy v. Ferguson* in 1896 was essentially another sectional compromise: North and South believed that if blacks would only be satisfied with the "separate but equal" status the Court had approved, the nation could imagine that the problem had been solved.[6] But a half century later, blacks weren't satisfied and the problem remained. *Brown* in 1954 not only reversed *Plessy* but forced the nation to face its failure to establish racial equality—a democratic value implicit if not specified in both the Declaration of Independence and the Constitution.

The Supreme Court has seldom performed such lofty service—and sometimes, as in choosing George W. Bush to be president, the justices have seemed mostly to reflect the political views of the presidents who nominated them. Presidents, in fact, exercise so much control over the makeup of the Court that its independence sometimes has been questioned. Not always, however. On occasion, the reverse happens. In 1952, during the Korean War, for instance, President Harry Truman, ostensibly acting to head off a threatened strike, seized the steel industry. In *Youngstown Sheet and Tube Company v. Sawyer*, the Court promptly ruled that he had no authority for such a drastic step and the president as promptly returned the steel mills to their private owners.[7] That Truman had appointed Fred M. Vinson, a poker-game crony from their Senate days, chief justice apparently did not sway the Court in the president's favor.

President Eisenhower chose several outstanding justices—among them John M. Harlan, William J. Brennan, Potter Stewart, and, perhaps most important, to succeed Vinson, Earl Warren—but failed to advance the Warren Court's most significant achievement, the unanimous *Brown* ruling. And despite his original high opinion of Warren, the president later told friends that nominating Warren was "the biggest damn fool mistake" he had ever made.

The Johnson administration was notable for its part in several Supreme Court developments: Johnson nominated Thurgood Marshall, the lead attorney in the *Brown* case, to be the first black member of the Supreme Court and talked President Kennedy's appointee, Arthur Goldberg, *off* the Court and into the ambassadorship to the United Nations—during the Vietnam War, theoretically a more important post. Johnson also named Earl Warren, while chief justice, to serve as chairman of the commission that investigated Kennedy's murder. The precedent of outside service had been set for the Court when Justice Robert H. Jackson served on the Nuremberg war crimes tribunal. Nevertheless, perhaps as a measure of growing public esteem for the Court's independence, the Warren appointment was criticized as establishing an improper role for a chief justice.

Two Republican presidents, however—Richard Nixon and Ronald Reagan—have most directly influenced today's Supreme Court, and their actions reach ahead to affect its future. Nixon had the distinction of nominating *two* chief justices—Warren E. Burger directly and William H. Rehnquist as an associate justice later named chief by Reagan. Nixon stumbled badly and twice in succession, however, when a first choice, Clement Haynsworth, and then a second, G. Harrold Carswell, were rejected by the Senate. Continuing to seek a Southerner for the Court, Nixon later nominated Lewis F. Powell, Jr., of Virginia, who was easily confirmed. Ironically, it was this Court that in effect forced Nixon to resign the presidency by ordering him to surrender what the press termed the "smoking gun" tape, which fixed his guilt in the Watergate coverup. An important distinction should be drawn, however. Nixon chose to resign. The Court was not seen as having directly forced him out, as later it was considered to have "chosen" Bush over Gore.

That Nixon in one and a half terms had six opportunities to nominate justices, four of whom were confirmed by the Senate, illustrates the erratic nature of Supreme Court nominations, as well as the unpredictable makeup of the Court itself. In ordinary circumstances, after all, such nominations can be made, and that makeup changed, only after the death or resignation of someone on the bench, a relatively in-frequent occurrence. Nixon's successor, the "accidental president" Ger-ald Ford, had only one chance to nominate a justice—John Paul Stevens. Jimmy Carter, the first Democrat in the White House after eight years of Nixon and Ford, had none. Carter did nominate many blacks and women to the lower courts, an indication of what he might have done in regard to the Supreme Court. Had Carter been given the opportunity to appoint a Supreme Court justice, it's not unreasonable to suppose that Al Gore rather than George Bush would be president today.

During his two terms, Ronald Reagan nominated and saw con-firmed three justices who remain on today's Court—the so-called Rehnquist Court because he also named William H. Rehnquist, a sit-ting associate justice for fourteen years, as chief justice. The first woman justice, Sandra Day O'Connor, joined the Court under Rea-gan's patronage. Reagan also put forward perhaps the most controver-sial nomination of modern times, perhaps ever—that of Robert Bork, a well-known conservative with views on civil rights and abortion that almost guaranteed opposition. Bork failed to win confirmation in a vi-cious Senate battle, and after Nixon's two failed nominations and Bork's defeat, judicial nominations became highly political actions. President Bush I and Bill Clinton seemed careful to choose moderates unlikely to evoke the fierce opposition Bork aroused. Bush's first choice, David Souter, though ostensibly a conservative, has compiled a rea-sonably liberal record and was not among the majority five that put Bush II in the White House; Bush's other choice, Clarence Thomas, has turned out to be probably the Court's most conservative member. Clinton nominated Ruth Bader Ginsburg, the second woman to join the Court, and Stephen Breyer, and both won fairly easy confirmation.

Clinton's nominations notwithstanding, Republican occupation of the White House in twenty of the last thirty-two years has resulted in at least nominal Republican dominance of the Supreme Court as measured by the party affiliations of the presidents who appointed the justices. Suffice it to say, today's Court is entirely a product of these thirty-two years. During that period, the Republicans won five presi-dential elections and the Democrats three. But during that same pe-riod, four Republican presidents (Nixon, Ford, Reagan, and Bush I) chose ten confirmed Supreme Court justices, including two chiefs (Burger and Rehnquist), while one Democratic president, Clinton, appointed only two justices and no chiefs. As a not entirely predictable result, the Rehnquist Court has a relatively stable but not fixed conservative majority of five: Rehnquist, Scalia, Thomas, Kennedy, and O'Connor. But since Justices Kennedy and O'Connor are sometimes "swing votes," the usual liberal four—Stevens, Souter, Ginsburg, and Breyer—are not invariably in the minority.

This philosophical lineup seems unlikely to change anytime soon, though the faces and names might. Rehnquist, O'Connor, and Stevens, owing to age, health, and length of service, might be among the earliest to leave the Court; if they do so within the next two years, however, their seats would be filled by Bush II, a Republican and a conservative. Of course, death is always unpredictable and so, sometimes, are resignations, and it's at least conceivable that a Democrat or a more liberal Republican (or, less likely, an Independent) could become president in 2004. The makeup of the Senate that must confirm any presidential nomination is also a variable. Further, the records of David Souter and, say, Byron White (President Kennedy's first appointee) are ample proof that justices do not always reflect the views and politics of the presidents who nominate them. For all these reasons, at least, it's impossible to predict the future makeup of the Supreme Court, much less its conservative/liberal division. On the evidence available, however, it can be predicted that whatever changes in the Court may occur in the future, and whatever rulings a Court at any given moment may render, the public is likely to accept both the Court and its decisions—with screams of agony, perhaps, as after *Brown* in the fifties, but without challenging a decision or causing effective political reprisal against the institution or the justices.

In fact, the Supreme Court—unelected and lofty as it is—seems to have reached a position that, if not untouchable, is at least as authoritative and accepted as that of any institution in the nation. The Court is not only peculiarly American, as often noted, but also peculiarly powerful.

Introduction

HERMAN SCHWARTZ

In the introduction to *The Burger Years* (1987), I wrote that the appointment of Associate Supreme Court Justice William H. Rehnquist as the sixteenth chief justice of the United States and the elevation of Court of Appeals Judge Antonin Scalia to the high court mark "the beginning of a reshaping of the Supreme Court, the contours of which are still unknown." Fifteen years later, we know those contours. The Rehnquist Court is the most conservative Supreme Court since before the New Deal. Ronald Reagan's efforts to reshape the American judiciary have succeeded.

For a half century, from 1937 until as late as 1987, the Court could be characterized as moderate to liberal, for even the Burger Court, the Rehnquist Court's predecessor, turned out to be far less conservative than had been anticipated after Nixon appointed four justices. But in 1988, Anthony Kennedy succeeded Justice Lewis F. Powell, Jr., who, though fundamentally conservative, had often voted with the Court's liberals on such issues as affirmative action and church-state separation. Kennedy has been more consistently conservative, which has produced a fairly firm five-justice majority. This majority has persistently used its one-vote margin to move the constitutional and legal clock back toward the 1920s and early 1930s. It has not been able to do so completely, and probably has not even wanted to in all respects. Indeed, in some areas, such as women's rights and to some extent the rights of gays and lesbians, the Court has consolidated earlier gains and even moved beyond them, though usually over the objections of Rehnquist, Scalia, Clarence Thomas, and either Kennedy or Sandra Day O'Connor. Nevertheless, the conservative bloc has moved as aggressively as its slim margin has allowed to undermine or restrict many of the gains for social justice and civil rights that the Court consolidated over the preceding fifty years.

Two events dominate this period, both coming at its end and within a year of each other: *Bush v. Gore* and the terrorist attacks on September 11, 2001.[1] Their long-term consequences for the future of the Supreme Court and the nation are still unclear, despite their immense immediate impact. There may not even be any real long-term consequences to *Bush v. Gore*, and the Court will probably not be harmed or even affected by the outrage that decision produced. Soon after the decision, most Americans appeared willing to forget and forgive whatever the Court did that was wrong. Moreover, impartial studies of the contested balloting indicate that although Vice President Al Gore would have won by a very narrow margin if all the votes cast in Florida had been recounted, the limited recount that the Court blocked—the only matter at issue before it—would not have changed the outcome.[2] This, of course, does not change the fact that in its handling of that case, the Court's conservative majority displayed blatant partisanship and judicial unscrupulousness, as John P. MacKenzie's essay in this collection demonstrates. But those studies make it less likely that the Court's public standing will be seriously undermined by its behavior.

In part, this is because the conventional wisdom that the Supreme Court has been hurt by a series of self-inflicted wounds (*Dred Scott* is the most frequently cited example) is wrong. The Court hasn't really suffered all that much from these "wounds." It has become so "peculiarly powerful," as Tom Wicker puts it, that it is less affected by public reaction than the other two branches of government. The Court's decisions since *Bush v. Gore* certainly show no tendency on its part to pull in its horns.

As to the consequences of September 11, it is certain that there will be important ones. At least some of the many intrusive security measures adopted by the Bush administration on its own and by Congress at its behest—surveillance of lawyer-client conversations of prisoners in custody, secret military commissions with the power of life and death over all noncitizens in deliberately hasty proceedings under rules made up by the secretary of defense, military detention of American citizens without access to counsel or a judicial hearing, expanded surveillance powers—will come before the Court.[3] And if history is any guide, these measures will almost always be upheld. The Supreme Court's record in defending our liberties at a time of foreign threat is not reassuring. If anything, the Court as a body and some justices individually have made things worse. From the Alien and Sedition Acts during the Napoleonic Wars through the Court-sanctioned punishment of dissent in World War I and the Palmer Raids in 1919–20, through World War II, the internment of the Japanese Americans (even after any danger of a West Coast invasion—the ostensible justification—was past), and the trial of General Yamashita, and on through the McCarthy years, the Court has rarely prevented or even criticized flagrant violations of fundamental rights.

Even when we haven't had a national emergency, the Supreme Court has not generally been in the forefront of the fight for liberty and equality. Because the Warren and Burger Courts were in the vanguard of this fight (with some backsliding by the Burger Court), many of us have come to think that the Court was always like that. But for most of its history the Supreme Court has been concerned more with protecting the interests of the haves and maintaining the status quo than with protecting the have-nots by advancing social justice and human freedom. As Wicker's brief historical survey notes, the Bill of Rights under which we live today is a largely modern creation, dating mostly from the 1930s. The first case in which the First Amendment's freedom of speech and press provisions were enforced against official action came in 1931 and the first decision protecting freedom of religion in 1940.[4] The Equal Protection Clause, the first constitutional effort to make a reality of the Declaration of Independence proclamation that "all men are created equal," was not fully enforced until the *Brown v. Board of Education* school desegregation cases in 1954.[5]

It is thus not unusual to find that the current Supreme Court majority is not interested in, and is even sometimes hostile to, promoting civil rights and civil liberties. And in light of the Court's treatment of blacks in America before 1938, it seems altogether fitting that one of the areas where it has done the most damage to progressive hopes is in the many decisions and settings where race is at issue—discrimination, affirmative action for racial minorities, criminal justice (including especially capital punishment) and the rights of prisoners. As William L. Taylor's contribution to this volume shows, in almost every area where progress in racial and other kinds of justice—education, employment, voting—was made, the five-member majority that currently dominates the Supreme Court, aided and abetted by conservative lower-court judges picked by Presidents Reagan and George H. W. Bush, has begun to implement William Rehnquist's original agenda: to undo the gains of the last fifty years by making it ever more difficult for racial and ethnic minorities, battered women, the disabled, the elderly, and the otherwise unfairly treated to achieve justice through the courts.

Stephen B. Bright's essay shows, in saddening detail, how the conservative justices have used their slim majority to allow the representation of people charged with capital offenses, a disproportionate number of whom are black, to be so minimal that it amounts to no representation at all. At the same time, they have shut off almost every avenue by which prisoners condemned to death can challenge their death sentences for constitutional defects. Yet it is becoming ever clearer that, as Justice Harry A. Blackmun said after hearing scores of capital cases, "the death penalty experiment has failed. . . . No combination of procedural rules or substantive regulations ever can save the death penalty from its constitutional deficiencies."[6]

Charles Ogletree's contribution broadens the picture to include other areas of criminal procedure in which the Supreme Court has narrowed the rights of the accused. The war on drugs has produced an especially large volume of Fourth Amendment search-and-seizure cases, where, because of the flagrant racial and ethnic discrimination endemic to the enforcement of drug laws, the impact of the Court's decisions falls most heavily on African Americans. Ogletree explains how the Court, without expressly overruling the most significant decisions of the Warren Court, such as *Miranda v. Arizona*, has whittled them down.[7] Recent decisions have also facilitated widespread use of racial profiling by allowing searches in connection with trivial traffic and other offenses. Some recent decisions, as Ogletree notes, do enhance the defendant's rights, but such decisions are few and far between.

Just as most of the capital punishment and criminal defense cases appear not to be race cases but are, so too for the prisoners' rights cases. In the late 1960s and early 1970s, the national conscience was shaken by the appalling conditions of our prisons, and although the criminal justice reform movement effectively ended in 1968, the prisoners' rights movement went into high gear almost immediately thereafter. Following some scattered rulings in 1964 and in 1968 on religion and on racial segregation in prison, in 1969 the Supreme Court issued a series of decisions that promised to improve living conditions, discipline, and medical care, to permit access to reading matter and to courts and legal services, and to rein in the near-total power of prison officials over the lives of prisoners. In 1972, however, Rehnquist and Powell joined the Court. By 1974, decisions favorable to prisoners dwindled and conditions dramatically worsened. The war on drugs produced a huge rise in the prisoner population, composed of a disproportionate number of racial and ethnic minorities, and terrible overcrowding. The Court began to turn away prisoner petitions with increasing regularity so that today, as William E. Hellerstein shows in his essay, almost all the decisions favorable to prisoners have been either overturned or substantially narrowed. A prisoner is again at the mercy of prison officials.

Speech, abortion, gay rights, and religion enjoyed greater solicitude from the Rehnquist Court. In such controversial areas as pornography on the Internet, flag burning, and political satire, the Supreme Court, as Jamin B. Raskin concedes, blocked efforts to interfere with someone's speech because of what was said. But when major public institutions like public television, schools, and the federal government have tried to control who uses their facilities or public money and how, this Court has given them virtual carte blanche. And the Court's apparent special concern for maintaining the two-party system, for which there is no constitutional basis, has worked to the detriment of minor parties.

Abortion issues also received a mixed reception from the Court. On the one hand, as Susan Estrich observes, *Roe v. Wade* was affirmed, and the ban on criminalizing abortion was kept in place.[8] And Estrich does not think this will change, since only justices appointed by a Republican president would be inclined to overrule *Roe*, and the Republican Party understands that the political damage of such a decision would be prohibitive. As *Bush v. Gore* showed, Republican judges can be very solicitous of Republican Party interests. But the chief beneficiaries of *Roe* are middle-class women, for violence by so-called prolife groups and other pressures have made it difficult for poor women to find doctors willing to perform abortions. Moreover, the Court's delphic utterances in the *Casey* case describing what restrictions may be imposed on abortions, have encouraged states and localities to create numerous obstacles to terminating a pregnancy.[9] Not surprisingly, the resulting burdens have fallen most heavily on the poor.

Gay rights is the one area where this Court has realized some, albeit halting, progress. We are indeed a long way from the open hostility toward gays reflected in the 5–4 majority in *Bowers v. Hardwick*, when the Supreme Court allowed states to criminalize consensual homosexual activity. Now, Chai R. Feldblum finds, the Court is showing greater respect for gay people's rights, evident not only in the 1996 decision striking down a Colorado constitutional amendment that denied gay people almost all legal protection against discrimination but even in decisions like *Boy Scouts v. Dale* and the Boston St. Patrick's Day parade case, both of which went against the gay litigants.[10] The essential question, according to Feldblum, is whether a majority of the Court and the country will come to believe that homosexual conduct is morally equivalent to heterosexual conduct, for judicial decisions are and always have been influenced by judges' moral perceptions.

A more confusing pattern is disclosed in Norman Redlich's comprehensive essay on church-state separation and the free exercise of religion. The decisions of the Warren and Burger Courts made it quite difficult to provide financial support for religious education or to allow official prayers in schools. (Voluntary student prayer that has no state involvement has always been permitted.) Demands for financing and officially sanctioned school prayer have continued, and the Rehnquist

Court has responded sympathetically to the first but not to the second. A major question is whether the Court's decision allowing publicly financed vouchers to be used for religious school attendance will extend to permitting public financing of other religious activities. Also, the Court's attitude toward school prayer is not unambiguous. The Court has treated prayer as speech and has viewed schools as public forums; consequently, public schools and colleges must provide religious groups with a place to pray or other school resources, including money, if the schools provide equivalent benefits to nonreligious groups.

Perhaps the most contentious area of the Rehnquist Court's jurisprudence has been its federalism decisions. In an astonishing display of judicial activism not seen since the 1930s, the Court's five conservatives have struck at the power of the federal government by annulling more federal statutes than any court in recent memory, almost always by 5–4 majorities and over outraged dissents. The claim that this has been done in the name of states' rights and federalism is a facade, one casually abandoned whenever federalism conflicts with more material interests like race, money, and power. Part of the conservative attack on federally created social programs, these decisions reflect the Reagan-Bush agenda that still animates the Republican Party. It is no coincidence that the losing litigants in these decisions are the disabled, the elderly, and working people. The nation and indeed much of Congress do not share the Court's Reaganite philosophy, but the fortuity of Supreme Court departures and appointments has allowed Republican presidents disproportionate opportunities to nominate justices, so that regardless of popular opinion, today's Supreme Court majority is able to further the Reagan social agenda. As Wicker's essay points out, this Supreme Court was put together during a period that covers eight presidential elections, of which the Republicans won five and the Democrats three. But during that same period, Republican presidents put all but two of the present justices on the Court, with Reagan appointing three, including Scalia, one of the most doctrinaire members of the Court, and with Nixon appointing the equally conservative Rehnquist in 1972.

The resulting hostility to social legislation is illustrated in Andrew J. Imparato's essay, which traces this Court's undermining of the Americans with Disabilities Act, the landmark statute that gave hope to so many who suffer from the indifference usually shown the disabled. Disability law is, however, developing swiftly, and since disability law is largely statutory, Congress may correct some of the Court's misinterpretations.

The disability cases are, however, but one group among many. The five conservatives on this Court are hostile not just to the welfare state but to the use of the courts by private citizens to enforce any of their constitutional and legal rights, as David C. Vladeck and Alan B. Morrison demonstrate and as the federalism cases illustrate. For example, the Freedom of Information Act is now riddled with judicially sanctioned exceptions; judicial review of regulatory action, except with respect to suits by business, is curtailed; and the majority has consistently overridden state regulatory laws that are tougher on business than on their federal counterparts.

The resistance to citizen suits also appears in the environmental context, as James Salzman documents. Although the Court's record on construing and applying substantive environmental laws does not show a consistent pattern, it has used environmental law cases to raise the barriers to citizen suits in general and to environmental suits in particular.

The tilt toward business interests is especially pronounced in the antitrust cases. Eleanor M. Fox shows how the Court has adopted the teaching of the Chicago School of Economics. This doctrine, the shortcomings of which are more and more apparent, presupposes that markets work efficiently and governmental intervention is harmful. It is totally indifferent to concentrations of economic power, even though it was the fear of such conglomerations of economic muscle that produced the Sherman, Clayton, and antimerger antitrust laws. As a result of the current Court's rulings, antitrust law today is largely probusiness and giant corporations like Microsoft are left largely unregulated.

The last essay, by Lawrence E. Mitchell, shows how the Court has cut back on the protective aspects of the securities laws, leaving the field to the courts of the state of Delaware. This is bad news for investors, for these courts are notoriously tender toward management. The need for federal supervision has recently been brought home with special force with the collapse of the giant Enron Corporation and the many other revelations of big business corruption, in which executives have walked off with millions, while investors lost huge amounts of money and many employees lost their life savings.

During the Rehnquist era, the Supreme Court has been hostile to minority aspirations and has cut back on the rights of the accused and the imprisoned; it has opened the doors of the execution chamber and shut the doors of the courthouse; it has chipped away at abortion rights, lowered the barrier between church and state, and undermined the free exercise of minority religions; it has allowed public institutions to discriminate; it has restricted the opportunities of students, minority candidates, federal fund recipients, and others to make their views known; it has shrunk federal power and narrowly interpreted federal social legislation by misreading congressional intent; and it has promoted business interests. On the positive side, it has kept alive efforts to fight discrimination against homosexuals, has maintained the ban on officially sanctioned school prayer, and has protected traditional speech.

By and large, these actions mirror the Reagan agenda for the courts. A 1984 study of the performance of Reagan appointees noted with satisfaction that these judges had dismissed suits by Medicare patients whose funding was terminated without a hearing, had prevented union members from suing their union, and had rejected claims by public assistance recipients, refugees, American Indians, handicapped children, the elderly, victims of Securities Act violations, public housing tenants, antitrust plaintiffs, and, of course, prisoners and others suing under any of the various civil rights acts.[11] Things haven't changed.

One of the more curious aspects of the Rehnquist era is the current Court's sharp cutback in its caseload. In 1985–86, the year before Rehnquist became chief justice, the Court decided 172 cases, with 159 opinions. During the 2001–2 term, it decided 76 with opinions. This drastic cutback will continue in part because of the Republican dominance of the lower courts established during the twelve Reagan-Bush years. Senate Republicans' obstruction during the Clinton presidency

ensured that this imbalance was not offset by liberal Clinton appointees, and so the lower courts' rulings are largely in line with the
high court's. Not surprisingly, it finds there is no need to review them.

During the 2001–04 presidential term, one or more Supreme
Court vacancies are virtually certain, for several of the justices are elderly and have served for many years. The next presidential term is
likely to see even more vacancies. The enormous role that the Supreme
Court now plays in American life guarantees that these nominations
will be controversial. Nevertheless, whoever survives the confirmation
process will almost certainly be moderately to very conservative.
Republicans have vowed there will be "no more Souters," and unless
Democrats decide to be far more confrontational on judicial appointments than they have been, nominees who are not glaringly far from
the mainstream will easily get through, especially if President Bush is
reelected. In her essay in this collection, Susan Estrich reports that
President Bill Clinton told her that he thought Bush was much more
conservative than people assumed. Judging by the Bush nominations
to the circuit courts as of this writing and other evidence, Clinton was
correct. The bizarre quirks of the 2000 presidential election may prove
to have long-term consequences little appreciated now, producing a
Court that for years to come will do what the Supreme Court has all
too often done in the past—helping the powers that be to comfort the
comfortable and afflict the afflicted.

Equal Protection for One Lucky Guy

JOHN P. MacKENZIE

"Our consideration is limited to the present circumstances, for the problem of equal protection in election processes generally presents many complexities."

That quiet sentence, in the unsigned opinion that stopped the recount and hastened to hand the presidency to George W. Bush, is very likely the most scandalous feature of the amazing case of *Bush v. Gore.*[1] More outlandish than the conservative majority's trashing of federalism principles and all the rules of restraint it usually lays claim to, this one-sentence disclaimer of legal principle was the linchpin of the majority's selective, inappropriate application of equal protection doctrine in favor of a presidential candidate whose claim would have been dismissed under the rules that apply to everyone else.

The Court was saying that this decision, purporting to enforce the Constitution's guarantee of equal protection of the laws, set no precedent. The statement was itself unprecedented. Before December 12, 2000, such a bald remark was unknown in Supreme Court annals; indeed, it was unthinkable. *Of course* a high court pronouncement on law or the Constitution sets a precedent for future cases. Not this time—at least not if the five-justice majority could help it. This decision, itself a legal orphan lacking a respectable precedent, is designed for one and only one beneficiary: George W. Bush.

That little sentence betrayed a Rehnquist Court self-portrait that is both ominous and damning. A court that will not be bound by its own decisions is a court that refuses, when it thinks necessary, to be a court at all—a tribunal that claims the right, when it thinks necessary, to be a law unto itself.

Although the nonprecedential statement has no precedent, it decidedly creates a dangerous one that points toward a lawless future. The majority of five gives every outward sign that it stands ready to repeat this performance if asked by the right parties. "When contending parties invoke the process of the courts," said the five, "it becomes our unsought responsibility to resolve the federal and constitutional issues the judicial system has been forced to confront." That grandiose assertion of power and right brings to mind the lament of Justice Robert Jackson, in the 1944 case that upheld the confinement of Americans with Japanese faces, that the Court had invested government with power that "then lies about like a loaded weapon ready for the hand of any authority that can bring forth a plausible claim of an urgent need."[2]

It does not redeem the five that Bush has turned out to be the "winner" in the news media ballot studies. What matters is what the justices knew and valued when they ruled. A consortium of large news organizations studied the ballots for many months and reached judgments about the probable outcome if certain ballots were recounted. But the Court did not allow the recounting. Nor does it matter that the political process of congressional counting of electoral votes probably would have elected Bush. It matters far more that the Supreme Court's lawless five prevented the constitutional, regular political process from operating. The survey results in late 2001 took some of the sting out of arguments that the Court stole the election for Bush, and President Bush's subsequent conduct in the White House has enhanced his personal claim to legitimacy, but that leaves the Supreme Court as the major institution whose legitimacy is deeply questioned. Far from vindicating the Court's actions, the ballot surveys emphasize how extreme was the Court's abuse of its discretion to intervene on Bush's behalf, since Bush was not the injured party in the case. People who wanted to vote for Gore, notably minorities, had thousands of ballots nullified, yet the Court assumed without justification that Bush had suffered the injury and thus had legal standing to complain.

Unique though it may be, this way of executing justice bears an ugly family resemblance to other aspects of the Court's regular business since 1991, when Clarence Thomas replaced Thurgood Marshall, creating a hard-core majority bent on radically altering the legal landscape with a series of increasingly high-handed, injudicious rulings. The five—Chief Justice William Rehnquist and Justices Sandra Day O'Connor, Antonin Scalia, Anthony Kennedy, and Thomas—have used their razor-thin majority to drive American jurisprudence far to the right of the centrist, moderate understandings of most Americans.

The decision ranks with history's worst. No, *Bush v. Gore* is not *Dred Scott* and it's not *Plessy v. Ferguson*.[3] It didn't consign black Americans to unendable slavery or render the Fourteenth Amendment moot by sanctioning racial apartheid in America. But it shares a salient characteristic with the *Dred Scott* decision of 1857. In reaching these decisions, both Courts decided matters beyond those necessary to resolving the case, cloaking themselves in the mantle of statesmanship, national savior, and crisis averter. The *Dred Scott* justices, seeking a politically smooth settlement of slavery issues, spoke well beyond the needs of the case and inflamed the nation, announcing not only that Dred Scott could not sue for his freedom but that he and other blacks in his situation could *never* win it. Another candidate for worst decision, *Plessy v. Ferguson*, the 1896 separate-but-equal ruling, was also tragically wrong. But at least in *Plessy* the Supreme Court was the proper decision maker. The Supreme Court never had any business in the cases that became *Bush I* and *Bush II.*

The Court had no business in *Bush I* for relatively technical, prosaic, but important reasons, even apart from its flimsy merits. Chiefly, the case was moot, legally dead. On November 24, when the Court agreed to review the Florida Supreme Court's extension of the election protest period, that extension had two days to run, and by the time the Court heard oral argument on December 1, that extended deadline had passed, ending the extension issue in favor of Bush, the plaintiff and Supreme Court petitioner who, despite the court-ordered extension, emerged from the protest period with a certified lead of 537 votes. The state system already had moved into the election law's court-administered contest period. When a controversy is over, the lack of a live case or controversy puts the dispute beyond the Court's power, a barrier the Court takes seriously most of the time. Not here. Instead the Court sent the case back to Florida for clarification.

As for *Bush II*, the review of Florida's Supreme Court order for a statewide manual recount, the larger reason why the highest court had no business there was that the Constitution and governing federal law assign it no role. Congress has a role: it counts electoral votes and, when necessary, decides between competing slates of electors. States have a role: their legislatures make the state rules and their courts, in Florida as in many other states, are assigned to interpret them and manage postelection judicial contests. As a nation we probably could have enlisted the Supreme Court for these tasks when we structured our government, but we never did.

The November 7 election was a tie, a phenomenon that apologists for the Court have used as a starting point in an argument that the Court heroically served as tiebreaker. Al Gore had half a million more votes nationwide than Bush, but both candidates needed Florida's 25 electoral votes and Bush led initially, it was said, by 1,784 votes, out of nearly 6 million recognized as cast. When the vote appears to be a tie, it's always possible that at some stage in a recount the lead will shift. From the initial mandatory recount through the protest period and the court contest period, an important and realistic goal for Gore, aside from ultimate victory, was to pull ahead if only temporarily, to show that Florida was still a jump ball and to make Bush abandon his stance that the election was over and the votes all counted. For Bush the name of the game was the reverse: stop the counting even when it appeared he led by as few as 154 votes. For Gore that meant to accelerate recounts, for Bush it meant to stall and run out the clock.

To understand the enormity of the Court's errors and their shock effect it is necessary to recognize how the law and federal litigation work normally. In our system a state's high court is the authoritative interpreter of that state's law so far as the United States Supreme Court is concerned. The U.S. high court does not interpret a state's law but takes it as expounded by the state's highest legal authority and only then decides whether that law squares with the U.S. Constitution or federal law. State supreme courts may interpret their state laws in ways that a justice in Washington would consider bizarre, yet that interpretation is binding. Even when a state high court seems to violate equal protection doctrine, the U.S. high court regularly ignores the case unless it is brought by a complaining party who has legal standing to complain, which usually means the party has been legally hurt.

These are not liberal inventions. They are the bedrock of the federal legal system. They help to explain why a broad consensus of legal specialists and experienced Court observers thought the justices would never hear Bush's claims, much less rule in his favor, and why literally hundreds of law professors protested the Court's actions. Liberal bias does not explain this reaction, notwithstanding apologists for Bush.

Hence the hostile reception of many outsiders to Bush's first petition and wonderment that the Supreme Court agreed to hear the case. The petition made three claims. First, that the Florida Supreme Court changed its state law, extending the protest period deadline so as to "violate" the governing 1887 Electoral Count Act. The act, said the petition, "requires that a state resolve controversies relating to the appointment of electors under 'laws enacted prior to' election day." Second, that the state court's decisions had so changed the duly enacted state election law that it violated the Constitution's Article II, Section 1, which provides that each state appoint its electors "in such manner as the Legislature thereof may direct." And third, that the court-ordered "arbitrary, standardless and selective manual recounts that threaten to overturn the results of the election" violated equal protection and due process rights.

"Court observers"—constitutional law teachers and practitioners, talking heads on television and the journalists who specialize in court coverage—mostly gave the petition no chance of winning Supreme Court review. First, courts don't "violate" that 1887 law and the law "requires" nothing; the worst a court can do is make it harder for a state to gain the law's so-called safe harbor—certain approval by Congress of electors chosen pursuant to laws enacted before the election. Second, the notion that Florida's high court had changed the state's law, as opposed to interpreting it, seemed loony; even legal neophytes knew full well that state high courts are the authentic interpreters of their states' laws. The United States Supreme Court may strike down a state law but will not second-guess the state court as to what that law says. The constitutional provision that the state's "Legislature" sets the state's election rules surely did not mean that there was no court review or interpretation permitted of the election code the legislature enacted. Or did it? Third, the equal protection argument seemed to take the Supreme Court into uncharted territory and at least the five most conservative justices had long been loath to expand those rights.

But Court observers were wrong. While the justices declined to consider the equal protection claim, on November 24 they did grant review on the first two questions and set a breakneck course for briefing and oral argument, scheduled for December 1. At the oral argument, what had seemed loony became surreal. The notion that Florida's highest court had changed rather than interpreted its state law struck some justices as compelling. Justice Scalia and Chief Justice Rehnquist were vocal about it, while the quiet Justice Thomas probably was a third vote. At times Justices O'Connor and Kennedy seemed challenged by the argument as well. Justices John Paul Stevens, David Souter, Ruth Bader Ginsburg, and Stephen Breyer seemed solidly of the traditional view that, ordinarily at least, a state high court's rulings on its state laws were authoritative.

Only Justice Breyer suggested the obvious, saying he guessed the case was moot since the secretary of state had already certified Bush the winner on November 26 so it didn't matter whether delaying the certification until that date had been proper. But no justice pressed the parties to explain why there might still be a live controversy.

Late in the argument Justice Ginsburg, perhaps sensing that Justice Scalia's reading of the Florida Supreme Court opinion was attracting votes, suggested remanding the case so the state justices could clarify their opinion. Three days later that is what the Court did in an unsigned opinion setting aside the Florida ruling and sending the case back to the state's high court.[4] It was now up to the Florida justices to say whether they had impermissibly changed state law and had failed to consider adequately the state's interest in reaching that safe harbor where its presidential electors could be counted by Congress without challenge.

When the protest period ended with the certification of Bush as winner by 537 votes and the court contest period began on November 27, Gore now sought court review of ballots allegedly legal but not tallied. Circuit Judge N. Sanders Sauls in Tallahassee repeatedly refused to look at the ballots. A week later, on December 4, Judge Sauls ruled that Gore had failed to carry the burden of proving that there were enough uncounted legal votes to *change* the election. The trouble was, as the state supreme court said on review of Sauls's decision on Friday, December 8, Sauls had misstated the legal test for deciding when to review the ballots, since the law required Gore to prove only that the number of legal disputed ballots was "sufficient to change *or place in doubt* the result of the election."[5] Judge Sauls's misreading of the statute was elementary, judicially substandard, and costly to the Gore forces in terms of time. If Judge Sauls had ordered ballot examinations on December 4, the job would have seemed much more doable before December 12 than it appeared with each passing day. Six of Florida's seven supreme court justices agreed that Sauls had erred, but the ultimate vote to order an immediate recount was 4–3.

The recount order was broader than Gore's requested four large counties. All the so-called undervotes—ballots that showed no vote for president for whatever reason—were to be examined. Amid complaints from Bush that the proposed recounting was standardless and vague, the state justices avoided decreeing a standard any more specific than state statutes mentioned: counters and a circuit judge must determine the intent of the voter. The state justices were very likely spooked by the arguments in the U.S. Supreme Court over the effect of court-induced changes in the state law. The demand for more specificity seemed a trap that the Bush forces would spring if the case got back to Washington, arguing that the state court had again "changed" the law.

Just as the manual recounting was getting under way on Saturday, December 9, came the Supreme Court's order to stop. The Court granted a Bush stay application and permitted review once again. The stay application in *Bush II* offered basically the same issues as *Bush I*, including the equal protection argument the Court had ignored in the earlier review. Under Supreme Court practice, such a stay would be granted only when a majority thought Bush would succeed and that he would be irreparably harmed if the ballot review continued while the case was being heard. The stay, carrying those implications, stunned many but the 5–4 lineup did not. Justice Stevens, joined by Justices Souter, Ginsburg, and Breyer, filed a pointed dissent that showed how issues and attitudes had hardened. The dissenters said the majority had already displayed disrespect for a state high court on questions of state law and abandoned traditional judicial caution on a matter that was ultimately for Congress to decide.

In caustic reply, Justice Scalia filed a concurring opinion warning that the stay did indeed indicate that five justices thought Bush would probably win. As for irreparable harm, that would flow from "the counting of votes that are of questionable legality," which would harm Bush "and the country by casting a cloud upon what he claims to be the legitimacy of his election." And Scalia flagged the equal protection issue: "the propriety, indeed the constitutionality, of letting the standard for determination of voters' intent—dimpled chads, hanging chads, etc.—vary from county to county."[6]

The oral arguments two days later, on December 11, showed no sign of a change in the now familiar lineup. If anything, Justices Souter and Breyer explored the equal protection issue in a way that pointed even further to a reversal of the Florida Supreme Court's December 8 judgment, though their questions envisioned fashioning a standard and proceeding with the ballot review. Justice Ginsburg questioned whether imposing a standard not set forth in preexisting state statutes wouldn't prompt the Bush forces to redouble their complaint that new law was being made in conflict with the safe harbor federal law.

Justice O'Connor expressed annoyance that the Florida court had not yet responded to the remand order calling for clarification of its November 21 opinion. That opinion was filed that evening.[7] It took the form of a substitute opinion that reiterated its basis in conventional statutory construction, the reconciling of conflicting provisions of the election code. This time it avoided mentioning the state constitution, apparently to appease any United States Supreme Court justice who thought it was making new law by using the state charter in interpreting the state statutes. The Florida justices indicated that they had been too swamped with election cases to respond earlier. There was a single, rather odd dissent by Chief Justice Charles Wells, who had been part of the unanimous court in the November 21 decision but who had dissented on December 8. "I dissent from issuing a new decision while the United States Supreme Court has under consideration *Bush v. Gore*," he said. In light of Justice O'Connor's expression of annoyance that this response had not yet been made, what was the problem with issuing it now? That was never explained. It is unclear whether the new Florida opinion changed any votes in Washington, for the Washington justices never discussed its significance.

Just before 10 p.m. on December 12, two hours before the safe harbor period would end, the Court came down with its judgment: no more counting, 5–4. That ended the 2000 election, unless the stay issued three days earlier had already dealt the death blow. Five justices, and you know who they are, accepted the equal-protection argument that varying counting procedures and too broad a definition of a valid ballot deprived someone—it was never clear exactly whom—of the right to equal treatment of his, her, or their ballot or ballots. Then, observing the lateness of the hour, the Court said the counting had to stop because Florida's legislature had expressed the desire to make the safe harbor and avoid any possible contest between competing slates in Congress. There wasn't time, they said, for Florida to arrange uniform ballot review standards.

Somewhere in the middle of the unsigned opinion they said, "Our consideration is limited to the present circumstances, for the problem of equal protection in election processes generally presents many complexities." Awkwardly out of place, this comment served to disengage the majority from their assigned duty to expound the Constitution and federal law and divert it to their present mission of breaking the national election tie at the behest of the only candidate who contended that the mission was legitimate.

Three of the five—Chief Justice Rehnquist and Justices Antonin Scalia and Clarence Thomas—accepted the argument that Florida's highest court had changed the state's laws in the guise of interpretation, "impermissibly distorted them beyond what is a fair reading," violating the directive of Article II, Section 1, of the Constitution that each state choose its presidential electors "in such manner as the Legislature thereof may direct."

Of the four dissenters, Justices David Souter and Stephen Breyer saw merit in the equal protection argument but dissented heartily from the decision to halt the counting. They said it was for Florida to decide if time was lacking and whether to seek greater accuracy even at the risk of losing the safe harbor of indisputable acceptance by Congress of its results. Like Justices John Paul Stevens and Ruth Bader Ginsburg, they contended the Court never should have taken *Bush II* or, for that matter, *Bush I*. They roasted the concurring three justices for disrespecting the Florida Supreme Court's interpretation of state law.

Three months later, Justices Kennedy and Thomas were before a House appropriations subcommittee on the Court's budget. As sometimes happens, subcommittee members like to talk about decisions. Representative José Serrano of the Bronx told the witnesses that he and his constituents were hurt and baffled by *Bush v. Gore*. Justice Kennedy said that he understood but that the Court had no choice but to hear the case. "Sometimes it is easy to enhance your prestige by not exercising your responsibility," he said, "but that has not been the tradition of our Court." He went on: "Ultimately, the power and the prestige and the respect of the Court depend on trust. My colleagues and I want to be the most trusted people in America." Justice Thomas said he, too, would have ducked "if there was a way," but there wasn't.

There was. It might have taken more courage, but the Court could have and should have sat idly by while the presidential election worked its political course. Florida had a messy decentralized system governed by sometimes confusing statutes, but its courts were working at their assigned duty. The state supreme court justices, while not steeped in the nuances of United States Supreme Court review, were diligently focused on the state's own law. In *Bush I* they construed reasonably the mosaic of state laws, and in their opinion they threw in the state's constitution and its high value on the right of the people to govern. That should not have fueled the federal justices' suspicions that they were "changing" the law. They were doing "what judges do," as Justice Stevens argued. If they got their state law wrong, the Supreme Court was supposed nevertheless to take the law as state-interpreted and not reinterpret it. Again, this norm is not some liberal invention. It is one of the building blocks of federalism.

By contrast, as the history of the 1887 federal electoral count law demonstrated, there was no assignment for the federal courts. The federal law with its safe harbor provision was a set of rules for Congress, created by Congress to guide its acceptance or rejection of sometimes competing electoral slates submitted from the states. Those rules were enacted more than a decade after the seismic battle over the Hayes-Tilden deadlock of 1876. To ease the task of deciding between conflicting slates, Congress sought to discourage maneuvers to change state laws during the postelection contests. The law gave conclusive status to slates of electors chosen six days before the Electoral College's votes were tallied in accordance with laws enacted before the election itself. A state having trouble deciding who won its vote for president might pass up the safe harbor provision if it wished, devoting the time to achieving a more accurate result.

Some have asked what a Supreme Court is for if not to settle national questions of this magnitude. The answer is plain: unless there is a major question of constitutional or federal law raised by someone with legal standing to raise it, the Supreme Court's duty is to do nothing. Some have said we mustn't have Congress mucking around in these matters, and the answer to that is: that's our system. Even if Congress wanted the system to be different, if it passed a law, for example, assigning the Supreme Court as the arbiter of disputed electoral slates, the Court probably would have to decline the task on the constitutional ground that it was a nonjudicial chore. But the Court showed distrust of our political arrangements and of the fitness of Congress to judge electoral disputes. It was not the first time this Court so dismissed Congress. Much of the Rehnquist Court's reputed emphasis on federalism is a retreat from generations of opinions that trusted Congress to regulate interstate commerce and to enforce the Fourteenth Amendment, as that amendment provides, "by appropriate legislation."

The Court's claim that it could decide this case without setting a precedent for others is of a piece with its refusal of late to give adequate leeway to Congress in matters of commerce and civil rights. It's a clumsy assertion of supremacy beyond the restraints the judiciary is supposed to observe. It's beyond activism—a refusal to be bound by the contours of the job of judging even at the high court's lofty level, indeed especially at that level, for the Supreme Court sits not as a court

of high correction but as an agency of high legal policy. Precedents are
the stuff of that job—setting them, recognizing them, even breaking
with them on rare occasions. Justices O'Connor, Kennedy, and
Souter paid their dues to precedent in their controlling 1992 opinion
refusing to overrule *Roe v. Wade*, saying, "the very concept of the rule of
law underlying our own Constitution requires such continuity over
time that a respect for precedent is, by definition, indispensable," but of
the three, only Souter did not join the unsigned "no precedent" opinion.[8]

Perhaps the most outspoken justice on the virtue of precedent as
limiting judicial excess is Scalia. He has noted that a Court that recog-
nizes the consequences of a decision on future cases is more likely to
take care not to decide too much in the case at hand. His statement in
his 1996 dissent from the decision desegregating the Virginia Military
Institute was correct (the dissent itself was not): "The Supreme Court
of the United States does not sit to announce 'unique' dispositions. Its
principal function is to establish precedent."[9] That statement alone
should have given Justice Scalia pause when joining the *Bush v. Gore*
majority in disavowing the setting of precedent—if the justice considered his own statements binding. Yet again, this is not a liberal or conservative position. It is quite common for justices of any philosophy to
point out to lawyers that a victory for their clients might set a precedent that may prove regrettable in cases down the road. That's what it
means to say, "Hard cases make bad law," that is, sympathetic cases
cause bad precedents.

It's also the significance of the quip that a Court decision of no lasting principle is like a ticket "good for this day and train only." Dissenters often use such barbs to charge that a majority's decision is one
of those without a respectable lasting principle and is doomed to an
early death, but until *Bush v. Gore*, majority justices had never so plainly
said that their own decision had no legs. True, some justices have a
greater tendency than others to stress the facts of a case in ways that
limit the future utility of the legal holding. I can think of a 1972 case,
Wisconsin v. Yoder, in which the majority was moved to uphold the religious free-exercise claims of Amish parents to keep their children out
of the public high schools.[10] The justices feared, with some reason, that
too broad a ruling would invite all kinds of claims that they were not

ready to recognize, like conscientious objection to paying taxes that help pay for war. So the Court laid out the facts in full array and observed that few could match the religious claims of the Amish in this regard. But there, by contrast to *Bush v. Gore*, the assumption was that the *Yoder* decision inescapably created a precedent.

The claim of power to deny precedential effect to a court's own opinion is a dangerous claim indeed. As it happens, lower federal courts are asserting it thousands of times a year, in the alleged superior interest of judicial economy. Many appellate court rules provide that a panel of judges may order that their opinions be neither published nor cited, which deprives many parties of the benefit of precedent. It will be interesting to see if the Supreme Court justices someday pass on the constitutionality of this practice and whether they will recognize it as kindred to their own audacious assertion in *Bush v. Gore*. Judge Richard Arnold of the Eighth U.S. Circuit Court of Appeals has written that the practice goes unconstitutionally beyond the judicial power, but his decision was vacated when the Internal Revenue Service rendered the controversy moot by changing the policy that was at issue in the case— insisting as it did so that it was not setting a precedent.[11]

Any one of a number of factors that counseled caution could have spared the majority justices such a flagrant assertion of power. They could have honored their own principle of deference to state courts about state law. They could have applied their traditionally conservative views of equal protection and long-standing neutral rules about legal standing—especially since George W. Bush had totally failed to demonstrate injury, irreparable or reparable, from the recounting. Or they could have shown awareness of the bad looks of it all: candidate Bush had praised Scalia and Thomas as his kind of justices, giving them every incentive to rule for the candidate more sympathetic to their kind of justice. Or they could have avoided the distrust springing from appearances: Scalia's son in a law firm representing Bush, Thomas's wife recruiting job candidates for a Bush administration. Or they could have averted the obvious perception that they would never have stretched their own rules for the candidate not named Bush. Did the four dissenters suffer from comparable appearance of bias? Even assuming they did, their opinions showed that they voted and reasoned without violating so many valued principles.

The kindest comment about *Bush v. Gore* was that of Richard Posner, a sitting federal judge, who said that the sloppy job had the "pragmatic" effect of averting a "crisis." But that alleged crisis was merely the prospect that the regular machinery would operate so that Congress, the constitutionally chosen instrument for counting electoral votes, could count them notwithstanding the Rehnquist Court's pathological distrust of that coordinate branch.

A number of law professors say that regardless of the Court's disclaimer, *Bush v. Gore* inevitably will spawn more equal protection rulings and potentially a new era for that right, especially in voting cases. Paul Freund used to tell his Harvard Law students that equal protection was "like a little boy who knew how to spell *banana* but didn't know when to stop." It may well develop that equal protection is not so casually limited. If so, it won't be the doing of the five, most of whom are not expansionist about equal protection except, perversely, in certain civil rights cases. (The five are often found recognizing the rights of white men, who were not the intended beneficiaries of the Fourteenth Amendment, to equal treatment when some rules are bent to diversify the workforce.)

The hope that *Bush v. Gore* has a silver lining is based not only on principle but also on an attitude that is respectful to the point of being patronizing. Will lower courts start enforcing equal protection based on emanations from *Bush v. Gore*, and if they do, will the five sit by and let it happen? Don't count on it. Anyone who was shocked by *Bush v. Gore* but expects the five to reform themselves into recognizable judges is better advised to prepare for more shock. Indeed, the five may look at the public's relatively tepid reaction to *Bush v. Gore* and perceive not condemnation but rather encouragement, while Bush's approval ratings, especially after September 11 and the findings of the press consortium on the news media ballot studies, may serve to mask the Court's performance and the election controversy itself. Will the justices reform and refrain from issuing decisions good for this day and train only? Don't count on that, either. This gang uses real bullets and they pack Justice Jackson's loaded weapon, ready to fire whenever they feel the need.

RACE AND
CRIMINAL JUSTICE

Racial Equality:
The World According to Rehnquist

WILLIAM L. TAYLOR

❦

During the sixteen years Earl Warren presided over the Supreme Court, from 1953 to 1969, constitutional rights and liberties flourished as never before in the nation's history. With its unanimous 1954 decision in *Brown v. Board of Education* striking down racial segregation laws in public education, the Court became a catalyst for a largely peaceful revolution in civil rights.[1] Resistance by Southern leaders to the Court's decree led to a peaceful protest movement. Violent repression of that movement brought about a national consensus in favor of equality of opportunity that found expression in the civil rights laws of the 1960s.

Toward the end of the Warren years, the Supreme Court, finally supported by the legislative and executive branches, felt able to provide effective desegregation remedies, to give new life to Reconstruction laws eviscerated by the Court in the nineteenth century, and to extend equal protection to other groups suffering discrimination. By 1969, we were a different nation. The formal racial caste system in the South was eliminated and new opportunities for black Americans and other people of color had opened in the North as well.

Between 1969 and 1986, during which Chief Justice Warren Burger presided, the Court was a study in contradictions. On the one hand, the Court sanctioned remedies for public school racial segregation that had been long deferred and that provided new opportunities for black youngsters throughout the South. The Court also extended protections against intentional racial segregation of students in the North and West in states that did not have segregation laws in 1954. And for the most part the Burger Court interpreted the new federal civil rights laws so as to enable them to achieve their purposes, notably in the *Griggs* case, in which it struck down practices that served as a barrier to the employment of black applicants where those practices could not be shown to be necessary to the operation of the business.[2]

On the other hand, in two major decisions, *San Antonio v. Rodriguez* in 1973 and *Milliken v. Bradley* in 1974, a narrow 5–4 majority of the Burger Court sanctioned the retention of major barriers to the educational progress of minority and poor students.[3] *Milliken*, by treating local school district lines as almost impermeable barriers, locked urban children of color and poor children out of the better opportunities provided in suburban schools. *Rodriguez*, by justifying state systems of financing public schools largely through property taxes, denied many poor urban students improvement of their segregated schools.

In addition, during the Burger years, the Court placed new emphasis on the need for proof of intent to sustain claims of constitutional violations in employment, housing, and voting, relegating remedies in these areas to liberal interpretation of civil rights statutes.[4]

In both the pro– and anti–civil rights decisions, the Burger majority paradoxically may have been drawing lessons from *Brown v. Board of Education*. In its desegregation remedy decisions, the Court majority may have been motivated in part by a perceived need to protect the Court as an institution from giving in to the body blows it received from so many sources in the years following the *Brown* decision. If after that stormy time a practical desegregation remedy was not available, what had the struggle been all about?

At the same time, some justices in the majority in *Rodriguez* and *Milliken*, notably Potter Stewart, who was the pivotal vote in each case, may have been motivated by another lesson drawn from *Brown*—that the Court encounters trouble whenever it ventures into areas that have large social consequences without some solid core of public support. In *Milliken*, the Court was being asked to call for urban-suburban school desegregation in the very state where George Wallace had made a strong showing in a presidential primary held less than two years earlier and in a national climate far less hospitable to the protection of civil rights than in the early 1960s. In *Rodriguez*, the Court was being asked to invalidate a state school financing system in ways that would have called for a major redistribution of public resources. As Justice Thurgood Marshall said of *Milliken*, the decision was "more a reflection of a perceived public mood that we have gone far enough in enforcing the Constitution than it is the product of neutral principles of law."[5] The same could be said of *Rodriguez*.

If there is ambivalence and conflict in the record of the Burger Court on civil rights, there is no such uncertainty in the record of the Rehnquist Court. Chief Justice William H. Rehnquist has led a working majority hostile to civil rights from almost the day of his ascent to that office in October 1986. Ever since Justice Clarence Thomas (succeeding Thurgood Marshall in 1991) joined the Court, a bloc of five justices (Rehnquist, Antonin Scalia, Sandra Day O'Connor, Anthony Kennedy, and Thomas) has worked assiduously to chip away at both the scope of the civil rights laws and the remedies for their violation. The most affected areas have been fair employment, equal educational opportunity, voting rights, and affirmative action.

Interestingly, to some extent, the damage done by the Court to the opportunities offered to African Americans and other people of color has been mitigated by Congress's willingness to correct some of the Court's restrictive readings. Also, other major institutions in society—among them major employers, colleges, and universities that had stood mute or in opposition to the holdings of the Warren Court—have come to embrace affirmative action policies to extend opportunities to minorities. That the progress has proved durable through the decades of Nixon, Reagan, and the two Bushes is testimony to the work of the civil rights movement and the Warren Court, to the claim of equal justice on the American conscience, and to the changing demography of the nation, which has resulted in a changing calculus for both our political and economic systems.

Nevertheless, civil rights progress has been stymied, particularly for the worst off in society. Moreover, the Rehnquist majority has recently grown bolder. No longer restricting itself to crabbed interpretations of civil rights statutes, it is inventing whole new doctrines under the Commerce Clause, the Eleventh Amendment, and Section 5 of the Fourteenth Amendment that severely constrict the other branches of the federal government in their capacity to act on behalf of minorities and the poor. Whether this latest trend will abate or intensify will depend on the next appointments to the Court. Although hard to predict, it could ultimately result in a clash with the Congress or the executive branch, as occurred during the New Deal. One thing does appear fairly certain: if the current trend continues, racial and socioeconomic isolation in the nation and the gap between haves and have-nots will increase, with a great potential for division and conflict.

The previous career of William Rehnquist unambiguously foreshadowed the imprint he would make as chief justice. As a law clerk to Robert Jackson, Rehnquist wrote a memorandum to the justice during the 1952 term of the Court to assist him in deciding the pending *Brown* case. In it he said:

> If this Court, because its members individually are liberals and dislike segregation, now chooses to strike it down, it differs from the McReynolds Court only in the kinds of litigants it favors and the kinds of special claims it protects.
>
> I realize that is an unpopular and unhumanitarian position . . . but I think *Plessy v. Ferguson* was right and should be reaffirmed.[6]

When Rehnquist returned to Arizona to practice law, his political activities included running "ballot security" programs for the Republican Party and, according to the testimony of several witnesses, challenging the literacy of black citizens at the polls.[7]

Once on the Court, Justice Rehnquist quickly staked out positions that he would follow throughout his judicial career. Much of the early work was summarized by Harvard professor David Shapiro in an incisive analysis of Rehnquist's opinions from March 1972 to July 1976. Among the characteristics noted by Shapiro are the following:

Too often, unyielding insistence on a particular result appears to have contributed to a wide discrepancy between theory and practice in matters of constitutional interpretation, to unwarranted relinquishment of federal responsibilities and deference to state law and institutions, to tacit abandonment of evolving protections of liberty and property, to sacrifice of craftsmanship, and to distortion of precedent.[8]

One example of these traits (not cited in Shapiro) is Justice Rehnquist's position on school desegregation. In 1973, he was the lone dissenter when the Court decided in *Keyes v. School District No. 1 of Denver* that the *Brown* decision could be applied to school districts in the North and West even absent formal statutes commanding segregation.[9] Four years later, Justice Rehnquist wrote for the Court in remanding a Dayton school desegregation case for further proceedings because of a failure of the lower courts to make proper findings. The decision was not controversial, but Justice Rehnquist could not resist a bit of extra verbiage:

> If [school segregation] violations are found, the District Court in the first instance . . . must determine how much incremental segregative effect these violations had on the racial distribution of the Dayton school population as presently constituted when their distribution is compared to what it would have been in the absence of such constitutional violations.[10]

Justice Rehnquist was asking the impossible. Assuming that some segregation would likely exist in public schools even if the government had never decreed it, there is no known method for extracting the effect of that segregation from the immeasurable consequences of a public order that had segregated and stigmatized black people for more than two centuries. Unless such a method is discovered, Justice Rehnquist's quest for the "incremental segregative effect" is an exercise in fiction.

In the film *It's a Wonderful Life*, the protagonist (played by James Stewart) considers his life a failure and is on the verge of suicide when a guardian angel intervenes. The angel (Clarence by name) is able to re-create the distressed circumstances of the hero's town, friends, and family as they would have been if the hero had never lived and thus demonstrates to him that he has not been a failure but has made a real contribution to the well-being and prosperity of all. The movie ends happily. Lacking such divine intervention, judges and lawyers in school segregation cases cannot re-create the situation that would have existed if the officially created segregation had never occurred. The party bearing the legal burden of persuasion—a burden that Rehnquist would place on the minority students—would always lose. Justice Rehnquist conveniently omitted any mention of the *Keyes* decision in which Justice William J. Brennan, writing for the majority, held that once a substantial violation is proved, the burden of justifying a limited remedy falls on school officials.

When the *Dayton* case came back to the Supreme Court in 1979 with proper findings made by the lower court, the majority rejected the Rehnquist view, saying that once deliberate practices of discrimination are proved, it is the defendant's burden to demonstrate that any segregation that is not to be subject to the court-ordered remedy was innocently caused.[11] But as will be seen below, as chief justice, Rehnquist has had what may be the last word, not just in erecting barriers to remedy in education but also in employment, affirmative action, and voting.

The first sustained application of the Rehnquist treatment of civil rights came in a series of fair-employment cases decided in 1989 and 1990. The most important of these decisions was *Wards Cove Packing Company v. Atonio.*[12] In *Griggs v. Duke Power Company*, a unanimous Court, in an opinion written by Chief Justice Warren Burger, had decided in 1971 that Title VII of the Civil Rights Act of 1964 could bar employment practices that had an adverse impact on minorities or women. Once plaintiffs proved that the practice adversely affected them as a group, the burden shifted to the employer to show that the practice was required by business necessity.

The *Griggs* decision was undergirded by a practical understanding of the barriers that had long faced people of color. The Court said:

Absence of discriminatory intent does not redeem employment procedures or testing mechanisms that operate as "built-in headwinds" for minority groups and are unrelated to measuring job capacity.

Two years later, the Court observed in another case:

> *Griggs* was rightly concerned that childhood deficiencies in the education and background of minority citizens resulting from forces beyond their control not be allowed to work a cumulative and invidious burden on such citizens for the remainder of their lives.[13]

Griggs brought about many new opportunities for minorities. Once paper-and-pencil tests and other qualifications that could not be shown to be related to job performance were dropped or reversed, minority applicants gained access to jobs as police officers, firefighters, over-the-road truckers, and a multiplicity of white-collar occupations.

Congress had been presented with a real opportunity to change the *Griggs* interpretation when it made major revisions to Title VII in 1972. Yet Congress left the law intact amid strong indications that many supported its approach. But this did not deter a bare 5–4 majority in *Wards Cove* from undermining *Griggs*. First, the Court said that, even after the establishment of adverse impact, the burden of persuasion with regard to the legitimacy of the business practice still resided with the plaintiff. Second, the majority said that business necessity did not mean that the practice must "be 'essential' or 'indispensable' to the employer's business for it to pass muster."[14] Thus the rule of *Griggs* was changed from business necessity to business convenience.

A second decision in 1989, *Patterson v. McClean Credit Union*, did much to rescind the promise of enforcing a post–Civil War statute that gave minorities the same right as white persons to make and enforce contracts.[15] While the statute had been eviscerated by post-Reconstruction decisions that refused to apply it to private discriminators, the Warren and Burger Courts had restored it to its original purpose by finding violations against realtors and private schools that engaged in discrimination.

In the *Patterson* case, Mrs. Patterson claimed she was verbally abused at her job as a bank teller because of her race. Justice Kennedy, writing for a 5–4 majority, rejected the claim, saying that on its face the statute covered only the making and enforcement of contracts and not their terms and conditions. In his dissent Justice Brennan pointed to legislative history that included concerns about freed slaves who were being whipped on the job. He also noted that if Mrs. Patterson had been explicitly advised that she could have the job but would be racially abused, she would not have the same rights as whites.

In 1991, after a two-year struggle, Congress revised the Court's interpretations of the law in *Wards Cove* and *Patterson*. In the process, Congress also reversed five other 1989 Court decisions that erected barriers to enforcement of federal fair employment.[16] President George H. W. Bush had threatened to veto the bill as favoring "quotas" but backed down when Republican senators said they might not vote to sustain his veto. They were concerned about both the growing influence of African Americans in elections and the danger of being viewed as outside the consensus favoring equality of opportunity.

This rebuke by Congress in the 1991 Civil Rights Act had little impact on the Rehnquist Court's determination to curb the application of civil rights laws. In the *Bakke* case in 1978, the Burger Court had left broad scope for race-conscious affirmative action policies as long as they were carefully crafted for remedial purposes or to further goals of achieving diversity.[17] But in striking down in 1995 the application of a federal program designed to promote affirmative action, the Rehnquist 5–4 majority in *Adarand Contractors v. Pena* held that, in order to pass constitutional muster, race-conscious programs designed for a remedial purpose must meet the same exacting standards of judicial review as those designed to subjugate minorities.[18] In the aftermath of *Adarand*, the Court left in place lower-court decisions aggressively attacking affirmative action, including a Fifth Circuit decision holding that Justice Powell's opinion in *Bakke* was "not binding precedent" and that discrimination lower down in the University of Texas's public education system was no justification for affirmative action at the university's law school.[19]

The *Hopwood* decision not only sought to divorce "societal" discrimination from government discrimination but to so compartmentalize government discrimination that one department or agency could not be held accountable for remedying wrongs committed by another. This approach was clearly inconsistent with the Warren Court's historic decision in the Little Rock case treating the state of Arkansas as a single entity in order to effectuate *Brown*.[20] It was also in direct conflict with the pragmatic philosophy of *Griggs* and its progeny that practices that disadvantaged children should "not be allowed to work a cumulative and invidious burden" on them for the rest of their lives.

But this new approach fit neatly with Rehnquist's view that private and public discrimination could be separated by a bright line and that the latter could and should be compartmentalized, sliced, and diced so as to limit government's duty to afford a remedy.[21]

With enactment of the Voting Rights Act of 1965, Congress and the Johnson administration took effective action to end century-old devices that disenfranchised black people in the South. Thereafter the major challenge became finding ways to deal with the myriad electoral practices that diluted the influence of newly enfranchised black voters. One classic device was electing candidates for office at large rather than through districts in which black voters would have the ability to elect one or more candidates of their choice.

When a 1980 decision of the Burger Court required proof that the dilution was intentional, it seemed that many such practices would survive judicial challenge.[22] To overcome the effects of that decision, when Congress in 1982 enacted an extension of the Voting Rights Act, it dispensed with the need to prove intent, stating that it was enough to show that the practice at issue had the effect of diluting minority votes.

In a series of cases beginning in 1993, however, the Rehnquist majority has whittled down the protections of the act. The key decision came in 1993 in *Shaw v. Reno*, in which white voters challenged a North Carolina reapportionment plan that, for the first time since Reconstruction, included two majority black congressional districts.[23] In the past, the Rehnquist majority had applied increasingly rigorous rules of standing to bar minorities from access to federal courts. In *Shaw*, however, the majority ignored those rules and allowed the white plaintiffs to pursue their case even though they did not claim that their ability to participate had been impaired or their votes diluted. Having decided that such claims would be heard by the federal courts, the majority insisted (and continues to insist) that race (i.e., the aggregation of black voters to elect a black candidate) not be the "predominant concern" over political and other factors traditionally used in the drawing of lines.

Districting cases like *Shaw v. Reno* are not free from complexity. The ultimate objective of the Voting Rights Act is to deal with practices that dilute the influence of minority voters. While districting that distributes black citizens among many districts may have a dilutive effect, so may practices that pack many black voters into a single district. The latter practices may ensure the election of a black candidate in a particular district, but they may rob voters of potential significant influence in surrounding areas. It is important that a fair balance be struck.

The influence of minority voters has indeed increased significantly since the 1982 extension of the Voting Rights Act, but the 2000 election—where many African-American and Latino voters were faced with inferior voting equipment, long lines at the polls, improper purges, and other problems—demonstrates the long distance that remains to be traveled to reach equal voting opportunity. For more than six decades during the last century, the Court, even during its years of countenancing segregation, was the strongest proponent of enforcing the Fourteenth and Fifteenth Amendments to eliminate discrimination in the electoral process. Now, as long as a Rehnquist majority prevails, the Court is more likely to be an impediment than an ally in overcoming remaining obstacles.

In the 1990s the Rehnquist Court turned its attention to the question of when federal court orders for school desegregation should be terminated, releasing states of the obligation to assist the desegregation process and leaving school districts free to pursue their own systems of student assignment.

During the Burger years, the Court had indicated that the test for government officials claiming to have eliminated their racially dual systems and reached "unitary" status would be rigorous. They would have to demonstrate that they had abolished both the trappings of segregation, such as one-race schools, and the vestiges of the segregated system. What were those vestiges? In the 1971 *Swann* case, the Court had found that planned segregation of schools led to segregated housing, with families clustering in residential patterns around schools that accepted their children.[24] And in *Milliken II* in 1977, a unanimous Court reinforced the findings of *Brown* concerning the damage done by segregation and concluded:

> Pupil assignment [for desegregation] alone does not automatically remedy the impact of previous, unlawful educational isolation; the consequences linger and can be dealt with only by independent measures.[25]

The language of *Swann* suggests that as long as substantial housing segregation persists and a return to "neighborhood schools" would mean a return to racial segregation, the vestiges of the old order remain and unitary status has not been attained. The language of *Milliken II* suggests that time is needed for both desegregation and state-financed school improvement measures to narrow the gap between black and white student achievement.

But in three cases in the 1990s, the Rehnquist majority gave short shrift to such considerations, indicating an impatience to return schools to local control.[26] In a 1992 case, *Freeman v. Pitts*, Justice Kennedy wrote for the majority that residential segregation might be a product more of differing preferences by blacks and whites on the racial composition of neighborhoods where they seek to locate than of state-fostered segregation. In the 1995 *Missouri v. Jenkins* case, the Rehnquist majority reached out to take on unitary issues that had not been litigated in the lower courts. Again, Chief Justice Rehnquist sounded his familiar theme of "incremental effect." Conceding that the district court had previously found that "segregation has caused a systemwide reduction in achievement in the schools [of Kansas City]," he replied that the lower court "never has identified the incremental effect that segregation has had on minority student achievement or the specific goals of the quality education programs."

In the Rehnquist worldview racial inequality is the "natural condition" and efforts to ameliorate it through government remedies demand strict proof that government created the inequality.

In his dissent in the 1991 *Dowell* case, Justice Marshall said that "a desegregation decree cannot be lifted so long as conditions likely to inflict the stigmatic injury in *Brown I* persist and there remain feasible methods of eliminating such conditions." For Rehnquist, however, it is clear that the stigma is gone (if it ever existed) and that we live in a color-blind society in which no special efforts are needed to redress past racial wrongs.

Beginning in 2000, the Rehnquist majority grew bolder both in its assault on congressional powers and in its efforts to curb judicial authority to provide civil rights remedies.

Until recently, the constitutional power of Congress to regulate commerce under Article I, Section 8 (a power whose broad reach had been affirmed in many New Deal–era cases), seemed a sturdy basis for dealing with many forms of discrimination by private institutions. In 1964, the Commerce Clause was a major predicate for those sections of the Civil Rights Act that barred discrimination in places of public accommodation and by private employers.

But in May 2000, a 5–4 majority informed the nation in *United States v. Morrison* that the clause did not allow Congress to provide a remedy to protect women against domestic violence because it did not extend to matters that are "non-economic in nature."[27] In doing so, the five justices spurned the traditional deference the Court gives to Congress, which had made extensive findings about the tangible effects of violence against women, calculating costs of about $3 billion in one year alone. Nor was the majority impressed by the fact that thirty-six states supported the Violence against Women Act before the Court.

Similarly, while the Eleventh Amendment affords states a "sovereign immunity" defense in some situations, students of the Constitution long had considered that these situations were very limited and did not preclude suits against states to enforce obligations imposed by federal statutes. Yet in *Kimel v. Florida Board of Regents*, the same five-member majority ruled that Congress could not invoke its explicit constitutional power to enforce the Fourteenth Amendment and override sovereign immunity so that state employees who had been victims of age discrimination could seek damages from their own state for the violation of federal law.[28] Age discrimination, the majority opined, is not as serious a matter as race and gender discrimination. Consequently, the Age Discrimination in Employment Act failed a test of "congruence and proportionality," a newly invented construct of the Rehnquist majority. Later the same majority used sovereign immunity to bar suits based on violation of the rights of persons with disabilities.[29] It remains to be seen whether the Spending Clause, which has provided a basis for suits against state agencies that receive federal money, will also be narrowed.

Finally, in April 2001, the Rehnquist majority renewed its war against discrimination cases that were based on disproportionate racial impact rather than intent. In 1964, Congress passed Title VI of the Civil Rights Act requiring nondiscrimination in programs and activities receiving federal funds. While the Supreme Court subsequently ruled that Title VI itself reached only acts of deliberate discrimination, it also allowed federal departments and agencies to go further in implementing regulations. In the very first regulation issued after enactment, the Justice Department in 1964 forbade fund recipients from utilizing "criteria or methods of administration which have the effect of subjecting individuals to discrimination."

Since the Court had explicitly ruled that individuals suffering discrimination under Title VI could seek redress in the federal courts, it was widely assumed that private individuals could also bring actions for violations of the regulations that simply implemented Title VI. But in April 2001, the Rehnquist majority ruled otherwise, rejecting a suit brought by a Latino resident of Alabama who was denied the opportunity to take an exam for a driver's license in Spanish.[30] While the Title VI regulations can still be enforced by federal agencies, there is no realistic prospect that the many violations that occur can be redressed even by federal officials more committed to civil rights than the Bush administration.

The consequences of this ruling are sweeping. Title VI regulations have been employed to help minorities gain more equal access to public transportation, to ensure that they are not relegated to dead-end classes for the mentally retarded based on faulty tests, and to deal with myriad other discriminatory practices. All are now in jeopardy.

Since discriminatory practices these days are rarely accompanied by neon signs advertising their invidious intent, the Court has made the struggle for equal opportunity more difficult for hundreds of thousands of people.

In writing the Court's opinion in *Brown*, Earl Warren forsook conventional constitutional analysis in a plea for public understanding of the flesh-and-blood realities facing the Court. "Look," he appeared to be saying to people in the South, "we know we are disturbing a set of mores and traditions that are deeply embedded in your life, but we must do so because segregation is damaging the lives and opportunities of little children."[31]

When William Brennan became a dominant force on the Court in the late 1960s and the 1970s, perhaps in response to attacks on the *Brown* opinion, he made more use of traditional legal principles in his decisions. So, in *Keyes*, he relied on rebuttable presumptions to derive the need for a systemwide desegregation remedy from a proven violation that affected only part of a district. But Brennan's presumptions were "common sense" and he explained why it was reasonable to infer that school authorities who deliberately segregated some schools should be held responsible for curing segregation that existed at others. He also was acutely aware of a judge's role in balancing competing interests and insisted that in examining challenges to affirmative action policies to benefit minorities, the court must determine whether the interests of whites are "unduly trammeled."

In contrast, a concern for flesh-and-blood realities, for common-sense analysis, and for weighing competing interests is what is absent from the arid legalisms of the Rehnquist approach. An analysis grounded in common sense and reality would not sustain Rehnquist's fanciful notion that it is possible to separate out with neat precision the consequences of persistent, unconstitutional state practices from conditions of inequity that would have existed without the unlawful practices. Sometimes the legal analysis borders on the absurd. For example, it has become accepted doctrine that racial practices that disadvantage minorities are subjected to the strictest judicial scrutiny because they are invidious and can be justified rarely, if ever. The Rehnquist Court has now extended that doctrine to hold that race-conscious efforts to *remedy* such invidious racial practices must also be subjected to strict scrutiny. So in the Rehnquist lexicon, the more severe the discrimination, the less one can do to remedy it.

Nor can the work of the Rehnquist majority be justified in the conventional parlance still used to praise conservative judges. It is not "strict constructionist," as witness the radical departure in *Kimel* from both the text and history of the Eleventh Amendment to erect new state sovereignty barriers to remedies for discrimination. It is not "respectful of precedent," as witness the readiness of the Court to overturn years of expansive interpretation of the Commerce Clause. And it most certainly does not exhibit "judicial restraint," as is apparent in the Court's willingness to disregard congressional findings and to exalt its own wisdom over that of any other branch of government.

Most of all, the Rehnquist majority seems willfully ignorant of the realities of life for many poor and struggling people. That was evident in a 5–4 decision of the Court in March 2002 in the case of *Hoffman Plastics Compounds v. National Labor Relations Board*.[32] The issue was whether to uphold an award of back pay by the NLRB to an unauthorized alien who had been illegally discharged by his employer for engaging in union activity. There was no specific provision in either the labor laws or the immigration laws prohibiting such awards and it appeared uncontested that back pay awards were one of the most effective ways of deterring illegal labor practices.

But Chief Justice Rehnquist, writing for the majority, said that "awarding back pay in a case like this not only trivializes the immigration laws, it also condones and encourages future violations." In dissent, Justice Stephen Breyer, with a firmer grasp on the real world where employers hire people they know or suspect are illegal aliens to secure cheap labor, wrote that "to *deny* the Board the power to award back pay" might increase the strength of "the magnetic force" that pulls illegal immigrants to the United States by lowering the cost to the employer of labor law violations (emphasis in original).

The decision stands in stark contrast to *Plyler v. Doe* two decades earlier, in which the Court struck down a Texas law barring the children of undocumented aliens from public schools.[33] Against similar claims that providing a free public education would encourage illegal immigration, Justice Brennan wrote that the law

> imposes a lifetime hardship on a discrete class of children not accountable for their disability status. The stigma of illiteracy will mark them for the rest of their lives. By denying these children a basic education, we deny them the ability to live within the structure of our civic institutions, and foreclose any realistic possibility that they will contribute in even the smallest way to the progress of our Nation.

While public officials of all political persuasions struggle with the issues surrounding illegal immigration, few outside the Rehnquist majority believe that large numbers of illegal aliens already here will leave, and that others will be deterred from coming, because of draconian measures affecting their employment or the education of their children.

In the new millennium the nation faces important challenges: how to avert racial and ethnic tensions in an increasingly diverse society, how to provide economic opportunity in a postindustrial age to those who have faced deprivation and discrimination, and how to encourage participating citizenship for all. In its policies fostering a renewal of racial isolation in our schools and public life, and in squelching efforts of other branches of government and private institutions to offer a helping hand to those worst off, the current Court majority has become one of the "built-in headwinds" that its predecessors recognized and deplored.[34] If the Rehnquist majority (or its successor) continues on its current course, the Court will have virtually abandoned its historic role of affording remedies for "discrete and insular minorities" who cannot rely on the ordinary political processes for their protection.

The Rehnquist Revolution in
Criminal Procedure

CHARLES J. OGLETREE, JR.

The Rehnquist Court has had a tremendous impact on criminal justice issues, significantly rolling back the procedural rights of criminal defendants. This result owes much to the leadership of Chief Justice William H. Rehnquist, as can be seen in the way many of the Court's recent decisions on matters of criminal procedure were foreshadowed by his dissenting opinions prior to 1986, as associate justice. However, it would be an overgeneralization to assert that all the decisions of the Rehnquist Court have restricted the rights of criminal defendants. Rather, the current era can be seen as one of ideological tension between competing and fluid understandings of the scope of constitutional protections of a criminal defendant's procedural rights. While a criminal defendant today would certainly enjoy narrower procedural protections than sixteen years ago, there has been a certain amount of ideological back-and-forth in the Court's decisions over that period. One example of how this ideological tension has played out is in the issue of racial profiling, and the same tension will no doubt inform the Court's approach to the challenging and pressing questions of constitutional criminal procedure that arose in the aftermath of the September 11, 2001, terrorist attacks in Washington and New York.

What does it mean to talk about the jurisprudence of the Rehnquist Court? What responsibility can we attribute to the chief justice for the decisions of "his" Court? Normally, when we talk about the decisions of a particular Court, invoking the name of the presiding chief justice simply sets historical limits on the decisions we are considering. We may, in addition, attempt to discern the dominant legal philosophy characterizing the Court's decisions during his tenure. This practice has its uses: it provides neat comparisons for different periods of legal history and focuses analysis on the opinions, dissents, and concurrences in each case, rather than purely on the holding.

But the Court is, after all, composed of nine individual justices, each with his or her own legal philosophy. Furthermore, the Rehnquist Court is an extremely fractured one, reaching consistent and relatively predictable 5–4 votes along many issues, which makes it all the more difficult to talk in terms of a unitary, dominant judicial philosophy. It is with these caveats, then, that we can analyze the decisions of the Rehnquist Court as creating an identifiable corpus of criminal procedure law.

To better understand the criminal jurisprudence of the Rehnquist Court, we might consider that there are two models of criminal justice for the Court to draw upon: the *crime-control* model, which promotes deterrence and punishment of crime as the most important end of the criminal justice system, and the *due process* model, which is concerned with vindicating constitutional rights and maximizing individual freedom from government control.[1] The crime-control model permits government agents considerable discretion in pursuing criminals, requires them to submit only to a relatively formal, uniform set of rules to control that discretion, and exhibits significant confidence in the government's identification of suspects as guilty of the crime with which they are charged. By contrast, the due process model requires stricter adherence to constitutional guarantees when the government is surveilling, detaining, and searching individuals; protects those constitutional guarantees through early judicial oversight of the police to ensure that the investigative process is free from bias or error; and emphasizes the presumption of innocence and the burden of proof in determining the guilt or innocence of a suspect.

While these models are neither exhaustive nor particularly sophisticated, they are useful as a framework for understanding different approaches to constitutional criminal procedure. To appreciate how these models apply in practice, it is worth considering the general features of a police investigation and arrest. The investigation typically begins with police observation of an individual's behavior. The Fourth Amendment's prohibition of unreasonable searches and seizures ensures that the police may not arrest people without good reason—what is commonly called "probable cause." A somewhat ambiguous and loosely defined concept, probable cause generally requires that the police have a "substantial basis" for believing that a search will provide evidence that the individual is guilty of an offense. A lesser standard is imposed when the search is likely to be less than ordinarily intrusive. For example, when an officer simply wishes to stop and perhaps frisk an individual at a roadblock or an airport security checkpoint, the less onerous "reasonable suspicion" standard is used. Reasonable suspicion requires no more than some articulable reason to believe that a crime has been or will be committed.[2]

Let us imagine that an officer has reasonable suspicion to stop and search you—she has information that someone driving the same make of car as you is planning to rob a department store, and you have driven slowly past that department store five times in the last half hour. With such evidence, the officer may detain you for a brief time, ask you questions, require you to exit your car, frisk you, and look around your car for weapons. You have a limited right to walk away, and at this stage of the investigation, anything you say to the police will be voluntary. If that investigation turns up sufficient information for the officer to establish that she has probable cause to believe that you plan to rob the store—for example, she sees a fake gun and a mask on the backseat—she may arrest you, impound your car, and take the mask and gun into police custody. To conduct a further search, including a search of your home, she must obtain a warrant from a magistrate, again based on probable cause.

Once she has decided to arrest you, the officer may continue to question you only after delivering a warning of your rights. This so-called *Miranda* warning—familiar to all viewers of TV cop shows—informs you of your Fifth Amendment right to avoid self-incrimination and the right to obtain the assistance of an attorney during any questioning that takes place. These rights, however, can be waived. If you continue to talk after the warning and without your attorney—perhaps to tell the police that the mask and gun are your son's Halloween costume and that you were only looking at a particular pair of shoes in the store window—the police can use anything you say as evidence against you in a criminal trial.

The checks on the power of the police to search and seize are of relatively recent vintage. Although they are based upon, and arguably required by, the Fourth, Fifth, and Sixth Amendments, the three cases that created these protections—*Miranda v. Arizona*, *Massiah v. United States*, and *Mapp v. Ohio*—were decided by the Warren Court in the 1960s.[3] They all reflected a marked shift in the Court's attitude toward the powers of the police vis-à-vis the rights of individual citizens and attempted to give some teeth to the elements of the due process model present in the Constitution. It is in contrast to the Warren Court in particular, with its emphasis on vindicating the individual constitutional rights of criminal defendants, that the Rehnquist Court is usually presented.

There is little doubt that the Rehnquist Court is particularly conservative in the field of criminal law and has strongly endorsed the crime-control model of criminal justice. In contrast to the Warren Court, with its due process leanings, the Rehnquist Court has, as Stanley H. Friedelbaum observes, "moved decisively to rework a wide array of judicially devised components of the criminal law by directly overturning or materially eroding their value as precedents."[4]

No Court has been perfectly consistent in its application of jurisprudential models or in its ideological approach, mainly because of the fact-specific nature of many adjudications as well as shifts in majorities based on where along the ideological spectrum a particular case falls. For example, consider *Terry v. Ohio*, ironically a Warren Court decision and one of the most important contributors to the conservative erosion of the Warren Court's legacy.[5] The facts presented in *Terry* are rather like the circumstances in the typical police investigation described above. An officer noticed Terry and another man on a street corner and observed an unusual pattern of behavior, in which they "pace[d] alternately along an identical route, pausing to stare in the same store window roughly twenty-four times; . . . followed immediately by a conference between the two men on the corner" and a discussion with a third man several blocks away. Based on these observations, the police officer stopped the three men and conducted a limited search for weapons. Guns were found, which formed the basis for Terry's conviction on charges of carrying a concealed weapon. The Court found that the police officer had acted reasonably in stopping the suspects, in part because the officer conducted not a full-blown search and seizure but only a "stop and frisk" for weapons. Although the Court limited the original rationale of *Terry* to a search for weapons and required some objective justification for the stop, subsequent decisions have substantially broadened its effect. The *Terry* decision has ultimately been used to authorize pretextual stops and has resulted in an increase in racial profiling.

In fact, this use of Warren-era precedent to erode Warren-era doctrine is a feature of the Rehnquist Court's conservative jurisprudence. Instead of disputing the content of the constitutional rights available to a citizen when stopped and questioned by the police, the Rehnquist Court has simply removed the adverse procedural consequences of police breaches of those rights.

For example, in *Caplin & Drysdale, Chartered v. United States*, a criminal defendant challenged a criminal forfeiture statute because, in taking his possessions, the state had left him without the means to retain the counsel of his choice.[6] He claimed that this violated his Sixth Amendment right to counsel. The Court disagreed, noting ,that he could retain an attorney—if one would work for free—and that the Sixth Amendment did not entitle him to the attorney of his choice, only to representation by counsel. The Court did not narrow the constitutional right to counsel—it simply adopted a rule that collaterally removed the defendant's meaningful enjoyment of the right.

The use of such judge-created procedural rules to limit the meaningfulness of constitutional rights is Chief Justice Rehnquist's own contribution to the jurisprudence of the Supreme Court. Three areas of law particularly demonstrate this impact: searches and seizures under the Fourth Amendment, the Fifth Amendment's right to avoid compelled self-incrimination, and the Eighth Amendment's prohibition on cruel and unusual punishment. In each area, Rehnquist's opinions during his tenure as an associate justice, often in dissent, foreshadowed the future direction of the Court.

The Warren Court determined that the only way to prevent police officers from violating the Fourth Amendment was to adopt a rule precluding the prosecution from using any evidence obtained in an unreasonable manner—in other words, without probable cause or without a validly issued warrant. That rule—called the exclusionary rule because such evidence was excluded from consideration at trial—is deeply unpopular with proponents of the crime-control model. Chief Justice Rehnquist has been extremely critical of the Fourth Amendment's exclusionary rule and has argued in dissent that *Mapp v. Ohio*, one of the principal Warren Court precedents developing this doctrine, be overruled.[7]

Of particular importance for the Fourth Amendment is the rule that searches and seizures may ordinarily be conducted only after obtaining a warrant from an impartial magistrate based on probable cause. The strictest application of the warrant requirement was given by the Warren Court, which held that "searches conducted outside the judicial process, without prior approval by judge or magistrate, are *per se* unreasonable under the Fourth Amendment—subject only to a few specifically established and well-delineated exceptions."[8] The contrary view, and one articulated strongly by Chief Justice Rehnquist, is that if the searches are "reasonable," the warrant requirement is redundant. Thus, if a suspect consents to a search, the officer may reasonably search anywhere he believes that consent would reach, including closed containers within the area to be searched.

The chief justice's adherence to the crime-control model of criminal justice and his disapproval of the due process model can be seen in his support for eliminating the exclusionary rule. His justification was based on a central element of the crime-control model: because admission of evidence from an unconstitutional search will injure only guilty defendants, not innocent ones, any evidence seized illegally should be permitted. In dissent, Rehnquist contended that "generally a warrant is not required to seize and search any movable property [such as "clothing, a briefcase or suitcase, packages, or a vehicle"] in the possession of a person properly arrested in a public place."[9] In *Delaware v. Prouse*, again contrary to the majority's view, he would also have allowed random stops of motorists in order to check driver's licenses and registration, finding that the state had an interest in preventing unlicensed, unsafe motorists from driving.[10] He has also argued that the police may execute an arrest warrant by searching the home of a third party even absent a search warrant, exigent circumstances, or consent and that police in carrying out a search warrant may frisk all patrons in a bar even without reasonable individualized suspicion that the patrons were armed.[11] In *Dunaway v. New York*, he argued in dissent that a defendant was not "seized" where he had "voluntarily accompanied the police to the station to answer their questions" and where the police behavior "was entirely free of physical force or show of authority."[12] Finally, he would have limited the circumstances in which courts may consider excluding evidence because of police misbehavior. In *Franks v. Delaware*, the central case entitling a defendant to a hearing to exclude or "suppress" illegally obtained police evidence, he would have held that probable cause could be based on a false statement and should not trigger an evidentiary hearing.[13]

The approach to criminal justice manifested in these dissenting opinions bore fruit in the majority opinions of the Court once Rehnquist became chief justice. For example, one way of getting around the warrant requirement is for the criminal suspect to waive those rights— so police often have an incentive to induce waiver or to "encourage consent." Many people do not realize that they have a right to refuse to consent to a search, or to limit the scope of a search, pending a warrant from a magistrate. So, in the example that began this chapter, if you were the car's driver, you could have refused to let the police officer search your car, particularly the trunk, without a warrant. However, if you mistakenly thought the officer was just being polite in asking and could search your car regardless of your consent, you might allow any search suggested by the officer. Chief Justice Rehnquist has not required that police inform suspects of their right to refuse consent: "The community has a real interest in encouraging consent, for the resulting search may yield necessary evidence for the solution and prosecution of crime, evidence that may ensure that a wholly innocent person is not wrongly charged with a criminal offense." So the chief justice's argument, which is now the law, is that "if [a suspect's] consent would reasonably be understood to extend to a particular [area or thing], the Fourth Amendment provides no grounds for requiring a more explicit authorization."[14] The scope of a search is determined not by where you would have drawn the line but by where a reasonable police officer would have done so. What matters is the officer's interpretation—given police priorities in searching—of your consent.

The Rehnquist Court has extended this principle even further in the case of searches outside the home—it has crafted an "exception" to the Fourth Amendment's warrant requirement for packages in a car. In *California v. Acevedo*, the Court permitted the police to search a container located within an automobile if they have probable cause to believe it held contraband or evidence but don't have a warrant for the package or probable cause to search the vehicle as a whole.[15] This is a direct application of the crime-control model that Chief Justice Rehnquist often articulated in dissent as an associate justice.

This same conception of criminal justice informs Chief Justice Rehnquist's approach to the Fifth Amendment. As an associate justice, Rehnquist often argued in dissent that the Fifth Amendment's protection against self-incrimination was being applied too broadly. One of the fundamental aspects of the right not to incriminate oneself (the "right to silence" or "taking the Fifth") is that a jury may not draw any adverse inferences from a defendant's refusal to testify. The burden is on the government to prove its case, not on the defendant to establish his or her innocence. In his dissenting opinion in *Carter v. Kentucky*, then-Justice Rehnquist would have eliminated this presumption and have held that there is no constitutional obligation on state trial judges to give "no adverse inference" instructions to the jury.[16] And in *Doyle v. Ohio*, he would have affirmed the defendants' convictions even though the prosecutor attempted to use their post-*Miranda* silence against them at trial.[17]

Under Chief Justice Rehnquist, the Court has evinced a deep skepticism about the validity of the *Miranda* decision itself. It has, for example, virtually eliminated the requirement that the *Miranda* waiver be given knowingly and intelligently. Such a requirement ensures that a suspect knows the consequences of starting to talk—that the evidence may be used to convict him—and so embodies a standard concern of the due process model of criminal justice. In *Colorado v. Connelly*, the Court refused to find that the waiver of a suspect's *Miranda* rights and his subsequent confession were involuntary, even though the suspect suffered from hallucinations rendering him unable "to make free and rational choices" at the time of his confession.[18] Chief Justice Rehnquist's use of the crime-control model changed the scope of the inquiry; the previous standard, which inquired whether a waiver had been knowing, intelligent, and voluntary, was abandoned for an analysis of police coercion: so long as the confession was not a product of police coercion, there was neither a *Miranda* nor a voluntariness violation.

The constitutionality of *Miranda* finally came before the Court in 2000 in *Dickerson v. United States*. This case dealt with the question of whether *Miranda* was simply a set of prophylactic judge-made rules that could be overruled by an act of Congress or was instead a constitutional basis for the exclusion of evidence. For years, the Rehnquist Court had indicated that the *Miranda* warnings had no firm basis in the Constitution. Rather, the decision was often characterized as a judge-created procedural rule that could be repealed by appropriate legislation. Although Chief Justice Rehnquist had frequently characterized *Miranda* the same way, in *Dickerson*, writing for the Court, he ultimately conceded the constitutionality of the *Miranda* decision. *Dickerson* thus seems, at first glance, to be an entrenchment of the due process model and an anomaly in the general approach of the Rehnquist Court's jurisprudence.[19]

Behind the chief justice's concession, however, stands a simple fact: the Court did not need to overrule *Miranda*, because it had already eviscerated most of its protections. The Rehnquist Court has burdened the assertion of *Miranda* rights with a variety of procedural impediments. One of the most important has been the "harmless error" rule—the legal equivalent of the phrase "no harm, no foul." Originally, where the courts found that evidence had been entered erroneously, they would reverse the verdict; the result was many technical acquittals. To evade this rule, subsequent courts developed the harmless-error doctrine: as long as a defendant's case is not substantially harmed by the introduction of tainted evidence, there is no reason for a court of appeals to reverse the conviction. The Supreme Court initially applied the federal harmless-error rule only to nonconstitutional errors. Under the Rehnquist Court, however, it was extended to include constitutional errors, even those that had previously been considered so fundamental as to require automatic reversal, such as the introduction into evidence of a coerced confession.

Confession evidence is often vital to a trial. Prosecutors will often not even go to trial without confession evidence because it establishes the government's case so compellingly. Coerced confessions, however, are unconstitutional—they have, by definition, been obtained in violation of the defendant's Fifth Amendment rights. And the confession has usually been coerced in a situation in which only the police and the defendant know the facts, and the defendant has just been discredited as a reliable witness because he has effectively convicted himself. If he retracts his testimony, he can be impeached because he must either be lying to the jury now or have lied to the police when he gave his initial testimony. How could such an error ever be harmless?

Chief Justice Rehnquist has argued that the answer to that question turns on the difference between "structural" and "trial" errors. Structural errors are those that make the trial as a whole a sham, such as a biased judge or the refusal to provide defense counsel. "Trial" errors do not render the trial qualitatively unjust, according to the chief justice, and can be cured—or rendered harmless—in a variety of ways, including permitting further cross-examination or by the judge's instructing the jury to ignore the error. There is thus no need for a per se rule of reversal for trial errors. So long as the evidence does not taint the jury's decision-making process, the error is in fact harmless and, because no legal "foul" has been committed, the verdict will be allowed to stand.

Given the inability of the defense to counter such evidence, the per se rule must apply to coerced confessions as well. Trials in which the verdict is premised upon unconstitutionally obtained evidence of the defendant that cannot effectively be challenged surely suffer from a structural defect every bit as damning as having a biased judge or being refused defense counsel. It is simply not true that "the admission of an involuntary confession is a 'trial error' similar both in degree and kind to the erroneous admission of other types of evidence," as Rehnquist claims. In most cases, the defense counsel must rely almost exclusively on procedural objections to the improper admission of the evidence. The trial becomes skewed, and appellate courts cannot meaningfully apply harmless-error analysis.[20]

Chief Justice Rehnquist's approach here is another example of the crime-control model applied through a jurisprudence of "procedural narrowing." The chief justice does not change the right of a defendant to have his involuntary confession declared unconstitutional, but he does significantly narrow the number of occasions upon which that unconstitutionality will matter in practice.

Rehnquist's dissenting opinions as an associate justice also demonstrate a focus on restricting the constitutional protections established by the Eighth Amendment prohibition of cruel and unusual punishment and on limiting the scope of federal habeas corpus rules establishing a defendant's right to challenge the legal basis of his or her imprisonment.

The Eighth Amendment is particularly important because it has been used to attack the constitutionality of capital punishment. During the brief period between 1972 and 1976 during which the administration of the death penalty was often declared to violate the Eighth Amendment, Rehnquist joined the dissent in *Roberts v. Louisiana*, which argued that mandatory imposition of the death penalty does not amount to cruel and unusual punishment.[21] He also would have upheld a state statute that eliminated a "guilty without capital punishment" verdict, the effect of which was a mandatory death sentence if the defendant was found guilty. Furthermore, he would have held that imposing the death penalty for rape, or for aiding and abetting a felony during the course of which a murder is committed, or on an insane prisoner, does not violate the Eighth Amendment.[22]

Federal habeas law provides another example of the limitation of the constitutional rights of criminal defendants. Often defendants are

represented by court-appointed counsel who—due to the lack of an effective public defender program, underfunding, or inexperience—are
unprepared to mount an adequate defense of their client. As a consequence, they fail to raise important issues at time of trial. The consequences of this failure can be significant. Prior to *Wainwright v. Sykes*,
the failure to raise a legal issue waived that issue only if there was an
intentional relinquishment or abandonment of a known right or privilege.[23] For example, if the failure to raise a claim was made for tactical
reasons, the issue could not be presented on appeal or during habeas
proceedings. If the issue was dropped inadvertently, however, it could
still be raised on appeal. In *Wainwright*, Justice Rehnquist overturned
this rule and instituted a new test for habeas claims, as a result of
which a defendant can raise a new issue for the first time during a
habeas proceeding only if he can establish some overriding reason why
he did not do so before—which is extremely difficult to satisfy unless
there has been a change in the law or the state has withheld facts—and
that the failure to raise the claim actually prejudiced his case.

This restriction of access to collateral review has been extended
even further during Rehnquist's tenure as chief justice. In *Teague v.
Lane*, the justices decided an issue not briefed by the parties that drastically narrowed the scope of habeas relief.[24] The issue was, again, a
procedural one: whether a new constitutional rule could be applied in
a petition for habeas corpus. *Teague* held that when a habeas petitioner
argued for the application of a newly established rule of constitutional
criminal procedure, a federal court could not decide the matter unless
the new rule was one that would be applied retroactively. Moreover, in
Teague and subsequent decisions, the Rehnquist Court has read the
retroactive application exception very narrowly. The dramatic restriction effected by *Teague* can be seen in Justice Brennan's dissenting opinion, which lists many rights that were recognized for the first time on
habeas corpus review.[25] As James S. Liebman states, "If Warren
Burger led 'The Counter-Revolution That Wasn't,' then *Teague* reveals
William Rehnquist in the vanguard of the Thermidor that is."[26]

Despite the general focus of its decisions on restricting the procedural
rights of criminal defendants, it bears reemphasizing that the Rehn-

quist Court is not a monolithic entity. In fact, some commentators contend that the Rehnquist Court's more recent decisions have "reflect[ed] [its] efforts to refine its established conservative criminal justice doctrine."[27] The Court has handed down a number of decisions that could be characterized as falling within the due process model of criminal procedure; in just the 1999–2000 term, for example, one observer notes, "the Rehnquist Court decided in favor of individuals in cases concerning such issues as Fourth Amendment searches and seizures, Sixth Amendment ineffective assistance of counsel, ex post facto laws, Miranda warnings, and the Fifth Amendment privilege against compelled self-incrimination."[28] In these cases, in which the Court upheld a criminal defendant's constitutional rights, Chief Justice Rehnquist, however, found himself with the dissenters.

One effect of the Court's criminal policy has been to enlarge the potential for the use of racial profiling by the police. Its decisions increase the power of the police to arrest and search individuals and their automobiles for baseless, pretextual offenses. Unfortunately, the temptation for the use of racially motivated arrests and stops has proven far too great, and minorities have suffered accordingly.

Two decisions of the Rehnquist Court in 1996 and 2000 have made it particularly easy for the police to engage in racial profiling. In the first, *Whren v. United States*, the Court allowed police to stop a car and arrest the occupants for a minor traffic violation, such as turning without signaling, in order to follow up a suspicion that the occupants were engaged in something more serious.[29] Since such minor violations are very common, the decision makes it very easy for the police to stop a car just because the occupants are black or Mexican. The lower courts, following the lead of the Supreme Court, have pushed the *Whren* case to its limits. In one case, they allowed police to arrest the driver of a truck with four black occupants for not signaling when changing lanes to avoid a police car deliberately driven close to the truck; in another case, a black driver was arrested for momentarily crossing a yellow line.

In the second case, *Illinois v. Wardlow*, a black man in "an area known for heavy narcotics trafficking"—a description of many African-American and Hispanic neighborhoods in the United States—looked in the direction of patrolling police officers and ran away.[30] That was all, but it was enough for a 5–4 majority of the Court, in an opinion by Chief Justice Rehnquist, to allow the police to stop and frisk the man. Rehnquist called the man's action "unprovoked flight." As the dissenters pointed out, however, "among some citizens, particularly minorities and those residing in high crime areas, there is also the possibility that the fleeing person is entirely innocent, but, with or without justification, believes that contact with the police can itself be dangerous, apart from any criminal activity associated with the officers' sudden presence. For such a person, unprovoked flight is neither 'aberrant' nor 'abnormal.' "

Data demonstrate that racial profiling is not an illusory concern. Racial profiling and pretextual traffic stops, enabled by the *Terry* decision and facilitated by *Whren* and *Wardlow*, have become so endemic in many cities and on many highways that the offense has been termed "Driving While Black." The ACLU recently reported that almost 73 percent of motorists stopped and searched on I-95 in Maryland in 1996 were black, even though black violators made up less than 17 percent of observed traffic violators.[31] A review of police videotapes of stops by a Florida drug squad showed that black and Hispanic motorists made up 70 percent of the stops and 80 percent of vehicle searches on the Florida Turnpike; only nine of the more than one thousand recorded stops resulted in traffic citations, despite a Florida Supreme Court decision that allows traffic stops only for legitimate traffic violations.[32]

Perhaps the most insidious application of racial profiling occurs when all members of a certain race are considered suspects for a crime committed by a person of color. In 1988, during a police hunt for a rapist known as the "Central City Stalker," described as an African-American man in his early twenties with a mustache, 5'6" to 5'8", weighing between 120 and 140 pounds, the police stopped and frisked several hundred men and arrested sixty more simply because they were African American.[33]

In 1992, Oneonta College in upstate New York gave the names of 125 black students, its entire black male student body, to police officers investigating the attempted rape of an elderly white woman who alleged her assailant was a young black man.[34] Thirty-seven of the students who were stopped and questioned by the police sued the city, and the lower courts denied their claims. Perhaps not surprisingly, the Supreme Court declined to review that decision.

After the September 11 terrorist attacks, many persons appearing to be of Arab descent or of the Muslim faith were treated as suspects by the government and by individual Americans. As of October 13, 2001, U.S. authorities had arrested or detained 698 people.[35] As of October 2, 2001, the Council on American-Islamic Relations had received 785 reports of anti-Muslim incidents.[36]

Laws have been proposed that would authorize the police and the federal government to restrict criminal procedure protections, beyond that which would normally be constitutional, in cases where a criminal investigation involves suspected terrorism. The Supreme Court's approach to the constitutionality of these proposed laws, as well as to the persistent and widespread practice of racial profiling of racial and ethnic minorities, will depend on whether it follows the dominant thread of the Rehnquist Court's decisions or some of the recent cases protecting constitutional rights.

No Rights of Prisoners

WILLIAM E. HELLERSTEIN

For much of America's history, prisoners had no rights to speak of. Even after slavery had been abolished, courts spoke of prisoners as slaves of the state, and well into the twentieth century courts adhered to a hands-off policy concerning prisoner complaints about their treatment. Between 1956 and 1969, however, the Warren Court produced a constitutional revolution in criminal procedure that extended to state criminal defendants almost all the procedural protections of the Bill of Rights. Although only a few of the Warren Court's decisions addressed the rights of prisoners as such, its concern with due process of law and equal protection created a much wider sensitivity to the rights of prisoners that was not easily cabined.[1] Thus, as the Warren Court era drew to a close, the lower federal courts began to display a considerable and expanding receptivity to inmate grievances, especially those arising due to the living conditions and disciplinary practices in some of the country's most notorious prison systems.[2] These developments were accompanied by prison disturbances and several bloody prison riots, including the one in September 1971 at New York's Attica State Prison that took the lives of forty-three people.

Keeping pace with these events, there emanated within a short period of time from the newly constituted Supreme Court, under Chief Justice Warren Earl Burger, a host of decisions involving prisoners' rights to freedom of religion, freedom of speech, procedural due process, and adequate medical care.[3] Although the Burger Court subsequently reined in the thrust of some of its earlier rulings, its first years remain the high-water mark for prisoners' rights.

The Rehnquist Court, in contrast, has had a unique two-pronged negative effect on prisoners' rights. First, through its own jurisprudence, it has cut back significantly on the progressive rulings of the Burger Court, with some exceptions. Second, and perhaps with greater lethal effect, its jurisprudence has carried an implicit message that prisoners' rights are fair game for further evisceration, a message that Congress was quick to embrace in the highly restrictive Prison Litigation Reform Act of 1996.[4] Although some Rehnquist Court decisions have been favorable to prisoners, in virtually every major segment of prisoners' rights jurisprudence the Court's impact has been devastating. Here I will deal with four of these areas: freedom of speech and religion, due process, access to the courts, and inhumane treatment.

Three of the Rehnquist Court's earliest prisoners' rights cases involved the First Amendment's free speech and free exercise of religion clauses, and the Court left little doubt as to its hostility to such claims. A Missouri prison regulation restricted the rights of inmates to correspond with inmates in other penal institutions. The lower courts, applying the strict scrutiny standard normally attendant upon free-speech cases and following Burger Court precedent, had declared the regulation unconstitutional because it was more restrictive than necessary to meet the prison's security concerns.

In the Rehnquist Court this traditional speech standard was abandoned. Writing for a 5–4 majority in *Turner v. Safley*, Justice Sandra Day O'Connor declared that "when a prison regulation impinges on inmates' constitutional rights, the regulation is valid if it is reasonably related to legitimate penological interests." She added, "In our view, such a standard is necessary if 'prison administrators, . . . and not the courts [are] to make the difficult judgments concerning institutional operations.' "[5]

Almost sixty years ago, in his dissent in the infamous Japanese internment case, Justice Robert H. Jackson warned that a principle as "elastic and deferential" as whether official conduct is reasonable can lie "about like a loaded weapon ready for the hand of any authority that can bring forth a plausible claim of an urgent need. Every repetition imbeds that principle more deeply into our law and thinking and expands to its new purposes."[6] The decision in *Turner* bears out Jackson's admonitions, for as Justice John Paul Stevens—joined in dissent by Justices William J. Brennan, Thurgood Marshall, and Harry Blackmun—pointed out, an "open-ended reasonableness standard makes it much too easy to uphold restrictions on prisoners' First Amendment rights on the basis of administrative concerns and speculation about possible security risks rather than on the basis of evidence that the restrictions are needed to further an important governmental interest."

Just two years later, in *Thornburgh v. Abbott*, Justice Stevens's fears were realized. Applying the *Turner* standard, the Court allowed prison officials to reject a publication sent to an inmate "if it is detrimental to the security, good order, or discipline of the institution or if it might facilitate criminal activity."[7] The feeble protection provided by the "reasonableness" standard applied by the Court in *Thornburgh* was apparent on the face of the trial record, for many of the rejected publications criticized prison conditions or presented points of view that prison administrators simply did not like. There was no evidence that the particular incoming publications, some of which had been delivered to inmates in other prisons, had ever caused a disciplinary or security problem.

With *Turner*'s highly deferential "reasonableness" standard firmly embedded in the Court's First Amendment prison jurisprudence, a prison inmate's assertion of a right to provide legal assistance to other inmates stood no chance of success. In *Shaw v. Murphy*, Justice Clarence Thomas, writing for a unanimous Court, framed the issue as "whether *Turner* permits an *increase* in constitutional protection whenever a prisoner's communication includes legal advice" (emphasis added). He concluded that it does not because the "*Turner* factors concern only the relationship between the asserted penological interests and the prison regulation," and affording "First Amendment protection for inmate legal advice would undermine prison officials' ability to address the 'complex and intractable' problems of prison administration."[8]

Religious freedom fared no better, and again the contrast with the Burger Court is marked. In 1972, in *Cruz v. Beto*, the Burger Court held that a Buddhist was entitled to a reasonable opportunity to pursue his Buddhist faith comparable to that offered prisoners who adhered to more conventional religious precepts.[9] A harbinger of what the future might hold was the lone dissent by the Court's new associate justice, William H. Rehnquist. He severely criticized the majority for being insufficiently deferential to the administrative discretion of prison officials and denounced the Court's liberal construction of *pro se* prisoner complaints, those filed by prisoners themselves. In his view, prisoners cared less about the merits of their case than they did about obtaining "a short sabbatical to the nearest federal courthouse."

Within a year of Rehnquist's confirmation as chief justice in 1986, a different approach to prisoners' rights became apparent. In *O'Lone v. Estate of Shabazz*, decided in 1987, a bitterly divided Court upheld prison policies that prevented Muslim prisoners on work detail from attending Jumu'ah, a weekly Muslim congregational service commanded by the Koran.[10] Rehnquist, writing for the five-member majority, conceded that the prisoners' sincerely held religious beliefs compelled attendance at Jumu'ah. Nonetheless, he found that the lower court had erred in placing the burden on prison officials to show that there existed no less restrictive ways to meet prison needs. In putting that burden on the prison officials, declared Rehnquist, the lower court had failed to show the respect and deference the Constitution allows for the judgment of prison administrators.

Following *O'Lone*, federal courts have allowed prison officials asserting debatable security concerns or merely administrative inconvenience to prohibit inmates from wearing head coverings required by their religions, to prohibit possession of rosaries, to deny religious dietary restrictions, and to require the cutting of hair or the shaving of beards in contravention of the legitimate precepts of the inmates' religions.[11]

Life in prison is hard, even if served without incident. But such uneventful prison time is rare, and there are many things that prison officials can do that make life in prison even harder. To prevent the arbitrary imposition of prison sanctions and other officially imposed hardships, the Burger Court gave a broad interpretation to the Due Process Clause of the Fourteenth Amendment that a state shall not "deprive any person of life, liberty, or property without due process of law." It focused on either the severity of the deprivation or whether state rules governing the imposition of the deprivation gave the prisoner certain rights.[12] In *Wolff v. McDonnell* (1974), for example, the Court held that inmates could not be punished without a fair hearing for infractions of prison rules that resulted in the deprivation of good time credit, including notice of the charges, an opportunity to be heard and to present evidence, and a written statement of reasons for the decision reached.[13] Later cases, which involved decisions to assign prisoners to harsher prisons or to administrative segregation units, focused on whether the state had established criteria or limited discretion in the matter. The result was to give prisoners some procedural protections even as to the denial of relatively small freedoms or privileges.

In 1995, in *Sandin v. Conner*, these gains were lost.[14] A five-member majority led by Chief Justice Rehnquist greatly reduced a prisoner's right to a fair decision-making process by holding that when a prisoner was sentenced to punitive segregation he or she did not have a "liberty interest," an interest worthy of protection by due process. This decision represented a sea change in the Court's jurisprudence. Prisoners, unlike everyone else seeking due process of law, must now plead and prove that they have suffered an "*atypical* and *significant* hardship . . . in relation to the ordinary incidents of prison life*"* (emphasis added). Prison litigation is different from other due process litigation, argued Rehnquist. Prison administrators need freedom to run secure prisons, and permitting them to punish inmates in ways that are not "atypical" or do not constitute "significant hardships" allows them the necessary flexibility.

As the impact of *Sandin v. Conner* continues to unfold, two consequences already are known. Prisoners can be sent to punitive segregation units regardless of a state's statutory law or regulations, without justification and even vindictively, without recourse to federal court because they have not suffered an "atypical" or "significant hardship."

Second, the decision has produced substantial confusion as federal judges try to figure out the meaning of those terms. Judging by the plethora of cases that still abound, all that the Court seems to have achieved is simply a reduction in the quantum of due process to which a prisoner is entitled.

A core principle of both the Warren and Burger Courts was that a prisoner had a right of access to the courts. Building on the 1969 Warren Court decision in *Johnson v. Avery* that prison officials could not interfere with a prisoner's right to prepare legal documents, in 1977 the Burger Court ruled in *Bounds v. Smith* that this included an affirmative right either to an adequate law library or to legal services to prepare legal documents.[15] In *Lewis v. Casey* in 1996, however, the Rehnquist Court seized the occasion to level a broadside against a prisoner's right to litigate in federal court.[16]

In *Lewis*, twenty-two inmates from Arizona prisons complained that Arizona's prison law libraries were inadequate to afford them access to the courts to which they were entitled. Their complaints included the inadequate training of library staff, insufficiently updated materials, and lack of assistance for illiterate or non-English-speaking inmates. After a three-month trial, the district court accepted their claims and appointed a special master to hold a hearing and draft an injunction that set forth standards and procedures for Arizona's prison law libraries.

All nine Supreme Court justices agreed that the injunction issued by the district court was overly broad. Rather than remand the case, however, Justice Antonin Scalia, for a five-member majority, complained about overuse of federal equitable power and the excessive reliance by federal judges on special masters, and he underscored the need for federal judges to defer to prison administrators and to be attentive to principles of federalism and the separation of powers. In the course of his opinion, Justice Scalia declared that prisoners did not have an abstract, freestanding right to a law library or legal assistance. To establish a constitutional violation, he said, an inmate must demonstrate that he or she suffered an actual injury brought about by shortcomings in the prison library or legal assistance program that have hindered, or are presently hindering, his efforts to pursue a nonfrivolous legal claim.

The conservative majority did not stop there. It had to dispose of affirmative language in the *Bounds* case that prison authorities must also enable a prisoner to determine the legitimacy of his grievances and to litigate effectively in court. It accomplished this simply by asserting that those principles had no antecedents in the Court's pre-*Bounds* cases and therefore should now be disclaimed. And to round out its circumscription of a prisoner's right of access to the courts, Justice Scalia added that *Bounds* also does not guarantee inmates the wherewithal to file any and every type of legal claim but requires only that they be provided with the tools to attack their sentences, directly or collaterally, and to challenge the conditions of their confinement. Insofar as a prisoner might be rendered unable to research or receive legal assistance with respect to other matters of importance, such as his or her parental or marital status, this language effectively imposes a form of civil death on a prisoner, a throwback to the days when states enacted civil death statutes.

Given the Rehnquist Court's diminution of prisoners' speech and religious rights, due process, and access to the courts, the Eighth Amendment's Cruel and Unusual Punishment Clause has taken on increasing importance as a bar to inhumane treatment. With but a few exceptions, however, the Court has rendered it more difficult for prisoners to seek redress under that amendment as well.

In 1976, the Burger Court's decision in *Estelle v. Gamble* made it possible for prisoners to win damages or obtain injunctive relief if prison officials were "deliberately indifferent" to their medical needs.[17] In *Hutto v. Finney*, decided two years later, the Court held that extensive confinement in an Arkansas prison's isolation unit constituted cruel and unusual punishment in light of the brutal conditions in that unit.[18] Because the conditions were so inhumane, the meaning of "deliberate indifference" was not an issue. Both decisions were of cardinal importance because the principles they announced became the foundation for lower federal court rulings that required prison officials to provide prisoners with basic human needs such as adequate food, clothing, shelter, and physical safety, including suicide-prevention procedures.

In *Wilson v. Seiter* the Rehnquist Court, in a majority opinion by Justice Scalia, turned the silk purse victory by prisoners in *Estelle v. Gamble* into a sow's ear.[19] Deliberate indifference, which requires proof of culpable intent, may be appropriate for measuring a discrete instance of the denial of medical care, as was the case in *Estelle*, but it is not meaningful to talk of the intent of prison officials when overall prison conditions are at issue. In *Wilson*, the Court treated them the same.

Wilson, an Ohio prison inmate, invoked the Cruel and Unusual Punishment Clause to challenge overcrowding, excessive noise, inadequate ventilation, unsanitary dining facilities and food preparation, and housing with mentally and physically ill inmates. Ignoring prior decisions that it was the objective nature of the conditions that determined whether they amounted to cruel and unusual punishment, the Court ruled that the prisoner must show that prison officials deliberately intended to create these conditions or were "deliberately indifferent" to their existence. But intent is often impossible to prove, especially where prison conditions are involved, for as the dissenters pointed out, "inhumane prison conditions often are the result of cumulative actions and inactions by numerous officials inside and outside a prison, sometimes over a long period of time. In those circumstances, it is far from clear whose intent should be examined."

Three years later, in *Farmer v. Brennan*, the Court explained what "deliberate indifference" meant: the prisoner has to show that prison officials actually knew the prisoner faced a substantial risk of harm and disregarded that risk by failing to take reasonable measures.[20] The result is that, as Justice Blackmun bitterly observed, if the "legislature refused to fund a prison adequately, the resulting barbaric conditions should not be immune from constitutional scrutiny simply because no prison official acted culpably."

In two Eighth Amendment rulings, the Rehnquist Court did provide prisoners with some added protection. In *Hudson v. McMillian*, the Court held that the use of excessive physical force against a prisoner can constitute cruel and unusual punishment even though the prisoner does not suffer serious injury.[21] At his Senate confirmation hearings the year before, Justice Clarence Thomas had testified that from his court of appeals windows he used to gaze upon lines of handcuffed prisoners and think "there but for the grace of God go I." Nevertheless, in solitary dissent he complained that "today's expansion of the Cruel and Unusual Punishment Clause beyond all bounds of history and precedent is, I suspect, yet another manifestation of the pervasive view that the Federal Constitution must address all ills in our society." He again dissented the following year, this time with Justice Scalia, when the Court in *Helling v. McKinney* allowed a Nevada prisoner to try to prove his claim that prison officials, with deliberate indifference, had exposed him to levels of tobacco smoke from other prisoners that posed an unreasonable risk to his health in violation of the Eighth Amendment.[22]

In 1996, Congress passed the Prison Litigation Reform Act (PLRA), which drastically curtails a prisoner's right to improve his conditions of confinement. The act includes significant limitations on the ability of prisoners to proceed without paying fees and on the award of attorneys' fees, thereby reducing prison inmates' ability to interest lawyers in their cases. In addition, the PLRA bars prisoners from bringing damages lawsuits for mental or emotional injuries "without a prior showing of physical injury." As recently interpreted by the Rehnquist Court in *Booth v. Churner*, the act also requires prisoners to exhaust administrative remedies, even when they are suing only for damages, a remedy that prison officials have no authority to provide.[23]

Furthermore, the act significantly circumscribes a federal court's remedial powers. It provides that prospective relief with respect to prison conditions shall not be granted "unless the court finds that such relief is narrowly drawn, extends no further than necessary to correct the violations of the Federal right, and is the least intrusive means necessary to correct violation of the Federal right." Courts are instructed not to construe the act "to order the construction of prisons or the raising of taxes, or to repeal or detract from otherwise applicable limitations on the remedial powers of courts." The act also restricts severely the effects of consent judgments, a large number of which are the result of settlements agreed upon by the parties rather than fully litigated cases.

For many years, federal courts have ordered prisoners released in order to remedy severe overcrowding. The act now explicitly limits this authority to cases in which a court must have previously ordered less intrusive relief that failed to remedy the situation. Also, these orders can now be issued only by three-judge district courts after a finding by "clear and convincing" evidence—rather than merely a preponderance—that "crowding is the primary cause of the violation of a Federal right and no other relief will remedy the violation of the Federal right." Finally, the act makes it much easier for prison officials to terminate injunctive relief obtained by prisoners and to even obtain a stay of such relief by simply filing a motion to terminate.

Under our Constitution's structured separation of powers, each branch of government is normally deemed responsible for its own actions. But the question can be asked whether the Prison Litigation Reform Act, whose draconian effect on the rights of prisoners is still unfolding, would have become law had the Rehnquist Court stood more firmly in defense of principles laid down by decisions of the Warren and Burger Courts. The question suggests at least two possible answers. On the one hand, Congress has every right to attempt to override a decision or a line of decisions of the Court that it disagrees with, as it did unsuccessfully when it legislatively sought to supersede the Court's landmark ruling in *Miranda v. Arizona*, an effort that was rebuffed by the Court in *Dickerson v. United States*.[24] On the other hand, Congress can proceed not only in a direction that it believes fits comfortably within the Court's jurisprudence but also where there is room for it to move beyond where the Court has gone. With respect to prisoners' rights, proving the existence of a direct causal link between the Rehnquist Court's decisions and the enactment of the Prison Litigation Reform Act may be difficult. It seems very likely, however, that those decisions, and perhaps even more importantly their language, mostly in dicta, in which the Court either trivialized or minimized the claims of prisoners, contributed significantly to a climate in which Congress felt exceptionally secure in its own programmatic savaging of a prisoner's right to redress in the federal courts.

Speculation on the future direction of the Supreme Court's jurisprudence in a particular area can often be a fool's game. But such speculation with regard to the Rehnquist Court's prisoners' rights jurisprudence incurs but slight risk. Without any changes in its membership, the Court will continue to be grudging in its willingness to value prisoners' concerns over prison officials' ability to run their institutions without interference from federal courts. The Court will probably remain protective of inmates when they are subjected to physical harm, as several of the Eighth Amendment cases suggest. But in virtually all other aspects of prison life, new ground will not be broken on behalf of prisoners; rather, prisoners will have their hands full merely retaining whatever gains have been secured. The Prison Litigation Reform Act undoubtedly will prevent many types of cases from even being heard in federal courts, let alone the Supreme Court.

The prisoners' rights "revolution," if it can even be called that, has been over for some time. To the extent that society was led to believe that it was all about whether a prisoner had a constitutional right to "chunky" rather than "smooth" peanut butter, the revolution had no chance. One can only hope that we are not on our way back to the bread-and-water stage.

Capital Punishment:

Accelerating the Dance with Death

STEPHEN BRIGHT

> Having virtually conceded that both fairness and rationality cannot be achieved in the administration of the death penalty, the Court has chosen to deregulate the entire enterprise, replacing, it would seem, substantive constitutional requirements with mere aesthetics, and abdicating its statutorily and constitutionally imposed duty to provide meaningful judicial oversight to the administration of death by the States. . . . The path the Court has chosen lessens us all.
> —Justice Harry A. Blackmun[1]

The Rehnquist Court has made it easier for states to carry out executions no matter how incompetent the lawyer appointed to defend the accused, no matter how clear the racial discrimination in the infliction of the death penalty, and regardless of whether the condemned was a child at the time the crime was committed, mentally ill, or even innocent. A return to states' rights has taken precedence over the vindication of the Bill of Rights, and "finality"—bringing proceedings to an end and carrying out executions—has taken precedence over fairness.

William H. Rehnquist has always been a strong supporter of the widest application and most expeditious imposition of the death penalty. In his first year on the Court, he dissented from *Furman v. Georgia* (1972), which declared the death penalty unconstitutional because of the arbitrariness and discrimination in its infliction.[2] Four years later, he voted to uphold five death penalty statutes enacted by the states in response to *Furman*. These included laws that made the death penalty mandatory for certain crimes and that the majority struck down because the laws ignored the individual circumstances of the person facing execution.[3]

In 1981, Rehnquist expressed concern over the delay caused by appellate review of capital cases and suggested that the Supreme Court review every case in order to expedite executions.[4] Although that suggestion was rejected by the other members of the Court, Rehnquist led a campaign to erect what Justice Harry Blackmun described as a "byzantine morass of arbitrary, unnecessary, and unjustifiable impediments to the vindication of federal rights."[5] Rehnquist has nevertheless prevailed. In a series of decisions—with Rehnquist often writing the majority opinion—the Court has imposed numerous barriers to federal court review of capital cases and drastically restricted the scope of that review.

Those efforts have been so successful in shredding the safety net of constitutional protections that even supporters of capital punishment have expressed grave concern about the lack of fairness and the risk of executing the innocent. Justices Blackmun and Lewis Powell, who voted with Rehnquist to uphold the death penalty in *Furman v. Georgia* in 1972 and to uphold even the mandatory laws in 1976, eventually came to the conclusion that capital punishment should be abandoned. Even Justice Sandra Day O'Connor, who joined the Court in 1981 and regularly votes to uphold death sentences and to restrict review of capital cases, noted that "serious questions were being raised about whether the death penalty is being fairly administered in this country." At the time she spoke, over ninety people sentenced to death had been exonerated since the death penalty was reinstated in 1976, leading Justice O'Connor to admit frankly, "If statistics are any indication, the system may well be allowing some innocent defendants to be executed."[6] And several years earlier, in a speech to the American Bar Association, Justice John Paul Stevens pointed out that scientific evidence had conclusively established that a number of innocent people had been sentenced to death; he suggested that one reason was the shabby legal representation appointed for defendants too poor to hire their own lawyers.

George Ryan, the Republican governor of Illinois, had supported the death penalty and other "tough on crime" measures as a member of the Illinois legislature. Early in 2000, however, he expressed dismay at his state's "shameful record of convicting innocent people and putting them on death row" and declared a moratorium on capital punishment.

By the time of these realizations, however, the Rehnquist Court had largely succeeded in giving the states free rein to carry out executions. And other governors not as concerned as Governor Ryan allow the machinery of death to chug on. Texas's busy execution chamber dispatched 152 people during the six-year period George W. Bush was governor. Brad Thomas, Florida Governor Jeb Bush's top policy adviser on capital punishment, expressed his enthusiasm for expediting executions with the comment "Bring in the witnesses, put [the defendants] on a gurney, and let's rock and roll."[7] For those who share such sentiments, the Rehnquist Court has made it easier than ever to dance with death.

Criminal cases, especially capital cases, are often affected by the passions of the moment. This and the enormity of a state's taking the life of a human being should result in more careful scrutiny by the courts of any case in which the death penalty is imposed. The Rehnquist Court, however, has steadily reduced the power of the federal courts to review capital cases and to set aside convictions and death sentences obtained in violation of the Bill of Rights. It has required strict compliance with various technical rules that are not even known by many of the court-appointed lawyers assigned to defend poor people. A lawyer's mistake can, therefore, cost a client his or her life. For example, the Court held that the federal courts could not review issues raised by Roger Keith Coleman, who was condemned to death in Virginia, because his lawyers were late in filing his notice of appeal. In that case, Justice O'Connor opened the majority opinion with the startling sentence "This is a case about federalism," to which Justice Blackmun responded in dissent:

> Federalism; comity; state sovereignty; preservation of state resources; certainty: The majority methodically inventories these

multifarious state interests. . . . One searches the majority's opinion in vain, however, for any mention of petitioner Coleman's right to a criminal proceeding free from constitutional defect or his interest in finding a forum for his constitutional challenge to his conviction and sentence of death.[8]

The Court has also ruled that federal courts may not even address some issues on habeas corpus review, making it easier, even where constitutional violations are found, for federal judges to shrug their shoulders, pronounce the violations "harmless," and affirm the conviction and sentence.[9]

The Rehnquist Court has restricted the power of courts to grant new trials even when it has been discovered after trial that egregious police or prosecutorial misconduct may have contributed to the conviction or that new evidence indicates that the defendant is actually innocent of the crime. In cases where prosecutors have refused to disclose evidence that cast doubt on the defendant's guilt or have misled the jury, the Court requires a showing that the misconduct actually affected the outcome, forcing courts to guess at what would or would not have mattered to a jury at trial and substituting trial by appellate judges for trial by jury. For example, the Court has held that a prosecutor's failure to disclose exculpatory evidence regarding the accuracy of an eyewitness's testimony does not require it to overturn a death sentence.[10]

Even innocence is irrelevant. In a case from Texas, the prosecutor expressly repudiated the version of events he had used to obtain defendant Jesse Dwayne Jacobs's conviction and death sentence. The prosecutor argued at Jacobs's trial that Jacobs had fired the fatal shot. The same prosecutor argued, however, at a subsequent trial involving a second person accused of the same crime that it was the second person who had fired the fatal shot. Indeed, the prosecutor now believed Jacobs's claim that he had not fired the shot or even anticipated that the victim would be shot; the prosecutor also agreed that parts of Jacobs's confession were false. Under the argument advanced at the second trial, Jacobs would not have been eligible for the death penalty under Texas law.[11] Nevertheless, only Justices Stevens, Ginsburg, and Breyer were willing to stay the execution, and Jacobs was executed.

In the few cases where prosecutorial misconduct was so egregious that the Court set aside the conviction, Rehnquist, Scalia, and Thomas dissented.[12] Justice Scalia has written that "in a sensible system of criminal justice" wrongful conviction is avoided at the trial level, not by appellate review. However, the exoneration of many people in noncapital as well as capital cases through the use of DNA evidence—and, in the cases of three persons sentenced to death in Illinois, by the findings of a journalism class at Northwestern University—demonstrates that trials often result in wrongful convictions, and evidence of police or prosecutorial misconduct, incompetent defense lawyering, and innocence sometimes surfaces after trial, during the appellate review and even later.

The Court's restrictions on federal habeas corpus review were not enough for Congress. In the Antiterrorism and Effective Death Penalty Act, which President Bill Clinton signed into law in 1996, Congress added still more procedural barriers, including a one-year time limit for filing federal habeas corpus petitions. These restrictions on federal habeas corpus review rest on the notion that state court judges will enforce the Constitution as well as their federal counterparts. This ignores political realities. An elected judge who suppresses evidence seized in an unlawful search or arrest or who even grants a change of venue to another part of the state where there has been no publicity about the crime, thereby depriving the local community of its chance to exact vengeance, may be ruining any hope of being reelected. More than a few judges have learned this lesson the hard way. In 1994, for example, after the Texas Court of Criminal Appeals reversed a conviction in a particularly notorious capital case, a former chairman of the state Republican Party called for Republicans to take over the court. The voters responded, and by 1998 the court, which had once been made up exclusively of Democrats, was composed entirely of Republicans who were all strong supporters of the death penalty.[13]

In 1996, Justice Penny White was voted off the Tennessee Supreme Court after a decision in a death penalty case led the Republican Party and other groups to oppose her retention. Immediately after the retention election, the governor of Tennessee, Don Sundquist, said, "Should a judge look over his shoulder [in making decisions] about whether they're going to be thrown out of office? I hope so."

Sundquist's effort to intimidate the state judiciary was similar to that of Governor George Deukmejian of California. In 1986, Deukmejian campaigned against three justices of the state supreme court because they had voted to overturn death sentences. All lost their seats, and Deukmejian appointed their replacements. Ever since, the California Supreme Court has had one of the highest affirmance rates in capital cases of any court in the country.

The courts in Texas, Tennessee, California, and other states have sacrificed the rule of law and the independence of their judiciaries to bring about executions. As Supreme Court Justice Stevens once remarked, "It was never contemplated that the individual who has to protect our individual rights would have to consider what decision would produce the most votes." Twenty years ago people sentenced to death in violation of the Constitution in those states could reasonably expect that a federal court, insulated from political pressures, would prevent their execution. As a result of Rehnquist Court decisions, they now have little hope that federal courts will surmount the many barriers and vindicate their constitutional rights.

Restrictions imposed by the Court and Congress on the power of federal courts to review capital cases represent not only a return to states' rights; such restrictions send the message that constitutional violations are inconsequential, show a willingness to tolerate departures from constitutional standards in the quest for convictions and death sentences, and reaffirm the notion voiced so often by politicians that the Bill of Rights is nothing more than a collection of "technicalities" that get in the way of convicting the accused and carrying out their sentences.

The death penalty is frequently imposed not because the defendant committed the worst crime but because he or she had the misfortune of being assigned the worst court-appointed lawyer. Poor people have no control over the legal representation they receive; judges appoint lawyers to defend them. Justice Ruth Bader Ginsburg said in 2001 that she had "yet to see a death case among the dozens coming to the Supreme Court . . . in which the defendant was well represented at trial. People who are well represented at trial do not get the death penalty."[14] At some later, critical stages of appellate review, the poor may not have a lawyer at all, making it impossible for them to gain access to courts that would be open to them if they could afford a lawyer. The Rehnquist Court is responsible for allowing this shameful lack of fairness and equal justice to worsen during a time of unprecedented prosperity in American society and the legal profession.

The right to counsel is the most fundamental constitutional right a person charged with a crime has, because every other right depends upon it. An attorney is also needed to conduct an independent investigation and present the evidence necessary for a fair and reliable determination of guilt or innocence and, in case of conviction, a proper sentence. But many states still do not have public defender systems and pay the lawyers assigned to defend the poor very little. Consequently, the most difficult cases, where the client's life is at stake, attract few lawyers willing to accept wages that are among the lowest in the legal profession. In many states, lawyers defending a capital case are paid less than a paralegal is paid for completing forms for a bankruptcy case. Lawyers appointed to represent the accused often lack the knowledge, skill, and resources and sometimes even the inclination to provide a competent defense. About one-third of the people sentenced to death in Illinois, Kentucky, and Texas were represented at their capital trials by lawyers who were later disbarred, suspended, or convicted of crimes. Courts have even upheld cases when lawyers appointed to represent the defendant were drunk or asleep during trial. One federal judge, in reluctantly upholding a death sentence, observed that, as interpreted by the Supreme Court, the Constitution "does not require that the accused, even in a capital case, be represented by able or effective counsel."[15]

While the Supreme Court has required since 1932 that a poor person facing the death penalty be provided a lawyer at trial, it was not until 1984 that the Supreme Court addressed the quality of legal representation. In the case of David Leroy Washington, who was sentenced to death in Florida, the Court held that, while an accused is entitled to a "reasonably competent" lawyer, a conviction or death sentence should not be overturned even if the lawyer's representation was deficient unless the defendant shows a "reasonable probability" that the lawyer's incompetence affected the outcome.[16] Justice Thurgood Marshall, in dissent, warned that this standard was so malleable that it was meaningless.

He was right. Several years later, Justice Marshall observed that "capital defendants frequently suffer the consequences of having trial counsel who are ill-equipped to handle capital cases" and pointed to numerous cases in which the lawyers "presented no evidence in mitigation of their clients' sentences because they did not know what to offer or how to offer it, or had not read the state's sentencing statute."[17] Justice O'Connor, who in 1984 authored the opinion setting the lax standard, later acknowledged the poor quality of representation, noting that in 2000 a defendant represented by court-appointed lawyers in Texas was 28 percent more likely to be convicted than one who retained private counsel and 44 percent more likely to receive the death penalty when convicted.[18]

Even though it has long been apparent that lower courts have been tolerating levels of representation that make a mockery of the right to counsel, the Rehnquist Court has refused to reexamine the standard. At the same time, the Court has tightened what Justice Marshall described as an "increasingly pernicious visegrip" by adopting strict rules prohibiting consideration of constitutional violations because a court-appointed attorney did not present critical evidence or was ignorant of the law or did not follow a state procedural rule. According to the Court, even when the ignorance or ineptitude of a court-appointed lawyer costs a client vindication of his or her constitutional rights— and thus his or her life—the client's right to counsel has not been violated. The Court has found only once in its history that a lawyer's poor performance violated the right to counsel. In that case, decided in 2000, the Court held that a man sentenced to death in Virginia was denied his right to counsel by the lawyer's failure to investigate the man's background and present evidence that was "indispensable" for the jury's sentencing decision. Even there, Rehnquist, Scalia, and Thomas dissented. They voted to allow Virginia to execute the man.[19]

There are important stages in the review of capital cases following trial at which, as a result of a decision by the Rehnquist Court, a poor person may have no lawyer at all. The Supreme Court held in the early

1960s that a poor person accused of a crime was constitutionally guaranteed a lawyer at trial and for one appeal.[20] After his appointment in 1972 as associate justice, Rehnquist wrote that a poor person is not entitled to a lawyer for the further appeals that many states provide or for petitions to review convictions.

In 1989, in an opinion by Chief Justice Rehnquist, the Court by a 5–4 vote refused to make an exception for people under sentence of death, rejecting the argument that those condemned to death had a special need for counsel in the later stages of review because of the complexity of capital cases, the enormity of the punishment, and the immense time pressures of preparing and filing a petition before an execution date. In *Murray v. Giarratano* Rehnquist wrote: "Virginia may quite sensibly decide to concentrate the resources it devotes to providing attorneys to capital defendants at the trial and appellate stages of a capital proceeding" instead of at later stages of review. At the time of the man's trial, however, Virginia paid lawyers appointed to defend people facing the death penalty less than any other state. It had decided not to apply its resources to providing adequate representation for the poor at *any* stage of the proceedings.[21]

As a result of that decision, Exzavious Gibson, whose I.Q. was found on different tests to be between 76 and 82, stood, totally bewildered and without a lawyer, in front of a judge at his first state postconviction hearing. The case went forward as follows:

> The Court: OK, Mr. Gibson, are you ready to proceed?
>
> Mr. Gibson: I don't have an attorney.
>
> The Court: I understand that.
>
> Mr. Gibson: I am not waiving my rights.
>
> The Court: I understand that. Do you have any evidence to put up?
>
> Mr. Gibson: I don't know what to plead.
>
> The Court: Huh?
>
> Mr. Gibson: I don't know what to plead.

Nevertheless, the hearing continued. The state of Georgia was represented by a lawyer who specializes in capital cases and who presented evidence that Gibson was helpless to challenge or cross-examine. Gibson offered no evidence, examined no witnesses, and made no objections. The judge denied Gibson relief by signing an order prepared by the attorney general's office without making a single change. The Georgia Supreme Court held that Gibson had no right to counsel and affirmed the denial of relief. And Gibson is in no way unique. People facing the death penalty in Alabama, Texas, and other states are frequently unable to find lawyers before their deadlines for filing petitions for review.

Thanks to the Rehnquist Court, whether people sentenced to death receive full review of their case before execution is a function of income and luck. A person wealthy enough to hire a lawyer can obtain full review. Virtually all of those on death row, however, are poor. If they are fortunate, a lawyer may volunteer to represent them for free or they may be in a state that provides lawyers during the later stages of review. Very frequently, however, the condemned face death alone without access to the legal system.

The criminal justice system is the part of society least affected by the civil rights movement in large measure because of the hands-off approach to racial discrimination in criminal cases taken by the Rehnquist Court in a capital case in 1987.

A person of color is more likely than a white person to be stopped by the police, to be abused by the police during that stop, to be taken into custody, to be denied bail, to be charged with a serious crime, and to be convicted. He or she is also apt to receive a harsher sentence than a white person. Although people of color are most likely to be victims of crime and to be charged with crime, there are few people of color among judges, prosecutors, and lawyers. Even in communities with substantial African-American or Hispanic populations, the jury may be all white. Often, the only person of color who sits in front of the bar in the courtroom is the person on trial.

Study after study has confirmed that race plays a role in capital sentencing. In 2000, the U.S. Department of Justice examined its own record and found that over three-fourths of the people given the death penalty were members of racial minorities. Over half were African

American. A major reason for these disparities is the vast and unchecked discretion afforded prosecutors. The two most important decisions in a death penalty case are made not by the jury or judge but by the prosecutor. First, the prosecutor decides whether to seek the death penalty, which is always a matter of discretion—the prosecutor is never required to seek death. Second, the prosecutor has complete discretion in deciding whether to offer a sentence less than death in exchange for the defendant's guilty plea. The overwhelming majority of all criminal cases, including capital cases, are resolved not by trials but by plea bargains. In the thirty-eight states that have the death penalty, 97.5 percent of the chief prosecutors are white. In eighteen of the states, all the prosecutors are white.

Although African Americans constitute only 12 percent of the national population, they are victims of half the murders that are committed in this country. Yet 80 percent of those on death row are there for crimes against white people. The discrepancy is even greater in the death-belt states of the South. In Georgia and Alabama, for example, African Americans are the victims of 65 percent of the homicides, yet 80 percent of those sentenced to death are sentenced for crimes against white persons. In Georgia, of the twenty-three people executed between 1976 (when the death penalty was reinstated) and 2000, twenty-one were executed for crimes against white victims.

The racial disparities are stark, undeniable, and disturbing in an increasingly diverse society. Courts seldom, however, address the extent to which those disparities are the result of racial prejudice, whether conscious or unconscious, because the Rehnquist Court held in 1987 that racial disparities in sentencing did not even raise an inference of discrimination. The Court allowed Georgia to continue to carry out executions despite substantial racial disparities in its infliction.[22] In a 5–4 opinion by Justice Powell, the Court found that such disparities were "inevitable" and rejected them as a basis for inferring discrimination. Instead, the Court required defendants to prove that the decision makers in their individual cases discriminated, a virtually impossible task unless the prosecutor or a juror admits as much. The Court justified this impossible burden in part because the claim of racial discrimination in capital cases, "taken to its logical conclusion, throws into serious question the principles that underlie our entire criminal justice system." Justice William Brennan, in dissent, characterized this concern as "a fear of too much justice."

The decision frustrated challenges to sentencing disparities in other areas and even to ugly racial incidents. The Georgia Supreme Court refused to allow a hearing into why 98 percent of those serving a life sentence for a second drug offense are African American. Two African-American men sentenced to death by an all-white jury in Utah were executed even though jurors received a note that contained the words "Hang the Nigger's" (*sic*) and a drawing of a figure hanging from a gallows. No court, state or federal, ever conducted a hearing on such questions as who wrote the note, what influence it had on the jurors, and how widely they may have discussed it.[23]

Although the Rehnquist Court held in a 5–4 opinion by Scalia in 1989 that mentally retarded persons were subject to capital punishment, the Court found in 2002 that much has changed and a national consensus had developed against execution of the mentally retarded.[24] The Court, by a 6–3 vote, concluded that the execution of mentally retarded people violates the Constitution, because the mentally retarded, owing to their limitations in the areas of reasoning, judgment, and control of impulses, lack the same degree of moral culpability as people who are not retarded.

Rehnquist and Scalia both filed dissents that were joined by Thomas. Scalia's dissent was arrogant, caustic, and sarcastic in its disdain for the majority's reasoning, the universal abandonment of executing the mentally retarded by other countries, and the opinions of professional and religious organizations. (Scalia dismissed the views of the leaders of his own religion, saying that Catholic bishops are so far from being representative, even of the views of Catholics, that they are currently the object of intense national—and even ecumenical—criticism.) He predicted that capital trials would become a game because defendants would feign mental retardation. However, a finding of mental retardation requires that limited intellectual functioning be apparent during childhood. Since mentally retarded persons have a history of low test scores and special education classes during childhood, it is virtually impossible to feign retardation. This did not prevent Scalia from cynically predicting that capital trials would become a game of those facing condemnation pretending to be retarded.

Scalia's view that world opinion and practices are irrelevant won the votes of four other justices in an earlier case that upheld the death penalty for children who were sixteen or seventeen at the time of their crimes.[25] As a result, since 1990 the United States is one of only six countries that have executed people who were under eighteen at the time of the crime—the other five are Iran, Nigeria, Pakistan, Saudi Arabia, and Yemen. Even in that rather undistinguished company, the United States leads by far in the number executed. The United States is one of only two countries that have not ratified the International Covenant on the Rights of the Child, which among other things would prohibit the execution of people who were children at the time of their crimes; the other country is Somalia.

In declaring a moratorium on executions in Illinois, Governor George Ryan said that the execution of an innocent person would be the "ultimate nightmare." Many supporters of capital punishment argue, however, that society is fighting a "war on crime," and, as in any other war, there will be some innocent casualties. An earlier notion of justice, that it was better for ten guilty people to go free than for an innocent person to be convicted, is being eclipsed. One legacy of the Rehnquist Court will be the replacement of that notion with another, that sacrificing a few innocent lives to wage a war on crime is more important than ensuring the fairness and reliability of a conviction and death sentence. It is a sad commentary on the Court, its members, and the times. Justice Brennan observed in one of his many eloquent dissents, "the way in which we choose those who will die reveals the depth of moral commitment among the living."[26] As Justice Blackmun ultimately concluded, the path the Court has chosen lessens us all.

INDIVIDUAL RIGHTS

The Religion Clauses:
A Study in Confusion

NORMAN REDLICH

When William H. Rehnquist became chief justice of the United States in 1986, the Supreme Court inherited a complicated framework of judicial doctrines developed over four decades of litigation involving the Religion Clauses. Despite the inevitable ebbs and flows in the interpretation of these doctrines, they are justly credited with providing this diverse country with a degree of protection for religious freedom, religious diversity, and religious peace that is unrivaled anywhere else in the world. The critical decisions that guided the Court's interpretations of the Religion Clauses during the first fifteen years of Rehnquist's tenure as chief justice were rooted and decided within the context of these same precedents, although different facts, changes in Court personnel, and the inevitable modifications in positions have left the seminal cases in a state of uncertainty, a result that may be traced in part to the countervailing doctrines these very decisions generated. Litigation has focused primarily on the Establishment Clause (the church-state separation provision), with "free exercise" concerns generally merged with, and subsumed by, issues involving freedom of speech.

When read carefully, the pivotal Establishment Clause decisions, partly because of their vagueness and generality of language, contain various doctrinal seeds that have allowed the Court broad flexibility to move in different directions on a host of issues. In the 1947 *Everson* case, for example, the Court proclaimed that the government could not pass laws "which aid one religion, aid all religions, or prefer one religion over another," but nevertheless upheld state financing of bus transportation to parents of parochial school students, thereby maintaining a degree of flexibility that may not have been predicted or fully understood at the time.[1]

The doctrines in the prayer cases were similarly untidy. In *Engel v. Vitale*, a 1962 case striking down a New York law directing the reading of a so-called nondenominational prayer at the beginning of each school day, the Court carefully limited the opinion to the precise facts before it, opening the way for religious teaching to reenter the public schools through persons distributing religious literature, engaging in prayer on college premises, or allowing student religious publications to be funded by the state and circulated on school grounds.[2]

In essence, then, the Rehnquist Court inherited constitutional doctrines that were sufficiently flexible so that a sharply divided Court could decide cases, even reaching seemingly contradictory results, without explicitly overruling any of the foundational cases that formed the jurisprudence bequeathed to it.

It would be a mistake, however, to view the Rehnquist years as a wholesale undermining of the judicial edifice created in prior years. The strong separationist dicta in *Everson* have not been overruled. Even with the narrowing of the traditional concept of separation of church and state by countervailing doctrines—the necessity of accommodating religious beliefs, concepts of so-called neutrality toward religion, expansion of speech-protecting principles to encompass religious activities that take place in public forums, including public schools—the Court has refused to erase the line prohibiting direct financial aid to religious schools or government promulgation of and support for prayers in schools. Instead we have a multitude of conflicting and contradictory principles that could either topple the delicate constitutional arrangement or reinvigorate the constitutional principles that the Rehnquist Court inherited. The interpretation of the Religion Clauses is still very much up for grabs.

The main building block of the establishment structure bequeathed to the Rehnquist Court was *Lemon v. Kurtzman*.[3] In *Lemon*, with its famous three-part test—secular purpose, religiously neutral effects, and no excessive entanglement with religion—the Court refused to allow the government to subsidize the salaries of teachers employed by parochial schools. Without addressing the question whether the principal or primary effect of the programs was the advancement of religion, the Court held that the "cumulative impact of the entire relationship arising under the statutes . . . involves excessive entanglement between government and religion." Because the teachers subsidized by the government could use the aid to engage in religious teaching rather than to cover textbook or transportation costs, as allowed in prior cases, the state was constitutionally obligated to take precautions to guard against that happening.

But by instituting needed safeguards to prevent government resources from being "diverted" for religious use, the state would inevitably run afoul of the "excessive entanglement" prong of the test. "These prophylactic contacts," the *Lemon* ruling held, "involve excessive and enduring entanglement between state and church." Some justices, prominent among whom was then-Justice Rehnquist, decried the Catch-22 thus created. In their view, government support provided to religious schools was deemed by the majority to create an impermissible risk of advancing religion through behind-the-door diversions of state resources to religious uses, thus running afoul of the "effects" test. Any attempt to prevent such a diversion, however, would be barred by concerns about "excessive entanglement."

Thus, courts were required to decide whether a particular form of aid fell on the textbook and transportation side of the line or whether it was sufficiently "divertible" to place it within the range of objections that applied to government subsidization of teacher salaries. The complexity of this line-drawing enterprise was well illustrated in *Wolman v. Walter*, a 1977 case in which the Court upheld government provision of secular textbooks, standardized testing and scoring, and therapeutic services but barred state aid in the form of loans of audiovisual equipment and transportation for field trips. The Court concluded that TVs and VCRs could be used for religious teaching and that field trips presented opportunities to inculcate religious lessons.[4]

The Rehnquist Court (or a majority therein) was clearly impatient with the approach it inherited, with its fine distinctions on the issue of

divertibility and its stringency. Yet the Court did not squarely overrule
Lemon. It did, however, substantially modify its application in various
contexts. Whereas the precedents in the pre-Rehnquist era had demonstrated a deep and abiding concern about the diversion of government resources for religious use, fearful that a message of symbolic
church-state union and government endorsement of religion might be
communicated, the Rehnquist majority was less troubled than its predecessors when the aid was first given to private individuals who then
decided to channel the aid to religious purposes. Hence, the Rehnquist
Court, with echoes of *Everson*, found no constitutional defects in a student's decision to use government vocational assistance to study at a
Christian college to become a pastor (*Witters*) or in a state's provision
of sign language interpreters for students who attended a Roman
Catholic high school (*Zobrest*).[5] The Court gave great weight to the fact
that the aid that ultimately flowed to religious institutions did so only as
a result of the genuinely independent and private choices of aid recipients, even though there was no dispute that the government-financed
interpreter would be "diverted" to translate the religious message
taught in class or that the vocational assistance might be "diverted" to
allow the aspiring pastor to attend a class on the New Testament
taught by a Baptist minister.

Perhaps the most important modification the Rehnquist Court effected in applying *Lemon* was a repudiation of the assumption that certain types of government aid are more "divertible"—and therefore
more objectionable—than others. In the process, the Court undid the
Catch-22 created by prior cases. Absent compelling evidence to the
contrary, the Rehnquist Court operated on the assumption that public
school and sectarian school teachers alike would heed constitutional
limits and not funnel government resources, of whatever form, toward
religious teaching. Pervasive monitoring was thus unnecessary, and the
possibility of excessive entanglement between church and state was
therefore eliminated. Using this modified framework, in 1997 the
Court, in *Agostini v. Felton*, overturned an injunction issued twelve years
earlier in *Aguilar v. Felton* that had barred the use of federal funds to pay
the salaries of public employees who taught in parochial schools.[6] There
would no longer be any per se legal bar to these forms of state aid.

Then, in *Mitchell v. Helms*, decided in 2000, a majority of the Court concluded that the Constitution does not prohibit the government from lending instructional materials and equipment to religiously affiliated schools—even in classes taught by teachers hired by, and under the supervision of, sectarian schools.[7] *Wolman*, with its classification of various types of aid depending on their "divertibility," was expressly overruled.

What the Rehnquist Court did not do, however, is as important as what it did do. While a plurality of the Court would elevate "neutrality" or "evenhandedness" as the sole inquiry—allowing government aid to be diverted to religious use as long as aid recipients are not defined by reference to their religion and the substance of the state aid itself does not contain religious content—this position failed to garner the requisite five votes. As a result, the doctrines in this area remain muddy and contentious. Both concurring and dissenting justices make clear that diversion of government resources to religious instruction, if the violation can be proved, is still barred under current law, with the possible exception being cases where the aid passes through a private party who independently decides to direct the government aid to religious use. Finally, the level of permissible constitutional violations remains uncertain. Notwithstanding verifiable instances of impermissible diversion in *Helms*, for example, the majority refused to invalidate the assistance program, finding these violations "de minimis."

Yet the basic *Lemon* approach survives. Neutrality has not triumphed as the ultimate touchstone, probably because it is unworkable. The wall of separation has, however, become conspicuously more porous. While the Rehnquist majority did not overrule the foundational cases in this area, other decisions—notably *Wolman* and *Aguilar*—that gave shape and content to that doctrinal foundation were unabashedly renounced.

Given this Court's willingness to overturn disfavored precedents, the future direction of religion-funding cases remains in doubt. Still, at least for now, the Establishment Clause has bite or at least a threatening bark. Direct cash grants to religious schools remain unconstitutional, even though similar secular organizations qualify. Widespread diversion of government aid to religious use, if the violations can be proven, continues to be constitutionally barred, even though the type of aid in question is distributed without regard to religious affiliation by the government under a broad-based secular program. As important as are the justices' disagreements in the funding cases, these disputes should not obscure the crucial role the Establishment Clause has played in separating politics and religion, despite the efforts of the Christian right and certain religious leaders and opportunistic politicians to breach the barrier the clause has erected.

In the 1962 case of *Engel v. Vitale*, the Supreme Court held that "it is no part of the business of government to compose official prayers for any group of the American people to recite as a part of a religious program carried on by government." New York, therefore, could not require a school prayer—even a nondenominational one (a religious impossibility)—to be recited in class at the beginning of each school day. Since then, the Court has been vigilant in guarding this clear prohibition from erosion. In *School District of Abington v. Schempp* (1963), the Court expanded the reach of *Engel* by invalidating a Pennsylvania law requiring "at least ten verses from the Holy Bible . . . be read, without comment, at the opening of each public school on each school day," even though the law provided that "any child shall be excused from such Bible reading, or attending such Bible reading, upon the written request of his parent or guardian" and even though the particular verses were to be chosen by the students reading the verses, without the participation of teachers.[8] The Court recognized this as an exercise with "a devotional and religious character." It was not designed to present the Bible objectively as a work of history or literature but was a state-sponsored religious observance.

These cases led to more subtle and sophisticated attempts by states to introduce religion back into the public schools. Alabama, for example, enacted a statute in 1981 providing for a moment of silence "for meditation or voluntary prayer." No religious exercise was involved, only a brief opportunity for students to pray if they so wished. Or so the state argued. In *Wallace v. Jaffree*, however, the Court carefully examined the background and legislative history behind the enactment and found that the goal was "an effort to return voluntary prayer to the public schools," with the explicit reference to "voluntary prayer" indicating the state's "endorsement"—a result at odds "with the established principle that the government must pursue a course of complete neutrality toward religion."[9]

These skeptical attitudes and probing examinations into the statutory purpose continued even after Rehnquist became chief justice. In *Edwards v. Aguillard* (1987), for example, the Court struck down Louisiana's Creationism Act, which required teachers who taught evolution to teach "creation science" as well.[10] The Court rejected the state's contention that the act, under the banner of academic freedom, merely sought to guarantee the evenhanded presentation of scientific evidence to schoolchildren. Cutting through the thicket of verbiage, the Court recognized that the act was intended "to narrow the science curriculum . . . by counterbalancing its teaching at every turn with the teaching of creationism."

Five years later, in *Lee v. Weisman*, the Court banned graduation prayers in a public school—even though the prayers were allegedly nondenominational and were delivered by invited members of the clergy otherwise unconnected to the school.[11] The Court expressed concern about the potential for coercion of high school students and about the symbolic message of state endorsement that might be communicated. In rejecting the school's free-speech claims, the Court recognized a special role for the Establishment Clause. "Speech is protected by ensuring its full expression even when the government participates," the Court wrote. "In religious debate or expression the government is not a prime participant. . . . The Establishment Clause is a specific prohibition on forms of state intervention in religious affairs with no precise counterpart in the speech provisions."

Given such strong language and the constraint imposed by a relatively unbroken line of precedents barring prayers and religious teaching in the public schools, the Court's recent decision in *Santa Fe Independent School District v. Doe* (2000) is unsurprising.[12] The Court refused to allow student-led, student-initiated prayers at football games, finding that these invocations were implicitly authorized by government policy and took place "on government property at government-sponsored school-related events." Echoing *Lee*'s concerns about coercion of students who might object to participating in the religious exercise and "the actual or perceived" endorsement of religion that would be conveyed by the intimate association of church and state, the Rehnquist Court refused to allow the prayers even though the students voted to have them. The government could not, in the Court's words, establish "a governmental electoral mechanism that turns the school into a forum for religious debate."

Despite these cases, it would be a mistake to conclude that prayers and religious instructions are now completely expelled from public schools. One cannot predict, for example, whether a pure moment of silence, without the incriminating bits of legislative history that infected the laws in *Wallace* and *Aguillard*, would withstand constitutional challenge. Moreover, recent developments have cast doubt on the scope of the Court's prayers cases, as schools throughout the country try various ways to evade the constitutional prohibition. In *Adler v. Duval County School Board*, high school seniors were permitted to vote on whether to include opening and closing "messages" at graduation and to elect the student speaker to deliver an uncensored speech.[13] The Eleventh Circuit approved this practice because it concerned only generic graduation "messages" not "invocations," religion was not at the core of the arrangement, and, unlike in *Santa Fe*, school officials could not censor the student's speech. Despite *Lee*, *Santa Fe*, and similar cases that appear to have established clear principles, another line of precedents seems to permit religion to reenter the public schools through another route.

Establishment concerns seem to retreat into the background when pitted against free-speech values. In *Widmar v. Vincent*, decided in 1981, the Court struck down a university regulation prohibiting the use of university buildings or grounds "for purposes of religious worship or religious teaching."[14] The university defended its policy on establishment grounds—maintaining church-state separation—but the Court found that there were no establishment dangers under the *Lemon* test and that the university's policy discriminated against religious groups on the basis of their religious message, thereby violating the Free Exercise and Free Speech Clauses. To accomplish this result, the Court in *Widmar* characterized prayers as ordinary speech and ignored the special role reserved for the Establishment Clause as evidenced in the school prayer cases. But religious speech, as we have seen, is different from secular speech when the government is involved. By conceptualizing prayers that take place in government-supported public forums as ordinary speech, the Court chipped away at the independent force of the Establishment Clause.

In addition to equating prayers with everyday speech, the Court, in requiring equal access to facilities by religious groups, concluded that "an open forum in a public university does not confer any imprimatur of state approval on religious sects or practices." This concept elevated neutrality as a crucial, if not decisive, factor in the inquiry. But neutrality in the prayers and funding cases is an elusive standard. Clearly, the government cannot pay the salaries of ministers and rabbis simply because there is a broad-based program distributing money to leaders of similarly situated secular groups. A principal cannot invite a cleric to lead a graduation prayer even if the school invites other prominent members of the community holding contrasting viewpoints to give graduation speeches. In emphasizing neutrality here, the Court has substituted confusion and uncertainty for reasoned analysis. Moreover, the presence of a "public forum"—the condition that triggers the requirement of neutrality in these cases—has defied clear definition despite decades of case law.

The confusion is evident in *Rosenberger v. Rector and Visitors of the University of Virginia*, a 1995 case invalidating the university's guidelines withholding support payments from any group that "primarily promotes or manifests a particular belief in or about a deity or an ultimate reality."[15] Invoking the regulation, the university denied financial assistance to a student newspaper, *Wide Awake*, that espoused a Christian perspective. In striking down the regulation on free-speech grounds, a 5–4 majority of the Court, arguing that the university had violated neutrality principles governing speech in "limited public forums," expanded the definition of "public forum" from a purely physical concept with tangible geographical boundaries (*Widmar*) to a more amorphous concept of support and assistance. By creating a common fund to support student activities, the university had created a "public forum," the Court found, rejecting the distinction advanced by the university between access to facilities and provision of funds. If, as *Rosenberger* strongly suggests, neutrality is the touchstone and the government must be neutral as between religious and secular groups in the provision of funds, nothing stands in the way of unrestricted state funding of religious activities, as long as religious groups are not favored.

The Rehnquist Court has done little to sort out the resulting confused state of affairs. In *Good News Club v. Milford Central School* (2001), the Court affirmed the reasoning of *Widmar* and *Rosenberger* without clarifying the relationship these public forum cases have with other doctrinal areas and without reconciling any of the tensions between establishment and free-speech concerns.[16] The policy in *Good News Club* authorized district residents to use the school building after school for, among other things, "instruction in education, learning, or the arts," as well as "social, civic, recreational, and entertainment uses pertaining to the community welfare." The school denied use of the facility to the Good News Club on the grounds that the club's purpose was to conduct religious instruction and that granting it access would violate the Establishment Clause. Following *Rosenberger*, the Court struck down the policy on free-speech grounds, finding that the school had created a limited public forum and that excluding the religious group would constitute impermissible viewpoint discrimination.

The Court in *Good News Club* ignored the factual similarity to the funding and prayers cases. Children were the primary members of the audience in *Good News Club*, as in *Lee* and *Santa Fe*, raising the distinct possibility that children might misperceive state endorsement of religion from the simple fact that religious activities were taking place on school premises. Moreover, there existed a potential for students to feel subtle coercion to participate, even though the afterschool lessons, like a graduation ceremony or a football game, were not technically part of the required curriculum.

Good News Club purported simply to follow *Rosenberger*'s neutrality requirement concerning "public forums," but it ignored the significance of the expansion of the public forum's concept to classroom space. Speech in a public school setting, however, troubled the Court in the funding and prayers cases because of the possible divisiveness and coercion when the *government* sponsors a public forum in which religious issues are debated—whether in the form of an electoral mechanism, as in *Santa Fe*, or in the form of an afterschool religion class outside the core curriculum, as in *Good News Club*.

Hence, despite the apparent neatness and consistency in the doctrines concerning school prayers (*Lee* and *Santa Fe*, which rather uniformly held that prayers are impermissible) and the doctrines concerning public forums (*Widmar*, *Rosenberger*, *Good News Club*, which rather uniformly held that public forums must be made available to religious groups), the doctrines, when viewed together, become very blurred. These two lines of cases cannot be hermetically sealed off. The Rehnquist Court's failure to address their relationship has maintained and increased chaos at the margin. While *Good News Club*, because of its similarity to *Rosenberger*, was treated as a public forum case, it could easily be viewed as a funding case, in which the religious group impermissibly "diverted" a government resource (classroom space) toward religious use, or a school prayers case, with all the attendant dangers of subtle coercion and symbolic union of church and state.

These public forum and free-speech cases, decided with broad church-state implications, demonstrate the confusion and uncertainty that results when cases are decided separately within the boundaries of artificial categories that lack defensible content or structure.

As in the free-speech and public forum cases, the Rehnquist Court has compartmentalized free-exercise claims without considering whether the recognition by a government of a "freedom of religion" exception to a statute constitutes an establishment of religion. Thus, the theoretical tension that may exist between free-exercise and establishment concerns does not appear to have caused the Court to deviate from its practice of evaluating free-exercise claims in terms that appear quite unrelated to the Establishment Clause. For example, when the Rehnquist Court, in perhaps its most important free-exercise case, the 1990 decision in *Employment Division, Department of Human Resources v. Smith*, upheld Oregon's denial of employment benefits to a Native American fired for ingesting peyote, it made no reference to the argument that granting the exception might constitute an establishment of religion.[17] Instead, the Court treated the free-exercise claim in isolation and considered only the question of whether, in evaluating free-exercise claims, it should apply a "compelling state interest" standard or the more lenient "rational relationship" standard. Departing from earlier cases that had invalidated state laws for failing to meet a "compelling state interest" test, the Rehnquist Court allowed states far more leeway in restricting religious practices as long as governments could provide a meaningful "rational relationship" for upholding the statute. Indeed, in its most prominent case upholding a free-exercise claim, *Church of the Lukumi Babalu Aye, Inc., v. City of Hialeah,* the Court struck down an ordinance enacted to prevent members of the Santeria faith from performing animal sacrifices, a principal tenet of their religion.[18] Since the ordinance was not a statute of general applicability and therefore differed from zoning or unemployment insurance laws, the Court had little difficulty concluding that the statute demonstrated hostility against the Santeria religion and therefore violated the Free Exercise Clause.

It is commonly asserted that the Free Exercise and Establishment Clauses are in conflict because a ruling that a government program violates the Establishment Clause arguably violates someone's free-exercise rights, and the recognition of a free-exercise claim usually creates a preference for a religious practice in violation of the Establishment Clause. As a result, the Court has not invoked the Establishment Clause as a basis for rejecting a free-exercise claim, and it has not invoked the Free Exercise Clause in rejecting an Establishment Clause claim. Instead, the Court seems determined to decide Free Exercise and Establishment Clause issues without consideration of the consequences that a decision under one clause might have on the other. For example, although *Smith* has been widely criticized for its cavalier treatment of the free-exercise claims of peyote users (applying a standard of mere rationality to laws that allegedly infringe on free exercise), the Court narrowed the scope of free-exercise protection and did not bolster its conclusion by arguing that the state's exemption might have created Establishment Clause problems. Similarly, in *City of Boerne v. Flores,* the Court rejected a federal statute, the Religious Freedom Restoration Act (RFRA), by significantly narrowing Congress's powers to enforce the Fourteenth Amendment and did not contend, as it was urged to, that RFRA was an unconstitutional establishment.[19] And, in the *Hialeah* case, the Court found a free-exercise violation without contending, as it might have done, that upholding the practice of ritual sacrifice would have violated the Establishment Clause. Although these three free-exercise cases—*Smith, Hialeah,* and *City of Boerne*—can be criticized for their failure to address the tension between establishment and free-exercise issues, they send a clear message that the Court intends to treat Free Exercise and Establishment Clause issues separately, without addressing the tension that the clauses create. Indeed, this compartmentalization may reflect the reality that the two clauses, which appear to be in conflict, are in their separate ways protective of religious freedom.

This theme of uncertainty continues as one examines cases dealing with the display of religious symbols in public places. In *Stone v. Graham* (1980), the Court invalidated a Kentucky statute requiring the display of the Ten Commandments in every public classroom, because the Court did not believe the posting had a legitimate secular purpose.[20] The significance of this ruling was quickly limited four years later, however, in *Lynch v. Donnelly*, in which the Court upheld the display of a crèche, or Nativity scene, as part of the city of Pawtucket's Christmas celebration.[21] The Court found that the display served a secular purpose: "celebrat[ing] the Holiday and . . . depict[ing] the origins of that Holiday." Even though the government-sponsored display might provide an "incidental benefit" to religion, this was not enough to invalidate the practice, and the display did not produce an excessive entanglement between church and state.

Once again, these pre–Rehnquist Court cases failed to lay down any bright-line rules, merely declaring that the issue is necessarily one of line drawing because "total separation [of church and state] is not possible in an absolute sense. Some relationship between government and religious organizations is inevitable."

The fact-intensive nature, as well as the hopelessly amorphous quality, of the inquiry became quite evident in the 1989 case *Allegheny County v. ACLU*.[22] The Rehnquist Court was faced with the constitutionality of two religious displays: a crèche on the grand staircase of the county courthouse, and an eighteen-foot menorah next to a forty-five-foot Christmas tree and a sign saluting liberty—all placed in front of the city-county building. After a detailed description of the decoration, the Court first found that the display of the crèche communicated impermissible government endorsement of "a patently Christian message." Among the factors analyzed were the floral arrangement surrounding the crèche and the location of the crèche in "the main and most beautiful part of the building."

With respect to the menorah, the Court reached the opposite conclusion. It found that "in the shadow of the tree, the menorah is readily understood as simply a recognition that Christmas is not the only traditional way of observing the winter-holiday season" and was unlikely to convey an impermissible message of endorsement.

Once again, while the structure of the *Lemon* test was preserved in this line of cases, its application, as evidenced by the Court's struggle to draw a principled line in *Allegheny*, is anything but straightforward. What seemed to be a clear-cut prohibition in *Stone* became a far more nebulous and unpredictable inquiry, with the ultimate outcome depending heavily on the particularities of each case—including details that one would think only interior decorators would notice and analyze—and the views of five justices at the particular moment.

At the end of the 2001–02 term, two issues in the area of religion remained heavily contested. The first was vouchers. The second was charitable choice. How would they fare constitutionally? Would the rush toward the elusive goal of "neutrality" sweep away the barriers created by the Court's interpretation of the Establishment Clause?

It is not difficult to understand the appeal of school vouchers to certain parents and politicians. Designed to maximize choice and competition, they would allow more parents the financial ability to make schooling decisions for their children, including placing them in religiously affiliated private schools. Also, the Rehnquist Court had made it much easier for vouchers to pass constitutional muster. *Mitchell v. Helms*, which allowed the government to lend equipment and instructional materials to private schools, widened the door. In addition, vouchers, unlike equipment loans, are given directly to parents, who then exercise the independent choice to direct the aid to religious educational institutions.

Not surprisingly, a narrowly divided Supreme Court, on the last day of the 2001–02 term, upheld the Cleveland school voucher program while at the same time distinguishing the voucher case from earlier cases that had invalidated direct financial assistance to religious schools. In his opinion in *Zelman v. Simmons-Harris*, Chief Justice Rehnquist, writing for a 5–4 majority, emphasized the concept of "neutrality," and the fact that the voucher program involved decisions by individual parents rather than direct grants, such as had been held invalid in *Lemon*. Relying on *Mueller v. Allen*, *Zobrest*, *Witters*, and *Agostini*, the chief justice's opinion upheld the voucher program without overruling or even mentioning *Lemon*. Both the opinion of the Court and Justice O'Connor's concurrence distinguished the voucher program from financial grants and argued that it was similar to other programs of direct financial assistance, disregarding the fact that the voucher program enabled substantial sums of money to flow directly to the religious schools. Thus, the most eagerly anticipated Establishment Clause case since *Lemon* was treated by the chief justice and by Justice O'Connor as a case that added nothing to Establishment Clause jurisprudence and, indeed, was compelled by precedents.[23]

As was to be expected, the four dissenting justices (Stevens, Souter, Ginsburg, and Breyer) emphasized in their opinions that the voucher program was a thinly disguised attempt to funnel public money directly to religious schools.

Having passed constitutional muster, voucher programs can be expected to flourish and, when combined with the types of financial assistance that were upheld in *Mitchell v. Helms*, direct extensive infusions of public money to religious schools. Only the financial and political limitations on state spending, as well as the continued objections to vouchers by advocates of public education and church-state separation, stand in the way of a drastic shift in the financing of primary education from public to religious schools.

These impediments may not apply to charitable choice, although that, too, has begun to encounter political resistance. Still, it is difficult for political leaders to object to programs that, for example, provide drug treatment assistance to heroin addicts or counsel teenage mothers in crisis.

Nevertheless, charitable choice programs are highly vulnerable on constitutional grounds—perhaps more so than school vouchers—for they place religion at the center of government-funded programs,

thereby raising major establishment concerns. According to preliminary details, the government, at least in some cases, would be directly
funneling money to religious organizations to help them provide useful
social services. Therefore, unlike the sign language assistance program
in *Zobrest,* the vocational assistance program in *Witters,* or even school
vouchers, there is no buffer between church and state.

Coercion, moreover, may be involved in some situations, as when a
homeless person, for example, is placed in a situation where he or she
feels a compulsion to join in a prayer before receiving a meal in a
soup kitchen. With the government's role in the welfare area rapidly
shrinking, the homeless person might not be able to find a nearby
government-run kitchen. And even if homeless persons are not required to pray—just as no one is required to bow one's head in the
pre–football game prayer—the element of coercion is undoubtedly
present, especially given the vulnerable position that the homeless frequently endure.

Another danger is the possibility of communicating a message of
state endorsement. The close partnership between church and state
conveys a symbol of church-state union that is not unlike the display of
a cross or a Nativity scene in front of city hall.

Mitchell v. Helms, Agostini, and *Zelman* indicate clearly that "neutrality"
can destroy rather than preserve the constitutional separation of
church and state. The Establishment Clause, apart and beyond the
free-speech and free-exercise provisions, must be kept as an independent barrier against the diversion of government funds to religious use.
The confused state of the law that the Rehnquist Court has left us gives
cause for concern, particularly since the constitutionality of charitable
choice remains very much an open question and the separationist position seems to command only a narrow and fluctuating Court majority.
Also open are the efforts of certain religious groups to seek government
money and to insert religion into various aspects of public life. To
those for whom the separation of church and state is a unique and important aspect of religious diversity, freedom, and peace, a future that
depends on the decisions of one or two Supreme Court justices is a ter-
rifying prospect.

The First Amendment:
The High Ground and the Low Road

JAMIN B. RASKIN

Compared with its astonishing decision in *Bush v. Gore*—which established that truth can do irreparable harm, burdens on pregnant chads are more suspect than burdens on pregnant women, poor dimpled chads have a right to equal treatment across county lines that poor dimpled children do not, the remedy for hypothetical potential variations in counting a few ballots is the disenfranchisement of tens of thousands of people, and Supreme Court decisions can be good for the evening of publication only—the Rehnquist Court's performance thus far in First Amendment cases would seem to merit something like a standing ovation.

Rather than turning back the clock on freedom of expression, in several landmark cases—especially *Hustler v. Falwell, Texas v. Johnson,* and *Rosenberger v. Rector and Visitors of the University of Virginia*—the Court has continued to spell out the commanding theme of modern free-speech jurisprudence: the state shall not deliberately repress expression, however extreme, based on its content or viewpoint.[1] It even propelled this principle into cyberspace with libertarian Internet decisions like *Reno v. ACLU,* which established that, when it comes to sex talk, grown-ups can take care of their own children and need not be treated like children themselves, and *Ashcroft v. Free Speech Coalition,* which struck as overbroad Congress's attempt to criminalize "computer-generated" images that create the appearance of minors having sex.[2]

At the level of principle and rhetoric, shifting majorities on the Court have thus far taken the high ground on speech, even when the hard-right justices, such as Chief Justice William H. Rehnquist, have filed curmudgeonly dissents. This rhetorical speech friendliness has both historical and contemporary causes. The Court's libertarian course was set in earlier cases like *New York Times v. Sullivan*, *Cohen v. California*, and *Brandenburg v. Ohio*.[3] In the Rehnquist Court, Justice David Souter is a powerful intellectual force for free expression, and Justice Anthony Kennedy, often joining with the moderate-liberal bloc, has emerged as a lucid champion of free speech and viewpoint neutrality—well, sometimes at least.

But for fascinating political reasons, even the authority-worshiping hard right of the Court occasionally finds itself defending free speech. The ferocious right-wing backlash against "political correctness" and campus hate-speech codes in the late 1980s and the 1990s gave free-speech grievances an unprecedented halo in conservative circles during the Rehnquist era. In *R.A.V. v. St. Paul*, where the Court unanimously struck down a municipal anti-cross-burning ordinance, Justice Antonin Scalia wrote a haughty opinion, clearly animated by anti-PC sentiment, insisting that, while fighting words generally can be criminalized, *racist* fighting words cannot be selectively targeted.[4] The conservative justices' plutocratic identification of unrestrained campaign spending with political expression, which dates back to *Buckley v. Valeo*, has further convinced them that they are now the true champions of free expression, holding the line against political censorship by liberal reformers.[5] For the antichoice justices—Rehnquist, Scalia, and Clarence Thomas—a number of edgy cases where obstructionist "prolife" street protestors have invoked the First Amendment against prosecution have clinched their sense of free-speech martyrdom on the cross of political correctness.[6]

These "culture war" crosscurrents came to a head in 2000 in *Boy Scouts of America v. Dale*, where the solid conservative bloc of five, over the dissent of Justices John Paul Stevens, David Souter, Ruth Bader Ginsburg, and Stephen Breyer, found that the Boy Scouts, as a private group exercising associational rights, could exclude gay scoutmasters.[7] The liberals argued, a bit oddly, that the Boy Scouts had never really taken an expressive position against homosexuality. But the real issue was not whether the exclusion of gays was an expressive associational statement but whether a state could treat the Boy Scouts as a public accommodation like a hotel or restaurant. There are interesting arguments both ways that never really appeared in the case, but the die had probably been cast already in *Hurley v. Irish-American Gay, Lesbian, and Bisexual Group of Boston*, where Justice Souter found that since the private organizers of the St. Patrick's Day parade in Boston had a right to define their own message, they could exclude an unwanted formal contingent from the Boston Gay, Lesbian, and Bisexual Group.[8] A good answer to these anachronistic homophobic expressions by private groups in civil society is political counterpressure and boycott, effective strategies that are currently costing the Boy Scouts dearly.

But the conservatives' preening free-speech rhetoric in high-profile pet cases where they *like* the speech they are protecting masks a complex and demoralizing system of speech repression they have shaped for the rest of society. When citizens have challenged censorship and viewpoint discrimination in major social institutions such as schools, public television networks, electoral systems, and federally funded programs, the Rehnquist majority has habitually deferred to government and rolled over the rights of the people. Thus, while certain kinds of extreme speech and exclusionary policies have won larger-than-life symbolic victories in the Rehnquist Court, ordinary speech has suffered terrible defeats and reversals at the level of institutional practices (including the practice of electoral democracy), where Americans need the First Amendment most. The Court has grabbed the rhetorical high ground but has usually taken the low road when it really counts.

To give the devil its due, however, the Rehnquist Court has quite faithfully rejected frontal attacks on offensive speech in public places by way of the criminal and civil law. The classic decision in this vein is *Texas v. Johnson* (1989), where a five-justice majority made up of Justices William Brennan, Thurgood Marshall, Harry Blackmun, Scalia, and Kennedy struck down the criminal conviction of Gregory Johnson, a member of the Revolutionary Communist Party, for "desecrating" an

American flag at the 1984 Republican National Convention.[9] In *Texas v. Johnson*, Justice Brennan revived the spirit of Justice Robert Jackson in his famous 1943 opinion in *West Virginia v. Barnette*, which invalidated West Virginia's compulsory Pledge of Allegiance and flag salute.[10] Echoing Jackson's syntax and enunciating a kind of political free-exercise principle, Justice Brennan wrote: "If there is a bedrock principle underlying the First Amendment, it is that the Government may not prohibit the expression of an idea simply because society finds the idea itself offensive or disagreeable."

Making essentially literary and sentimental arguments, the dissenters wanted the Court to elevate its loyalty to the flag over its loyalty to free speech. Rehnquist, joined by Byron White and Sandra Day O'Connor, excerpted flowery passages of flag-related poetry and fiction to show that "the American flag has occupied a unique position as the symbol of our Nation, a uniqueness that justifies a governmental prohibition against flag burning in the way Johnson did here." It evidently did not matter to them that the First Amendment contains no exception for censorship of speech about "unique" patriotic symbols, because, as Rehnquist put it, "millions and millions of Americans regard [the flag] with an almost mystical reverence."

Also dissenting, Justice John Paul Stevens, ordinarily well grounded in the First Amendment, echoed the call to suspend conventional rules of constitutional analysis: "Even if flag burning could be considered just another species of symbolic speech under the *logical* application of the rules that the Court has developed in its interpretation of the First Amendment in other contexts, this case has an *intangible* dimension that makes those rules inapplicable." He likened the claimed right to burn flags in protest to "a federal right to post bulletin boards and graffiti on the Washington Monument." The problem with the analogy is that we have but one Washington Monument, all of it public property; if it is defaced, it is ruined for all. But we have tens of millions of flags, the private property of citizens who can do with them what they will without harming their fellow citizens' enjoyment of their own flags or the government's control of its own supply.

In 1988, the year before *Texas v. Johnson*, the conservatives joined the liberals in deciding *Hustler v. Falwell*, which will be another enduring statement of free-speech values. In *Hustler*, there was no American flag to hypnotize the conservatives, and Chief Justice Rehnquist actually wrote the opinion for a unanimous Court. *Hustler* had lampooned Jerry Falwell, leader of the Moral Majority, insinuating in an advertisement that parodied celebrity "first times" that a drunken Falwell had lost his virginity to his mother in an outhouse. The piece had a disclaimer reading "ad parody, not to be taken seriously," so it was clearly not meant to be taken as a statement of biographical fact. But Falwell sued *Hustler* in Virginia and recovered on the nouveau tort of intentional infliction of emotional distress.[11]

Rehnquist found that the right of political cartoonists and satirists to poke fun at public figures was at stake even if the caricature of Falwell in *Hustler* was "at best a distant cousin" to most journalistic cartoons. There was, he said, no coherent way to "separate" the political highbrow from the pornographic lowbrow and "the pejorative description 'outrageous' does not supply one."[12] Because the right of aggressive political satire is protected, the Court found that public figures could not recover for the intentional infliction of emotional distress—this is what comedians, cartoonists, and satirists do for a living—without first proving that a false statement of fact had been made with "actual malice," as *New York Times v. Sullivan* puts it. Here, the Court edged toward the epiphany that the First Amendment protects *all* speech against purposeful government efforts to silence it.

In *Rosenberger v. Rector and Visitors of the University of Virginia*, the Court in 1995 struck down the University of Virginia's practice of reimbursing the publishing costs of all student-produced newspapers and magazines except those having a religious purpose or identification. In a 5–4 split, with the conservatives now on the free-speech side, Justice Kennedy held that the university's publishing program established a limited public forum for student speech and its policy disfavoring religiously inflected speech was viewpoint discrimination.

In a speech market dominated by secular viewpoints, Justice Kennedy wrote, religion furnishes an alternative premise and perspective, a different "standpoint from which a variety of subjects may be discussed and considered." Despite the fact that the university thought it was avoiding Establishment Clause problems by refusing to subsidize publications like the plaintiff's *Wide Awake* Christian newspaper, it was actually effecting "a sweeping restriction on student thought and student inquiry." This understanding followed from the Court's 1981 holding in *Widmar v. Vincent*, which invalidated a public university's exclusion of religious groups from use of school facilities held open to all other student groups.[13] Although the liberals in dissent—Justices Souter, Stevens, Ginsburg, and Breyer—thought the university's selective ban was indeed required by the Establishment Clause to prevent state funding of religious proselytization, the majority found there was no compelling interest in excluding religious publications because a program that funded all journals equally would actually be "neutral toward religion." It is a First Amendment requirement, not offense, to allow religious speakers to have their say in public forums.

While the Court in *Rosenberger* determined that stripping certain subjects and speakers from a public forum is, almost by definition, the suppression of speech, the conservatives' understanding of this point has vanished in major institutional settings where they want to defer to administrative power over unwelcome expression. This acquiescence to bureaucratic censorship has dramatic antidemocratic consequences throughout society.

For example, in *Arkansas Educational Television Commission v. Forbes* (1998), the Court's conservatives and Justice Breyer (unfortunately) upheld by a 6–3 vote the commission's exclusion of Ralph Forbes, an Independent running for Congress, from a televised debate on its public TV channel that included his Democratic and Republican rivals.[14] This was a disappointing decision, not just because the censorship of political viewpoint was so blatant but because the government's interference in the campaign almost certainly changed the outcome of the election.

Forbes had been an irritant to the Republican Party establishment before leaving the party, but he was not a joke, as Justice Kennedy portrayed him. In 1990, Forbes had run for lieutenant governor on a hard-right platform and captured a winning 46.8 percent of the vote in a three-way Republican primary race, taking a clean majority in fifteen of sixteen counties in his congressional district. Thus, when he sued the public cable TV network *pro se* in his First Amendment case—to which he gave the irresistible caption *Forbes v. The Arrogant Orwellian Bureaucrats of the AETN, the Crooked Lying Politicians, and the Special Interests*— he won in the Eighth Circuit Court of Appeals, where Chief Judge Richard Arnold found that the televised debate was a "limited public forum."[15] In such a forum, a speaker may not be excluded without compelling reason. As a balloted candidate, Forbes properly belonged to the class of speakers invited, and AETN's rationale for excluding him—its standardless and tautological judgment about his political "viability"—violated the First Amendment because his viability was a "judgment to be made by the people of the Third Congressional District, not by officials of the government in charge of channels of communication."

Justice Kennedy did not see things this way. Squinting hard, he wrote that AETN "did not make its debate generally available to candidates for Arkansas' Third Congressional District seat" but rather "reserved eligibility for participation in the debate to candidates for the Third Congressional District seat [as opposed to some other seat]. At that point . . . [AETN] made candidate-by-candidate determinations as to which of the eligible candidates would participate in the debate." Thus, the debate was really a "nonpublic forum."[16]

In the "nonpublic forum," government can make "reasonable" and viewpoint-neutral exclusions. But why was the exclusion of Forbes reasonable and viewpoint-neutral? No policy or criteria for invitation were ever announced. AETN simply invited the major party candidates and rejected the Independent. The freewheeling "candidate-by-candidate determination" method that Justice Kennedy invoked as proof that the debate was a nonpublic forum was itself the essential violation of Forbes's First Amendment rights. For there were no objective viewpoint-neutral standards used in making these selections, only unregulated and standardless decisions.

Justice Kennedy dangerously eroded the doctrine of viewpoint neutrality by sanctioning the practice of government officials making ad hoc judgments about a balloted candidate's "viability." Of course, even assuming that the officials were clairvoyant and could foretell the elec-

tion results, what made Forbes not "viable" was his perceived unpopu-
larity. But *Texas v. Johnson* taught us that unpopular viewpoints must receive equal free-speech protection. So what is the relevance of viability
anyway? Even in a two-person race, one candidate is certain to lose,
but we do not consider the debate a waste of time for that reason. After facing Stephen Douglas in eight celebrated debates all over the
state of Illinois in the 1858 Senate race, Abraham Lincoln lost the election. But his debate performance laid the groundwork for his successful
presidential run two years later.

Justice Kennedy thought there was no viewpoint discrimination because the trial jury determined that Forbes's exclusion was not based
on "objections or opposition to his views."[17] But this reliance badly
confused the doctrine of viewpoint discrimination. The factual question of whether the network objected to Forbes's views does not control
the legal question of whether his exclusion was viewpoint-based. The
test of First Amendment viewpoint neutrality is an objective test that
focuses on the nature of a governmental classification treating two
classes of speakers differently, not a subjective test that focuses on the
motivations of specific government actors in suppressing someone's
speech. Subjective animus may be evidence of objective viewpoint discrimination, but it is not an element of it.

In *Rosenberger*, for example, there was no allegation of animosity toward religious students, but Justice Kennedy himself found that religiously motivated expression provided a distinctive viewpoint that
could not be blocked from public debate. The University of Virginia
bore no malice toward religion, but its rule effectively silenced a distinctive body of opinion. In the same way, the whole purpose and effect of excluding Forbes was to block out presentation of a political
viewpoint and candidate deemed unpopular. This is the essence of
viewpoint discrimination, which is the cardinal First Amendment sin.

The Court's transparent embrace of the Democratic-Republican
"two-party system" in *Forbes* permeates its treatment of election cases.
In *Timmons v. Twin Cities Area New Party* (1997), the New Party challenged Minnesota's 1901 "anti-fusion" law as a violation of the First
Amendment associational rights of party members who wanted to
cross-nominate a Democratic-Farmer-Labor candidate, State Repre-

sentative Andy Dawkins, on the New Party line. Dawkins agreed but faced a law that prevented "fusion" candidacies, the kind that gave life in the nineteenth century to numerous progressive and populist parties in the Midwest and West.[18] The Eighth Circuit upheld the challenge, finding that the fusion ban was a "severe" burden on the New Party's "freedom to select" its own "standard-bearer" and its right to "broaden the base of public participation in and support for [its] activities."[19]

But by a vote of 6–3, the Supreme Court reversed and rejected the plaintiffs' claims. Slicing the bologna very fine, Rehnquist distinguished the conceded right of the New Party to nominate its own standard-bearer from its right to place its nominee's name on the ballot, a right that he said is not absolute. The New Party could endorse Dawkins and campaign for him, but Minnesota could keep his name off the New Party's ballot line. In other words, the ballot belongs to the government, not the people. In this sense, the decision echoes the equally troubling *Burdick v. Takushi*, where the conservatives upheld Hawaii's ban on write-in votes, finding that the government could shape the ballot to provide for selection among preapproved candidates.[20]

Although the Constitution says nothing of a two-party system, Chief Justice Rehnquist in *Timmons* came close to constitutionalizing it: "The Constitution permits the Minnesota legislature to decide that political stability is best served through a healthy two-party system." Of course, a "healthy two-party system" is a fluid arrangement open to challenge, the kind that gave rise to Lincoln's Republican Party prior to the Civil War. But the kind that Minnesota sought to entrench is a fortified political establishment built on violation of other citizens' rights. Many people were shocked by the Rehnquist Court's partisan intervention into the 2000 election in *Bush v. Gore*, but why should a Court that had already gone beyond the text of the Constitution effectively to establish a two-party system have any qualms about maintaining that system and simply dropping one of the parties?

No case better exemplifies the shift from the Warren Court's defense of speech in America's institutions to the Rehnquist Court's acquiescence to administrative censorship than the 1988 decision in *Hazelwood School District v. Kuhlmeier*, which sharply undercut the Court's watershed 1969 holding in *Tinker v. Des Moines School District*.[21] In *Tinker*, the Court reversed the suspension of thirteen-year-old Mary Beth Tinker, a Quaker who wore a black armband to school to protest the Vietnam War. The Court found that "state-operated schools may not be enclaves of totalitarianism" and that students enjoy "freedom of expression" unless it "materially" disrupts the educational process or violates other students' rights. Justice Abe Fortas, writing for the majority, was emphatic that students must be able to bring their own thoughts and feelings to school and "may not be confined to the expression of those sentiments that are officially approved."

This understanding began to unravel in 1986 with Chief Justice Burger's decision in *Bethel School District No. 403 v. Fraser*, which upheld discipline against a student for making lewd remarks in a student council nominating address.[22] But in *Hazelwood*, the Court set up a far more sweeping counterprinciple to the famous *Tinker* rule. There, the conservative majority upheld a principal's censorship of two student-written articles that were scheduled for publication in the school newspaper, one about the impact of parental divorce on high school students and the other about the problems faced by teenage mothers. The articles were deemed "inappropriate." The students felt their worthy journalistic efforts gave them an open-and-shut case on *Tinker* grounds, but the Court held that school officials can "exercise editorial control" over the "content of student speech" in all "school-sponsored activities," including newspapers, yearbooks, and theater, for any "legitimate pedagogical" purpose at all. The message sent to students is that their schools are training them not for participatory citizenship but for submission to bureaucratic power. The result in many parts of the country has been a crackdown on student speech and the development of private Web sites by students to castigate their censors, a trend that has predictably produced a lot of district court litigation.

The principles of viewpoint and content neutrality, embraced by majorities of five justices each in *Texas v. Johnson* and *Rosenberger*, lose their hold when government discriminates against speech in programs it funds, especially where conservatives favor the discrimination. This is the lesson of *Rust v. Sullivan*, where the Court upheld antiabortion regulations promulgated by the first President Bush's Department of Health and Human Services regarding family-planning groups that receive Title X funding.[23] The so-called gag rules banned all abortion counseling and referrals of pregnant patients by doctors, required physicians to refer pregnant clients "for appropriate prenatal and/or social services by furnishing a list of available providers that promote the welfare of the mother and the unborn child," and prohibited any projects receiving Title X funds from engaging in activities that "encourage, promote or advocate abortion as a method of family planning." The Court viewed these restrictions not as unconstitutional conditions compelling speech or forbidding it but rather as a funding and policy choice to prefer childbirth over abortion. As Chief Justice Rehnquist put it, "The Government has not discriminated on the basis of viewpoint; it has merely chosen to fund one activity to the exclusion of another."

In a powerful dissent joined by Justices Marshall and Brennan and in part by O'Connor, Justice Blackmun argued that the ban on abortion counseling was a direct assault on the free-speech and privacy rights of both women and their physicians. He also stated, "By refusing to fund those family-planning projects that advocate abortion *because* they advocate abortion, the Government plainly has targeted a particular viewpoint."[24] Reliance on the fact that these are funding decisions "simply begs the question," he wrote, since it is clear that the government could not, for example, distribute funds to clinics "upon considerations of race." According to Justice Blackmun, "ideological viewpoint is a similarly repugnant ground upon which to base funding decisions."

In fairness, it should be said that abortion politics have also at times distorted the free-speech principles of liberals on the Court. In one significant case, the liberals let their fears of admittedly spooky antiabortion protestors dilute their commitment to free speech in the "traditional public forum" of the public sidewalk. In the rather shocking 5–4 decision of *Hill v. Colorado* (2000), where they were joined by Justice O'Connor, the liberals upheld a remarkable state law ban in Colorado against "knowingly approach[ing] another person within eight feet of such person . . . for the purpose of passing a leaflet or handbill to, displaying a sign to, or engaging in oral protest, education, or counseling with such person in the public way or sidewalk area within a radius of one hundred feet from any entrance door to a health care facility."[25] Everything about this law, from its legislative history to its text to its enforcement, tells us that it was a content- and viewpoint-based effort to suppress antiabortion activities outside of clinics. But the majority, validating for the first time in the First Amendment context a social interest in being left alone (outside the home), upheld the law as a reasonable place-and-manner regulation. *Hill* now stands as a template for local governments to develop regulations to stifle the expression of unpopular views in public places. One assumes the liberals will quickly return to their senses, but in the meantime the labor movement should beware.

The case that might have forced the justices to choose loyalties between the viewpoint-discrimination principle upheld in *Rosenberger* and the principle that government may selectively subsidize speech activities was *National Endowment for the Arts v. Finley.* The case brought to a head a decade-long public controversy over provocative NEA-funded art, such as Robert Mapplethorpe's homoerotic photography and Andres Serrano's much-maligned *Piss Christ.* Congress passed a statutory provision requiring the chairperson of the National Endowment for the Arts to ensure that, in the grants application process, "artistic excellence and artistic merit are the criteria by which applications are judged, taking into consideration general standards of decency and respect for the diverse beliefs and values of the American public."[26] An overly eager challenge to the law brought before it took effect by performance artist Karen Finley and other NEA-grant hopefuls elicited an ambiguous result. By an 8–1 vote, the majority upheld the new standard on the theory that the NEA, reading the provision as "merely hortatory," viewed it as stopping "well short of an absolute restriction." The majority thus interpreted the language only to make the NEA take "decency and respect" (whatever the terms might mean) into consideration in a general way in forming selection panels and not on a dispositive case-by-case basis with respect to applications.[27] If the NEA converted the general admonition into a specific "penalty on disfavored viewpoints, then we would confront a different case."

Justice Scalia, joined by Justice Thomas, concurred in the result but slammed the majority for changing the plain meaning of the act. He wrote: " 'The operation was a success, but the patient died.' What such a procedure is to medicine, the Court's opinion in this case is to law. . . . The most avid congressional opponents of the provision could not have asked for more." He viewed it as "100% clear that decency and respect are to be taken into account in evaluating applications" and found there to be absolutely nothing wrong with this kind of viewpoint discrimination.[28] Indeed, his opinion is a panegyric to the virtues of viewpoint discrimination in government-funded programs, where the government can spend its money however it wants.

Justice Souter's lone dissent provided the most intellectually honest perspective in the case. He agreed strongly with Justice Scalia that the statute embodied a requirement of viewpoint discrimination in consideration of specific grant applications, but he saw this as blatantly unlawful. Even if interpreted to be a command of only general and diffuse consideration by the NEA, Justice Souter argued, the "decency and respect" provision was no more legitimate than a requirement of "taking into consideration the centrality of Christianity to the American cultural experience," or "taking into consideration whether the artist is a communist," or "taking into consideration the political message conveyed by the art," or "taking into consideration the superiority of the white race." Justice Souter rejected Justice Scalia's claim that this was just a case of government itself being the speaker, the conservative paradigm in *Rust*, since it was clearly acting as an arts patron subsidizing private speech by artists. The NEA was in the same position as the University of Virginia when it paid for student speech. Justice Souter's unflinching defense of free speech and his unwillingness to paper things over mark him as the great champion of the First Amendment on the Rehnquist Court and the proper heir to Justice Brennan.

The most recent government funding case, *Legal Services Corporation v. Velazquez*, was a 5–4 win for free speech when Justice Kennedy joined the liberals to invalidate outrageous restrictions Congress imposed on the Legal Services Corporation, which distributes federal funds to groups providing free legal assistance to the poor.[29] Congress blocked any funding of groups that represent clients challenging the validity or constitutionality of a welfare law, and if a problem with the law surfaced after representation began, Congress required the lawyer to withdraw from representation. Finding that this restriction caused a "severe impairment of the judicial function," the majority saw it as "designed to insulate the Government's interpretation of the Constitution from judicial challenge." Amazingly but not uncharacteristically, the four other conservatives who defended the fundamentalist Christian student newspaper in *Rosenberger* against government manipulation of speech found the legal services restriction to be an unobjectionable *Rust*-style decision by government on how to spend its own funds.

There are enough historical and ideological forces at work to keep Chief Justice Rehnquist and his allies from gutting the First Amendment in the way they have worked over equal protection. Indeed, because of the politics of antiabortion protest, campaign finance reform, hate-speech regulation, and the always simmering controversy over "political correctness," conservatives both on and off the Court have of late affected a kind of wounded First Amendment pride about standing up for unpopular speech. This microchip on the shoulder is all to the good, and we can only hope (against hope) that their newfound interest in free expression lasts during the speech-hostile environment accompanying the war on terrorism.

The problem is that the healthy doctrines of viewpoint and content neutrality sketched out in cases like *Rosenberger* never go to work for ordinary people who dare to challenge the authority of those who run our social institutions. You are far better off appearing before this Court as a student editing a fundamentalist Christian newspaper or even a hopeless teenage Maoist burning flags in the street than as an organizer of a new political party that might threaten the two-party system, an intellectually engaged student speaking uncomfortable truths to the community in the high school campus newspaper, or a poor woman in a federally funded family-planning clinic who wants to talk to her doctor about a life choice the conservatives wish would just go away. The problem with the Rehnquist Court lies not so much in its high principles and rhetoric but rather in its malleable, unsystematic doctrines and its concrete sympathies, which tilt hard to the right and remain depressingly constant over time.

Gay Rights

CHAI FELDBLUM

Shortly before William Rehnquist became chief justice, the Supreme Court issued an opinion in the case of *Bowers v. Hardwick* that upheld the constitutionality of Georgia's sodomy law.[1] In the years of the Rehnquist Court, it has decided only three other cases dealing with gay rights. The pace and substance of change in this country's attitudes toward equality for gay people are well reflected in these cases, however. The tone of the Court's opinions, whether the result has been a "win" for the gay rights party or not, has been relatively respectful of those who are gay, lesbian, or bisexual. Moreover, the increasing number of cases that have come to the Supreme Court raising issues of gay equality reflect the rise in gay rights activism and visibility. But the narrow loss for James Dale, the openly gay scoutmaster who lost his bid to remain in the Boy Scouts by a one-vote margin in the Supreme Court, reflects as well how the next few appointments to the Supreme Court will shape the future of gay legal rights.[2]

The underlying theme in these Supreme Court cases has been the justices' views regarding the morality of gay sexual conduct. As long as most of them believed homosexual conduct was *inherently* immoral, gay rights claims were necessarily doomed to failure. But as the country's attitudes began to shift regarding the inexorable connection between immorality and gay sexual conduct and, with them, the attitudes of some of the justices, the outcomes of gay rights cases became less easy to predict. No justice has yet been willing to write a decision based on a stated belief that homosexual conduct is morally equivalent to heterosexual conduct. But a majority of the justices are no longer willing to accept that homosexual conduct is inherently and necessarily *immoral*.

Of course, liberals like to believe that moral judgments should ordinarily have little relevance anyway for purposes of governmental actions and judicial decisions. Under a liberal view of "equality" and "individual rights," individuals should have a right to intimate association and privacy that should not be restricted by the government, as long as the individual's behavior harms no one else. A majority of people in a society may dislike, or even hate, a particular behavior in question, but a liberal, neutral government is designed to protect the right of an individual to engage in such behavior, regardless of how morally perverse it may seem to others in society.

In reality, however, legislative and judicial decision making is often shaped by the moral assessments of legislators and judges. Thus, if gay sexual conduct is viewed by a majority in the society as morally reprehensible, and consequently to be condemned if not eradicated, it will be next to impossible for individuals engaged in such conduct to gain nondiscrimination protection based on sexual orientation in either the legislative or the judicial arena. The only way they can achieve acceptance, tolerance, and ultimately true equality is for the public moral assessment of homosexuality to change. Nothing makes this clearer than the progression of Supreme Court cases dealing with gay rights.

In 1986, in *Bowers v. Hardwick*, the Supreme Court considered the constitutionality of a Georgia sodomy statute that criminalized oral or anal sex engaged in by any two individuals, regardless of the individuals' gender or sexual orientation. Thus, under Georgia law, a married couple who engaged in oral or anal sex were engaging in as equally criminal activity as a gay man who had oral or anal sex with another man.

The question whether the Georgia statute was constitutional would not necessarily have been an easy question to answer under the Court's constitutional jurisprudence to date. The Court had previously found a general "right to privacy" in the Constitution, which has been held to prohibit a state from criminalizing the use of contraception, abortion, or other family-planning decisions—for married couples or unmarried couples. The question in *Bowers v. Hardwick*, therefore, should have been whether this "right to privacy" also prohibited a state from criminalizing certain types of sexual conduct—that is, oral or anal sex—whether practiced by married or unmarried couples or by gay or heterosexual couples.

But Justice Byron White, who wrote the Court's majority opinion, framed the question in a manner that made the answer obvious to him (and presumably, any reader) as soon as he posed the question. To Justice White, the question in the case was whether "the Federal Constitution confers a fundamental right for *homosexuals* to engage in *sodomy*." As Justice White explained, the right of privacy had previously been extended by the Court to protect such areas as child rearing, family relationships, marriage, and procreation. The moral distinction between such areas of life and the relationships engaged in by gay people was patently clear to him. As he noted, "no connection between family, marriage, or procreation on the one hand and homosexual activity on the other has been demonstrated." Therefore the answer to the question had to be no.

Justice White was also not willing to extend a more limited "right to be let alone" to protect any consensual gay sexual conduct practiced in the privacy of a home. The Court had previously recognized such a right in prohibiting a state from criminalizing the reading of obscene materials inside the privacy of one's home. But Justice White could not envision how homosexual conduct would then be distinguished, "except by fiat," from private sexual conduct such as "adultery, incest, and other sexual crimes committed in the home."

Justice Blackmun's dissenting opinion in *Hardwick* was a remarkably progressive one in many ways. It is worth observing, however, that he did not argue that gay sexual conduct should be protected under the right of privacy because gay couples embody the same moral values as heterosexual couples. In a previous case, in which the government had been constitutionally prohibited from interfering with family and marriage relationships, the Court had waxed eloquent on the virtues of heterosexual coupling within the marriage context: "Marriage is a coming together for better or for worse, hopefully enduring, and intimate to the degree of being sacred. It is an association that promotes a way of life, not causes; a harmony in living, not political faiths; a bilateral loyalty, not commercial or social projects."[3] But Justice Blackmun did not invoke this opinion to argue that committed gay couplings should be protected against government intrusion because such relationships partake equally of the importance and good of heterosexual couplings within marriage. Instead, he focused on the "right to be let alone" aspect of the right of privacy. As noted, under this aspect of privacy, the government is constitutionally prohibited from interfering with those activities that occur in the privacy of one's home and do not harm others (such as reading pornography at home). As Justice Blackmun put it, quoting an earlier case, " 'a way of life that is odd or even erratic but interferes with no rights or interests of others is not to be condemned because it is different.' "[4]

Almost ten years passed before the Supreme Court again considered a gay rights case fully on its merits. During that time (1986–95), the country witnessed an increase in activism and visibility on the part of the gay community, as deaths from AIDS ravaged it, encouraging increased fear and prejudice. But the disease also politicized hundreds of individuals and involuntarily "outed" many others as gay. Thousands of people were suddenly confronted with the fact that they *did* know someone who was gay, often a close family member or personal friend. Gay people who had been hiding their sexual orientation for years began to "come out," trading invisibility for integrity and pride.

One symbolic aspect of this push for visibility was efforts by gay, lesbian, and bisexual descendants of Irish immigrants to march in the St. Patrick's Day parades in New York City and Boston. The message these marchers intended to send was clear: "Irish is good. Gay is good. Irish gay is good." Each year, however, parade organizers excluded the gay Irish groups. Clearly, they wanted nothing to do with the message conveyed by such groups. In 1995, the Supreme Court concluded in *Hurley v. Irish-American Gay, Lesbian, and Bisexual Group of Boston* that the Boston parade organizers had a constitutional right not to be forced by a state antidiscrimination law to include a gay Irish group among its march contingents.[5] Although the decision was greeted with dismay by some gay rights advocates, its tone reflected a sea change in the Court's attitude toward homosexuality.

Justice David Souter, writing for a unanimous Court, explained that most parades are intended to express something. And although the Boston St. Patrick's Day parade hosted various and often cacophonous contingents and messages, each contingent's expression, at least in the eyes of the parade's organizers, comported with what merited celebration on that day. The gay Irish group had a message as well. The presence of organized marchers under the gay Irish banner, Justice Souter explained, would "suggest their view that people of their sexual orientations have as much claim to unqualified social acceptance as heterosexuals and indeed as members of parade units organized around other identifying characteristics."[6]

It is hard to imagine the majority in *Hardwick* understanding that gay people might want to march in a parade to convey the message that gay people are morally and socially equivalent to heterosexuals. That would have seemed preposterous. It would have seemed to the *Hardwick* majority like a group of adulterers or a group of people who engage in incest marching to send a message of pride and integrity about adultery or incest! But to Justice Souter, it seemed reasonable that a contingent of gay people would want to march to express a message of pride and integrity about being gay and Irish. Moreover, he described that desire respectfully and thoughtfully. The problem, from his perspective, was that the parade organizers did not wish to send such a message, and the First Amendment precludes the government from forcing people to utter speech they do not wish to utter.

Justice Souter emphasized that the objective of the state's antidiscrimination law based on sexual orientation was legitimate: to ensure that individuals are not denied access to private businesses and groups simply because they are gay. But in this case, the parade organizers had not barred individual gay people from marching in the parade. Rather, they had a rule barring an organized gay Irish *group* from marching in order to send a message through the parade about the goodness of being Irish and gay. Under the First Amendment, a state antidiscrimination law could not force a private entity to send such a message.

While gay Irish groups never managed to obtain permission from parade organizers to march in either the Boston or the New York parade, the acceptance of gay people living their lives openly and with integrity increased over time. Together with visibility and a sense of "belonging" came the passage of local and state antidiscrimination laws that prohibited government, private employers, and private businesses from using sexual orientation as a basis for adverse actions. Between 1990 and 1995, approximately 80 cities, counties, or localities passed such laws and ordinances; by 2001, the number had reached 134 (prohibiting discrimination in private employment) and 239 (prohibiting discrimination in public employment).

Proponents of these antidiscrimination laws do not argue for their passage on the grounds that homosexual conduct is morally equivalent to heterosexual conduct. Rather, they take pains to assert that such laws are neutral regarding the morality of being gay and that they simply ensure equality for all people—gay or straight. Nevertheless, there has often been a backlash to these laws, spurred in part because the liberal rhetoric of neutrality used in advocating them ignores the moral disagreements that still exist over gay sexual conduct. That is, people who believe homosexuality is morally wrong also believe employers and businesses should be able to refuse to associate with people whose conduct they find morally reprehensible.

Interestingly enough, the opponents of these laws have rarely attempted to get them repealed by asserting a virulent view regarding the immorality of homosexuality. (This is a mirror image of the reticence of gay rights supporters who do not advocate the passage of such laws because of a putative moral equivalence of homosexuality and heterosexuality.) The fact is, as more gay people have begun to live ordinary, honest, and open lives, the previously assumed societal belief that homosexuality is inherently immoral has itself come under question. Most people in America today do not believe that homosexuality is an inherent evil that must be eradicated. Most people also do not believe that responsible gay sexual conduct is morally equivalent to responsible heterosexual conduct (and thus, for example, should be supported by the government in the way that heterosexual coupling is supported through marriage and other benefits). But a clear majority are now uncomfortable with the idea that private parties should be allowed to deny individuals housing or employment based solely on their sexual orientation.[7]

Thus, the approach taken by those who oppose antidiscrimination laws is to describe them as bestowing "special rights" for gay people. For example, in Colorado, where the cities of Aspen and Boulder and the city and county of Denver banned discrimination based on sexual orientation in a range of areas, opponents sponsored a ballot initiative to amend the Colorado constitution to repeal all such existing protections and to preclude the adoption of any further protections. Known as Amendment 2 and passed by a vote of 54 percent, the provision precluded Colorado, all its localities, and any of its agencies from adopting any rule that provided "homosexual, lesbian, or bisexual orientation, conduct, practice, or relationships" any claim of "minority status, quota preferences, protected status, or claim of discrimination." The campaign to pass Amendment 2 was peppered with claims that gay people were seeking to obtain special rights through the passage of such laws.

In 1996, in the case of *Romer v. Evans*, six justices of the Supreme Court concluded that the people of Colorado had violated the Constitution's guarantee of "equal protection under the law" when they passed Amendment 2. The opinion, written by Justice Anthony Kennedy, stressed the breadth of the protection removed by the amendment and the narrowness of its focus on gay people. Unlike any other group that might need protection from discrimination and could approach their cities, localities, and state for such protection, gay people were precluded from seeking it. Justice Kennedy concluded that the sheer breadth of the amendment seemed "inexplicable by anything but animus toward the class it affects; it lacks a rational relationship to legitimate state interests."[8]

Justice Antonin Scalia, joined by Justices Rehnquist and Clarence Thomas, was vigorous in his dissent and incredulous at the majority's reasoning. From the dissent's perspective, the Court's opinion in *Hardwick* had pronounced it constitutionally permissible for a state to make homosexual conduct criminal. Given that, surely it was permissible for a state to pass laws that simply disfavored homosexual conduct; even further, surely it was permissible for a state not to confer special pro-

tection on homosexual conduct by prohibiting discrimination specifically on that characteristic.

It also seemed eminently reasonable to Justice Scalia that the people of a state might want to ensure that special protections based on
sexual orientation were never passed anywhere in their state. He noted
that the majority opinion had contained grim, disapproving hints that
the people of Colorado were guilty of "animus" toward homosexuality,
"as though that has been established as un-American." But, as he
observed, "I had thought that one could consider certain conduct reprehensible—murder, for example, or polygamy, or cruelty to animals—
and could exhibit even 'animus' toward such conduct. Surely that is
the only sort of 'animus' at issue here: moral disapproval of homosexual conduct, the same sort of moral disapproval that produced the
centuries-old criminal laws that we held constitutional in [*Hardwick*]."[9]

Justice Scalia was absolutely correct, of course, that certain animus
is permissible in our society. That is why the liberal rhetoric of neutrality that asserts that antidiscrimination laws simply establish basic
equality and nothing more is somewhat disingenuous. While such laws
may not condone any particular behavior, they certainly establish that
particular types of animus are no longer considered permissible. Indeed, as Justice Scalia correctly noted, they effectively stand for the
proposition that discrimination based on homosexuality is as reprehensible as discrimination based on race or gender.

But the majority justices in *Romer*, presumably reflecting public
opinion in the country by 1996, presumed that a locality might indeed
wish to make animus based on sexual orientation illegal in its jurisdiction. Moreover, they presumed that a state constitutional amendment
that broadly denied gay people in that locality, and all other localities,
the right to seek and benefit from such laws reflected inappropriate animus for purposes of the Equal Protection Clause.

These justices never said they believed homosexuality and heterosexuality were morally equivalent, nor did they probably even view
their opinion as morally condoning homosexual conduct. Nevertheless,
the logic of their opinion required them to view gay sexual conduct as
morally distinct from the immorality of murder, polygamy, or cruelty
to animals.

The breadth of Colorado's Amendment 2 and the fact that gay people were denied the right to seek protection from their own local, friendly localities were clearly factors for Justices Kennedy and Sandra Day O'Connor in joining the *Romer* majority. Indeed, while it was deciding *Romer*, the Supreme Court had pending before it a case that raised essentially identical issues to those presented in *Romer*. In *Equality Foundation of Greater Cincinnati, Inc. v. City of Cincinnati*, the appellate court upheld the validity of an amendment to Cincinnati's city charter that repealed a city council ordinance prohibiting discrimination based on sexual orientation and denying the council the right to pass such ordinances in the future.[10] Ordinarily, one would have expected the Supreme Court to summarily reverse the *Equality Foundation* case, based on its recently released *Romer* decision. Instead, the Court sent it back to the appellate court for "further review" in light of *Romer*.

The appellate court's subsequent review and decision were a shock to gay rights advocates. The court concluded that the *narrowness* of the city charter amendment (all it did was affect the city council ordinances) distinguished it from Amendment 2 in Colorado and that it was reasonable for the people of Cincinnati to want to eliminate the public and private costs that might accrue from lawsuits arising under the council's ordinance. Indeed, a significant portion of Justice Scalia's legal reasoning in his *Romer* dissent made its way into the appellate court's majority decision, which largely parroted Justice Scalia's opinion, also in dissent (joined in by the other *Romer* dissenters), from the Supreme Court's remand decision.[11]

Gay rights advocates sought review of the second *Equality Foundation* ruling in the Supreme Court, but the Court refused to hear the case, thus letting the appellate court ruling stand. In the ordinary course of events, not too much should be read into the Supreme Court's refusal to hear a case. Indeed, in this instance three justices (John Paul Stevens, Souter, and Ruth Bader Ginsburg) wrote an accompanying statement pointing out that the Court may refuse to hear a case simply because specific facts make it inappropriate for Supreme Court review. But the fact that the Supreme Court allowed the ruling in *Equality Foundation* to stand felt like a splash of cold water to gay rights advocates after the euphoria of the *Romer* decision. To some observers, it seemed to indicate that Justices Kennedy and O'Connor, the two moderate justices who had respectively written and joined *Romer*, were not willing to extend gay rights too far.

This interpretation seemed to be validated in the case the Supreme Court decided in June 2000, *Boy Scouts of America v. Dale*. New Jersey had passed a public accommodations law that prohibited a range of businesses and associations from discriminating on the basis of sexual orientation. The New Jersey Supreme Court concluded that the Boy Scouts of America were covered under that law as a public accommodation, a ruling the Supreme Court had no authority to review because it was based on an interpretation of state law. But the Boy Scouts argued to the Supreme Court that the Constitution precluded the state from forcing the organization to comply with a state antidiscrimination law that required it to retain an openly gay scoutmaster, James Dale. The Boy Scouts viewed themselves as like the St. Patrick's Day parade organizers in *Hurley*. If the Boy Scouts were forced to retain James Dale, they would be forced to send a moral message about homosexuality that was contrary to their own chosen and expressed viewpoint about homosexuality.

Chief Justice Rehnquist, joined by Justices Kennedy, O'Connor, Scalia, and Thomas, agreed. He concluded that the Boy Scouts needed to exclude James Dale as a scoutmaster to preserve their expressive views regarding homosexuality and that the government's interest in prohibiting discrimination was not sufficient to override the Boy Scouts' First Amendment expressive rights.

The Boy Scouts' actual view on homosexuality, however, was a seriously contested issue in the case. According to the Boy Scout Oath and Law, scouts must be "morally straight" and "clean." "Morally straight" is defined in the *Boy Scout Handbook* as being a "person of strong character," and "guid[ing] your life with honesty, purity, and justice." There was nothing in the Scout Oath or *Handbook* that stated that being gay was incompatible with being "morally straight." Writing for the majority in *Dale*, Chief Justice Rehnquist was forced to observe that the Scout Oath never expressly mentioned either sexuality or sexual orientation and indeed that the terms "morally straight" and "clean" were not self-defining. As he explained, "Some people may believe that engaging in homosexual conduct is not at odds with being 'morally straight' and 'clean.' And others may believe that engaging in homosexual conduct is contrary to being 'morally straight' and 'clean.' "

Having acknowledged that there was not a universal societal view regarding the immorality of gay sexual conduct, Rehnquist then simply asserted that the Boy Scouts fell into the latter category of those who believe homosexual conduct is inconsistent with being morally straight and clean. To Rehnquist and his colleagues, this conclusion was simple: the organization had stated such a position about homosexuality in a memo to the Boy Scouts executive committee and had told the Supreme Court in its brief that this was its view.

In previous cases, in which groups such as the Rotary Club or the United States Jaycees had been forced to defend their policies of excluding women as members, the Court had been able to identify specific practices on the part of the organization (such as inviting women as junior members or as guests) that undermined their asserted expressive interests in excluding women as full members. By contrast, in *Dale*, all the Supreme Court had before it was the Boy Scouts' bald assertion that admitting homosexuals as scoutmasters would be incompatible with the organization's mission. Nevertheless, given the current public state of moral views on homosexuality, these five justices presumably considered it reasonable that a respected American organization would consider gay sexual conduct to be incompatible with being "morally straight," and hence it was easier for these justices to accept the Boy Scouts' simple assertion to that effect.

In response, the four dissenting justices, led by Justice Stevens, took the majority to task for accepting, with little critical analysis, the Boy Scouts' assertion that they had a clear, coherent viewpoint that being gay was morally wrong. The dissenting justices did not doubt that many people held such a view, including people who were senior Boy Scouts officials. Nor did they believe that whether such a view was correct or reasonable was relevant to the Court's legal analysis, a point Justice Souter emphasized in a separate opinion. The problem for them was that it was difficult to discern this viewpoint about homosexuality from the way values were actually taught in Boy Scouts settings. There was no mention of homosexuality in the Scout Oath or *Hand-*

book; scoutmasters were told to refer questions about sexuality generally to those better able to handle them (religious counselors or parents), and a number of the entities that sponsored Boy Scouts chapters had expressed policies of nondiscrimination based on sexual orientation and, hence, presumably did not share the same moral views on homosexuality as did the Boy Scouts executive committee.

As the dissenting justices emphasized, it was irrelevant to their legal analysis whether they agreed with the Boy Scouts' moral message. The First Amendment protects the rights of groups to organize in order to convey their viewpoints—even viewpoints that might be heartily disliked by others. But society's changing moral assessment of homosexuality meant that the Boy Scouts could not simply require that scouts live lives of "honesty, purity, and justice" and then presume that this was understood to include a requirement not to engage in gay conduct. As Justice Stevens observed, although unfavorable opinions about gay people are ancient and "like equally atavistic opinions about certain racial groups . . . have been nourished by sectarian doctrine," over the years "interaction with real people, rather than mere adherence to traditional ways of thinking about members of unfamiliar classes, have modified those opinions." For example, he noted, some religious communities had clearly altered their views on the morality of homosexuality, including some of the religious groups that sponsor Boy Scouts chapters.

Despite the loss for James Dale and other gay scoutmasters, the fact that the issue of whether gay conduct was contrary to being "morally straight" and "clean" was seriously contested is itself an important reflection of society's changing moral assessments of homosexuality. These changing assessments are a direct reaction to the real lives of gay people—lives that are lived openly, honestly, and right next door in suburbia, urban areas, and the countryside. Moreover, the continued visibility of such lives—both in the media and in real life—shows no sign of decreasing.

The narrow victory for the Boy Scouts in *Dale* has not ended the public conversation regarding gay conduct and morality. To the contrary, the Boy Scouts' position that engaging in gay conduct is necessarily contrary to being moral has come under attack—or, at least, strict scrutiny—by parents, boys, and families across the country. Once one accepts that individuals do not choose to be gay (a fact validated by all reputable scientific and psychological work), it is hard to justify the morality of denying gay people the opportunity to love other human beings. The public conversations about Boy Scouts, morality, and love will ultimately only enhance the possibility of equality for all gay people.

The courts have always been a locus of public debate, both as a reflection of the current state of beliefs on a particular issue and as a catalyst for further examination of such beliefs. In the area of gay rights, everything from membership in the Boy Scouts to recognition of same-sex marriage has been debated in the courts. In each case, legal decisions have helped move the conversation forward, even if the particular outcome has not been favorable to the gay plaintiff's position. For example, in 1999, the Vermont Supreme Court ruled that gay couples in Vermont have a right under the state constitution to have their relationships recognized by the state in some form equal to that of heterosexual relationships.[12] This decision was possible only because the conversation on the morality of gay coupling shifted.

Future rulings from the Supreme Court will in large part depend on future appointments of justices. Socially conservative justices will presumably be more willing to assume that homosexuality is immoral and hence that discrimination based on sexual orientation is legitimate; liberal or moderate justices may be more skeptical of the assumption that gay conduct is necessarily immoral. But regardless of the composition of the Supreme Court, as an increasing number of gay people live open and honest lives, the public view of the morality of gay conduct will continue to undergo change. And that change, ultimately, will be the most revolutionary one of all.

The Politics of Abortion

SUSAN ESTRICH

For the last two decades of the twentieth century, feminists sought to draw a link between the presidential election, the Supreme Court, and reproductive freedom. "You vote for the Court when you vote for president. You're voting on *Roe v. Wade*."[1] That's what they say, every four years. And we said it again in 2000.

In one sense, of course, it was immediately true this time around: the Supreme Court did decide the election and, depending on your perspective, it did so on a partisan or at least a political basis. Would the same majority have stepped in to block a recount ordered by the state court if doing so would have made Al Gore president? It was remarkable enough that they did it for George Bush, ideologically speaking.

But as a strategy, tying an election to the Supreme Court and thence to *Roe v. Wade* rarely works, and as a prediction, it oversteps the mark. In the 2000 election, while there was certainly a significant gender gap and certainly a correlation between views on abortion and voting, Al Gore got fewer votes than the prochoice position does on most polls. Ralph Nader's support was almost entirely composed of prochoice voters who were reconciled to Bush's election, and Bush received substantial backing among prochoice white women, particularly those who were married.

As a political matter, the last thing President George Bush wants is to turn either future mid-term elections, and particularly the 2004 reelection, into an actual referendum on abortion, which is why the prediction is part doomsday, part wishful thinking.

The good news is that middle-class women are unlikely to lose their rights to a safe early abortion. The bad news is that they are unlikely to rise up politically to demand their rights, much less the rights of less fortunate women.

Legally speaking, the story of abortion can be seen as a tale of two cases. The first was *Roe v. Wade*, decided in 1973. Prior to *Roe*, each state decided for itself whether to allow abortion; Massachusetts didn't (unless you had two doctors attesting to mental instability) and New York did, and women used to chip in to buy bus tickets when girls got pregnant.

Then everything changed. In one of the most criticized opinions in modern jurisprudence, the United States Supreme Court held that a Texas law prohibiting all abortions except when necessary to save the life of the mother violated the Constitution. Justice Harry Blackmun's painstaking opinion divided a pregnancy into trimesters, holding that during the first trimester state prohibitions could not limit a woman's right to choose, in consultation with her doctor, to terminate a pregnancy; that during the second trimester this right could be limited only to protect her health; and that only after the fetus reached the stage of viability in the third trimester, the stage where the baby could survive outside the womb, did the state have a compelling interest in protecting potential human life.

The smart boys had a field day with *Roe*. A generation of young constitutional scholars ate Justice Blackmun for lunch, finding nothing in the Constitution or its penumbra to justify the Court's articulation of a constitutional right to choose. The trimester approach was criticized as having neither a medical nor a legal basis; it is a construct, an invention, testament to the legislative judgments that inform abortion regulation. What kind of constitutional right comes with a trimester analysis? None, of course.

Yet there was always a logic to *Roe* that was more substantial than its doctrinal basis. Years of discussing, debating, and teaching abortion have taught me that this is not a subject where anyone changes anyone else's mind, where intelligent argument is anything more than that, where politics works. It is a matter of belief, tempered with experience, almost immune from outside influence. The decision to terminate a pregnancy is one that in our society can only be left to the individual: there is no collective judgment that could be tolerably enforced. The argument against *Roe* in the academy was never that the Court had reached the wrong result but rather that someone else should have reached it. The inelegant answer to that complaint and the ultimate raison d'être for the decision was that unfortunately no one else was stepping up to the plate. Justice Blackmun did what needed to be done, inelegantly, perhaps, but effectively. This is why *Roe* has survived, despite itself.

In 1989, in *Webster v. Reproductive Health Services*, four justices of the Supreme Court seemed to give notice that they were ready to overrule *Roe*.[2] The Missouri law at issue in *Webster* declared that life begins at conception, prohibited using government funds or facilities for the purpose of "encouraging or counseling" a woman to have an abortion, and required a test of "viability" before abortions would be allowed after twenty weeks of pregnancy. The Court upheld the statute, without a majority opinion. Chief Justice William Rehnquist, writing for himself and Justices Byron White and Anthony Kennedy, criticized the twin pillars of *Roe*: trimesters and viability. The rigid *Roe* framework, he wrote, is hardly consistent with the notion of a Constitution cast in general terms. As for viability, Rehnquist opined, "we do not see why the State's interest in protecting potential human life should come into existence only at the point of viability, and that there should therefore be a rigid line allowing state regulation after viability, but prohibiting it before viability." Justice Antonin Scalia wrote separately, emphasizing that the plurality opinion "effectively would overrule *Roe v. Wade*. . . . I think that should be done," he added, "but would do it more explicitly." In Scalia's judgment, the failure to overrule *Roe* "needlessly prolongs this Court's self-awarded sovereignty over a field where it has little proper business since the answers to most of the cruel questions posed are political and not juridical."

And so prochoice activists raised the alarm, louder than ever. Four votes to overrule *Roe*. And that didn't include Sandra Day O'Connor, who concurred in the result with the Rehnquist group but refused to enter the discussion as to whether or not *Roe* should be overruled, saying there would be "time enough to reexamine *Roe*" when a state passed a law, presumably one prohibiting abortion, whose constitutionality actually turned on *Roe*. And it didn't take account of the newly appointed justices: between the time of the Court's *Webster* decision and its ruling three years later in *Planned Parenthood of Southern Pennsylvania v. Casey*, Justices William Brennan and Thurgood Marshall had been replaced by Justices David Souter and Clarence Thomas.[3] The solicitor general of the United States used the Pennsylvania law at issue in *Casey* as an opportunity to argue that the Court should overrule *Roe*.

"Liberty finds no refuge in a jurisprudence of doubt." In a joint opinion by Justices O'Connor, Kennedy, and Souter, the Court upheld not the logic of *Roe*, not its doctrine, not its approach, but its result. Throwing away trimesters, but bowing to precedent and affirming the value of a woman in the room, the Court held that a woman retained a right to decide whether to terminate a pregnancy prior to viability and that the state, while free to pursue its preference for birth over abortion, could not impose an "undue burden" on the woman's right to decide for herself.

In states whose legislatures are antichoice, abortion statutes are regularly loaded with all kinds of time, place, and manner restrictions, consent forms and waiting periods, and even bans on procedures, like the legal creation of the concept of a "partial-birth abortion."[4] Then the Supreme Court sorts them out, upholding most, throwing out only the very worst. In *Casey* itself, the Court upheld a waiting period for adult abortions; earlier, it had upheld informed-consent provisions that, in the eyes of some, constitute nothing less than a sermon against abortion. Parental-consent laws, provided there is some form of judicial override, have been upheld now for most of the last two decades. Since *Casey*, it is only the prohibition of "partial-birth abortion" that has risen to the level of an undue burden.

"Life's not fair," Jimmy Carter declared when the Supreme Court upheld the right of state and local governments to deny public funding to poor women seeking abortions. In the years since, it's gotten more unfair, but the truth is that law is only part of the problem. The continued vitality of *Roe v. Wade* means that if you're lucky enough to live in a place where doctors aren't afraid to do abortions and you have the money to pay for one, you don't have to bring cash in a plain envelope. If it's provided and you can pay for it, an abortion is safe and legal, until viability. In Los Angeles, you can open the phone book, make an appointment, and bring a credit card.

On the other hand, if the Catholic hospital is the only one in town, or you're under eighteen or poor, or live in North Dakota rather than Santa Monica, or don't notice your period is late because you're just a kid, you may have real troubles. You may have to bring suit if you're a teenager, even if it's a relative who raped you; you may be too late for an early abortion and then have to sort through the obstacles and regulations that start kicking in with force. In most states, if you're poor and depend on Medicaid for health care, it'll provide everything but an abortion. In much of the country, outside urban areas, access matters more than law: finding a local doctor, hospital, or clinic is simply impossible; in 86 percent of all counties, most of them rural, and in some states, there are none. If you have money, you can go to another state.

It is said that the country is less prochoice than it used to be, and that's probably so. It's easy to be troubled by the idea of abortion when it's a theoretical issue for you or when you have in your mind's eye the image of a much-wanted baby on a sonogram. I have lost babies at seven and twelve weeks, and they were in my soul. Then again, I'm not fourteen, or a college freshman on the verge of her life, or an at-the-end-of-her-rope struggling mother of four or five. I'm not the girl in the dorm room next door who hemorrhaged on the way home in the bus.

Today's young people may be less ardently prochoice, but they have also grown up in a world in which the choices are theirs to make. Take that away and see if they still feel the same.

Now imagine that the Court had come down the other way in *Casey*. Imagine that the Court were to revisit its decision. The impact on the political sphere would be enormous. Overruling *Roe* would make politics matter more. If *Roe* were actually to be overruled, every state would be required to go through a full-blown debate about whether and when to permit or prohibit abortions. Congress would have to go through the same sort of debate.

Such a debate would have to empower women. Could a room full of men get away with deciding whether to make abortion a crime without even pretending to listen to a woman now and again? Imagine what would happen if they tried. Every time a man stood up to give a speech about what he thinks, there'd be women laughing in beauty shops across America. I can't think of an easier way to motivate women to take over American politics, to recognize that they have the power to do it.

And then imagine what a real movement of women using their power could accomplish—not only on the issue of reproductive freedom but on issues of health care, education, the environment, human rights . . . That's my pipedream of course, what's behind those election-year speeches every four years.

Which is reason enough that it won't happen. Consider the abortion issue from George W. Bush's perspective. I believe that he really is against abortion. I saw former President Bill Clinton shortly after his first Oval Office meeting with his successor, and his assessment of then-Governor Bush rings true: he thought Bush was much more conservative than people assumed, and also much cannier.

Antiabortion activists value the fight for its own sake, even if, indeed sometimes especially if, they lose. Is there any explanation, after all, for the fact that they so often refuse to add the mediating "life and health of the mother" language that would render their restrictions less vulnerable to constitutional attack? Unlike politicians, who prefer to ask for less and win, activists often opt to demand more, even if it means grabbing defeat from the jaws of victory, in the hopes of pushing the larger debate forward.

Would antiabortion activists like to make presidential campaigns referendums on abortion? Certainly, even if they lose them. It puts their issue at the center of the fight, holds everyone's feet to the fire, allows them to demonstrate their clout and make their case.

At the 1992 Republican convention, only the pragmatists, the hacks, the nonbelievers viewed the takeover by the religious right as a signal of doom. Everyone else there had a great time. Best convention ever, people kept telling me, at least the ones who didn't call me a "babykiller." George W. Bush was also there, first learning the lesson that Karl Rove, now his senior political adviser, would repeat afterward, that his father had been undermined by his loss of support on the right, a mistake Rove was determined not to repeat. The younger President Bush has been very good to the religious right on abortion, giving them John Ashcroft as attorney general and the executive orders they wanted, not to mention a decision on stem-cell research that positioned the administration substantially to the right of that well-known liberal Orrin Hatch. But none of that has served to turn abortion into a highly salient issue for the broader public, a fact that is also a measure of Rove's political skill. The first round of the Bush administration's antiabortion executive orders, limiting the ability of international family-planning organizations that accept federal funds to use their own money for abortion, came on the same day that Ashcroft was pledging allegiance to *Roe v. Wade* as the law of the land in his confirmation hearings on Capitol Hill. The stem-cell decision, welcomed by antiabortion activists who saw it as the victory it was, was packaged with enough care to make it appear far more generous to researchers than it was.

As for the rank inconsistency between Bush's support for government aid to churches, where the answer to the entanglement argument is that the church uses government funds for its public activities and private funds for its religious ones, and his refusal to apply the same approach to family-planning organizations—his administration simply chooses to ignore it. And to a large extent, the issue does go away. Thus far, those most harmfully affected by the administration's actions on abortion are poor women abroad and United States servicewomen, who can no longer get a safe abortion at a military hospital. Previously, at least the option existed even though they were required to pay for it themselves. Exactly where does a servicewoman in Saudi Arabia go if not to a military facility? Or how about Pakistan? Still, foreign women and women serving abroad hardly provide the needed fodder, or army, for a domestic political revolution. Something akin to the fight over Robert Bork's nomination might stoke the flames, which is why we are unlikely to see a Robert Bork. Conservatives, absolutely. But a closely divided Senate only makes it easier for Bush to resist the calls for the most conservative nominees in favor of a relative liberal like Orrin Hatch. Code language like "respect for precedent" will signal a nominee who will ultimately toe the Anthony Kennedy line on abortion, uphold virtually all restrictions, but maintain the basic constitutional right recognized in *Roe v. Wade.*

I worked on my first abortion case twenty-three years ago when I was a law clerk for Justice John Paul Stevens; the issue was Massachusetts's parental-consent law. My students are now litigating parental-consent laws across the country; what is striking to me is how little has changed in two decades, legally speaking—same sorts of issue, same sorts of argument, with more and more of the effort reserved for the swing votes in the middle who are engaged in that precarious task of burden measuring. The promise of a solution in the form of RU-486 has yet to materialize; administration of the oral abortion pill still requires medical supervision and in any event is not appropriate except in the early weeks.

Meanwhile, the political climate has changed dramatically. During the Carter administration, feminists fought to include in the Democratic platform, over the opposition of President Carter himself, the same language that Attorney General Ashcroft has used. Today, Democratic candidates trumpet their support for abortion rights, while Republicans at the national level are struggling to figure out how to hold on to the right without losing the middle, particularly the moderate, female middle. Democrats win not because abortion is an issue but because for most voters it isn't one; since their rights are protected, such voters are free to think what they want and vote how they choose, and they feel no need to give high priority to an issue that could affect them but doesn't. Can you blame them for ignoring activists who make the prochoice argument every four years? When I say, on the eve of an election, that *Roe* is on the ballot, it is not because I really think I or my students will lose their rights. It is because for me it is enough that poor women and foreign women and teenage girls continue to lose their rights. The political majorities don't exist for taking our rights away, and the courts—the "rule of law"—provide ample cover for Republican politicians like Bush and Ashcroft to avoid the attempt.

This campaign dilemma inevitably raises the question of whether we on the prochoice side have actually succeeded in the courts too well. We have taken advantage of the right wing's unwillingness to add the clauses that could save their statutes and thus have won more than we have lost in the lower courts and even in the Supreme Court. The surprise here is not that we are still fighting the same war but that after so much time with the Rehnquist Court, with six of its members appointed by Republicans, we haven't lost it yet.

Overruling *Roe v. Wade* would mean turning abortion exclusively into a political issue, a result that might, both in the short term and in the long run, aid in the election of prochoice candidates. But it would come at the expense of the life and health of those women who still depend on the law and on the courts, even if the protection is tattered. And for most of us, who are in fact very much both prochoice and prolife, that would be an unacceptable trade-off.

THE ASSAULT ON FEDERAL POWER

The States' Rights Assault on Federal Authority

HERMAN SCHWARTZ

The five conservative justices on the Rehnquist Supreme Court have intensified Ronald Reagan's assault on the New Deal, on the Great Society, and on other congressional efforts to improve the lives of ordinary Americans. Their weapon of choice has been a professed passion for states' rights in the name of liberty, democracy, and efficiency. But just as the states' rights doctrine was used during the New Deal to block federal efforts to combat with the Depression, the Rehnquist Court's embrace of this constitutional theory, which seems nonideological, is merely a fig leaf to cover up more tangible interests like race, wealth, and power. As *Bush v. Gore* so clearly shows, the devotion to states' rights is quickly abandoned when vital interests are at stake like winning a presidential election and determining one's own successors on the Court.

This is not new. Though states' rights is a very pliable doctrine and liberals are not averse to invoking it, federalism has been used most often for regressive causes. It was the slaveholders' favorite strategy before the Civil War and the segregationists' after it and a weapon in the judicial assault on the New Deal. But concern for states' rights was noticeably absent when the states themselves passed social legislation intended to deal with the ravages of America's post–Civil War industrialization and conservative judges, again led by the Supreme Court, struck down almost two hundred of these laws.

By the beginning of the twentieth century it was obvious that the problems of a huge, modern industrial society could be dealt with only on a national scale, and the federal government began to enact legislation to correct some of the worst abuses. One was child labor, which the states had been unable to cope with on their own. In 1916, Congress passed the Child Labor Act, but it was quickly struck down as unconstitutional in 1918 by a 5–4 majority, over a Holmes-Brandeis dissent. Child labor was a "purely local matter . . . entrusted to local authority," declared the Court, and the federal government had no business dealing with it. A second effort to restrict child labor through the taxing power met the same fate four years later.[1]

Then the Depression came. To pull the nation out of it, President Franklin D. Roosevelt's administration created the New Deal with its many federal programs and agencies. One result was a massive transfer of power to the federal government.

The New Deal was intended to do more than bring recovery to the economy and restore the status quo. FDR wanted also to provide basic economic security for the average American and to prevent a repeat of the Depression's ravages. This obviously required a bigger government, higher taxes, and a redistribution of wealth. It inevitably outraged conservatives and produced a deep political cleavage that persists to this day.

During FDR's first term (1933–36) a five-member conservative majority of the Supreme Court consistently struck down his programs and policies for purportedly exceeding federal authority and encroaching on states rights.[2] In 1937, things changed, as Justice Owen Roberts switched sides, voting to uphold New Deal initiatives like minimum-wage laws, Social Security, and other economic programs. Then, as the conservative justices left the Court and New Deal appointees took their places, the Commerce Clause of the Constitution was interpreted to allow federal regulation to extend to anything even marginally affecting the economy.[3] Over the next six decades, the Supreme Court used both the Commerce Clause and the post–Civil War Fourteenth Amendment to confirm the New Deal's shift of power to the national government. The matter seemed to be settled.

But not really. Though the states' rights resurgence attained its full vigor only with the Rehnquist Court, conservative sniping at federal authority began with the Burger Court in the early 1970s, especially after William H. Rehnquist and Lewis Powell became justices in 1972. Raised in a Roosevelt-hating family, Rehnquist has been an archconservative since childhood. While a law clerk to Justice Robert H. Jackson in 1952, he argued that the separate-but-equal doctrine "was right and should be reaffirmed." At his confirmation hearing as chief justice in 1986, he denied that this represented his own view, but lied about this, as Jackson's secretary and others have confirmed and as his whole career shows. Additional evidence comes from a memo he wrote in a case that year, which did not come to light during the 1986 hearings:

> It is about time the court faced the fact that the white people in the South don't like the colored people; the Constitution restrains them from effecting this dislike through state action, but it most assuredly did not appoint the court as a sociological watchdog to rear up every time private discrimination raised its admittedly ugly head.[4]

And while a lawyer in Phoenix, Arizona, he opposed modest public accommodation and school desegregation proposals.

Rehnquist's first opportunity to strike at federal power came in 1976, in *National League of Cities v. Usery*, a case involving the 1974 amendments to the Fair Labor Standards Act, which extended minimum-wage and maximum-hours requirements to state and local governments.[5] Cobbling together a 5–4 majority, Rehnquist got the Court to strike down the 1974 amendments. For authority, he looked to the Tenth Amendment, which provides that "the powers not delegated to the United States by the Constitution . . . are reserved to the states." Since the amendment does not specify what is in fact "reserved," Rehnquist created a new doctrine based on the "policy" of the Tenth Amendment, which he said authorized judges to prohibit Congress and the federal government from regulating the states' "traditional functions," if doing so "impaired their sovereignty" and "their ability to function effectively in a federal system." The result was judicial confusion, as courts struggled with these vacuous criteria. After nine years, the Court overruled the decision in *Garcia v. San Antonio Metropolitan Transit Authority* (1985).[6]

National League of Cities was not Rehnquist's first use of states' rights against social welfare legislation. Two years earlier, in anticipation of cases using the Eleventh Amendment to expand state sovereign immunity, he had written for a 5–4 majority in *Edelman v. Jordan* an opinion that denied aged, blind, and disabled Social Security recipients the right to sue Illinois officials for wrongfully withholding their payments.[7] And in 1985, the same year that the Court decided *Garcia* and overturned *National League of Cities*, the four dissenters in *Garcia*, now joined by the increasingly conservative Byron White (virtually the same majority as in *Edelman*), dismissed a Rehabilitation Act suit against a state hospital for discriminating against a partially blind diabetic, because Congress had not *explicitly* authorized such a suit even though Congress's intent to allow such suits was clear.[8] Congress could not, of course, have anticipated that the Court would require it to go further and make an explicit statement to that effect when its intent was obvious, but the diabetic still lost his lawsuit.

In 1991, Clarence Thomas joined Rehnquist, Anthony Kennedy, Sandra Day O'Connor, and Antonin Scalia, making a virtually solid conservative majority. The constitutional assault on federal power now went into high gear with two targets: federal power and use of the courts by private individuals and public interest organizations—often called "private attorneys general"—to enforce federally created rights, especially those related to social welfare. This attack on private suits, a vital component in the enforcement of such laws, has long been championed by Justice Scalia, who seems to believe that only the executive branch should have that authority—even though (or perhaps because) it is clear that the executive branch has neither the resources nor sometimes even the will to enforce these laws effectively.

The first target came in 1992, the year after Thomas joined the Court: a statute regulating disposal of radioactive waste. No state wants to have radioactive waste stored on its territory. To forestall direct federal regulation, the states bargained among themselves and with the federal government, working out a plan proposed by the National Governors Association that called for various interstate agreements and obligations. An appropriate law was passed, but after it went into effect, New York changed its mind and challenged the statute. It won in *New York v. United States.*[9]

As in *National League of Cities,* the conservatives were unable to rely on any provision in the Constitution, so this time they used their own new conception of the constitutional "framework" and "structure" to bar the federal government from "commandeering" state officials to implement federal laws, in the process ignoring numerous historical examples of state implementation of federal laws. "Accountability is . . . diminished" by such state enforcement, wrote Justice O'Connor, because state officers who have to implement burdensome federal directives would be blamed for them. The Court used the same "accountability" reasoning five years later in *Printz v. United States* to slap down the Brady gun control bill's requirement that local law enforcement officers check the backgrounds of prospective gun purchasers, even though the argument is patently ludicrous—people in the radioactive-waste business knew the rules were set by the federal government, and are there gun owners or buyers anywhere who don't know the Brady bill is a federal law?[10] If there are, surely a sign to that effect would give enough notice, and local officials would certainly not be bashful about telling them.

Four years after *New York v. United States,* the trickle of antifederal decisions became a flood.

The Commerce Clause is the source of federal power over the national economy. Recognizing the interrelatedness of almost all parts of the economy, the Supreme Court had upheld every assertion of federal power under the Commerce Clause since 1937. In 1995, that changed. In *United States v. Lopez,* the now-usual 5–4 majority, again in a Rehnquist opinion, struck down a federal law criminalizing the possession of guns in a school zone because the justices saw no "economic" transaction in the situation and there was no specific congressional finding of an effect on interstate trade.[11] The obvious impact of school violence on the national economy was dismissed, and the fact that most guns moved in interstate trade was ignored.[12] In 2000, the same 5–4 majority used the same argument to strike down the Violence against Women Act (VAWA). Domestic violence is not an "economic" matter, wrote Rehnquist, even though there was, in Justice Souter's words, "a mountain of data" that violence against women costs the economy billions each year. The Court also ignored overwhelming state support for the act.[13]

The Constitution does presuppose a line between interstate and local commerce, but in today's world it is impossible to draw the line with any precision. There is also no way to distinguish clearly between "economic" and "noneconomic" matters, as the VAWA case makes clear, for any large-scale phenomenon will have economic effects and there are no manageable judicial standards for drawing the line between inter- and intrastate commerce in any but the easiest cases. Whenever the Court has tried to draw a line limiting federal authority over the economy on behalf of states' rights, reality has soon washed it away.

The implication is that virtually everything is subject to federal power and that in practice the federal government is not really a government of limited powers. That is probably true for the national economy, which can be dealt with only on a national scale. We act on that understanding all the time. As the Court recognized in *Garcia*, meaningful protections for the states can only be political and they are usually quite sufficient.

But there is one instance in which the courts can impose meaningful limits on the national government and that is when federal power encroaches on individual rights. Then the Court can indeed impose limits that are both needed and usually workable.

In 1996, the Rehnquist Court turned its fire on a private person's ability to enforce his or her rights against state violations, the private attorney general suit, resurrecting the Eleventh Amendment and a state sovereign immunity doctrine that had been repudiated just seven years earlier. The amendment denies *federal* courts jurisdiction over suits by citizens of *one state* against *another* state. Nevertheless, over the next five years the conservative bloc developed a state sovereign immunity doctrine that is based on the discredited "The king can do no wrong" philosophy, allowing a state to prevent money damage suits against itself, even by its *own* citizens, even in *state* courts, and even if the state engages in ordinary private business activities that wrongly damage a private competitor and violate federal law.[14] Although nothing in the language of the Constitution touches on any of these three situations, and certainly not for rights created by Congress, that did not faze these justices, each of whom has regularly excoriated liberal judges as "activists" when they sought to promote individual rights or did not stick closely to the text of the Constitution.[15]

Despite this ban on private suits against states, since 1908 people injured by state officials who violate either the Constitution or federal law have been able to get a federal court order against those officials to prevent continuing violations.[16] This doctrine, the so-called *Ex parte Young* remedy, has never been challenged. Yet even that is being chipped away by a new rule that if the federal law in question establishes a particular structure for enforcing that law, the remedy is not available unless Congress makes clear that it is.[17] Those special statutory enforcement structures are, however, often unavailable to private parties, being reserved to the federal government. The practical effect is to deny any private remedy for violations of rights by state administrators even though victims of such violations have long relied on such remedies; several lower courts have used this new doctrine this way, though at this writing, one has been reversed.[18] And since the federal government is usually too busy or has other reasons for not strictly enforcing the statutory remedy, the effect is to deny any relief at all, no matter how blatant or egregious the violation.

Suits by the federal government against a state are not supposed to be affected by sovereign immunity, but even when there is federal enforcement, the conservative justices have managed to strike at national authority. In *Federal Maritime Commission v. South Carolina State Ports Authority* (2002),[19] the commission tried to enforce the antidiscrimination provisions of the federal Shipping Act of 1984. The commission used a trial-type hearing between the complainant and the Ports Authority as a way for the commission to decide whether to get a court order against the authority. This, Justice Thomas wrote for the usual 5–4 majority, was like a private suit against a state defendant and therefore barred by state sovereign immunity. But as Justice Breyer's dissent pointed out, it was still the federal executive agency that decided whether and how to enforce the act. It could have used other methods but these would have required use of the commission staff, and like most enforcement agencies, the commission is understaffed. The Court's approach, Breyer warned, could undermine enforcement of many worker safety and health laws as well as the effective handling of complaints against state hospitals for improper medical care.

In their assault on private enforcement suits, the conservatives have also turned on the Reconstruction Amendments. Section 5 of the Fourteenth Amendment empowers Congress to enforce the provisions of that amendment "by appropriate legislation." In 1976, the Court declared that because these amendments effected a major transfer of power to the federal government from the states, suits against states brought under them and under laws passed pursuant to Section 5 (and Amendment XV, Section 2) would be exempt from Eleventh Amendment immunity. This seemed like a likely vehicle for the survival of many private suits, since the Fourteenth Amendment and the Civil Rights Act of 1983 cover a great many areas, particularly unlawful discrimination. That door to the federal courts was soon shut.

In 1990, in *Employment Division v. Smith*, the Court narrowly adopted a Scalia opinion overturning a twenty-seven-year-old rule that allowed religious groups not to comply with generally applicable statutes if those laws imposed unnecessary burdens on important religious practices. The case involved the Native American Church's sacramental use of peyote, a drug banned by the Oregon drug law (though not in other states or by the federal government). Congress responded by promptly and almost unanimously passing the Religious Freedom Restoration Act (RFRA) to reinstate the pre-*Smith* rule.

But RFRA didn't last long. In *City of Boerne v. Flores* (1997), the Court first cut back on congressional power by ruling that Section 5 gave Congress no right to "interpret" the Constitution by protecting religious freedom beyond the limits the Court had set in *Smith*—a view contested by many constitutional experts.[20] Moreover, the Court said, even if RFRA involved no new interpretation but only a remedy under Section 5 for judicially established interpretations, it failed in that regard as well because it went too far, burdening too many state activities too heavily. A Section 5 remedy had to be "proportionate and congruent," wrote Justice Kennedy for the usual five-member majority. And here the obligations that RFRA imposed on the states were considered too burdensome, even though the states had lived comfortably for more than a quarter century with the pre-*Smith* rule that RFRA tried to reinstate.

During the next four years, the conservative majority turned back efforts to use Section 5 in suits under the Age Discrimination in Employment Act, the Violence against Women Act, the Americans with Disabilities Act, and the patent and trademark laws.[21] In the VAWA case, the 5–4 majority ruled that Section 5 did not apply to the states' unconstitutional *failures* to enforce their own laws on violence against women, even though the attorneys general of thirty-eight states supported the federal act because, as they told Congress, those failures resulted from sex discrimination. According to Chief Justice Rehnquist, relying in his argument on now-discredited 1875 cases that had not involved the state in any way, Section 5 was limited to affirmative state abuses.

In *Garrett*, a Disabilities Act case, Rehnquist, again writing for the majority, recognized that Section 5 gives Congress leeway in how to enforce the Fourteenth Amendment, particularly when it comes to finding the facts and shaping a remedy. But then he cavalierly dismissed thirteen congressional hearings, a report by a national task force that heard more than thirty thousand people in all fifty states, census results, and other studies, as well as three hundred specific examples of state discrimination against the disabled (all laid out in Justice Stephen Breyer's dissent). Even if all this did show a pattern of discrimination, Rehnquist wrote, Congress hadn't proved either that the discrimination was "irrational," which the Court has defined as "patently arbitrary," or that there were a great many such instances. But to provide such proof, Congress would have to hold the equivalent of a full-blown trial for a very large number of cases of discrimination, an obvious impossibility never before demanded of any legislative body. As a result, states can now violate with impunity many congressionally created rights for the elderly, pregnant women, the mentally retarded, the mentally ill, and others.

There have been a few isolated losses for the states' rights bloc: Kennedy jumped ship to make a 5–4 majority to strike down a state term limits law, and in 2000 the Court upheld a law banning the sale by states of private data collected from driver's license applications.[22] But such decisions have been few and far between.[23]

Is there any justification for this exaltation of states' rights at the expense of the federal government? In her opinion for the Court in *Gregory v. Ashcroft*, Justice O'Connor set forth the advantages she saw in strong state sovereignty:

> This federalist structure of joint sovereigns preserves to the people numerous advantages. It assures a decentralized government that will be more sensitive to the diverse needs of a heterogeneous society; it increases opportunity for citizen involvement in democratic processes; it allows for more innovation and experimentation in government; and it makes government more responsive by putting the States in competition for a mobile citizenry. . . . Perhaps the principal benefit of the federalist system is a check on abuses of government power.[24]

Unfortunately, these "advantages" are frequently unrealized and offset by very real disadvantages. Unless they are directly involved, few citizens pay much attention to state issues or even to local ones. Media coverage of state activities is spotty at best and often nonexistent. Voter turnout in state and local elections is even lower than in national elections. Indeed, few voters even know the names of their local representatives other than their mayor, and they know even less about their state representatives. Most voters, however, know who their congressional representatives and senators are and what they are doing. Whatever the opportunities for citizen involvement at the state and local levels, few seem interested in taking advantage of them.

Moreover, state sovereignty is hardly necessary either for citizen involvement or for most of what states do. Decentralization without sovereignty offers many opportunities for meaningful local participation and governmental responsiveness.[25] Indeed, we have two ubiquitous examples in this country—city and county government, including school and zoning boards. Yet both cities and counties are but creatures of the state, without sovereignty or indeed any constitutional status at all.

As for the "principal benefit" of checking "abuses of power," historically that kind of check has come not from the states on the federal government but the reverse, as James Madison predicted in *Federalist Paper* No. 10; discrimination against blacks, women, and gays and encroachments on free speech are obvious examples. In fact, much and perhaps most of the time, states' rights have been a weapon of reaction. Moreover, when the national government suffered from McCarthyism and similar "abuses of government power," the states did not check the abuses but exacerbated them.[26]

There is, however, one area where state sovereignty is necessary: social and other experimentation, especially where the federal government is unable to act. State and local action on tobacco, gun control, prescription drug pricing, consumer safety, campaign finance, and other issues requires truly independent state authority, for decentralization alone would subject these initiatives to the same forces that block national action. These instances do not justify the Supreme Court's states' rights decisions, however, for they have been made in cases where the federal government has indeed acted. Moreover, on more than a few occasions the states have sued the federal government for relaxing environmental standards and other matters.[27]

Nor is experimentation always a good thing. At least some state experimentation has involved a "race to the bottom," not only in corporate affairs, as in Delaware, but in lowered wages, worse safety conditions, child labor, discrimination, and other matters.

There are also issues of efficiency and of corruption. Although many state legislators now work full-time their sessions are still relatively short—the Texas legislature, for example, meets only once every two years for just four months. Much important legislation is rushed through in the waning minutes of a session, unread by most legislators. Conflicts of interest are rife: a recent study found that 20 percent of state legislators "help regulate their own business or professional interests, [or] have financial ties to organizations that lobby state governments, and many receive income from agencies they oversee."[28]

State and local governments are often hostile to those down on their luck, particularly if they are racial minorities. That is one reason the Republican Party's Contract with America pushed so strongly for more state and local control at the expense of the federal government.[29] For example, in 1999 New York City conceded in court that workers at "job centers," formerly welfare offices, illegally prevented or discouraged people from applying for food stamps and Medicaid. Despite a court order, the city was still doing so a year later.[30] Many states have made it so onerous to apply for food stamps, which the states administer, that many needy people do not even apply.[31]

The hollowness of the conservatives' concern for states' rights was revealed in *New York v. United States*. The radioactive waste law was not a federal initiative but was conceived and promoted by the states. When the dissenters on the Supreme Court pointed this out, Justice O'Connor responded that the anticommandeering principle was not for the benefit of the states but to preserve "the liberties" of the people; the states' consent to the law was irrelevant. But how are the people's liberties protected when the wishes of their elected representatives are ignored? And is not accountability diminished if those representatives cannot act as they believe their constituents want?

This indifference to state interests is not a rare phenomenon. The Court's conservatives struck down hundreds of state and local affirmative action plans, voluntary desegregation plans, and electoral districting plans that created majority-black districts. Nor have Rehnquist, Scalia, and the others hesitated either to strike down zoning and environmental laws in order to protect property rights or to rule that federal law has preempted state tort law when business interests are at stake. Their allies in Congress, who also proclaim their undying loyalty to states' rights, likewise have no problem with proposing legislation barring assisted suicide, gay marriage, limits on tort recovery, and other matters that are usually considered quintessentially local.[32]

Academic commentators disagree on how harmful the conservatives' federalism rulings have been. They have unquestionably spawned confusion and litigation, thereby overburdening a federal judiciary that is already creaking. Moreover, conservative judges on the lower courts have used the Supreme Court decisions that blurred established law on *Ex parte Young* and the Spending Clause to dismiss class action suits by Medicaid and Social Security Act beneficiaries.[33] If the decisions taken by these lower courts are approved by the Supreme Court, the effects could be devastating for the poor, the disabled, and all the other intended beneficiaries of the New Deal and Great Society programs.

Some years ago, a University of Chicago law professor, one of the leaders of the current states' rights movement, announced the goal of the movement in unequivocal terms: to overturn the New Deal and to shrink the federal government to just a few functions. Given the accumulated history and law of the last sixty years, as well as the events of September 11, 2001, that goal is not likely to be achieved. But except in certain areas directly related to national defense, the Supreme Court's conservative majority is also not likely to abandon its campaign against federal power and citizen suits. Enemies of federal authority on and off the Court rarely abandon their crusade, as history shows again and again. In 1918, while German armies were rolling toward Paris, the Supreme Court's five-member conservative majority struck down the Child Labor Act. During the worst of the Depression, conservative justices struck down almost every major federal effort to pull us out of it. Moreover, Rehnquist, Scalia, and their colleagues are not likely to see much of a link between suits by welfare, Social Security, and Medicaid beneficiaries, or victims of discrimination, and war-induced needs.[34]

Because of *Bush v. Gore*, the next appointments to the Supreme Court may not differ much from the current Court majority. It may take a constitutional crisis similar to that of the 1930s and a change in the White House before the current assault on those shortchanged by birth and by fortune is thwarted.

The Roles, Rights, and Responsibilities of the Executive Branch

DAVID C. VLADECK AND ALAN B. MORRISON

In a democratic system governed by the rule of law, government—and particularly the executive branch—must be accountable to the citizenry for its policies and actions. Under our constitutional system of checks and balances, Congress can impose a direct check on specific executive branch actions by oversight and legislation, but citizens can do so only indirectly, either by voting the president out of office or by invoking the power of the judiciary to review executive action. For the latter approach to be successful, however, citizens must know what the executive branch is doing, must have the right to use the courts to challenge actions they believe violate the law, and must have judges willing to compel the executive branch to obey the law.

The 1966 Freedom of Information Act (FOIA) is arguably the most important tool ordinary Americans have to oversee the workings of their government. The Rehnquist Court has made it increasingly difficult for citizens to use the act. At the same time, by narrowing the rules of standing and in some cases overturning congressional efforts to broaden access, the Court has made it harder for private citizens to challenge illegal government actions in federal court. Also, it has increasingly insulated agency action from judicial review when the challenges are made by public interest plaintiffs, while it has expanded judicial review when the challenges come from business interests. Its sympathy for business has also led it to ignore the federalist inclinations that it professes in other contexts and frequently to strike down state regulations when they are more rigorous than federal ones. All in all, the Rehnquist Court has been a boon to business and not a friend to the ordinary citizen.

Under the FOIA, any person has the right to request any record in the hands of a federal agency other than the president, Congress, or the judiciary, subject to nine exemptions that permit the government to withhold sensitive records. The hostile attitude of the Burger Court toward the public's efforts to obtain government documents has been adopted by the Rehnquist Court. In no more than a handful of the thirty-two FOIA cases decided by the Court since 1966 has it sided, even in part, with the requester.

Under the FOIA, courts are supposed to balance privacy rights against the public's right to know, tipping the scale toward disclosure in close cases. Nevertheless, the Court has often accepted claims that disclosure might jeopardize an individual's privacy rights that, to put it charitably, are far-fetched. A low point came with *Department of Justice v. Reporters Committee for Freedom of the Press* (1989).[1] The Reporters Committee asked for the arrest records of certain persons alleged to have been involved in organized crime and illegal dealings with a corrupt congressman. Holding that the records were exempt from disclosure under the FOIA's privacy exemption, the Court dismissed the fact that the information had already been made public. Most significantly, however, it narrowed the scope of the public interest to be considered in the FOIA balancing process by limiting it to "the core purpose of the FOIA," namely, to "shed light on an agency's performance of its statutory duties." Thus, even if government documents are important for other reasons, such as exposing corruption or even criminal misconduct, they may be withheld so long as the government can point to virtually any privacy interest, no matter how remote or implausible.

The Court more fully developed the rule of *Reporters Committee* in its follow-up decision in *Department of State v. Ray* (1991).[2] At issue in *Ray* were notes made by State Department personnel on the treatment of Haitian refugees who had been involuntarily returned to Haiti. The request was made by an immigration lawyer who wanted the notes, including the names of the returnees, both to bolster the claim that returnees were being subjected to political reprisal and to facilitate their reinterview by human rights advocates. Applying *Reporters Committee*, the Court allowed the State Department to withhold the names to protect the privacy of the interviewees because the release of personal identifiers "would not shed any additional light on the Government's conduct of its obligation." In a classic Catch-22, the refugees' own privacy interests were cited as justification to thwart access to their records by lawyers trying to assist them in developing their cases for asylum.

There is one significant Rehnquist Court FOIA ruling that benefits requesters, but it has a limited reach. In *Department of the Interior v. Klamath Water Users Protective Association* (2001), the Court rejected the government's argument that the FOIA's exemption for intraagency records shielded from public disclosure documents exchanged between the Department of the Interior and the Klamath and other Indian tribes regarding disputed water rights because the department's special role as trustee to Indian tribes made the tribes more like government consultants than like outsiders.[3] The Court rejected this and other prosecrecy arguments. Though this suggests that the Court will not automatically rubber-stamp government claims, it does not signal any measurable shift in the Court's FOIA cases.

Following the Supreme Court's lead, lower courts have clamped down on access under the FOIA, weakening significantly the ability of the citizenry to hold their government accountable. The tragic events of September 11 have only accelerated this trend.

The Rehnquist Court has left a mark on the judicial review of federal agency decisions in two distinct ways. First, it has further insulated the executive branch from attack by cutting back on the Court's "standing" jurisprudence, which makes it harder for parties complaining of noneconomic harm (such as environmental groups) to get into court; second, it has redefined the law relating to deference to agency action in a way that frees the courts, in cases brought mainly by business interests, to superintend the regulatory process more closely.

Under Article 3 of the Constitution, federal courts may adjudicate

only actual "cases" and "controversies." Injuries that neither have occurred nor are imminent are not sufficient to trigger the exercise of
federal judicial power. A party who cannot show actual or imminent
"injury," as defined by the Court, lacks "standing" and may not sue in
federal court. Until 1990, the Court had held that someone contesting
an agency's decision in environmental cases could generally establish
personal injury and overcome the standing hurdle by showing that the
challenged conduct was likely to harm the environment. But then the
Rehnquist Court repudiated this liberal standing doctrine, and it is
now much more difficult for a party claiming noneconomic harm to be
heard in court, primarily as a result of *Lujan v. National Wildlife Federation*
(*Lujan I*) and *Lujan v. Defenders of Wildlife* (*Lujan II*).[4]

Justice Antonin Scalia, writing for the Court in both cases, brushed
aside the plaintiffs' arguments on injury. In *Lujan I*, he faulted the plaintiffs, who alleged that they used a park for hiking and other recreational purposes, for not specifying that they actually used the very
portions of the park that the Department of the Interior had opened
up to mining. In *Lujan II*, the plaintiffs were wildlife experts who had
regularly traveled abroad to view species threatened with extinction in
their natural habitats. Rejecting the plaintiffs' claim that they were
harmed because they would not be able to see the species endangered
by a proposed Egyptian dam rehabilitation project, Scalia observed
that it is "pure speculation and fantasy" to "say that anyone who observes or works with an endangered species, anywhere in the world, is
appreciably harmed by a single project affecting some portion of that
species."

When Congress passed the Endangered Species Act it recognized
that the law was not self-enforcing and that court compulsion might be
necessary. To enable individual citizens to serve as private attorneys
general to force compliance with important laws, Congress often en-
acts "citizen suit" provisions, and the Endangered Species Act contains
such a provision. Prior to *Lujan II*, the Supreme Court had accepted
the proposition that Congress could confer such a right, the deprivation of which gave rise to injury sufficient to provide standing. But in
Lujan II the Court ruled that Congress could not "convert the undifferentiated public interest in executive officers' compliance with the law

into an 'individual right' vindicable in the courts." In so ruling, the Court made it far more difficult for ordinary citizens to compel the executive branch to obey the law.

Six years later, the Court reaffirmed its get-tough policy in *Steel Company v. Citizens for a Better Environment*.[5] The Steel Company had repeatedly failed to comply with the reporting requirements of the Emergency Planning and Community Right-to-Know Act, and the citizens group alerted the company of its intention to bring suit to force it to obey the law. The company then submitted its reports to the Environmental Protection Agency—six years after they were due but before the suit was filed. When citizens sued to ensure future compliance with the act, the Court, again in an opinion by Justice Scalia, ruled that past harms were not sufficient to constitute present injury, even though there was no assurance that the company would not again disregard the law as soon as the lawsuit was dismissed.

The Court somewhat tempered this ruling in *Friends of the Earth, Inc. v. Laidlaw Environmental Services (TOC), Inc.*[6] There the Court held, over a Scalia-Thomas dissent, that the plaintiffs had standing to maintain a suit under the Clean Water Act where the defendant ceased its violations *after* the lawsuit was brought. But nothing in *Laidlaw* prevents companies from ignoring their legal obligations until they learn of a potential lawsuit and then, before the suit is filed, bringing themselves into compliance and thereby avoiding litigation, with little risk of sanction.

Another opinion curtailing the right of citizens to have a court check agency action is just as important. In *Ohio Forestry Association, Inc. v. Sierra Club* (1998), the Court rejected, on "ripeness" grounds, a challenge to the EPA's overall land-use plan for a major forest area in Ohio because only the *implementation* of certain aspects of the plan could trigger harm, according to the Court, not just the adoption of the plan.[7] Litigation would have to wait until the logging and road-building activities that the plaintiffs wanted to prevent were imminent.

Taken together, these cases deal a serious blow to the ability of citizens who suffer noneconomic injuries at the hands of executive branch agencies to bring suit, particularly environmentalists, preservationists, and animal rights activists.

The Court's decisions on judicial deference to administrative agencies, however, suggest that the Court is not willing to protect these executive branch agencies when businesses challenge their actions. The terrain in this area of law was marked, some thought for good, by the Supreme Court's 1984 ruling in *Chevron, U.S.A., Inc. v. Natural Resources Defense Council, Inc.*, which held that courts owe considerable deference to any authoritative agency interpretation of the statutes the agency administers.[8] Statutory ambiguities were to be left to resolution by the executive branch, so long as the agency's interpretation was consistent with a reasonable reading of the statute.[9]

The first crack in the *Chevron* wall was the Court's 2000 ruling in *Christensen v. Harris County*, where the Court suggested that an informal agency position, as set forth in a letter, for example, may not warrant *Chevron*-style deference.[10] The wall did not crumble, however, until 2001 and *United States v. Mead Corporation*.[11] That case involved the mundane question of what deference, if any, should be given to rulings made by the United States Customs Service. Mead imports diaries and day planners, merchandise that for years entered the country duty-free. Then the Customs Service's headquarters office shifted ground and classified Mead's three-ring binder products as "bound diaries" subject to tariff. Mead challenged the ruling and succeeded. Formally adopted agency positions, either through a notice-and-comment rule making or through an adjudicatory proceeding, the Court ruled, are entitled to *Chevron* deference, but informal agency statements, such as in an opinion letter, policy statement, or amicus brief, are not; at most they deserve respect based on the persuasive power of their reasoning. In other words, unless an agency position is formally adopted, reviewing courts will no longer be obligated to uphold it even though that position is reasonable and not at odds with the text of the statute.

The consequences of *Mead* are far-reaching, as Justice Scalia pointed out in his lone dissent. The decision tells courts to give far greater scrutiny to agency action, at least in those cases where the agency's position has not been formally adopted. Indeed, *Mead* can be seen as uprooting part of *Chevron*'s foundation because it suggests that, at least where the agency has not officially adopted an interpretation, it is the courts and not the executive branch that should take the lead in resolving statutory ambiguities. Since many if not most agency pronouncements fall into the informal category, the court's powers are vastly enlarged under *Mead*.

Mead is a big victory for any party challenging agency action, especially big business. Because the Rehnquist Court's standing restrictions have driven down the number of nonbusiness challenges to agency action, most lawsuits against federal agencies are now filed by businesses complaining of overregulation. *Mead* gives those challengers a boost because it tells reviewing courts that they have an important role to play in ensuring the fairness and rationality of the regulatory process and that they need not tilt the scale in favor of government. It remains to be seen whether challenges from environmental and consumer advocates will benefit from *Mead* as well.

Two pre-*Mead* cases also warrant mention. First is the Court's controversial 5–4 decision in 2000 in *FDA v. Brown & Williamson Tobacco Corporation*.[12] The FDA claimed authority to regulate tobacco products as "drugs" under the Food, Drug and Cosmetic Act because of the industry's manipulation of the nicotine content in cigarettes and chewing tobacco. This is a question on which the agency would ordinarily receive substantial deference under *Chevron*. Nevertheless, the Court ruled that the FDA lacked authority over tobacco products because Congress had never explicitly given the agency the power to regulate them.

The ruling is result-oriented adjudication at its worst. Congress does not usually specify the products an agency may regulate; it describes them categorically and lists any exclusions, and the Food, Drug and Cosmetic Act is no exception. The majority could not plausibly find that nicotine failed to meet the statutory definition of a drug because, in fact, it is a drug, and even the industry did not seriously contest that fact. Instead, the Court pieced together a congressional "intent" to *deny* the FDA authority over tobacco even though, despite many opportunities to do so, Congress had never said in a statute or other pronouncement that tobacco was off-limits to the FDA. A more charitable explanation is that tobacco regulation is so politically volatile that the Court thought that Congress, not an administrative agency, ought to tackle the job. If so, *Brown & Williamson* is an unalloyed act of judicial activism, the sort of activism that conservatives normally decry.

Despite its probusiness tilt, this Court has its limits. In *Whitman v.*

American Trucking Associations (2001), the question was whether Congress intended that when the EPA sets air quality standards under the Clean Air Act, it may look at health concerns alone, or must also consider the costs of regulation.[13] The Court unanimously upheld the EPA on this key question, ruling that the text of the act did not permit a reviewing court to read in a cost-consideration requirement. Had industry prevailed, cost/benefit concerns would have inevitably dwarfed other factors in rule making, and unless an agency could justify its regulatory decisions in hard economic terms, those decisions would have been at high risk of judicial invalidation.

The Constitution divides government into three parts and envisions that each branch will operate in a way that checks the inevitable tendency of institutions—here, the other branches of government—to aggrandize their own power. The Burger Court had been accused of reinvigorating the separations of powers doctrine by being overly rigid and formalistic in keeping each branch within its respective spheres. In a pair of celebrated cases the Court had overturned efforts by Congress to give power to the executive branch but to retain control over the exercise of that power.[14]

The Rehnquist Court has shown a more pragmatic and flexible approach in evaluating the constitutionality of claimed interbranch encroachments. In *Morrison v. Olson* (1988), it upheld the independent counsel law against claims that denying the president and attorney general control over the appointment, the supervision, and, to a significant degree, the firing of a high-level prosecutor to investigate and, if necessary, prosecute charges of criminal wrongdoing by senior government officials fundamentally interfered with the powers of the executive branch.[15] Written by Chief Justice Rehnquist, *Morrison* rejected the Burger Court's notion of iron-clad separation and sustained a scheme that, everyone acknowledged, permitted the judiciary to carry out powers—like appointing and supervising a prosecutor—that historically had been the responsibility of the executive branch. The Court was obviously influenced by Congress's determination that an independent prosecutor was essential to a public perception that the laws were being equally and fairly enforced in the course of investigations of high-ranking administration officials, including the president.

The Rehnquist Court's pragmatist bent has its limits, however. In 1996, Congress gave President Clinton what presidents have wanted for many decades—a line-item veto. The constitutions of more than forty states give their governor some form of line-item veto, but there is no comparable provision in the U.S. Constitution. Congress understood that the bill had serious constitutional problems, and so it included a special provision allowing an immediate and expedited challenge by members of Congress, who would be injured in their capacity as legislators by the grant of power to the president. A suit was filed, but the Supreme Court ruled in *Raines v. Byrd* (1997) that members of Congress lacked standing.[16] According to the opinion written by Chief Justice Rehnquist, they suffered no personal injury, and any harm to them in their legislative capacities was not the kind of injury that could be redressed in the federal courts. This was an important victory for the executive branch because it sharply limited, if not eliminated, cases in which members of Congress might sue the executive branch for violations of the Constitution.

The president's victory, however, was short-lived. A year later, in *Clinton v. City of New York*, the Court agreed that the line-item veto statute was an unauthorized end run around the Constitution.[17] Although counter to the Rehnquist Court's emerging pragmatism, the decision was clearly influenced by the majority's concern that the law shifted to the president unprecedented and excessive power that Congress could not effectively check.

Finally, in 2001, in *Whitman v. American Trucking Associations*, the Court unanimously rejected the claim that Congress had failed to give the EPA sufficient guidance on how to write pollution standards under the Clean Air Act and that the EPA regulations should therefore be struck down. Industry's main argument was that Congress, in directing the EPA to reduce air pollution without reference to the costs involved, failed to give the agency sufficiently concrete principles within which to act, thereby conferring on it the power to regulate the economy "back to the stone age."

Justice Scalia's opinion seems to put to rest, perhaps permanently, the notion that the courts should tell Congress how it should delegate its rule-making power to executive agencies. As he put it, the Court has "almost never felt qualified to second-guess Congress regarding the permissible degree of policy judgment that can be left to those executing or applying the law." So long as the delegation falls somewhere between these distant poles, the Court will uphold it.

This ruling's implications go well beyond the confines of the case and solidify the view that the Rehnquist Court will not usually tread on power-sharing arrangements between the branches. Congress routinely identifies a difficult problem and gives the agency some degree of direction, but leaves many of the hard choices to the agency to decide. To have agreed with industry in this case would have forced Congress to fine-tune each delegation of authority to an agency—a process that would tie Congress in knots and render it unable to tackle the difficult issues that face our nation, like fighting air pollution.

Preemption is a lawyer's word—no ordinary person would use it in conversation. But the concept is simple: the Supremacy Clause of the Constitution says that if there is a conflict between state and federal law (the Constitution, a statute passed by Congress, or a rule of a federal agency), federal law controls or "preempts" state law. Cases arise because Congress or a federal agency has been unclear about whether the federal and state schemes can coexist. These disputes generally fall into two categories: first, where a state wants to regulate activities or conduct (such as the sale of cigarettes to minors) that is also subject to federal regulation; second, where a person is suing for damages under state law for injuries caused by conduct of the defendant and the defendant claims that, because the conduct is regulated by federal law, state law cannot be the basis for liability.

The executive branch plays a pivotal role in this dynamic between the application of federal or local law. Most statutes enacted by Congress are not self-executing; they are implemented and enforced only when a federal agency takes some form of regulatory action. Congress, for example, may decree that no car may be sold in the United States unless it meets safety standards issued by the National Highway Traffic

Safety Administration (NHTSA), the federal agency that regulates auto safety. But until NHTSA takes action, the statute has little practical meaning. Moreover, because the federal agencies are presumed to understand the relationship between their rules and local law, the Supreme Court looks to the agencies to provide guidance on whether they intend that their regulation preempt state law.

The main battle in regulatory preemption cases is between businesses that are regulated by both the federal and the state governments and state governments that want to enforce their laws. States often seek to do this in instances where their laws are more stringent than the federal ones and they are concerned that the lax federal rules may not provide sufficient protection. Almost invariably, the defendant will claim that federal law trumps state law and that the state is foreclosed from enforcing its law. Time and again, the Rehnquist Court has sided with business (often supported by the federal government) to find state laws preempted.

A cigarette advertising case best illustrates this point. On the final day of the 2000–01 term, the Court concluded in *Lorillard Tobacco Company v. Reilly* that the Federal Cigarette Labeling Act preempted efforts by Massachusetts to limit cigarette advertising near parks and playgrounds.[18] The federal law was designed to ensure that the warnings set forth on cigarette packaging and labeling were uniform and not subject to diverse content requirements by states. The Court concluded that the federal law applied as well to the location of advertising and that it barred states from imposing limitations on where cigarette advertising could be placed. Under the Court's ruling, states would be disabled from preventing tobacco companies from erecting billboards across the street from elementary schools and playgrounds.

Lorillard typifies the problems with the Court's regulatory preemption cases. The Court's mechanical and wooden reading of the labeling law is wholly divorced from any appreciation of the purpose of the law or the adverse consequences of its own ruling. It bodes ill for future cases of this kind and suggests that the Rehnquist Court, despite its professed allegiance to states' rights, will be quite willing to find for regulatory preemption, especially when that frees business from regulation it finds burdensome.

In claims for damages, when injured consumers are pitted against the manufacturers of federally regulated products, the manufacturers almost invariably argue that federal law preempts state tort law. The function for the Supreme Court in these cases is to determine whether Congress, when it enacted the federal regulatory program, intended to displace state law remedies. Historically, the Court has been wary of finding preemption under these circumstances because tort law has long been seen as a necessary state law supplement, providing compensation to injured parties and imposing another discipline on the marketplace.

The Rehnquist Court's approach in this area can be seen in two recent cases. In *Buckman Company v. Plaintiffs' Legal Committee*, it rejected a state tort claim by an individual injured by defective orthopedic bone screws who argued that a company acting on behalf of the manufacturers of the defective device had committed fraud on the FDA in gaining approval for the device and should be held liable.[19] The Court, backed by the FDA, concluded that policing fraud against the FDA was up to the agency alone and not a matter of local concern, even where, as here, the fraud allegedly allowed a defective device on the market that resulted in serious injuries to thousands of people.

In *Geier v. American Honda Motor Corporation*, the Court upheld a preemption claim, wiping out the state tort law claim of a young woman injured in a car accident where the car had only a manual seat belt and no air bag.[20] The issue was whether a federal standard, which required some but not all cars to have either a passive seat belt or an air bag during the early 1990s, preempted a state law claim that the manufacturer should have installed an air bag in the woman's car. The federal agency involved, the NHTSA, did not purport to preempt state tort laws when it issued the standard gradually requiring air bags. Nonetheless, the Court held that state tort law was inconsistent with the NHTSA phase-in approach, leaving the victim without any legal claim.

These cases suggest that where Congress's instructions about preemption are less than crystal-clear, the Court may be shifting away from safeguarding the rights of injured parties to seek compensation under state law and toward the idea that federal regulation frees corporations of tort liability under state law. This is disturbing. Federal agencies cannot provide the protection the public needs, and state tort law is necessary not just to provide remedies to injured parties but to impose discipline on the market and impose safety across the board.

Many of the cases discussed here were decided by a razor-thin 5–4 margin, and the replacement of a single sitting justice could have profound effects. Even with that cautionary note in mind, two overarching conclusions may be drawn about the Rehnquist Court and its relation to the executive branch.

First, it is sympathetic to big business. It has moved decisively to insulate commercial interests from tort litigation in damages preemption cases, it has shielded business from simultaneous federal and state regulation in its regulatory preemption cases, and it has enabled business to challenge federal regulation more effectively by stripping away the judicial deference that historically has been accorded to agency action. Second, the Rehnquist Court has hobbled the ability of ordinary citizens seeking stricter regulation of commercial activity to sue federal agencies, showing little sympathy for the role citizens play in shaping our democracy.

Individually, the Court's rulings are troubling. But taken as a whole, they signal a real hostility to allowing courts to hold the government accountable under the laws and the Constitution on behalf of ordinary citizens.

Environmental Law

JAMES SALZMAN

Modern environmental law is now more than thirty years old, no longer a new legal field but a mature area with its own practicing bar, shelves of regulations and statutes, and thousands of reported opinions. Environmental law's radical innovation of the "citizen suit" has created a key role for ordinary citizens, not just for the government, to use the courts as private attorneys general to enforce our laws. Its integration of ecological principles into legal doctrine has helped reshape our conceptions of legitimate restrictions on the use of private property. These developments, just to mention a few, have contributed greatly to our legal system, forcing a reassessment of basic assumptions. This may well explain why the most influential decisions in the field of administrative law have been environmental cases.

Unlike many of the other topics covered in this volume, the Rehnquist Court's treatment of environmental law defies meaningful labeling. Indeed, the best description that comes to mind is neither "proenvironment" nor "prodevelopment" but, rather, "indifferent." Despite the indisputable rise of environmental concerns on the public agenda, environmental law has played the role of Zelig in the Supreme Court's chambers, observing great events but playing little part in their unfolding.

Consider the research findings of Professor Richard Lazarus, who has analyzed the Supreme Court's decisions over the past three decades, covering all of the Rehnquist Court and almost all of the Burger Court. In reviewing more than 240 cases where environmental issues were raised, Lazarus concluded that "environmental protection concerns implicated by a case appear, at best, to play no favored role in shaping the outcome, which is a sharp departure from what many judges in the 1970s conceived of as the proper judicial function in environmental law. . . . [For] most of the Court most of the time environmental law raises no special issues or concerns worthy of distinct treatment as a substantive area of the law."[1] Deputy Solicitor General Edwin Kneedler shared this view, observing that "in almost every case, the environmental issue is overtaken by some other aspect of the Court's jurisprudence which disposes of the case."[2]

As evidence of the Rehnquist Court's lack of environmental focus, can you guess who has written the most environmental opinions, by far, over the past thirty years? Not Justice William O. Douglas, whose proud rhetoric championing environmental protection on behalf of the public interest is still reprinted in many environmental law casebooks. No, the prize for the leading opinion writer goes to Justice Byron White, hardly one identified with an environmental agenda of *any* kind. And his environmental opinions seem no different from his Commerce Clause, First Amendment, or equal protection opinions—unemotional, analytic, and workmanlike.

In the Rehnquist Court (and Burger Court, for that matter), environmental law has largely served as nondescript wrapping paper, delivering issues for the Court to consider but torn off and discarded while the Court assesses the administrative law, standing, criminal law, and other doctrinal fields contained within them. To be fair, advocates before the Court on environmental issues have not been ideologically consistent, either. In the Reagan era, for example, out of concern that the federal government lacked the will to enforce environmental laws aggressively, states led the way in strengthening environmental protections and environmental groups championed federalism arguments for greater state authority. Under the Clinton administration nearly the opposite was true, with these same groups arguing for stronger federal powers.

This is not to say, however, that particular justices' decisions in environmental cases have been random; it is just that their traditional labels as "liberal" or "conservative" provide little predictive power of how they will vote. Lazarus found only two justices with consistent voting records in environmental cases—Justices Antonin Scalia and Clarence Thomas. Their consistent antienvironment votes, and the voting patterns of other justices, can better be explained by focusing on more basic views rather than on overarching political alignments. As a general guide, justices who believe in a preeminent role for the executive branch in enforcing the law, in a sharp limit on the power of Congress to regulate at the state level, and in the primacy of private property rights over state uses will more likely decide cases against environmental protection. This can be seen in debates over three major issues reshaping environmental law—citizens' access to courts, the scope of private property rights, and Commerce Clause jurisprudence.

Environmental law's greatest contribution to our legal system has likely been its development of the citizen suit, allowing people to sue polluters when they cause harm and the government when it fails to fulfill its mandate of environmental protection. Virtually all our major environmental laws contain citizen suit provisions, creating a legion of private attorneys general to supplement the government's role in enforcing our laws. The once radical idea that private citizens, not just the government, can use the courts to enforce the range of environmental laws has been a powerful force for protection over the last thirty years, ensuring the compliance, both directly and indirectly, of literally thousands of companies and our most powerful government agencies.

For citizen suits to vindicate the protections promised by our laws, however, private parties must be able to get into court in the first place. And to do that they must satisfy the requirements of a doctrine known as "standing." Plaintiffs must demonstrate (1) that they have suffered a recognized harm, (2) that they have suffered it by an act forbidden under the law, and (3) that the court can provide redress. While seemingly easy to satisfy as a result of decisions over the last decade these three requirements have in fact become increasingly difficult for environmental plaintiffs to meet.

Environmental harms fit awkwardly within our common-law notions of injury. Unlike traditional tort harms, like whacking someone on the head, environmental harms are often attenuated, resulting from cumulative, multiple causes over some time. It is unusual for a harm resulting from pollution to be traced back to a single emission source. More generally, the degradation of air and water quality occurs over a long period of extended pollution from multiple sources. Given such remote causation, and wanting to achieve an overall "acceptable" level of pollution, environmental law generally regulates specific emissions at classes of sources, therefore not having to prove the harm caused by each specific emission. In simple terms, it has transformed the common law of nuisance into a comprehensively regulated field that avoids the harm *ex ante* by limiting pollution at its source.

Environmental harms do not just include harm from pollution, of course. What about injuries people sense from the commercial development of a forest or mountainside? Since the landmark 1972 case *Sierra Club v. Morton*, such nonphysical harms have satisfied standing's injury requirements.[3] In that case, the Sierra Club sued to prevent Disney from constructing a ski resort in the Sequoia National Forest. Broadening the scope of harm to include noneconomic injury, the Court held that the requirements of standing may be satisfied by injury to aesthetic and environmental values, even if suffered by many. Over time, however, this standard has been cut back.

In two of the Court's most significant decisions of the nineties, the *Lujan* cases, Justice Scalia, writing for the majority, stated that plaintiffs must demonstrate specific links of causation between the challenged act and the claimed harm to them.[4] In the case of actions alleged to threaten endangered species, he required them to show they had a particular economic or physical connection to the species, and he expressly ruled out aesthetic or recreational injuries. The net effect was to restrict citizens' access to the courts. Some lower courts have since denied standing to plaintiffs unable to show particular harm from a polluter's specific discharge. But we know that this is well-nigh impossible because the harm resulting from pollution can rarely be traced to a single source.

The doors to the courthouse became even tougher to open in the 1998 case *Steel Company v. Citizens for a Better Environment*.[5] In 1995, Citizens for a Better Environment (CBE) filed a citizen suit against the Steel Company for its failure over the previous six years to submit a series of compliance forms required by law. In a citizen suit of this kind, plaintiffs must first inform a defendant of its alleged violations and then wait sixty days before filing suit. During the sixty days before CBE filed its suit, Steel Company submitted its long-overdue forms. CBE went ahead with the case, but on appeal to the Supreme Court it was told that it had failed to meet the redressability requirement for standing. In a Scalia opinion, the Court held that the remedy available in this case, payment of civil penalties to the U.S. Treasury, could not redress injury to CBE or its members. As he put it, "Although a suitor may derive great comfort and joy from the fact that the United States Treasury is not cheated, that a wrongdoer gets his just desserts, or that the nation's laws are faithfully enforced, that psychic satisfaction is not an acceptable Article III remedy because it does not redress a cognizable Article III injury." In other words, because the statute required penalties to be paid to the Treasury rather than to the plaintiffs, the redressability requirement of standing could not be met for the simple reason that the harms suffered by the plaintiffs would not be compensated.

This decision was a body blow to the whole concept of citizen suits, where the primary goal is environmental protection rather than personal enrichment. If the EPA and state agencies presented little credible threat of enforcement to certain industries (and this has certainly happened), companies could simply violate environmental laws and come into compliance, perhaps just temporarily, when forewarned of a citizen suit.

Consistent in its lack of consistency, the Court then reversed its holdings on environmental standing in midstride. In *Friends of the Earth, Inc. v. Laidlaw Environmental Services (TOC), Inc.* (2000), the Court breathed new life into citizen suits.[6] Friends of the Earth had brought a citizen suit under the Clean Water Act against Laidlaw, the operator of a hazardous-waste incinerator that discharged wastewater into the Tyger River in South Carolina. The organization alleged that the facility had violated its permit requirements hundreds of times. It submitted affidavits of several of its members stating that they had stopped using the Tyger River because of health concerns. The district court had found that Laidlaw had violated the mercury effluent permit limits 489 times, the monitoring requirements 420 times, and the reporting requirements 503 times and had been assessed $405,800 in civil penalties. The Fourth Circuit Court of Appeals, though, following the holding of *Steel Company v. Citizens for a Better Environment*, vacated this opinion, in part because the civil penalties awarded in citizen suits did not meet the redressability requirement of standing.

Laidlaw provided a stark example of how, if the government did not act, the Supreme Court's decisions could eviscerate the protection of citizen suits and effectively allow polluters to violate requirements with impunity. Perhaps shocked by the consequence of their earlier decision, the Court now reaffirmed the status of aesthetic and recreational injuries that it had recognized in earlier cases such as *Sierra Club v. Morton*. Eliminating the need for precise tracing of cause and physical effect, the Court stated that the plaintiff's reasonable concern about the effects of toxic pollutants released by Laidlaw on recreational, aesthetic, or economic interests was sufficient for standing. This would make it easier for a plaintiff to demonstrate injury. As to redressability, the Court argued that all civil penalties have a deterrent effect. *Steel Company* was distinguished rather than overturned, with the Court noting that *Steel Company* had denied standing for citizen suits seeking civil penalties for *wholly past* violations, whereas the violations in this case were ongoing and could continue undeterred. Thus plaintiffs must be able to show the likelihood that violations will continue in the future. Justices Scalia and Thomas, it should be noted, strongly dissented, arguing that the Court had sanctioned a "generalized remedy" and ignored the *Steel Company* decision.

While *Laidlaw* reversed the trend of weakening citizen suits, the issue is far from resolved, for it is driven by a fundamental disagreement. The underlying logic for closing the courtroom doors to many environmental concerns lies in differing conceptions of the separation of powers. In his opinions on standing, Justice Scalia has argued that the burden to ensure that laws are faithfully executed lies solely with the executive branch, not the public or the courts. If citizens are concerned over agencies' poor compliance with statutory mandates, the opinions have suggested, they should go to Congress for a legislative fix or the executive branch for a political resolution. As Scalia wrote in *Laidlaw*, "in seeking to overturn that tradition by giving an individual plaintiff the power to invoke a public remedy, Congress has done precisely what we have said it cannot do: convert an 'undifferentiated public interest' into an 'individual right' vindicable in the courts. . . . By permitting citizens to pursue civil penalties payable to the Federal Treasury, the Act . . . turns over to private citizens the function of enforcing the law."[7]

The problem with this pat answer is that Congress provided for citizen suits expressly to ensure that the executive branch *did* enforce the laws. Had the Reagan administration's neutering of the EPA under Anne Gorsuch been forgotten in the mists of time? Citizen suits certainly can force agency agendas, and this does raise concerns over whether the executive branch's discretion to enforce the laws has been unduly limited. But citizen suits normally arise when the government is *not* enforcing the laws. Indeed, usually the federal government can overfile and take over the case. Scalia's advice that, in the face of nonenforcement, citizens should go to Congress or the executive branch for a political resolution rings hollow. Why go to Congress when it has already provided for citizen suits to address this very situation? Why go to the executive branch when it already is not enforcing the law? All that's left of Scalia's strategy is to vote the bums out of office.

The second major fault line—protection of private property rights—runs through what are called takings cases. The Fifth Amendment of the Constitution provides that private property cannot be taken for public use without just compensation. Environmental law raises takings concerns precisely because it alters our vision of property and the legitimacy of government's constraints on its use. As the public's appreciation of and demands for environmental quality increase, our notions of what constitutes reasonable use evolve as well. Use of a private resource, such as housing construction along a coastline, can adversely affect the environment by increasing coastline erosion. To protect the public's interests, the government may restrict such property development for the public benefit of coastal conservation. Yet if the government had to compensate every landowner whose property value diminished *at all* as a result of such zoning, the cost of enforcing such restrictions would be prohibitive and could never take place because of the costs. The difficulty of line drawing, of course, lies in determining when restrictions are so complete and unfair that they constitute a "taking" for which the property owner must be compensated.

The Rehnquist Court has applied the Takings Clause aggressively and shifted the balance toward greater compensation for property owners. For example, in the important decision *Lucas v. South Carolina Coastal Council*, written by Justice Scalia in 1992, the Court required compensation for regulations that deprive the property owner of all economically valuable use of the land unless the government can prove the restriction is necessary to prevent what has traditionally been recognized as a common-law nuisance.[8] This not only switched the burden of proof onto the government to justify its restrictions but, in another part of the opinion, left the lower courts the option of requiring compensation for less than total diminution (and some are already doing so). The net result has been expanded protections for private property owners and cost constraints on legislatures seeking to protect public resources. The case had a slim majority, so new appointments to the Supreme Court will surely affect the trajectory of future takings jurisprudence.

The third major debate shaping environmental law is the reach of congressional authority. This plays out through the Commerce Clause of the Constitution. The Constitution grants Congress several sources of authority to regulate activities in the states, including the power to tax and spend and the power to provide for the common defense. The single most important source of authority for environmental law has been the power to regulate interstate commerce, provided by the Commerce Clause. Congressional reliance on the Commerce Clause seems obvious in a statute like the Clean Air Act, for instance, since air pollution routinely travels across state lines. The same is true for water pollution as well. The Commerce Clause has also been used to justify protection of isolated wetlands. The Clean Water Act forbids the dredging and filling of navigable waters without a permit. How, though, could this be justified under the Commerce Clause if the wet-lands are not linked to other waters—such as prairie potholes or other seasonal wetlands? The answer, traditionally, has been migratory wa-terfowl. Duck hunting is a multibillion-dollar business. Because ducks and geese stop off in such wetlands to feed during their migration, un-der the Migratory Bird Rule the EPA and the Army Corps of Engi-neers have justified protection of wetlands as a significant concern of interstate commerce.

In 1995, the expansive breadth of the Commerce Clause was di-rectly challenged for the first time in more than fifty years in *United States v. Lopez*.[9] The Court held that a federal statute regulating private activity exceeded the authority of the Commerce Clause. The chal-lenged statute, the Gun-Free School Zones Act, prohibited the posses-sion of firearms within a thousand feet of a school. In a 5–4 majority, Rehnquist wrote that the activity of possessing a gun in or near a school is not inherently economic or commercial in nature; that the act in question had no express element that explicitly affected interstate commerce; that Congress made no specific findings that possessing a gun in or near a school would affect interstate commerce; and that the suggested connections to interstate commerce were extremely attenu-ated and could "destroy the Framers' system of enumerated and re-served state powers." The Court went on to hold that the Commerce Clause covers only activities that "substantially affect" interstate com-merce. This decision sent shock waves through the environmental com-munity for the same reasons that the *Lujan* decisions had. Direct causation is exceedingly difficult to prove in the environmental context.

The holding of *Lopez* was driven home in the 2000 case *United States v. Morrison*, which struck down part of the Violence against Women Act.[10] Writing for the same five-member majority as in *Lopez*, Rehn-quist held that neither law was directed at regulating economic or commercial activities. Despite several years of data gathering by Con-gress to document the interstate economic effects of violence against women, the Court argued that, in order to maintain the "distinction between what is truly national and what is truly local," the threshold of substantially affecting interstate commerce must be high.[11] If after *Lopez* the Court's scrutiny of Congressional enactments under the

Commerce Clause was unclear, after *Morrison* it was plainly evident. It was also historic. As Professor Michael Gerhardt has observed, "In the past 5 years, the Rehnquist Court has struck down 23 federal laws, including 11 for exceeding Congress' authority under the U.S. Commerce Clause, section 5 of the Fourteenth Amendment, or both. Not since the titanic conflict between Congress and the Court in the 1930s over the fate of the New Deal has the Court been as active as it has in recent years in enforcing federalism-based limitations on Congressional power."[12] Shortly after *Lopez* was decided, Justice Thomas commented that he believed the Migratory Bird Rule fails to satisfy the Commerce Clause.[13] Five years later, it appeared that the entire Court would face this issue when certiorari was granted in *Solid Waste Agency of Northern Cook County (SWANCC) v. U.S. Army Corps of Engineers*.[14] SWANCC, a consortium of twenty-three suburban Chicago cities and villages, had petitioned to develop a disposal site for solid waste in a 553-acre former sand and gravel pit that had been abandoned for almost thirty years. The site had gradually developed into a successional stage forest, with the old trenches turning into permanent and seasonal ponds that ranged in size from one-tenth of an acre to several acres. The Army Corps of Engineers refused to issue a permit to fill the ponds, stating that as many as 121 bird species, including both endangered and migratory birds, had been observed at the site.

In a 1985 decision, *United States v. Riverside Bayview Homes*, the Court had held that the Clean Water Act covered wetlands adjacent to navigable waters.[15] In *SWANCC*, Rehnquist, writing again for the same 5–4 majority as in the *Lopez* and *Morrison* cases, sidestepped the Commerce Clause issue and decided the case on statutory grounds, distinguishing the *Riverside* decision by holding that the Migratory Bird Rule applied only to navigable waters and that waters with no hydrologic connection to open waters (that is, isolated wetlands) were not "navigable waters." The decision has been decried by environmental groups, concerned that it may have put one-fifth of America's bodies of water in jeopardy. The decision also raises the question of whether any of the Clean Water Act (including its pollution provisions) applies to isolated waters. In a district court case in New Jersey, for example, lawyers argued that the Army Corps of Engineers lacked jurisdiction over wetlands owned by a company because they were geographically distant from navigable waters.

While not a Commerce Clause decision, *SWANCC* raises similar concerns over federalism. The Court held that the agency was not entitled to the deference courts normally give to administrative agencies that promulgate federal regulations under *Chevron*.[16] In dicta, the Court noted that a broad reading of the Clean Water Act could impinge upon states' rights to control land and water issues. As Rehnquist wrote,

> Where an administrative interpretation of a statute invokes the outer limits of Congress' power, we expect a clear indication that Congress intended that result. This requirement stems from our prudential desire not to needlessly reach constitutional issues and our assumption that Congress does not casually authorize administrative agencies to interpret a statute to push the limit of congressional authority. This concern is heightened where the administrative interpretation alters the federal-state framework by permitting federal encroachment upon traditional state power. . . . Twice in the past six years we have reaffirmed the proposition that the grant of authority to Congress under the Commerce Clause, though broad, is not unlimited. See *United States v. Morrison*, 529 U.S. 598 (2000) and *United States v. Lopez*, 514 U.S. 549 (1995).[17]

Echoes of the *Lopez* decision continue to sound. Whether undercutting laws by statutory interpretation or Commerce Clause jurisprudence (or Article 5 of the Fourteenth Amendment, for that matter), the Court's majority views the issue as the same—the allocation of authority between the states and federal government. Notwithstanding its contrary decision in *Bush v. Gore*, the Rehnquist Court has established a clear preference to favor state over federal exercise of authority. What are the implications for environmental protection?

From a historical perspective, one would conclude that environmental protection will suffer. One of the main reasons for the development of federal environmental law in the 1970s was the historic failure of states to implement and enforce tough environmental standards. State agencies have traditionally been threatened by the possibility of co-optation by the industries they are supposed to regulate. Perhaps things have changed, though, in the last thirty years. After all, today political candidates reflexively define themselves as environmentalists. The most recent test for the greening of local politics has been the response of states to the *SWANCC* decision. According to the Environmental Law Institute, at least nineteen states reacted to the newly created gap in Clean Water Act protection of isolated wetlands by either enacting or recommending the enactment of laws to protect these areas. While that is a promising development, it is worth remembering that not all these proposed laws will be enacted and that over half the states still have not responded. Overall, then, it seems likely that the transfer of environmental protection authority from the federal government to the states will lead to less protection.

Environmental protection has surely been affected by the Rehnquist Court, but apparently not because of concerns about or antipathy toward the environment. Rather, decisions on "environmental cases" have been made on the grounds of fundamental political issues such as the separation of powers, protection of private property rights, and federalism. These cases have determined the shape of environmental protection and the shape of a wide range of other fields as well. And what of the future? As Richard Lazarus concludes, "It will be the rare candidate that will have a clear environmental track record from which we can readily predict future votes as a justice in environmental cases."[18] It seems a safe bet, however, that justices who share the views of Scalia and Thomas on rigid separation of powers and strong property rights will provide a stronger majority for decisions that weaken environmental protection. Beyond that predictor, however, all bets are off.

The "Miserly" Approach to Disability Rights

ANDREW J. IMPARATO

In the decades since World War II, disabled Americans have worked to change the public perception of disability from a charity model, where the disabled person is a source of pity evoking paternalism, to a civil rights or social model, where the focus is on removing barriers to participation. Many have also advocated moving away from the medical model, where the disabled person is a patient in need of treatments, more research, and ultimately a "cure." In both the charity and the medical models, disability is viewed as an inherently negative or tragic status and disabled people are often portrayed as helpless victims of fate. In contrast, in the social or civil rights model, disabled people are full citizens seeking self-determination along with economic and political power.

In the civil rights paradigm for disability, the goal is to fix the society, not the disabled person. Many limitations associated with disabling conditions may more accurately be attributed to the interaction between these conditions and the physical and social environment. When the environment is made accessible, disabled people can participate fully notwithstanding their impairments. Supporters of disability rights have emphasized that employers, governments at all levels, and public accommodations should make reasonable adjustments so that disabled people will not be excluded; schools must educate all pupils so that disabled children need not go without schooling, as they once did; and transportation and telecommunications systems should accommodate disabled users so that the infrastructure for commerce and community works for everyone.

Although disability rights advocates achieved important legislative and court victories in the 1970s and 1980s, the civil rights model was not wholeheartedly embraced until Congress enacted the Americans with Disabilities Act (ADA) in 1990.[1] To be sure, signs of the charity model, like Jerry Lewis's annual telethons for the Muscular Dystrophy Association, vex disability rights advocates, and the medical model continues to influence funding for research budgets, most recently concerning efforts to develop genetically engineered humans free of disabling conditions. And yet the ADA has helped refocus Americans on the important goals of equality of opportunity, full participation, independent living, and economic self-sufficiency for the more than 56 million disabled children and adults living in the United States.

Upon signing the ADA into law, President George H. W. Bush remarked, "With today's signing . . . every man, woman and child with a disability can now pass through once-closed doors, into a bright new era of equality, independence and freedom."[2] Unfortunately, since William H. Rehnquist became chief justice of the Supreme Court, the bipartisan congressional and administrative efforts to open those doors have been undermined and sometimes nullified by him and his increasingly activist colleagues. Instead of embracing the civil rights model embodied in the ADA, the Rehnquist Court has repeatedly demonstrated an outdated and offensive paternalism in its approach to disability. To a large extent, Americans with disabilities are still waiting for a landmark Supreme Court decision that truly accelerates their cause in the manner that *Brown v. Board of Education* altered American consciousness around race.

In his concurrence and dissent in an important 1985 case involving a challenge to a zoning ordinance impeding the establishment of a group home for people with cognitive disabilities, Justice Thurgood Marshall discussed the subtleties of analyzing equal protection issues in a disability context.[3] One issue in the case was whether a law that allegedly denies equal protection to people with cognitive disabilities deserved "heightened" scrutiny, like laws challenged by women and racial and ethnic minorities under the Equal Protection Clause of the Fourteenth Amendment. The greater the scrutiny, the greater the chance that the challenged law or activity will be found to violate the Constitution. Discussing how judges determine when a minority is sufficiently discrete and insular to merit a "more searching judicial inquiry into laws adversely affecting it," Justice Marshall noted their ability to apply lessons from history and their own experience:

> Because prejudice spawns prejudice, and stereotypes produce limitations that confirm the stereotype on which they are based, a history of unequal treatment requires sensitivity to the prospect that its vestiges endure. In separating those groups that are discrete and insular from those that are not, as in many important distinctions, "a page of history is worth a volume of logic."[4]

Unfortunately, under the leadership of Chief Justice Rehnquist, the Supreme Court has frequently applied quite faulty logic, demonstrating an appalling insensitivity to the shameful history and ongoing vestiges of disability discrimination in the United States. Its jurisprudence in three critical areas makes this glaringly evident: new constitutional limitations on laws protecting the individual rights of children and adults with disabilities; statutory interpretations dramatically shrinking the protected class under the ADA and other disability rights laws; and a dangerous tendency to defer to bureaucratic prerogatives and "professional" judgments when human rights issues are at stake.

In 1985, the year before Justice Rehnquist was elevated by President Ronald Reagan to serve as chief justice, he joined in Justice Byron White's majority opinion in *Cleburne v. Cleburne Living Center*, holding that the application of a municipal zoning ordinance requiring that a proposed group home for adults with mental retardation had to obtain a special-use permit violated the Equal-Protection Clause of the Fourteenth Amendment.[5] Justice White's opinion (joined also by Justices

Lewis F. Powell, John Paul Stevens, and Sandra Day O'Connor) used an unusually rigorous "rational basis" test to overturn the challenged ordinance's application in that case and held that the Texas municipality at issue had not proffered a rational basis for believing that the proposed group home would pose any special threat to the city's legitimate interests.

Under a traditional "rational basis" test, when a citizen seeks to challenge a law or ordinance under the Equal Protection Clause of the Constitution, he or she must show that the challenged law is not rationally or reasonably related to a legitimate government purpose. If the government can show that the challenged law serves a legitimate policy goal or has a "rational basis," then the law is upheld as a legitimate exercise of the government's power to legislate. Some categories of laws are subjected to more searching review or stricter scrutiny because the constitutional interests at stake require a more substantial showing to justify the challenged unequal treatment. Justice Stevens, joined by Chief Justice Warren Burger, filed a concurring opinion in *Cleburne* asserting that the three standards of equal protection review described in Justice White's opinion more appropriately should be thought of as "a continuum of judgmental responses to differing classifications which have been explained in opinions by terms ranging from 'strict scrutiny' at one extreme to 'rational basis' on the other."[6] Justice Stevens went on to reason that the challenged zoning ordinance was unconstitutional as applied to the group home, noting his unwillingness to believe "that a rational member of this disadvantaged class [people with cognitive disabilities] could ever approve of the discriminatory application of the city's ordinance in this case."[7]

The most cogent and convincing opinion in the *Cleburne* case was filed by Justice Thurgood Marshall, joined by Justices William J. Brennan and Harry A. Blackmun. Justice Marshall, describing his opinion as "concurring in the judgment in part and dissenting in part," argued for an intermediate level of review for equal protection cases involving people with cognitive disabilities similar to the standard the Court had developed for women and for children born out of wedlock. In a passage representing a high-water mark for constitutional jurisprudence in the disability rights arena, Justice Marshall wrote:

For the retarded, just as for Negroes and women, much has changed in recent years, but much remains the same; outdated statutes are still on the books, and irrational fears or ignorance, traceable to the prolonged social and cultural isolation of the retarded, continue to stymie recognition of the dignity and individuality of retarded people. Heightened judicial scrutiny of action appearing to impose unnecessary barriers to the retarded is required in light of increasing recognition that such barriers are inconsistent with evolving principles of equality embedded in the Fourteenth Amendment.[8]

When Congress passed the ADA five years after the *Cleburne* decision, it made explicit findings intended to signify to the federal courts that allegedly discriminatory laws affecting people with disabilities deserved heightened scrutiny under the Constitution. Congress made it clear that it considered people with disabilities to be a "discrete and insular minority" occupying a "position of political powerlessness," that "discrimination against individuals with disabilities continue[s] to be a serious and pervasive social problem," and that people with disabilities have historically been subjected to "purposeful unequal treatment" on the basis of their immutable human characteristics.[9]

In 1993, the Rehnquist Court revisited this issue in an equal protection case challenging the state of Kentucky's procedures for determining when a person with mental retardation may be committed involuntarily to an institution. In *Heller v. Doe*, Justice Anthony Kennedy wrote a majority opinion (joined by Chief Justice Rehnquist and Justices White, Antonin Scalia, and Clarence Thomas) applying a "rational basis" standard and upholding Kentucky's system of involuntary commitment, which made it easier to institutionalize adults with cognitive disabilities than to commit adults with mental illness. Because the former group had not argued for heightened scrutiny in the lower courts, Justice Kennedy wrote that it would be inappropriate to apply a different standard in the Supreme Court. In a separate dissent, Justice Blackmun noted his "continuing adherence to the view that laws that discriminate against individuals with mental retardation, or infringe upon fundamental rights, are subject to heightened scrutiny."[10]

Peculiarly, Justice Blackmun did not cite the congressional findings in the ADA to add weight to his argument.

Justifying a rational basis standard in *Heller*, Justice Kennedy (joined by Justices Rehnquist, White, Scalia, and Thomas) noted that "a classification neither involving fundamental rights nor proceeding along suspect lines is accorded a strong presumption of validity."[11] For the five justices in the *Heller* majority, it appears that the right of an adult with cognitive disabilities to live in a place of his or her choosing was not a "fundamental right." If avoiding involuntary commitment was not a fundamental right for such a person, it would be difficult to discern what would be. Applying the rational basis test, the majority in *Heller* accepted the basis for the challenged distinctions, making it easier to involuntarily lock up Kentucky residents with mental retardation than to involuntarily commit Kentuckians with mental illness.

Justice David Souter, joined (on this issue) by Justices Blackmun, Stevens, and O'Connor, filed a dissent in *Heller* concluding that, even under a rational basis standard, "Kentucky's provision of different procedures for the institutionalization of the mentally retarded and the mentally ill is not supported by any rational justification."[12] Applying a rigorous review reminiscent of the beefed-up rational basis test used by the majority in *Cleburne*, Justice Souter noted that an important "individual liberty" interest was at stake in *Heller* that "encompasses both freedom from restraint and freedom from the stigma that restraint and its justifications impose on an institutionalized person." He concluded that Kentucky should not be permitted under the Equal Protection Clause of the Fourteenth Amendment "to draw a distinction that is difficult to see as resting on anything other than the stereotypical assumption that the retarded are 'perpetual children,' an assumption that has historically been taken to justify the disrespect and 'grotesque mistreatment' to which the retarded have been subjected."[13]

Ironically, whereas the majority in *Heller* went out of its way to avoid deciding the appropriate standard of review for the challenged Kentucky law in that case, in 2001 the Rehnquist Court took pains to announce the appropriateness of a rational basis standard of review for equal protection challenges on the basis of disability. The case, *University of Alabama v. Garrett*, involved allegations of employment discrimination under the ADA by two disabled employees of the state of Alabama.[14]

The real issue in *Garrett* was whether Congress had the authority under Section 5 of the Fourteenth Amendment to abrogate Alabama's Eleventh Amendment immunity to suits for damages by private individuals. Although no state law or regulation was being challenged on constitutional grounds in *Garrett*, and even though Alabama did not even try to argue that the alleged discriminatory treatment of two of its disabled employees was rational, Chief Justice Rehnquist (joined by Justices O'Connor, Scalia, Kennedy, and Thomas) reached the standard of review issue in the context of his discussion of the "limitations that the court's interpretation of the equal protection clause of section § 1 of the Fourteenth Amendment places upon States' treatment of the disabled." Citing and quoting from Justice White's majority opinion in *Cleburne*, he declared that state conduct that discriminates on the basis of disability "incurs only the minimum 'rational-basis' review applicable to general social and economic legislation."

A basic tenet of disability civil rights law that distinguishes it from other civil rights laws is that providing equal opportunity to an employee or customer with a disability sometimes requires the employer or business to treat that employee or customer differently and make a reasonable accommodation or an adjustment—a necessary change from standard operating procedures. For example, an employer may need to purchase a screen reader to enable a blind employee to use his or her computer or a business may need to make an exception to its prohibition on animals in the store for a customer with a service animal. Under the ADA, the failure to make this kind of reasonable accommodation or modification amounts to discrimination.

This important baseline principle of disability discrimination law seems to have been completely missed by the majority in *Garrett*. Chief Justice Rehnquist asserted for the majority in *Garrett*:

The result of *Cleburne* is that States are not required by the Fourteenth Amendment to make special accommodations for the disabled, so long as their actions toward such individuals are rational. They could quite hard headedly—and perhaps hard-heartedly—hold to job-qualification requirements which do not make allowance for the disabled. If special accommodations are to be required, they have to come from positive law and not through the Equal Protection Clause.[15]

This analysis completely misses the point that a failure to provide a *reasonable* accommodation is an *irrational* act that results in a denial of equal opportunity for a disabled employee or job applicant. Moving on from its analysis of the constitutional underpinnings of "special accommodations for the disabled," the majority in *Garrett* then struck down those provisions of the ADA that allow individuals with disabilities to bring damage actions against a state when it discriminates in employment on the basis of disability because Congress had failed to document "a pattern of discrimination" in employment by the states that violates the Fourteen Amendment.[16]

In a blistering dissent, Justice Stephen Breyer, joined by Justices Stevens, Souter, and Ruth Bader Ginsburg, offered a detailed review of the legislative findings that would justify a reasonable determination by Congress that there was indeed a widespread problem of unconstitutional disability discrimination in employment by the states in 1990.[17] Breyer strongly took issue with the sleight of hand Chief Justice Rehnquist used to undermine the ADA's constitutionality by applying the rational basis standard of review:

> The problem with the Court's approach is that neither the "burden of proof" that favors States nor any other rule of restraint applicable to *judges* applies to *Congress* when it exercises its § 5 power. "Limitations stemming from the nature of the judicial process . . . have no application to Congress." Rational-basis review—with its presumptions favoring constitutionality—is a "paradigm of *judicial* restraint." And the Congress of the United States is not a lower court. . . .[18]

Justice Breyer is exactly right. The Court failed to recognize that a legislative body is not limited to a record put together by lawyers and a lower court the way the Supreme Court is. Congress can obtain information from all sources, including the victims of discrimination. Congress also reflects public attitudes and beliefs about the nature of disability discrimination and the most appropriate legal remedy for victims. By its indifference toward Congress's superior competence in such matters, the Court, as Breyer said, "improperly invades a power that the Constitution assigns to Congress."

In lamenting the majority's power grab in *Garrett*, Breyer perhaps unintentionally reminds us that the same five activist justices who undermined Congress's constitutional authority in *Garrett* also usurped the role of the electorate and (if necessary) Congress in deciding the outcome of the 2000 presidential election.

As *Garrett* makes clear, the conservative majority on the Rehnquist court has demonstrated a strong unwillingness to use the Equal Protection Clause of the Fourteenth Amendment to safeguard individual rights at the hands of a discriminatory state actor. On the contrary, reinvigorating states' rights sensibilities that the Civil War and the modern civil rights movement apparently have not put to rest, it has gone out of its way to eviscerate whatever protections the Equal Protection Clause might have afforded Americans with disabilities. To be sure, the loss of justices like Marshall, Brennan, and Blackmun dealt a profound blow to anyone who valued the Supreme Court's role as a champion of the civil rights of individuals under the Constitution. Although Justices Stevens and Breyer have supported disability rights more often than not, no justice has emerged as a consistent champion, bringing sensitivity and understanding to the constitutional jurisprudence of disability rights in the manner of a Justice Thurgood Marshall.

The Rehnquist Court also demonstrated breathtaking arrogance when it disregarded congressional intent, unanimous administrative agency interpretations, and the overwhelming majority of federal courts of appeal when it removed civil rights protections from large segments of the ADA's protected class in *Sutton v. United Airlines* (1999) and two related cases.[19] In this *Sutton* trilogy, Justice O'Connor, joined by all but Justices Stevens and Breyer, ruled that individuals with disabilities who can correct their impairments through mitigating measures such as medications and assistive devices do not meet the statutory definition of "individual with a disability" under the ADA. In other words, the ADA no longer protects disabled people who, with treatment and/or assistive devices, are able to function well but nonetheless experience discrimination because of irrational employer behavior. In a case decided early in 2002, the Rehnquist Court further narrowed the scope of the protected class.[20]

Apparently unconcerned that the ADA is a remedial statute that should be "construed broadly to effectuate its purposes," the majority in *Sutton* decided to narrowly limit who gets to bring a claim under the ADA.[21] The ADA defines a disability as a physical or mental impairment that substantially limits one or more major life activities of such individual; a record of such an impairment; or being regarded as having such an impairment.[22] The key issue in the *Sutton* trilogy was straightforward: when a court determines whether an individual has a disability for purposes of the ADA, does it make that assessment based on the individual's natural or "unmitigated" state, or should it take into account how that individual is able to function with the assistance of "mitigating measures" like medication, assistive technology, or prosthetics?

Until the Court's decision in *Sutton*, eight of the nine federal courts of appeal that had addressed the matter, all three executive agencies that had issued regulations or interpretive bulletins under the ADA, and all the key congressional committees that wrote the ADA agreed that a court should determine whether an individual has a disability by assessing the person in his or her unmitigated state.[23] Nevertheless, trying hard to keep the protected class from exceeding the figure of 43 million used in one of Congress's hortatory findings in the ADA, the *Sutton* majority decided to ignore Congress's express instruction that the "purpose of [the ADA is] to provide a clear and comprehensive national mandate for the elimination of discrimination against individuals with disabilities."[24] In her opinion for the majority, Justice O'Connor contrasted the "work disability" approach, which focuses on the individual's reported ability to work, with the "health conditions" approach, which looks at all conditions that impair the health or typical functional abilities of an individual. Then, delving into arcane policy documents to determine the origins of the 43 million figure identified in the ADA's findings, the majority decided incomprehensibly that a slightly smaller figure used in an early version of the ADA "clearly reflects an approach to defining disabilities that is closer to the work disabilities approach than the health conditions approach."[25]

The work disabilities approach is inappropriate in the civil rights context. A good example of a federal disability law that takes a work disabilities approach to determining eligibility is the Social Security Act. To be eligible for disability retirement benefits or Supplemental Security Income benefits under this law, an individual must show an "inability to engage in any substantial gainful activity by reason of any . . . physical or mental impairment which can be expected to result in death or which has lasted or can be expected to last for a continuous period of not less than 12 months."[26] By making an analogy with this work disability definition in the Social Security Act, the *Sutton* majority missed the critical distinction between a narrow statutory definition appropriate for a program providing retirement benefits to support someone who can no longer work and a broad definition appropriate for a civil rights law intended to prohibit acts of disability-related discrimination against people who can work.[27]

As Justice Stevens observes in his *Sutton* dissent, a broad definition of the protected class does not guarantee a job to unqualified job applicants with disabilities.[28] The case simply asked whether people who function well should be able to assert disability discrimination when their condition substantially limits them in the absence of a mitigating measure. Does the ADA let people with correctable conditions "in the door" of civil rights protection? Why not? As Justice Stevens notes, "Inside that door is nothing more than basic protection from irrational and unjustified discrimination because of a characteristic that is beyond a person's control."[29]

Citing the landmark 1987 decision in *School Board of Nassau County v. Arline*, Justice Stevens went on to note that one of the ADA's purposes is to "dismantle employment barriers based on society's accumulated myths and fears."[30] Given this purpose, he pointed out, "It is especially ironic to deny protection for persons with substantially limiting impairments that, when corrected, render them fully able and employable." The majority's decision in *Sutton*, Justice Stevens concluded, "may have the perverse effect of denying coverage for a sizeable portion of the core group of 43 million" people with disabilities that Congress declared its intention to protect.[31] That group includes people with controlled conditions like epilepsy and diabetes, people with prosthetic legs and arms that restore functioning, and people with psychiatric and other health conditions that are well controlled.

This bizarre result was entirely unnecessary. "In order to be faithful to the remedial purposes of the Act," wrote Justice Stevens, "we should give it a generous, rather than a miserly, construction."[32] Sadly, thanks to the Rehnquist Court's "miserly" interpretation of the definition of disability, millions of disabled Americans have been stripped of their civil rights protections.[33]

In January 2002, the Rehnquist Court further narrowed the scope of the ADA's protected class in *Toyota v. Williams*, a case involving an autoworker with carpal tunnel syndrome.[34] The autoworker had successfully argued to the appeals court that her condition met the ADA's definition of disability because it substantially limited her ability to perform manual tasks. In a unanimous decision written by Justice O'Connor, the Rehnquist Court disagreed, holding that to be substantially limited in performing manual tasks, an individual must have an impairment that prevents or severely restricts him or her from doing activities that are of central importance to most people's daily lives.[35] The Court reasoned that Williams had failed to make this showing as a matter of law, in part because of evidence demonstrating that she was able to bathe, brush her teeth, and perform housework notwithstanding her impairments. Questioning the importance of the Equal Employment Opportunity Commission's interpretation of the statute, the Court decided that the statute's reference to "substantially limits" meant "prevents or severely restricts" and its reference to "major" life activities meant activities "of central importance to most people's daily lives." Because Williams was still able to brush her teeth, she failed to demonstrate the kind of impairment that would have invoked the protections of the ADA.[36]

The practical impact of decisions like *Williams* and the *Sutton* trilogy is that disabled plaintiffs find it harder and harder to challenge employment discrimination. Either they lose on the issue of whether they have a disability or the evidence they submit to demonstrate the severity of their impairments is used to question their qualifications for the job. This no-win situation was never intended by Congress, and it leaves millions of disabled Americans without an effective remedy for discrimination.[37]

When Congress enacted the ADA, it found that "historically, society has tended to isolate and segregate individuals with disabilities, and, despite some improvements, such forms of discrimination against individuals with disabilities continue to be a serious and pervasive social problem. . . . Discrimination against individuals with disabilities persists in such critical areas as employment, housing, public accommodations, education, transportation, communication, recreation, institutionalization, health services, voting, and access to public services."[38] Given that much of this discrimination falls within the purview of bureaucracies overseeing programs that serve disabled people, it follows that one good way to address disability discrimination is to challenge discriminatory behavior by those bureaucracies. In two cases where such challenges have been made, the Rehnquist Court has been reluctant to question the judgments of bureaucrats and professionals who make the rules.

In the *Heller* case, a class of plaintiffs with cognitive disabilities sought to challenge Kentucky's system for involuntary commitment, which made it easier to confine these people than to confine adults with mental illness. In defense of their scheme, Kentucky argued that the lower standard of proof followed from the fact that this disability is easier to diagnose than mental illness; that it is easier to determine whether a person with a cognitive disability presents a danger or a threat of danger to self, family, or others than it is to make such a determination for a person with mental illness; and that prevailing methods of treatment for people with disabilities are, as a general rule, less invasive than those for people with mental illness.[39]

Noting that "differences in treatment between the mentally retarded and the mentally ill have long existed in Anglo-American law," and "continu[e] to the present day" in many states, the Court concluded that Kentucky had proffered a rational basis for its challenged commitment standards.[40] The analysis in *Heller* implied that a history of discriminatory treatment that continues to the present can and will be used to justify the continuation of the challenged discriminatory conduct under the Constitution. What are the limits of this bizarre calculation? In *Buck v. Bell* (1927), the Supreme Court held that sterilization of "feeble-minded" individuals was permissible under the Constitution.[41] Should this history be used to justify a state law requiring sterilization of adults with mental retardation in 2002?

As Justice Souter noted in his dissent,

> Surely the Court does not intend to suggest that the irrational and scientifically unsupported beliefs of pre–19th century England can support any distinction in treatment between the mentally ill and the mentally retarded today. At that time, "lunatics" were "[s]een as demonically possessed or the products of parental sin [and] were often punished or left to perish. . . ." The primary purpose of an adjudication of "idiocy" appears to have been to "depriv[e] [an individual] of [his] property and its profits."[42]

Interestingly, Souter disparages the particular history referenced by the majority in *Heller* as "irrational and scientifically unsupported." The notion that reason and science will consistently lead one to the right answer in a disability discrimination case, however, is suspect. As Justice Marshall pointed out in his concurrence and dissent in *Cleburne*, "Fueled by the rising tide of Social Darwinism, the 'science' of eugenics, and the extreme xenophobia of [the late nineteenth and early twentieth centuries], leading medical authorities and others began to portray the 'feeble-minded' as a 'menace to society and civilization' . . . responsible in a large degree for many, if not all, of our social problems."[43]

Making reference to the troubling history of eugenic marriage and sterilization laws, Justice Marshall updated the problem by noting modern laws that exclude individuals with cognitive disabilities from voting. "Courts . . . do not sit or act in a social vacuum. Moral philosophers may debate whether certain inequalities are absolute wrongs, but history makes clear that constitutional principles of equality, like constitutional principles of liberty, property, and due process, evolve over time; what once was a 'natural' and 'self-evident' ordering later comes to be seen as an artificial and invidious constraint on human potential and freedom."[44]

It is precisely this understanding of historical and social context that is missing from the Rehnquist Court's analysis of disability discrimination in cases like *Heller* and *Garrett*. When disability discrimination is alleged, more often than not the Court both sits and acts "in a social vacuum." Rather than recognizing the inherent human right to be free from involuntary confinement, particularly after Congress's findings in the ADA, it has sought refuge in the professional opinions of the state bureaucrats and medical authorities in whose care severely disabled people are often placed.

In 1999, in *Olmstead v. L.C.*, the Supreme Court revisited the issue of institutionalization involved in *Heller*.[45] Two Georgia women with mental disabilities challenged their continued care in a segregated institutional setting. Both plaintiffs were determined by Georgia to be ready for community-based care but had to remain in an institution because of a lack of community-based options. In a plurality opinion, Justice Ginsburg held that the ADA "may require placement of persons with mental disabilities in community settings rather than institutions" when "the State's treatment professionals have determined that community placement is appropriate, the transfer from institutional care to a less restrictive setting is not opposed by the affected individual, and the placement can be reasonably accommodated, taking into account the resources available to the State and the needs of others with mental disabilities."[46] In other words, if you need long-term services and supports, you may have a right to get them in the community, provided you can convince your treating professionals that you are ready to leave the institution and the bureaucracy can accommodate your request within its budgetary limitations.

It is worth noting how the holding in *Olmstead* got watered down as the case made its way through the federal courts. In the district court, Georgia tried to argue that the only reason the plaintiffs were stuck in an institution was inadequate funding, not discrimination, but the court rejected the state's argument, holding that "unnecessary institutional segregation of the disabled constitutes discrimination *per se*, which cannot be justified by a lack of funding." Revisiting the possibility of a cost-based defense by the state, the Eleventh Circuit Court of Appeals decided that such a defense was possible, but that Congress would permit such a defense "only in the most limited of circumstances." A cost-based justification would fail, the Eleventh Circuit reasoned, "unless the State can prove that requiring it to [expend additional funds in order to provide the plaintiffs with integrated services] would be so unreasonable given the demands of the State's mental health budget that it would fundamentally alter the service [the State] provides."[47]

Once *Olmstead* reached the Supreme Court, the state's bureaucratic prerogatives took on greater importance.[48] Although Justice Ginsburg held that "unjustified isolation . . . is properly regarded as discrimination based on disability," she recognized "the State's need to maintain a range of facilities for the care and treatment of persons with diverse mental disabilities, and the State's obligation to administer services with an even hand." Holding that the Eleventh Circuit's remand instruction was "unduly restrictive," she ruled that the lower court must consider "not only the cost of providing community-based care to the litigants, but also the range of services the State provides others with mental disabilities, and the State's obligation to mete out those services equitably."[49]

Throughout her opinion, Justice Ginsburg noted the appropriateness of the reliance by the state on "the reasonable assessments of its own professionals" and the need for the state to have a "comprehensive, effectively working plan for placing qualified persons with mental disabilities in less restrictive settings, and a waiting list that moved at a reasonable pace."[50] In other words, as long as the bureaucracy is functioning properly, the ADA may not require any extraordinary effort on behalf of individuals with disabilities seeking to escape institutional confinement. The approach taken in the lower courts is more consistent with Congress's stated desire to enact a "clear and comprehensive national mandate for the elimination of discrimination against individuals with disabilities."[51]

Not satisfied that the level of deference set out in Justice Ginsburg's opinion was great enough, Justice Kennedy (joined by Justice Breyer)

launched into a laborious discussion of the history of deinstitutional-
ization of people with mental illness and the danger that states may in-
appropriately release people with mental disabilities into substandard
care in the community. "It is of central importance," he opined, "that
courts apply today's decision with great deference to the medical decisions of the responsible, treating physicians and . . . with appropriate
deference to the program funding decisions of state policymakers."[52]
In a dissenting opinion, Justice Thomas (joined by Justices Rehnquist
and Scalia), went even further, saying that "the appropriate course
would be to respect the States' historic role as the dominant authority
responsible for providing services to individuals with disabilities."[53] In
other words, whatever the state decides is good enough.

As the opinions in *Heller* and *Olmstead* demonstrate, when the rights
of disabled individuals to live outside of institutions are at stake, the
Rehnquist Court is reluctant to question the prerogatives of state officials and treating professionals to determine how best to distribute
these freedoms. Its overblown deference to bureaucratic prerogatives
means that disabled people will continue to experience unnecessary
segregation and institutionalization for many years to come.

In 2002, the Supreme Court applied its predisposition to defer to
professionals in two employment cases. The first, *U.S. Airways v. Barnett,*
involved a challenge to an employer's voluntary seniority system that
had resulted in a qualified disabled worker being bumped out of a
job.[54] The majority ruled that the employer's professional obligation to
honor its voluntary seniority system trumps the the disabled employee's
right under the ADA to be reassigned to a vacant position for which he
is qualified. The second case, *Chevron, U.S.A., Inc. v. Echazabal,* was a
challenge to the EEOC's regulation permitting employers to reject a
job applicant who, because of his or her disability, would pose a direct
threat to the employee's own health or safety. The unanimous Court in
Echazabal upheld the challenged regulation, noting in part that an employer's professional obligation to ensure the health and safety of his
workers under the Occupational, Safety, and Health Act was greater
than a disabled employee's right "to operate on equal terms within the
workplace."[55]

Ironically, in a case brought by a disabled golfer seeking access to a
golf cart between shots on the PGA tour, the Rehnquist Court was

much more willing to scrutinize the rationale for the decision to exclude the disabled person.[56] In *PGA Tour, Inc. v. Martin*, Justice Stevens (joined by Justices Rehnquist, O'Connor, Kennedy, Souter, Ginsburg, and Breyer) ruled that an elite golfer with a disability was entitled to a waiver of the rule barring golf carts on the PGA tour. Because the prohibition was designed to highlight the fatigue factor for competitors in a professional tournament, the Court reasoned that the plaintiff, Casey Martin, was entitled to a waiver of the rule given that he had demonstrated in the lower court that he experiences more fatigue even with a golf cart than most players do without. The Court ruled that Martin's opportunity to compete was more important than the administrative burden their holding placed on tour operators. Although Martin's victory was rightly hailed by disability advocates, the unique circumstances of his case will likely limit its impact. And the juxtaposition of the strong holding in *Martin* with the timid analysis in *Olmstead* is troubling. After these two rulings, if you are locked in an institution, the ADA may be little comfort; but, if you are being excluded from an elite sporting event, the ADA may open the doors. Unfortunately, the liberty interests at stake in cases like *Olmstead* and *Heller* and the employment issues in *Garrett*, *Barnett*, and *Echazabal* affect many more Americans than the atypical issues presented in the *Martin* case.

Still reeling from *Garrett* and subsequent losses in the 2001–02 term, disability rights advocates are worried about where the activist Rehnquist Court may strike next. Will they hold Title II of the ADA unconstitutional, thereby gutting what little protection the *Olmstead* decision afforded recipients of state services? In their efforts to rein in congressional authority, will they move on to the Spending Clause, calling into question the constitutionality of decades-old laws like Section 504 of the Rehabilitation Act and the Individuals with Disabilities Education Act?[57] Will they continue to chip away at the scope of the protected class in the ADA, and will we need new laws to redefine that group? Presented a historic opportunity to breathe life into constitutional and statutory protections of the rights of disabled people, the Rehnquist Court has instead harmed the cause of disability rights for generations to come.

Antitrust and Business Power

ELEANOR M. FOX

For most of ninety years, the U.S. antitrust laws stood against private power. Senator John Sherman, father of the Sherman Antitrust Act, spoke of the problems that agitate "the popular mind": "Among them all none is more threatening than the inequality of condition, of wealth, and opportunity that has grown within a single generation out of the concentration of capital into vast combinations."[1] President Woodrow Wilson, in support of the 1914 Clayton Bill, called for a law that "will open the field . . . to scores of men who had been obliged to serve when their abilities entitled them to direct."[2] In 1949, Congressman Emanuel Celler vowed, in support of his bill to strengthen the merger law, to stop the increasing industrial concentration in order to prevent another Hitler from arising.[3]

The first merger challenged under the 1950 merger law came before the Warren Court in 1962, and a unanimous Court applied the law faithfully to its legislative mandate and statutory spirit: Congress sought to prevent the "rising tide of economic concentration" for social and political reasons. "It resolved these competing considerations [pluralism and efficiency] in favor of decentralization."[4]

These statutes have not since been amended by Congress in any significant way. And yet neither Senator Sherman nor Congressman Celler nor Chief Justice Warren would recognize the modern case law of antitrust as having very much affinity to the laws they wrote or applied. As a result of judicial decision making, the U.S. antitrust law is no longer antipower. The law, the jurists say, is proefficiency and pro-consumer. In fact, the law is probusiness freedom (it assumes business acts efficiently), subject to a few limiting principles whose purview continually shrinks. The Burger Court set the stage for the U-turn in antitrust; the Rehnquist Court executed the turn.

Since the days of the Warren Court, conservative and libertarian lawyers, economists, and policy makers who identified themselves with a philosophy called the Chicago School sought to take the reins of antitrust. The Chicago School opposes microeconomic intervention by the government. In its strongest form, it presumes that markets nearly always work to keep business responsive to consumers and that government intervention (including antitrust action) nearly always obstructs markets, hurting consumers and impairing the freedom of people in their economic activity. Some Chicago School advocates treat competitor cartels (for example, price-fixing agreements) as an exception that warrants government intervention because cartels are a means to control the market and are inefficient. Others believe that cartels are so fragile in the face of market forces that they will quickly self-destruct. Most Chicago School advocates believe that all people, other than undeserving laggards, are better off with policies that maximize aggregate wealth, and they oppose the use of antitrust laws to achieve a fairer distribution of wealth, a fairer distribution of economic opportunity, or fairer rules of the game; they see no connection between democratic values and market rules that control private power.

These would-be policy makers were not immediately successful. In effect, the Chicago School lay in wait until, first, economic recession and the Nixon era, when the Burger Court put a lid on the expanding proplaintiff antitrust rulings of the 1960s, and, second, the Reagan era, when the Supreme Court, following the lead of Reagan's antitrust chiefs, reformulated the raison d'être of antitrust law. The only reason for antitrust law, they announced, is to remove market obstructions so that business can be more efficient and consumers can get more goods at lower prices, increasing the size of the economic pie. The only proper target of antitrust, they said, is private power that artificially limits the output of goods or services across an entire market; moreover, private power seldom exists unless aided by government.

The Rehnquist Court rhetoric recalls the words, now more than a century old, of the most famous jurist to scorn the Sherman Act, Oliver Wendell Holmes. "State interference is an evil, where it cannot be shown to be a good," he said. "Its cumbrous and expensive machinery ought not to be set in motion unless some clear benefit is to be derived from disturbing the status quo."[5] And he seldom found clear benefit.

Three major antitrust decisions of the Rehnquist Court and the dictum in a dissenting opinion by Justice Antonin Scalia illustrate the enterprise to deflate antitrust.

The first case is *Business Electronics Corporation v. Sharp Electronics Corporation*, a typical example of the use of conservative economic assumptions to change the compass course of U.S. antitrust law.[6] Sharp, a manufacturer of electronic calculators, sold its product through two retailers in the Houston, Texas, area. One of those retailers, Business Electronics, offered the calculators at discount prices; the other retailer, Hartwell, complained to Sharp, which agreed to cut off Business Electronics. Business Electronics sued Sharp and won a jury verdict, on the strength of the case law that proscribed agreements to cut off a discounter in order to eliminate low prices. The Supreme Court reversed this verdict.

As Justice Scalia noted in his opinion in *Sharp*, the case was about a *vertical* restraint. These restraints are in the seller-buyer chain, and usually concern the suppliers' restriction of the freedom of their resellers, such as the freedom to charge low prices. Before *Sharp*, the law contained a strong rule against resale price agreements on grounds that they unduly restrict the freedom of the reseller to make price choices. The freedom to discount and the growth of discounting as a way of business had been shown empirically to lower prices by as much as 20 percent.

Justice Scalia and the Rehnquist Court majority jettisoned the law's preference for freedom of discounting, and reformulated upside down the basis of the rule against vertical price fixing. Scalia not only rejected the terminated discounter's claim but also eradicated the law's protection of the right to discount, undercut the rule against resale price agreements, and trivialized even the concern that such agreements facilitate competitor cartels.

First, the agreement to cut off the discounter concerned only one brand, Sharp calculators; thus it was an "intrabrand" restraint, Scalia said. The antitrust laws do not protect intrabrand competition, he said, but only "interbrand" competition (competition among Sharp and other makers of calculators). "So long as interbrand competition existed, that would provide a 'significant check' on any attempt to exploit intrabrand market power." Second, the Court said (counterhistorically), the support for the rule against vertical price restraints was based on their role in facilitating cartels among producers. That is, if Sharp and its competitors wanted to fix the price of calculators, they might enforce their cartel by agreeing also to require their dealers to charge a specified price. The resale price agreements would reduce the producers' incentive to cheat on their cartel (that is, secretly to charge a lower price to get more business) because the retailer could not in turn charge lower prices to its customers. But, said Justice Scalia, simply disciplining discounters cannot facilitate cartelizing: "Cartels are neither easy to form nor easy to maintain" (a bold statement for a justice to make without evidence). Cartels self-destruct in the face of uncertainty over their terms, and intolerance for discounters fails to supply the price certainty needed to form a cartel.

Moreover, a firm in the position of Sharp may "legitimately" desire a higher price to induce its resellers to provide more service; it may wish to get rid of discounters because of the discounters free ride on the services of full pricers. For example, their customers can get free information from Hartwell and then buy the product from no-frills Business Electronics, undermining Hartwell's incentives to invest in providing service. Therefore, said Scalia, a law against agreements to cut off discounters could "penalize perfectly legitimate conduct." Thus, in *Sharp*, the Supreme Court turned the law's preference for discounting into a preference for producer's freedom to squash discounting.

The second case is *Brooke Group v. Brown & Williamson Tobacco Corporation*.[7] Liggett, predecessor to Brooke Group, had launched a generic (no-frills, no-brand) cigarette, which it offered at a price 30 percent lower than branded cigarettes. This new competition challenged the entrenched four-firm tobacco oligopoly. The smallest of the four firms, Brown & Williamson, had the most to lose and took action. It introduced a directly competing brand and gave discriminatory rebates to those of its large distributors that aggressively fought the war. For eighteen months, Brown & Williamson sold its fighting brand—Black & Whites—to these favored distributors at prices below its marginal cost, incurring a loss of $15 million and inflicting on Liggett a loss of $50 million. Eventually, as expected, Liggett could no longer afford to stay in the war. It was forced to raise its prices high enough to remove the generic threat to the branded oligopoly.

Since, under prior case law, Brown & Williamson's acts appeared to be illegal price discrimination and price predation, Liggett sued. It won a jury verdict. The trial court, however, gave judgment notwithstanding verdict to Brown & Williamson. The Supreme Court affirmed the dismissal of the case on grounds that largely wipe out predatory pricing cases.

Writing for the Court, Justice Anthony Kennedy first commented that price cutting is good. True, to be sure, but not consistent with *Sharp*. "Discouraging a price cut . . . does not constitute sound antitrust policy." The Court argued that the object of predatory pricing is to get rid of the competitor and charge yet higher prices in the future, which assumes recoupment of the investment in price predation, but the cost of predatory pricing is huge and seldom recoupable, argued Kennedy, because the firm loses money on the predatory campaign, and when it tries to recoup by raising prices, new competition swoops in. "Predatory pricing schemes are rarely tried, and even more rarely successful," said Kennedy. Moreover, a failed predatory strategy is entirely good for consumers, who benefit from below-cost prices and never face monopoly prices.

Suggesting that Liggett nonetheless may have regarded Brown &

Williamson's long-enduring below-cost strategy as unfair, the Court said:

> That below-cost pricing may impose painful losses on its target is of no moment to the antitrust laws if competition is not injured. . . .
>
> Even an act of pure malice by one competitor against another does not, without more, state a claim under the federal antitrust laws; those laws do not create a federal law of unfair competition.

Most nations of the world disagree that predation without recoupment is rarely tried and rarely successful. They also disagree that predation is good for competition. They believe that persistent below-marginal-cost pricing, especially as a response to a maverick competitor, deters mavericks and harms competition.

The third case that dramatizes the turn of the Court is *California Dental Association v. Federal Trade Commission*, a case about advertising restraints.[8] Prior to the time of the Rehnquist Court, the law had been harsh on agreements between doctors, dentists, and other professionals that tended to raise prices for their professional services. Since the late 1960s, the Federal Trade Commission and the Department of Justice observed time and again that such professionals, in the name of ethics, enforced gentlemen's agreements not to advertise, solicit, or discount; not to entice away clients; and not to engage in any other commercial practices that threatened to break the pricing structure, thus perpetuating a professional mystique that insulated price gouging.

Three-quarters of California's dentists belonged to the California Dental Association, which had a code of ethics, supported by guidelines. In the name of prohibiting false and misleading advertising, the guidelines forbade simple advertisements such as "10% discount to seniors" or "quality services" at "reasonable prices." The Federal Trade Commission and the appellate court found the guidelines to be anticompetitive by their nature and required the dentists to justify their guidelines as procompetitive or efficient, which they could not do. The Supreme Court reversed this ruling. It said that the likelihood of anticompetitive effects from such advertising bans was not obvious, that the dentists' guidelines might just as well have had net procompetitive effects or no competitive effect at all, and that, without empirical evidence of the likelihood that advertising limitations decreased the quantity of dental services demanded, the government would fail to make its case.

The Court, in an opinion by Justice David Souter, found "puzzling" the appellate court's conclusion that advertising bans, by their nature, are anticompetitive. It said that the appellate court erred because it

> gave no weight to the countervailing, and at least equally plausible, suggestion that restricting difficult-to-verify claims about quality or patient comfort would have a procompetitive effect by preventing misleading or false claims that distort the market. It is, indeed, entirely possible to understand the CDA's restrictions on unverifiable quality and comfort advertising as nothing more than a procompetitive ban on puffery.

This is a very important and dangerous point. The Court appears to have specified the criterion for "harming competition," and it is that which artificially limits market output. Lessening rivalry itself no longer qualifies as anticompetitive. And the Court appears to have placed burdens of proof on plaintiffs and even on the Federal Trade Commission that cannot be met. Predictions from economic theory may not even be enough. Empirical evidence, though unavailable, may be necessary. Moreover, given the indeterminacy of economics, whoever has the burden of proof will lose.

It might be comforting to imagine that the ruling of the *California Dental* case will be confined to professionals. Perhaps the Court would shield professionals from antitrust on the somewhat suspect presumption that we can trust them to do what is best for patients or clients. Perhaps the case will not be the blueprint for steel or software producers. But perhaps it will.

In a fourth opinion, though a dissenting one, Justice Scalia seems to articulate the current Court's philosophy. For some years after Eastman

Kodak entered the market for medical imaging machinery, it encouraged the growth of an entrepreneurial industry to service and repair its machines and it supplied independent service organizations (ISOs) with repair parts to facilitate their task. When the business of repairing and servicing the machines became lucrative, Kodak stopped supplying repair parts to ISOs, required manufacturers of Kodak parts to boycott them, and raised the price of its own aftermarket service to its customers. The ISOs sued. Kodak moved to dismiss on grounds that its conduct was just an intrabrand restraint, it had no power in the imaging machine market, and the imaging machine market was competitive and therefore could be trusted to punish and thus prevent anticompetitive behavior in the aftermarket. The majority of the Court, in an opinion by Justice Harry Blackmun, disagreed. Justice Blackmun said that the case must go to trial because the ISOs had raised material issues of fact, supported by an economic theory, concerning Kodak's power and exploitation in the aftermarket. Justice Scalia, joined by Justices Sandra Day O'Connor and Clarence Thomas, dissented. Kodak's acts, said Scalia, were "potentially procompetitive arrangements." Moreover, the "interbrand market will generally punish intrabrand restraints that consumers do not find in their interest," and Kodak did not have "the sort of 'monopoly power' sufficient to bring the sledgehammer of [Section 2 of the Sherman Act] into play."

The Rehnquist Court can indeed be expected to view Section 2 of the Sherman Act, which prohibits monopolization, as a sledgehammer. The Court's deep skepticism that private power exists, its belief that single-firm (noncartel) acts are virtually always procompetitive, and its belief in the changing, dynamic, and disciplining nature of markets would lead it almost always to reject a case against a monopolist.

It may have been a blessing to antitrust believers that the Supreme Court declined to hear a direct appeal from the district court in *United States and 19 States v. Microsoft*, for there is a significant possibility that the Supreme Court would have accepted at least one of two arguments Microsoft made: first, that Microsoft had no monopoly power because high tech markets are dynamic and fast-moving, and the threat of being overtaken by outsiders' innovations constrained it always to act like a competitor, and second, that Microsoft, while it may have harmed competitors, never harmed consumers. Output of computer software was always on the increase; competition was not restrained.

Microsoft controls more than 95 percent of operating systems for personal computers. Netscape pioneered the browser and, using the new language, Java, threatened to innovate a software product and platform ("middleware") that would be transportable to any operating system. If successful cross-platform middleware could be launched, applications makers would no longer be enticed into writing their applications for Microsoft; they could profitably write to the middleware, which would function on any operating system. This would break the barriers to entry into the operating system market and dissolve Microsoft's monopoly power.

Microsoft discerned the middleware threat and sprang into action. It designed and carried out a strategy to prevent the Netscape/Java innovation from taking root. Netscape needed access to a critical mass of operating system users, which it would get if users and PC makers could freely choose Netscape's Navigator as their browser for Microsoft's Windows. Microsoft succeeded in closing off all Netscape Navigator's most efficient channels of access to customers. It developed its own browser, the Internet Explorer, which it tied to its operating system, preventing the browser's removal without downgrading other functions. It prevented PC makers from loading Navigator on their PCs along with Windows. It prevented or deterred the major Internet service providers and content providers from including or featuring the Navigator browser. It splintered the Java language, depriving it of its promise to be a cross-platform language that would facilitate the development of middleware.

The Justice Department and states sued and won all aspects of their lawsuit, and the district court entered an order to break Microsoft in two. Microsoft appealed, and the Justice Department sought to channel the appeal directly to the Supreme Court, which declined to hear the case. The appeal was heard by the D.C. Circuit Court of Appeals.

On the appeal, Microsoft's principal ammunition was political philosophy; it tried to set the stage by selling a perspective. The perspective was forcefully presented on the Microsoft Web site as well as in its legal briefs: antitrust intervention into new-economy markets tramples on property rights and personal freedoms, harms innovation and progress, and sets back American competitiveness in the world economy. New-economy markets are different, Microsoft argued. The competition is *for* the market, not *in* the market. The incumbent, having provisionally won, can never rest on its laurels. It must be paranoid to survive. It must always compete hard or it will be instantaneously dislodged. Microsoft articulated this argument in its brief on appeal:

> Dramatic improvements in microprocessors regularly alter the entire competitive landscape of the industry. . . . As Intel chairman Dr. Andrew Grove described in his book, *Only the Paranoid Survive: How to Exploit the Crisis Points That Challenge Every Company*, such technological advances—known as "inflection points" or "paradigm shifts"—can quickly diminish the value of (or eliminate altogether) entire categories of products, making the computer industry inherently unpredictable. . . . Hence, the greatest competitive threat to a leading product frequently comes not from another product within the same category, "but rather a technological advance that renders the boundaries defining the category obsolete."[9]

If accepted the only-the-paranoid-survive theory had three devastating implications for the government's case. First, the trial judge, Thomas Penfield Jackson, would have misdefined the market. The antitrust market had to include all sources of pressure on Microsoft—thus, UNIX, LINUX, Apple, hand-held computers, portal Web sites, and middleware. Second, Judge Jackson would have wrongly held that Microsoft had monopoly power. It had to act like a competitor to survive. And, finally, Judge Jackson would have wrongly held that Microsoft's acts caused harm to competition and consumers. So important is it for a high-tech firm to be free to compete in the gale-tossed world, and so harmful is it to mistake a procompetitive for an anticompetitive act (the theory goes), that courts must be demanding in their requirement of proof that the challenged acts were anticompetitive and harmed consumers. The only theory of harm to consumers depended on proof that Microsoft's strategies actually held at bay competitive technologies that would have overtaken Microsoft in its operating system competition. The government had failed to prove that such technologies (that is, the middleware of Netscape and Java) actually would have materialized and taken root but for Microsoft's acts. Thus, there was no proof of causation. Had any one of these three points prevailed, Microsoft would have won its case. None did.

A major question was whether the government had to prove that Microsoft's exclusionary acts in fact increased Microsoft's power over operating systems. There was no proof that it did. Netscape's threat to innovate middleware and break the back of Microsoft's operating system monopoly may have been only a phantom. The court of appeals resolved this issue—as to whether the government must prove actual harm to competition—against Microsoft. It held that the court could presume that Microsoft's acts caused antitrust harm as long as the anticompetitive conduct "reasonably appeared [at the time of the acts] capable of making a significant contribution to . . . maintaining monopoly power. . . . We may infer causation when exclusionary conduct is aimed at producers of nascent competitive technologies." A more demanding rule "would only encourage monopolists to take more and earlier anticompetitive action. . . . Suffice it to say that it would be inimical to the purpose of the Sherman Act to allow monopolists free rein to squash nascent, albeit unproven, competitors at will—particularly in industries marked by rapid technological advance and frequent paradigm shifts."[10]

The Court thus took a pragmatic and progressive stand. It upheld the monopoly maintenance charges while it reversed other claims and remanded the issue of the appropriate remedy. Had it accepted Microsoft's invitation to abstain from intervention in e-markets, or even to demand proof that Microsoft's illegal acts actually suppressed the quantity of computer operating software on the market (output limitation), the plaintiffs would have lost. The whole brilliantly won government victory would have been undone, and Microsoft, and the next Microsofts, would have been given license to be predatory. Judgment for Microsoft would have been the death of the law against monopolization.

If the Supreme Court had taken the case on direct appeal, bypassing the appellate court, there is reason to believe that a majority of the justices—attracted to Microsoft's theme song, "Only the Paranoid Survive"—would have joined Justice Scalia in seeing Microsoft as a vigorous competitor, in puzzling over how competition could have been harmed in the face of increasing software sales, and in avoiding at all costs "the sledgehammer" of Section 2.

Even now, the victory for the government against Microsoft may be squandered. The Department of Justice in the George W. Bush administration has agreed with Microsoft to settle for little more than a Band-Aid, and a Band-Aid of doubtful adhesion, given the difficulties of enforcing the final decree. Microsoft has accepted the proposal; nine plaintiff states oppose the Microsoft–federal government agreement. The judge—newly assigned because Judge Jackson compromised his impartiality by giving interviews to the press—must determine whether the agreed settlement is in the public interest. But whatever the specific result in *Microsoft*, the language of the appellate court will stand as precedent. It should have value in reining in future predatory monopolists, even if *United States v. Microsoft* should take its place as one of the Pyrrhic victories of antitrust.

In 1976, Ralph Nader, Mark Green, and Joel Seligman wrote *The Taming of the Giant Corporation*. The title itself suggested the powerful image of the antitrust laws as enacted by Congress and as interpreted by the Supreme Court. In this dawn of the twenty-first century, a counterimage has emerged in the federal agencies and the Supreme Court. It may be called *The Unleashing of the Giant Corporation*. The image-makers argue that business freedom, even for the largest firms, will increase efficiency and bolster American competitiveness in the world. They equate liberalization with freedom from government regulation. Globalization reinforces the laissez-faire stance of twenty-first century U.S. antitrust law.

Business power may outstrip, perhaps already has outstripped, the power of governments. Business firms and networks rise above and spread beyond national borders. National law and its guardians (for example, the Supreme Court) are seriously challenged to contain private power in global markets. Meanwhile, the problem of private power, even more modestly located, is eluding the Rehnquist Court.

No Business like No Business

LAWRENCE E. MITCHELL

Analyzing the Supreme Court's jurisprudence of securities regulation is a bit like studying a dog's tail. Partly for policy reasons and partly by default, the main source of law dealing with the organization, finance, and governance of American corporations is state law, not federal law, and the Supreme Court therefore has little to say about these matters. It's well known that the law of the state of incorporation governs any company's internal relations and that Delaware is the state of incorporation for almost half of all publicly traded companies (which are, for the most part, the companies governed by the securities laws). This has made Delaware the Supreme Court of corporate law and a powerful influence on the majority of the other states.

Federal securities law is, in a real sense, largely external to these workings, as it regulates the selling and buying of securities and the conduct of brokers and dealers in the market. In that way, it is external to the corporation much as antitrust law or labor law might be. But unlike these and other areas of external regulation, it has significant intersections with state law, through its rules prohibiting fraud and its disclosure and reporting requirements regulating the conduct of corporations; here it often touches up against, if it does not intersect or parallel, state law. As a result, the Supreme Court can't help some degree of involvement in matters that we would consider to be corporate governance. At various times in the history of securities law the Court has been more or less willing to attempt to impose some federal uniformity over the behavior of public corporations to depose the rule of one of our smallest states. During the Rehnquist years, in contrast, the Court has significantly pulled back from securities protections, deregulating public corporations and clearing the path for Delaware to maintain its supreme rule. At the same time, the Court has been ever more willing to diminish the external protections for investors in public markets that the securities laws were designed to provide. The importance of this trend can hardly be overstated. A (very) brief history of securities law will help place this Court's work in context.

Much of the work immediately following the enactment of the securities laws involved cleaning up the mess from the stock market crash of 1929 and rectifying the abuses that led to it. Before too long, however, prosperity and economic stability began to return, and enforcement was steady if uninteresting. The securities laws were used to regulate markets, while corporate governance was left to the states. By the mid-1960s it had become apparent that the dominant force in corporate law, the state of Delaware, had pretty much abrogated any responsibility to enforce the fiduciary obligations that officers and directors had to stockholders, an observation documented by William Cary in a famous 1974 *Yale Law Journal* article.[1] Agree with its policy conclusions or not, Cary's article highlighted an oddity of our federal system: the regulation of major multistate and multinational corporations had been left by Congress to the states in which they were incorporated, and tiny Delaware, seizing an opportunity in the early part of the twentieth century, had become home to a disproportionate number of giant corporations and therefore, by default, the arbiter of United States corporate law.[2] As Cary pointed out, the revenues from the chartering business and all that went with it (including the guaranteed employment of Wilmington lawyers as local counsel for big-city corporate firms) gave the Delaware courts every incentive to keep corporate managements happy, and they did so by regularly and consistently (while not quite invariably) limiting managerial obligations.[3]

Cary had an opportunity to attempt to rectify what he saw as the illegitimate federalization of Delaware law. As chairman of the Securities and Exchange Commission in the Kennedy administration, he embarked on an enforcement program designed to use the securities laws (principally their disclosure and antifraud provisions) to place meaningful obligations on directors and officers. This effort was picked up by the Second Circuit Court of Appeals in New York (which, until the maturity of Silicon Valley and the consequent increasing involvement of the Ninth Circuit in securities matters, was considered the Supreme Court of securities law) and by the Supreme Court itself, and in a series of decisions beginning in the mid-1960s and continuing to 1975, the disclosure and fiduciary-like protections of the federal securities laws became a powerful tool to keep managerial misconduct in check.

The brakes were put on by the Supreme Court in 1975, which in respect to securities law can be seen as the real beginning of the Rehnquist Court. The opening salvos of the battle took place principally between Justices Lewis Powell (a former corporate lawyer), for restricting the reach of the securities laws, and Harry Blackmun, for continuing the expansion. And they fought on a battlefield of policy. Broadly stated, Powell's approach to securities jurisprudence was to require some form of serious misconduct on the part of defendant corporations, or their officers or directors, before holding them liable to plaintiffs. He did so by introducing the technique of narrow statutory interpretation, first announced in a 1975 concurrence to a rare opinion by Rehnquist (whose presence in securities matters is almost always as a voter rather than a writer), in a sentence that has become the rallying cry in virtually all the Rehnquist Court's securities opinions: "The starting point in every case involving construction of a statute is the language itself."[4] Blackmun, in contrast and taking his cue from the remedial and market-protective purposes of the laws, was more concerned with the effect on the markets of managerial mistakes, even if the level of misconduct fell short of fraud and even if the statute required an expansive reading to reach the result.

Statutory interpretation may have been the methodology of these opinions, but reading them makes clear that the Supreme Courts that decided these cases understood the policy implications of their actions in terms of the legislature's goals and their effects upon the market and were, appropriately for the Supreme Court, driven by them. Of course it's no surprise that the Supreme Court should be driven by policy; after all, while it decides cases, it does so on the matrix of the larger purposes for which our laws are enacted. This is true even of relatively strict constructionists on the Court, who have a legitimate argument that lawmaking (at least nonconstitutional, regulatory-type lawmaking) ought to be left to Congress. But the Rehnquist Court has gone beyond this, discarding any pretense of finding intent in favor of tortured statutory readings. Not surprisingly, the opinions often make for very bad, or at least confusing, policy.

A case in point is a decision that actually tightens regulation, this one in the area of insider trading. Despite the good outcome, it's fair to say that *United States v. O'Hagan* is one of the most confusing of the Rehnquist Court opinions.[5] I like the decision as a policy matter because I believe in an expansive reading of the securities laws to aim at untoward market effects; I dislike the opinion as both a jurisprudential and a policy matter because it makes no sense either as an opinion protecting markets from unfair trading advantage or as an opinion tying securities violations to relevant illegal conduct. It is a halfway measure resulting from precisely the interpretive problems I'm describing.

The facts in the case are simple. O'Hagan was a partner at Dorsey & Whitney, the firm that represented Grand Metropolitan in its bid to acquire Pillsbury. Although O'Hagan didn't work on the deal, he bought call options on Pillsbury stock as well as stock itself. (A call option is the right to buy stock from the seller of the option at a preset price.) His firm later withdrew from the representation, and O'Hagan sold his stock and options at a profit of more than $4 million. He was convicted by a jury for criminal insider trading, a conviction overturned by the Eighth Circuit Court of Appeals. The Supreme Court reversed the Eighth Circuit and remanded the case for its reconsideration, after which the conviction was affirmed.

The legal issue wasn't too complicated, but it was one with which the Court had struggled on and off for seventeen years, namely whether the insider trading laws developed under the statute and its regulations ought to be interpreted to include what has become known as the misappropriation theory of insider trading. Very briefly, insider trading law traditionally covered the trading activity of those whom the word "insider" would, in common parlance, seem to cover, officers and directors of the company in whose stock they traded. The idea was that such people, because they owe a fiduciary obligation to their corporations' stockholders (which includes the obligation not to profit personally by using corporate assets), were prohibited from using corporate information (a corporate asset) that was not publicly available ("inside information") to trade against their corporations' stockholders (that is, to buy or sell stock in trades with the corporations' stockholders). This is straightforward, and while it required a few judicial twists and turns in light of the breadth and brevity of the statute, it indisputably comports with Congress's intent to prevent fraud and ensure fair markets. Until the 1980s, insider trading wasn't perceived as a serious problem, in part perhaps because insiders had relatively few opportunities to make profits that justified the risk; after all, big price-moving corporate information is not an everyday occurrence. What changed in the 1980s was the explosion of corporate takeovers at substantial premia over stock prices. This was the kind of information that could dramatically alter a stock's price on a given day. The takeover boom provided tempting illicit opportunities that some insiders found impossible to resist, and when these temptations ran into the political ambitions of the United States attorney for the Southern District of New York, Rudolph Giuliani, a number of high-profile prosecutions and convictions resulted.

The problem was that traditional insider trading law didn't always seem to get the bad guys. In the hostile-takeover case, the only traditional insiders were the officers and directors of the unwitting target company, who presumably had no advance notice of the takeover before the rest of the market and therefore no opportunity to profit from the information. But a lot of other people were involved in takeovers, including insiders of the hostile bidder, as well as all the retainers—lawyers, investment bankers, financial printers, and the like. These were the people who knew about the bids in advance of the market, and among these groups emerged a class of people who bought stock in the target companies before takeover bids were announced. Having had no prior relation with the companies, they were not insiders.

Although there was academic debate over whether insider trading was, as an aggregate matter, economically efficient and whether it ought to be permitted, there was no debate that the activities of these people brought them substantial profits at the expense of other (if unidentified) traders. And there was little question that the trading public perceived these people as taking advantage of the rest of us. So a doctrine developed, initially in the Second Circuit, holding that these "tippees" or "outsiders" or "temporary insiders" could be liable for insider trading if they breached a fiduciary duty to someone—usually the bidding company—in using its inside information for their advantage. But the area of criminal liability remained open.

And thus came O'Hagan. He was not an insider of Pillsbury. And while technically he was not an insider of Grand Met either, his firm was a temporary insider or an outsider with fiduciary obligations in its representation of the hostile bidder. O'Hagan, as a partner of the firm, was bound by the fiduciary duty owed by Dorsey & Whitney as Grand Met's agent and lawyer not to use its property for his own purposes, as well as by his fiduciary duty to his partners. Thus, he was in the sight lines of the misappropriation theory.

So far this makes sense. There is some legitimate argument against the misappropriation theory based in the ambiguous language of the statute, but the interesting point for our purpose is the way the Court rationalized the adoption of the misappropriation theory in criminal insider trading cases and, perhaps even more significantly, the parameters they imposed on the theory. For this is where legal technique blinks business sense.

The misappropriation theory comes in two flavors. The first, articulated by Chief Justice Burger, concurring in a 1980 insider trading decision, held that anyone who *stole* inside information was prohibited from using it to trade (unless he first disclosed the information publicly, which of course would defeat the purpose). Burger's theory made good business and legal sense; the offense was the distorting effect that the insider trading had on the market, the unfairness of its tilting the playing field in favor of people in privileged positions, exactly the kind of problem the securities laws were aimed at.

The variant adopted by the current Supreme Court differs. It is, like the rest of the Court's opinions, justifiable only as an elevation of interpretive technique over common sense and policy.

The Court's misappropriation theory holds as follows: only a person who breaches a fiduciary duty to the source of inside information in using that information to trade violates the insider trading laws. The doctrine thus exempts from liability other traders who, by virtue of a privileged (but nonfiduciary) position giving them access to nonpublic information, similarly distort the market. Thus O'Hagan, as a temporary insider of Grand Met and as a fiduciary of his partners at Dorsey & Whitney, committed a crime in trading on the information. This would have been covered under Burger's theory as well as the theory the Court chose to adopt, for O'Hagan was in a privileged position and to allow him to use that position would be to create unfairness in the trading market.

But why is it necessary to find that O'Hagan breached a fiduciary duty to anybody? Anyone with a privileged market position could take advantage of those who don't simply by using that position to obtain secret information. To so hold, as Burger would, that such behavior is prohibited has the policy coherence of looking to the effects of privileged trading on the market (and there is no doubt, given the way that markets work, that such privileged trading could well have market effects). One could argue that such a person ought not to be held liable if there was nothing illegal about the way in which the information was obtained, and this, too, would have a certain policy coherence—it would look to the conduct of persons in the market as the determining factor of liability rather than to the effect on the market, thus elevating traditional notions of criminal law over the concept of regulatory crimes. Were the Court to have held this way, it would at least have alerted the trading public to the possibility that sometimes there is structural unfairness in the markets, allowing traders to make their own decisions about whether they want to play the game and perhaps affecting stock prices.

To understand the silliness of the Court's position, look at what it doesn't cover (the Court acknowledges this gap, if not its silliness). If Dorsey & Whitney had given permission to O'Hagan to use the information (perhaps in lieu of a larger partnership draw) and had informed Grand Met of this fact, O'Hagan's trading would not have breached his fiduciary duty and he would thus have been free of criminal liability *even though the effect of his conduct on the market would have been identical*.[6]

Thus, the Court's attempt to create an effect-based jurisprudence fails because of its insistence on misconduct that has nothing to do with the offense. After all, Dorsey & Whitney wasn't harmed (except, perhaps, in its reputation, although one doubts whether people hold the actions of a rogue partner against an entire firm), and Grand Met wasn't harmed either—there was no evidence that as a result of O'Hagan's actions it paid more to acquire Pillsbury than it had been planning to pay. Finally, and most importantly, the harm on which the violation is based—O'Hagan's breach of fiduciary duty to Dorsey & Whitney and Grand Met—has nothing to do with the harm targeted by the antifraud provisions on which insider trading law is based, that is, distortion of the market by fraudulent trading. So why the half-baked result?

The answer lies in the Court's approach to statutory interpretation and its own precedent. The statute requires "manipulation or deception." The Court could have held that trading on information that was not publicly available was intrinsically manipulative, as when an analyst obtains secret information by talking to a corporate employee. But it had precedents that held that manipulation had a limited technical meaning (principally wash sales and similar prearranged false trades) and that deception required breach of a preexisting duty, such as a fiduciary duty. The kind of insider trading we have been considering does not fit within this narrow understanding of manipulation. So it focused on the word "deception," which implicates fraud. Breach of fiduciary duty is considered constructive fraud, so breach of fiduciary duty amounts to "deception" and criminal liability exists. This makes sense in the case of traditional insiders—the people they are hurting are their own stockholders, and the connection between their deceptive conduct and the harm is clear. To sustain this interpretation in the case of a conduct-based jurisprudence makes sense. But the Court stretched the statutory language in attempting to develop an effect-based theory that makes the violation turn on whether the temporary insider (or "outsider," as the Court put it) had the permission of somebody who had no relationship to the relevant market, in this case traders in Pillsbury stock, to distort the market.

The statutory linchpin is the requirement that the manipulation or deception be "in connection with" the purchase or sale of securities. This requirement has been treated very broadly, and the Court continued to stretch it in *O'Hagan*. The most tenuous connection suffices. For example, O'Hagan's breach—the theft of information—is tied to securities fraud because he used it to buy Pillsbury securities. But because those most likely to be harmed by the theft of information, Dorsey & Whitney and Grand Met, were completely unrelated to the persons harmed by O'Hagan's trades, the sellers of call options on Pillsbury stock and Pillsbury stockholders, his theft of information is deemed unrelated to the statute's goal of preventing market distortion and harm to traders.[7] If the Court had understood its own implicit concern with market effect and simply acknowledged that the policy of the statute was to establish an even playing field, it could have concluded that the use of privilege to obtain, and trade on, information not available to others distorted that playing field and thus was manipulative. This would have corrected the market distortions with which the insider trading rules are concerned. Conversely, the Court could have held that such behavior was neither manipulative nor deceptive with respect to securities markets and therefore was no violation. The halfway measure which Justice Clarence Thomas in dissent rightly called "incoherent," simply confuses the law in the name of the statute and leads to a result where market protection is as much a function of the accident of circumstances as it is anything else.

O'Hagan may be tortured and silly, but at least it has the excuse of arising from prior and long-standing interpretations of an admittedly broad and arguably uncertain statute. Justice Anthony Kennedy's opinion in *Gustafson v. Alloyd* has no similar excuse and presents itself as sheer nonsense.[8] The issue was the much more technical one of whether a prospectus issued in connection with the private offering of securities was a "prospectus" within the meaning of the 1933 Securities Act. That act provides a long series of definitions intended to apply throughout unless otherwise indicated. One of those definitions, appearing in Section 2(10), is of a prospectus, which is said to be "any prospectus, notice, circular, advertisement, letter, or communication, written or by radio or television, which offers any security for sale or confirms the sale of any security."[9] A definition of prospectus is important because it goes directly to the heart of the act, Section 5, which prohibits the offering or sale of any security without an effective registration statement filed with the SEC unless another provision of the act exempts it (there is a statutorily interpreted exemption for so-called private placements, the type of sale at issue in *Gustafson*). And there are very detailed requirements for the form and content of prospectuses to be filed with the SEC. There is also, as a matter of practice, a similarly stylized approach to information distributed in connection with private placements, including the type and form of information contained in a private contract for the sale of stock in an entire company, the issue in *Gustafson*. Practicing lawyers, keenly aware of the legal proscriptions on incomplete or misleading information, as well as of their own potential liability, take as much care with these private documents as they do with public registration statements.

It is almost painfully obvious that the purpose of the statute is to prevent the use of unregulated types of information in connection with the offering and sale of securities, and the securities bar has always been mindful of this in drafting the documents used for that purpose. Not only "prospectuses" (an obviously generic term as it appears in the definition of "prospectus" itself) but advertisements, letters, and even sales confirmations come within the sweep of the definition. Thus, when the issue arose in the case of whether a stock purchase agreement containing allegedly material misinformation was a "prospectus," the answer should have been obvious. The contract was, after all, a "writing" that "offers any security for sale or confirms the sale of any security." And it would be difficult to find many securities lawyers who disagree with that proposition.

Not so the Court. Justice Kennedy, avoiding the definitional section (which corporate practitioners understand provides a substantial part of the action in any corporate document) until he had established his conclusion, began in the middle of the statute with Section 10, which provides that a prospectus is required to contain the information provided in the registration statement, from which he concluded that because there is no registration statement for privately issued securities, no document containing information relating to those securities can be a prospectus.

Now wait. The 1933 Securities Act deals with registration requirements but also provides exemptions from registration (both explicitly
and by judicial interpretation). And there is absolutely nothing in the
definition, Section 2(10), that limits the term "prospectus" to registered
securities. Nor is there anything in Section 12(2), which protects
against negligently misleading statements. In fact, one could argue
that, given the nature of business, this protection is even more necessary in the case of private sales because of the lack of public information, the absence of analysts following the stock and investment
bankers underwriting it, and the likely inability of a purchaser to get
the information unless the seller provides it. These realities, however,
didn't bother the Court. Instead, Justice Kennedy reached his conclusion despite the commonsensical reading that prospectuses for registered offerings are required to contain the information provided in
the registration statement whereas prospectuses for private offerings
had no particular form but, whatever the form, were required to be
negligence-free. In the guise of providing a statutory interpretation, he
simply wrote the definition of a prospectus out of the statute.

Why did the Court reach this conclusion? Had any of the justices
practiced securities law, the correct answer to the problem would have
been obvious. But it is clear that the Court did not understand the way
securities practice is done or what the legitimate concerns of buyers
and sellers are. Kennedy notes, in an attempt at policy defense, "It is
understandable that Congress would provide buyers with a right to rescind . . . [with respect to] a document prepared with care, following
well-established procedures relating to investigations with due diligence. . . . It is not plausible to infer that Congress created this extensive liability for every casual communication between buyer and seller
in the secondary market."

What is plausible, indeed almost certainly correct, is that Congress
attempted to *eliminate* the use of casual communications in the purchase and sale of securities and to promote a great deal of care precisely to preclude the use of misinformation. And the quoted sentence
reveals a stunning ignorance of actual practice—any first-year associate in a law firm could have told Kennedy that virtually the same due
diligence done in every public offering is regularly performed in all pri-

vate offerings, including those of all the stock of a business, if for no
other reason than to protect the lawyers themselves from liability.

Instead of following common sense, as to policy and practice, the
Court was driven by Kennedy's insistence on a statutory interpretation
that preserved "a symmetrical and coherent regulatory scheme in
which the operative words have a consistent meaning throughout."[10]
But the preservation of a coherent *regulatory* scheme does not necessarily depend on symmetry, no matter how much a sense of statutory ele-
gance might demand it. The world, and certainly the world of
business, does not operate with such artifice. Kennedy approaches the
problem as if he were a general contractor hell-bent on building a
Georgian mansion from a set of Frank Gehry blueprints. Or a physicist
manipulating results to avoid experimental protocols, in this case the
definitional section designed to infuse the statute with meaning. The
order he attempts to enforce upon the form of the statute has nothing
to do with the practical realities underlying the regulatory scheme.[11]

Another significant opinion, this one written, surprisingly, by Justice
Blackmun—joined by Rehnquist, White, and Marshall, with a partial
concurrence by Scalia and dissents by Stevens (joined by Souter),
O'Connor (joined by Kennedy), and Kennedy (joined by O'Connor)—suggests, if nothing else, that bad jurisprudence makes strange
bedfellows. The case is the 1991 *Lampf, Pleva, et al. v. Gilbertson*, and the
issue was the appropriate statute of limitations to apply.[12] Since the
1934 Securities Act did not provide for an express private cause of action but rather one had been implied by the courts, there clearly was
no express statute of limitations that went with it. The traditional procedure when a federal statute does not have an express statute of limitations is to borrow the most analogous state statute of limitations. In
rejecting this rule and instead creating a federal statute of limitations
from the corners of the 1934 act, the Court admitted it was taking an
unusual step, especially in light of the fact that Congress was aware of
the general rule and presumably expected that it would be applied in
cases like this. Since, however, the 1934 act does contain express causes
of action with their own statutes of limitations, the Court chose to look

within the statute in the interests of creating a more consistent statutory approach.

Of course, as Emerson said, "a foolish consistency is the hobgoblin of little minds." For the sake of consistency, the Court created a statute of limitations for this antifraud provision that runs one year from the discovery of the fraud but with an absolute three-year limit of repose. In other words, if the fraud is not discovered within three years, the plaintiff is out of luck.

The Court's reasoning is tortuous, but its general direction is apparent. It is intriguing to note, however, that in the interests of consistency, perhaps the most plaintiff-friendly securities justice on the Court created a rule that, as Justice Kennedy wrote, "conflicts with traditional limitations periods for fraud-based actions, frustrates the usefulness of Section 10(b) in protecting defrauded investors, and imposes severe practical limitations on a federal implied cause of action that has become an essential component of the protection the law gives to investors who have been injured by unlawful practices."

Why? Because the essence of fraud is concealment. It is entirely possible for far longer than three years to pass before the discovery of a fraud. Indeed, in the Enron case, assuming that fraudulent nondisclosure is found to exist, it is probable that at least some of that fraud occurred outside the three-year limitations period. In fact, although Enron was only a pipeline company at the time of the opinion, the impact of the holding on that case is echoed in Justice Kennedy's remark: "Ponzi schemes, for example, can maintain the illusion of a profit-making enterprise for years, and sophisticated investors might not be able to discover the fraud until long after its perpetration." Using a technical approach rather than a realistic approach to statutory interpretation, the Court again forecloses the possibility of remedies for a large class of investors.

The Rehnquist Court's poor record in interpreting securities law is again evident in the 1994 opinion in *Central Bank of Denver v. First Interstate Bank of Denver.*[13] Justice Kennedy, joined by Rehnquist, O'Connor, Scalia, and Thomas, held that Section 10(b) did not impose civil liability on those who aided and abetted violations of the statute. Invoking the talismanic phrase "the starting point in every case involving construction of a statute is the language itself," Kennedy concluded that since the language of this admittedly broad and ambiguous statute didn't expressly provide for aiding and abetting liability, the game was over and such liability didn't exist. He did go on to address arguments plaintiffs had made but concluded again with the assertion that the statutory language was enough.

The logic is ridiculous. While it's true that the statute is the starting point, the Court has always recognized (as the lower courts generally have as well) that Section 10(b) is more in the nature of an antifraud *principle* than an outcome determinative rule. The Court virtually ignores the development of aiding and abetting liability in common law and insists on an explicit statutory source. It does recognize the existence of one in a 1909 act of Congress providing for aiding and abetting liability for all federal crimes, which of course would pick up criminal violations of Section 10(b), but dismisses without any policy justification other than a felt need to protect potential defendants the possibility that the principle logically could extend to civil actions as well. The Court's main concern is that extending aiding and abetting liability to civil actions under Section 10(b) would reach people who had not engaged in the conduct prohibited by Section 10(b), without recognizing that aiding and abetting liability exists *precisely* to extend liability to people who didn't commit the primary violation but provided significant help to others in committing the prohibited act. The Court fails to acknowledge that Section 10(b) violations frequently involve the knowing and essential input of people—accountants, lawyers, investment bankers, and, in this case, indenture trustees—other than the primary violators. Thus, the case significantly limits the efficacy of the statute in prohibiting fraud.

I've saved the best for last, an opinion by a justice I generally admire, David Souter. The case is *Virginia Bankshares v. Sandberg,* and it involved a suit by stockholders of First American Bank of Virginia who were frozen out in a merger of the bank with Virginia Bankshares, which owned 85 percent of the bank's stock.[14] The stockholders complained that the proxy statement sent out by First American was materially misleading because in it the directors said that the stockholders would be receiving a "high price" for their stock, a statement a jury found to be untrue. Misleading proxy statements are prohibited by Section 14(a) of the 1934 Securities Act and the rules the SEC has adopted to implement it. First American and its directors were found liable, a judgment affirmed by the Fourth Circuit. The Supreme Court reversed, with the relevant portion of the opinion joined by Rehnquist, White, O'Connor, and Scalia and dissented from by Blackmun and Stevens (with Marshall and Kennedy joining in various aspects of the dissent).

The legal problem arose because Virginia law did not require that the directors send out a proxy statement in this sort of merger. As a result, the Court concluded that the misleading proxy statement could not have "caused" the merger to occur. Of course, in one sense, even had the proxy statement been legally required, it could not have caused the merger since Virginia Bankshares owned well more than enough stock to approve the merger without a single vote of minority stockholders. But twenty-one years earlier, Justice John Marshall Harlan, Jr., writing for the Court in *Mills v. Electric Auto-Lite Company*, concluded that since the purpose of the proxy rules was to prevent misleading information in proxy statements, and even a proxy statement in the case of a controlled corporation could have adverse effects upon plaintiffs (and, I note, on the market prices of the subsidiary's stock prior to the merger), such statements were indeed causative in a legal sense if the proxy statement was an "essential link in the accomplishment of the transaction."[15] Because the minority's votes were not legally required in this case, the Court held that the proxy statement could not be seen as an essential link in the transaction. Thus a narrow notion of tortlike proximate causation was imported into a remedial statutory scheme clearly designed to protect stockholders in a complex market in which proximate cause is almost always difficult to prove.

The Court overlooked some significant practical aspects of the deal. In the first place, a major reason for the proxy solicitation was that First American and Virginia Bankshares had a director in common and disinterested stockholder ratification was necessary to insulate the transaction from invalidation on conflict-of-interest grounds. The Court declined to decide this argument because it appeared that the merger didn't preclude stockholder pursuit of the state remedy, thus making the argument irrelevant, even though First American's board of directors evidently thought it materially important enough to incur the time and cost of issuing a proxy statement. And even though the proxy statement wasn't legally required, this doesn't alter the fact that the directors actually issued it. Once a misleading proxy statement asking for stockholder approval of the merger had been issued, the damage was done.

This fact was clearly recognized by Stevens, Blackmun, and Marshall in a dissent written by Justice Kennedy in which they noted that, regardless of the state legal requirement, the "real question ought to be whether an injury was shown by the effect the nondisclosure had on the entire merger process, including the period before votes are cast." This showed some understanding of business and market behavior. The dissent recognized that the directors could stop the merger if it was too unpopular with minority stockholders. The "including" phrase showed an appreciation of the effect that proxy misstatements could have on the trading price of First American stocks prior to the merger, harming traders relying on that information. Finally, it acknowledged the practical lack of protection for minority stockholders if thousands of them were required to prove how they would have voted if the information had been accurate. "Those who lack the strength to vote down a proposal have all the more need of disclosure," the dissent noted, demonstrating a clear understanding of the practical realities of being a minority stockholder and the securities law policy of protecting precisely those people. By contrast, the majority rested the bulk of its opinion on the fact that the cause of action under Section 14(a) was implied by the courts rather than being explicit in the statute, and thus as a matter of statutory interpretation limited (although as a matter of statutory interpretation it should also be noted that the statute and rule are very broadly worded and prohibit the use of misleading statements in any proxy statement involving registered securities—and it is clear that First American's shares were registered securities).

The dissent was refreshing in its common sense, but the opinion occurred rather early in the Rehnquist Court, when Blackmun and Marshall could lend weight to Stevens's business understanding. The Court as constituted in 2002 has only the greatly outnumbered Stevens to keep it honest, with the voice of common sense and business sense buried in a battle over statutory interpretation techniques.

There have been some advances in the Court's use of the protective aspects of the securities law but, with the exception of *O'Hagan*, these mostly occurred in the early years of the Rehnquist Court, when Blackmun and Marshall were prominent voices. The clear trend in recent years has been to cut back these protections wherever possible, a trend justified by a dogmatic reliance on statutory language without much regard to the purposes of the statutes or the way they function in the real world of securities trading. It seems obvious that the Court's general purpose is to limit severely the scope of the securities laws, but the justices seem to do so without any real appreciation of the effects on market efficiency. After all, one of the preconditions of an efficient market is an honest market. Moreover, their use of highly artificial and often illogical statutory technique constitutes its own form of deception: if the Court intends to cut back on the securities laws for some policy reason, it ought to be frank and tell us—and tell us why. One suspects that a major reason the Court hasn't done this is that the justices themselves don't quite know why, other than perhaps a knee-jerk attempt to provide benefits to business, benefits that are questionable in a market stripped of investor protections. If the trend continues, not only will the Court leave the markets in a less regulated and therefore riskier condition but it will likely complete the process of leaving virtually all important business policy to the state of Delaware.

Notes

TOM WICKER: *Foreword: Reflections of a Court Watcher*

1. *Worcester v. State of Georgia*, 31 U.S. 515 (1832).
2. 347 U.S. 483 (1954).
3. *Bush v. Gore*, 531 U.S. 98 (2000).
4. *Marbury v. Madison*, 5 U.S. (1 Cranch) 137 (1803).
5. *Dred Scott v. Sandford*, 60 U.S. 393 (1857).
6. 163 U.S. 537 (1896).
7. 343 U.S. 579 (1952).

HERMAN SCHWARTZ: *Introduction*

1. *Bush v. Gore*, 531 U.S. 98 (2000).
2. Ford Fessenden and John M. Broder, "Examining the Vote: The Overview; Study of Disputed Florida Ballots Finds Justices Did Not Cast the Deciding Vote," *New York Times*, Nov. 12, 2001, p. A1.
3. On the military tribunals, see Herman Schwartz, "These Secret Tribunals Ignore Due Process and Treat Suspects As If They Are Presumed Guilty before Trial," *Insight on the News*, Jan. 28, 2002, p. 43, and "Tribunal Injustice," *The Nation*, Jan. 21, 2002.
4. *Near v. Minnesota*, 283 U.S. 697 (1931); *Cantwell v. Connecticut*, 310 U.S. 296 (1940).
5. *Brown v. Board of Education*, 347 U.S. 483 (1954).
6. *Callins v. Collins*, 510 U.S. 1141, 1145 (1994) (Blackmun, J., dissenting).
7. 384 U.S. 436 (1966).
8. 410 U.S. 113 (1973).

9. *Planned Parenthood of Southeastern Pennsylvania v. Casey*, 505 U.S. 833 (1992).

10. *Romer v. Evans*, 517 U.S. 620 (1996); *Boy Scouts v. Dale*, 530 U.S. 640 (2000); *Hurley v. Irish-American Gay, Lesbian, and Bisexual Group of Boston*, 515 U.S. 557 (1995).

11. Craig A. Stern, "Judging the Judges: The First Two Years of the Reagan Bench," *Benchmark* 1 (July–Oct. 1984): 3.

JOHN P. MacKENZIE: *Equal Protection for One Lucky Guy*

1. *Bush v. Gore*, 531 U.S. 98 (2000).

2. *Korematsu v. United States*, 323 U.S. 214 (1944).

3. *Dred Scott v. Sandford*, 60 U.S. 393 (1857); *Plessy v. Ferguson*, 163 U.S. 537 (1896).

4. *Bush v. Palm Beach County Canvassing Board*, 531 U.S. 70 (2000).

5. See *Gore v. Harris*, 772 So. 2d 1243, 1252 (Fla. 2000).

6. See *Bush v. Gore*, 531 U.S. 1046 (2000) (Scalia, J., concurring).

7. *Palm Beach County Canvassing Board. v. Harris*, 772 So. 2d 1292 (Fla. 2000).

8. *Planned Parenthood of Southeastern Pennsylvania v. Casey*, 505 U.S. 833, 854 (1992).

9. *United States v. Virginia*, 518 U.S. 515, 596 (1996) (Scalia, J., dissenting).

10. 406 U.S. 205 (1972).

11. See *Anastasoff v. United States*, 223 F., 3d 898 (8th Cir. 2000).

WILLIAM L. TAYLOR: *Racial Equality: The World According to Rehnquist*

1. 347 U.S. 483 (1954).

2. *Griggs v. Duke Power Company*, 401 U.S. 424 (1971).

3. *San Antonio Independent School District v. Rodriguez*, 411 U.S. 1 (1973); *Milliken v. Bradley*, 418 U.S. 717 (1974).

4. *Washington v. Davis*, 426 U.S. 229 (1976); *Arlington Heights v. Metropolitan Housing Development Corporation*, 429 U.S. 252 (1977); *Mobile v. Bolden*, 446 U.S. 55 (1980).

5. 418 U.S. at 814.

6. See Richard Kluger, *Simple Justice: The History of* Brown v. Board of Education *and Black America's Struggle for Equality* (New York, 1975), pp. 605–09. While Rehnquist claimed during his 1971 confirmation hearings that the memo was prepared to reflect Jackson's views rather than his own, Kluger's review of the circumstances provides strong evidence that this is simply not so.

7. *Washington Post*, July 25, 1986.

8. David Shapiro, "Mr. Justice Rehnquist: A Preliminary View," *Harvard Law Review* 90 (1976): 293, 298.

9. *Keyes v. School District No. 1 of Denver*, 413 U.S. 189 (1973).

10. 422 U.S. 406, 420 (1977).

11. *Dayton II*, 443 U.S. 526 (1979).

12. 490 U.S. 642 (1989).

13. *McDonnell Douglas v. Green*, 411 U.S. 792 (1973).

14. 490 U.S. at 659–60.

15. 491 U.S. 164 (1989).

16. See William Taylor, "The Civil Rights Act of 1991," *Touro Law Review* 9 (1992): 157.

17. *Regents of the University of California v. Bakke*, 483 U.S. 265 (1978).

18. *Adarand Contractors v. Pena*, 515 U.S. 200 (1995).

19. *Hopwood v. Texas*, 78 F. 3d 932, *certiorari denied*, 116 Sup. Ct. 2581 (1996).

20. *Cooper v. Aaron*, 358 U.S. 1 (1958).

21. Another example of Rehnquist's prestidigitation came in *Dayton I* when he held that rescision by a school board of a voluntary desegregation policy was not a violation of the Fourteenth Amendment if the policy had not been implemented. The fact that the policy was rescinded after a successful campaign laced with racial rhetoric to replace the board members who voted for the original policy was deemed irrelevant because it was not "state action."

22. *Mobile v. Bolden*, 446 U.S. 55 (1980).

23. 509 U.S. 630 (1993).

24. *Swann v. Charlotte-Mecklenburg Board of Education*, 402 U.S. 1 (1971).

25. *Milliken v. Bradley*, 433 U.S. 288 (1977).

26. *Oklahoma City Board of Education v. Dowell*, 498 U.S. 237 (1991); *Freeman v. Pitts*, 503 U.S. 467 (1992); *Missouri v. Jenkins*, 515 U.S. 70 (1995).

27. 529 U.S. 598 (2000).

28. 528 U.S. 62 (2000).

29. *Board of Trustees of the University of Alabama v. Garrett*, 531 U.S. 356 (2001).

30. *Alexander v. Sandoval*, 532 U.S. 275 (2001).

31. The more conventional constitutional analysis was provided in the accompanying District of Columbia case, *Bolling v. Sharpe*, 347 U.S. 497 (1954).

32. 115 Sup. Ct. 1275 (2002).

33. 457 U.S. 202 (1982).

34. *Griggs v. Duke Power Company*, 401 U.S. 424, 432 (1971).

CHARLES J. OGLETREE, JR.: *The Rehnquist Revolution in Criminal Procedure*

1. See Herbert L. Packer, "Two Models of the Criminal Process," *University of Pennsylvania Law Review* 113 (1964): 1.

2. For probable cause, see *Illinois v. Gates*, 462 U.S. 213 (1983); for reasonable suspicion, see *United States v. Sokolow*, 490 U.S. 1 (1989).

3. 384 U.S. 436 (1966); 377 U.S. 201 (1964); 367 U.S. 643 (1961).

4. Stanley H. Friedelbaum, *The Rehnquist Court: In Pursuit of Judicial Conservatism* (Westport, 1994), p. 129.

5. 392 U.S. 1 (1968).

6. 491 U.S. 617 (1989).

7. See *Robbins v. California*, 453 U.S. 420, 437 (1981) (Rehnquist, J., dissenting), over-

ruled by *United States v. Ross*, 456 U.S. 798 (1982). See also *Arkansas v. Sanders*, 442 U.S. 753 (1979) (Blackmun, J., and Rehnquist, J., dissenting), modified by *United States v. Ross*, 456 U.S. 798 (1982).

8. See *Katz v. United States*, 389 U.S. 347 (1967).

9. *United States v. Chadwick*, 433 U.S. 1, 19 (1977), abrogated by *California v. Acevedo*, 500 U.S. 565 (1991).

10. 440 U.S. 648, 664–67 (1979) (Rehnquist, J., dissenting).

11. See *Steagald v. United States*, 451 U.S. 204, 223–31 (1981) (Rehnquist, J., dissenting); *Ybarra v. Illinois*, 440 U.S. 85, 98–110 (1979) (Rehnquist, J., dissenting).

12. 442 U.S. 200, 222–23 (1979) (Rehnquist, J., dissenting).

13. 438 U.S. 154, 182 (1978) (Rehnquist, J., dissenting).

14. *Florida v. Jimeno*, 500 U.S. 248, 252 (1991).

15. 500 U.S. 565 (1991).

16. 450 U.S. 288 (1981). As an associate justice, Rehnquist also supported the restriction of double-jeopardy protections, which prevent individuals being tried twice for the same offense. See *Crist v. Bretz*, 437 U.S. 28, 40–53 (1978) (Powell, J., dissenting).

17. 426 U.S. 610, 620–34 (1976).

18. 479 U.S. 157, 170 (1986).

19. "As the Court today acknowledges, since *Miranda* we have explicitly, and repeatedly, interpreted that decision as having announced, not the circumstances in which custodial interrogation runs afoul of the Fifth or Fourteenth Amendment, but rather only 'prophylactic' rules that go beyond the right against compelled self-incrimination" 530 U.S. 428, 450 (2000) (Scalia, J., dissenting).

20. For a critique of Chief Justice Rehnquist's harmless-error analysis, see Charles J. Ogletree, Jr., "The Supreme Court, Comment: *Arizona v. Fulminante*: The Harm of Applying Harmless Error to Coerced Confessions," *Harvard Law Review* 105 (1991): 152.

21. For the death penalty as violating the Eighth Amendment, see 428 U.S. 325, 337–63 (1976) (White, J., dissenting).

22. See *Coker v. Georgia*, 433 U.S. 584, 604–22 (1977) (Burger, C. J., dissenting); *Enmund v. Florida*, 458 U.S. 782, 801–31 (1982) (O'Connor, J., dissenting); *Ford v. Wainwright*, 477 U.S. 399, 431–35 (1986) (Rehnquist, J., dissenting).

23. 433 U.S. 72 (1977).

24. 489 U.S. 288 (1989).

25. *Id.* at 334–45 (Brennan, J., dissenting).

26. James S. Liebman, "More Than 'Slightly Retro': The Rehnquist Court's Rout of Habeas Corpus Jurisdiction in *Teague v. Lane*," *New York University Review of Law and Social Change* 18 (1991): 540–41.

27. Staci Rosche, "How Conservative Is the Rehnquist Court? Three Issues, One Answer," *Fordham Law Review* 65 (1997): 2719.

28. Christopher E. Smith, "Criminal Justice and the U.S. Supreme Court's 1999–2000 Term," *North Dakota Law Review* 77 (2001): 25.

29. 517 U.S. 806 (1996).

30. 528 U.S. 119 (2000).

31. See David A. Harris, "Driving While Black: Racial Profiling on Our Nation's Highways," *American Civil Liberties Union Special Report,* June 1999, http://www.aclu.org/profiling/report/index.html.

32. See Edward Walsh, "The Racial Issue Looming in the Rear-View Mirror; Activists Seek Data on Police 'Profiling,' " *Washington Post,* May 19, 1999, p. A3.

33. Nat Hentoff, "Forgetting the Fourth Amendment in Philadelphia," *Washington Post,* Apr. 16, 1988, p. A25.

34. Diana Jean Schemo, "Singling Out Blacks Where Few Are to Be Found," *New York Times,* Oct. 20, 1992, p. B1.

35. Jim McGee, "In Federal Law Enforcement 'All the Walls Are Down'; Personnel from Assorted Agencies Work Together at FBI Headquarters," *Washington Post,* Oct. 14, 2001, p. A16.

36. For a further discussion of racial profiling, see Charles J. Ogletree, Jr., "Fighting a Just War without an Unjust Loss of Freedom," *Africana.com,* Oct. 11, 2001.

WILLIAM E. HELLERSTEIN: *No Rights of Prisoners*

1. In *Cooper v. Pate,* 378 U.S. 546 (1964) (per curiam), the Court ruled that a prisoner's claim that he had been punished for exercising his religious beliefs could not be dismissed outright. In *Lee v. Washington,* 390 U.S. 333 (per curiam), the Court prohibited the racial segregation of prisoners. In *Johnson v. Avery,* 393 U.S. 483 (1969), the Court ruled that a regulation that prohibited inmates from assisting other inmates in the preparation of habeas corpus petitions was an unconstitutional interference with access to the courts.

2. *Holt v. Sarver,* 309 F. Supp. 367 (E.D. Ark. 1970).

3. *Cruz v. Beto,* 405 U.S. 319 (1972); *Procunier v. Martinez,* 416 U.S. 396 (1974); *Wolff v. McDonnell,* 418 U.S. 539 (1974); *Estelle v. Gamble,* 429 U.S. 97 (1976).

4. Public Law 104–134, 110 Stat. 1321.

5. 482 U.S. 78 (1987).

6. *Korematsu v. United States,* 323 U.S. 214, 246 (1944).

7. 490 U.S. 401 (1989).

8. 121 Sup. Ct. 1475 (2001).

9. 405 U.S. 319 (1972).

10. 482 U.S. 342 (1987).

11. *Young v. Lane,* 922 F. 2d 370 (7th Cir. 1991); *Friend v. Kolodzieczak,* 923 F. 2d 126 (9th Cir. 1991); *Kahey v. Jones,* 836 F. 2d 948 (5th Cir. 1988); *Fromer v. Scully,* 874 F. 2d 69 (2d Cir. 1989); and *Pollock v. Marshall,* 845 F. 2d 656 (6th Cir.), certiorari denied, 488 U.S. 987 (1988).

12. For severity of deprivation, see *Morrisey v. Brewer,* 408 U.S. 471 (1972).

13. 418 U.S. 539 (1974).

14. 515 U.S. 472 (1995).

15. *Johnson v. Avery*, 393 U.S. 483 (1969); *Bounds v. Smith*, 430 U.S. 817 (1977).

16. 518 U.S. 343 (1996).

17. 429 U.S. 97 (1976).

18. 437 U.S. 678 (1978).

19. 501 U.S. 294 (1991).

20. 511 U.S. 294 (1994).

21. 503 U.S. 1 (1992).

22. 509 U.S. 25 (1993).

23. 532 U.S. 731 (2001).

24. *Miranda v. United States*, 384 U.S. 436 (1966); *Dickerson v. United States*, 530 U.S. 428 (2000).

STEPHEN BRIGHT: *Capital Punishment: Accelerating the Dance with Death*

1. *Callins v. Collins*, 510 U.S. 1141 (1994) (Blackmun, J., dissenting from denial of certiorari).

2. *Furman v. Georgia*, 408 U.S. 238 (1972).

3. *Woodson v. North Carolina*, 428 U.S. 280 (1976); *Roberts v. Louisiana*, 428 U.S. 325 (1976).

4. *Coleman v. Balkcom*, 451 U.S. 949 (1981) (Rehnquist, J., dissenting from denial of certiorari).

5. *Coleman v. Thompson*, 501 U.S. 722, 758–59 (1991) (Blackmun, J., dissenting).

6. "Justice O'Connor Expresses New Doubts about Fairness of Capital Punishment," *Baltimore Sun*, July 4, 2001, p. A3.

7. "Florida Lets Speed Govern Executions," *Chicago Tribune*, Feb. 28, 2000, p. N1.

8. 501 U.S. 722, 758 (Blackmun, J., dissenting).

9. *Teague v. Lane*, 489 U.S. 288 (1989); *Brecht v. Abrahamson*, 507 U.S. 619 (1993).

10. *Strickler v. Greene*, 527 U.S. 263 (1999); *Sawyer v. Whitley*, 505 U.S. 333 (1992).

11. *Jacobs v. Scott*, 513 U.S. 1067 (1995).

12. See, e.g., *Schlup v. Delo*, 513 U.S. 298 (1995); *Kyles v. Whitley*, 514 U.S. 419 (1995).

13. Stuart Eskenazi, "Strong Convictions," *Houston Press*, Nov. 18, 1998.

14. "Oklahoma Governor Commutes Death Case; Texas Bill Boosts Defense for the Poor," *Chicago Tribune*, Apr. 11, 2001, p. N8.

15. *Riles v. McCotter*, 799 F. 2d 947, 955 (5th Cir. 1986) (Rubin, J., concurring).

16. *Strickland v. Washington*, 466 U.S. 668 (1984).

17. Remarks of Justice Thurgood Marshall at the Second Circuit Judicial Conference (Sept. 1988), reprinted in 125 F.R.D. 201, 202–03 (1988).

18. "Justice O'Connor Expresses New Doubts about Fairness of Capital Punishment," *op. cit.*

19. *Williams (Terry) v. Taylor*, 529 U.S. 362 (2000).

20. *Gideon v. Wainwright*, 372 U.S. 335 (1963); *Douglas v. California*, 372 U.S. 353 (1963).

21. *Murray v. Giarratano*, 492 U.S. 1 (1989).

22. *McCleskey v. Kemp*, 481 U.S. 279 (1987).

23. *Andrews v. Shulsen*, 485 U.S. 919 (1988).

24. *Perry v. Lynaugh*, 492 U.S. 302 (1989); *Atkins v. Virginia*, 122 Sup. Ct. 2242 (2002).

25. *Stanford v. Kentucky*, 492 U.S. 361 (1989).

26. *McCleskey v. Kemp*, 481 U.S. 279, 344 (1987) (Brennan, J., dissenting).

NORMAN REDLICH: *The Religion Clauses: A Study in Confusion*

1. *Everson v. Board of Education*, 330 U.S. 1 (1947).

2. *Engel v. Vitale*, 370 U.S. 421 (1962).

3. 403 U.S. 602 (1971).

4. 433 U.S. 229 (1977).

5. *Witters v. Washington Department of Services for the Blind*, 474 U.S. 481 (1986); *Zobrest v. Catalina Foothills School District*, 509 U.S. 1 (1993).

6. *Agostini v. Felton*, 521 U.S. 203 (1997); *Aguilar v. Felton*, 473 U.S. 402 (1985).

7. 530 U.S. 793 (2000).

8. 374 U.S. 203 (1963).

9. 472 U.S. 38 (1985).

10. 482 U.S. 578 (1987).

11. 505 U.S. 577 (1992).

12. 530 U.S. 290 (2000).

13. 250 F. 3d 1330 (11th Cir. 2001), certiorari denied, 122 Sup. Ct. 579 (2001).

14. 454 U.S. 263 (1981).

15. 515 U.S. 819 (1995).

16. 533 U.S. 98 (2001).

17. 494 U.S. 872 (1990).

18. 508 U.S. 520 (1993).

19. 521 U.S. 507 (1997).

20. 449 U.S. 39 (1980).

21. 465 U.S. 668 (1984).

22. 492 U.S. 573 (1989).

23. *Zelman v. Simmons-Harris*, 122 Sup. Ct. 2460 (2002).

JAMIN B. RASKIN: *The First Amendment: The High Ground and the Low Road*

1. *Hustler v. Falwell*, 485 U.S. 46 (1988); *Texas v. Johnson*, 491 U.S. 397 (1989); *Rosenberger v. Rector and Visitors of the University of Virginia* 515 U.S. 819 (1995).

2. 521 U.S. 844 (1997), invalidating as both vague and overboard the Communications Decency Act, which criminalized knowing transmission on the Internet of indecent messages to minors and knowing display of patently offensive messages accessible to minors, 122 Sup. Ct. 1389 (2002). A similar opinion was *Sable Communications of California, Inc. v. FCC*, 492 U.S. 115 (1989), striking down congressional restrictions on interstate "dial-a-porn" messages.

3. *New York Times v. Sullivan*, 376 U.S. 254 (1964), holds that public figures may recover in state libel actions only if they can show "actual malice" by defendants, meaning knowledge or reckless disregard of the falsity of alleged defamatory statements. *Cohen v. California*, 403 U.S. 15 (1971), invalidates the criminal conviction of a young man who wore "Fuck the Draft" on his jacket into a courtroom, finding that "one man's vulgarity is another's lyric" and political "cacophony" is a sign of "strength." *Brandenburg v. Ohio*, 395 U.S. 444 (1969), holds that advocacy of the use of illegal force is constitutionally protected "except where such advocacy is directed to inciting or producing imminent lawless action and is likely to incite or produce such action."

4. 505 U.S. 377 (1992).

5. *Buckley v. Valeo*, 424 U.S. 1 (1976).

6. See, e.g., *Schenck v. Pro-Choice Network*, 117 Sup. Ct. 855, 867 (1997), in which Chief Justice Rehnquist upheld an injunctive-fixed buffer zone outside abortion clinics but struck down a "floating" fifteen-foot buffer zone, stating that "speech in public areas is at its most protected on public sidewalks."

7. 530 U.S. 640 (2000).

8. 515 U.S. 557 (1995).

9. Texas law made it a crime to "deface, damage or otherwise physically mistreat" the American flag "in a way that the actor knows will seriously offend one or more persons likely to observe or discover his action," 491 U.S. 397, 435 (1989).

10. 319 U.S. 624 (1943).

11. 485 U.S. 48, 46–48 (1988).

12. *Id.* at 55.

13. 454 U.S. 263 (1981).

14. 523 U.S. 666 (1998). Jamin B. Raskin filed an amicus brief in this case on behalf of Perot '96, Ross Perot's 1996 presidential campaign organization.

15. *Arkansas Educational Television Commission v. Forbes*, 93 F. 3d 497 (8th Cir. 1996).

16. 523 U.S. 666, 680 (1993).

17. 93 F. 3d at 497.

18. *Timmons v. Twin Cities Area New Party*, 520 U.S. 351, 356 (1997).

19. 73 F. 3d 196, 198 (8th Cir., 1997).

20. 505 U.S. 222 (1992).

21. *Hazelwood School District v. Kuhlmeier, Tinker v. Des Moines School District*, 484 U.S. 260 (1988); 393 U.S. 503 (1969).

22. 478 U.S. 675 (1986).

23. 500 U.S. 173 (1991).

24. 500 U.S. at 210 (Blackmun, J., and Marshall, J., dissenting).

25. 530 U.S. 703 (2000); Colorado Revised Statutes, sec. 18–9–122(3) (2000).

26. 524 U.S. 569 (1998), quoting 20 U.S.C. sec. 954(d)(1).

27. *Id.* at 581.

28. *Id.* at 590, 591 (Scalia, J., and Thomas, J., concurring).

29. 531 U.S. 533 (2001).

CHAI FELDBLUM: *Gay Rights*

1. 478 U.S. 186 (1986).
2. *Boy Scouts of America v. Dale*, 530 U.S. 640 (2000).
3. *Griswold v. Connecticut*, 381 U.S. 479 (1965).
4. *Hardwick*, 478 U.S. at 206, quoting *Wisconsin v. Yoder*, 406 U.S. 205, 223–24 (1972).
5. *Hurley v. Irish-American Gay, Lesbian, and Bisexual Group of Boston*, 515 U.S. 557 (1995).
6. *Id.* at 574.
7. *Inside-OUT: A Report on the Experiences of Lesbians, Gays and Bisexuals in America and the Public's Views on Issues and Policies Related to Sexual Orientation.* Kaiser Family Foundation Pub. 3193, available at http://www.kff.org.
8. *Romer v. Evans*, 517 U.S. 620, 632 (1996).
9. *Id.* at 644 (Scalia, J., dissenting).
10. *Equality Foundation of Greater Cincinnati, Inc. v. City of Cincinnati*, 54 F. 3d 261 (6th Cir. 1995).
11. 525 U.S. 943 (1998). *Equality Foundation of Greater Cincinnati, Inc. v. City of Cincinnati*, 128 F. 3d 289 (6th Cir. 1997), certiorari denied, 525 U.S. 943 (1998).
12. *Baker v. State of Vermont*, 744 A. 2d 864 (Sup. Ct. Vt. 1999).

SUSAN ESTRICH: *The Politics of Abortion*

1. 410 U.S. 113 (1973).
2. 492 U.S. 490 (1989).
3. 505 U.S. 833 (1992).
4. *Stenberg v. Carhart*, 530 U.S. 914 (2000).

HERMAN SCHWARTZ: *The States' Rights Assault on Federal Authority*

1. *Hammer v. Dagenhart*, 247 U.S. 251 (1918); *Bailey v. Drexel Furniture Company*, 259 U.S. 20 (1922).
2. *United States v. Butler*, 297 U.S. 1 (1936); *Carter v. Carter Coal Company*, 298 U.S. 238 (1936).
3. *Wickard v. Filburn*, 317 U.S. 111 (1942).
4. George Lardner, Jr., and Saundra Saperstein, "A Chief Justice-Designate with Big Ambitions Even as a Boy, Rehnquist Hoped to Change the Government," *Washington Post*, July 6, 1986, p. 8, available at 1986 WC 2035528. See also Richard Kluger, *Simple Justice: The History of* Brown v. Board of Education *and Black America's Struggle for Equality* (New York, 1975), pp. 605–09.
5. *National League of Cities v. Usery*, 426 U.S. 833 (1976).
6. *Garcia v. San Antonio Metropolitan Transit Authority*, 469 U.S. 528 (1985).
7. 415 U.S. 651 (1974).
8. *Atascadero State Hospital v. Scanlon*, 473 U.S. 234 (1985).
9. 505 U.S. 144 (1992).

10. *Printz v. United States*, 521 U.S. 898 (1997).

11. 514 U.S. 549 (1995).

12. Congress promptly amended the law to reflect the fact that most guns move in interstate commerce, and the amended law has not been challenged. See Seth P. Waxman, "Symposium: Shifting the Balance of Power? The Supreme Court, Federalism and State Sovereign Immunity." Foreword: "Does the Solicitor General Matter?" *Stanford Law Review* 53 (2001): 1125.

13. *United States v. Morrison*, 529 U.S. 598 (2000).

14. *Seminole Tribe of Florida v. Florida*, 517 U.S. 44 (1996); *Alden v. Maine*, 527 U.S. 706 (1999); *College Savings Bank v. Florida*, 527 U.S. 666 (1999).

15. *Seminole Tribe*, 517 U.S. at 57.

16. *Ex parte Young*, 209 U.S. 123 (1908).

17. *Seminole Tribe*, 517 U.S. at 76.

18. *Westside Mothers v. Haveman*, 133 F. Supp. 2d 549 (E.D. Mich. 2001), *reversed*, 289 F. 3d 852 (6th Cir. 2002); *Joseph A. ex rel Wolfe v. Ingram*, 262 F. 3d 1113 (10th Cir. 2001).

19. 2002 U.S. Lexis 3794 (May 28, 2002).

20. *Employment Division v. Smith*, 494 U.S. 872 (1990) *City of Boerne v. Flores*, 521 U.S. 507 (1997).

21. *Kimel v. Florida Board of Regents*, 528 U.S. 62 (2000); *Morrison*, 529 U.S. at 620; *Board of Trustees v. Garrett*, 531 U.S. 356 (2001).

22. *U.S. Term Limits, Inc. v. Thornton*, 514 U.S. 779 (1995); *Reno v. Condon*, 528 U.S. 141 (2000).

23. *Gregory v. Ashcroft*, 501 U.S. 452, 458, 1991.

24. *Id.* at 501 U.S. at 456.

25. Edward L. Rubin, "Puppy Federalism and the Blessings of America," *Annals*, March 2001, p. 37. See also Herman Schwartz, "The Supreme Court's Federalism: Fig Leaf for Conservatives," *Annals*, March 2001, p. 119.

26. Harold Hyman, *A More Perfect Union: The Impact of the Civil War and Reconstruction on the Constitution* (New York, 1973), p. 12, n. 18. See, e.g., *Slochower v. Board of Education*, 350 U.S. 551 (1956); *Stuyvesant Town Corporation v. United States*, 346 U.S. 864 (1953).

27. Stephen Labaton, "States Seek to Counter U.S. Deregulation," *New York Times*, Jan. 13, 2002, sect. 1, p. 22.

28. "State Legislators Mix Public and Private Business," *New York Times*, May 21, 2001, p. A26.

29. Sheryll D. Cashin, "Federalism, Welfare Reform and the Minority Poor: Accounting for the Tyranny of State Majorities," *Columbia Law Review* 99 (1999): 552–53, n. 6.

30. Editorial, "Turning Away the Needy," *New York Times*, July 31, 2000, p. A18.

31. Nina Bernstein, "Bingo, Blood and Burial Plots in the Quest for Food Stamps," *New York Times*, Aug. 13, 2000, p. A1.

32. Despite the urgency of the terrorism threat, in October and November 2001, Attorney General John Ashcroft decided, despite strongly supported legislation in Oregon, California, and elsewhere, to go after doctors who assist terminally ill pa-

tients to die or who prescribe marijuana for medical reasons. See Sam Howe Ver-hovek, "U.S. Acts to Stop Assisted Suicides," *New York Times*, Nov. 7, 2001, p. A1.

33. *Westside Mothers*, 133 F. Supp. 2d at 562; *Joseph A.*, 262 F. 3d at 1123.

34. For example, even in the immediate aftermath of the World Trade Center tragedy, conservative Republicans in the House of Representatives and President Bush op-posed federalizing airport security because it would create a federal entity, despite the obvious and continuing failures of private security arrangements. See Lizette Alvarez, "A Nation Challenged: Airport Security; Bush Seeking House Allies on Airport Security Plan," *New York Times*, Nov. 1, 2001, p. B1.

DAVID C. VLADECK and ALAN B. MORRISON: *The Roles, Rights, and Responsibilities of the Executive Branch*

1. *Department of Justice v. Reporters Committee for Freedom of the Press*, 489 U.S. 749 (1989).

2. *Department of State v. Ray*, 502 U.S. 164 (1991).

3. *Department of the Interior v. Klamath Water Users Protective Association*, 532 U.S. 1 (2001).

4. *Lujan v. National Wildlife Federation*, 497 U.S. 871 (1990); *Lujan v. Defenders of Wildlife*, 504 U.S. 555 (1992).

5. *Steel Company v. Citizens for a Better Environment*, 523 U.S. 83 (1998).

6. *Friends of the Earth, Inc. v. Laidlaw Environmental Services (TOC), Inc.*, 528 U.S. 167 (2000).

7. *Ohio Forestry Association, Inc. v. Sierra Club*, 523 U.S. 726 (1998).

8. *Chevron, U.S.A., Inc. v. Natural Resources Defense Council, Inc.*, 467 U.S. 837 (1984).

9. See *United States v. Mead Corporation*, 533 U.S. 218, 231, at nn. 12 and 13 and ac-companying text (2001).

10. *Christensen v. Harris County*, 529 U.S. 576 (2000).

11. 533 U.S. 218.

12. *FDA v. Brown & Williamson Tobacco Corporation*, 529 U.S. 120 (2000).

13. *Whitman v. American Trucking Associations*, 531 U.S. 457 (2001).

14. *INS v. Chadha*, 462 U.S. 919 (1983); *Bowsher v. Synar*, 478 U.S. 714 (1986).

15. *Morrison v. Olson*, 487 U.S. 654 (1988). The "Morrison" in this case was Alexia Morrison, independent counsel, not Alan B. Morrison, coauthor of this chapter.

16. *Raines v. Byrd*, 521 U.S. 811 (1997).

17. *Clinton v. City of New York*, 524 U.S. 417 (1998).

18. *Lorillard Tobacco Company v. Reilly*, 532 U.S. 956 (2001).

19. *Buckman Company v. Plaintiffs' Legal Committee*, 531 U.S. 341 (2001).

20. *Geier v. American Honda Motor Corporation*, 529 U.S. 861 (2000).

JAMES SALZMAN: *Environmental Law*

1. Richard J. Lazarus, "Restoring What's Environmental about Environmental Law in the Supreme Court," *UCLA Law Review* 47 (2000): 737.

2. Edwin Kneedler, "It's Not about the Environment Anymore," *Environmental Forum* 17 (2000): 46.

3. 405 U.S. 727 (1972).

4. *Lujan v. National Wildlife Federation*, 497 U.S. 871 (1990); *Lujan v. Defenders of Wildlife*, 504 U.S. 555 (1992).

5. 523 U.S. 83 (1998).

6. 528 U.S. 167 (2000).

7. *Id.* at 204–05, 209.

8. 505 U.S. 1003 (1992). See also *Palazzolo v. Rhode Island*, 533 U.S. 606 (2001) (holding that "post-enactment purchasers," those who acquire title after the effective date of a state-imposed land-use restriction, may still recover under *Lucas*).

9. 514 U.S. 549 (1995).

10. 529 U.S. 598 (2000).

11. *Id.* at 599.

12. Michael J. Gerhardt, "Federal Environmental Regulation in a Post-*Lopez* World: Some Questions and Answers," *Environmental Law Reporter* 30 (2000): 10980.

13. In dissenting from the denial of certiorari, Justice Thomas wrote that "the Corps' basis for jurisdiction rests entirely on the actual or potential presence of migratory birds on petitioner's land. In light of *Lopez*, I have serious doubts about the propriety of the Corps' assertion of jurisdiction over petitioner's land in this case" (*Cargill, Inc. v. United States*, 516 U.S. 955, 958 [1995]).

14. 531 U.S. 159 (2001).

15. 474 U.S. 121 (1985).

16. 531 U.S. 159, 160–61 (2001).

17. *Id.* at 172–73.

18. Lazarus, "Restoring What's Environmental," p. 764, n. 1.

ANDREW J. IMPARATO: *The "Miserly" Approach to Disability Rights*

1. 42 U.S.C. Sect. 12101(a)(8).

2. *Equality of Opportunity: The Making of the Americans with Disabilities Act* (Washington, D.C.: National Council on Disability, 1997), appendix G.

3. *Cleburne v. Cleburne Living Center*, 473 U.S. 432 (1985).

4. *Id.* at 473, quoting *New York Trust Company v. Eisner*, 256 U.S. 345, 349 (1921) (Holmes, J.).

5. *Id.*

6. *Id.* at 451 (Stevens, J., concurring).

7. *Id.* at 455.

8. *Id.* at 467.

9. 42 U.S.C. Sect. 12101(a)(7), (a)(2), (a)(7).

10. *Heller v. Doe*, 509 U.S. 312, 335 (1993) (Blackmun J., dissenting). Internal citations omitted.

11. *Id.* at 319, citing *FCC v. Beach Communications, Inc.*, 508 U.S. 307, 314–15 (1993).

12. *Id.* at 335 (Souter, J., dissenting).

13. *Id.* at 348.

14. *Board of Trustees of University of Alabama v. Garrett*, 121 Sup. Ct. 955 (2001). Patricia

Garrett, a nurse who was treated for breast cancer, alleged that she was demoted by the University of Alabama Hospital in Birmingham because of her cancer. The other employee whose suit was consolidated with Garrett's, Milton Ash, was a security officer with the Alabama Department of Youth Services. Ash, who had chronic asthma, challenged his employer's denial of a request to modify his duties to minimize his exposure to carbon monoxide and cigarette smoke. Ash also challenged his employer's denial of a reassignment to a daytime shift to accommodate his sleep apnea. Alabama successfully moved for summary judgment in both cases in the trial court on the ground that the ADA exceeded Congress's authority to abrogate the state's Eleventh Amendment immunity to these types of suits. See 989 F. Supp. 1409, 1410 (N.D. Ala. 1998). After the cases were consolidated on appeal, the Eleventh Circuit Court of Appeals reversed, holding that the ADA validly abrogates the state's Eleventh Amendment immunity. See 193 F. 3d 1426, 1433 (C.A. 11 1998).

15. *Id.* at 964.

16. *Id.* at 967–68.

17. See, e.g., *id.* at 972 (Breyer, J., dissenting).

18. *Id.* at 972–73. Emphasis in original.

19. *Sutton v. United Airlines*, 527 U.S. 471 (1999). See also *Murphy v. United Parcel Service, Inc.*, 527 U.S. 516 (1999), and *Albertson's, Inc. v. Kirkingburg*, 527 U.S. 555 (1999). *Sutton* involved twin sisters with severe myopia fully correctable with eyeglasses who challenged their rejection for positions as commercial airline pilots. *Murphy* involved a UPS mechanic with high blood pressure that was responsive to medication. *Kirkingburg* involved a truck driver with monocular vision. In both *Murphy* and *Kirkingburg*, plaintiffs challenged their terminations by alleging discrimination on the basis of disability.

20. *Toyota v. Williams*, 534 U.S. 184 (2002).

21. *Tcherepnin v. Knight*, 389 U.S. 332, 336 (1967), quoted by Justice Stevens in his dissenting opinion in *Sutton*, 527 U.S. at 504. The narrow approach adopted in the *Sutton* trilogy can be contrasted with a broader approach applied in a 1998 case called *Bragdon v. Abbott*, 524 U.S. 624. In that case, with Justice Kennedy writing for the majority, the Court ruled that a dental patient with asymptomatic HIV infection was covered by the ADA because she was limited in the major life activity of reproduction. Deferring to the opinions of the administrative enforcement agencies and court interpretations of similar language defining disability under the Rehabilitation Act, the *Bragdon* Court reasoned that Congress clearly intended that asymptomatic HIV-positive individuals be covered by the ADA. Just one year after *Bragdon*, the Court felt free to disregard similar interpretations and precedents that would have weighed in support of the plaintiffs in the *Sutton* trilogy. See *Chevron, U.S.A., Inc. v. Echazabal*, 536 U.S. 122 Sup. Ct. 2045 (June 10, 2002) (discussed below).

22. 42 U.S.C. Sect. 12102(2).

23. See *Sutton*, 527 U.S. at 495–96 (Stevens, J., dissenting).

24. 42 U.S.C. Sect. 12101(b)(1).

25. *Sutton*, 527 U.S. at 485.

26. 42 U.S.C. Sect. 423(d)(1)(A).

27. See *Cleveland v. Policy Management Systems Corporation*, 526 U.S. 795 at 801 (Breyer, J., noting for a unanimous Court that the "Social Security Act and the ADA both help individuals with disabilities, but in different ways").

28. See *Sutton*, 527 U.S. at 503–04.

29. *Id.* at 504. The equal opportunity "door" can be contrasted with other "doors" of eligibility that enable a severely disabled young person to retire at age eighteen (the Social Security Act) or enable a person to park in a specially designated space for people with mobility impairments. In the former case, there is no down side to opening the door wide. In the latter case, there are good reasons carefully to limit who gets in the door.

30. *Id.* at 509–10, citing 480 U.S. 273 (1987), involving a teacher with tuberculosis who challenged discriminatory termination.

31. *Id.* at 510, 512.

32. *Id.* at 495.

33. For an analysis of lower court decisions in the aftermath of *Sutton*, see Chai Feldblum, "Honey, They Shrunk Our Law: Ways the Courts Have Systematically Denied the Civil Rights of Persons Intended to Be Protected by the ADA," covering cases through the year 2000, available at www.aapd-dc.org.

34. 534 U.S. 184 (2002).

35. *Id.*, slip op. at 13.

36. *Id.*, slip op. at 9–17.

37. In a newspaper article published shortly after the decision, Congressman Steny Hoyer, who managed passage of the bill in the House, criticized the decision for misconstruing what Congress had actually intended: "43 million people . . . seemed like a lot and we thought that showed we intended the law to be broad rather than narrow" ("Not Exactly What We Intended, Justice O'Connor," *Washington Post*, Jan. 20, 2002, pp. B1, B5.)

38. 42 U.S.C. Sect. 12101(a)(2), (a)(3).

39. *Heller*, 509 U.S. at 321–26.

40. *Id.* at 326, 327. "At English common law there was a 'marked distinction' in the treatment accorded 'idiots' (the mentally retarded) and 'lunatics' (the mentally ill)," the Court observed, citing F. Pollock and F. Maitland, *The History of English Law* (Boston, 1909), vol. 1, p. 481.

41. 274 U.S. 200, 207 (1927) (Holmes, J.).

42. *Heller*, 509 U.S. at 346, n. 6 (Souter, J., dissenting, citing S. Herr, *Rights and Advocacy for Retarded People* [Lexington, MA, 1983], p. 9.)

43. *Cleburne*, 473 U.S. at 461–62.

44. *Id.* at 464, 466, comparing *Plessy v. Ferguson*, 163 U.S. 537 (1896), with *Brown v. Board of Education*, 347 U.S. 483 (1954).

45. 527 U.S. 581 (1999).

46. *Id.* at 587.

47. *Id.* at 594; 595, citing 138 F. 3d at 902; 595, citing 138 F. 3d at 905.

48. Only Justice Stevens, filing a separate concurrence, supported the analysis of the Eleventh Circuit, 527 U.S. at 607–08.

49. *Id.* at 597.

50. *Id.* at 602, 605–06.

51. 42 U.S.C. Sect. 12101(b)(1).

52. 527 U.S. at 608–10 (Kennedy, J., concurring).

53. *Id.* at 625 (Thomas, J., dissenting).

54. 122 Sup. Ct. 1516 (2002).

55. 122 Sup. Ct. 2045 (2002).

56. *PGA Tour, Inc. v. Martin*, 121 Sup. Ct. 1879 (2001), allowing Casey Martin to use a golf cart would not fundamentally alter the tournament.

57. For a harbinger of narrow interpretations of Congress's powers under the Spending Clause, see *Barnes v. Gorman*, 536 U.S. 122 Sup. Ct. 2097 (June 17, 2002) (punitive damages not available to injured parties suing under Title II of the ADA and Sect. 504 of the Rehabilitation Act.)

ELEANOR M. FOX: *Antitrust and Business Power*

1. *Congressional Record* 2460 (1890).

2. *Address by the President on Trusts and Monopolies before the Joint Session of Congress (Jan. 20, 1914)*, 63d Cong., 2d sess. 1914, H. Doc. 625, 5.

3. 95 *Congressional Record* 11486 (1949).

4. *Brown Shoe Company v. United States*, 370 U.S. 294 (1962).

5. Oliver Wendell Holmes, *The Common Law* (1881), p. 96. The Sherman Act itself he famously called "economic humbug."

6. 485 U.S. 717 (1988).

7. 509 U.S. 209 (1993).

8. 526 U.S. 756 (1999).

9. Brief of Microsoft Corporation on appeal to D.C. Circuit, Nov. 27, 2000, at 16.

10. *United States v. Microsoft Corporation*, 253 F. 3d 34 (D.C. Cir.), certiorari denied, 122 Sup. Ct. 350 (2001).

LAWRENCE E. MITCHELL: *No Business like No Business*

1. William L. Cary, Federalism and Corporate Law: Reflections Upon Delaware 83 Yale L. J. 663 (1974). That abrogation was again affirmed in an article by three sitting Delaware judges, reported in *The New York Times* on June 15, 2001, in which they suggested that managers should be more free to manage than they are, an argument that would, from a doctrinal perspective, diminish fiduciary obligations. I actually agree with this conclusion, although with a different implementation that retains supporting duties. See Lawrence E. Mitchell, *Corporate Irresponsibility: America's Newest Export* (New Haven, 2002).

2. Delaware's primacy is aided by a rule of law known as the internal affairs doctrine, which holds that the law of the state of incorporation governs the relation-

ships among directors, officers, and stockholders, no matter where the corporation actually does its business and no matter where the case is adjudicated. Thus a corporation incorporated in Delaware with offices and facilities in New York, Tennessee, Texas, California, Illinois, London, Hong Kong, and Singapore will be governed by Delaware law, no matter which court (at least in the United States) hears the case and even though it does no business in Delaware.

3. The debate over Cary's views is principally about whether these limitations have been economically efficient and therefore presumably beneficial. Nobody seriously disputes the proposition that the duties of directors and officers in Delaware corporations are far from rigorous.

4. *Blue Chip Stamps v. Manor Drug Stores*, 421 U.S. 723 (1975). In light of what I shall have to say about the Rehnquist Court I do want to make it clear that for Powell, who understood perfectly well what he was doing as a policy matter, the statutory language was indeed the starting point and not, as it is for the current Court, the whole point.

5. 521 U.S. 642 (1997).

6. It's not clear from the opinion whether Grand Met could have overridden this permission by objecting—it seems that O'Hagan's primary breach was to Dorsey & Whitney. At the very least, Grand Met could have fired the firm and sought an injunction against O'Hagan's using the information.

7. Justice Thomas's dissent (joined by Rehnquist), in one of the few bright lights (from a policy perspective) of this Court's securities jurisprudence, understands the way the Court's stretch of the "in connection with" requirement creates an incoherent result.

8. 513 U.S. 561 (1995).

9. The statute has been renumbered since this decision. I adhere to the numbering in use at the time of the case.

10. Underlying this approach is also the Court's desire to cut back dramatically on the scope of the securities laws. Even when it doesn't succeed (see *O'Hagan*), there nonetheless seems to be a Court-side insistence on technical manipulation, despite the fact that the opinions are also laden with policy talk with respect to the effect of the interpretation at issue. The policy talk is almost always dicta, as any law student can see, and, as in *Gustafson*, frequently devoid of any meaningful understanding of markets or business. The real action lies within the statute.

11. Justice Thomas completely eschews policy or any mention of the practices and operations of the secondary markets in a dissenting opinion that never for a moment strays beyond the techniques of statutory interpretation, making it no better in terms of business policy even though reaching what I believe to be the right result.

12. 501 U.S. 350 (1991).

13. 511 U.S. 164 (1994).

14. 501 U.S. 1083 (1991).

15. 396 U.S. 375 (1970). *Mills* was arguably distinguishable from *Virginia Bankshares* in that in the former case, the controlling stockholder held over a majority of the stock but two-thirds of the stockholders were required to approve the merger, a fact that required that at least some of the minority votes be counted.

Contributors

STEPHEN BRIGHT has been the Director of the Southern Center for Human Rights in Atlanta since 1982, and teaches courses on the death penalty and criminal law at the Harvard and Yale Law Schools.

SUSAN ESTRICH was the first woman president of the Harvard Law Review and the first woman to run a Presidential campaign. Formerly a tenured professor of law at Harvard, she is currently the Robert Kingsley Professor of Law and Political Science at the University of Southern California, a commentator for Fox News, and the author of five books, including *Sex & Power* (2000). She graduated from Wellesley College and Harvard Law School.

CHAI FELDBLUM teaches at the Georgetown University Law Center. A former law clerk to Justice Harry Blackmun, she has been legal counsel to the National Gay and Lesbian Task Force and President of the Disability Rights Counsel.

ELEANOR M. FOX is the Walter J. Derenberg Professor of Trade Regulation at New York University School of Law, where she teaches and writes on antitrust law, European Union law, and issues of globalization.

WILLIAM E. HELLERSTEIN is a professor of law at Brooklyn Law School and director of the Brooklyn Law School Second Look Program Clinic. He teaches constitutional law, criminal procedure, and civil rights law. He was the attorney-in-charge of the Criminal Appeals Bureau of the New York Legal Aid Society for seventeen years and is a former staff attorney with the United States Commission on Civil Rights. He has written and lectured extensively on the rights of criminal defendants and the rights of prisoners.

ANDREW J. IMPARATO is the president and chief executive officer of the American Association of People with Disabilities (AAPD), a national membership organization based in Washington, D.C. AAPD advocates for public policies that promote the goals of the Americans with Disabilities Act. Prior to joining AAPD, Imparato worked as an attorney with the National Council on Disability, the U.S. Equal Employment Opportunity Commission, the U.S. Senate Subcommittee on Disability Policy, and the Disability Law Center in Boston, Massachusetts. He acknowledges the assistance of Jacqueline Okun, American University Law School, Class of 2002, and Adam Jed, Yale University, Class of 2002.

JOHN P. MacKENZIE covered the Supreme Court for *The Washington Post* from 1965 to 1977 and wrote editorials for *The New York Times* from 1977 to 1997. He is the author of *The Appearance of Justice* (1974).

LAWRENCE E. MITCHELL is John Theodore Fey Research Professor of Law at The George Washington University, where he is also Founding Director of the Sloan Program for the Study of Business in Society and the International Institute for Corporate Governance and Accountability. He is the author of numerous scholarly articles on corporate governance and responsibility, a casebook on corporate finance, and *Stacked Deck: A Story of Selfishness in America* (1998) and *Corporate Irresponsibility: America's Newest Export* (2001).

ALAN B. MORRISON founded the Public Citizen Litigation Group with Ralph Nader in 1972. In addition to the more than forty cases that he and his colleagues have argued in the Supreme Court (winning more than 60 percent), they also run a project in which they help several dozen lawyers each year, most with limited Supreme Court experience, brief and argue their cases. Mr. Morrison is currently teaching at Stanford Law School, and in the past has taught at Harvard, New York University, Tulane University, and University of Hawaii Law Schools.

CHARLES J. OGLETREE, JR., is the Jesse Climenko Professor of Law at Harvard Law School, where he has taught for the past eighteen years. Professor Ogletree has appeared as the moderator of many public television programs and as a commentator on national television and public radio information shows. He is the author and co-author of numerous articles and books on a wide variety of issues concerning the criminal justice system.

JAMIN B. RASKIN is a professor of constitutional law at American University's Washington College of Law and founder of its Marshall-Brennan Fellowship Program, which sends law students into public high schools to teach a course in constitutional literacy. He is the author of *We the Students* (2000) and the forthcoming, *Overruling Democracy: The Supreme Court Versus the American People* (Routledge 2003). Raskin is a former assistant attorney general of Massachusetts and has written widely about the First Amendment.

NORMAN REDLICH is dean emeritus and Judge Edward Weinfeld Professor of Law Emeritus at New York University Law School. He is chair of the American Jewish Congress's Governing Council, co-chair of the American Jewish Congress's Commission on Law and Social Action, and in 2002 he received the Lifetime Achievement Award from the Lawyers' Committee for Civil Rights Under Law. Dean Redlich acknowledges the assistance of Chi T. Steve Kwok, class of 2002, Yale Law School.

JAMES SALZMAN is a professor of law at American University's Washington College of Law. He has lectured on environmental law and policy in the Americas, Europe, Asia, Australia, and Africa and has served as a visiting professor at Harvard and Stanford Law Schools.

HERMAN SCHWARTZ is a professor of law at American University's Washington College of Law. He is a civil rights and civil liberties activist who has written extensively on constitutional law and human rights in the United States and abroad, and has served in both federal and state government. His books include *Packing the Courts: The Conservative Campaign to Rewrite the Constitution* (1988) and *The Struggle for Constitutional Justice in Post-Communist Europe* (2000) and he is the editor of *The Burger Years: Rights and Wrongs of the Supreme Court, 1969–1986* (1987). He lives in Washington, D.C.

WILLIAM L. TAYLOR is a Washington, D.C., lawyer who has been a civil rights advocate for more than four decades. He was a staff lawyer for Thurgood Marshall at the NAACP Legal Defense Fund in the 1950s and general counsel and staff director for the U.S. Commission on Civil Rights in the 1960s. He is an adjunct professor at the Georgetown Law School and is president of the Leadership Conference Education Fund. He has filed briefs in the Supreme Court in the Warren, Burger, and Rehnquist eras.

DAVID C. VLADECK teaches at Georgetown University Law Center. He is counsel to Public Citizen Litigation Group, where he, and his coauthor Alan B. Morrison, litigated a number of the constitutional and administrative law cases discussed in their chapter.

TOM WICKER is a former columnist for *The New York Times* and is the author of many essays and more than 15 books, including *Dwight D. Eisenhower* (2002) and *JFK and LBJ: The Influence of Personality upon Politics* (1991). He has received numerous awards for journalism and literature, and holds several honorary degrees.

Index